D1171979

THE LOEB CLASSICAL LIBRARY

FOUNDED BY JAMES LOEB

LUCIAN

III

LCL 130

LUCIAN

VOLUME III

WITH AN ENGLISH TRANSLATION BY

A. M. HARMON

HARVARD UNIVERSITY PRESS
CAMBRIDGE, MASSACHUSETTS
LONDON, ENGLAND

First published 1921
Reprinted 1947, 1960, 1969, 1995

ISBN 0-674-99144-3

Printed in Great Britain by St Edmundsbury Press Ltd,
Bury St Edmunds, Suffolk, on acid-free paper.
Bound by Hunter & Foulis Ltd, Edinburgh, Scotland.

CONTENTS

LIST OF LUCIAN'S WORKS

SHOWING THEIR DIVISION INTO VOLUMES IN THIS EDITION

VOLUME I

Phalaris I and II—Hippias or the Bath—Dionysus—Heracles—Amber or The Swans—The Fly—Nigrinus—Demonax—The Hall—My Native Land—Octogenarians—A True Story I and II—Slander—The Consonants at Law—Symposium or The Lapiths.

VOLUME II

The Downward Journey or The Tyrant—Zeus Catechized—Zeus Rants—The Dream or The Cock—Prometheus—Icaromenippus or The Sky-man—Timon or The Misanthrope—Charon or the Inspector—Philosophies for Sale.

VOLUME III

The Dead Come to Life or The Fisherman—The Double Indictment or Trials by Jury—On Sacrifices—The Ignorant Book Collector—The Dream or Lucian's Career—The Parasite—The Lover of Lies—The Judgement of the Goddesses—On Salaried Posts in Great Houses.

VOLUME IV

Anacharsis or Athletics—Menippus or The Descent into Hades—On Funerals—A Professor of Public Speaking—Alexander the False Prophet—Essays in Portraiture—Essays in Portraiture Defended—The Goddess of Surrye.

VOLUME V

The Passing of Peregrinus—The Runaways—Toxaris or Friendship—The Dance—Lexiphanes—The Eunuch—Astrology—The Mistaken Critic—The Parliament of the Gods—The Tyrannicide—Disowned.

VOLUME VI

Historia—Dipsades—Saturnalia—Herodotus—Zeuxis—Pro Lapsu—Apologia—Harmonides—Hesiodus—Scytha—Hermotimus—Promethus Es—Navigium.

VOLUME VII

Dialogues of the Dead—Dialogues of the Sea—Gods—Dialogues of the Gods (exc. Deorum Judicium cf. Vol. III)—Dialogues of the Courtesans.

VOLUME VIII

Soloecista—Lucius or the Ass—Amores—Demosthenes—Halcyon—Podagra—Ocypus—Cyniscus—Philopatris—Charidemus—Nero—Epigram.

THE WORKS OF LUCIAN

THE DEAD COME TO LIFE, OR THE FISHERMAN

This is Lucian's reply to the storm of angry protest which he had evoked from the schoolmen with his *Philosophies for Sale* (II. 450 ff.), wherein, to their mind, he had unwarrantably and outrageously ridiculed the ancient philosophers and their doctrines.

The scene is in Athens. The dead who have come to life are the ancient philosophers, bent upon wreaking vengeance on Frankness, which is Lucian's alias here.

Eventually conceded a formal trial before Philosophy, he is acquitted on the plea that his ridicule had not been aimed at the ancient worthies but at their unworthy successors of his own time. As these impostors cannot be induced to stand trial, Frankness is empowered to go about and brand them, so that people can tell them from the genuine philosophers. Before departing on his mission, he fishes up, with a bait of figs and gold, typical representatives of the chief schools for the inspection of their founders.

Lucian's plea is specious, for in *Philosophies for Sale* he had certainly shown scant regard for those whom he now professes to hold in such high esteem. But it is not meant to be taken seriously; it is put forward with a wink at the audience for the sake of turning the tables on his critics. His new-found deference, moreover, is well seasoned with irony, and quite offset by the pose of urbane and patronizing superiority which he assumes in feigned unconsciousness. The piece is almost all persiflage, and maddeningly unanswerable for that reason.

The dialogue is strikingly like an Aristophanic comedy in its construction, especially in the fact that it has a clearly marked second part, somewhat loosely attached to the first, which develops a series of incidents after the plot has been worked out. Because of this similarity, and for many other reasons too, none of Lucian's writings better serves to introduce and illustrate the *Double Indictment*, which follows it.

ΑΝΑΒΙΟΥΝΤΕΣ Η ΑΛΙΕΥΣ[1]

ΣΩΚΡΑΤΗΣ

1 Βάλλε βάλλε τὸν κατάρατον ἀφθόνοις τοῖς λίθοις· ἐπίβαλλε τῶν βώλων· προσεπίβαλλε καὶ τῶν ὀστράκων· παῖε τοῖς ξύλοις τὸν ἀλιτήριον· ὅρα μὴ διαφύγῃ· καὶ σὺ βάλλε, ὦ Πλάτων· καὶ σύ, ὦ Χρύσιππε, καὶ σὺ δέ, καὶ πάντες ἅμα·[2] συνασπίσωμεν ἐπ' αὐτόν,

ὡς πήρη πήρηφιν ἀρήγῃ, βάκτρα δὲ βάκτροις,

κοινὸς γὰρ πολέμιος, καὶ οὐκ ἔστιν ἡμῶν ὅντινα οὐχ ὕβρικε. σὺ δέ, ὦ Διόγενες, εἴ ποτε καὶ ἄλλοτε, χρῶ τῷ ξύλῳ· μηδὲ ἀνῆτε· διδότω τὴν ἀξίαν βλάσφημος ὤν. τί τοῦτο; κεκμήκατε, ὦ Ἐπίκουρε καὶ Ἀρίστιππε; καὶ μὴν οὐκ ἐχρῆν.

ἀνέρες ἔστε, σοφοί, μνήσασθε δὲ θούριδος ὀργῆς.

2 Ἀριστότελες, ἐπισπούδασον· ἔτι θᾶττον.[3] εὖ ἔχει· ἑάλωκεν τὸ θηρίον. εἰλήφαμέν σε, ὦ μιαρέ. εἴσῃ γοῦν αὐτίκα οὕστινας ἡμᾶς ὄντας ἐκακηγό-

MSS. available in photographs: Γ, UPN.

[1] ΑΝΑΒΙΟΥΝΤΕΣ Η ΑΛΙΕΥΣ γ (and Thomas Magister): ΑΛΙΕΥΣ Η ΑΝΑΒΙΟΥΝΤΕΣ β.

[2] Punctuation A.M.H.: καὶ σὺ δὲ καὶ πάντες ἅμα συν. γ; καὶ σὺ δέ. πάντες ἅμα συν. β, edd.

[3] Punctuation K. Schwartz: ἐπισπούδασον ἔτι θᾶττον MSS.

THE DEAD COME TO LIFE, OR THE FISHERMAN

SOCRATES

PELT, pelt the scoundrel with plenty of stones! Heap him with clods! Pile him up with broken dishes, too! Beat the blackguard with your sticks! Look out he doesn't get away! Throw, Plato; you too, Chrysippus; you too; everybody at once! Let's charge him together.

"Let wallet to wallet give succour, and cudgel to
cudgel,"[1]

for he is our joint enemy, and there is not a man of us whom he has not outraged. Diogenes, ply your stick, if ever you did before; let none of you weaken; let him pay the penalty for his ribaldry. What is this? Have you given out, Epicurus and Aristippus? Come, that is too bad!

"Show yourselves men, ye sages, and call up the
fury of battle."[2]

Aristotle, make haste! Still faster! That's well; the game is bagged. We have you, villain! you shall soon find out what sort of men you have been

[1] *Iliad* 2, 363:
κρῖν' ἄνδρας κατὰ φῦλα, κατὰ φρήτρας, Ἀγάμεμνον,
ὡς φρήτρη φρήτρηφιν ἀρήγῃ, φῦλα δὲ φύλοις.

[2] *Iliad* 6, 112; Homer has "friends," not "sages."

ρεις. τῷ τρόπῳ δέ τις αὐτὸν καὶ μετέλθῃ; ποικίλον γάρ τινα θάνατον ἐπινοῶμεν κατ' αὐτοῦ πᾶσιν ἡμῖν ἐξαρκέσαι δυνάμενον· καθ' ἕκαστον γοῦν ἑπτάκις δίκαιός ἐστιν ἀπολωλέναι.

ΦΙΛΟΣΟΦΟΣ

Ἐμοὶ μὲν ἀνασκολοπισθῆναι δοκεῖ αὐτόν.

ΑΛΛΟΣ

Νὴ Δία, μαστιγωθέντα γε πρότερον.

ΑΛΛΟΣ

Πολὺ πρότερον τοὺς ὀφθαλμοὺς ἐκκεκολάφθω.

ΑΛΛΟΣ

Τὴν γλῶτταν αὐτὴν ἔτι πολὺ πρότερον ἀποτετμήσθω.

ΣΩΚΡΑΤΗΣ

Σοὶ δὲ τί, Ἐμπεδόκλεις, δοκεῖ;

ΕΜΠΕΔΟΚΛΗΣ

Εἰς τοὺς κρατῆρας ἐμπεσεῖν αὐτόν, ὡς μάθῃ μὴ λοιδορεῖσθαι τοῖς κρείττοσιν.

ΠΛΑΤΩΝ

Καὶ μὴν ἄριστον ἦν καθάπερ τινὰ Πενθέα ἢ Ὀρφέα

λακιστὸν ἐν πέτραισιν εὑρέσθαι μόρον,

ἵνα ἂν καὶ τὸ μέρος αὐτοῦ ἕκαστος ἔχων ἀπηλλάττετο.

ΠΑΡΡΗΣΙΑΔΗΣ

3 Μηδαμῶς· ἀλλὰ πρὸς Ἱκεσίου φείσασθέ μου.

insulting. But how *are* we to punish him, to be sure? Let us invent a complex death for him, such as to satisfy us all; in fact he deserves to die seven times over for each of us.

PHILOSOPHER

I suggest he be crucified.

ANOTHER

Yes, by Heaven; but flogged beforehand.

ANOTHER

Let him have his eyes put out long beforehand.

ANOTHER

Let him have that tongue of his cut off, even longer beforehand.

SOCRATES

And you, Empedocles—what do you suggest?

EMPEDOCLES

That he be thrown into my crater,[1] so that he may learn not to abuse his betters.

PLATO

Indeed, the best suggestion would have been for him, like another Pentheus or Orpheus,

"To find among the crags a riven doom," [2]

so that each of us might have gone off with a scrap of him.

FRANKNESS

No, no! In the name of Him who hears the suppliant,[3] spare me!

[1] Aetna, into which Empedocles is said to have leapt.

[2] Both Pentheus and Orpheus were torn to pieces by Maenads. The verse is from a lost tragedy (Nauck, *Tr. Gr. Fragm.* p. 895).

[3] Zeus.

ΠΛΑΤΩΝ

Ἄραρεν· οὐκ ἂν ἀφεθείης ἔτι. ὁρᾷς δὲ δὴ καὶ τὸν Ὅμηρον ἅ φησιν,

ὡς οὐκ ἔστι λέουσι καὶ ἀνδράσιν ὅρκια πιστά.

ΠΑΡΡΗΣΙΑΔΗΣ

Καὶ μὴν καθ᾽ Ὅμηρον ὑμᾶς καὶ αὐτὸς ἱκετεύσω· αἰδέσεσθε γὰρ ἴσως τὰ ἔπη καὶ οὐ παρόψεσθε ῥαψῳδήσαντά με·

ζωγρεῖτ᾽ οὐ κακὸν ἄνδρα καὶ ἄξια δέχθε ἄποινα,
χαλκόν τε χρυσόν τε, τὰ δὴ φιλέουσι σοφοί περ.

ΠΛΑΤΩΝ

Ἀλλ᾽ οὐδὲ ἡμεῖς ἀπορήσομεν πρὸς σὲ Ὁμηρικῆς ἀντιλογίας. ἄκουε γοῦν·

μὴ δή μοι φύξιν γε, κακηγόρε, βάλλεο θυμῷ
χρυσόν περ λέξας, ἐπεὶ ἵκεο χεῖρας ἐς ἁμάς.

ΠΑΡΡΗΣΙΑΔΗΣ

Οἴμοι τῶν κακῶν. ὁ μὲν Ὅμηρος ἡμῖν ἄπρακτος, ἡ μεγίστη ἐλπίς. ἐπὶ τὸν Εὐριπίδην δή μοι καταφευκτέον· τάχα γὰρ ἂν ἐκεῖνος σώσειέ με.

μὴ κτεῖνε· τὸν ἱκέτην γὰρ οὐ θέμις κτανεῖν.

ΠΛΑΤΩΝ

Τί δέ; οὐχὶ κἀκεῖνα Εὐριπίδου ἐστίν,

οὐ δεινὰ πάσχειν δεινὰ τοὺς εἰργασμένους;

PLATO

Your doom is sealed: you cannot be let go now. You know, of course, what Homer says:

"Since between lions and men there exist no bonds
of alliance."[1]

FRANKNESS

Indeed, I myself will quote Homer in begging you for mercy. Perhaps you will revere his verses and will not ignore me when I have recited them:

"Save me, for I am no churl, and receive what is
fitting in ransom,
Copper and gold, that in truth are desirable even
to sages."[2]

PLATO

But we ourselves shall not be at a loss for a Homeric reply to you; listen to this, for instance:

"Think not now in your heart of escape, you
speaker of slander,
Even by talking of gold, once into our hands you
have fallen."[3]

FRANKNESS

Oh, what wretched luck! Homer, in whom I had my greatest hope, is useless to me. I suppose I must take refuge with Euripides; perhaps he might save me:

"Slay not! The suppliant thou shalt not slay."[4]

PLATO

Ah, but is not this by Euripides, too?

"No harm for them that wrought to suffer harm."[5]

[1] *Iliad* 22, 262. [2] A cento; *Iliad* 6, 46, 48; 20, 65.
[3] *Iliad* 10, 447–8, with alterations.
[4] Nauck, p. 663. Cf. *Ion* 1553. [5] *Orestes* 413.

ΠΑΡΡΗΣΙΑΔΗΣ

Νῦν οὖν ἕκατι ῥημάτων κτενεῖτέ[1] με;

ΠΛΑΤΩΝ

Νὴ Δία· φησὶ γοῦν ἐκεῖνος αὐτός,

ἀχαλίνων στομάτων
ἀνόμου τ' ἀφροσύνας
τὸ τέλος δυστυχία.

ΠΑΡΡΗΣΙΑΔΗΣ

4 Οὐκοῦν ἐπεὶ δέδοκται πάντως ἀποκτιννύναι καὶ οὐδεμία μηχανὴ τὸ διαφυγεῖν με, φέρε τοῦτο γοῦν εἴπατέ μοι, τίνες ὄντες ἢ τί πεπονθότες ἀνήκεστον πρὸς ἡμῶν ἀμείλικτα ὀργίζεσθε καὶ ἐπὶ θανάτῳ συνειλήφατε;

ΠΛΑΤΩΝ

Ἅτινα μὲν εἴργασαι ἡμᾶς τὰ δεινά, σεαυτὸν ἐρώτα, ὦ κάκιστε, καὶ τοὺς καλοὺς ἐκείνους σου λόγους ἐν οἷς φιλοσοφίαν τε αὐτὴν κακῶς ἠγόρευες καὶ εἰς ἡμᾶς ὕβριζες, ὥσπερ ἐξ ἀγορᾶς ἀποκηρύττων σοφοὺς ἄνδρας, καὶ τὸ μέγιστον, ἐλευθέρους· ἐφ' οἷς ἀγανακτήσαντες ἀνεληλύθαμεν ἐπὶ σὲ παραιτησάμενοι πρὸς ὀλίγον τὸν Ἀϊδωνέα, Χρύσιππος οὑτοσὶ καὶ Ἐπίκουρος καὶ ὁ Πλάτων ἐγὼ καὶ Ἀριστοτέλης ἐκεῖνος καὶ ὁ σιωπῶν οὗτος Πυθαγόρας καὶ Διογένης καὶ ἅπαντες ὁπόσους διέσυρες ἐν τοῖς λόγοις.

ΠΑΡΡΗΣΙΑΔΗΣ

5 Ἀνέπνευσα· οὐ γὰρ ἀποκτενεῖτέ με, ἢν μάθητε ὁποῖος ἐγὼ περὶ ὑμᾶς ἐγενόμην· ὥστε ἀπορρίψατε τοὺς λίθους, μᾶλλον δὲ φυλάττετε. χρήσεσθε γὰρ αὐτοῖς κατὰ τῶν ἀξίων.

[1] κτενεῖτέ Guyet; κτείνετέ βγ.

FRANKNESS

"Then will ye slay me now, because of words?"[1]

PLATO

Yes, by Heaven! Anyhow, he himself says:

"Of mouths that are curbless
And fools that are lawless
The end is mischance."[2]

FRANKNESS

Well, then, as you are absolutely determined to kill me and there is no possibility of my escaping, do tell me at least who you are and what irreparable injuries you have received from me that you are irreconcilably angry and have seized me for execution.

PLATO

What dreadful wrongs you have done us you may ask yourself, you rascal, and those precious dialogues of yours in which you not only spoke abusively of Philosophy herself, but insulted us by advertising for sale, as if in a slave-market, men who are learned, and what is more, free-born. Indignant at this, we requested a brief leave of absence from Pluto and have come up to get you—Chrysippus here, Epicurus, Plato (myself), Aristotle over there, Pythagoras here, who says nothing, Diogenes, and everyone that you vilified in your dialogues.

FRANKNESS

I breathe again, for you will not put me to death if you understand how I have acted as regards you. So throw away your stones; or better, keep them. You will make use of them against those who deserve them.[3]

[1] Euripides? Nauck, p. 663. [2] *Bacchae* 386 ff.
[3] It is curious that this suggestion, though emphasized by being repeated (§ 11), is not worked out.

ΠΛΑΤΩΝ

Ληρεῖς. σὲ δὲ χρὴ τήμερον ἀπολωλέναι, καὶ ἤδη γε

λάϊνον ἕσσο χιτῶνα κακῶν ἕνεχ' ὅσσα ἔοργας.

ΠΑΡΡΗΣΙΑΔΗΣ

Καὶ μήν, ὦ ἄριστοι, ὃν ἐχρῆν μόνον ἐξ ἁπάντων ἐπαινεῖν οἰκεῖόν τε ὑμῖν ὄντα καὶ εὔνουν καὶ ὁμογνώμονα καί, εἰ μὴ φορτικὸν εἰπεῖν, κηδεμόνα τῶν ἐπιτηδευμάτων εὖ ἴστε ἀποκτενοῦντες, ἢν ἐμὲ ἀποκτείνητε τοσαῦτα ὑπὲρ ὑμῶν πεπονηκότα. ὁρᾶτε οὖν μὴ κατὰ τοὺς πολλοὺς[1] τῶν νῦν φιλοσόφων αὐτοὶ[2] ποιεῖτε, ἀχάριστοι καὶ ὀργίλοι καὶ ἀγνώμονες φαινόμενοι πρὸς ἄνδρα εὐεργέτην.

ΠΛΑΤΩΝ

Ὢ τῆς ἀναισχυντίας. καὶ χάριν σοι τῆς κακηγορίας προσοφείλομεν; οὕτως ἀνδραπόδοις ὡς ἀληθῶς[3] οἴει διαλέγεσθαι; ἢ καὶ εὐεργεσίαν καταλογιῇ πρὸς ἡμᾶς ἐπὶ τῇ τοσαύτῃ ὕβρει καὶ παροινίᾳ τῶν λόγων;

ΠΑΡΡΗΣΙΑΔΗΣ

6 Ποῦ γὰρ ἐγὼ ὑμᾶς ἢ πότε ὕβρικα, ὃς ἀεὶ φιλοσοφίαν τε θαυμάζων διατετέλεκα καὶ ὑμᾶς αὐτοὺς ὑπερεπαινῶν καὶ τοῖς λόγοις οἷς καταλελοίπατε ὁμιλῶν; αὐτὰ γοῦν ἃ φημι ταῦτα, πόθεν ἄλλοθεν ἢ παρ' ὑμῶν λαβὼν καὶ κατὰ τὴν μέλιτταν ἀπανθισάμενος ἐπιδείκνυμαι τοῖς ἀνθρώποις; οἱ δὲ ἐπαινοῦσι καὶ γνωρίζουσιν ἕκασ-

[1] κατὰ τοὺς πολλοὺς γN: not in BU.
[2] αὐτοὶ Cobet: αὐτὸ MSS.
[3] οὕτως ἀνδραπόδοις (sicine cum servis —?) ὡς ἀληθῶς K. Schwartz: οὕτως ἀνδραπόδοις ἀληθῶς γ; οὕτως ὡς ἀνδραπόδοις ἀληθῶς β, edd. since Jacobitz.

PLATO

Nonsense: you must die to-day. Yes, forthwith

"Don your tunic of stone on account of the wrongs you have done us!"[1]

FRANKNESS

Truly, gentlemen, you will put to death, you may depend upon it, the one man in the world whom you ought to commend as your friend, well-wisher, comrade in thought, and, if it be not in bad taste to say so, the defender of your teachings, if you put me to death after I have laboured so earnestly in your behalf. Take care, then, that you yourselves are not acting like most of our present-day philosophers by showing yourselves ungrateful and hasty and inconsiderate toward a benefactor.

PLATO

O what impudence! So we really owe you gratitude for your abuse, into the bargain? Are you so convinced that you are truly talking to slaves? Will you actually set yourself down as our benefactor, on top of all your insolent and intemperate language?

FRANKNESS

Where, pray, and when have I insulted you? I have always consistently admired philosophy and extolled you and lived on intimate terms with the writings that you have left behind. These very phrases that I utter—where else but from you did I get them? Culling them like a bee, I make my show with them before men, who applaud and recognize where and

[1] *Iliad* 3, 57.

τον τὸ ἄνθος ὅθεν καὶ παρ' ὅτου καὶ ὅπως ἀνελεξάμην, καὶ λόγῳ μὲν ἐμὲ ζηλοῦσι τῆς ἀνθολογίας, τὸ δ' ἀληθὲς ὑμᾶς καὶ τὸν λειμῶνα τὸν ὑμέτερον, οἳ τοιαῦτα ἐξηνθήκατε ποικίλα καὶ πολυειδῆ τὰς βαφάς, εἴ τις ἀναλέξασθαί τε αὐτὰ ἐπίσταιτο καὶ ἀναπλέξαι καὶ ἁρμόσαι, ὡς μὴ ἀπᾴδειν θάτερον θατέρου. ἔσθ' ὅστις οὖν ταῦτα εὖ πεπονθὼς παρ' ὑμῶν κακῶς ἂν εἰπεῖν ἐπιχειρήσειεν εὐεργέτας ἄνδρας, ἀφ' ὧν εἶναί τις ἔδοξεν; ἐκτὸς εἰ μὴ κατὰ τὸν Θάμυριν ἢ τὸν Εὔρυτον εἴη τὴν φύσιν, ὡς ταῖς Μούσαις ἀντᾴδειν, παρ' ὧν εἴληφε τὴν ᾠδήν, ἢ τῷ Ἀπόλλωνι ἐριδαίνειν ἐναντία τοξεύων, καὶ ταῦτα δοτῆρι ὄντι τῆς τοξικῆς.

ΠΛΑΤΩΝ

7 Τοῦτο μέν, ὦ γενναῖε, κατὰ τοὺς ῥήτορας εἴρηταί σοι· ἐναντιώτατον δ' οὖν[1] ἐστι τῷ πράγματι καὶ χαλεπωτέραν σου ἐπιδείκνυσι τὴν τόλμαν, εἴ γε τῇ ἀδικίᾳ καὶ ἀχαριστία πρόσεστιν, ὃς παρ' ἡμῶν τὰ τοξεύματα, ὡς φής, λαβὼν καθ' ἡμῶν ἐτόξευες, ἕνα τοῦτον ὑποθέμενος τὸν σκοπόν, ἅπαντας ἡμᾶς ἀγορεύειν κακῶς· τοιαῦτα παρὰ σοῦ ἀπειλήφαμεν ἀνθ' ὧν σοι τὸν λειμῶνα ἐκεῖνον ἀναπετάσαντες οὐκ ἐκωλύομεν δρέπεσθαι καὶ τὸ προκόλπιον ἐμπλησάμενον ἀπελθεῖν· ὥστε διά γε τοῦτο μάλιστα δίκαιος ἂν εἴης ἀποθανεῖν.

ΠΑΡΡΗΣΙΑΔΗΣ

8 Ὁρᾶτε· πρὸς ὀργὴν ἀκούετε καὶ οὐδὲν τῶν δικαίων προσίεσθε. καίτοι οὐκ ἂν ᾠήθην ποτὲ ὡς ὀργὴ Πλάτωνος ἢ Χρυσίππου ἢ Ἀριστοτέλους ἢ τῶν ἄλλων ὑμῶν καθίκοιτο ἄν, ἀλλά μοι

[1] δ' οὖν Fritzsche: γοῦν MSS.

from whom and how I gathered each flower; and although ostensibly it is I whom they admire for the bouquet, as a matter of fact it is you and your garden, because you have put forth such blossoms, so gay and varied in their hues—if one but knows how to select and interweave and combine them so that they will not be out of harmony with one another. Would any man, after receiving this kindly treatment at your hands, attempt to speak ill of benefactors to whom he owes his reputation? Not unless he be like Thamyris or Eurytus in his nature, so as to raise his voice against the Muses from whom he had the gift of song, or to match himself against Apollo in archery—and he the giver of the bow!

PLATO

That speech of yours is good rhetoric, my fine fellow; but it is directly against your case and only makes your presumptuousness appear more staggering, since ingratitude is now added to injustice. For you got your shafts from us, as you admit, and then turned them against us, making it your only aim to speak ill of us all. That is the way you have paid us for opening that garden to you and not forbidding you to pick flowers and go away with your arms full. For that reason, then, above all else, you deserve to die.

FRANKNESS

See! You give me an angry hearing, and you reject every just plea! Yet I should never have supposed that anger could affect Plato or Chrysippus or Aristotle or the rest of you; it seemed to me that

ἐδοκεῖτε μόνοι δὴ πόρρω εἶναι τοῦ τοιούτου. πλὴν ἀλλὰ μὴ ἄκριτόν γε, ὦ θαυμάσιοι, μηδὲ πρὸ δίκης ἀποκτείνητέ με. ὑμέτερον γοῦν καὶ τοῦτο ἦν, μὴ βίᾳ μηδὲ κατὰ τὸ ἰσχυρότερον πολιτεύεσθαι, δίκῃ δὲ τὰ διάφορα λύεσθαι διδόντας λόγον καὶ δεχομένους ἐν τῷ μέρει. ὥστε δικαστὴν ἑλόμενοι κατηγορήσατε μὲν ὑμεῖς ἢ ἅμα πάντες ἢ ὅντινα ἂν χειροτονήσητε ὑπὲρ ἁπάντων, ἐγὼ δὲ ἀπολογήσομαι πρὸς τὰ ἐγκλήματα. κᾆτα ἢν μέν τι ἀδικῶν φαίνωμαι καὶ τοῦτο περὶ ἐμοῦ γνῷ τὸ δικαστήριον, ὑφέξω δηλαδὴ τὴν ἀξίαν· ὑμεῖς δὲ βίαιον οὐδὲν τολμήσετε· ἢν δὲ τὰς εὐθύνας ὑποσχὼν καθαρὸς ὑμῖν καὶ ἀνεπίληπτος εὑρίσκωμαι, ἀφήσουσί με οἱ δικασταί, ὑμεῖς δὲ εἰς τοὺς ἐξαπατήσαντας ὑμᾶς καὶ παροξύναντας καθ' ἡμῶν τὴν ὀργὴν τρέψετε.

ΠΛΑΤΩΝ

9 Τοῦτ' ἐκεῖνο· εἰς πεδίον τὸν ἵππον, ὡς παρακρουσάμενος τοὺς δικαστὰς ἀπέλθῃς. φασὶ γοῦν ῥήτορά σε καὶ δικανικόν τινα εἶναι καὶ πανοῦργον ἐν τοῖς λόγοις. τίνα δὲ καὶ δικαστὴν ἐθέλεις γενέσθαι, ὅντινα μὴ σὺ δωροδοκήσας, οἷα πολλὰ ποιεῖτε, ἄδικα πείσεις ὑπὲρ σοῦ ψηφίσασθαι;

ΠΑΡΡΗΣΙΑΔΗΣ

Θαρρεῖτε τούτου γε ἕνεκα· οὐδένα τοιοῦτον διαιτητὴν ὕποπτον ἢ ἀμφίβολον ἀξιώσαιμ' ἂν

you, and you alone, were surely far away from anything of that kind. But, however that may be, my masters, do not put me to death unsentenced and unheard. This too was once a trait of yours, not to deal with fellow-citizens on a basis of force and superior strength, but to settle your differences by course of law, according a hearing and in your turn receiving one. So let us choose a judge, and then you may bring your complaint either jointly or through anyone whom you may elect to represent you all; and I will defend myself against your charges. Then, if I am proven guilty, and the court passes that verdict upon me, I will submit, of course, to the punishment that I deserve, and you will not have taken it upon yourselves to do anything high-handed. But if after I have undergone my investigation I am found innocent and irreproachable, the jury will discharge me, and you will turn your anger against those who have misled you and set you against me.

PLATO

There we have it! "Cavalry into the open," so that you may give the slip to the jury and get away.[1] At any rate, they say that you are an orator and a lawyer and a wizard at making speeches. And whom do you wish to be judge, what is more? It must be someone whom you cannot influence by a bribe, as your sort often do, to cast an unjust ballot in your favour.

FRANKNESS

Do not be alarmed on that score. I should not care to have any such referee of suspicious or doubtful

[1] As cavalry seeks open country to manœuvre in, so the lawyer seeks the courtroom. Compare Plato, *Theaetetus*, 183 d: *ἱππέας εἰς πεδίον προκαλεῖ, Σωκράτη εἰς λόγους προκαλούμενος.*

γενέσθαι καὶ ὅστις ἀποδώσεταί μοι τὴν ψῆφον. ὁρᾶτε γοῦν, τὴν Φιλοσοφίαν αὐτὴν μεθ' ὑμῶν ποιοῦμαι δικάστριαν ἔγωγε.

ΠΛΑΤΩΝ

Καὶ τίς ἂν κατηγορήσειεν, εἴ γε ἡμεῖς δικάσομεν;

ΠΑΡΡΗΣΙΑΔΗΣ

Οἱ αὐτοὶ κατηγορεῖτε καὶ δικάζετε· οὐδὲν οὐδὲ τοῦτο δέδια. τοσοῦτον ὑπερφέρω τοῖς δικαίοις καὶ ἐκ περιουσίας ἀπολογήσεσθαι ὑπολαμβάνω.

ΠΛΑΤΩΝ

10 Τί ποιοῦμεν, ὦ Πυθαγόρα καὶ Σώκρατες; ἔοικε γὰρ ἀνὴρ οὐκ ἄλογα προκαλεῖσθαι δικάζεσθαι ἀξιῶν.

ΣΩΚΡΑΤΗΣ

Τί δὲ ἄλλο ἢ βαδίζωμεν ἐπὶ τὸ δικαστήριον καὶ τὴν Φιλοσοφίαν παραλαβόντες ἀκούσωμεν ὅ τι καὶ ἀπολογήσεται· τὸ πρὸ δίκης γὰρ οὐχ ἡμέτερον, ἀλλὰ δεινῶς ἰδιωτικόν, ὀργίλων τινῶν ἀνθρώπων καὶ τὸ δίκαιον ἐν τῇ χειρὶ τιθεμένων. παρέξομεν οὖν ἀφορμὰς τοῖς κακηγορεῖν ἐθέλουσιν καταλεύσαντες ἄνδρα μηδὲ ἀπολογησάμενον ὑπὲρ ἑαυτοῦ, καὶ ταῦτα δικαιοσύνῃ χαίρειν αὐτοὶ λέγοντες. ἢ τί ἂν εἴποιμεν Ἀνύτου καὶ Μελήτου πέρι, τῶν ἐμοῦ κατηγορησάντων, ἢ τῶν τότε δικαστῶν, εἰ οὗτος τεθνήξεται μηδὲ τὸ παράπαν ὕδατος μεταλαβών;

ΠΛΑΤΩΝ

Ἄριστα παραινεῖς, ὦ Σώκρατες· ὥστε ἀπίωμεν ἐπὶ τὴν Φιλοσοφίαν. ἡ δὲ δικασάτω, καὶ ἡμεῖς ἀγαπήσομεν οἷς ἂν ἐκείνη διαγνῷ.

character, who would sell me his vote. See, for my part I nominate Philosophy herself to the bench, and you yourselves also!

PLATO

And who can conduct the prosecution if we are to be jurors?

FRANKNESS

Be prosecutors and jurors at the same time. Even that arrangement has no terrors for me, since I have so much the better of you in the justice of my case and expect to be so over-stocked with pleas.

PLATO

What shall we do, Pythagoras and Socrates? Really, the man seems to be making a reasonable request in demanding a trial.

SOCRATES

What *can* we do but go to court, taking Philosophy with us, and hear his defence, whatever it may be. Prejudgment is not our way; it is terribly unprofessional, characteristic of hot-headed fellows who hold that might is right. We shall lay ourselves open to hard words from those who like to deal in them if we stone a man who has had no opportunity even to plead his case, especially as we ourselves maintain that we delight in just dealing. What could we say of Anytus and Meletus, who prosecuted me, or of the jurors on that occasion, if this fellow is to die without getting any hearing at all? [1]

PLATO

Excellent advice, Socrates; so let us go and get Philosophy. She shall judge, and we shall be content with her decision, whatever it may be.

[1] Literally, "without getting any water at all"; *i.e.* any of the time ordinarily allowed for court speeches, which was apportioned with a water-clock.

ΠΑΡΡΗΣΙΑΔΗΣ

11 Εὖ γε, ὦ σοφώτατοι, ἀμείνω ταῦτα καὶ νομιμώτερα. τοὺς μέντοι λίθους φυλάττετε, ὡς ἔφην· δεήσει γὰρ αὐτῶν μικρὸν ὕστερον ἐν τῷ δικαστηρίῳ.

Ποῦ δὲ τὴν Φιλοσοφίαν εὕροι τις ἄν; οὐ γὰρ οἶδα ἔνθα οἰκεῖ· καίτοι πάνυ πολὺν ἐπλανήθην χρόνον ἀναζητῶν τὴν οἰκίαν, ὡς συγγενοίμην αὐτῇ. εἶτα ἐντυγχάνων ἄν τισι τριβώνια περιβεβλημένοις καὶ πώγωνας βαθεῖς καθειμένοις παρ' αὐτῆς ἐκείνης ἥκειν φάσκουσιν, οἰόμενος εἰδέναι αὐτοὺς ἀνηρώτων· οἱ δὲ πολὺ μᾶλλον ἐμοῦ ἀγνοοῦντες ἢ οὐδὲν ὅλως ἀπεκρίναντό μοι, ὡς μὴ ἐλέγχοιντο οὐκ εἰδότες, ἢ ἄλλην θύραν ἀντ' ἄλλης ἐπεδείκνυον. οὐδέπω γοῦν καὶ τήμερον ἐξευρεῖν δεδύνημαι τὴν οἰκίαν.

12 Πολλάκις δὲ ἢ αὐτὸς εἰκάσας ἢ ξεναγήσαντός τινος ἧκον ἂν ἐπί τινας θύρας βεβαίως ἐλπίσας τότε γοῦν εὑρηκέναι, τεκμαιρόμενος τῷ πλήθει τῶν εἰσιόντων τε καὶ ἐξιόντων, ἁπάντων σκυθρωπῶν καὶ τὰ σχήματα εὐσταλῶν καὶ φροντιστικῶν τὴν πρόσοψιν· μετὰ τούτων οὖν συμπαραβυσθεὶς καὶ αὐτὸς εἰσῆλθον ἄν. εἶτα ἑώρων γύναιόν τι οὐχ ἁπλοϊκόν, εἰ καὶ ὅτι μάλιστα εἰς τὸ ἀφελὲς καὶ ἀκόσμητον ἑαυτὴν ἐπερρύθμιζεν, ἀλλὰ κατεφάνη μοι αὐτίκα οὐδὲ τὸ ἄνετον δοκοῦν τῆς κόμης ἀκαλλώπιστον ἐῶσα οὐδὲ τοῦ ἱματίου τὴν ἀναβολὴν ἀνεπιτηδεύτως περιστέλλουσα· πρόδηλος δὲ ἦν κοσμουμένη αὐτοῖς καὶ πρὸς εὐπρέπειαν τῷ ἀθεραπεύτῳ δοκοῦντι προσχρωμένη. ὑπεφαίνετο δέ τι καὶ ψιμύθιον καὶ φῦκος, καὶ τὰ ῥήματα πάνυ ἑταιρικά, καὶ ἐπαινουμένη ὑπὸ τῶν ἐρασ-

FRANKNESS

Well done, most learned sirs; this course is better and more legal. Keep your stones, however, as I said; for you will need them presently at court.

But where is Philosophy to be found? For my part I do not know where she lives. Yet I wandered very long in search of her dwelling, so that I might study with her. Then I met men with short cloaks and long beards who professed to come directly from her; and thinking that they knew, I questioned them. But they were far more at a loss than I, and either made no answer, in order that they might not be convicted of ignorance, or else pointed out one door after another. Even to this day I have been unable to find her house.

Often, either by guesswork on my own part or under the guidance of someone else, I would go to a door in the firm belief that at last I had found it, drawing my conclusion from the number of men that came and went, all solemn of countenance, decorous in dress, and studious in looks. So I would thrust myself among them and enter also. Then I always saw a hussy who was far from ingenuous, however much she strove to bring herself into harmony with simplicity and plainness. On the contrary, I perceived at once that she did not leave the apparent disorder of her hair unenhanced by art, nor let her mantle hang about her in unstudied folds. It was patent that she used it all as a make-up and employed her seeming negligence to heighten her attractiveness. There were also evidences of enamel and rouge; her talk was quite that of a courtesan; she delighted in being praised by her lovers for her

τῶν εἰς κάλλος ἔχαιρε, καὶ εἰ δοίη τις προχείρως ἐδέχετο, καὶ τοὺς πλουσιωτέρους ἂν παρακαθισαμένη πλησίον τοὺς πένητας τῶν ἐραστῶν οὐδὲ προσέβλεπεν. πολλάκις δὲ καὶ γυμνωθείσης αὐτῆς κατὰ τὸ ἀκούσιον ἑώρων περιδέραια χρυσᾶ τῶν κλοιῶν[1] παχύτερα. ταῦτα ἰδὼν ἐπὶ πόδα[2] ἂν εὐθὺς ἀνέστρεφον, οἰκτείρας δηλαδὴ τοὺς κακοδαίμονας ἐκείνους ἑλκομένους πρὸς αὐτῆς οὐ τῆς ῥινὸς ἀλλὰ τοῦ πώγωνος καὶ κατὰ τὸν Ἰξίονα εἰδώλῳ ἀντὶ τῆς Ἥρας συνόντας.

ΠΛΑΤΩΝ

13 Τοῦτο μὲν ὀρθῶς ἔλεξας· οὐ γὰρ πρόδηλος οὐδὲ πᾶσι γνώριμος ἡ θύρα. πλὴν ἀλλὰ οὐδὲν δεήσει βαδίζειν ἐπὶ τὴν οἰκίαν· ἐνταῦθα γὰρ ἐν Κεραμεικῷ ὑπομενοῦμεν αὐτήν. ἡ δὲ ἤδη που ἀφίξεται ἐπανιοῦσα ἐξ Ἀκαδημίας, ὡς περιπατήσειε καὶ ἐν τῇ Ποικίλῃ· τοῦτο γὰρ ὁσημέραι ποιεῖν ἔθος αὐτῇ· μᾶλλον δὲ ἤδη πρόσεισιν. ὁρᾷς τὴν κόσμιον, τὴν ἀπὸ τοῦ σχήματος, τὴν προσηνῆ τὸ βλέμμα, τὴν ἐπὶ συννοίας ἠρέμα βαδίζουσαν;

ΠΑΡΡΗΣΙΑΔΗΣ

Πολλὰς ὁμοίας ὁρῶ τό γε σχῆμα καὶ τὸ βάδισμα καὶ τὴν ἀναβολήν. καίτοι μία πάντως ἥ γε ἀληθὴς Φιλοσοφία καὶ ἐν αὐταῖς.

ΠΛΑΤΩΝ

Εὖ λέγεις. ἀλλὰ δηλώσει ἥτις ἐστὶ φθεγξαμένη μόνον.

ΦΙΛΟΣΟΦΙΑ

14 Παπαῖ· τί Πλάτων καὶ Χρύσιππος ἄνω καὶ Ἀριστοτέλης καὶ οἱ λοιποὶ ἅπαντες, αὐτὰ δὴ τὰ

[1] κλοιῶν β: ἐγχέλεων γ (eels).
[2] ἐπὶ πόδα Cobet: ἐπὶ πόδας MSS.

beauty; she took eagerly any presents that were offered; and she would let her wealthy lovers sit close beside her, but would not even look at those who were poor. And often when she exposed her throat as if by accident, I saw gold necklaces thicker than shackles. On observing all this I would withdraw at once, pitying, as you may well believe, those poor unfortunates whom she was leading, not by the nose, but by the beard, and who, like Ixion, embraced but a phantom and not Hera.

PLATO

You are right in one point: the door is not conspicuous and not known to all. However, there will be no need to go to her house. We shall wait for her here in the Potters' Quarter. She will come here presently, no doubt, on her way back from the Academy, to stroll in the Painted Porch also, for it is her custom to do so every day. In fact, here she comes now. Do you see her, the mannerly one, the one in the mantle, soft of eye, walking slowly, rapt in thought?

FRANKNESS

I see many who are alike in mantle, walk, and fashion. Yet surely only one, even among them, is the true Philosophy.

PLATO

Right, but she will show you who she is, just by speaking.

PHILOSOPHY

Ah! What are you all doing in the upper world, Plato and Chrysippus and Aristotle and the rest of

κεφάλαιά μου τῶν μαθημάτων; τί αὖθις εἰς τὸν βίον; ἆρά τι ὑμᾶς ἐλύπει τῶν κάτω; ὀργιζομένοις γοῦν ἐοίκατε. καὶ τίνα τοῦτον συλλαβόντες ἄγετε; ἦ που τυμβωρύχος τις ἢ ἀνδροφόνος ἢ ἱερόσυλός ἐστιν;

ΠΛΑΤΩΝ

Νὴ Δία, ὦ Φιλοσοφία, πάντων γε ἱεροσύλων ἀσεβέστατος, ὃς τὴν ἱερωτάτην σὲ κακῶς ἀγορεύειν ἐπεχείρησεν καὶ ἡμᾶς ἅπαντας, ὁπόσοι τι παρὰ σοῦ μαθόντες τοῖς μεθ' ἡμᾶς καταλελοίπαμεν.

ΦΙΛΟΣΟΦΙΑ

Εἶτα ἠγανακτήσατε λοιδορησαμένου τινός, καὶ ταῦτα εἰδότες ἐμέ, οἷα πρὸς τῆς Κωμῳδίας ἀκούουσα ἐν Διονυσίοις ὅμως φίλην τε αὐτὴν ἥγημαι καὶ οὔτε ἐδικασάμην οὔτε ᾐτιασάμην προσελθοῦσα, ἐφίημι δὲ παίζειν τὰ εἰκότα καὶ τὰ συνήθη τῇ ἑορτῇ; οἶδα γὰρ ὡς οὐκ ἄν τι ὑπὸ σκώμματος χεῖρον γένοιτο, ἀλλὰ τοὐναντίον ὅπερ ἂν ᾖ καλόν, ὥσπερ τὸ χρυσίον ἀποσμώμενον τοῖς κόμμασι, λαμπρότερον ἀποστίλβει καὶ φανερώτερον γίγνεται. ὑμεῖς δὲ οὐκ οἶδα ὅπως ὀργίλοι καὶ ἀγανακτικοὶ γεγόνατε. τί δ' οὖν αὐτὸν ἄγχετε;

ΠΛΑΤΩΝ

Μίαν ἡμέραν ταύτην παραιτησάμενοι ἥκομεν ἐπ' αὐτὸν ὡς ὑπόσχῃ τὴν ἀξίαν ὧν δέδρακεν. φῆμαι γὰρ ἡμῖν διήγγελλον οἷα ἔλεγεν εἰς τὰ πλήθη καθ' ἡμῶν.

ΦΙΛΟΣΟΦΙΑ

15 Εἶτα πρὸ δίκης οὐδὲ ἀπολογησάμενον ἀποκτενεῖτε; δῆλος γοῦν ἐστιν εἰπεῖν τι θέλων.

you, the very fore-front of my studies? Why have you come back to life? Did anything in the under-world distress you? You certainly appear to be angry. And who is this man whom you have taken into custody? Some ghoul or murderer or profaner of holiness, I suppose.

PLATO

Yes, indeed, Philosophy, the most impious of all profaners, for he made bold to speak ill of you, than whom nothing is more holy, and of us, one and all, who learned something from you and have left it to those who came after us.

PHILOSOPHY

Then it made you angry to be vituperated? And yet you knew that in spite of the hard names which Comedy calls me during the festival of Dionysus, I have held her my friend, and neither sued her at law nor berated her in private, but permit her to make the fun that is in keeping and customary at the festival. I am aware, you see, that no harm can be done by a joke; that, on the contrary, whatever is beautiful shines brighter and becomes more conspicuous, like gold cleansed by its minting. But you, for some reason or other, have grown hot-tempered and violent. Tell me, why do you throttle him?

PLATO

Obtaining leave of absence for this one day, we came to get him, so that he may pay the penalty for what he has done; for rumours repeatedly told us what sort of language he used in public against us.

PHILOSOPHY

Then you intend to put him to death before trial, without even a chance to defend himself? It is certainly clear that he wants to make a statement.

ΠΛΑΤΩΝ

Οὔκ, ἀλλ' ἐπὶ σὲ τὸ πᾶν ἀνεβαλόμεθα, καὶ σοὶ ὅτι ἂν δοκῇ, τοῦτο ποιήσῃ τέλος τῆς δίκης.

ΦΙΛΟΣΟΦΙΑ

Τί φὴς σύ;

ΠΑΡΡΗΣΙΑΔΗΣ

Τοῦτο αὐτό, ὦ δέσποινα Φιλοσοφία, ἥπερ καὶ μόνη τἀληθὲς ἂν ἐξευρεῖν[1] δύναιο· μόλις γοῦν εὑρόμην πολλὰ ἱκετεύσας τὸ σοὶ φυλαχθῆναι τὴν δίκην.

ΠΛΑΤΩΝ

Νῦν, ὦ κατάρατε, δέσποιναν αὐτὴν καλεῖς; πρῴην δὲ τὸ ἀτιμότατον Φιλοσοφίαν ἀπέφαινες ἐν τοσούτῳ θεάτρῳ ἀποκηρύττων κατὰ μέρη δύ' ὀβολῶν ἕκαστον εἶδος αὐτῆς τῶν λόγων.

ΦΙΛΟΣΟΦΙΑ

Ὁρᾶτε μὴ οὐ Φιλοσοφίαν οὗτός γε ἀλλὰ γόητας ἄνδρας ἐπὶ τῷ ἡμετέρῳ ὀνόματι πολλὰ καὶ μιαρὰ πράττοντας ἠγόρευεν κακῶς.

ΠΑΡΡΗΣΙΑΔΗΣ

Εἴσῃ αὐτίκα, ἢν ἐθέλῃς ἀπολογουμένου ἀκούειν μόνον.

ΦΙΛΟΣΟΦΙΑ

Ἀπίωμεν εἰς Ἄρειον πάγον, μᾶλλον δὲ εἰς τὴν ἀκρόπολιν αὐτήν, ὡς ἂν ἐκ περιωπῆς ἅμα κατα-16 φανείη πάντα ἐν τῇ πόλει. ὑμεῖς δέ, ὦ φίλαι, ἐν τῇ Ποικίλῃ τέως περιπατήσατε· ἥξω γὰρ ὑμῖν ἐκδικάσασα τὴν δίκην.

ΠΑΡΡΗΣΙΑΔΗΣ

Τίνες δέ εἰσιν, ὦ Φιλοσοφία; πάνυ γάρ μοι κόσμιαι καὶ αὗται δοκοῦσιν.

[1] ἂν ἐξευρεῖν A.M.H.: ἐξευρεῖν γ, ἂν εὑρεῖν β.

PLATO

No: we have referred the whole matter to you, and you are to conclude the trial as you think best.

PHILOSOPHY

You, there, what do you say?

FRANKNESS

Precisely what they do, my Lady Philosophy; for you, even without aid, could discover the truth. In fact, it was only with difficulty, after a deal of entreaty, that I secured the reservation of the case for you.

PLATO

Now, you scoundrel, you call her "My Lady," do you? Just the other day you made her out to be utterly contemptible by offering every form of her doctrines for sale at two obols apiece before so large an audience

PHILOSOPHY

Careful! Perhaps *his* abuse was not directed against Philosophy, but against impostors who do much that is vile in our name.

FRANKNESS

You shall see at once, if you will only hear my defence.

PHILOSOPHY

Let us go to the Areopagus, or rather, to the Acropolis itself, so that at the same time we may get a bird's eye view of everything in the city. You, my dears, may walk about in the Painted Porch meanwhile: I shall join you after concluding the trial.

FRANKNESS

Who are they, Philosophy? They too seem very mannerly.

ΦΙΛΟΣΟΦΙΑ

Ἀρετὴ μὲν ἡ ἀνδρώδης αὕτη, Σωφροσύνη δὲ ἐκείνη καὶ Δικαιοσύνη ἡ[1] παρ' αὐτήν. ἡ προηγουμένη δὲ Παιδεία, ἡ ἀμυδρὰ δὲ καὶ ἀσαφὴς τὸ χρῶμα ἡ Ἀλήθειά ἐστιν.

ΠΑΡΡΗΣΙΑΔΗΣ

Οὐχ ὁρῶ ἥντινα καὶ λέγεις.

ΦΙΛΟΣΟΦΙΑ

Τὴν ἀκαλλώπιστον ἐκείνην οὐχ ὁρᾷς, τὴν γυμνήν, τὴν ὑποφεύγουσαν ἀεὶ καὶ διολισθάνουσαν;

ΠΑΡΡΗΣΙΑΔΗΣ

Ὁρῶ νῦν μόλις. ἀλλὰ τί οὐχὶ καὶ ταύτας ἄγεις, ὡς πλῆρες γένοιτο καὶ ἐντελὲς τὸ συνέδριον; τὴν Ἀλήθειαν δέ γε καὶ συνήγορον ἀναβιβάσασθαι πρὸς τὴν δίκην βούλομαι.

ΦΙΛΟΣΟΦΙΑ

Νὴ Δία, ἀκολουθήσατε καὶ ὑμεῖς· οὐ βαρὺ γὰρ μίαν δικάσαι δίκην, καὶ ταῦτα περὶ τῶν ἡμετέρων ἐσομένην.

ΑΛΗΘΕΙΑ

17 Ἄπιτε ὑμεῖς· ἐγὼ γὰρ οὐδὲν δέομαι ἀκούειν ἃ πάλαι οἶδα ὁποῖά ἐστιν.

ΦΙΛΟΣΟΦΙΑ

Ἀλλ' ἡμῖν, ὦ Ἀλήθεια, ἐν δέοντι συνδικάζοις ἂν καὶ καταμηνύοις ἕκαστα.

ΑΛΗΘΕΙΑ

Οὐκοῦν ἐπάγωμαι καὶ τὼ θεραπαινιδίω τούτω εὐνοϊκοτάτω μοι ὄντε;

ΦΙΛΟΣΟΦΙΑ

Καὶ μάλα ὁπόσας ἂν ἐθέλῃς.

[1] ἡ Fritzsche: not in MSS.

PHILOSOPHY

This one with the masculine air is Virtue; yonder is Temperance, and there beside her Justice; the one in advance is Culture, and she that is faint and indistinct in colour is Truth.

FRANKNESS

I do not see which one you really mean.

PHILOSOPHY

Do you not see the unadorned one over there, naked, always shrinking into the background and slipping away?

FRANKNESS

I can just see her now. But why not bring them also, in order that the meeting may be full and perfect? As to Truth, indeed, I wish to introduce her into the trial as an advocate.

PHILOSOPHY

To be sure. (*To the others*) Come with us also. It is not a hard matter to try a single case, particularly one that will involve our own interests.

TRUTH

You others go: I do not need to hear what I have long known all about.

PHILOSOPHY

But it would help us, Truth, if you should join in the trial and give us information on each point.

TRUTH

Then shall I bring along these two waiting-women, who are in very close sympathy with me?

PHILOSOPHY

Yes, indeed, as many as you wish.

ΑΛΗΘΕΙΑ

Ἕπεσθον, ὦ Ἐλευθερία καὶ Παρρησία, μεθ' ἡμῶν, ὡς τὸν δείλαιον τουτονὶ ἀνθρωπίσκον ἐραστὴν ἡμέτερον ὄντα καὶ κινδυνεύοντα ἐπὶ μηδεμιᾷ προφάσει δικαίᾳ σῶσαι δυνηθῶμεν. σὺ δέ, ὦ Ἔλεγχε, αὐτοῦ περίμεινον.

ΠΑΡΡΗΣΙΑΔΗΣ

Μηδαμῶς, ὦ δέσποινα, ἡκέτω δὲ καὶ οὗτος, εἰ καί τις ἄλλος·[1] οὐ γὰρ τοῖς τυχοῦσι θηρίοις προσπολεμῆσαι δεήσει με, ἀλλ'[2] ἀλαζόσιν ἀνθρώποις καὶ δυσελέγκτοις, ἀεί τινας ἀποφυγὰς εὑρισκομένοις, ὥστε ἀναγκαῖος ὁ Ἔλεγχος.

ΕΛΕΓΧΟΣ[3]

Ἀναγκαιότατος μὲν οὖν· ἄμεινον δέ, εἰ καὶ τὴν Ἀπόδειξιν παραλάβοις.

ΑΛΗΘΕΙΑ

Ἕπεσθε πάντες, ἐπείπερ ἀναγκαῖοι δοκεῖτε πρὸς τὴν δίκην.

ΠΛΑΤΩΝ

18 Ὁρᾷς; προσεταιρίζεται καθ' ἡμῶν, ὦ Φιλοσοφία, τὴν Ἀλήθειαν.

ΦΙΛΟΣΟΦΙΑ

Εἶτα δέδιτε, ὦ Πλάτων καὶ Χρύσιππε καὶ Ἀριστότελες, μή τι ψεύσηται ὑπὲρ αὐτοῦ Ἀλήθεια οὖσα;

ΠΛΑΤΩΝ

Οὐ τοῦτο, ἀλλὰ δεινῶς πανοῦργός ἐστιν καὶ κολακικός· ὥστε παραπείσει αὐτήν.

[1] εἰ καί τις ἄλλος Fritzsche : καὶ εἴ τις ἄλλος γ ; not in β.
[2] ἀλλ' edd.: not in MSS.
[3] ΕΛΕΓΧΟΣ Gesner : ΦΙΛΟΣ. vulg.

TRUTH

Come with us, Liberty and Free-speech, so that we may be able to rescue this poor creature, our admirer, who is facing danger for no just reason. You, Investigation, may stay where you are.

FRANKNESS

Hold, my lady: let him come too, if anyone is to come. Those whom I shall have to fight to-day are none of your ordinary cattle, but pretentious fellows, hard to argue down, always finding some loophole or other, so that Investigation is necessary.

INVESTIGATION

Yes, most necessary: and you had better take Proof along too.

TRUTH

Come, all of you, since you appear to be necessary to the case.

PLATO

Do you see that? He is suborning Truth against us, Philosophy.

PHILOSOPHY

Then you, Plato and Chrysippus and Aristotle, are afraid that she, Truth, may tell some lie in his behalf?

PLATO

It isn't that, but he is terribly unprincipled and smooth-tongued, so that he will seduce her.

ΦΙΛΟΣΟΦΙΑ

Θαρρεῖτε· οὐδὲν μὴ γένηται ἄδικον, Δικαιο-
19 σύνης ταύτης συμπαρούσης. ἀνίωμεν οὖν. ἀλλὰ εἰπέ μοι σύ, τί σοι τοὔνομα;

ΠΑΡΡΗΣΙΑΔΗΣ

Ἐμοί; Παρρησιάδης Ἀληθίωνος τοῦ Ἐλεγξικλέους.

ΦΙΛΟΣΟΦΙΑ

Πατρὶς δέ;

ΠΑΡΡΗΣΙΑΔΗΣ

Σύρος, ὦ Φιλοσοφία, τῶν Ἐπευφρατιδίων. ἀλλὰ τί τοῦτο; καὶ γὰρ τούτων τινὰς οἶδα τῶν ἀντιδίκων μου οὐχ ἧττον ἐμοῦ βαρβάρους τὸ γένος· ὁ τρόπος δὲ καὶ ἡ παιδεία οὐ κατὰ Σολέας ἢ Κυπρίους ἢ Βαβυλωνίους ἢ Σταγειρίτας. καίτοι πρός γε σὲ οὐδὲν ἂν ἔλαττον γένοιτο οὐδ' εἰ τὴν φωνὴν βάρβαρος εἴη τις, εἴπερ ἡ γνώμη ὀρθὴ καὶ δικαία φαίνοιτο οὖσα.

ΦΙΛΟΣΟΦΙΑ

20 Εὖ λέγεις· ἄλλως γοῦν ἠρόμην. ἡ τέχνη δέ σοι τίς; ἄξιον γὰρ ἐπίστασθαι τοῦτό γε.

ΠΑΡΡΗΣΙΑΔΗΣ

Μισαλαζών εἰμι καὶ μισογόης καὶ μισοψευδὴς καὶ μισότυφος καὶ μισῶ πᾶν τὸ τοιουτῶδες εἶδος τῶν μιαρῶν ἀνθρώπων· πάνυ δὲ πολλοί εἰσιν, ὡς οἶσθα.

ΦΙΛΟΣΟΦΙΑ

Ἡράκλεις, πολυμισῆ τινα μέτει τὴν τέχνην.

PHILOSOPHY

Have no fear. No injustice will be done while we have Justice here with us. Let us go up, then. But tell me, what is your name?

FRANKNESS

Mine? Frankness, son of Truthful, son of Renowned Investigator.

PHILOSOPHY

And your country?

FRANKNESS

I am a Syrian, Philosophy, from the banks of the Euphrates. But what of that? I know that some of my opponents here are just as foreign-born as I: but in their manners and culture they are not like men of Soli or Cyprus or Babylon or Stageira.[1] Yet as far as you are concerned it would make no difference even if a man's speech were foreign, if only his way of thinking were manifestly right and just.

PHILOSOPHY

True: it was a needless question, to be sure. But what is your calling? That at least is worth knowing.

FRANKNESS

I am a bluff-hater, cheat-hater, liar-hater, vanity-hater, and hate all that sort of scoundrels, who are very numerous, as you know.

PHILOSOPHY

Heracles! You follow a hateful calling!

[1] Although they were born there: Chrysippus in Soli, Aristotle in Stageira. No philosopher mentioned by name in this piece came from Cyprus or from Babylon, and these allusions are not clear. Perhaps Lucian has in mind Zeno of Citium and Poseidonius of Seleucia on the Tigris.

ΠΑΡΡΗΣΙΑΔΗΣ

Εὖ λέγεις· ὁρᾷς γοῦν ὁπόσοις ἀπεχθάνομαι καὶ ὡς κινδυνεύω δι' αὐτήν.

Οὐ μὴν ἀλλὰ καὶ τὴν ἐναντίαν αὐτῇ πάνυ ἀκριβῶς οἶδα, λέγω δὲ τὴν ἀπὸ τοῦ φιλο[1] τὴν ἀρχὴν ἔχουσαν· φιλαλήθης τε γὰρ καὶ φιλόκαλος καὶ φιλαπλοϊκὸς καὶ ὅσα τῷ φιλεῖσθαι συγγενῆ. πλὴν ἀλλ' ὀλίγοι πάνυ ταύτης ἄξιοι τῆς τέχνης, οἱ δὲ ὑπὸ τῇ ἐναντίᾳ ταττόμενοι καὶ τῷ μίσει οἰκειότεροι πεντακισμύριοι. κινδυνεύω τοιγαροῦν τὴν μὲν ὑπ' ἀργίας ἀπομαθεῖν ἤδη, τὴν δὲ πάνυ ἠκριβωκέναι.

ΦΙΛΟΣΟΦΙΑ

Καὶ μὴν οὐκ ἐχρῆν· τοῦ γὰρ αὐτοῦ καὶ τάδε, φασί, καὶ τάδε· ὥστε μὴ διαίρει τὼ τέχνα· μία γὰρ ἐστὸν δύ' εἶναι δοκοῦσα.

ΠΑΡΡΗΣΙΑΔΗΣ

Ἄμεινον σὺ ταῦτα οἶσθα, ὦ Φιλοσοφία. τὸ μέντοι ἐμὸν τοιοῦτόν ἐστιν, οἷον τοὺς μὲν πονηροὺς μισεῖν, ἐπαινεῖν δὲ τοὺς χρηστοὺς καὶ φιλεῖν.

ΦΙΛΟΣΟΦΙΑ

21 Ἄγε δή, πάρεσμεν γὰρ ἔνθα ἐχρῆν, ἐνταῦθά που ἐν τῷ προνάῳ τῆς Πολιάδος δικάσωμεν. ἡ Ἱέρεια διάθες ἡμῖν τὰ βάθρα, ἡμεῖς δὲ ἐν τοσούτῳ προσκυνήσωμεν τὴν θεόν.

[1] φιλο Halm: φιλῶ γ, φίλου β. Cf. Arist. *Vesp.* 77, Luc. *adv. Ind.* 20.

FRANKNESS

You are right. You see, in fact, how many have come to dislike me and how I am imperilled because I follow it.

However, I am very well up in the opposite calling, too: I mean the one with love for a base; for I am a truth-lover, a beauty-lover, a simplicity-lover, and a lover of all else that is kindred to love. But there are very few who deserve to have this calling practised upon them, while those who come under the other and are closer akin to hatefulness number untold thousands. So the chances are that by this time I have lost my skill in the one calling for lack of practice, but have become very expert in the other.

PHILOSOPHY

But that ought not to be so, for if a man can do the one, they say, he can do the other. So do not distinguish the two callings; they are but one, though they seem two.

FRANKNESS

You know best as to that, Philosophy. For my part, however, I am so constituted as to hate rascals and to commend and love honest men.

PHILOSOPHY

Come, now, since we are where we planned to be, let us hold our court somewhere hereabouts in the portico of Our Lady of the Citadel.[1] Priestess, arrange the benches for us. Let us in the meantime pay our homage to the goddess.

[1] Athena Polias, who shared with Erechtheus the temple now known as the Erechtheum.

ΠΑΡΡΗΣΙΑΔΗΣ

Ὦ Πολιάς, ἐλθέ μοι κατὰ τῶν ἀλαζόνων σύμμαχος ἀναμνησθεῖσα ὁπόσα ἐπιορκούντων ὁσημέραι ἀκούεις αὐτῶν· καὶ ἃ πράττουσι δὲ μόνη ὁρᾷς ἅτε δὴ ἐπὶ σκοπῆς οἰκοῦσα.[1] νῦν καιρὸς ἀμύνασθαι αὐτούς. ἐμὲ δὲ ἤν που κρατούμενον ἴδῃς καὶ πλείους ὦσιν αἱ μέλαιναι, σὺ προσθεῖσα τὴν σεαυτῆς σῶζέ με.

ΦΙΛΟΣΟΦΙΑ

22 Εἶεν· ἡμεῖς μὲν ὑμῖν καὶ δὴ καθήμεθα ἕτοιμοι ἀκούειν τῶν λόγων, ὑμεῖς δὲ προελόμενοί τινα ἐξ ἁπάντων, ὅστις ἄριστα κατηγορῆσαι ἂν δοκεῖ, συνείρετε τὴν κατηγορίαν καὶ διελέγχετε· πάντας γὰρ ἅμα λέγειν ἀμήχανον.[2] σὺ δέ, ὦ Παρρησιάδη, ἀπολογήσῃ τὸ μετὰ τοῦτο.

ΠΛΑΤΩΝ

Τίς οὖν ὁ ἐπιτηδειότατος ἐξ ἡμῶν ἂν γένοιτο πρὸς τὴν δίκην;

ΧΡΥΣΙΠΠΟΣ

Σύ, ὦ Πλάτων. ἥ τε γὰρ μεγαλόνοια θαυμαστὴ καὶ ἡ καλλιφωνία δεινῶς Ἀττικὴ καὶ τὸ κεχαρισμένον καὶ πειθοῦς μεστὸν ἥ τε σύνεσις καὶ τὸ ἀκριβὲς καὶ τὸ ἐπαγωγὸν ἐν καιρῷ τῶν ἀποδείξεων, πάντα ταῦτά σοι ἀθρόα πρόσεστιν· ὥστε τὴν προηγορίαν δέχου καὶ ὑπὲρ ἁπάντων εἰπὲ τὰ εἰκότα. νῦν ἀναμνήσθητι πάντων ἐκείνων καὶ συμφόρει εἰς τὸ αὐτό, εἴ τί σοι πρὸς Γοργίαν ἢ Πῶλον ἢ Πρόδικον ἢ Ἱππίαν εἴρηται· δεινότερος οὗτός ἐστιν. ἐπίπαττε οὖν καὶ τῆς εἰρω-

[1] ἐπίσκοπος οὖσα β.
[2] οὐ γὰρ οἷόν τε πάντας ἅμα λέγειν γ.

FRANKNESS

Lady of the Citadel, come to my aid against the pretenders, remembering how many oaths thou dost hear them make and break each day, and what they do thou alone seest, dwelling as thou dost upon a lookout. Now is thine hour to requite them. If thou seest that I am being overborne, and that the black ballots are more than the half, add thou thine own and set me free.[1]

PHILOSOPHY

Well and good. Here we are for you, gentlemen, all seated in readiness to hear the speeches. Choose one of your number who in your opinion can best conduct the prosecution, and when you have done so, build up your complaint and establish your charge; it is not feasible for all to speak at once. You, Frankness, shall make your defence thereafter.

PLATO

Which of us, I wonder, would be the best fitted to handle the case?

CHRYSIPPUS

You, Plato. Marvellous sublimity, superlatively Attic elegance, charm and persuasiveness, insight, subtlety, opportune seductiveness in demonstration—all this is yours to the full. Accept the spokesmanship, therefore, and say whatever is appropriate in behalf of us all. Remember now all your former successes and put together any points you have urged against Gorgias or Polos or Hippias or Prodicus: this man is more able than they. So apply a light

[1] Frankness asks of Athena more aid than she generally gave; for the proverbial ballot of Athena merely decided a tie vote in favour of the defendant, as in the trial of Orestes.

νείας καὶ τὰ κομψὰ ἐκεῖνα καὶ συνεχῆ ἐρῶτα, κἄν σοι δοκῇ, κἀκεῖνό που παράβυσον, ὡς "ὁ μέγας ἐν οὐρανῷ Ζεὺς πτηνὸν ἅρμα ἐλαύνων" ἀγανακτήσειεν ἄν, εἰ μὴ οὗτος ὑπόσχοι τὴν δίκην.

ΠΛΑΤΩΝ

23 Μηδαμῶς, ἀλλά τινα τῶν σφοδροτέρων προχειρισώμεθα, Διογένη τοῦτον ἢ Ἀντισθένη ἢ Κράτητα ἢ καὶ σέ, ὦ Χρύσιππε· οὐ γὰρ δὴ κάλλους ἐν τῷ παρόντι καὶ δεινότητος συγγραφικῆς ὁ καιρός, ἀλλά τινος ἐλεγκτικῆς καὶ δικανικῆς παρασκευῆς· ῥήτωρ δὲ ὁ Παρρησιάδης ἐστίν.

ΔΙΟΓΕΝΗΣ

Ἀλλ' ἐγὼ αὐτοῦ κατηγορήσω· οὐδὲ γὰρ πάνυ μακρῶν οἶμαι τῶν λόγων δεήσεσθαι. καὶ ἄλλως ὑπὲρ ἅπαντας ὕβρισμαι δύ' ὀβολῶν πρῴην ἀποκεκηρυγμένος.

ΠΛΑΤΩΝ

Ὁ Διογένης, ὦ Φιλοσοφία, ἐρεῖ τὸν λόγον ὑπὲρ ἁπάντων. μέμνησο δέ, ὦ γενναῖε, μὴ τὰ σεαυτοῦ μόνον πρεσβεύειν ἐν τῇ κατηγορίᾳ, τὰ κοινὰ δὲ ὁρᾶν· εἰ γάρ τι καὶ πρὸς ἀλλήλους διαφερόμεθα ἐν τοῖς δόγμασι, σὺ δὲ τοῦτο μὲν μὴ ἐξέταζε, μηδὲ ὅστις ἐστὶν ὁ ἀληθέστερος νῦν λέγε, ὅλως δὲ ὑπὲρ Φιλοσοφίας αὐτῆς ἀγανάκτει περιυβρισμένης καὶ κακῶς ἀκουούσης ἐν τοῖς Παρρησιάδου λόγοις, καὶ τὰς προαιρέσεις ἀφείς, ἐν αἷς διαλλάττομεν, ὃ κοινὸν ἅπαντες ἔχομεν, τοῦτο ὑπερμάχει. ὅρα· σὲ μόνον προεστησάμεθα καὶ ἐν σοὶ τὰ πάντα ἡμῶν νῦν κινδυνεύεται, ἢ σεμνότατα δόξαι ἢ τοιαῦτα πιστευθῆναι οἷα οὗτος ἀπέφηνε.

sprinkling of irony, too, put those clever, incessant questions of yours, and if you think best, also slip it in somewhere that "great Zeus in heaven driving his winged car" would be angry if this man should not be punished.

PLATO

No, let us make use of someone more strenuous—Diogenes here, or Antisthenes, or Crates, or you yourself, Chrysippus. For surely what the occasion demands now is not elegance and literary distinction, but some degree of argumentative and forensic equipment: Frankness is a professional speaker.

DIOGENES

Well, then, I will be prosecutor, for we shall not require speeches of any great length, I suppose: and besides, I have been insulted beyond all of you, since I was auctioned off the other day for two obols.

PLATO

Diogenes will make the speech, Philosophy, for all of us. Remember, friend, not just to speak for yourself in the complaint, but to keep our common interests in view. If we do disagree with one another a little in our doctrines, you must not examine into that, or attempt to say who is the nearer right, but, in general, make an impassioned plea for Philosophy herself, because she has been heaped with insult and shamefully abused in the dialogues of Freespeaker; ignore the personal views wherein we differ, and fight for what we all have in common. Take note, you are our sole representative and it rests with you whether all our teachings are to seem worthy of high reverence or to be thought no better than this man made them out to be.

ΔΙΟΓΕΝΗΣ

24 Θαρρεῖτε, οὐδὲν ἐλλείψομεν· ὑπὲρ ἁπάντων ἐρῶ. κἂν ἡ Φιλοσοφία δὲ πρὸς τοὺς λόγους ἐπικλασθεῖσα—φύσει γὰρ ἥμερος καὶ πρᾶός ἐστιν—ἀφεῖναι διαβουλεύηται αὐτόν, ἀλλ᾽ οὐ τὰ ἐμὰ ἐνδεήσει· δείξω γὰρ αὐτῷ ὅτι μὴ μάτην ξυλοφοροῦμεν.

ΦΙΛΟΣΟΦΙΑ

Τοῦτο μὲν μηδαμῶς, ἀλλὰ τῷ λόγῳ μᾶλλον· ἄμεινον γὰρ ἤπερ τῷ ξύλῳ. μὴ μέλλε δ᾽ οὖν. ἤδη γὰρ ἐγκέχυται τὸ ὕδωρ καὶ πρὸς σὲ τὸ δικαστήριον ἀποβλέπει.

ΠΑΡΡΗΣΙΑΔΗΣ

Οἱ λοιποὶ καθιζέτωσαν, ὦ Φιλοσοφία, καὶ ψηφοφορείτωσαν μεθ᾽ ὑμῶν, Διογένης δὲ κατηγορείτω μόνος.

ΦΙΛΟΣΟΦΙΑ

Οὐ δέδιας οὖν μή σου καταψηφίσωνται;

ΠΑΡΡΗΣΙΑΔΗΣ

Οὐδαμῶς· πλείοσι γοῦν κρατῆσαι βούλομαι.

ΦΙΛΟΣΟΦΙΑ

Γενναῖά σου ταῦτα· καθίσατε δ᾽ οὖν. σὺ δέ, ὦ Διόγενες, λέγε.

ΔΙΟΓΕΝΗΣ

25 Οἷοι μὲν ἡμεῖς ἄνδρες ἐγενόμεθα παρὰ τὸν βίον, ὦ Φιλοσοφία, πάνυ ἀκριβῶς οἶσθα καὶ οὐδὲν δεῖ λόγων· ἵνα γὰρ τὸ κατ᾽ ἐμὲ σιωπήσω, ἀλλὰ Πυθαγόραν τοῦτον καὶ Πλάτωνα καὶ Ἀριστοτέλη καὶ Χρύσιππον καὶ τοὺς ἄλλους τίς οὐκ οἶδεν ὅσα εἰς τὸν βίον καλὰ εἰσεκομίσαντο; ἃ

DIOGENES

Do not be alarmed; we shall not come short: I will speak in behalf of all. Even if Philosophy, swayed by his eloquence—for she is naturally kindly and gentle—determines to acquit him, I for my part shall not be found wanting, for I will show him that we do not carry sticks for nothing!

PHILOSOPHY

Not by any means! Use arguments, rather, for that is better. But do not delay. The water already has been poured in,[1] and the jury has its eyes upon you.

FRANKNESS

Let the others[2] take seats, Philosophy, and cast their votes with your company, and let Diogenes be the only prosecutor.

PHILOSOPHY

Then are you not afraid they may find you guilty?

FRANKNESS

Not at all. In fact, I wish to win by a larger majority.

PHILOSOPHY

That is handsome of you. Well, then, take your seats, and you, Diogenes, begin your speech.

DIOGENES

What sort of men we were in life, Philosophy, you know right well, and I need not discuss that point at all; for who is not aware how much beauty was brought into life by Pythagoras here, Plato, Aristotle, Chrysippus and the others, to say nothing of myself?

[1] *i.e.* the water-clock has been filled.

[2] The rest of the philosophers, who are to sit on the jury (§ 9).

δὲ τοιούτους ὄντας ἡμᾶς ὁ τρισκατάρατος οὑτοσὶ Παρρησιάδης ὕβρικεν ἤδη ἐρῶ.

Ῥήτωρ γάρ τις, ὥς φασιν, ὤν, ἀπολιπὼν τὰ δικαστήρια καὶ τὰς ἐν ἐκείνοις εὐδοκιμήσεις, ὁπόσον ἢ δεινότητος ἢ ἀκμῆς ἐπεπόριστο ἐν τοῖς λόγοις, τοῦτο πᾶν ἐφ' ἡμᾶς συσκευασάμενος οὐ παύεται αὐτὸς[1] μὲν ἀγορεύων κακῶς γόητας καὶ ἀπατεῶνας ἀποκαλῶν, τὰ πλήθη δὲ ἀναπείθων καταγελᾶν ἡμῶν καὶ καταφρονεῖν ὡς τὸ μηδὲν ὄντων· μᾶλλον δὲ καὶ μισεῖσθαι πρὸς τῶν πολλῶν ἤδη πεποίηκεν αὐτούς τε ἡμᾶς καὶ σὲ τὴν Φιλοσοφίαν, φληνάφους καὶ λήρους ἀποκαλῶν τὰ σὰ καὶ τὰ σπουδαιότατα ὧν ἡμᾶς ἐπαίδευσας ἐπὶ χλευασμῷ διεξιών, ὥστε αὐτὸν μὲν κροτεῖσθαι καὶ ἐπαινεῖσθαι πρὸς τῶν θεατῶν, ἡμᾶς δὲ ὑβρίζεσθαι. φύσει γὰρ τοιοῦτόν ἐστιν ὁ πολὺς λεώς, χαίρουσι τοῖς ἀποσκώπτουσιν καὶ λοιδορουμένοις, καὶ μάλισθ' ὅταν τὰ σεμνότατα εἶναι δοκοῦντα διασύρηται, ὥσπερ ἀμέλει καὶ πάλαι ἔχαιρον Ἀριστοφάνει καὶ Εὐπόλιδι Σωκράτη τουτονὶ ἐπὶ χλευασίᾳ παράγουσιν ἐπὶ τὴν σκηνὴν καὶ κωμῳδοῦσιν ἀλλοκότους τινὰς περὶ αὐτοῦ κωμῳδίας.

Καίτοι ἐκεῖνοι μὲν καθ' ἑνὸς ἀνδρὸς ἐτόλμων τοιαῦτα, καὶ ἐν Διονυσίοις ἐφειμένον αὐτὸ ἔδρων, καὶ τὸ σκῶμμα ἐδόκει μέρος τι τῆς ἑορτῆς, καὶ

ὁ θεὸς ἴσως ἔχαιρε[2] φιλόγελώς τις ὤν.

26 ὁ δὲ τοὺς ἀρίστους συγκαλῶν, ἐκ πολλοῦ φροντίσας καὶ παρασκευασάμενος καὶ βλασφημίας

[1] αὐτὸς inserted by A.M.H.: ἡμᾶς Bekker; παύεται μὲν MSS. [2] ἔχαιρε Bekker, K. Schwartz; χαίρει MSS.

I shall proceed to speak of the insults which, in spite of our merit, this double-dyed scoundrel Frankness has dealt us.

He is a public speaker, they say: but abandoning the courts and the successes to be gained therein, he concentrated upon us all the eloquence and power that he had acquired in rhetoric, and not only unceasingly abuses us himself by calling us cheats and liars, but induces the public to laugh and sneer at us as if we amounted to nothing at all. More than that, he has at last made people actually hate you, Philosophy, as well as us by dubbing your doctrines stuff and nonsense and rehearsing in mockery all that is most serious in what you taught us, so as to get applause and praise from his audience for himself and contumely for us. The common sort are that way by nature; they delight in jesters and buffoons, and most of all when they criticise what is held in high reverence. Just so in days gone by they took delight in Aristophanes and Eupolis, who brought Socrates on the stage to make fun of him and got up monstrous farces about him.

The playwrights, however, showed their boldness against only one man, and at the Dionysia, when it was permissible to do so, and the joking was considered part of the holiday, and

The god, who loves his joke, no doubt was pleased.[1]

But this man brings the best people together, after a long period of thinking and preparing and writing

[1] Author unknown.

τινὰς εἰς παχὺ βιβλίον ἐγγράψας, μεγάλῃ τῇ φωνῇ ἀγορεύει κακῶς Πλάτωνα, Πυθαγόραν, Ἀριστοτέλη τοῦτον, Χρύσιππον ἐκεῖνον, ἐμὲ καὶ ὅλως ἅπαντας οὔτε ἑορτῆς ἐφιείσης οὔτε ἰδίᾳ τι πρὸς ἡμῶν παθών· εἶχε γὰρ ἄν τινα συγγνώμην αὐτῷ τὸ πρᾶγμα, εἰ ἀμυνόμενος, ἀλλὰ μὴ ἄρχων αὐτὸς ἔδρα.

Ὃ δὲ πάντων δεινότατον, ὅτι τοιαῦτα ποιῶν καὶ τὸ σὸν ὄνομα,[1] ὦ Φιλοσοφία, ὑποδύεται καὶ ὑπελθὼν τὸν Διάλογον ἡμέτερον οἰκέτην ὄντα, τούτῳ συναγωνιστῇ καὶ ὑποκριτῇ χρῆται καθ' ἡμῶν, ἔτι καὶ Μένιππον ἀναπείσας ἑταῖρον ἡμῶν ἄνδρα συγκωμῳδεῖν αὐτῷ τὰ πολλά, ὃς μόνος οὐ πάρεστιν οὐδὲ κατηγορεῖ μεθ' ἡμῶν, προδοὺς τὸ κοινόν.

27 Ἀνθ' ὧν ἁπάντων ἄξιόν ἐστιν ὑποσχεῖν αὐτὸν τὴν δίκην. ἢ τί γὰρ ἂν εἰπεῖν ἔχοι τὰ σεμνότατα διασύρας ἐπὶ τοσούτων μαρτύρων; χρήσιμον γοῦν καὶ πρὸς ἐκείνους τὸ τοιοῦτον, εἰ θεάσαιντο αὐτὸν κολασθέντα, ὡς μηδὲ ἄλλος τις ἔτι καταφρονοίη Φιλοσοφίας· ἐπεὶ τό γε τὴν ἡσυχίαν ἄγειν καὶ ὑβριζόμενον ἀνέχεσθαι οὐ μετριότητος, ἀλλὰ ἀνανδρίας καὶ εὐηθείας εἰκότως ἂν νομίζοιτο. τὰ μὲν γὰρ τελευταῖα τίνι φορητά; ὃς καθάπερ τὰ ἀνδράποδα παραγαγὼν ἡμᾶς ἐπὶ τὸ πωλητήριον καὶ κήρυκα ἐπιστήσας ἀπημπόλησεν, ὥς φασιν, τοὺς μὲν ἐπὶ πολλῷ, ἐνίους δὲ μνᾶς Ἀττικῆς, ἐμὲ δὲ ὁ παμπονηρότατος οὗτος δύ' ὀβολῶν· οἱ παρόντες δὲ ἐγέλων.

Ἀνθ' ὧν αὐτοί τε ἀνεληλύθαμεν ἀγανακτήσαντες καὶ σὲ ἀξιοῦμεν τιμωρήσειν ἡμῖν τὰ ἔσχατα ὑβρισμένοις.

[1] τὸ σὸν ὄνομα K. Schwartz: ὑπὸ τὸ σὸν ὄνομα MSS.

down slanders in a thick roll, and then loudly abuses Plato, Pythagoras, Aristotle here, Chrysippus there, myself, and in a word, one and all, without the sanction of a holiday and without having had anything done to him personally by us. He would have some excuse for the thing, of course, if he had acted in self-defence instead of starting the quarrel.

What is worst of all, in doing this sort of thing, Philosophy, he shelters himself under your name, and he has suborned Dialogue, our serving-man, employing him against us as a helper and a spokesman. Moreover, he has actually bribed Menippus,[1] a comrade of ours, to take part in his farces frequently; he is the only one who is not here and does not join us in the prosecution, thereby playing traitor to our common cause.

For all this he ought to be punished. What, pray, can he have to say for himself after ridiculing all that is most holy before so many witnesses? In fact, it would be a good thing for them, too, if they were to see him punished, so that no other man might ever again sneer at Philosophy; for to keep quiet and pocket insults might well be thought to betoken weakness and simplicity rather than self-control. And who could put up with his last performances? Bringing us like slaves to the auction-room and appointing a crier, he sold us off, they say, some for a high price, some for an Attic mina, and me, arrant scoundrel that he is, for two obols! And those present laughed!

On account of this, we ourselves have come up here in a rage, and we think it right that you for your part should avenge us because we have been insulted to the limit.

[1] The Cynic, of Gadara: Lucian's chief predecessor in satirical prose.

ΠΛΑΤΩΝ

28 Εὖ γε, ὦ Διόγενες, ὑπὲρ ἁπάντων καλῶς ὁπόσα ἐχρῆν ἅπαντα εἴρηκας.

ΦΙΛΟΣΟΦΙΑ

Παύσασθε ἐπαινοῦντες· ἔγχει τῷ ἀπολογουμένῳ. σὺ δὲ ὁ Παρρησιάδης λέγε ἤδη ἐν τῷ μέρει· σοὶ γὰρ τὸ νῦν ῥεῖ. μὴ μέλλε οὖν.

ΠΑΡΡΗΣΙΑΔΗΣ

29 Οὐ πάντα μου, ὦ Φιλοσοφία, κατηγόρησε Διογένης, ἀλλὰ τὰ πλείω καὶ ὅσα ἦν χαλεπώτερα οὐκ οἶδα ὅ τι παθὼν παρέλιπεν. ἐγὼ δὲ τοσούτου δέω ἔξαρνος γενέσθαι ὡς οὐκ εἶπον αὐτά, ἢ ἀπολογίαν τινὰ μεμελετηκὼς ἀφῖχθαι, ὥστε καὶ εἴ τινα ἢ αὐτὸς ἀπεσιώπησεν ἢ ἐγὼ μὴ πρότερον ἔφθην εἰρηκώς, νῦν προσθήσειν μοι δοκῶ. οὕτως γὰρ ἂν μάθοις οὕστινας ἀπεκήρυττον καὶ κακῶς ἠγόρευον ἀλαζόνας καὶ γόητας ἀποκαλῶν. καί μοι μόνον τοῦτο παραφυλάττετε, εἰ ἀληθῆ περὶ αὐτῶν ἐρῶ. εἰ δέ τι βλάσφημον ἢ τραχὺ φαίνοιτο ἔχων ὁ λόγος, οὐ τὸν διελέγχοντα ἐμέ, ἀλλ' ἐκείνους ἂν οἶμαι δικαιότερον αἰτιάσαισθε,[1] τοιαῦτα ποιοῦντας.

Ἐγὼ γὰρ ἐπειδὴ τάχιστα συνεῖδον ὁπόσα τοῖς ῥητορεύουσιν ἀναγκαῖον τὰ δυσχερῆ προσεῖναι, ἀπάτην καὶ ψεῦδος καὶ θρασύτητα καὶ βοὴν καὶ ὠθισμοὺς καὶ μυρία ἄλλα, ταῦτα μέν, ὥσπερ εἰκὸς ἦν, ἀπέφυγον, ἐπὶ δὲ τὰ σά, ὦ Φιλοσοφία, καλὰ ὁρμήσας ἠξίουν ὁπόσον ἔτι μοι λοιπὸν τοῦ βίου καθάπερ ἐκ ζάλης καὶ κλύδωνος εἰς εὔδιόν

[1] αἰτιάσαισθε Dindorf: αἰτιάσεσθαι B, αἰτιάσασθαι P, αἰτιάσεσθε UN, αἰτιᾶσθε γ.

PLATO

Good, Diogenes! You have splendidly said all that you ought on behalf of us all.

PHILOSOPHY

Stop applauding! Pour in the water for the defendant. Now, Frankness, make your speech in turn, for the water now is running for you. Don't delay, then.

FRANKNESS

Diogenes did not complete the complaint against me, Philosophy. He left out, for some reason or other, the greater part of what I said, and everything that was very severe. But I am so far from denying that I said it all and from appearing with a studied defence that whatever he passed over in silence or I neglected previously to say, I purpose to include now. In that way you can find out whom I put up for sale and abused, calling them pretenders and cheats. And I beg you merely to note throughout whether what I say about them is true. If my speech should prove to contain anything shocking or offensive, it is not I, their critic, but they, I think, whom you would justly blame for it, acting as they do.

As soon as I perceived how many disagreeable attributes a public speaker must needs acquire, such as chicanery, lying, impudence, loudness of mouth, sharpness of elbow, and what all besides, I fled from all that, as was natural, and set out to attain your high ideals, Philosophy, expecting to sail, as it were, out of stormy waters into a peaceful haven

τινα λιμένα ἐσπλεύσας ὑπὸ σοὶ σκεπόμενος καταβιῶναι.

30 Κἀπειδὴ *μόνον παρέκυψα εἰς τὰ ὑμέτερα, σὲ μέν, ὥσπερ ἀναγκαῖον ἦν, καὶ τούσδε ἅπαντας ἐθαύμαζον ἀρίστου βίου νομοθέτας ὄντας καὶ τοῖς ἐπ' αὐτὸν ἐπειγομένοις χεῖρα ὀρέγοντας, τὰ κάλλιστα καὶ συμφορώτατα παραινοῦντας, εἴ τις μὴ παραβαίνοι αὐτὰ μηδὲ διολισθάνοι, ἀλλ' ἀτενὲς ἀποβλέπων εἰς τοὺς κανόνας οὓς προτεθείκατε, πρὸς τούτους ῥυθμίζοι καὶ ἀπευθύνοι τὸν ἑαυτοῦ βίον, ὅπερ νὴ Δία καὶ τῶν καθ' ὑμᾶς*[1] *αὐτοὺς ὀλίγοι ποιοῦσιν.*

31 Ὁρῶν *δὲ πολλοὺς οὐκ ἔρωτι φιλοσοφίας ἐχομένους ἀλλὰ δόξης μόνον τῆς ἀπὸ τοῦ πράγματος ἐφιεμένους, καὶ τὰ μὲν πρόχειρα ταῦτα καὶ δημόσια καὶ ὁπόσα παντὶ μιμεῖσθαι ῥᾴδιον εὖ μάλα ἐοικότας ἀγαθοῖς ἀνδράσι, τὸ γένειον λέγω καὶ τὸ βάδισμα καὶ τὴν ἀναβολήν, ἐπὶ δὲ τοῦ βίου καὶ τῶν πραγμάτων ἀντιφθεγγομένους τῷ σχήματι καὶ τἀναντία ὑμῖν ἐπιτηδεύοντας καὶ διαφθείροντας τὸ ἀξίωμα τῆς ὑποσχέσεως, ἠγανάκτουν, καὶ τὸ πρᾶγμα ὅμοιον ἐδόκει μοι καθάπερ ἂν εἴ τις ὑποκριτὴς τραγῳδίας μαλθακὸς αὐτὸς ὢν καὶ γυναικεῖος* Ἀχιλλέα *ἢ* Θησέα *ἢ καὶ τὸν* Ἡρακλέα *ὑποκρίνοιτο αὐτὸν μήτε βαδίζων μήτε βοῶν ἡρωϊκόν, ἀλλὰ θρυπτόμενος ὑπὸ τηλικούτῳ προσωπείῳ, ὃν οὐδ' ἂν ἡ* Ἑλένη *ποτὲ ἢ* Πολυξένη *ἀνάσχοιντο πέρα τοῦ μετρίου αὐταῖς προσεοικότα, οὐχ ὅπως ὁ* Ἡρακλῆς *ὁ* Καλλίνικος, *ἀλλά μοι δοκεῖ τάχιστ' ἂν ἐπιτρῖψαι τῷ ῥοπάλῳ*

[1] ἡμᾶς β: see opposite note.

and to live out the rest of my life under your protection.

Hardly had I caught a glimpse of your doctrines when I conceived admiration for you, as was inevitable, and for all these men, who are the lawgivers of the higher life and lend a helping hand to those who aspire to it by giving advice which is extremely good and extremely helpful if one does not act contrary to it or falter, but fixedly regards the principles which you have established and tries to bring his life into harmony and agreement with them—a thing, to be sure, which very few, even of your own disciples, do![1]

When I saw, however, that many were not in love with Philosophy, but simply coveted the reputation of the thing, and that although in all the obvious, commonplace matters which anyone can easily copy they were very like worthy men (in beard, I mean, and walk and garb), in their life and actions, however, they contradicted their outward appearance and reversed your practice and sullied the dignity of the profession, I became angry. The case seemed to me to be as if some actor in tragedy who was soft and womanish should act the part of Achilles or Theseus, or even Heracles himself, without either walking or speaking as a hero should, but showing off airs and graces in a mask of such dignity. Even Helen or Polyxena would never suffer such a man to resemble them too closely, let alone Heracles, the conquering hero, who, in my opinion, would very soon

[1] I give Fritzsche's interpretation of this last clause, though I fear it strains the Greek and is foreign to Lucian's thought. Another, and I think a better, solution is to excise the clause as an early gloss, reading ἡμᾶς and interpreting it more naturally, "a thing which very few, even in our own time, do." Compare the late gloss in β: τὶ ταῦτα τοῖς καθ' ἡμᾶς ἔοικε μονάχοις.

παίων τοῦτον αὐτόν τε καὶ τὸ προσωπεῖον, οὕτως ἀτίμως κατατεθηλυμμένος πρὸς αὐτοῦ.

32 Τοιαῦτα καὶ αὐτὸς ὑμᾶς πάσχοντας ὑπ' ἐκείνων ὁρῶν οὐκ ἤνεγκα τὴν αἰσχύνην τῆς ὑποκρίσεως, εἰ πίθηκοι ὄντες ἐτόλμησαν ἡρώων προσωπεῖα περιθέσθαι ἢ τὸν ἐν Κύμῃ ὄνον μιμήσασθαι, ὃς λεοντῆν περιβαλόμενος ἠξίου λέων αὐτὸς εἶναι, πρὸς ἀγνοοῦντας τοὺς Κυμαίους ὀγκώμενος μάλα τραχὺ καὶ καταπληκτικόν, ἄχρι δή τις αὐτὸν ξένος καὶ λέοντα ἰδὼν καὶ ὄνον πολλάκις ἤλεγξε καὶ ἀπεδίωξε παίων τοῖς ξύλοις.

Ὃ δὲ μάλιστά μοι δεινόν, ὦ Φιλοσοφία, κατεφαίνετο, τοῦτο ἦν· οἱ γὰρ ἄνθρωποι εἴ τινα τούτων ἑώρων πονηρὸν ἢ ἄσχημον ἢ ἀσελγές τι ἐπιτηδεύοντα, οὐκ ἔστιν ὅστις οὐ Φιλοσοφίαν αὐτὴν ᾐτιᾶτο καὶ τὸν Χρύσιππον εὐθὺς ἢ Πλάτωνα ἢ Πυθαγόραν ἢ ὅτου ἐπώνυμον αὐτὸν ὁ διαμαρτάνων ἐκεῖνος ἐποιεῖτο καὶ οὗ τοὺς λόγους ἐμιμεῖτο·[1] καὶ ἀπὸ τοῦ κακῶς βιοῦντος πονηρὰ περὶ ὑμῶν εἴκαζον τῶν πρὸ πολλοῦ τεθνηκότων· οὐ γὰρ παρὰ ζῶντας ὑμᾶς ἡ ἐξέτασις αὐτοῦ ἐγίγνετο, ἀλλ' ὑμεῖς μὲν ἐκποδών, ἐκεῖνον δὲ ἑώρων σαφῶς ἅπαντες δεινὰ καὶ ἄσεμνα ἐπιτηδεύοντα, ὥστε ἐρήμην ἡλίσκεσθε μετ' αὐτοῦ καὶ ἐπὶ τὴν ὁμοίαν διαβολὴν συγκατεσπᾶσθε.

33 Ταῦτα οὐκ ἤνεγκα ὁρῶν ἔγωγε, ἀλλ' ἤλεγχον αὐτοὺς καὶ διέκρινον ἀφ' ὑμῶν· ὑμεῖς δέ, τιμᾶν ἐπὶ τούτοις δέον, εἰς δικαστήριόν με ἄγετε. οὐκοῦν ἤν τινα καὶ τῶν μεμυημένων ἰδὼν ἐξαγορεύοντα ταῖν θεαῖν τὰ ἀπόρρητα καὶ ἐξορχούμενον ἀγανακτήσω καὶ διελέγξω, ἐμὲ τὸν ἀσεβοῦντα

[1] ἐμιμεῖτο Seager: ἐποιεῖτο γβ.

smash both man and mask with a few strokes of his club for making him out so disgracefully effeminate.

Just so with me; when I saw you so treated by those others, I could not brook the shame of their impersonation when they made bold, though but apes, to wear heroic masks, or to copy the ass of Cumae who put on a lion's skin and claimed to be himself a lion, braying in a very harsh and fearsome way at the ignorant Cumaeans, until at length a foreigner, who had often seen lions and asses, exposed him and chased him away by beating him with sticks.

But what seemed to me most shocking, Philosophy, was this, that if people saw any one of these fellows engaged in any wicked or unseemly or indecent practice, every man of them at once laid the blame upon Philosophy herself, and upon Chrysippus or Plato or Pythagoras or whichever one of you furnished that sinner with a name for himself and a model for his harangues; and from him, because he was leading an evil life, they drew sorry conclusions about you others, who died long ago. For as you were not alive, he could not be compared with you. You were not there, and they all clearly saw him following dreadful and discreditable practices, so that you suffered judgment by default along with him and became involved in the same scandal.

I could not endure this spectacle, but set about exposing them and distinguishing them from you; and you, who ought to reward me for it, bring me into court! Then if I observed one of the initiates disclosing the mysteries of the Goddesses Twain and rehearsing them in public, and became indignant and showed him up, would you consider *me* the impious

ἡγήσεσθε εἶναι; ἀλλ' οὐ δίκαιον. ἐπεὶ καὶ οἱ ἀθλοθέται μαστιγοῦν εἰώθασιν, ἤν τις ὑποκριτὴς Ἀθηνᾶν ἢ Ποσειδῶνα ἢ τὸν Δία ὑποδεδυκὼς μὴ καλῶς ὑποκρίνηται μηδὲ κατ' ἀξίαν τῶν θεῶν, καὶ οὐ δή που ὀργίζονται αὐτοῖς ἐκεῖνοι, διότι τὸν περικείμενον αὐτῶν τὰ προσωπεῖα καὶ τὸ σχῆμα ἐνδεδυκότα ἐπέτρεψαν παίειν τοῖς μαστιγοφόροις, ἀλλὰ καὶ ἥδοιντ' ἄν, οἶμαι, μᾶλλον[1] μαστιγουμένῳ·[2] οἰκέτην μὲν γάρ τινα ἢ ἄγγελον μὴ δεξιῶς ὑποκρίνασθαι μικρὸν τὸ πταῖσμα, τὸν Δία δὲ ἢ τὸν Ἡρακλέα μὴ κατ' ἀξίαν ἐπιδείξασθαι τοῖς θεαταῖς, ἀποτρόπαιον ὡς αἰσχρόν.

34 Καὶ γὰρ αὖ καὶ τόδε πάντων ἀτοπώτατόν ἐστιν, ὅτι τοὺς μὲν λόγους ὑμῶν πάνυ ἀκριβοῦσιν οἱ πολλοὶ αὐτῶν, καθάπερ δὲ ἐπὶ τοῦτο μόνον ἀναγιγνώσκοντες αὐτοὺς καὶ μελετῶντες, ὡς τἀναντία ἐπιτηδεύοιεν, οὕτως βιοῦσιν. τὸ μὲν γὰρ βιβλίον χρημάτων φησὶ δεῖν καταφρονεῖν[3] καὶ δόξης καὶ μόνον τὸ καλὸν ἀγαθὸν οἴεσθαι καὶ ἀόργητον εἶναι καὶ τῶν λαμπρῶν τούτων ὑπερορᾶν καὶ ἐξ ἰσοτιμίας αὐτοῖς διαλέγεσθαι, καλά,[4] ὦ θεοί, καὶ σοφὰ καὶ θαυμάσια λέγον[5] ὡς ἀληθῶς. οἱ δὲ καὶ αὐτὰ ταῦτα ἐπὶ μισθῷ διδάσκουσιν καὶ τοὺς πλουσίους τεθήπασιν καὶ πρὸς τὸ ἀργύριον κεχήνασιν, ὀργιλώτεροι μὲν τῶν κυνιδίων ὄντες, δειλότεροι δὲ τῶν λαγωῶν, κολακικώτεροι δὲ τῶν πιθήκων, ἀσελγέστεροι δὲ τῶν ὄνων, ἁρπακτικώτεροι δὲ τῶν γαλῶν, φιλονεικότεροι δὲ τῶν ἀλεκτρυόνων. τοιγαροῦν γέλωτα ὀφλισκάνουσιν ὠθιζόμενοι ἐπ' αὐτὰ καὶ περὶ τὰς τῶν

[1] οἶμαι μᾶλλον Jacobs: οἶμαι β, μᾶλλον γ.
[2] μαστιγουμένῳ Bekker: μαστιγουμένων MSS.

one? It would not be just. Certainly the officials of the games always flog an actor if he takes the part of Athena or Poseidon or Zeus and does not play it well and in accordance with the dignity of the gods; and the gods themselves are surely not angry at them for letting the scourgers whip a man wearing their masks and dressed in their clothing. On the contrary, they would be gratified, I take it, if he were flogged more soundly. Not to act a servant's or a messenger's part cleverly is a trivial fault, but not to present Zeus or Heracles to the spectators worthily—Heaven forfend! how shameful!

It is most extraordinary, too, that most of them are thoroughly up in your writings, but live as if they read and studied them simply to practise the reverse. Their book tells them they must despise wealth and reputation, think that only what is beautiful is good, be free from anger, despise these people of eminence, and talk with them as man to man; and its advice is beautiful, as Heaven is my witness, and wise and wonderful, in all truth. But they teach these very doctrines for pay, and worship the rich, and are agog after money; they are more quick-tempered than curs, more cowardly than hares, more servile than apes, more lustful than jackasses, more thievish than cats, more quarrelsome than game-cocks. Consequently, they let themselves in for ridicule when they hustle

---

[3] Text γ: πάντα μὲν γὰρ ὅσα φασὶν οἷον χρημάτων καταφρονεῖν β, edd.
[4] ἀλλ' γ. [5] λέγον A.M.H.: λέγοντες γ, λίαν β.

πλουσίων πυλῶνας ἀλλήλους παραγκωνιζόμενοι καὶ δεῖπνα πολυάνθρωπα δειπνοῦντες καὶ ἐν αὐτοῖς τούτοις ἐπαινοῦντες φορτικῶς καὶ πέρα τοῦ καλῶς ἔχοντος ἐμφορούμενοι καὶ μεμψίμοιροι φαινόμενοι καὶ ἐπὶ τῆς κύλικος ἀτερπῆ καὶ ἀπῳδὰ φιλοσοφοῦντες καὶ τὸν ἄκρατον οὐ φέροντες· οἱ ἰδιῶται δὲ ὁπόσοι πάρεισιν, γελῶσι δηλαδὴ καὶ καταπτύουσιν φιλοσοφίας, εἰ τοιαῦτα καθάρματα ἐκτρέφει.

35 Τὸ δὲ πάντων αἴσχιστον, ὅτι μηδενὸς δεῖσθαι λέγων ἕκαστος αὐτῶν, ἀλλὰ μόνον πλούσιον εἶναι τὸν σοφὸν κεκραγὼς μικρὸν ὕστερον προσελθὼν αἰτεῖ καὶ ἀγανακτεῖ μὴ λαβών, ὅμοιον ὡς εἴ τις ἐν βασιλικῷ σχήματι ὀρθὴν τιάραν ἔχων καὶ διάδημα καὶ τὰ ἄλλα ὅσα βασιλείας γνωρίσματα προσαιτοίη τῶν ὑποδεεστέρων δεόμενος.

Ὅταν μὲν οὖν λαβεῖν αὐτοὺς δέῃ, πολὺς ὁ περὶ τοῦ κοινωνικὸν εἶναι δεῖν λόγος καὶ ὡς ἀδιάφορον ὁ πλοῦτος καί, "Τί γὰρ τὸ χρυσίον ἢ τἀργύριον, οὐδὲν τῶν ἐν τοῖς αἰγιαλοῖς ψήφων διαφέρον;" ὅταν δέ τις ἐπικουρίας δεόμενος ἑταῖρος ἐκ παλαιοῦ καὶ φίλος ἀπὸ πολλῶν ὀλίγα αἰτῇ προσελθών, σιωπὴ καὶ ἀπορία καὶ ἀμαθία καὶ παλινῳδία τῶν δογμάτων πρὸς τὸ ἐναντίον· οἱ δὲ πολλοὶ περὶ φιλίας ἐκεῖνοι λόγοι καὶ ἡ ἀρετὴ καὶ τὸ καλὸν οὐκ οἶδα ὅποι ποτὲ οἴχεται ταῦτα ἀποπτάμενα πάντα, πτερόεντα ὡς ἀληθῶς ἔπη, μάτην ὁσημέραι πρὸς αὐτῶν ἐν ταῖς διατριβαῖς σκιαμαχούμενα. 36 μέχρι γὰρ τούτου φίλος ἕκαστος αὐτῶν, εἰς ὅσον ἂν μὴ ἀργύριον ἢ χρυσίον ᾖ προκείμενον ἐν τῷ μέσῳ· ἢν δέ τις ὀβολὸν ἐπιδείξῃ μόνον, λέλυται μὲν ἡ εἰρήνη, ἄσπονδα δὲ κακή-

after it all and elbow one another at the portals of the rich and take part in great banquets, where they pay vulgar compliments, stuff themselves beyond decency, grumble openly at their portions, vent their philosophy disagreeably and discordantly over their cups, and fail to carry their drink well. All those present who are not of the profession laugh at them, naturally, and spit philosophy to scorn for breeding up such beasts.

Most shameless of all, though each one of them says he needs nothing and bawls it abroad that only the wise man is rich, after a little he presents himself and asks for something, and is angry if he does not get it. It is just as if someone in royal robes, with a high turban and a diadem and all the other marks of kingly dignity, should play the mendicant, begging of men worse off than himself.

When they must needs receive a present, there is a great deal of talk to the effect that a man should be ready to share what he has, and that money does not matter: "What, pray, does gold or silver amount to, since it is not in any way better than pebbles on the sea-shore!" But when someone in want of help, an old-time comrade and friend, goes and asks for a little of their plenty, he encounters silence, hesitancy, forgetfulness, and complete recantation of doctrines. Their numerous speeches about friendship, their "virtue" and their "honour" have all gone flying off, I know not whither, winged words for certain, idly bandied about by them daily in their class-rooms. Each of them is your friend as long as silver and gold are not in sight on the table; but if you merely give them a glimpse of an obol, the peace is broken, it is war without truce or parley

ρυκτα πάντα, καὶ τὰ βιβλία ἐξαλήλιπται καὶ ἡ ἀρετὴ πέφευγεν. οἷόν τι καὶ οἱ κύνες πάσχουσιν ἐπειδάν τις ὀστοῦν εἰς μέσους αὐτοὺς ἐμβάλῃ· ἀναπηδήσαντες δάκνουσιν ἀλλήλους καὶ τὸν προαρπάσαντα τὸ ὀστοῦν ὑλακτοῦσιν.

Λέγεται δὲ καὶ βασιλεύς τις Αἰγύπτιος πιθήκους ποτὲ πυρριχίζειν διδάξαι καὶ τὰ θηρία—μιμηλότατα δέ ἐστι τῶν ἀνθρωπίνων—ἐκμαθεῖν τάχιστα καὶ ὀρχεῖσθαι ἁλουργίδας ἀμπεχόμενα καὶ προσωπεῖα περικείμενα, καὶ μέχρι γε πολλοῦ εὐδοκιμεῖν τὴν θέαν, ἄχρι δὴ θεατής τις ἀστεῖος κάρυα ὑπὸ κόλπου[1] ἔχων ἀφῆκεν εἰς τὸ μέσον· οἱ δὲ πίθηκοι ἰδόντες καὶ ἐκλαθόμενοι τῆς ὀρχήσεως, τοῦθ' ὅπερ ἦσαν, πίθηκοι ἐγένοντο ἀντὶ πυρριχιστῶν καὶ συνέτριβον τὰ προσωπεῖα καὶ τὴν ἐσθῆτα κατερρήγνυον καὶ ἐμάχοντο περὶ τῆς ὀπώρας πρὸς ἀλλήλους, τὸ δὲ σύνταγμα τῆς πυρρίχης διελέλυτο καὶ κατεγελᾶτο ὑπὸ τοῦ θεάτρου.

37 Τοιαῦτα καὶ οὗτοι ποιοῦσιν, καὶ ἔγωγε τοὺς τοιούτους κακῶς ἠγόρευον καὶ οὔποτε παύσομαι διελέγχων καὶ κωμῳδῶν, περὶ ὑμῶν δὲ ἢ τῶν ὑμῖν παραπλησίων—εἰσὶ γάρ, εἰσί τινες ὡς ἀληθῶς φιλοσοφίαν ζηλοῦντες καὶ τοῖς ὑμετέροις νόμοις ἐμμένοντες—μὴ οὕτως μανείην ἔγωγε ὡς βλάσφημον εἰπεῖν τι ἢ σκαιόν. ἢ τί γὰρ ἂν εἰπεῖν ἔχοιμι; τί γὰρ ὑμῖν τοιοῦτον βεβίωται; τοὺς δὲ ἀλαζόνας ἐκείνους καὶ θεοῖς ἐχθροὺς ἄξιον οἶμαι μισεῖν. ἢ σὺ γάρ, ὦ Πυθαγόρα καὶ Πλάτων καὶ Χρύσιππε καὶ Ἀριστότελες, τί φατε; προσήκειν ὑμῖν τοὺς τοιούτους ἢ οἰκεῖόν τι καὶ

[1] κόλπου du Soul: κόλπον MSS.

everywhere, the pages of their books have become blank, and Virtue has taken to her heels. So it is with dogs, when you toss a bone among them; they spring to their feet and begin biting each other and barking at the one that was first to snatch the bone.

It is said, too, that a king of Egypt once taught apes to dance, and that the animals, as they are very apt at imitating human ways, learned quickly and gave an exhibition, with purple mantles about them and masks on their faces. For a long time the show, they say, went well, until a facetious spectator, having nuts in his pocket, tossed them into the midst. On catching sight of them, the monkeys forgot their dance, changed from artists of the ballet to the simians that they really were, smashed their masks, tore their costumes, and fought with each other for the nuts; whereby the carefully planned ballet was entirely broken up, and was laughed at by the spectators.

These self-styled philosophers do just that, and I for my part abused their sort, and shall never stop criticizing and ridiculing them. But as for you and those who resemble you—for there are, there are some who truly cultivate philosophy and abide by your laws—may I never be so insane as to say anything abusive or unkind of you! What could I say? What is there of that nature in the lives that you have led? But those pretenders and miscreants deserve in my opinion to be hated. Come, now, Pythagoras, Plato, Chrysippus, Aristotle—what do you say? Have their sort anything to do with you,

συγγενὲς ἐπιδείκνυσθαι τῷ βίῳ; νὴ Δί᾿ Ἡρακλῆς, φασίν, καὶ πίθηκος. ἢ διότι πώγωνας ἔχουσι καὶ φιλοσοφεῖν φάσκουσι καὶ σκυθρωποί εἰσι, διὰ τοῦτο χρὴ ὑμῖν εἰκάζειν αὐτούς; ἀλλὰ ἤνεγκα ἄν, εἰ πιθανοὶ γοῦν ἦσαν καὶ ἐπὶ τῆς ὑποκρίσεως αὐτῆς· νῦν δὲ θᾶττον ἂν γὺψ ἀηδόνα μιμήσαιτο ἢ οὗτοι φιλοσόφους.

Εἴρηκα ὑπὲρ ἐμαυτοῦ ὁπόσα εἶχον. σὺ δέ, ὦ Ἀλήθεια, μαρτύρει πρὸς αὐτοὺς εἰ ἀληθῆ ἐστιν.

ΦΙΛΟΣΟΦΙΑ

38 Μετάστηθι, ὦ Παρρησιάδη· ἔτι πορρωτέρω. τί ποιῶμεν ἡμεῖς; πῶς ὑμῖν εἰρηκέναι ἀνὴρ ἔδοξεν;

ΑΛΗΘΕΙΑ

Ἐγὼ μέν, ὦ Φιλοσοφία, μεταξὺ λέγοντος αὐτοῦ κατὰ τῆς γῆς δῦναι εὐχόμην· οὕτως ἀληθῆ πάντα εἶπεν. ἐγνώριζον γοῦν ἀκούουσα ἕκαστον τῶν ποιούντων αὐτὰ καὶ ἐφήρμοζον μεταξὺ τοῖς λεγομένοις, τοῦτο μὲν εἰς τόνδε, τοῦτο δὲ ὁ δεῖνα ποιεῖ· καὶ ὅλως ἔδειξε τοὺς ἄνδρας ἐναργῶς καθάπερ ἐπί τινος γραφῆς τὰ πάντα προσεοικότας, οὐ τὰ σώματα μόνον ἀλλὰ καὶ τὰς ψυχὰς αὐτὰς εἰς τὸ ἀκριβέστατον ἀπεικάσας.

ΑΡΕΤΗ

Κἀγὼ πάνυ ἠρυθρίασα ἡ Ἀρετή.[1]

ΦΙΛΟΣΟΦΙΑ

Ὑμεῖς δὲ τί φατέ;

[1] ἡ Ἀρετή B: ὦ Ἀρετή other MSS.

or have they displayed any similarity or kinship in their mode of life? Aye, "Heracles and the monkey," as the proverb has it![1] Because they have long beards and claim to be philosophers and look sour, ought they to be compared with you? I could have put up with it if they were at least convincing in their roles, but as things are, it would be easier for a buzzard to imitate a nightingale than for them to imitate philosophers.

I have said all that I had to say in my own defence. Truth, tell them whether it is true.

PHILOSOPHY

Stand aside, Frankness; still farther . . . What are we to do? What did you think of the man's speech?

TRUTH

For my part, Philosophy, while he was speaking I prayed that I might sink into the earth, so true was everything that he said. In fact, as I listened, I recognized each of the men who act that way and applied his remarks to them: "That refers to this man; so-and-so does that." In short, he portrayed the gentlemen to the life, as in a painting, accurate likenesses in every respect, depicting not only their persons, but their very souls as faithfully as could be.

VIRTUE

I, Virtue, also had to blush for shame.

PHILOSOPHY

And what say *you*?

[1] You are no more like these men than Heracles was like the monkey that wore the lion's skin. Cf. § 32, and *Lover of Lies*, § 5.

ΠΛΑΤΩΝ

Τί δὲ ἄλλο ἢ ἀφεῖσθαι αὐτὸν τοῦ ἐγκλήματος καὶ φίλον ἡμῖν καὶ εὐεργέτην ἀναγεγράφθαι; τὸ γοῦν τῶν Ἰλιέων ἀτεχνῶς πεπόνθαμεν· τραγῳδόν τινα τοῦτον ἐφ' ἡμᾶς κεκινήκαμεν ᾀσόμενον τὰς Φρυγῶν συμφοράς. ᾀδέτω δ' οὖν καὶ τοὺς θεοῖς ἐχθροὺς ἐκτραγῳδείτω.

ΔΙΟΓΕΝΗΣ

Καὶ αὐτός, ὦ Φιλοσοφία, πάνυ ἐπαινῶ τὸν ἄνδρα καὶ ἀνατίθεμαι τὰ κατηγορούμενα καὶ φίλον ποιοῦμαι αὐτὸν γενναῖον ὄντα.

ΦΙΛΟΣΟΦΙΑ

39 Εὖ ἔχει· πρόσιθι Παρρησιάδη· ἀφίεμέν σε τῆς αἰτίας, καὶ ἁπάσαις κρατεῖς, καὶ τὸ λοιπὸν ἴσθι ἡμέτερος ὤν.

ΠΑΡΡΗΣΙΑΔΗΣ

Προσεκύνησα τήν γε πρώτην·[1] μᾶλλον δέ, τραγικώτερον αὐτὸ ποιήσειν μοι δοκῶ· σεμνότερον γάρ·

ὦ μέγα σεμνὴ Νίκη, τὸν ἐμὸν
βίοτον κατέχοις
καὶ μὴ λήγοις στεφανοῦσα.

ΑΡΕΤΗ

Οὐκοῦν δευτέρου κρατῆρος ἤδη καταρχώμεθα· προσκαλῶμεν κἀκείνους, ὡς δίκην ὑπόσχωσιν ἀνθ' ὧν εἰς ἡμᾶς ὑβρίζουσι· κατηγορήσει δὲ Παρρησιάδης ἑκάστου.

[1] τὴν Πτερωτὴν Madvig, *i.e.* Victory. But for τήν γε πρώτην cf. Xen. *Mem.* 3, 6, 10: and *Demosth. Enc.* 30.

PLATO

What else but to acquit him of the charge and set him down as our friend and benefactor? Indeed, just what happened to the Ilians[1] has happened to us—we have brought down upon ourselves an actor of tragedies to hold forth about the woes of the Trojans! Let him hold forth, then, and make tragedies out of these miscreants.

DIOGENES

I, too, Philosophy, commend the man highly, take back my complaint and count him a friend, for he is a gallant fellow.

PHILOSOPHY

Good! Come, Frankness. We acquit you of the charge; you have an unanimous verdict in your favour, and from now on you may count yourself one of my household.

FRANKNESS

I pay my homage at once. (*He kisses his hand.*) But no! I think I shall do it more as they do in a play, for that will be more reverential:

"O Victory, goddess so greatly revered,
Take my life in thy care
And cease not to crown me with garlands."[2]

VIRTUE

Well, then, let us now initiate our second bowl of wine. Let us summon up those others to be punished for the insults they are inflicting upon us. Frankness shall accuse each of them.

[1] The latter-day Trojans.
[2] Euripides, close of *Phoenissae*, *Orestes*, *Iphigenia in Tauris*.

ΦΙΛΟΣΟΦΙΑ

Ὀρθῶς, ὦ Ἀρετή, ἔλεξας. ὥστε σύ, παῖ Συλλογισμέ, κατακύψας εἰς τὸ ἄστυ προσκήρυττε τοὺς φιλοσόφους.

ΣΥΛΛΟΓΙΣΜΟΣ

40 Ἄκουε, σίγα· τοὺς φιλοσόφους ἥκειν εἰς ἀκρόπολιν ἀπολογησομένους ἐπὶ τῆς Ἀρετῆς καὶ Φιλοσοφίας καὶ Δίκης.

ΠΑΡΡΗΣΙΑΔΗΣ

Ὁρᾷς; ὀλίγοι ἀνίασι γνωρίσαντες τὸ κήρυγμα, καὶ ἄλλως δεδίασι τὴν Δίκην· οἱ πολλοὶ δὲ αὐτῶν οὐδὲ σχολὴν ἄγουσιν ἀμφὶ τοὺς πλουσίους ἔχοντες. εἰ δὲ βούλει πάντας ἥκειν, κατὰ τάδε, ὦ Συλλογισμέ, κήρυττε—

ΣΥΛΛΟΓΙΣΜΟΣ[1]

Μηδαμῶς, ἀλλὰ σύ, ὦ Παρρησιάδη, προσκάλει καθ' ὅ τι σοι δοκεῖ.

ΠΑΡΡΗΣΙΑΔΗΣ

41 Οὐδὲν τόδε χαλεπόν. Ἄκουε, σίγα. ὅσοι φιλόσοφοι εἶναι λέγουσιν καὶ ὅσοι προσήκειν αὐτοῖς οἴονται τοῦ ὀνόματος, ἥκειν εἰς ἀκρόπολιν ἐπὶ τὴν διανομήν. δύο μναῖ ἑκάστῳ δοθήσονται καὶ σησαμαῖος πλακοῦς· ὃς δ' ἂν πώγωνα βαθὺν ἐπιδείξηται, καὶ παλάθην ἰσχάδων οὗτός γε προσεπιλήψεται. κομίζειν δ' ἕκαστον σωφροσύνην μὲν ἢ δικαιοσύνην ἢ ἐγκράτειαν μηδαμῶς· οὐκ ἀναγκαῖα γὰρ ταῦτά γε, ἢν μὴ παρῇ· πέντε δὲ συλλογισμοὺς ἐξ ἅπαντος· οὐ γὰρ θέμις ἄνευ τούτων εἶναι σοφόν.

κεῖται δ' ἐν μέσσοισι δύο χρυσοῖο τάλαντα,
τῷ δόμεν, ὃς μετὰ πᾶσιν ἐριζέμεν ἔξοχος εἴη.

[1] ΣΥΛΛΟΓΙΣΜΟΣ A.M.H.: ΦΙΛ. edd.

PHILOSOPHY

Quite right, Virtue; so slip down into the town, Syllogism, my lad, and summon the philosophers.

SYLLOGISM

Oyez! Silence! Let the philosophers come to the Acropolis to present their defence before Virtue, Philosophy, and Justice.

FRANKNESS

Do you see! Very few of them understood the summons and are coming up. Besides, they fear Justice, and most of them are actually too busy because of their attentions to the rich. If you wish them all to come, Syllogism, make your proclamation like this—

SYLLOGISM

No! You summon them, Frankness, in the way you think best.

FRANKNESS

Nothing hard about that. Oyez! Silence! All who assert that they are philosophers, and all who think that they have any connection with the name, come to the Acropolis for a distribution of gifts! Two minas will be given to every man, and a seed-cake also; and whoever displays a long beard shall receive a basket of figs into the bargain. Never mind temperance or justice or self-control, as these qualities are not essential if they are not available; but let each bring with him five syllogisms by all means, for without these it is impossible to be wise.

"Lo, we have set up as prize two talents of gold for
the contest;
These shall we give unto him who prevails over all
in debating!"[1]

[1] Cf. *Iliad* 18, 507–8.

ΦΙΛΟΣΟΦΙΑ[1]

42 Βαβαί, ὅσοι· πλήρης μὲν ἡ ἄνοδος ὠθιζομένων ἐπὶ τὰς δύο μνᾶς, ὡς ἤκουσαν μόνον· παρὰ δὲ τὸ Πελασγικὸν ἄλλοι καὶ κατὰ τὸ Ἀσκληπιεῖον ἕτεροι καὶ παρὰ τὸν Ἄρειον πάγον[2] ἔτι πλείους, ἔνιοι δὲ καὶ κατὰ τὸν Τάλω τάφον, οἱ δὲ καὶ πρὸς τὸ Ἀνακεῖον προσθέμενοι κλίμακας ἀνέρπουσι βομβηδὸν νὴ Δία καὶ βοτρυδὸν ἑσμοῦ δίκην, ἵνα καὶ καθ᾽ Ὅμηρον εἴπω· ἀλλὰ κἀκεῖθεν εὖ μάλα πολλοὶ κἀντεῦθεν

μυρίοι, ὅσσα τε φύλλα καὶ ἄνθεα γίνεται ὥρῃ.

μεστὴ δὲ ἡ ἀκρόπολις ἐν βραχεῖ κλαγγηδὸν προκαθιζόντων καὶ πανταχοῦ πήρα κολακεία, πώγων ἀναισχυντία, βακτηρία λιχνεία, συλλογισμὸς φιλαργυρία· οἱ ὀλίγοι δέ, ὁπόσοι πρὸς τὸ πρῶτον κήρυγμα ἐκεῖνο ἀνῄεσαν, ἀφανεῖς καὶ ἄσημοι, ἀναμιχθέντες τῷ πλήθει τῶν ἄλλων, καὶ λελήθασιν ἐν τῇ ὁμοιότητι τῶν ἄλλων σχημάτων.

ΠΑΡΡΗΣΙΑΔΗΣ[3]

Τοῦτο γοῦν τὸ δεινότατόν ἐστιν, ὦ Φιλοσοφία, καὶ ὅ τις ἂν μέμψαιτο μάλιστά σου, τὸ μηδὲν ἐπιβαλεῖν γνώρισμα καὶ σημεῖον αὐτοῖς· πιθανώτεροι γὰρ οἱ γόητες οὗτοι πολλάκις τῶν ἀληθῶς φιλοσοφούντων.

[1] ΦΙΛΟΣΟΦΙΑ A.M.H.; double point U: no change of speaker in ΓN, edd.
[2] πάγον vulg.: not in γβ.
[3] ΠΑΡΡΗΣΙΑΔΗΣ A.M.H.; double point Γ: no change of speaker in UN, edd.

---

[1] The prehistoric wall of the Acropolis. Only tumbledown pieces were then to be seen (cf. § 47). The bit referred

PHILOSOPHY

Aha! What a lot of them! The road up to the gate is full of men hustling after the two minas, as soon as they heard of them; others are coming up beside the Pelasgicon;[1] others by the precinct of Asclepius;[2] even more of them along the Areopagus;[3] some, too, by the tomb of Talus;[4] and some have set ladders against the temple of the Twin Brethren[5] and are climbing up with a hum, by Heaven, and "in clusters" like swarming bees, to use the words of Homer;[6] from that side right many, and from the other

"Thousands of men, like the leaves and the flowers that come in the springtime."[7]

The Acropolis is full in a trice as they "noisily settle in place,"[8] and everywhere are begging-bags and flattery, beards and shamelessness, staves and gluttony, syllogisms and avarice. The few that came up in answer to the first summons are obscure and inconspicuous, intermingled with the crowd of others, and they escape the eye in the general similarity of garb.

FRANKNESS

In fact, that is the worst feature of it all, Philosophy, and the one for which you could be most criticized, that you have set no mark and token upon them. These cheats are often more convincing than the genuine philosophers.

to here was at the north-west corner, by the cave of Pan (*Double Indictment*, § 9).

[2] On the south slope, near the theatre of Dionysus.

[3] To the west, near the main entrance.

[4] Talus (or Calus) was nephew of Daedalus, who out of jealousy threw him down the cliff. Certain stones at the back of the theatre of Dionysus are thought to belong to his. tomb. [5] North side: exact site uncertain.

[6] *Iliad* 2, 89. [7] *Iliad* 2, 468. [8] *Iliad* 2, 463.

ΦΙΛΟΣΟΦΙΑ

Ἔσται τοῦτο μετ' ὀλίγον, ἀλλὰ δεχώμεθα ἤδη αὐτούς.

ΠΛΑΤΩΝΙΚΟΣ

43 Ἡμᾶς πρώτους χρὴ τοὺς Πλατωνικοὺς λαβεῖν.

ΠΥΘΑΓΟΡΙΚΟΣ

Οὔκ, ἀλλὰ τοὺς Πυθαγορικοὺς ἡμᾶς· πρότερος γὰρ ὁ Πυθαγόρας ἦν.

ΣΤΩΙΚΟΣ

Ληρεῖτε· ἀμείνους ἡμεῖς οἱ ἀπὸ τῆς Στοᾶς.

ΠΕΡΙΠΑΤΗΤΙΚΟΣ

Οὐ μὲν οὖν, ἀλλ' ἔν γε τοῖς χρήμασι πρῶτοι ἂν ἡμεῖς εἴημεν οἱ ἐκ τοῦ Περιπάτου.

ΕΠΙΚΟΥΡΕΙΟΣ

Ἡμῖν τοῖς Ἐπικουρείοις τοὺς πλακοῦντας δότε καὶ τὰς παλάθας· περὶ δὲ τῶν μνῶν περιμενοῦμεν, κἂν ὑστάτους δέῃ λαβεῖν.

ΑΚΑΔΗΜΑΙΚΟΣ

Ποῦ τὰ δύο τάλαντα; δείξομεν γὰρ οἱ Ἀκαδημαϊκοὶ ὅσον τῶν ἄλλων ἐσμὲν ἐριστικώτεροι.

ΣΤΩΙΚΟΣ

Οὐχ ἡμῶν γε τῶν Στωϊκῶν παρόντων.

ΦΙΛΟΣΟΦΙΑ

44 Παύσασθε φιλονεικοῦντες· ὑμεῖς δὲ οἱ Κυνικοὶ μήτε ὠθεῖτε ἀλλήλους μήτε τοῖς ξύλοις παίετε· ἐπ' ἄλλα γὰρ ἴστε κεκλημένοι. καὶ νῦν ἔγωγε ἡ Φιλοσοφία καὶ Ἀρετὴ αὕτη καὶ Ἀλήθεια δικάσομεν οἵτινες οἱ ὀρθῶς φιλοσοφοῦντές εἰσιν. εἶτα ὅσοι μὲν ἂν εὑρεθῶσιν κατὰ τὰ ἡμῖν δοκοῦντα βιοῦντες, εὐδαιμονήσουσιν ἄριστοι κεκριμένοι· τοὺς γόητας δὲ καὶ οὐδὲν ἡμῖν προσήκοντας κακοὺς

PHILOSOPHY

That shall be seen to presently; but let us welcome them now.

PLATONIST

We Platonists should get our share first.

PYTHAGOREAN

No! we Pythagoreans, for Pythagoras was earlier.

STOIC

Nonsense! we of the Porch are better.

PERIPATETIC

Not at all; in matters of money we of the Walk should be first.

EPICUREAN

Give us Epicureans the cakes and the figs, but we will wait for the money, even if we have to be the last to get it.

ACADEMIC

Where are the two talents? We Academics will show you how much better debaters we are than the rest!

STOIC

Not while we Stoics are here!

PHILOSOPHY.

Stop your bickering! You Cynics, do not jostle one another or strike each other with your staves. You were asked here for a different purpose, let me assure you! And now I, Philosophy, and Virtue here and Truth will decide who are the genuine philosophers. Then all who are found to be living by our rules shall be pronounced superior and will be happy ever after, but as for the cheats and all those who have nothing in common with us, we shall put

κακῶς ἐπιτρίψομεν, ὡς μὴ ἀντιποιῶνται τῶν ὑπὲρ αὐτοὺς ἀλαζόνες ὄντες. τί τοῦτο; φεύγετε; νὴ Δία, κατὰ τῶν γε κρημνῶν οἱ πολλοὶ ἀλλόμενοι. κενὴ δ' οὖν ἡ ἀκρόπολις, πλὴν ὀλίγων τούτων ὁπόσοι μεμενήκασιν οὐ φοβηθέντες τὴν
45 *κρίσιν. οἱ ὑπηρέται ἀνέλεσθε τὴν πήραν, ἣν ὁ Κυνικὸς ἀπέρριψεν ἐν τῇ τροπῇ. φέρ' ἴδω τί καὶ ἔχει· ἦ που θέρμους ἢ βιβλίον ἢ ἄρτους τῶν αὐτοπυριτῶν;*

ΥΠΗΡΕΤΗΣ[1]

Οὔκ, ἀλλὰ χρυσίον τουτὶ καὶ μύρον καὶ μαχαίριον κουρευτικὸν[2] *καὶ κάτοπτρον καὶ κύβους.*

ΦΙΛΟΣΟΦΙΑ

Εὖ γε, ὦ γενναῖε. τοιαῦτα ἦν σοι τὰ ἐφόδια τῆς ἀσκήσεως καὶ μετὰ τούτων ἠξίους λοιδορεῖσθαι πᾶσιν καὶ τοὺς ἄλλους παιδαγωγεῖν;

ΠΑΡΡΗΣΙΑΔΗΣ

Τοιοῦτοι μὲν οὖν ὑμῖν οὗτοι. χρὴ δὲ ὑμᾶς σκοπεῖν ὅντινα τρόπον ἀγνοούμενα ταῦτα πεπαύσεται καὶ διαγνώσονται οἱ ἐντυγχάνοντες, οἵτινες οἱ ἀγαθοὶ αὐτῶν εἰσι καὶ οἵτινες αὖ πάλιν οἱ τοῦ ἑτέρου βίου.

ΦΙΛΟΣΟΦΙΑ[3]

Σύ, ὦ Ἀλήθεια, ἐξεύρισκε· ὑπὲρ σοῦ γὰρ τοῦτο γένοιτ' ἄν, ὡς μὴ ἐπικρατῇ σου τὸ Ψεῦδος μηδὲ ὑπὸ τῇ Ἀγνοίᾳ λανθάνωσιν οἱ φαῦλοι τῶν ἀνδρῶν σε τοὺς χρηστοὺς μεμιμημένοι.

[1] ΥΠΗΡΕΤΗΣ A.M.H.; cf. *οἱ ὑπηρέται*: ΠΑΡΡ. vulg.
[2] *καὶ μαχαίριον κουρευτικὸν* A.M.H. (*κουρικὸν* du Soul): *καὶ μαχαίριον θυτικὸν* γ; not in β. Cf. Olympiodorus, *Vit. Platon.* 4.
[3] ΦΙΛΟΣΟΦΙΑ Bekker; double point after *βίου* in ΓU.

the wretches to a wretched end, so that they may not claim any part in things that are over their heads, false pretenders that they are! What is this? Are you running away? By Heaven, they are, most of them jumping over the cliffs! The Acropolis is empty except for these few who have remained because they did not fear the trial. Attendants, pick up the bag which the Cynic threw away in the rout. Come, let me see what is in it; probably lupines, or a book, or some whole-wheat bread.

ATTENDANT

No! gold—see here!—perfume, a razor, a mirror, and a set of dice!

PHILOSOPHY

Good for you, my fine fellow! Were these your instruments for the mortification of the flesh, and did you think that with the aid of these you could abuse all mankind and instruct the rest of the world?

FRANKNESS

Well, there you see what they are like. You must consider how all this is to stop going on unobserved, and how those who come into contact with them are to tell which of them are the good and which, on the contrary, the followers of the other life.

PHILOSOPHY

Invent a plan, Truth; for it would be in your own interest to do so, in order that Falsehood may not prevail over you, and bad men, under the cloak of Ignorance, escape your eye when they imitate the good.

ΑΛΗΘΕΙΑ

46 Ἐπ' αὐτῷ, εἰ δοκεῖ, Παρρησιάδη ποιησώμεθα τὸ τοιοῦτον, ἐπεὶ χρηστὸς ὦπται καὶ εὔνους ἡμῖν καὶ σέ, ὦ Φιλοσοφία, μάλιστα θαυμάζων, παραλαβόντα μεθ' ἑαυτοῦ τὸν Ἔλεγχον ἅπασι τοῖς φάσκουσι φιλοσοφεῖν ἐντυγχάνειν. εἶθ' ὃν μὲν ἂν εὕρῃ γνήσιον ὡς ἀληθῶς φιλόσοφον, στεφανωσάτω θαλλοῦ στεφάνῳ καὶ εἰς τὸ Πρυτανεῖον καλεσάτω, ἢν δέ τινι—οἷοι πολλοί εἰσι—καταράτῳ ἀνδρὶ ὑποκριτῇ φιλοσοφίας ἐντύχῃ, τὸ τριβώνιον περισπάσας ἀποκειράτω τὸν πώγωνα ἐν χρῷ πάνυ τραγοκουρικῇ μαχαίρᾳ καὶ ἐπὶ τοῦ μετώπου στίγματα ἐπιβαλέτω ἢ ἐγκαυσάτω κατὰ τὸ μεσόφρυον· ὁ δὲ τύπος τοῦ καυτῆρος ἔστω ἀλώπηξ ἢ πίθηκος.

ΦΙΛΟΣΟΦΙΑ

Εὖ γε, ὦ Ἀλήθεια, φής· ὁ δὲ ἔλεγχος, Παρρησιάδη, τοιόσδε ἔστω, οἷος ὁ τῶν ἀετῶν πρὸς τὸν ἥλιον εἶναι λέγεται, οὐ μὰ Δί' ὥστε κἀκείνους ἀντιβλέπειν τῷ φωτὶ καὶ πρὸς ἐκεῖνο δοκιμάζεσθαι, ἀλλὰ προθεὶς χρυσίον καὶ δόξαν καὶ ἡδονὴν ὃν μὲν ἂν αὐτῶν ἴδῃς ὑπερορῶντα καὶ μηδαμῶς ἑλκόμενον πρὸς τὴν ὄψιν, οὗτος ἔστω ὁ τῷ θαλλῷ στεφόμενος, ὃν δ' ἂν ἀτενὲς ἀποβλέποντα καὶ τὴν χεῖρα ὀρέγοντα ἐπὶ τὸ χρυσίον, ἀπάγειν ἐπὶ τὸ καυτήριον τοῦτον ἀποκείρας[1] πρότερον τὸν πώγωνα ὡς ἔδοξεν.

ΠΑΡΡΗΣΙΑΔΗΣ

47 Ἔσται ταῦτα, ὦ Φιλοσοφία, καὶ ὄψει αὐτίκα μάλα τοὺς πολλοὺς αὐτῶν ἀλωπεκίας ἢ πιθηκο-

[1] ἀποκείρας Fritzsche: ἀποκείραντα γN; ἀποκείραντας BU.

TRUTH

If you think best, let us empower Frankness himself to do this, since we have seen that he is honest and in sympathy with us, and that he particularly admires you, Philosophy—to take along Investigation and put himself in the way of all who claim to be philosophers. Then, whenever he finds a truly legitimate son of Philosophy, let him crown the man with a wreath of green olive and invite him to the Prytaneum;[1] and if he meets a scoundrel whose philosophy is but stage-play—there are many of that sort—let him tear his mantle, cut off his beard close to the skin with goat-shears, and stamp or brand a mark on his forehead, between the eyebrows; let the pattern of the brand be a fox or an ape.

PHILOSOPHY

Good for you, Truth! Let the test, Frankness, be like the test of the eaglets against the sun. Not that they, like the eaglets, are to stare at the light and be put to the proof in that way; but set gold and fame and pleasure in their view, and whomsoever of them you see paying no attention and in no way attracted to the spectacle, let him be the one to wear the crown of green olive; but whomever you see gazing fixedly at the gold and reaching his hand out after it, hale him off to the branding-place, after first cutting off his beard in accordance with our decision.

FRANKNESS

It shall be done, Philosophy. You shall very soon see most of them wearing the fox-brand or the ape-

[1] To be maintained at public expense, as Socrates thought he should have been.

φόρους, ὀλίγους δὲ καὶ ἐστεφανωμένους· εἰ βούλεσθε μέντοι, κἀνταῦθα ὑμῖν ἀνάξω τινὰς ἤδη αὐτῶν.

ΦΙΛΟΣΟΦΙΑ

Πῶς λέγεις; ἀνάξεις τοὺς φυγόντας;

ΠΑΡΡΗΣΙΑΔΗΣ

Καὶ μάλα, ἤνπερ ἡ ἱέρειά μοι ἐθελήσῃ πρὸς ὀλίγον χρῆσαι τὴν ὁρμιὰν ἐκείνην καὶ τὸ ἄγκιστρον, ὅπερ ὁ ἁλιεὺς ἀνέθηκεν ὁ ἐκ Πειραιῶς.

ΙΕΡΕΙΑ

Ἰδοὺ δὴ λαβέ, καὶ τὸν κάλαμόν γε ἅμα, ὡς πάντα ἔχῃς.

ΠΑΡΡΗΣΙΑΔΗΣ

Οὐκοῦν, ὦ ἱέρεια, καὶ ἰσχάδας μοί τινας δὸς ἀνύσασα καὶ ὀλίγον τοῦ χρυσίου.

ΙΕΡΕΙΑ

Λάμβανε.

ΦΙΛΟΣΟΦΙΑ

Τί πράττειν ἀνὴρ διανοεῖται; δελεάσας τὸ ἄγκιστρον ἰσχάδι καὶ τῷ χρυσίῳ καθεζόμενος ἐπὶ τὸ ἄκρον τοῦ τειχίου καθῆκεν εἰς τὴν πόλιν. τί ταῦτα, ὦ Παρρησιάδη, ποιεῖς; ἦ που τοὺς λίθους ἁλιεύσειν διέγνωκας ἐκ τοῦ Πελασγικοῦ;

ΠΑΡΡΗΣΙΑΔΗΣ

Σιώπησον, ὦ Φιλοσοφία, καὶ τὴν ἄγραν περίμενε· σὺ δέ, ὦ Πόσειδον ἀγρεῦ καὶ Ἀμφιτρίτη 48 φίλη, πολλοὺς ἡμῖν ἀνάπεμπε τῶν ἰχθύων. ἀλλ' ὁρῶ τινα λάβρακα εὐμεγέθη, μᾶλλον δὲ χρύσοφρυν· οὔκ, ἀλλὰ γαλεός ἐστιν. πρόσεισι γοῦν τῷ ἀγκίστρῳ κεχηνώς· ὤσφραται τοῦ χρυσίου· πλησίον

brand, and but few crowned with wreaths. If you like, however, I will bring you up some of them here and now.

PHILOSOPHY

What! you will bring up the runaways?

FRANKNESS

Yes, indeed, if the priestess will be good enough to lend me for a moment that hook and line which the fisherman from the Peiraeus dedicated.

PRIESTESS

There, take it, and the rod too, so that you may have a complete outfit.

FRANKNESS

And now, priestess, give me some figs quickly and a little of your gold.

PRIESTESS

Take them.

PHILOSOPHY

What does the man intend to do? Baiting the hook with the fig and the gold, and taking his seat on the crest of the wall, he has made a cast into the town! Why are you doing that, Frankness? Have you made up your mind to fish up the stones out of the Pelasgicon?

FRANKNESS

Hush, Philosophy; wait and see my catch. Poseidon, god of fishermen, and dear Amphitrite, send us up quantities of fish! Ah! I see a fine big pike, or rather, a golden carp.—No, it is a cat-fish. Anyhow, he is coming up to the hook with his mouth open. He has scented the gold; now he is close by; he

ἤδη ἐστίν· ἔψαυσεν· εἴληπται· ἀνασπάσωμεν. καὶ σύ, ὦ Ἔλεγχε, ἀνάσπα· Ἔλεγχε,[1] συνεπιλαβοῦ τῆς ὁρμιᾶς.

ΕΛΕΓΧΟΣ

Ἄνω ἐστί. φέρ' ἴδω τίς εἶ, ὦ βέλτιστε ἰχθύων; κύων οὗτός γε.[2] Ἡράκλεις τῶν ὀδόντων. τί τοῦτο, ὦ γενναιότατε; εἴληψαι λιχνεύων περὶ τὰς πέτρας, ἔνθα λήσειν ἤλπισας ὑποδεδυκώς; ἀλλὰ νῦν ἔσῃ φανερὸς ἅπασιν ἐκ τῶν βραγχίων ἀπηρτημένος. ἐξέλωμεν τὸ ἄγκιστρον καὶ τὸ δέλεαρ. μὰ Δί' ἔπιεν.[3] τουτὶ κενόν σοι τὸ ἄγκιστρον· ἡ δ' ἰσχὰς ἤδη προσέσχηται καὶ τὸ χρυσίον ἐν τῇ κοιλίᾳ.

ΠΑΡΡΗΣΙΑΔΗΣ

Ἐξεμεσάτω νὴ Δία, ὡς καὶ ἐπ' ἄλλους δελεάσωμεν. εὖ ἔχει· τί φής, ὦ Διόγενες; οἶσθα τοῦτον ὅστις ἐστίν, ἢ προσήκει τί σοι ἀνήρ;

ΔΙΟΓΕΝΗΣ

Οὐδαμῶς.

ΠΑΡΡΗΣΙΑΔΗΣ

Τί οὖν; πόσου ἄξιον αὐτὸν χρὴ φάναι; ἐγὼ μὲν γὰρ δύ' ὀβολῶν πρῴην αὐτὸν ἐτιμησάμην.

ΔΙΟΓΕΝΗΣ

Πολὺ λέγεις· ἄβρωτός τε γάρ ἐστιν καὶ εἰδεχθὴς καὶ σκληρὸς καὶ ἄτιμος· ἄφες αὐτὸν ἐπὶ κεφαλὴν κατὰ τῆς πέτρας· σὺ δὲ ἄλλον ἀνάσπασον καθεὶς τὸ ἄγκιστρον. ἐκεῖνο μέντοι· ὅρα, ὦ Παρρησιάδη, μὴ καμπτόμενός σοι ὁ κάλαμος ἀποκλασθῇ.

[1] ἀνάσπα· Ἔλεγχε γ: not in β, vulg.
[2] κύων οὗτός γε ς, L. Bos: αὔων οὗτός γε γ: not in β.
[3] μὰ Δί' ἔπιεν: γ, but after κοιλίᾳ: after δέλεαρ A.M.H. Previous edd. omit. β omits καὶ τὸ δέλεαρ . . . ἄγκιστρον.

struck; he is on; let's pull him up. You pull too, Investigation. Investigation, take hold of the line with me!

INVESTIGATION

He is up! Come, let me see what you are, my good fish. A dogfish![1] Heracles, what teeth! How about it, my fine fellow? Caught, were you, gormandizing about the rocks, where you hoped to slip under cover and keep out of sight? But now you will be in public view, hung up by the gills! Let us take out the hook and the bait. No, by Zeus, he has swallowed it! Here is your hook, all bare; the fig and the gold are secure in his insides.

FRANKNESS

Let him spew them up, by Zeus, so that we may bait for others. That's well. What say you, Diogenes; do you know who this fellow is, and has he anything in common with you?

DIOGENES

Not in the least!

FRANKNESS

Well, how much ought we to call him worth? For my part, I valued him at two obols the other day.

DIOGENES

A high price. He is inedible and ugly and tough and worthless. Throw him down the cliff head first. Let down your hook and pull up another. But I say: look out, Frankness, not to let your rod bend till it breaks.

[1] *i.e.* a Cynic.

ΠΑΡΡΗΣΙΑΔΗΣ

Θάρρει, ὦ Διόγενες· κοῦφοί εἰσι καὶ τῶν ἀφύων ἐλαφρότεροι.

ΔΙΟΓΕΝΗΣ

Νὴ Δί', ἀφυέστατοί γε· ἀνάσπα δὲ ὅμως.

ΠΑΡΡΗΣΙΑΔΗΣ

49 Ἰδού τις ἄλλος ὑπόπλατος ὥσπερ ἡμίτομος ἰχθὺς πρόσεισιν, ψῆττά τις, κεχηνὼς εἰς τὸ ἄγκιστρον· κατέπιεν, ἔχεται, ἀνεσπάσθω. τίς ἐστιν;

ΕΛΕΓΧΟΣ

Ὁ Πλατωνικὸς εἶναι λέγων.

ΠΑΡΡΗΣΙΑΔΗΣ

Καὶ σύ, ὦ κατάρατε, ἥκεις ἐπὶ τὸ χρυσίον; τί φής, ὦ Πλάτων; τί ποιῶμεν αὐτόν;

ΠΛΑΤΩΝ

50 Ἀπὸ τῆς αὐτῆς πέτρας καὶ οὗτος· ἐπ' ἄλλον καθείσθω.

ΠΑΡΡΗΣΙΑΔΗΣ

Καὶ μὴν ὁρῶ τινα πάγκαλον προσιόντα, ὡς ἂν ἐν βυθῷ δόξειεν, ποικίλον τὴν χρόαν, ταινίας τινὰς ἐπὶ τοῦ νώτου ἐπιχρύσους ἔχοντα. ὁρᾷς, ὦ Ἔλεγχε;

ΕΛΕΓΧΟΣ

Ὁ τὸν Ἀριστοτέλη προσποιούμενος οὗτός ἐστιν.

FRANKNESS

Have no fear, Diogenes. They are light, and pull no harder than weakfish.[1]

DIOGENES

Aye, they are mighty weak, for certain ; pull them up, however.

FRANKNESS

See ! Here comes another fish that looks like a plate,[2] as if he were sliced lengthways, a sort of flatfish, opening his mouth for the hook. He has swallowed it ; he is caught. Up with him ! What is he ?

INVESTIGATION

The kind that styles itself Platonic.

FRANKNESS

So you came to get the gold too, confound you ? What do you say, Plato ? What are we to do with him ?

PLATO

Over the same cliff with him ! Let down for another.

FRANKNESS

Ah, I see a very handsome one coming up, as far as can be judged in the deep water ; of many colours, with golden stripes on his back.[3] Do you see him, Investigation ?

INVESTIGATION

He is the kind that claims the name of Aristotle.

[1] Lucian puns upon ἀφύη (a small fish, sprat) and ἀφυής (dull, stupid).

[2] The pun here is upon Πλάτων and πλατύς (flat).

[3] The Peripatetics were criticized for love of gay clothing and gold.

ΠΑΡΡΗΣΙΑΔΗΣ[1]

Ἦλθεν, εἶτα πάλιν ἄπεισιν. περισκοπεῖ[2] ἀκριβῶς, αὖθις ἐπανῆλθεν, ἔχανεν, εἴληπται, ἀνιμήσθω.

ΑΡΙΣΤΟΤΕΛΗΣ

Μὴ ἀνέρῃ με, ὦ Παρρησιάδη, περὶ αὐτοῦ· ἀγνοῶ γὰρ ὅστις ἐστίν.

ΠΑΡΡΗΣΙΑΔΗΣ

Οὐκοῦν καὶ οὗτος, ὦ Ἀριστότελες, κατὰ τῶν 51 πετρῶν. ἀλλ' ἢν ἰδού, πολλούς που τοὺς ἰχθῦς ὁρῶ κατὰ ταὐτὸν ὁμόχροας, ἀκανθώδεις καὶ τὴν ἐπιφάνειαν ἐκτετραχυσμένους, ἐχίνων δυσληπτοτέρους. ἦ που σαγήνης ἐπ' αὐτοὺς δεήσει;

ΦΙΛΟΣΟΦΙΑ[3]

Ἀλλ' οὐ πάρεστιν. ἱκανὸν εἰ κἂν ἕνα τινὰ ἐκ τῆς ἀγέλης ἀνασπάσαιμεν. ἥξει δὲ ἐπὶ τὸ ἄγκιστρον δηλαδὴ ὃς ἂν αὐτῶν θρασύτατος ᾖ.

ΕΛΕΓΧΟΣ

Κάθες, εἰ δοκεῖ, σιδηρώσας γε πρότερον ἐπὶ πολὺ τῆς ὁρμιᾶς, ὡς μὴ ἀποπρίσῃ τοῖς ὀδοῦσι καταπιὼν τὸ χρυσίον.

ΠΑΡΡΗΣΙΑΔΗΣ

Καθῆκα. καὶ σὺ δέ, ὦ Πόσειδον, ταχεῖαν ἐπιτέλει τὴν ἄγραν. βαβαί, μάχονται περὶ τοῦ δελέατος, καὶ οἱ μὲν συνάμα πολλοὶ περιτρώγουσι τὴν ἰσχάδα, οἱ δὲ προσφύντες ἔχονται τοῦ χρυσίου. εὖ ἔχει· περιεπάρη τις μάλα καρτερός. φέρ' ἴδω τίνος ἐπώνυμον σεαυτὸν εἶναι λέγεις;

[1] ΠΑΡΡ. A.M.H.: no change of speaker in MSS.
[2] περισκοπεῖ Seybold, Fritzsche: περισκόπει MSS.
[3] ΦΙΛ. A.M.H.: double point after δεήσει in Γ.

FRANKNESS

He came up and then swam away again. He is making a careful survey. Now he has come back again; he has opened his mouth; he is caught. Up with him.

ARISTOTLE

Don't ask me about him, Frankness. I don't know who he is.

FRANKNESS

Then he too shall go over the cliff, Aristotle. But look here! I see a great number of fish closely alike in colour, spiny and rough-skinned, harder to grasp than sea-urchins.[1] Shall we need a seine for them?

PHILOSOPHY

But we haven't any. It will be enough if we land only one out of the school. The one that comes to the hook will of course be the boldest of them.

INVESTIGATION

Let down your line, if you want, but first arm it with iron for some distance, so that he may not saw it off with his teeth after he has swallowed the gold.

FRANKNESS

It is down. Poseidon, grant us a quick catch! Aha! they are fighting over the bait; some are nibbling the fig in schools and some have taken firm hold of the gold. Good! A very powerful one is on the hook! Come, let me see whose namesake you

[1] Stoics, then the most numerous school. They themselves were uncouth, and their doctrines spiny.

καίτοι γελοῖός εἰμι ἀναγκάζων ἰχθὺν λαλεῖν· ἄφωνοι γὰρ οὗτοί γε. ἀλλὰ σύ, ὦ Ἔλεγχε, εἰπὲ ὅντινα ἔχει διδάσκαλον αὐτοῦ.

ΕΛΕΓΧΟΣ

Χρύσιππον τουτονί.

ΠΑΡΡΗΣΙΑΔΗΣ

Μανθάνω· διότι χρυσίον προσῆν, οἶμαι, τῷ ὀνόματι. σὺ δ' οὖν, Χρύσιππε, πρὸς τῆς Ἀθηνᾶς εἰπέ, οἶσθα τοὺς ἄνδρας ἢ τοιαῦτα παραινεῖς αὐτοῖς ποιεῖν;

ΧΡΥΣΙΠΠΟΣ

Νὴ Δί', ὑβριστικὰ ἐρωτᾷς, ὦ Παρρησιάδη, προσήκειν τι ἡμῖν ὑπολαμβάνων τοιούτους ὄντας.

ΠΑΡΡΗΣΙΑΔΗΣ

Εὖ γε, ὦ Χρύσιππε, γενναῖος εἶ. οὗτος δὲ καὶ αὐτὸς ἐπὶ κεφαλὴν μετὰ τῶν ἄλλων, ἐπεὶ καὶ ἀκανθώδης ἐστί, καὶ δέος μὴ διαπαρῇ τις τὸν λαιμὸν ἐσθίων.

ΦΙΛΟΣΟΦΙΑ

52 Ἅλις, ὦ Παρρησιάδη, τῆς ἄγρας, μὴ καί τίς σοι, οἷοι πολλοί εἰσιν, οἴχηται ἀποσπάσας τὸ χρυσίον καὶ τὸ ἄγκιστρον, εἶτά σε ἀποτῖσαι τῇ ἱερείᾳ δεήσῃ. ὥστε ἡμεῖς μὲν ἀπίωμεν περιπατήσουσαι· καιρὸς δὲ καὶ ὑμᾶς ἀπιέναι ὅθεν ἥκετε, μὴ καὶ ὑπερήμεροι γένησθε τῆς προθεσμίας. σφὼ δέ, σὺ καὶ ὁ Ἔλεγχος, ὦ Παρρησιάδη, ἐν κύκλῳ ἐπὶ πάντας αὐτοὺς ἰόντες ἢ στεφανοῦτε ἢ ἐγκάετε, ὡς ἔφην.

say you are. But it is silly of me to try to make a fish talk; these anyhow are certainly dumb! Come, Investigation, tell us whom he has for master.

INVESTIGATION

Chrysippus here.

FRANKNESS

I understand: because there was gold in the name, I take it. Well, Chrysippus, in the name of the Goddess of Wisdom tell us, do you know these fellows, and do you advise them to do as they do?

CHRYSIPPUS

By Zeus, your questions are insulting, Frankness, if you imply that we have anything in common with that sort.

FRANKNESS

Good, Chrysippus: that is handsome of you. He too shall go head first after the rest, as he is spiny and there is danger that anyone who should try to eat him might get a hole in his gullet.

PHILOSOPHY

Enough of fishing, Frankness. One of them—there are many capable of it—may snatch off the gold and the hook and make away with them, and then you will have to settle with the priestess. So let us go away to take our stroll, and as for you (*to the* PHILOSOPHERS), it is high time you went where you came from, that you may not overstay your leave. Frankness, you and Investigation seek them all out on every hand and either crown or brand them, as I said.

ΠΑΡΡΗΣΙΑΔΗΣ

Ἔσται ταῦτα, ὦ Φιλοσοφία. χαίρετε, ὦ βέλτιστοι ἀνδρῶν. ἡμεῖς δὲ κατίωμεν, ὦ Ἔλεγχε, καὶ τελῶμεν τὰ παρηγγελμένα.

ΕΛΕΓΧΟΣ

Ποῖ δὲ καὶ πρῶτον ἀπιέναι δεήσει; μῶν εἰς τὴν Ἀκαδημίαν ἢ εἰς τὴν Στοὰν ἢ[1] ἀπὸ τοῦ Λυκείου ποιησώμεθα τὴν ἀρχήν;

ΠΑΡΡΗΣΙΑΔΗΣ

Οὐδὲν διοίσει τοῦτο. πλὴν οἶδά γε ἐγὼ ὡς ὅποι ποτ' ἂν ἀπέλθωμεν, ὀλίγων μὲν τῶν στεφάνων, πολλῶν δὲ τῶν καυτηρίων δεησόμεθα.

[1] ἢ Seybold: not in MSS.

FRANKNESS

It shall be done, Philosophy. Good-bye, gentlemen. Let us go down into the town, Investigation, and carry out our orders.

INVESTIGATION

Where shall we go first? To the Academy, or to the Porch? Or shall we begin with the Lyceum?

FRANKNESS

It will make no difference. I am sure, however, that wherever we go we shall need few crowns of olive, but many brands.

THE DOUBLE INDICTMENT

Again we have a reply to criticism, this time largely of an aesthetic nature. Lucian had been assailed from both sides, by the rhetoricians for abandoning speech-making and essay-writing and going over to dialogue, consecrated, since Plato's time, to the service of Philosophy, and by the philosophers for not handling dialogue in the traditional way. It is the usual reception accorded to innovators. Lucian's response is characteristically novel and effective. Using the form which he is censured for employing in precisely the way that he is censured for employing it, he insinuates himself into the favour of his audience by taking them first to Heaven to overhear a conversation between Zeus and Hermes, then in company with Hermes and Justice to the Areopagus, where Justice, after a brief and amusing colloquy with Pan, presides over a series of mock-trials (always a delectable entertainment to Greeks), culminating in the two that give the piece its name, Lucian *v.* Oratory and Lucian *v.* Dialogue, from which his audience is delighted to see him come off triumphant. The result is that rhetoric and philosophy *à la mode*, who have brought him before the bar of public opinion, are laughed out of court.

The Dialogue was composed, Lucian tells us (§ 32), when he was about forty years old, therefore probably not far from the year 165 A.D.

ΔΙΣ ΚΑΤΗΓΟΡΟΥΜΕΝΟΣ[1]

ΖΕΥΣ

1 Ἀλλ' ἐπιτριβεῖεν ὁπόσοι τῶν φιλοσόφων παρὰ μόνοις τὴν εὐδαιμονίαν φασὶν εἶναι τοῖς θεοῖς. εἰ γοῦν ᾔδεσαν ὁπόσα τῶν ἀνθρώπων ἕνεκα πάσχομεν, οὐκ ἂν ἡμᾶς τοῦ νέκταρος ἢ τῆς ἀμβροσίας ἐμακάριζον Ὁμήρῳ πιστεύσαντες ἀνδρὶ τυφλῷ καὶ γόητι, μάκαρας ἡμᾶς καλοῦντι καὶ τὰ ἐν οὐρανῷ διηγουμένῳ, ὃς οὐδὲ τὰ ἐν τῇ γῇ καθορᾶν ἐδύνατο. αὐτίκα γέ τοι ὁ μὲν Ἥλιος οὑτοσὶ ζευξάμενος τὸ ἅρμα πανήμερος τὸν οὐρανὸν περιπολεῖ πῦρ ἐνδεδυκὼς καὶ τῶν ἀκτίνων ἀποστίλβων, οὐδ' ὅσον κνήσασθαι τὸ οὖς, φασί, σχολὴν ἄγων· ἢν γάρ τι κἂν ὀλίγον ἐπιρραθυμήσας λάθῃ, ἀφηνιάσαντες οἱ ἵπποι καὶ τῆς ὁδοῦ παρατραπόμενοι κατέφλεξαν τὰ πάντα. ἡ Σελήνη δὲ ἄγρυπνος καὶ αὐτὴ περίεισιν φαίνουσα τοῖς κωμάζουσιν καὶ τοῖς ἀωρὶ ἀπὸ τῶν δείπνων ἐπανιοῦσιν. ὁ Ἀπόλλων τε αὖ πολυπράγμονα τὴν τέχνην ἐπανελόμενος ὀλίγου δεῖν τὰ ὦτα ἐκκεκώφηται πρὸς τῶν ἐνοχλούντων κατὰ χρείαν τῆς μαντικῆς, καὶ ἄρτι μὲν αὐτῷ ἐν Δελφοῖς ἀναγκαῖον εἶναι, μετ' ὀλίγον δὲ εἰς Κολοφῶνα θεῖ, κἀκεῖθεν εἰς Ξάνθον μεταβαίνει καὶ δρομαῖος

Available in photographs: Γ, UPN.

[1] ΔΙΣ ΚΑΤΗΓΟΡΟΥΜΕΝΟΣ Η ΔΙΚΑΣΤΗΡΙΑ β.

THE DOUBLE INDICTMENT

ZEUS

Plague take all philosophers who say that bliss is to be found only among the gods! If they but knew all that we endure for the sake of men, they would not envy us our nectar and ambrosia, putting their trust in Homer, a blind man and a fraud, who called us blissful and told about what is in heaven when he could not even see what is on earth. Here is an example right at hand: Helius puts his team to his chariot and traverses the sky all day long, clad in a garment of fire and resplendent with rays, not even getting leisure enough to scratch his ear, as they say: for if he unconsciously relaxes the least bit, his horses run away, turn out of the road, and burn everything up. Selene, too, goes about without a wink of sleep, giving light to night-roisterers and people returning late from dinners. Apollo, again, has taken up a very active profession, and has been deafened almost completely by people besetting him with requests for prophecies. One moment he has to be in Delphi; the next, he runs to Colophon; from there he crosses to Xanthus, and again at full speed

αὖθις εἰς Δῆλον ἢ εἰς Βραγχίδας· καὶ ὅλως ἔνθα ἂν ἡ πρόμαντις πιοῦσα τοῦ ἱεροῦ νάματος καὶ μασησαμένη τῆς δάφνης καὶ τὸν τρίποδα διασείσασα κελεύῃ παρεῖναι, ἄοκνον χρὴ αὐτίκα μάλα παρεστάναι συνείροντα τοὺς χρησμοὺς ἢ οἴχεσθαί οἱ τὴν δόξαν τῆς τέχνης. ἐῶ γὰρ λέγειν ὁπόσα ἐπὶ πείρᾳ τῆς μαντικῆς ἐπιτεχνῶνται αὐτῷ ἄρνεια κρέα καὶ χελώνας εἰς τὸ αὐτὸ ἕψοντες, ὥστε εἰ μὴ τὴν ῥῖνα ὀξὺς ἦν, κἂν ἀπῆλθεν αὐτοῦ ὁ Λυδὸς καταγελῶν. ὁ μὲν γὰρ Ἀσκληπιὸς ὑπὸ τῶν νοσούντων ἐνοχλούμενος "ὁρῇ τε δεινὰ θιγγάνει τε ἀηδέων ἐπ' ἀλλοτρίῃσί τε συμφορῇσιν ἰδίας καρποῦται λύπας." τί γὰρ ἂν ἢ[1] τοὺς Ἀνέμους φυτουργοῦντας λέγοιμι καὶ παραπέμποντας τὰ πλοῖα καὶ τοῖς λικμῶσιν ἐπιπνέοντας, ἢ τὸν Ὕπνον ἐπὶ πάντας πετόμενον, ἢ τὸν Ὄνειρον μετὰ τοῦ Ὕπνου διανυκτερεύοντα καὶ ὑποφητεύοντα αὐτῷ; πάντα γὰρ ταῦτα ὑπὸ φιλανθρωπίας οἱ θεοὶ πονοῦσιν, πρὸς τὸν ἐπὶ τῆς γῆς βίον ἕκαστος[2] συντελοῦντες.

2 Καίτοι τὰ μὲν τῶν ἄλλων μέτρια· ἐγὼ δὲ αὐτὸς ὁ πάντων βασιλεὺς καὶ πατὴρ ὅσας μὲν ἀηδίας ἀνέχομαι, ὅσα δὲ πράγματα ἔχω πρὸς τοσαύτας φροντίδας διῃρημένος· ᾧ πρῶτα μὲν τὰ τῶν ἄλλων θεῶν ἔργα ἐπισκοπεῖν ἀναγκαῖον ὁπόσοι τι ἡμῖν συνδιαπράττουσι τῆς ἀρχῆς, ὡς μὴ βλακεύωσιν ἐν αὐτοῖς, ἔπειτα δὲ καὶ αὐτῷ μυρία ἄττα πράττειν καὶ σχεδὸν ἀνέφικτα ὑπὸ λεπτότητος· οὐ γὰρ μόνον τὰ κεφάλαια ταῦτα τῆς

[1] ἢ C. F. Hermann (and Ψ ?): εἰ γUN.
[2] ἕκαστος Cobet (ἕκαστός τι): ἕκαστοι β, ἑκάστοις γ.

to Delos or to Branchidae. In a word, wherever his prophetess, after drinking from the holy well and chewing laurel and setting the tripod ashake, bids him appear, there is no delaying—he must present himself immediately to reel off his prophecies, or else it is all up with his reputation in the profession. I say nothing of the devices they get up to test his powers of divination, cooking mutton and turtle together, so that if he had not a good nose, that Lydian would have gone off laughing at him.[1] As for Asclepius, he is pestered by the sick: "Dire sights he sees, and touches what he loathes, and in the woes of others finds a crop of sorrow for himself."[2] Why should I refer either to the Winds, that aid the crops and speed the ships on their courses and blow upon the winnowers, or to Sleep, that wings his way to everyone, or to Jack-of-dreams, that keeps vigil all night long with Sleep and serves as his interpreter? All this work the gods do out of love for man, each contributing to life on earth.

And yet the others are not so badly off in comparison with myself. I am the monarch and father of all: but how many discomforts I put up with and how many bothers I have, distracted as I am by such a number of things to think of! First, I must oversee the work of all the other gods who help me in any way in administering my sovereignty, in order that they may not be remiss in it. Then I myself have to do any number of tasks that are almost impossible to carry out on account of their minuteness; for it is not to be supposed that I

[1] Croesus, who got up the device, according to Herodotus, to see which oracle was the most trustworthy (Herod. 1, 46–49).

[2] Hippocrates *de Flatibus*, 1, 6; said of the physician.

διοικήσεως, ὑετοὺς καὶ χαλάζας καὶ πνεύματα καὶ ἀστραπὰς αὐτὸς οἰκονομησάμενος καὶ διατάξας πέπαυμαι τῶν ἐπὶ μέρους φροντίδων ἀπηλλαγμένος, ἀλλά με δεῖ καὶ ταῦτα μὲν ποιεῖν ἀποβλέπειν δὲ κατὰ τὸν αὐτὸν χρόνον ἁπανταχόσε καὶ πάντα ἐπισκοπεῖν ὥσπερ τὸν ἐν τῇ Νεμέᾳ βουκόλον, τοὺς κλέπτοντας, τοὺς ἐπιορκοῦντας, τοὺς θύοντας, εἴ τις ἔσπεισε, πόθεν ἡ κνῖσα καὶ ὁ καπνὸς ἀνέρχεται, τίς νοσῶν ἢ πλέων ἐκάλεσεν, καὶ τὸ πάντων ἐπιπονώτατον, ὑφ' ἕνα καιρὸν ἔν τε Ὀλυμπίᾳ τῇ ἑκατόμβῃ παρεῖναι καὶ ἐν Βαβυλῶνι τοὺς πολεμοῦντας ἐπισκοπεῖν καὶ ἐν Γέταις χαλαζᾶν καὶ ἐν Αἰθίοψιν εὐωχεῖσθαι.

Τὸ δὲ μεμψίμοιρον οὐδὲ οὕτω διαφυγεῖν ῥᾴδιον, ἀλλὰ πολλάκις οἱ μὲν ἄλλοι θεοί τε καὶ ἀνέρες ἱπποκορυσταὶ εὕδουσι παννύχιοι, τὸν Δία δὲ ἐμὲ οὐκ ἔχει νήδυμος ὕπνος· ἢν γάρ τί που καὶ μικρὸν ἐπινυστάσωμεν, ἀληθὴς εὐθὺς ὁ Ἐπίκουρος, ἀπρονοήτους ἡμᾶς ἀποφαίνων τῶν ἐπὶ γῆς πραγμάτων. καὶ ὁ κίνδυνος οὐκ εὐκαταφρόνητος εἰ ταῦτα οἱ ἄνθρωποι πιστεύσουσιν αὐτῷ, ἀλλ' ἀστεφάνωτοι μὲν ἡμῖν οἱ ναοὶ ἔσονται, ἀκνίσωτοι δὲ αἱ ἀγυιαί, ἄσπονδοι δὲ οἱ κρατῆρες, ψυχροὶ δὲ οἱ βωμοί, καὶ ὅλως ἄθυτα καὶ ἀκαλλιέρητα πάντα[1] καὶ ὁ λιμὸς πολύς. τοιγαροῦν ὥσπερ οἱ κυβερνῆται ὑψηλὸς μόνος ἐπὶ τῆς πρύμνης ἕστηκα τὸ πηδάλιον ἔχων ἐν ταῖν χεροῖν, καὶ οἱ μὲν ἐπιβάται μεθύοντες εἰ τύχοι ἐγκαθεύδουσιν,

[1] πάντα Guyet: not in MSS.

simply manage and direct in person the principal features of my administration, such as rain, hail, wind, and lightning, and that then I am through, being dispensed from thinking of details. No, not only must I do all that, but I must look in all directions at the same time and keep an eye on everybody, just like the herdsman at Nemea,[1] to see who is stealing, who is committing perjury, who is offering sacrifice, whether anybody has poured a drink-offering, from what quarter the steam and the smoke of burnt-offerings rise, who has called upon me in sickness or at sea. What is most laborious of all, at one and the same moment I must attend the great sacrifice at Olympia, keep an eye on the armies at war near Babylon, send hail in the country of the Getae, and attend a banquet among the Ethiopians.

At that, it is not easy to escape criticism. It often happens that the others, "the gods and the warriors crested with horse-tails," sleep all through the night, while I, though Zeus, am not "held in the sweetness of slumber,"[2] for if I drowse off, even for an instant, Epicurus is instantly confirmed in his assertion that we exercise no providence over what happens on earth. And we cannot make light of the danger if men are going to take his word for this : our temples will have no wreaths, our wayside shrines no savoury steam, our wine-bowls no drink-offerings, our altars will be cold, and in short there will be general dearth of sacrifices and oblations, and famine will be rife. For that reason, like the master of a ship, I stand by myself high up on the stern with the tiller in my hands, and everybody else aboard gets drunk, perhaps, and goes to sleep, whereas I,

[1] Argus. [2] Partial paraphrase of *Iliad* 2, 1–2.

ἐγὼ δὲ ἄγρυπνος καὶ ἄσιτος ὑπὲρ ἁπάντων "μερμηρίζω κατὰ φρένα καὶ κατὰ θυμὸν" μόνῳ
3 τῷ δεσπότης εἶναι δοκεῖν τετιμημένος. ὥστε ἡδέως ἂν ἐροίμην τοὺς φιλοσόφους, οἳ μόνους τοὺς θεοὺς εὐδαιμονίζουσιν, πότε καὶ σχολάζειν ἡμᾶς τῷ νέκταρι καὶ τῇ ἀμβροσίᾳ νομίζουσι μυρία ὅσα ἔχοντας πράγματα.

Ἰδού γέ τοι ὑπ' ἀσχολίας τοσαύτας ἑώλους δίκας φυλάττομεν ἀποκειμένας ὑπ' εὐρῶτος ἤδη καὶ ἀραχνίων διεφθαρμένας, καὶ μάλιστα ὁπόσαι ταῖς ἐπιστήμαις καὶ τέχναις πρὸς ἀνθρώπους τινὰς συνεστᾶσιν, πάνυ παλαιὰς ἐνίας αὐτῶν. οἱ δὲ κεκράγασιν ἁπανταχόθεν καὶ ἀγανακτοῦσιν καὶ τὴν δίκην ἐπιβοῶνται κἀμὲ τῆς βραδυτῆτος αἰτιῶνται, ἀγνοοῦντες ὡς οὐκ ὀλιγωρίᾳ τὰς κρίσεις ὑπερημέρους συνέβη γενέσθαι, ἀλλ' ὑπὸ τῆς εὐδαιμονίας ᾗ συνεῖναι ἡμᾶς ὑπολαμβάνουσιν. τοῦτο γὰρ τὴν ἀσχολίαν καλοῦσιν.

ΕΡΜΗΣ

4 Καὐτός, ὦ Ζεῦ, πολλὰ τοιαῦτα ἐπὶ τῆς γῆς ἀκούων δυσχεραινόντων λέγειν πρὸς σὲ οὐκ ἐτόλμων. ἐπεὶ δὲ σὺ περὶ τούτων τοὺς λόγους ἐνέβαλες, καὶ δὴ λέγω. πάνυ ἀγανακτοῦσιν, ὦ πάτερ, καὶ σχετλιάζουσιν καὶ εἰς τὸ φανερὸν μὲν οὐ τολμῶσι λέγειν, ὑποτονθορύζουσι δὲ συγκεκυφότες αἰτιώμενοι τὸν χρόνον· οὓς ἔδει πάλαι τὰ καθ' αὑτοὺς εἰδότας στέργειν ἕκαστον τοῖς δεδικασμένοις.

ΖΕΥΣ

Τί οὖν, ὦ Ἑρμῆ, δοκεῖ; προτίθεμεν αὐτοῖς ἀγορὰν δικῶν, ἢ θέλεις εἰς νέωτα παραγγελοῦμεν;

without closing my eyes or eating, "ponder in heart and in soul"[1] for the benefit of all, rewarded only by being considered captain. So I should like to ask the philosophers, who say that only the gods are happy, when they suppose we really find leisure for our nectar and our ambrosia in the midst of our countless bothers.

Now, here is a case in point: for lack of spare time we are keeping all these stale lawsuits filed away, already spoiled by mildew and spiders' webs, especially those brought against certain persons by the sciences and the arts—some of these are very antiquated.[2] People are making an outcry on all sides and losing patience and hurling reproaches at Justice and blaming me for my slowness, not knowing that the hearings have not been postponed, as it happens, on account of our negligence, but on account of the bliss in which they imagine we exist: for that is what they call our press of business.

HERMES

I myself hear a great many complaints of that sort on earth, Zeus, but I did not venture to mention them to you. Now, however, I shall do so, as you began the discussion of this topic. They are indeed out of patience and indignant, father, and although they do not venture to talk openly, they put their heads together and grumble, finding fault with the delay. These men should have known long ago how things stood with them and should have acquiesced in the verdict in each case.

ZEUS

Well, what do you think, Hermes? Shall we open a session of court for them, or do you wish we should announce it for next year?

[1] *Iliad* 2, 3. [2] What these are becomes clear later (p. 109)

ΕΡΜΗΣ

Οὐ μὲν οὖν, ἀλλὰ ἤδη προθῶμεν.

ΖΕΥΣ

Οὕτω ποίει· σὺ μὲν κήρυττε καταπτάμενος ὅτι ἀγορὰ δικῶν ἔσται κατὰ τάδε. πάντας ὁπόσοι τὰς γραφὰς ἀπενηνόχασιν, ἥκειν τήμερον εἰς Ἄρειον πάγον, ἐκεῖ δὲ τὴν μὲν Δίκην ἀποκληροῦν σφίσι τὰ δικαστήρια κατὰ λόγον τῶν τιμημάτων ἐξ ἁπάντων Ἀθηναίων· εἰ δέ τις ἄδικον οἴοιτο γεγενῆσθαι τὴν κρίσιν, ἐξεῖναι ἐφέντι ἐπ' ἐμὲ δικάζεσθαι ἐξ ὑπαρχῆς, ὡς εἰ μηδὲ τὸ παράπαν ἐδεδίκαστο. σὺ δέ, ὦ θύγατερ, καθεζομένη παρὰ τὰς σεμνὰς θεὰς ἀποκλήρου τὰς δίκας καὶ ἐπισκόπει τοὺς δικάζοντας.

ΔΙΚΗ

5 Αὖθις εἰς τὴν γῆν, ἵν' ἐξελαυνομενη πρὸς αὐτῶν δραπετεύω πάλιν ἐκ τοῦ βίου τὴν Ἀδικίαν ἐπιγελῶσαν οὐ φέρουσα;

ΖΕΥΣ

Χρηστὰ ἐλπίζειν σε δεῖ· πάντως γὰρ ἤδη πεπείκασιν αὐτοὺς οἱ φιλόσοφοι σὲ τῆς Ἀδικίας προτιμᾶν, καὶ μάλιστα ὁ τοῦ Σωφρονίσκου τὸ δίκαιον ὑπερεπαινέσας καὶ ἀγαθῶν τὸ μέγιστον ἀποφήνας.

ΔΙΚΗ

Πάνυ γοῦν ὃν φῂς αὐτὸν ἐκεῖνον ὤνησαν οἱ περὶ ἐμοῦ λόγοι, ὃς παραδοθεὶς τοῖς ἕνδεκα καὶ εἰς τὸ δεσμωτήριον ἐμπεσὼν ἔπιεν ἄθλιος τοῦ κωνείου, μηδὲ τὸν ἀλεκτρυόνα τῷ Ἀσκληπιῷ

HERMES

No, indeed; let us open it now.

ZEUS

Do so. Fly down and proclaim that there will be a session of court under the following regulations. All who have entered suit are to come to the Areopagus to-day; at that place Justice is to empanel juries for them out of the entire body of Athenians, the number of jurymen to depend upon the penalty involved; and if anyone thinks that his hearing has been unjust, he is to be allowed to appeal to me and have the case tried afresh, just as if it had not been tried at all. (*To* JUSTICE) Daughter, take your place beside the Dread Goddesses,[1] empanel the juries and have an eye on the trials.

JUSTICE

Back to earth once more, to be driven off by them and to flee from the world again because I cannot stand being laughed at by Injustice?

ZEUS

You must be of good hope. Certainly by now the philosophers have persuaded them to regard you more highly than Injustice; especially the son of Sophroniscus,[2] who praised just dealing to the skies and declared it the greatest of blessings.

JUSTICE

Truly the very man you mention profited greatly by his talk about me! He was handed over to the Eleven, thrown into prison, and drank hemlock, poor fellow, before he had even paid that cock to

[1] The Eumenides, since the trial of Orestes, had an altar on the Areopagus. [2] Socrates.

ἀποδεδωκώς· παρὰ τοσοῦτον ὑπερέσχον οἱ κατήγοροι τἀναντία περὶ τῆς Ἀδικίας φιλοσοφοῦντες.

ΖΕΥΣ

6 Ξένα ἔτι τοῖς πολλοῖς τὰ τῆς φιλοσοφίας ἦν τότε, καὶ ὀλίγοι ἦσαν οἱ φιλοσοφοῦντες, ὥστε εἰκότως εἰς τὸν Ἄνυτον καὶ Μέλητον ἔρρεπεν τὰ δικαστήρια. τὸ δὲ νῦν εἶναι, οὐχ ὁρᾷς ὅσοι τρίβωνες καὶ βακτηρίαι καὶ πῆραι; καὶ ἁπανταχοῦ πώγων βαθὺς καὶ βιβλίον ἐν τῇ ἀριστερᾷ, καὶ πάντες ὑπὲρ σοῦ φιλοσοφοῦσι, μεστοὶ δὲ οἱ περίπατοι κατὰ ἴλας καὶ φάλαγγας ἀλλήλοις ἀπαντώντων, καὶ οὐδεὶς ὅστις οὐ τρόφιμος τῆς ἀρετῆς εἶναι δοκεῖν βούλεται. πολλοὶ γοῦν τὰς τέχνας ἀφέντες ἃς εἶχον τέως, ἐπὶ τὴν πήραν ᾄξαντες καὶ τὸ τριβώνιον, καὶ τὸ σῶμα πρὸς τὸν ἥλιον εἰς τὸ Αἰθιοπικὸν ἐπιχράναντες αὐτοσχέδιοι φιλόσοφοι ἐκ σκυτοτόμων ἢ τεκτόνων περινοστοῦσι σὲ καὶ τὴν σὴν ἀρετὴν ἐπαινοῦντες. ὥστε κατὰ τὴν παροιμίαν, θᾶττον ἄν τις ἐν πλοίῳ πεσὼν διαμάρτοι ξύλου ἢ ἔνθα ἂν ἀπίδῃ ὁ ὀφθαλμός, ἀπορήσει φιλοσόφου.

ΔΙΚΗ

7 Καὶ μὴν οὗτοί με, ὦ Ζεῦ, δεδίττονται πρὸς ἀλλήλους ἐρίζοντες καὶ ἀγνωμονοῦντες ἐν αὐτοῖς οἷς περὶ ἐμοῦ διεξέρχονται. φασὶ δὲ καὶ τοὺς πλείστους αὐτῶν ἐν μὲν τοῖς λόγοις προσποιεῖσθαί με, ἐπὶ δὲ τῶν πραγμάτων μηδὲ τὸ παράπαν εἰς τὴν οἰκίαν παραδέχεσθαι, ἀλλὰ δήλους εἶναι ἀποκλείσοντας ἤν ἀφίκωμαί ποτε αὐτοῖς ἐπὶ τὰς θύρας· πάλαι γὰρ τὴν Ἀδικίαν προεπεξενῶσθαι αὐτοῖς.

Asclepius;[1] so much the better of the argument had his accusers, whose philosophy was directly opposed to his, and favoured Injustice.

ZEUS

The people were still unfamiliar with the teachings of philosophy at that time, and there were few that pursued it, so it was natural that the juries inclined towards Anytus and Meletus. But at present, do not you see how many short cloaks and staves and wallets there are? On all sides there are long beards, and books in the left hand, and everybody preaches in favour of you; the public walks are full of people assembling in companies and in battalions, and there is nobody who does not want to be thought a scion of Virtue. In fact, many, giving up the trades that they had before, rush after the wallet and the cloak, tan their bodies in the sun to Ethiopian hue, make themselves extemporaneous philosophers out of cobblers or carpenters, and go about praising you and your virtue. Consequently, in the words of the proverb, it would be easier for a man to fall in a boat without hitting a plank than for your eye to miss a philosopher wherever it looks.

JUSTICE

Yes, but those very men frighten me, Zeus, by quarrelling with each other and showing unfairness even in their discussions of me. It is rumoured, too, that while most of them claim kinship with me in words, when it comes to facts they do not even open their house to me at all, but make it plain that they will lock me out if ever I come to their door; for they made Injustice their bosom friend long ago.

[1] His last words were: "Crito, we owe a cock to Asclepius. Do pay it without fail." (End of *Phaedo*).

ΖΕΥΣ

Οὐ πάντες, ὦ θύγατερ, μοχθηροί εἰσιν· ἱκανὸν δὲ κἂν ἐνίοις τισὶν χρηστοῖς ἐντύχῃς. ἀλλ' ἄπιτε ἤδη, ὡς κἂν ὀλίγαι τήμερον ἐκδικασθῶσιν.

ΕΡΜΗΣ

8 Προΐωμεν, ὦ Δίκη, ταύτῃ εὐθὺ τοῦ Σουνίου μικρὸν ὑπὸ τὸν Ὑμηττὸν ἐπὶ τὰ λαιὰ τῆς Πάρνηθος, ἔνθα αἱ δύο ἐκεῖναι ἄκραι· σὺ γὰρ ἔοικας ἐκλελῆσθαι πάλαι τὴν ὁδόν. ἀλλὰ τί δακρύεις καὶ σχετλιάζεις; μὴ δέδιθι· οὐκέθ' ὅμοια τὰ ἐν τῷ βίῳ· τεθνᾶσιν ἐκεῖνοι πάντες οἱ Σκείρωνες καὶ Πιτυοκάμπται καὶ Βουσίριδες καὶ Φαλάριδες οὓς ἐδεδίεις τότε, νυνὶ δὲ Σοφία καὶ Ἀκαδήμεια καὶ Στοὰ κατέχουσι πάντα καὶ πανταχοῦ σε ζητοῦσιν καὶ περὶ σοῦ διαλέγονται, κεχηνότες εἴ ποθεν εἰς αὐτοὺς καταπτοῖο πάλιν.

ΔΙΚΗ

Σὺ γοῦν μοι τἀληθές, ὦ Ἑρμῆ, ἂν εἴποις μόνος, ἅτε συνὼν αὐτοῖς τὰ πολλὰ καὶ συνδιατρίβων ἔν τε γυμνασίοις καὶ ἐν τῇ ἀγορᾷ—καὶ ἀγοραῖος γὰρ εἶ καὶ ἐν ταῖς ἐκκλησίαις κηρύττεις—ὁποῖοι γεγένηνται καὶ εἰ δυνατή μοι παρ' αὐτοῖς ἡ μονή.

ΕΡΜΗΣ

Νὴ Δία, ἀδικοίην γὰρ ἂν πρὸς ἀδελφήν σε οὖσαν μὴ λέγων. οὐκ ὀλίγα πρὸς τῆς φιλοσοφίας

---

[1] Lycabettus and the Acropolis. The promontory of Sunium is the most conspicuous landmark because Hermes

ZEUS

They are not all bad, my daughter, and it is enough if you find some that are good. But go now, so that a few cases, at least, may be heard to-day.

HERMES

Let us set out in this direction, Justice, straight for Sunium, not far from the foot of Hymettus, to the left of Parnes, where you see those two heights[1]; you have probably forgotten the way long since. But why are you crying and taking it hard? Don't be afraid: things are no longer the same in life. All those Scirons and Pinebenders and Busirises and Phalarises whom you used to fear in former days are dead, and now Wisdom and the Academy and the Porch are in full sway, seek for you everywhere, and hold conversations about you, in open-mouthed expectation that, from some quarter or other, you may perhaps come flying down to them once more.

JUSTICE

Well, Hermes, you are the only person who can tell me the truth, inasmuch as you associate with them a great deal, passing your days with them in the athletic clubs and in the market-place; for you are the god of the market, as well as being crier in the meetings of the assembly. What sort of people are they, and is it possible for me to abide among them?

HERMES

To be sure; I should not be treating you fairly if I did not tell you, since you are my sister. Most of

and Justice are coming down from above, and from seaward (cf. below, ἐν δεξιᾷ). Lucian's gods live in Heaven, not on Olympus or Ida.

ὠφέληνται οἱ πολλοὶ αὐτῶν· καὶ γὰρ εἰ μηδὲν ἄλλο, αἰδοῖ γοῦν τοῦ σχήματος μετριώτερα διαμαρτάνουσιν. πλὴν ἀλλὰ καὶ μοχθηροῖς τισιν ἐντεύξῃ αὐτῶν--χρὴ γάρ, οἶμαι, τἀληθῆ λέγειν—ἐνίοις δὲ ἡμισόφοις καὶ ἡμιφαύλοις. ἐπεὶ γὰρ αὐτοὺς μετέβαπτεν ἡ σοφία παραλαβοῦσα, ὁπόσοι μὲν εἰς κόρον ἔπιον τῆς βαφῆς, χρηστοὶ ἀκριβῶς ἀπετελέσθησαν ἀμιγεῖς ἑτέρων χρωμάτων, καὶ πρός γε τὴν σὴν ὑποδοχὴν οὗτοι ἑτοιμότατοι· ὅσοι δὲ ὑπὸ τοῦ πάλαι ῥύπου μὴ εἰς βάθος παρεδέξαντο ὁπόσον δευσοποιὸν τοῦ φαρμάκου, τῶν ἄλλων ἀμείνους, ἀτελεῖς δὲ ὅμως καὶ μιξόλευκοι καὶ κατεστιγμένοι καὶ παρδαλωτοὶ τὴν χρόαν. εἰσὶ δ' οἳ καὶ μόνον ψαύσαντες ἔκτοσθεν τοῦ λέβητος ἄκρῳ τῷ δακτύλῳ καὶ ἐπιχρισάμενοι τῆς ἀσβόλου ἱκανῶς οἴονται καὶ οὗτοι μεταβεβάφθαι. σοὶ μέντοι δῆλον ὅτι μετὰ τῶν ἀρίστων ἡ διατριβὴ ἔσται.

9 Ἀλλὰ μεταξὺ λόγων ἤδη πλησιάζομεν τῇ Ἀττικῇ· ὥστε τὸ μὲν Σούνιον ἐν δεξιᾷ καταλείπωμεν, εἰς δὲ τὴν ἀκρόπολιν ἀπονεύωμεν ἤδη. καὶ ἐπείπερ καταβεβήκαμεν, αὐτὴ μὲν ἐνταῦθά που ἐπὶ τοῦ πάγου κάθησο εἰς τὴν πνύκα ὁρῶσα καὶ περιμένουσα ἔστ' ἂν κηρύξω τὰ παρὰ τοῦ Διός, ἐγὼ δὲ εἰς τὴν ἀκρόπολιν ἀναβὰς ῥᾷον οὕτως ἅπαντας ἐκ τοῦ ἐπηκόου προσκαλέσομαι.

ΔΙΚΗ

Μὴ πρότερον ἀπέλθῃς, ὦ Ἑρμῆ, πρὶν εἰπεῖν ὅστις οὗτος ὁ προσιών ἐστιν, ὁ κερασφόρος, ὁ τὴν σύριγγα, ὁ λάσιος ἐκ τοῖν σκελοῖν.

them have been helped not a little by philosophy: for if it goes no further, at least regard for their cloth makes them more circumspect in sinning. However, you will come upon a few rascals among them—I *must* tell the truth, I suppose—and some who are partly wise and partly foolish. You see, when Wisdom took them in hand and dyed them over, all those who thoroughly absorbed the dye were made entirely serviceable, without any intermixture of other hues, and they are quite ready to receive you; while those who because of their ingrained filth were not deeply penetrated by the colouring matter of the dyestuff are better than the rest, to be sure, but unfinished products, half-white, blemished, and spotted like the pard. And there are some who have only touched the kettle on the outside with a finger-tip and smeared on some of the soot, yet think that they too are well enough dyed over. You, however, will of course pass your time with the best of them.

But in the course of our talk we are already drawing near to Attica, so let us leave Sunium on our right, and now let us glide down to the Acropolis. . . . Now that we have alighted, you sit down here on the Areopagus somewhere, facing the Pnyx, and wait until I give out the proclamation from Zeus. If I climb the Acropolis it will be easier for me to summon everybody from that point of vantage for the voice.

JUSTICE

Don't go, Hermes, until you have told me who comes here, the person with the horns and the shepherd's pipe and the hairy legs.

ΕΡΜΗΣ

Τί φής; ἀγνοεῖς τὸν Πᾶνα, τῶν Διονύσου θεραπόντων τὸν βακχικώτατον; οὗτος ᾤκει μὲν τὸ πρόσθεν ἀνὰ τὸ Παρθένιον, ὑπὸ δὲ τὸν Δάτιδος ἐπίπλουν καὶ τὴν Μαραθῶνάδε τῶν βαρβάρων ἀπόβασιν ἧκεν ἄκλητος τοῖς Ἀθηναίοις σύμμαχος, καὶ τὸ ἀπ' ἐκείνου τὴν ὑπὸ τῇ ἀκροπόλει σπήλυγγα ταύτην ἀπολαβόμενος οἰκεῖ μικρὸν ὑπὲρ τοῦ Πελασγικοῦ εἰς τὸ μετοίκιον συντελῶν. καὶ νῦν ὡς τὸ εἰκὸς ἰδὼν ἡμᾶς ἐκ γειτόνων πρόσεισι δεξιωσόμενος.

ΠΑΝ

10 Χαίρετε, ὦ Ἑρμῆ καὶ Δίκη.

ΕΡΜΗΣ

Καὶ σύ γε, ὦ Πάν, μουσικώτατε καὶ πηδητικώτατε Σατύρων ἁπάντων, Ἀθήνησι δὲ καὶ πολεμικώτατε.

ΠΑΝ

Τίς δὲ ὑμᾶς, ὦ Ἑρμῆ, χρεία δεῦρο ἤγαγεν;

ΕΡΜΗΣ

Αὕτη σοι διηγήσεται τὰ πάντα· ἐγὼ δὲ ἐπὶ τὴν ἀκρόπολιν ἄπειμι[1] καὶ τὸ κήρυγμα.

ΔΙΚΗ

Ὁ Ζεύς, ὦ Πάν, κατέπεμψέ με ἀποκληρώσουσαν τὰς δίκας. σοὶ δὲ πῶς τὰ ἐν Ἀθήναις ἔχει;

ΠΑΝ

Τὸ μὲν ὅλον οὐ κατ' ἀξίαν πράττω παρ' αὐτοῖς, ἀλλὰ πολὺ καταδεέστερον τῆς ἐλπίδος, καὶ ταῦτα

[1] ἄπειμι N: not in other MSS. Probably a conjecture, and more than one word may have been lost.

HERMES

What! Don't you know Pan, the most bacchanalian of the servants of Dionysus? He formerly lived on Parthenion,[1] but at the time of the approach of Datis by sea and the landing of the barbarians at Marathon, he came unasked to fight on the side of the Athenians; and since then, accepting this cavern under the Acropolis, a little above the Pelasgicon,[2] he lives in it, paying the usual tax as a resident alien. Very likely he has seen us near and is coming up to greet us.

PAN

Good day to you, Hermes and Justice.

HERMES

The same to you, Pan, most musical and most frolicsome of all satyrs, and at Athens the most bellicose!

PAN

What business brought you two here, Hermes?

HERMES

She will tell you the whole story; I am going to the Acropolis, to make my proclamation.

JUSTICE

Zeus sent me down, Pan, to empanel juries for the lawsuits. But how do you find things in Athens?

PAN

On the whole, I do not get on as well as I ought here—much worse than I expected; and yet I dis-

[1] A mountain in Arcadia.

[2] The cave of Pan, being in the N.W. corner of the Acropolis, can be pointed out (ταύτην) from the Areopagus, which is close by (ἐκ γειτόνων). For the bit of the prehistoric wall below it (Pelasgicon), see p. 63, note 1, and p. 71.

τηλικοῦτον ἀπωσάμενος κυδοιμὸν τὸν ἐκ τῶν βαρβάρων. ὅμως δὲ δὶς ἢ τρὶς τοῦ ἔτους ἀνιόντες ἐπιλεξάμενοι τράγον ἔνορχην θύουσί μοι πολλῆς τῆς κινάβρας ἀπόζοντα, εἶτ' εὐωχοῦνται τὰ κρέα, ποιησάμενοί με τῆς εὐφροσύνης μάρτυρα καὶ ψιλῷ τιμήσαντες τῷ κρότῳ. πλὴν ἀλλ' ἔχει τινά μοι ψυχαγωγίαν ὁ γέλως αὐτῶν καὶ ἡ παιδιά.

ΔΙΚΗ

11 Τὰ δ' ἄλλα, ὦ Πάν, ἀμείνους πρὸς ἀρετὴν ἐγένοντο ὑπὸ τῶν φιλοσόφων;

ΠΑΝ

Τίνας λέγεις τοὺς φιλοσόφους; ἆρ' ἐκείνους τοὺς κατηφεῖς, τοὺς συνάμα πολλούς, τοὺς τὸ γένειον ὁμοίους ἐμοί, τοὺς λάλους;

ΔΙΚΗ

Καὶ μάλα.

ΠΑΝ

Οὐκ οἶδα ὅλως ὅ τι καὶ λέγουσιν οὐδὲ συνίημι τὴν σοφίαν αὐτῶν· ὄρειος γὰρ ἔγωγε καὶ τὰ κομψὰ ταῦτα ῥημάτια καὶ ἀστικὰ οὐ μεμάθηκα, ὦ Δίκη. πόθεν γὰρ ἐν Ἀρκαδίᾳ σοφιστὴς ἢ φιλόσοφος; μέχρι τοῦ πλαγίου καλάμου καὶ τῆς σύριγγος ἐγὼ σοφός, τὰ δ' ἄλλα αἰπόλος καὶ χορευτὴς καὶ πολεμιστής, ἢν δέῃ. πλὴν ἀλλ' ἀκούω γε αὐτῶν ἀεὶ κεκραγότων καὶ ἀρετήν τινα καὶ ἰδέας καὶ φύσιν καὶ ἀσώματα διεξιόντων, ἄγνωστα ἐμοὶ καὶ ξένα ὀνόματα. καὶ τὰ πρῶτα μὲν εἰρηνικῶς ἐνάρχονται τῶν πρὸς ἀλλήλους λόγων, προιούσης δὲ τῆς συνουσίας ἐπιτείνουσι τὸ φθέγμα μέχρι πρὸς τὸ ὄρθιον, ὥστε ὑπερδιατεινομένων καὶ ἅμα λέγειν ἐθελόντων τό τε πρό-

pelled the mighty hue and cry of the barbarians. In spite of that, they come up only two or three times a year, pick out and sacrifice in my honour a he-goat with a powerful goatish smell, and then feast on the meat, making me a mere witness of their good cheer and paying their respects to me only with their noise. However, their laughter and fun afford me some amusement.

JUSTICE

In general, Pan, have they been improved in virtue by the philosophers?

PAN

What do you mean by philosophers? Those gloomy fellows, flocking together, with beards like mine, who talk so much?

JUSTICE

To be sure.

PAN

I do not know at all what they mean and I do not understand their wisdom, for I am a mountaineer and I have not studied those clever, citified, technical terms, Justice. How could a literary man or a philosopher possibly come from Arcadia? My wisdom does not go beyond the flute and the pipes; for the rest I am a goatherd, a dancer, and if need be a fighter. However, I hear them bawling continually and talking about "virtue" (whatever that means) and "ideas" and "nature" and "things incorporeal," terms that are to me unknown and outlandish. They begin their discussions peaceably, but as the conference proceeds they raise their voices to a high falsetto, so that, what with their excessive straining and their endeavour to talk at the same time, their

σωπον ἐρυθριᾷ καὶ ὁ τράχηλος οἰδεῖ καὶ αἱ φλέβες ἐξανίστανται ὥσπερ τῶν αὐλητῶν ὁπόταν εἰς στενὸν τὸν αὐλὸν ἐμπνεῖν βιάζωνται. διαταράξαντες γοῦν τοὺς λόγους καὶ τὸ ἐξ ἀρχῆς ἐπισκοπούμενον συγχέαντες ἀπίασι λοιδορησάμενοι ἀλλήλοις οἱ πολλοί, τὸν ἱδρῶτα ἐκ τοῦ μετώπου ἀγκύλῳ τῷ δακτύλῳ ἀποξυόμενοι, καὶ οὗτος κρατεῖν ἔδοξεν ὃς ἂν μεγαλοφωνότερος αὐτῶν ᾖ καὶ θρασύτερος καὶ διαλυομένων ἀπέλθῃ ὕστερος. πλὴν ἀλλ' ὅ γε λεὼς ὁ πολὺς τεθήπασιν αὐτούς, καὶ μάλιστα ὁπόσους μηδὲν τῶν ἀναγκαιοτέρων ἀσχολεῖ, καὶ παρεστᾶσι πρὸς τὸ θράσος καὶ τὴν βοὴν κεκηλημένοι. ἐμοὶ μὲν οὖν ἀλαζόνες τινὲς ἐδόκουν ἀπὸ τούτων καὶ ἠνιώμην ἐπὶ τῇ τοῦ πώγωνος ὁμοιότητι. εἰ δέ γε δημωφελές τι ἐνῆν τῇ βοῇ αὐτῶν καί τι ἀγαθὸν ἐκ τῶν ῥημάτων ἐκείνων ἀνεφύετο αὐτοῖς, οὐκ ἂν εἰπεῖν ἔχοιμι. πλὴν ἀλλ' εἴ γε δεῖ μηδὲν ὑποστειλάμενον τἀληθὲς διηγήσασθαι—οἰκῶ γὰρ ἐπὶ σκοπῆς, ὡς ὁρᾷς—πολλοὺς αὐτῶν πολλάκις ἤδη ἐθεασάμην περὶ δείλην ὀψίαν—

ΔΙΚΗ

12 Ἐπίσχες, ὦ Πάν. οὐχ ὁ Ἑρμῆς σοι κηρύττειν ἔδοξεν;

ΠΑΝ

Πάνυ μὲν οὖν.

ΕΡΜΗΣ

Ἀκούετε λεῴ,[1] ἀγορὰν δικῶν ἀγαθῇ τύχῃ καταστησόμεθα τήμερον Ἐλαφηβολιῶνος ἑβδόμῃ ἱσταμένου. ὁπόσοι γραφὰς ἀπήνεγκαν, ἥκειν εἰς Ἄρειον πάγον, ἔνθα ἡ Δίκη ἀποκληρώσει τὰ

[1] λεῴ Dindorf, Cobet: λεώς MSS.

faces get red, their necks get swollen, and their veins stand out like those of flute-players when they try to blow into a closed flute. In fact, they spoil their arguments, confuse the original subject of inquiry, and then, after abusing one another, most of them, they go away wiping the sweat off their foreheads with their bent fingers; and the man that is most loud-mouthed and impudent and leaves last when they break up is considered to have the best of it. However, the common people admire them, especially those who have nothing more pressing to do, and stand there enchanted by their impudence and their shouting. For my part, I considered them impostors in consequence of all this, and was annoyed at the resemblance in beard. But perhaps there was something beneficial to the common weal in their shouting and some good sprang from those technical terms of theirs—I can't say. However, if I am to tell the truth without any reserve—for I dwell on a look-out, as you see—I have often seen many of them in the dark of the evening—

JUSTICE

Hush, Pan; didn't it seem to you that Hermes is making a proclamation?

PAN

Why, yes.

HERMES

Oyez, oyez! Under the blessing of Heaven, we shall hold a session of court to-day, the seventh of Elaphebolion.[1] All who have entered suits are to come to the Areopagus, where Justice will empanel the juries

[1] The seventh of Elaphebolion was not far from the first of April.

δικαστήρια καὶ αὐτὴ παρέσται τοῖς δικάζουσιν· οἱ δικασταὶ ἐξ ἁπάντων Ἀθηναίων· ὁ μισθὸς τριώβολον ἑκάστης δίκης· ἀριθμὸς τῶν δικαστῶν κατὰ λόγον τοῦ ἐγκλήματος. ὁπόσοι δὲ ἀποθέμενοι γραφὴν πρὶν εἰσελθεῖν ἀπέθανον, καὶ τούτους ὁ Αἰακὸς ἀναπεμψάτω. ἢν δέ τις ἄδικα δεδικάσθαι οἴηται, ἐφέσιμον ἀγωνιεῖται τὴν δίκην· ἡ δὲ ἔφεσις ἐπὶ τὸν Δία.

ΠΑΝ

Βαβαὶ τοῦ θορύβου· ἡλίκον, ὦ Δίκη, ἀνεβόησαν, ὡς δὲ καὶ σπουδῇ συνθέουσιν ἕλκοντες ἀλλήλους πρὸς τὸ ἄναντες εὐθὺ τοῦ Ἀρείου πάγου. καὶ ὁ Ἑρμῆς δὲ ἤδη πάρεστιν. ὥστε ὑμεῖς μὲν ἀμφὶ τὰς δίκας ἔχετε καὶ ἀποκληροῦτε καὶ διακρίνατε ὥσπερ ὑμῖν νόμος, ἐγὼ δὲ ἐπὶ τὸ σπήλαιον ἀπελθὼν συρίξομαί τι μέλος τῶν ἐρωτικῶν ᾧ τὴν Ἠχὼ εἴωθα ἐπικερτομεῖν· ἀκροάσεων δὲ καὶ λόγων τῶν δικανικῶν ἅλις ἔχει μοι ὁσημέραι τῶν ἐν Ἀρείῳ πάγῳ δικαζομένων ἀκούοντι.

ΕΡΜΗΣ

13 Ἄγε, ὦ Δίκη, προσκαλῶμεν.

ΔΙΚΗ

Εὖ λέγεις. ἀθρόοι γοῦν, ὡς ὁρᾷς, προσίασι θορυβοῦντες, ὥσπερ οἱ σφῆκες περιβομβοῦντες τὴν ἄκραν.

ΑΘΗΝΑΙΟΣ

Εἴληφά σε, ὦ κατάρατε.

ΑΛΛΟΣ

Συκοφαντεῖς.

ΑΛΛΟΣ

Δώσεις ποτὲ ἤδη τὴν δίκην.

and be present in person at the trials. The jurors will be drawn from the entire body of Athenians; the pay will be three obols a case, and the number of jurors will be in accordance with the charge. All those who have entered suits but have died before they came to trial are to be sent back to earth by Aeacus. If anyone thinks he has had an unjust hearing, he is to appeal the case, and the appeal will be to Zeus.

PAN

Heavens, what a hubbub! What a shout they raised, Justice, and how eagerly they are gathering at a run, dragging each other up the hill, straight for the Areopagus! Hermes, too, is here already, so busy yourselves with the cases, empanel your juries and give your verdicts as usual; I am going back to the cave to pipe one of the passionate melodies with which I am in the habit of provoking Echo. I am sick of trials and speeches, for I hear the pleaders on the Areopagus every day.

HERMES

Come, Justice, let's call them to the bar.

JUSTICE

Quite right. Indeed they are approaching in crowds, as you see, with a great noise, buzzing about the hilltop like wasps.

ATHENIAN

I've got you, curse you!

SECOND ATHENIAN

You are a blackmailer!

THIRD ATHENIAN

At last you are going to pay the penalty!

ΑΛΛΟΣ

Ἐξελέγξω σε δεινὰ εἰργασμένον.

ΑΛΛΟΣ

Ἐμοὶ πρώτῳ ἀποκλήρωσον.

ΑΛΛΟΣ

Ἕπου, μιαρέ, πρὸς τὸ δικαστήριον.

ΑΛΛΟΣ

Μὴ ἄγχε με.

ΔΙΚΗ

Οἶσθα ὃ δράσωμεν, ὦ Ἑρμῆ; τὰς μὲν ἄλλας δίκας εἰς τὴν αὔριον ὑπερβαλώμεθα, τήμερον δὲ κληρῶμεν τὰς τοιαύτας ὁπόσαι τέχναις ἢ βίοις ἢ ἐπιστήμαις πρὸς ἄνδρας εἰσὶν ἐπηγγελμέναι. καί μοι ταύτας ἀνάδος τῶν γραφῶν.

ΕΡΜΗΣ

Μέθη κατὰ τῆς Ἀκαδημείας περὶ Πολέμωνος ἀνδραποδισμοῦ.

ΔΙΚΗ

Ἑπτὰ κλήρωσον.

ΕΡΜΗΣ

Ἡ Στοὰ κατὰ τῆς Ἡδονῆς ἀδικίας, ὅτι τὸν ἐραστὴν αὐτῆς Διονύσιον ἀπεβουκόλησεν.

ΔΙΚΗ

Πέντε ἱκανοί.

---

[1] As Hermes gives each writ to Justice, he reads the heading and she tells him how many jurors are to be drawn. Her orders are carried out in silence, and the juries are all in readiness when the first case is called, which is not until she has filled the docket for the day (§ 15).

[2] Polemo, intemperate in his youth, went to a lecture by Xenocrates to create a disturbance, but was converted to

FOURTH ATHENIAN

I will prove that you have committed horrible crimes!

FIFTH ATHENIAN

Empanel my jury first!

SIXTH ATHENIAN

Come to court with me, scoundrel!

SEVENTH ATHENIAN

Stop choking me!

JUSTICE

Do you know what we ought to do, Hermes? Let us put off the rest of the cases until to-morrow, and to-day let us provide only for those entered by professions or pursuits or sciences against men. Pass me up the writs of that description.[1]

HERMES

Intemperance *v.* the Academy *in re* Polemo: kidnapping.[2]

JUSTICE

Draw seven jurors.

HERMES

Stoa *v.* Pleasure: alienation of affections—because Pleasure coaxed away her lover, Dionysius.[3]

JUSTICE

Five will do.

philosophy by what he heard. He succeeded Xenocrates as head of the Academy (Diog. L. iv. 1 ff.).

[3] Dionysius the Convert was a pupil of Zeno, but became a Cyrenaic, "being converted to pleasure; for sore eyes gave him so much trouble that he could not bring himself to maintain any longer that pain did not matter" (Diog. L. vii. 1, 31; cf. vii. 4).

ΕΡΜΗΣ

Περὶ Ἀριστίππου Τρυφὴ πρὸς Ἀρετήν.

ΔΙΚΗ

Πέντε καὶ τούτοις δικασάτωσαν.

ΕΡΜΗΣ

Ἀργυραμοιβικὴ δρασμοῦ Διογένει.

ΔΙΚΗ

Τρεῖς ἀποκλήρου μόνους.

ΕΡΜΗΣ

Γραφικὴ κατὰ Πύρρωνος λιποταξίου.

ΔΙΚΗ

Ἐννέα κρινάτωσαν.

ΕΡΜΗΣ

14 Βούλει καὶ ταύτας ἀποκληρῶμεν, ὦ Δίκη, τὰς δύο, τὰς πρῴην ἀπενηνεγμένας κατὰ τοῦ ῥήτορος;

ΔΙΚΗ

Τὰς παλαιὰς πρότερον διανύσωμεν· αὗται δὲ εἰς ὕστερον δεδικάσονται.

ΕΡΜΗΣ

Καὶ μὴν ὅμοιαί γε καὶ αὗται καὶ τὸ ἔγκλημα, εἰ καὶ νεαρόν, ἀλλὰ παραπλήσιον τοῖς προαποκεκληρωμένοις· ὥστε ἐν τούτοις δικασθῆναι ἄξιον.

---

[1] Follower of Socrates; later, founder of the Cyrenaic School.

[2] Diogenes the Cynic was son and partner of the banker Hicesias in Sinope. They were caught making counterfeit

HERMES

High-living *v.* Virtue, *in re* Aristippus.[1]

JUSTICE

Let five sit in this case too.

HERMES

Banking *v.* Diogenes: absconding.[2]

JUSTICE

Draw only three.

HERMES

Painting *v.* Pyrrho: breach of contract.[3]

JUSTICE

Let nine sit on jury.

HERMES

Do you want us to provide juries for these two cases also, recorded yesterday against the public speaker?[4]

JUSTICE

Let us first finish up the cases of long-standing; these can go over until to-morrow for trial.

HERMES

Why, these are of the same nature, and the complaint, although recent, is very like those for which we have already provided juries, so that it ought to be tried along with them.

coin; the father was put to death, and the son fled to Athens (Diog. L. vii. 2, 1).

[3] Pyrrho the Sceptic began life as an artist (Diog. L. ix. 11).

[4] Lucian; coming from Samosata on the Euphrates, he is presently called "the Syrian."

ΔΙΚΗ

Ἔοικας, ὦ Ἑρμῆ, χαριζομένῳ τὴν δέησιν. ἀποκληρῶμεν δ' ὅμως, εἰ δοκεῖ, πλὴν ἀλλὰ ταύτας μόνας· ἱκαναὶ γὰρ αἱ ἀποκεκληρωμέναι. δὸς τὰς γραφάς.

ΕΡΜΗΣ

Ῥητορικὴ κακώσεως τῷ Σύρῳ· Διάλογος τῷ αὐτῷ ὕβρεως.

ΔΙΚΗ

Τίς δὲ οὗτός ἐστιν; οὐ γὰρ ἐγγέγραπται τοὔνομα.

ΕΡΜΗΣ

Οὕτως ἀποκλήρου, τῷ ῥήτορι τῷ Σύρῳ· κωλύσει γὰρ οὐδὲν καὶ ἄνευ τοῦ ὀνόματος.

ΔΙΚΗ

Ἰδοῦ, καὶ τὰς ὑπερορίους ἤδη Ἀθήνησιν ἐν Ἀρείῳ πάγῳ ἀποκληρώσομεν, ἃς ὑπὲρ τὸν Εὐφράτην καλῶς εἶχε δεδικάσθαι; πλὴν ἀλλὰ κλήρου ἕνδεκα τοὺς αὐτοὺς ἑκατέρᾳ τῶν δικῶν.

ΕΡΜΗΣ

Εὖ γε, ὦ Δίκη, φείδῃ μὴ πολὺ ἀναλίσκεσθαι τὸ δικαστικόν.

ΔΙΚΗ

15 Οἱ πρῶτοι καθιζέτωσαν τῇ Ἀκαδημείᾳ καὶ τῇ Μέθῃ· σὺ δὲ τὸ ὕδωρ ἔγχει. προτέρα δὲ σὺ λέγε ἡ Μέθη. τί σιγᾷ καὶ διανεύει; μάθε, ὦ Ἑρμῆ, προσελθών.

ΕΡΜΗΣ

"Οὐ δύναμαι," φησί, "τὸν ἀγῶνα εἰπεῖν ὑπὸ τοῦ ἀκράτου τὴν γλῶτταν πεπεδημένη, μὴ γέλωτα

JUSTICE

You appear to have been unduly influenced to make the request, Hermes. Let us make the drawing, however, since you wish; but only for these two cases; we have enough on the docket. Give me the writs.

HERMES

Oratory *v.* the Syrian: neglect. Dialogue *v.* the same: maltreatment.

JUSTICE

Who is this man? His name is not recorded.

HERMES

Empanel a jury for him as it stands in the writ—for the public speaker, the Syrian. There is nothing to hinder its being done anonymously.

JUSTICE

Look here, are we really to try cases from over the border here in Athens, on the Areopagus? They ought to have been tried on the other side of the Euphrates. However, draw eleven jurors, the same to sit for both cases.

HERMES

You are right, Justice, to avoid spending too much in jury-fees.

JUSTICE

Let the first jury sit, in the case of the Academy *v.* Intemperance. Fill the water-clock. Plead first, Intemperance . . . Why does she hold her tongue and shake her head? Go to her and find out, Hermes.

HERMES

She says that she cannot plead her case because her tongue is tied with drink and she is afraid of getting

ὄφλω ἐν τῷ δικαστηρίῳ." μόλις δὲ καὶ ἕστηκεν,[1] ὡς ὁρᾷς.

ΔΙΚΗ

Οὐκοῦν συνήγορον ἀναβιβασάσθω τῶν κοινῶν[2] τούτων τινά· πολλοὶ γὰρ οἱ κἂν ἐπὶ τριωβόλῳ διαρραγῆναι ἕτοιμοι.

ΕΡΜΗΣ

Ἀλλ' οὐδὲ εἷς ἐθελήσει ἔν γε τῷ φανερῷ συναγορεῦσαι Μέθῃ. πλὴν εὐγνώμονά γε ταῦτα ἔοικεν ἀξιοῦν.

ΔΙΚΗ

Τὰ ποῖα;

ΕΡΜΗΣ

"Ἡ Ἀκαδήμεια πρὸς ἀμφοτέρους ἀεὶ παρεσκεύασται τοὺς λόγους καὶ τοῦτ' ἀσκεῖ τἀναντία καλῶς δύνασθαι λέγειν. αὕτη τοίνυν," φησίν, "ὑπὲρ ἐμοῦ πρότερον εἰπάτω, εἶτα ὕστερον ὑπὲρ ἑαυτῆς ἐρεῖ."

ΔΙΚΗ

Καινὰ μὲν ταῦτα, εἰπὲ δὲ ὅμως, ὦ Ἀκαδήμεια, τὸν λόγον ἑκάτερον, ἐπεί σοι ῥᾴδιον.

ΑΚΑΔΗΜΕΙΑ

16 Ἀκούετε, ὦ ἄνδρες δικασταί, πρότερα τὰ ὑπὲρ τῆς Μέθης· ἐκείνης γὰρ τό γε νῦν ῥέον.

Ἠδίκηται ἡ ἀθλία τὰ μέγιστα ὑπὸ τῆς Ἀκαδημείας ἐμοῦ, ἀνδράποδον ὃ μόνον εἶχεν εὔνουν καὶ πιστὸν αὐτῇ, μηδὲν αἰσχρὸν ὧν προστάξειεν οἰόμενον, ἀφαιρεθεῖσα τὸν Πολέμωνα ἐκεῖνον, ὃς μεθ' ἡμέραν ἐκώμαζεν διὰ τῆς ἀγορᾶς μέσης, ψαλτρίαν ἔχων καὶ καταδόμενος ἕωθεν εἰς ἑσπέραν, μεθύων ἀεὶ καὶ κραιπαλῶν καὶ τὴν κεφαλὴν τοῖς

[1] ἕστηκα γ. [2] δεινῶν β; cf. *Jup. Trag.* 29.

laughed at in court. She can hardly stand, as you see.

JUSTICE

Then let her have an advocate appear, one of these public pleaders. There are plenty of them ready to split their lungs for three obols!

HERMES

But not one will care to espouse the cause of Intemperance, not openly, at any rate. However, this request of hers seems reasonable.

JUSTICE

What request?

HERMES

"The Academy," she says, "is always ready to argue on both sides and trains herself to be able to speak eloquently both pro and con. Therefore let her plead first for me, and then after that she will plead for herself."

JUSTICE

That is unprecedented. Nevertheless, make both speeches, Academy, since it is easy for you.

ACADEMY

Listen first, gentlemen of the jury, to the plea of Intemperance, as the water now runs for her.

The poor creature has been treated with the greatest injustice by me, the Academy. She has been robbed of the only friendly and faithful slave she had, who thought none of her orders unbecoming, Polemo yonder, who used to go roistering through the middle of the square in broad day, who kept a music-girl and had himself sung to from morning to night, who was always drunk and debauched and

στεφάνοις διηνθισμένος. καὶ ταῦτα ὅτι ἀληθῆ, μάρτυρες Ἀθηναῖοι ἅπαντες, οἳ μηδὲ πώποτε νήφοντα Πολέμωνα εἶδον. ἐπεὶ δὲ ὁ κακοδαίμων ἐπὶ τὰς τῆς Ἀκαδημείας θύρας ἐκώμασεν, ὥσπερ ἐπὶ πάντας εἰώθει, ἀνδραποδισαμένη αὐτὸν καὶ ἀπὸ τῶν χειρῶν τῆς Μέθης ἁρπάσασα μετὰ βίας καὶ πρὸς αὐτὴν ἀγαγοῦσα ὑδροποτεῖν τε κατηνάγκασεν καὶ νήφειν μετεδίδαξεν καὶ τοὺς στεφάνους περιέσπασεν καὶ δέον πίνειν κατακείμενον, ῥημάτια σκολιὰ καὶ δύστηνα καὶ πολλῆς φροντίδος ἀνάμεστα ἐπαίδευσεν· ὥστε ἀντὶ τοῦ τέως ἐπανθοῦντος αὐτῷ ἐρυθήματος ὠχρὸς ὁ[1] ἄθλιος καὶ ῥικνὸς τὸ σῶμα γεγένηται, καὶ τὰς ᾠδὰς ἁπάσας ἀπομαθὼν ἄσιτος ἐνίοτε καὶ διψαλέος εἰς μέσην ἑσπέραν κάθηται ληρῶν ὁποῖα πολλὰ ἡ Ἀκαδήμεια ἐγὼ ληρεῖν διδάσκω. τὸ δὲ μέγιστον, ὅτι καὶ λοιδορεῖται τῇ Μέθῃ πρὸς ἐμοῦ ἐπαρθεὶς καὶ μυρία κακὰ διέξεισι περὶ αὐτῆς.

Εἴρηται σχεδὸν τὰ ὑπὲρ τῆς Μέθης. ἤδη καὶ ὑπὲρ ἐμαυτῆς ἐρῶ, καὶ τὸ ἀπὸ τούτου ἐμοὶ ῥευσάτω.

ΔΙΚΗ

Τί ἄρα πρὸς ταῦτα ἐρεῖ; πλὴν ἀλλ' ἔγχει τὸ ἴσον ἐν τῷ μέρει.

ΑΚΑΔΗΜΕΙΑ

17 Οὑτωσὶ μὲν ἀκοῦσαι πάνυ εὔλογα, ὦ ἄνδρες δικασταί, ἡ συνήγορος εἴρηκεν ὑπὲρ τῆς Μέθης, ἢν[2] δὲ κἀμοῦ μετ' εὐνοίας ἀκούσητε, εἴσεσθε ὡς οὐδὲν αὐτὴν ἠδίκηκα.

Τὸν γὰρ Πολέμωνα τοῦτον, ὃν φησιν ἑαυτῆς οἰκέτην εἶναι, πεφυκότα οὐ φαύλως οὐδὲ κατὰ τὴν

[1] ὁ du Soul; not in MSS. [2] ἢν Fritzsche: εἰ MSS.

had garlands of flowers on his head. That this is true, all the Athenians will testify; for they never saw Polemo sober. But when the unhappy man went rollicking to the Academy's door, as he used to go to everybody's, she claimed him as her slave, snatched him out of the hands of Intemperance by main strength, and took him into her house. Then she forced him to drink water, taught him to keep sober, stripped off his garlands: and when he ought to have been drinking at table, she made him study intricate, gloomy terms, full of profound thought. So, instead of the flush that formerly glowed upon him, the poor man has grown pale, and his body is shrivelled; he has forgotten all his songs, and he sometimes sits without food or drink till the middle of the evening, talking the kind of balderdash that I, the Academy, teach people to talk unendingly. What is more, he even abuses Intemperance at my instigation and says any number of unpleasant things about her.

I have said about all that there is to say for Intemperance. Now I will speak for myself, and from this point let the water run for me.

JUSTICE

What in the world will she say in reply to that? Anyhow, pour in the same amount for her in turn.

ACADEMY

Heard casually, gentlemen of the jury, the plea which the advocate has made in behalf of Intemperance is quite plausible, but if you give an unprejudiced hearing to my plea also, you will find out that I have done her no wrong at all.

This man Polemo, who, she says, is her servant, was not naturally bad or inclined to Intemperance,

Μέθην, ἀλλ' οἰκεῖον ἐμοὶ τὴν φύσιν, προαρπάσασα νέον ἔτι καὶ ἁπαλὸν ὄντα συναγωνιζομένης τῆς Ἡδονῆς, ἥπερ αὐτῇ τὰ πολλὰ ὑπουργεῖ, διέφθειρε τὸν ἄθλιον τοῖς κώμοις καὶ ταῖς ἑταίραις παρασχοῦσα ἔκδοτον, ὡς μηδὲ μικρὸν αὐτῷ τῆς αἰδοῦς ὑπολείπεσθαι. καὶ ἅ γε ὑπὲρ ἑαυτῆς λέγεσθαι μικρὸν ἔμπροσθεν ᾤετο, ταῦτα ὑπὲρ ἐμοῦ μᾶλλον εἰρῆσθαι νομίσατε· περιῄει γὰρ ἕωθεν ὁ ἄθλιος ἐστεφανωμένος, κραιπαλῶν, διὰ τῆς ἀγορᾶς μέσης καταυλούμενος, οὐδέποτε νήφων, κωμάζων ἐπὶ πάντας, ὕβρις τῶν προγόνων καὶ τῆς πόλεως ὅλης καὶ γέλως τοῖς ξένοις.

Ἐπεὶ μέντοι γε παρ' ἐμὲ ἧκεν, ἐγὼ μὲν ἔτυχον, ὥσπερ εἴωθα ποιεῖν, ἀναπεπταμένων τῶν θυρῶν πρὸς τοὺς παρόντας τῶν ἑταίρων λόγους τινὰς περὶ ἀρετῆς καὶ σωφροσύνης διεξιοῦσα· ὁ δὲ μετὰ τοῦ αὐλοῦ καὶ τῶν στεφάνων ἐπιστὰς τὰ μὲν πρῶτα ἐβόα καὶ συγχεῖν ἡμῶν ἐπειρᾶτο τὴν συνουσίαν ἐπιταράξας τῇ βοῇ· ἐπεὶ δὲ οὐδὲν ἡμεῖς ἐπεφροντίκειμεν αὐτοῦ, κατ' ὀλίγον—οὐ γὰρ τέλεον ἦν διάβροχος τῇ Μέθῃ—ἀνένηφε πρὸς τοὺς λόγους καὶ ἀφῃρεῖτο τοὺς στεφάνους καὶ τὴν αὐλητρίδα κατεσιώπα καὶ ἐπὶ τῇ πορφυρίδι ᾐσχύνετο, καὶ ὥσπερ ἐξ ὕπνου βαθέος ἀνεγρόμενος ἑαυτόν τε ἑώρα ὅπως διέκειτο καὶ τοῦ πάλαι βίου κατεγίγνωσκεν. καὶ τὸ μὲν ἐρύθημα τὸ ἐκ τῆς Μέθης ἀπήνθει καὶ ἠφανίζετο, ἠρυθρία δὲ κατ' αἰδῶ τῶν δρωμένων· καὶ τέλος ἀποδρὰς ὥσπερ εἶχεν ηὐτομόλησεν παρ' ἐμέ, οὔτε ἐπικαλεσαμένης οὔτε βιασαμένης, ὡς αὕτη[1] φησίν, ἐμοῦ, ἀλλ' ἑκὼν αὐτὸς ἀμείνω ταῦτα εἶναι ὑπολαμβάνων.

[1] αὕτη Fr.: αὐτή MSS.

but had a nature like mine. But while he was still young and impressionable she preëmpted him, with the assistance of Pleasure, who usually helps her, and corrupted the poor fellow, surrendering him unconditionally to dissipation and to light women, so that he had not the slightest remnant of shame. In fact, what she thought was said on her behalf a moment ago, you should consider said on my behalf. The poor fellow went about from early to late with garlands on his head, flushed with wine, attended by music right through the public square, never sober, making roisterous calls upon everybody, a disgrace to his ancestors and to the whole city and a laughing-stock to strangers.

But when he came to my house, it chanced that, as usual, the doors were wide open and I was discoursing about virtue and temperance to such of my friends as were there. Coming in upon us with his flute and his garlands, first of all he began to shout and tried to break up our meeting by disturbing it with his noise. But we paid no attention to him, and as he was not entirely sodden with Intemperance, little by little he grew sober under the influence of our discourses, took off his garlands, silenced his flute-player, became ashamed of his purple mantle, and, awaking, as it were, from profound sleep, saw his own condition and condemned his past life. The flush that came from Intemperance faded and vanished, and he flushed for shame at what he was doing. At length he abandoned her then and there, and took up with me, not because I either invited or constrained him, as this person says, but voluntarily, because he believed the conditions here were better.

Καί μοι ἤδη κάλει αὐτόν, ὅπως καταμάθητε ὃν τρόπον διάκειται πρὸς ἐμοῦ.—τοῦτον, ὦ ἄνδρες δικασταί, παραλαβοῦσα γελοίως ἔχοντα, μήτε φωνὴν ἀφιέναι μήτε ἑστάναι ὑπὸ τοῦ ἀκράτου δυνάμενον, ὑπέστρεψα καὶ ἀνένηψα καὶ ἀντὶ ἀνδραπόδου κόσμιον ἄνδρα καὶ σώφρονα καὶ πολλοῦ ἄξιον τοῖς Ἕλλησιν ἀπέδειξα· καί μοι αὐτός τε χάριν οἶδεν ἐπὶ τούτοις καὶ οἱ προσήκοντες ὑπὲρ αὐτοῦ.

Εἴρηκα· ὑμεῖς δὲ ἤδη σκοπεῖτε ποτέρᾳ ἡμῶν ἄμεινον ἦν αὐτῷ συνεῖναι.

ΔΙΚΗ

18 Ἄγε δή, μὴ μέλλετε, ψηφοφορήσατε, ἀνάστητε· καὶ ἄλλοις χρὴ δικάζειν.

ΕΡΜΗΣ

Πάσαις ἡ Ἀκαδήμεια κρατεῖ πλὴν μιᾶς.

ΔΙΚΗ

Παράδοξον οὐδέν, εἶναί τινα καὶ τῇ Μέθῃ 19 τιθέμενον. καθίσατε οἱ τῇ Στοᾷ πρὸς τὴν Ἡδονὴν λαχόντες περὶ τοῦ ἐραστοῦ δικάζειν· ἐγκέχυται τὸ ὕδωρ. ἡ κατάγραφος ἡ τὰ ποικίλα σὺ ἤδη λέγε.

ΣΤΟΑ

20 Οὐκ ἀγνοῶ μέν, ὦ ἄνδρες δικασταί, ὡς πρὸς εὐπρόσωπόν μοι τὴν ἀντίδικον ὁ λόγος ἔσται, ἀλλὰ καὶ ὑμῶν τοὺς πολλοὺς ὁρῶ πρὸς μὲν ἐκείνην ἀποβλέποντας καὶ μειδιῶντας πρὸς αὐτήν, ἐμοῦ δὲ καταφρονοῦντας, ὅτι ἐν χρῷ κέκαρμαι καὶ ἀρρενωπὸν βλέπω καὶ σκυθρωπὴ δοκῶ. ὅμως δέ,

---

[1] An allusion to the famous frescoes of the Painted Porch; Polygnotus' *Taking of Troy*, *Theseus and the Amazons*, and

Please summon him now, that you may see how he has fared at my hands. . . . Taking this man, gentlemen of the jury, when he was in a ridiculous plight, unable either to talk or to stand on account of his potations, I converted him and sobered him and made him from a slave into a well-behaved, temperate man, very valuable to the Greeks; and he himself is grateful to me for it, as are also his relatives on his account.

I have done. It is for you now to consider which of us it was better for him to associate with.

JUSTICE

Come, now, do not delay; cast your ballots and get up; others must have their hearing.

HERMES

The Academy wins by every vote but one.

JUSTICE

It is not at all surprising that there should be one man to vote for Intemperance. Take your seats, you who have been drawn to hear Stoa *v.* Pleasure *in re* a lover. The clock is filled. You with the paint upon you and the gaudy colours, make your plea now.[1]

STOA

I am not unaware, gentlemen of the jury, that I shall have to speak against an attractive opponent; indeed, I see that most of you are gazing at her and smiling at her, contemptuous of me because my head is close-clipped, my glance is masculine, and I seem dour. Nevertheless, if you are willing to hear me

Battle of Marathon. Lucian brings in a bit of fun by deliberately using language which suggests a painted face and a gay dress and is in this sense so incongruous as to be comical.

ἣν ἐθελήσητε ἀκοῦσαί μου λεγούσης, θαρρῶ πολὺ δικαιότερα ταύτης ἐρεῖν.

Τοῦτο γάρ τοι καὶ τὸ παρὸν ἔγκλημά ἐστιν, ὅτι οὕτως ἑταιρικῶς ἐσκευασμένη τῷ ἐπαγωγῷ τῆς ὄψεως ἐραστὴν ἐμὸν ἄνδρα τότε σώφρονα τὸν Διονύσιον φενακίσασα πρὸς ἑαυτὴν περιέσπασεν, καὶ ἥν γε οἱ πρὸ ὑμῶν δίκην ἐδίκασαν τῇ Ἀκαδημείᾳ καὶ τῇ Μέθῃ, ἀδελφὴ τῆς παρούσης δίκης ἐστίν· ἐξετάζεται γὰρ ἐν τῷ παρόντι πότερα χοίρων δίκην κάτω νενευκότας ἡδομένους χρὴ βιοῦν μηδὲν μεγαλόφρον ἐπινοοῦντας ἢ ἐν δευτέρῳ τοῦ καλῶς ἔχοντος ἡγησαμένους τὸ τερπνὸν ἐλευθέρους ἐλευθέρως φιλοσοφεῖν, μήτε τὸ ἀλγεινὸν ὡς ἄμαχον δεδιότας μήτε τὸ ἡδὺ ἀνδραποδωδῶς προαιρουμένους καὶ τὴν εὐδαιμονίαν ζητοῦντας ἐν τῷ μέλιτι καὶ ταῖς ἰσχάσιν. τὰ τοιαῦτα γὰρ αὕτη δελέατα τοῖς ἀνοήτοις προτείνουσα καὶ μορμολυττομένη τῷ πόνῳ προσάγεται αὐτῶν τοὺς πολλούς, ἐν οἷς καὶ τὸν δείλαιον ἐκεῖνον ἀφηνιάσαι ἡμῶν πεποίηκεν, νοσοῦντα τηρήσασα· οὐ γὰρ ἂν ὑγιαίνων ποτὲ προσήκατο τοὺς παρὰ ταύτης λόγους.

Καίτοι τί ἂν ἔγωγε ἀγανακτοίην κατ' αὐτῆς, ὅπου μηδὲ τῶν θεῶν φείδεται, ἀλλὰ τὴν ἐπιμέλειαν αὐτῶν διαβάλλει; ὥστε εἰ σωφρονεῖτε, καὶ ἀσεβείας ἂν δίκην λάβοιτε παρ' αὐτῆς. ἀκούω[1] δὲ ἔγωγε ὡς οὐδὲ αὐτὴ παρεσκεύασται ποιήσασθαι τοὺς λόγους, ἀλλὰ τὸν Ἐπίκουρον ἀναβιβάσεται

[1] ἤκουον β.

---

[1] In this debate the word πόνος sometimes means "pain," as here, sometimes "toil," and sometimes both; thus

speak, I am confident that my plea will be far more just than hers.

As a matter of fact, the present charge is that by getting herself up in this courtesan style she beguiled my lover, Dionysius, a respectable man until then, by the seductiveness of her appearance, and drew him to herself. Furthermore, the suit which your predecessors decided between the Academy and Intemperance was the twin-sister of the present suit. For the point at issue now is whether we should live like swine with our noses to the ground in the enjoyment of pleasure, without a single noble thought, or whether, considering what is enjoyable secondary to what is right, we should follow philosophy in a free spirit like free men, neither fearing pain as invincible nor giving preference to pleasure in a servile spirit and seeking happiness in honey and in figs. By holding out such bait to silly people and by making a bogey out of pain,[1] my opponent wins over the greater part of them, and this poor man is one; she made him run away from me by keeping an eye upon him until he was ill, for while he was well he would never have accepted her arguments.

After all, why should *I* be indignant at her? Forsooth, she does not even let the gods alone, but slanders their management of affairs! If you are wise, then, you will give her a sentence for impiety also. I hear, too, that she is not even prepared to plead in person, but will have Epicurus appear as her

illustrating the point that Cicero makes in the *Tusculans* (ii. 15): Haec duo (*i.e.* laborem *et* dolorem) Graeci illi, quorum copiosior est lingua quam nostra, uno nomine appellant . . . O verborum inops interdum, quibus abundare te semper putas, Graecia!

συναγορεύσοντα· οὕτως ἐντρυφᾷ τῷ δικαστηρίῳ. πλὴν ἀλλὰ ἐκεῖνά γε· αὐτὴν ἐρωτᾶτε, οἵους ἂν οἴεται γενέσθαι τὸν Ἡρακλέα καὶ τὸν ὑμέτερον Θησέα, εἰ προσθέντες[1] τῇ ἡδονῇ ἔφυγον τοὺς πόνους· οὐδὲν γὰρ ἂν ἐκώλυεν μεστὴν ἀδικίας εἶναι τὴν γῆν, ἐκείνων μὴ πονησάντων.

Ταῦτα εἶπον οὐ πάνυ τοῖς μακροῖς τῶν λόγων χαίρουσα. εἰ δέ γε ἐθελήσειε κατὰ μικρὸν ἀποκρίνασθαί μοι συνερωτωμένη, τάχιστα ἂν γνωσθείη τὸ μηδὲν οὖσα. πλὴν ἀλλὰ ὑμεῖς γε τοῦ ὅρκου μνημονεύσαντες ψηφίσασθε ἤδη τὰ εὔορκα μὴ πιστεύσαντες Ἐπικούρῳ λέγοντι μηδὲν ἐπισκοπεῖν τῶν παρ᾽ ἡμῖν γιγνομένων τοὺς θεούς.

ΔΙΚΗ

Μετάστηθι. ὁ Ἐπίκουρος ὑπὲρ τῆς Ἡδονῆς λέγε.

ΕΠΙΚΟΥΡΟΣ

21 Οὐ μακρά, ὦ ἄνδρες δικασταί, πρὸς ὑμᾶς ἐρῶ· δεῖ γὰρ οὐδὲ πολλῶν μοι τῶν λόγων.

Ἀλλ᾽ εἰ μὲν ἐπῳδαῖς τισιν ἢ φαρμάκοις ὅν φησιν ἐραστὴν ἑαυτῆς ἡ Στοὰ τὸν Διονύσιον κατηνάγκασεν ταύτης μὲν ἀπέχεσθαι, πρὸς ἑαυτὴν δὲ ἀποβλέπειν ἡ Ἡδονή, φαρμακὶς ἂν εἰκότως ἔδοξεν καὶ ἀδικεῖν ἐκέκριτο ἐπὶ τοὺς ἀλλοτρίους ἐραστὰς μαγγανεύουσα. εἰ δέ τις ἐλεύθερος ἐν ἐλευθέρᾳ τῇ πόλει, μὴ ἀπαγορευόντων τῶν νόμων, τὴν παρὰ ταύτης ἀηδίαν μυσαχθεὶς καὶ ἣν φησι κεφάλαιον[2] τῶν πόνων τὴν εὐδαιμονίαν παραγίγνεσθαι λῆρον οἰηθείς, τοὺς μὲν ἀγκύλους ἐκείνους λόγους καὶ λαβυρίνθοις ὁμοίους ἀπέφυγε, πρὸς δὲ τὴν Ἡδονὴν ἄσμενος ἐδραπέτευσεν ὥσπερ δεσμά τινα διακόψας

[1] πεισθέντες β. [2] φασιν ἐπὶ κεφαλαίῳ β.

advocate, such contempt does she show the court! But see here—ask her what kind of men she thinks Heracles and your own[1] Theseus would have been if they had allied themselves to Pleasure and had shirked pain and toil. Nothing would hinder the earth from being full of wrong-doing if they had not toiled painfully.

This is all I have to say, for I am not at all fond of long speeches. But if she should consent to let me put questions and to give a brief reply to each, it would very soon be evident that she amounts to nothing. However, remember your oath and vote in accordance with it now, putting no faith in Epicurus, who says that the gods take no note of what happens among us.

JUSTICE

Stand aside. Epicurus, speak for Pleasure.

EPICURUS

I shall not address you at length, gentlemen of the jury, for I myself do not need many words.

If Pleasure had used charms or philtres to constrain Dionysius, whom Stoa claims to be her lover, to desert Stoa and to centre his regard upon her, she might fairly have been held a sorceress and might have been found guilty of using undue influence upon the lovers of others. But suppose a free man in a free city, unstopped by the laws, hating the tedium of life with her and thinking that the happiness which comes, she says, as the consummation of pain is stuff and nonsense, made his escape from her thorny, labyrinthine reasonings and ran away to Pleasure of his own free will, cutting the meshes of

[1] Athenian.

τὰς τῶν λόγων πλεκτάνας, ἀνθρώπινα καὶ οὐ βλακώδη φρονήσας καὶ τὸν μὲν πόνον, ὅπερ ἐστί, πονηρόν, ἡδεῖαν δὲ τὴν ἡδονὴν οἰηθείς, ἀποκλείειν ἐχρῆν αὐτόν, ὥσπερ ἐκ ναυαγίου λιμένι προσνέοντα καὶ γαλήνης ἐπιθυμοῦντα συνωθοῦντας ἐπὶ κεφαλὴν εἰς τὸν πόνον, καὶ ἔκδοτον τὸν ἄθλιον παρέχειν ταῖς ἀπορίαις, καὶ ταῦτα ὥσπερ ἱκέτην ἐπὶ τὸν τοῦ Ἐλέου βωμὸν ἐπὶ τὴν Ἡδονὴν καταφεύγοντα, ἵνα τὴν πολυθρύλητον ἀρετὴν δηλαδὴ ἐπὶ τὸ ὄρθιον ἱδρῶτι πολλῷ ἀνελθὼν ἴδῃ κᾆτα δι' ὅλου πονήσας τοῦ βίου εὐδαιμονήσῃ μετὰ τὸν βίον;

Καίτοι τίς ἂν κριτὴς δικαιότερος δόξειεν αὐτοῦ ἐκείνου, ὃς τὰ παρὰ τῆς Στοᾶς εἰδώς, εἰ καί τις ἄλλος, καὶ μόνον τέως τὸ καλὸν ἀγαθὸν οἰόμενος εἶναι, μεταμαθὼν ὡς κακὸν ὁ πόνος ἦν, τὸ βέλτιον ἐξ ἀμφοῖν δοκιμάσας εἵλετο; ἑώρα γάρ, οἶμαι, τούτους περὶ τοῦ καρτερεῖν καὶ ἀνέχεσθαι τοὺς πόνους πολλὰ διεξιόντας, ἰδίᾳ δὲ τὴν Ἡδονὴν θεραπεύοντας, καὶ μέχρι τοῦ λόγου νεανιευομένους, οἴκοι δὲ κατὰ τοὺς τῆς Ἡδονῆς νόμους βιοῦντας, αἰσχυνομένους μὲν εἰ φανοῦνται χαλῶντες τοῦ τόνου καὶ προδιδόντες τὸ δόγμα, πεπονθότας δὲ ἀθλίους τὸ τοῦ Ταντάλου, καὶ ἔνθα ἂν λήσειν καὶ ἀσφαλῶς παρανομήσειν ἐλπίσωσιν, χανδὸν ἐμπιμπλαμένους τοῦ ἡδέος. εἰ γοῦν τις αὐτοῖς τὸν τοῦ Γύγου δακτύλιον ἔδωκεν, ὡς περιθεμένους μὴ ὁρᾶσθαι, ἢ τὴν τοῦ Ἄϊδος κυνῆν, εὖ οἶδ' ὅτι μακρὰ

her logic as if they were bonds, because he had the spirit of a human being, not of a clod, and thought pain painful, as indeed it is, and pleasure pleasant, in that case would it have been right to bar him out, plunging him head over ears into a sea of pain when he was swimming from a wreck to a haven and yearned for calm water—to put the poor fellow at the mercy of her dilemmas in spite of the fact that he was seeking asylum with Pleasure like a suppliant at the Altar of Mercy—in order that he might climb "the steep" with copious sweat, cast eyes upon that famous Virtue,[1] and then, after toiling painfully his whole life long, be happy when life is over?

Who should be considered a better judge than this man himself, who knew the teachings of Stoa if ever a man did, and formerly thought that only what was right was good, but now has learnt that pain is bad, and so has chosen what he has determined to be the better? He saw, no doubt, that her set make a great deal of talk about fortitude and endurance of pain, but privately pay court to Pleasure; that they are bold as brass in the lecture-room, but live under the laws of Pleasure at home; that they are ashamed, of course, to let themselves be seen "lowering their pitch" and playing false to their tenets, but suffer the tortures of Tantalus, poor fellows, so that wherever they think they will be unobserved and can transgress their laws with safety, they eagerly glut themselves with pleasure. In fact, if they should be given the ring of Gyges, so that they could put it on and be unseen, or the Cap of Darkness, without a doubt they would bid good-bye

[1] For the Hill of Virtue, see Hesiod, *Works and Days*, 289 ff., and Simonides, 41.

χαίρειν τοῖς πόνοις φράσαντες ἐπὶ τὴν Ἡδονὴν ὠθοῦντο ἂν καὶ ἐμιμοῦντο ἅπαντες τὸν Διονύσιον, ὃς μέχρι μὲν τῆς νόσου ἤλπιζεν ὠφελήσειν τι αὐτὸν τοὺς περὶ τῆς καρτερίας λόγους· ἐπεὶ δὲ ἤλγησεν καὶ ἐνόσησεν καὶ ὁ πόνος ἀληθέστερος αὐτοῦ καθίκετο, ἰδὼν τὸ σῶμα τὸ ἑαυτοῦ ἀντιφιλοσοφοῦν τῇ Στοᾷ καὶ τἀναντία δογματίζον, αὐτῷ μᾶλλον ἢ τούτοις ἐπίστευσεν καὶ ἔγνω ἄνθρωπος ὢν καὶ ἀνθρώπου σῶμα ἔχων, καὶ διετέλεσεν οὐχ ὡς ἀνδριάντι αὐτῷ χρώμενος, εἰδὼς ὅτι ὃς ἂν ἄλλως λέγῃ καὶ Ἡδονῆς κατηγορῇ,

λόγοισι χαίρει, τὸν δὲ νοῦν ἐκεῖσ' ἔχει.[1]

Εἴρηκα· ὑμεῖς δ' ἐπὶ τούτοις ψηφοφορήσατε.

ΣΤΟΑ

22 Μηδαμῶς, ἀλλ' ὀλίγα μοι συνερωτῆσαι ἐπιτρέψατε.

ΕΠΙΚΟΥΡΟΣ

Ἐρώτησον· ἀποκρινοῦμαι γάρ.

ΣΤΟΑ

Κακὸν ἡγῇ τὸν πόνον;

ΕΠΙΚΟΥΡΟΣ

Ναί.

ΣΤΟΑ

Τὴν ἡδονὴν δὲ ἀγαθόν;

ΕΠΙΚΟΥΡΟΣ

Πάνυ μὲν οὖν.

ΣΤΟΑ

Τί δέ; οἶσθα τί διάφορον καὶ ἀδιάφορον καὶ προηγμένον καὶ ἀποπροηγμένον;[2]

---

[1] Euripides, *Phoenissae* 360.
[2] Stoic technical terms: see vol. ii, p. 488. Stoa intends

to pain for ever and would go crowding after Pleasure, one and all, imitating Dionysius who, until he was ill, expected to get some benefit from their discourses about fortitude, but when he encountered suffering and illness, and pain came closer home to him, he perceived that his body was contradicting Stoa and maintaining the opposite side. So he put more trust in it than in her set, decided that he was a man, with the body of a man, and thenceforward treated it otherwise than as if it were a statue, well aware that whoever maintains any other view and accuses Pleasure

"Doth like to talk, but thinks as others do!"[1]

I have done. Cast your ballots with this understanding of the case.

STOA

No, no! Let me cross-question him a little.

EPICURUS

Put your questions: I will answer them.

STOA

Do you consider pain bad?

EPICURUS

Yes.

STOA

And pleasure good?

EPICURUS

Certainly.

STOA

Well, do you know the meaning of "material" and "immaterial," of "approved" and "disapproved"?[2]

to prove that pleasure and pain are alike "immaterial," and neither "approved" nor "disapproved," because they neither help nor hinder the effort to attain Virtue.

ΕΠΙΚΟΥΡΟΣ

Μάλιστα.

ΕΡΜΗΣ

Οὔ φασιν, ὦ Στοά, συνιέναι οἱ δικασταὶ τὰ δισύλλαβα ταῦτα ἐρωτήματα· ὥστε ἡσυχίαν ἄγετε. ψηφοφοροῦσι γάρ.

ΣΤΟΑ

Καὶ μὴν ἐκράτησα ἄν, εἰ συνηρώτησα ἐν τῷ τρίτῳ τῶν ἀναποδείκτων σχήματι.

ΔΙΚΗ

Τίς ὑπερέσχεν;

ΕΡΜΗΣ

Πάσαις ἡ Ἡδονή.

ΣΤΟΑ

Ἐφίημι ἐπὶ τὸν Δία.

ΔΙΚΗ

Τύχῃ τῇ ἀγαθῇ. σὺ δὲ ἄλλους κάλει.

ΕΡΜΗΣ

23 Περὶ Ἀριστίππου Ἀρετὴ καὶ Τρυφή, καὶ Ἀρίστιππος δὲ αὐτὸς παρέστω.

ΑΡΕΤΗ

Προτέραν ἐμὲ χρὴ τὴν Ἀρετὴν λέγειν· ἐμὸς γάρ ἐστιν Ἀρίστιππος, ὡς δηλοῦσιν οἱ λόγοι καὶ τὰ ἔργα.

ΤΡΥΦΗ

Οὐ μὲν οὖν, ἀλλ' ἐμὲ τὴν Τρυφήν· ἐμὸς γὰρ ὁ ἀνήρ, ὡς ἔστιν ὁρᾶν ἀπὸ τῶν στεφάνων καὶ τῆς πορφυρίδος καὶ τῶν μύρων.

---

[1] The five "indemonstrables" of Chrysippus, so called because they are self-evident and require no proof, were all hypothetical or disjunctive syllogisms; examples are: (1) "if it is day, it is light; it is light, ∴ it is day"; (2) "if it

EPICURUS

Certainly.

HERMES

Stoa, the jurors say they can't understand these dissyllabic questions, so be silent; they are voting.

STOA

I should have won if I had put him a question in the form of the "third indemonstrable."[1]

JUSTICE

Who won?

HERMES

Pleasure, unanimously.

STOA

I appeal to Zeus!

JUSTICE

Good luck to you! Hermes, call another case.

HERMES

Virtue *v.* High-living, *in re* Aristippus. Let Aristippus appear in person.

VIRTUE

I ought to speak first; I am Virtue, and Aristippus belongs to me, as his words and his deeds indicate.

HIGH-LIVING

No, indeed; I ought to speak first; I am High-living, and the man is mine, as you can see from his garlands, his purple cloak and his perfumes.

is day, it is light; it is dark, ∴ it is not day"; (3) "Plato is not both dead and alive; he is dead, ∴ he is not alive"; (4) "it is either day or night; it is day, ∴ it is not night"; (5) "it is either day or night; it is not night, ∴ it is day." Cf. Diog. Laert. *Vit. Phil.* 7, 1, 49; Sext. Emp. *adv. Math.* 7.

ΔΙΚΗ

Μὴ φιλονεικεῖτε· ὑπερκείσεται γὰρ καὶ αὕτη ἡ δίκη ἔστ' ἂν ὁ Ζεὺς δικάσῃ περὶ τοῦ Διονυσίου· παραπλήσιον γάρ τι καὶ τοῦτο ἔοικεν εἶναι. ὥστ' ἐὰν μὲν ἡ Ἡδονὴ κρατήσῃ, καὶ τὸν Ἀρίστιππον ἕξει ἡ Τρυφή· νικώσης δὲ αὖ τῆς Στοᾶς, καὶ οὗτος ἔσται τῆς Ἀρετῆς κεκριμένος. ὥστε ἄλλοι παρέστωσαν. τὸ δεῖνα μέντοι, μὴ λαμβανέτωσαν οὗτοι τὸ δικαστικόν· ἀδίκαστος γὰρ ἡ δίκη μεμένηκεν αὐτοῖς.

ΕΡΜΗΣ

Μάτην οὖν ἀνεληλυθότες ὦσι γέροντες ἄνδρες οὕτω μακρὰν τὴν ἀνάβασιν;

ΔΙΚΗ

Ἱκανόν, εἰ τριτημόριον λάβοιεν. ἄπιτε, μὴ ἀγανακτεῖτε, αὖθις δικάσετε.

ΕΡΜΗΣ

24 Διογένη Σινωπέα παρεῖναι καιρός, καὶ σὺ ἡ Ἀργυραμοιβικὴ λέγε.

ΔΙΟΓΕΝΗΣ

Καὶ μὴν ἄν γε μὴ παύσηται ἐνοχλοῦσα, ὦ Δίκη, οὐκέτι δρασμοῦ δικάσεταί μοι, ἀλλὰ πολλῶν καὶ βαθέων τραυμάτων· ἐγὼ γὰρ αὐτίκα μάλα πατάξας[1] τῷ ξύλῳ—

ΔΙΚΗ

Τί τοῦτο; πέφευγεν ἡ Ἀργυραμοιβική, ὁ δὲ διώκει ἐπηρμένος τὸ βάκτρον. οὐ μέτριόν τι κακὸν ἡ ἀθλία ἔοικε λήψεσθαι. τὸν Πύρρωνα κήρυττε.

[1] πατάξω γ.

JUSTICE

Do not wrangle; this case will stand over until Zeus decides the case of Dionysius, for this seems to be similar. Consequently, if Pleasure wins, High-living shall have Aristippus, but if Stoa prevails, he shall be adjudged to Virtue. So let others appear. Look here, though—these jurors are not to get the fee, for their case has not come to trial.

HERMES

Then are they to have come up here for nothing, old as they are, and the hill so high?

JUSTICE

It will be enough if they get a third. Go your ways; don't be angry, you shall serve another day.

HERMES

It is time for Diogenes of Sinope to appear. Make your complaint, Banking.

DIOGENES

I protest, if she does not stop bothering me, Justice, it will not be running away that she will have me up for, but aggravated assault and battery, for I shall mighty soon take my staff and. . . .

JUSTICE

What have we here? Banking has run away, and he is making after her with his stick raised. The poor creature is likely to catch it pretty badly! Call Pyrrho.

ΕΡΜΗΣ

25 Ἀλλ' ἡ μὲν Γραφικὴ πάρεστιν, ὦ Δίκη, ὁ Πύρρων δὲ οὐδὲ τὴν ἀρχὴν ἀνελήλυθεν, καὶ ἐῴκει τοῦτο πράξειν.

ΔΙΚΗ

Διὰ τί, ὦ Ἑρμῆ;

ΕΡΜΗΣ

Ὅτι οὐδὲν ἡγεῖται κριτήριον ἀληθὲς εἶναι.

ΔΙΚΗ

Τοιγαροῦν ἐρήμην αὐτοῦ καταδικασάτωσαν. τὸν λογογράφον ἤδη κάλει τὸν Σύρον. καίτοι πρῴην ἀπηνέχθησαν κατ' αὐτοῦ αἱ γραφαί, καὶ οὐδὲν ἤπειγεν ἤδη κεκρίσθαι. πλὴν ἀλλ' ἐπεὶ ἔδοξεν, προτέραν εἰσάγαγε τῆς Ῥητορικῆς τὴν δίκην. βαβαί, ὅσοι συνεληλύθασιν ἐπὶ τὴν ἀκρόασιν.

ΕΡΜΗΣ

Εἰκότως, ὦ Δίκη· τό τε γὰρ μὴ ἕωλον εἶναι τὴν κρίσιν, ἀλλὰ καινὴν καὶ ξένην,[1] χθές, ὥσπερ ἔφης, ἐπηγγελμένην,[2] καὶ τὸ ἐλπίζειν ἀκούσεσθαι Ῥητορικῆς μὲν καὶ Διαλόγου ἐν τῷ μέρει κατηγορούντων, ἀπολογουμένου δὲ πρὸς ἀμφοτέρους τοῦ Σύρου, τοῦτο πολλοὺς ἐπήγαγε τῷ δικαστηρίῳ. πλὴν ἀλλὰ ἄρξαι ποτέ, ὦ Ῥητορική, τῶν λόγων.

ΡΗΤΟΡΙΚΗ

26 Πρῶτον μέν, ὦ ἄνδρες Ἀθηναῖοι, τοῖς θεοῖς εὔχομαι πᾶσι καὶ πάσαις, ὅσην εὔνοιαν ἔχουσα διατελῶ τῇ τε πόλει καὶ πᾶσιν ὑμῖν, τοσαύτην ὑπάρξαι μοι παρ' ὑμῶν εἰς τουτονὶ τὸν ἀγῶνα, ἔπειθ' ὅπερ ἐστὶ μάλιστα δίκαιον, τοῦτο παραστῆσαι τοὺς θεοὺς ὑμῖν, τὸν μὲν ἀντίδικον σιωπᾶν

[1] καὶ ξένην not in γ. [2] χθές—ἐπηγγελμένην not in β.

HERMES

Painting is here, Justice, but Pyrrho has not come up at all. It might have been expected that he would do this.

JUSTICE

Why, Hermes?

HERMES

Because he does not believe there is any true standard of judgment.

JUSTICE

Then let them bring in a verdict by default against him. Now call the speech-writer, the Syrian. After all, it was only recently that the writs were lodged against him, and there was no pressing need to have tried the cases now. However, since that point has been decided, introduce the suit of Oratory first. Heavens, what a crowd has come together for the hearing!

HERMES

Naturally, Justice. The case is not stale, but new and unfamiliar, having been entered only yesterday, as you said, and they hope to hear Oratory and Dialogue bringing charges in turn and the Syrian defending himself against both; this has brought crowds to court. But do begin your speech, Oratory.

ORATORY

In the first place, men of Athens, I pray the gods and goddesses one and all that as much good will as I steadily entertain toward the city and toward all of you may be shown me by you in this case, and secondly that the gods may move you to do what is above all the just thing to do—to bid my

κελεύειν, ἐμὲ δὲ ὡς προῄρημαι καὶ βεβούλημαι τὴν κατηγορίαν ἐᾶσαι ποιήσασθαι. οὐχὶ δὲ ταὐτὰ παρίσταταί μοι γιγνώσκειν ὅταν τε εἰς ἃ πέπονθα ἀποβλέψω καὶ ὅταν εἰς τοὺς λόγους οὓς ἀκούω· τοὺς μὲν γὰρ λόγους ὡς ὁμοιοτάτους τοῖς ἐμοῖς οὗτος ἐρεῖ πρὸς ὑμᾶς, τὰ δὲ πράγματα εἰς τοῦτο προήκοντα ὄψεσθε ὥστε ὅπως μὴ χεῖρόν τι πείσομαι πρὸς αὐτοῦ σκέψασθαι δέον. ἀλλὰ γὰρ ἵνα μὴ μακρὰ προοιμιάζωμαι τοῦ ὕδατος πάλαι εἰκῇ ῥέοντος, ἄρξομαι τῆς κατηγορίας.

27 Ἐγὼ γάρ, ὦ ἄνδρες δικασταί, τουτονὶ κομιδῇ μειράκιον ὄντα, βάρβαρον ἔτι τὴν φωνὴν καὶ μονονουχὶ κάνδυν ἐνδεδυκότα εἰς τὸν Ἀσσύριον τρόπον, περὶ τὴν Ἰωνίαν εὑροῦσα πλαζόμενον ἔτι καὶ ὅ τι χρήσαιτο ἑαυτῷ οὐκ εἰδότα παραλαβοῦσα ἐπαίδευσα. καὶ ἐπειδὴ ἐδόκει μοι εὐμαθὴς εἶναι καὶ ἀτενὲς ὁρᾶν εἰς ἐμέ—ὑπέπτησσε γὰρ τότε καὶ ἐθεράπευεν καὶ μόνην ἐθαύμαζεν—ἀπολιποῦσα τοὺς ἄλλους ὁπόσοι ἐμνήστευόν με πλούσιοι καὶ καλοὶ καὶ λαμπροὶ τὰ προγονικά, τῷ ἀχαρίστῳ τούτῳ ἐμαυτὴν ἐνεγγύησα πένητι καὶ ἀφανεῖ καὶ νέῳ προῖκα οὐ μικρὰν ἐπενεγκαμένη πολλοὺς καὶ θαυμασίους λόγους. εἶτα ἀγαγοῦσα αὐτὸν εἰς τοὺς φυλέτας τοὺς ἐμοὺς παρενέγραψα καὶ ἀστὸν ἀπέφηνα, ὥστε τοὺς διαμαρτόντας[1] τῆς ἐγγύης ἀποπνίγεσθαι. δόξαν δὲ αὐτῷ περινοστεῖν ἐπιδειξομένῳ τοῦ γάμου τὴν εὐποτμίαν, οὐδὲ τότε

[1] ἁμαρτάνοντας γ.

opponent hold his tongue and to let me make the complaint in the way that I have preferred and chosen. I cannot come to the same conclusion when I contemplate my own experiences and the speeches that I hear, for the speeches that he will make to you will be as like as can be to mine, but his actions, as you shall see, have gone so far that measures must be taken to prevent my experiencing worse injury at his hands[1] . . . But not to prolong my introduction when the water has been running freely this long time, I will begin my complaint.

When this man was a mere boy, gentlemen of the jury, still speaking with a foreign accent and I might almost say wearing a caftan in the Syrian style, I found him still wandering about in Ionia, not knowing what to do with himself; so I took him in hand and gave him an education. As it seemed to me that he was an apt pupil and paid strict attention to me—for he was subservient to me in those days and paid court to me and admired none but me—I turned my back upon all the others who were suing for my hand, although they were rich and good-looking and of splendid ancestry, and plighted myself to this ingrate, who was poor and insignificant and young, bringing him a considerable dowry consisting in many marvellous speeches. Then, after we were married, I got him irregularly registered among my own clansmen and made him a citizen, so that those who had failed to secure my hand in marriage choked with envy. When he decided to go travelling in order to show how happily married he was, I did not

[1] Oratory, more concerned about form than content, borrows her prooemium from Demosthenes, adding the first sentence of the Third Olynthiac to the first sentence of the oration on the Crown, and adapting both as best she can.

ἀπελείφθην, ἀλλὰ πανταχοῦ ἑπομένη ἄνω καὶ κάτω περιηγόμην· καὶ κλεινὸν αὐτὸν καὶ ἀοίδιμον ἐποίουν κατακοσμοῦσα καὶ περιστέλλουσα. καὶ τὰ μὲν ἐπὶ τῆς Ἑλλάδος καὶ τῆς Ἰωνίας μέτρια, εἰς δὲ τὴν Ἰταλίαν ἀποδημῆσαι θελήσαντι αὐτῷ τὸν Ἰόνιον συνδιέπλευσα καὶ τὰ τελευταῖα μέχρι τῆς Κελτικῆς συναπάρασα εὐπορεῖσθαι ἐποίησα.

Καὶ μέχρι μὲν πολλοῦ πάντα μοι ἐπείθετο καὶ συνῆν ἀεί, μηδεμίαν νύκτα γιγνόμενος ἀπόκοιτος 28 παρ' ἡμῶν. ἐπεὶ δὲ ἱκανῶς ἐπεσιτίσατο καὶ τὰ πρὸς εὐδοξίαν εὖ ἔχειν αὐτῷ ὑπέλαβεν, τὰς ὀφρῦς ἐπάρας καὶ μέγα φρονήσας ἐμοῦ μὲν ἠμέλησεν, μᾶλλον δὲ τέλεον εἴασεν, αὐτὸς δὲ τὸν γενειήτην ἐκεῖνον, τὸν ἀπὸ τοῦ σχήματος, τὸν Διάλογον, Φιλοσοφίας υἱὸν εἶναι λεγόμενον, ὑπεραγαπήσας μάλα ἐρωτικῶς πρεσβύτερον αὐτοῦ ὄντα, τούτῳ σύνεστιν. καὶ οὐκ αἰσχύνεται τὴν μὲν ἐλευθερίαν καὶ τὸ ἄνετον τῶν ἐν ἐμοὶ λόγων συντεμών, εἰς μικρὰ δὲ καὶ κομματικὰ[1] ἐρωτήματα κατακλείσας ἑαυτόν, καὶ ἀντὶ τοῦ λέγειν ὅ τι βούλεται μεγάλῃ τῇ φωνῇ βραχεῖς τινας λόγους ἀναπλέκων καὶ συλλαβίζων, ἀφ' ὧν ἀθρόος μὲν ἔπαινος ἢ κρότος πολὺς οὐκ ἂν ἀπαντήσειεν αὐτῷ, μειδίαμα δὲ παρὰ τῶν ἀκουόντων καὶ τὸ ἐπισεῖσαι τὴν χεῖρα ἐντὸς τῶν ὅρων καὶ μικρὰ ἐπινεῦσαι τῇ κεφαλῇ καὶ ἐπιστενάξαι τοῖς λεγομένοις. τοιούτων ἠράσθη ὁ γενναῖος ἐμοῦ καταφρονήσας. φασὶν δὲ αὐτὸν μηδὲ πρὸς τὸν ἐρώμενον τοῦτον εἰρήνην ἄγειν, ἀλλὰ ὅμοια[2] καὶ ἐκεῖνον ὑβρίζειν.

[1] κωμικά β.

[2] ὅμοια Fritzsche: οἶμαι MSS. (Fritzsche writes τὰ ὅμοια, but the article is not necessary: *Salt.* 63.)

desert him even then, but trailed up and down after him everywhere and made him famous and renowned by giving him finery and dressing him out. On our travels in Greece and in Ionia I do not lay so much emphasis; but when he took a fancy to go to Italy, I crossed the Adriatic with him, and at length I journeyed with him as far as Gaul, where I made him rich.

For a long time he took my advice in everything and lived with me constantly, never spending a single night away from home: but when he had laid in plenty of the sinews of war and thought that he was well off for reputation, he became supercilious and vain and neglected me, or rather deserted me completely. Having conceived an inordinate affection for that bearded man in the mantle, Dialogue, who is said to be the son of Philosophy and is older than he is, he lives with him. Showing no sense of shame, he has curtailed the freedom and the range of my speeches and has confined himself to brief, disjointed questions: and instead of saying whatever he wishes in a powerful voice, he fits together and spells out short paragraphs, for which he cannot get hearty praise or great applause from his hearers, but only a smile, or a restrained gesture of the hand, an inclination of the head, or a sigh to point his periods. That is the sort of thing this gallant gentleman fell in love with, despising me! They say, too, that he is not at peace with this favourite, either, but insults him in the same way.

29 Πῶς οὖν οὐκ ἀχάριστος οὗτος καὶ ἔνοχος τοῖς περὶ τῆς κακώσεως νόμοις, ὃς τὴν μὲν νόμῳ γαμετὴν παρ' ἧς τοσαῦτα εἴληφεν καὶ δι' ἣν ἔνδοξός ἐστιν οὕτως ἀτίμως ἀπέλιπεν, καινῶν δὲ ὠρέχθη πραγμάτων, καὶ ταῦτα νῦν ὁπότε μόνην ἐμὲ θαυμάζουσιν καὶ ἐπιγράφονται ἅπαντες προστάτιν ἑαυτῶν; ἀλλ' ἐγὼ μὲν ἀντέχω τοσούτων μνηστευόντων, καὶ κόπτουσιν αὐτοῖς τὴν θύραν καὶ τοὔνομα ἐπιβοωμένοις μεγάλῃ τῇ φωνῇ οὔτε ἀνοίγειν οὔτε ὑπακούειν βούλομαι· ὁρῶ γὰρ αὐτοὺς οὐδὲν πλέον τῆς βοῆς κομίζοντας. οὗτος δὲ οὐδὲ οὕτως ἐπιστρέφεται πρὸς ἐμέ, ἀλλὰ πρὸς τὸν ἐρώμενον βλέπει, τί, ὦ θεοί, χρηστὸν παρ' αὐτοῦ λήψεσθαι προσδοκῶν, ὃν οἶδε τοῦ τρίβωνος οὐδὲν πλέον ἔχοντα;

Εἴρηκα, ὦ ἄνδρες δικασταί, ὑμεῖς δέ, ἢν εἰς τὸν ἐμὸν τρόπον τῶν λόγων ἀπολογεῖσθαι θέλῃ, τοῦτο μὲν μὴ ἐπιτρέπετε,—ἄγνωμον γὰρ ἐπ' ἐμὲ τὴν ἐμὴν μάχαιραν ἀκονᾶν—κατὰ δὲ τὸν αὐτοῦ ἐρώμενον τὸν Διάλογον οὕτως ἀπολογείσθω, ἢν δύνηται.

ΕΡΜΗΣ

Τοῦτο μὲν ἀπίθανον· οὐ γὰρ οἷόν τε, ὦ Ῥητορική, μόνον αὐτὸν ἀπολογεῖσθαι κατὰ σχῆμα τοῦ Διαλόγου, ἀλλὰ ῥῆσιν καὶ αὐτὸς εἰπάτω.

ΣΥΡΟΣ

30 Ἐπεὶ καὶ τοῦτο, ὦ ἄνδρες δικασταί, ἡ ἀντίδικος ἠγανάκτησεν, εἰ μακρῷ χρήσομαι τῷ λόγῳ, καὶ ταῦτα τὸ δύνασθαι λέγειν παρ' ἐκείνης λαβών, πολλὰ μὲν οὐκ ἐρῶ πρὸς ὑμᾶς, τὰ κεφάλαια δὲ αὐτὰ ἀπολυσάμενος[1] τῶν κατηγορηθέντων ὑμῖν

[1] ἀπολυσάμενος Herwerden: ἐπιλυσάμενος MSS.

Is he not, then, ungrateful and subject to punishment under the laws that concern desertion, inasmuch as he so disgracefully abandoned his lawful wife, from whom he received so much and through whom he is famous, and sought a new arrangement, now of all times, when I alone am admired and claimed as patroness by everyone? For my part I hold out against all those who court me, and when they knock at my door and call my name at the top of their lungs, I have no desire either to open or to reply, for I see that they bring with them nothing but their voices. But this man even then does not come back to me: no, he keeps his eyes upon his favourite. Ye gods, what good does he expect to get from him, knowing that he has nothing but his short cloak?

I have finished, gentlemen of the jury. But I beg you, if he wishes to make his defence in my style of speaking, do not permit that, for it would be unkind to turn my own weapon against me; let him defend himself, if he can, in the style of his favourite, Dialogue.

HERMES

That is unreasonable. It is not possible, Oratory, for him, all by himself, to make his defence after Dialogue's manner. Let him make a speech as you did.

THE SYRIAN

Gentlemen of the jury, as my opponent was indignant at the thought of my using a long speech when I acquired my power of speaking from her, I shall not say much to you, but shall simply answer the main points of her complaint and then

ἀπολείψω σκοπεῖν περὶ ἁπάντων. πάντα γὰρ ὁπόσα διηγήσατο περὶ ἐμοῦ ἀληθῆ ὄντα διηγήσατο· καὶ γὰρ ἐπαίδευσεν καὶ συναπεδήμησεν καὶ εἰς τοὺς Ἕλληνας ἐνέγραψεν, καὶ κατά γε τοῦτο χάριν ἂν εἰδείην τῷ γάμῳ. δι' ἃς δὲ αἰτίας ἀπολιπὼν αὐτὴν ἐπὶ τουτονὶ τὸν Διάλογον ἐτραπόμην, ἀκούσατε, ὦ ἄνδρες δικασταί, καί με μηδὲν τοῦ χρησίμου ἕνεκα ψεύδεσθαι ὑπολάβητε.

31 Ἐγὼ γὰρ ὁρῶν ταύτην οὐκέτι σωφρονοῦσαν οὐδὲ μένουσαν ἐπὶ τοῦ κοσμίου σχήματος οἷόν ποτε ἐσχηματισμένην αὐτὴν ὁ Παιανιεὺς ἐκεῖνος ἠγάγετο, κοσμουμένην δὲ καὶ τὰς τρίχας εὐθετίζουσαν εἰς τὸ ἑταιρικὸν καὶ φυκίον ἐντριβομένην καὶ τὠφθαλμὼ ὑπογραφομένην, ὑπώπτευον εὐθὺς καὶ παρεφύλαττον ὅποι τὸν ὀφθαλμὸν φέρει. καὶ τὰ μὲν ἄλλα ἐῶ· καθ' ἑκάστην δὲ τὴν νύκτα ὁ μὲν στενωπὸς ἡμῶν ἐνεπίμπλατο μεθυόντων ἐραστῶν κωμαζόντων ἐπ' αὐτὴν καὶ κοπτόντων τὴν θύραν, ἐνίων δὲ καὶ εἰσβιάζεσθαι σὺν οὐδενὶ κόσμῳ τολμώντων. αὐτὴ δὲ ἐγέλα καὶ ἥδετο τοῖς δρωμένοις καὶ τὰ πολλὰ ἢ παρέκυπτεν ἀπὸ τοῦ τέγους ᾀδόντων ἀκούουσα τραχείᾳ τῇ φωνῇ ᾠδάς τινας ἐρωτικὰς ἢ καὶ παρανοίγουσα τὰς θυρίδας ἐμὲ οἰομένη λανθάνειν ἠσέλγαινε καὶ ἐμοιχεύετο πρὸς αὐτῶν. ὅπερ ἐγὼ μὴ φέρων γράψασθαι μὲν αὐτὴν μοιχείας οὐκ ἐδοκίμαζον, ἐν γειτόνων δὲ οἰκοῦντι τῷ Διαλόγῳ προσελθὼν ἠξίουν καταδεχθῆναι ὑπ' αὐτοῦ.

32 Ταῦτά ἐστιν ἃ τὴν Ῥητορικὴν ἐγὼ μεγάλα ἠδίκηκα. καίτοι εἰ καὶ μηδὲν αὐτῇ τοιοῦτο ἐπέπρακτο, καλῶς εἶχέ μοι ἀνδρὶ ἤδη τετταράκοντα ἔτη σχεδὸν γεγονότι θορύβων μὲν ἐκείνων καὶ

leave it to you to weigh the whole question. In all that she told about me she told the truth. She gave me an education and went abroad with me and had me enfranchized as a Greek, and on this account, at least, I am grateful to her for marrying me. Why I left her and took to my friend here, Dialogue, listen, gentlemen of the jury, and you shall hear; and do not imagine that I am telling any falsehood for the sake of advantage.

Seeing that she was no longer modest and did not continue to clothe herself in the respectable way that she did once when Demosthenes took her to wife, but made herself up, arranged her hair like a courtesan, put on rouge, and darkened her eyes underneath, I became suspicious at once and secretly took note where she directed her glances. I pass over everything else, but every night our street was full of maudlin lovers coming to serenade her, knocking at the door, and sometimes even venturing to force an entrance in disorderly fashion. She herself laughed and enjoyed these performances, and generally, when she heard them singing love-songs in a hoarse voice, she either peeped over the edge of the roof or else even slyly opened the windows, thinking that I would not notice it, and then wantoned and intrigued with them. I could not stand this, and as I did not think it best to bring an action for divorce against her on the ground of adultery, I went to Dialogue, who lived near by, and requested him to take me in.

That is the great injustice that I have done Oratory. After all, even if she had not acted as she did, it would have been proper that I, a man already about forty years of age, should take my leave of her

δικῶν ἀπηλλάχθαι καὶ τοὺς ἄνδρας τοὺς δικαστὰς ἀτρεμεῖν ἐᾶν, τυράννων κατηγορίας καὶ ἀριστέων ἐπαίνους ἐκφυγόντα, εἰς δὲ τὴν Ἀκαδήμειαν ἢ εἰς τὸ Λύκειον ἐλθόντα τῷ βελτίστῳ τούτῳ Διαλόγῳ συμπεριπατεῖν ἠρέμα διαλεγομένους, τῶν ἐπαίνων καὶ κρότων οὐ δεομένους.

Πολλὰ ἔχων εἰπεῖν ἤδη παύσομαι. ὑμεῖς δὲ εὔορκον τὴν ψῆφον ἐνέγκατε.

ΔΙΚΗ

Τίς κρατεῖ;

ΕΡΜΗΣ

Πάσαις ὁ Σύρος πλὴν μιᾶς.

ΔΙΚΗ

Ῥήτωρ τις ἔοικεν εἶναι ὁ τὴν ἐναντίαν θέμενος. 33 ὁ Διάλογος ἐπὶ τῶν αὐτῶν λέγε. ὑμεῖς δὲ περιμείνατε, διπλάσιον ἀποισόμενοι τὸν μισθὸν ἐπ' ἀμφοτέραις ταῖς δίκαις.

ΔΙΑΛΟΓΟΣ

Ἐγὼ δέ, ὦ ἄνδρες δικασταί, μακροὺς μὲν ἀποτείνειν τοὺς λόγους οὐκ ἂν ἐβουλόμην πρὸς ὑμᾶς, ἀλλὰ κατὰ μικρὸν ὥσπερ εἴωθα. ὅμως δὲ ὡς νόμος ἐν τοῖς δικαστηρίοις, οὕτω ποιήσομαι τὴν κατηγορίαν ἰδιώτης παντάπασιν καὶ ἄτεχνος τῶν τοιούτων ὤν· καί μοι τοῦτο ἔστω πρὸς ὑμᾶς τὸ προοίμιον.

Ἃ δὲ ἠδίκημαι καὶ περιύβρισμαι πρὸς τούτου, ταῦτά ἐστιν, ὅτι με σεμνὸν τέως ὄντα καὶ θεῶν τε πέρι καὶ φύσεως καὶ τῆς τῶν ὅλων περιόδου σκοπούμενον, ὑψηλὸν ἄνω που τῶν νεφῶν ἀεροβα-

stormy scenes and lawsuits, should let the gentlemen of the jury rest in peace, refraining from accusations of tyrants and laudations of princes, and should betake myself to the Academy or the Lyceum to walk about with this excellent person Dialogue while we converse quietly without feeling any need of praise and applause.

Though I have much to say, I will stop now. Cast your vote in accordance with your oath.

(*The votes are counted.*)

JUSTICE

Who is the winner?

HERMES

The Syrian, with every vote but one.

JUSTICE

Very likely it was a public speaker who cast the vote against him. Let Dialogue plead before the same jury. (*To the* JURORS) Wait, and you shall get double pay for the two cases.

DIALOGUE

For my part, gentlemen of the jury, I should prefer not to make you a long speech, but to discuss the matter a little at a time, as is my wont. Nevertheless I will make my complaint in the way that is customary in courts of law, although I am completely uninformed and inexperienced in such matters. Please consider this my introduction.

The wrongs done me and the insults put upon me by this man are these. I was formerly dignified, and pondered upon the gods and nature and the cycle of the universe, treading the air[1] high up above the

[1] In the *Clouds* of Aristophanes (225) Socrates says: "I tread the air and contemplate the sun."

τοῦντα, ἔνθα ὁ μέγας ἐν οὐρανῷ Ζεὺς πτηνὸν ἅρμα ἐλαύνων φέρεται, κατασπάσας αὐτὸς ἤδη κατὰ τὴν ἀψῖδα πετόμενον καὶ ἀναβαίνοντα ὑπὲρ τὰ νῶτα τοῦ οὐρανοῦ καὶ τὰ πτερὰ συντρίψας ἰσοδίαιτον τοῖς πολλοῖς ἐποίησεν, καὶ τὸ μὲν τραγικὸν ἐκεῖνο καὶ σωφρονικὸν προσωπεῖον ἀφεῖλέ μου, κωμικὸν δὲ καὶ σατυρικὸν ἄλλο ἐπέθηκέ μοι καὶ μικροῦ δεῖν γελοῖον. εἶτά μοι εἰς τὸ αὐτὸ φέρων συγκαθεῖρξεν τὸ σκῶμμα καὶ τὸν ἴαμβον καὶ κυνισμὸν καὶ τὸν Εὔπολιν καὶ τὸν Ἀριστοφάνη, δεινοὺς ἄνδρας ἐπικερτομῆσαι τὰ σεμνὰ καὶ χλευάσαι τὰ ὀρθῶς ἔχοντα. τελευταῖον δὲ καὶ Μένιππόν τινα τῶν παλαιῶν κυνῶν μάλα ὑλακτικὸν ὡς δοκεῖ καὶ κάρχαρον ἀνορύξας, καὶ τοῦτον ἐπεισήγαγεν μοι φοβερόν τινα ὡς ἀληθῶς κύνα καὶ τὸ δῆγμα λαθραῖον, ὅσῳ καὶ γελῶν ἅμα ἔδακνεν.

Πῶς οὖν οὐ δεινὰ ὕβρισμαι μηκέτ' ἐπὶ τοῦ οἰκείου διακείμενος,[1] ἀλλὰ κωμῳδῶν καὶ γελωτοποιῶν καὶ ὑποθέσεις ἀλλοκότους ὑποκρινόμενος αὐτῷ; τὸ γὰρ πάντων ἀτοπώτατον, κρᾶσίν τινα παράδοξον κέκραμαι καὶ οὔτε πεζός εἰμι οὔτε ἐπὶ τῶν μέτρων βέβηκα, ἀλλὰ ἱπποκενταύρου δίκην σύνθετόν τι καὶ ξένον φάσμα τοῖς ἀκούουσι δοκῶ.

ΕΡΜΗΣ

34 Τί οὖν πρὸς ταῦτα ἐρεῖς, ὦ Σύρε;

ΣΥΡΟΣ

Ἀπροσδόκητον, ὦ ἄνδρες δικασταί, τὸν ἀγῶνα τοῦτον ἀγωνίζομαι παρ' ὑμῖν· πάντα γοῦν μᾶλ-

[1] ἐπὶ τοῦ οἰκείου σχήματος διαμένων β.

clouds where "great Zeus in heaven driving his winged car"[1] sweeps on; but he dragged me down when I was already soaring above the zenith and mounting on "heaven's back,"[2] and broke my wings, putting me on the same level as the common herd. Moreover, he took away from me the respectable tragic mask that I had, and put another upon me that is comic, satyr-like, and almost ridiculous. Then he unceremoniously penned me up with Jest and Satire and Cynicism and Eupolis and Aristophanes, terrible men for mocking all that is holy and scoffing at all that is right. At last he even dug up and thrust in upon me Menippus, a prehistoric dog,[3] with a very loud bark, it seems, and sharp fangs, a really dreadful dog who bites unexpectedly because he grins when he bites.

Have I not been dreadfully maltreated, when I no longer occupy my proper rôle but play the comedian and the buffoon and act out extraordinary plots for him? What is most monstrous of all, I have been turned into a surprising blend, for I am neither afoot nor ahorseback, neither prose nor verse, but seem to my hearers a strange phenomenon made up of different elements, like a Centaur.[4]

HERMES

What are you going to say to this, Master Syrian?

THE SYRIAN

Gentlemen of the jury, the suit that I am contesting now before you is unexpected. In fact, I should

[1] Plato, *Phaedrus* 246 E.
[2] Plato, *Phaedrus* 247 B. [3] Cynic.
[4] This refers to the practice of mingling verse and prose, borrowed by Lucian from Menippus. For good illustrations see the beginning of *Zeus Rants* and of *The Double Indictment.*

λον ἂν ἤλπισα ἢ τὸν Διάλογον τοιαῦτα ἐρεῖν περὶ ἐμοῦ, ὃν παραλαβὼν ἐγὼ σκυθρωπὸν ἔτι τοῖς πολλοῖς δοκοῦντα καὶ ὑπὸ τῶν συνεχῶν ἐρωτήσεων κατεσκληκότα, καὶ ταύτῃ αἰδέσιμον μὲν εἶναι δοκοῦντα, οὐ πάντῃ δὲ ἡδὺν οὐδὲ τοῖς πλήθεσι κεχαρισμένον, πρῶτον μὲν αὐτὸν ἐπὶ γῆς βαίνειν εἴθισα εἰς τὸν ἀνθρώπινον τοῦτον τρόπον, μετὰ δὲ τὸν αὐχμὸν τὸν πολὺν ἀποπλύνας καὶ μειδιᾶν καταναγκάσας ἡδίω τοῖς ὁρῶσι παρεσκεύασα, ἐπὶ πᾶσι δὲ τὴν κωμῳδίαν αὐτῷ παρέζευξα, καὶ κατὰ τοῦτο πολλήν οἱ μηχανώμενος τὴν εὔνοιαν παρὰ τῶν ἀκουόντων, οἳ τέως τὰς ἀκάνθας τὰς ἐν αὐτῷ δεδιότες ὥσπερ τὸν ἐχῖνον εἰς τὰς χεῖρας λαβεῖν αὐτὸν ἐφυλάττοντο.

Ἀλλ' ἐγὼ οἶδ' ὅπερ μάλιστα λυπεῖ αὐτόν, ὅτι μὴ τὰ γλίσχρα ἐκεῖνα καὶ λεπτὰ κάθημαι πρὸς αὐτὸν σμικρολογούμενος, εἰ ἀθάνατος ἡ ψυχή, καὶ πόσας κοτύλας ὁ θεὸς ὁπότε τὸν κόσμον εἰργάσατο τῆς ἀμιγοῦς καὶ κατὰ ταὐτὰ ἐχούσης οὐσίας ἐνέχεεν εἰς τὸν κρατῆρα ἐν ᾧ τὰ πάντα ἐκεράννυτο, καὶ εἰ ἡ Ῥητορικὴ πολιτικῆς μορίου εἴδωλον, κολακείας τὸ τέταρτον. χαίρει γὰρ οὐκ οἶδ' ὅπως τὰ τοιαῦτα λεπτολογῶν καθάπερ οἱ τὴν ψώραν ἡδέως κνώμενοι, καὶ τὸ φρόντισμα ἡδὺ αὐτῷ δοκεῖ καὶ μέγα φρονεῖ ἢν λέγηται ὡς οὐ παντὸς ἀνδρός ἐστι συνιδεῖν ἃ περὶ τῶν ἰδεῶν ὀξυδορκεῖ.

Ταῦτα δηλαδὴ καὶ παρ' ἐμοῦ ἀπαιτεῖ καὶ τὰ πτερὰ ἐκεῖνα ζητεῖ καὶ ἄνω βλέπει τὰ πρὸ τοῖν

have looked for anything else in the world sooner than that Dialogue should say such things about me. When I took him in hand, he was still dour, as most people thought, and had been reduced to a skeleton through continual questions. In that guise he seemed awe-inspiring, to be sure, but not in any way attractive or agreeable to the public. So first of all I got him into the way of walking on the ground like a human being; afterwards by washing off all his accumulated grime and forcing him to smile, I made him more agreeable to those who saw him: and on top of all that, I paired him with Comedy, and in this way too procured him great favour from his hearers, who formerly feared his prickles and avoided taking hold of him as if he were a sea-urchin.

I know, however, what hurts him most. It is that I do not sit and quibble with him about those obscure, subtle themes of his, like "whether the soul is immortal," and "when God made the world, how many pints of pure, changeless substance he poured into the vessel in which he concocted the universe,"[1] and "whether rhetoric is the false counterpart of a subdivision of political science, the fourth form of parasitic occupation."[2] Somehow he delights in dissecting such problems, just as people like to scratch where it itches. Reflection is sweet to him, and he sets great store by himself if they say that not every-one can grasp his penetrating speculations about "ideas."

That is what he expects of me, naturally; and he demands those wings of his and gazes on high without

[1] Cf. Plato, *Timaeus* 35 A and 41 D.
[2] Cf. Plato, *Gorgias* 463 B, D, 465 C.

ποδοῖν οὐχ ὁρῶν. ἐπεὶ τῶν γε ἄλλων ἕνεκα οὐκ ἂν οἶμαι μέμψαιτό μοι, ὡς θοἰμάτιον τοῦτο τὸ Ἑλληνικὸν περισπάσας αὐτοῦ βαρβαρικόν τι μετενέδυσα, καὶ ταῦτα βάρβαρος αὐτὸς εἶναι δοκῶν· ἠδίκουν γὰρ ἂν τὰ τοιαῦτα εἰς αὐτὸν παρανομῶν καὶ τὴν πάτριον ἐσθῆτα λωποδυτῶν.

Ἀπολελόγημαι ὡς δυνατὸν ἐμοί· ὑμεῖς δὲ ὁμοίαν τῇ πάλαι τὴν ψῆφον ἐνέγκατε.

ΕΡΜΗΣ

35 Βαβαί, δέκα ὅλαις κρατεῖς· ὁ γὰρ αὐτὸς ἐκεῖνος ὁ πάλαι οὐδὲ νῦν ὁμόψηφός ἐστιν. ἀμέλει τοῦτο ἔθος ἐστίν, καὶ πᾶσι τὴν τετρυπημένην οὗτος φέρει· καὶ μὴ παύσαιτο φθονῶν τοῖς ἀρίστοις. ἀλλ' ὑμεῖς μὲν ἄπιτε ἀγαθῇ τύχῃ, αὔριον δὲ τὰς λοιπὰς δικάσομεν.

seeing what lies at his feet. As far as the rest of it goes, he cannot complain, I am sure, that I have stripped him of that Greek mantle and shifted him into a foreign one, even though I myself am considered foreign. Indeed I should be doing wrong to transgress in that way against him and to steal away his native costume.

I have made the best defence that I can. Please cast the same ballot as before.

(*The votes are counted.*)

HERMES

Well, well! You win by all of ten votes! The same one who voted against you before will not vote as the rest even now. Without doubt it is a habit, and the man always casts the ballot that has a hole in it.[1] I hope he will keep on envying men of standing. Well, go your ways, and good luck to you. To-morrow we shall try the rest of the cases.

[1] Each juror was given two ballots of metal shaped like a Japanese top, a flat circular disk, pierced perpendicularly at its centre by a cylindrical axis, which in the one for acquittal was solid, in the other, tubular.

ON SACRIFICES

In matter and manner, this little skit approximates very closely to the Cynic diatribe as exemplified in the fragments of Teles and in some portions of Epictetus.

It has a counterpart in the piece, *On Funerals*, so close that one is tempted to believe them both parts of the same screed, although they now stand some distance apart in Lucian's works; it may be, however, that this is simply a pendant to the other. They certainly belong together in some sense.

ΠΕΡΙ ΘΥΣΙΩΝ

1 Ἃ μὲν γὰρ ἐν ταῖς θυσίαις οἱ μάταιοι πράττουσι καὶ ταῖς ἑορταῖς καὶ προσόδοις τῶν θεῶν καὶ ἃ αἰτοῦσι καὶ ἃ εὔχονται καὶ ἃ γιγνώσκουσι περὶ αὐτῶν, οὐκ οἶδα εἴ τις οὕτως κατηφής ἐστι καὶ λελυπημένος ὅστις οὐ γελάσεται τὴν ἀβελτερίαν ἐπιβλέψας τῶν δρωμένων. καὶ πολύ γε, οἶμαι, πρότερον τοῦ γελᾶν πρὸς ἑαυτὸν ἐξετάσει πότερον εὐσεβεῖς αὐτοὺς χρὴ καλεῖν ἢ τοὐναντίον θεοῖς ἐχθροὺς καὶ κακοδαίμονας, οἵ γε οὕτω ταπεινὸν καὶ ἀγεννὲς τὸ θεῖον ὑπειλήφασιν ὥστε εἶναι ἀνθρώπων ἐνδεὲς καὶ κολακευόμενον ἥδεσθαι καὶ ἀγανακτεῖν ἀμελούμενον.

Τὰ γοῦν Αἰτωλικὰ πάθη καὶ τὰς τῶν Καλυδωνίων συμφορὰς καὶ τοὺς τοσούτους φόνους καὶ τὴν Μελεάγρου διάλυσιν, πάντα ταῦτα ἔργα φασὶν εἶναι τῆς Ἀρτέμιδος μεμψιμοιρούσης ὅτι μὴ παρελήφθη πρὸς τὴν θυσίαν ὑπὸ τοῦ Οἰνέως· οὕτως ἄρα βαθέως καθίκετο αὐτῆς ἡ τῶν ἱερείων διαφορά.[1] καί μοι δοκῶ ὁρᾶν αὐτὴν ἐν τῷ οὐρανῷ τότε μόνην τῶν ἄλλων θεῶν εἰς Οἰνέως πεπορευμένων, δεινὰ ποιοῦσαν καὶ σχετλιάζουσαν οἵας ἑορτῆς ἀπολειφθήσεται.

Available in photographs: ΓN.

[1] ἱερείων διαφορά γ: ἱερῶν διαμαρτία β; ἱερείων διαμαρτία edd.

ON SACRIFICES

In view of what the dolts do at their sacrifices and their feasts and processions in honour of the gods, what they pray for and vow, and what opinions they hold about the gods, I doubt if anyone is so gloomy and woe-begone that he will not laugh to see the idiocy of their actions. Indeed, long before he laughs, I think, he will ask himself whether he should call them devout or, on the contrary, irreligious and pestilent, inasmuch as they have taken it for granted that the gods are so low and mean as to stand in need of men and to enjoy being flattered and to get angry when they are slighted.

Anyhow, the Aetolian incidents—the hardships of the Calydonians, all the violent deaths, and the dissolution of Meleager—were all due, they say, to Artemis, who held a grudge because she had not been included in Oeneus' invitation to his sacrifice; so deeply was she impressed by the superiority of his victims! Methinks I can see her in Heaven then, left all by herself when the other gods and goddesses had gone to the house of Oeneus, fussing and scolding about being left out of such a feast!

2 Τοὺς δ' αὖ Αἰθίοπας καὶ μακαρίους καὶ τρισευδαίμονας εἴποι τις ἄν, εἴ γε ἀπομνημονεύει τὴν χάριν αὐτοῖς ὁ Ζεὺς ἣν[1] πρὸς αὐτὸν ἐπεδείξαντο δώδεκα ἑξῆς ἡμέρας ἑστιάσαντες, καὶ ταῦτα ἐπαγόμενον καὶ τοὺς ἄλλους θεούς.

Οὕτως οὐδέν, ὡς ἔοικεν, ἀμισθὶ ποιοῦσιν ὧν ποιοῦσιν, ἀλλὰ πωλοῦσιν τοῖς ἀνθρώποις τἀγαθά, καὶ ἔνεστι πρίασθαι παρ' αὐτῶν τὸ μὲν ὑγιαίνειν, εἰ τύχοι, βοϊδίου, τὸ δὲ πλουτεῖν βοῶν τεττάρων, τὸ δὲ βασιλεύειν ἑκατόμβης, τὸ δὲ σῶον ἐπανελθεῖν ἐξ Ἰλίου εἰς Πύλον ταύρων ἐννέα, καὶ τὸ ἐκ τῆς Αὐλίδος εἰς Ἴλιον διαπλεῦσαι παρθένου βασιλικῆς. ἡ μὲν γὰρ Ἑκάβη τὸ μὴ ἁλῶναι τὴν πόλιν τότε ἐπρίατο παρὰ τῆς Ἀθηνᾶς βοῶν δώδεκα καὶ πέπλου. εἰκάζειν δὲ χρὴ πολλὰ εἶναι ἀλεκτρυόνος καὶ στεφάνου καὶ λιβανωτοῦ μόνου παρ' αὐτοῖς ὤνια.

3 Ταῦτά γε, οἶμαι, καὶ ὁ Χρύσης ἐπιστάμενος ἅτε ἱερεὺς ὢν καὶ γέρων καὶ τὰ θεῖα σοφός, ἐπειδὴ ἄπρακτος ἀπῄει παρὰ τοῦ Ἀγαμέμνονος, ὡς ἂν καὶ προδανείσας τῷ Ἀπόλλωνι τὴν χάριν δικαιολογεῖται καὶ ἀπαιτεῖ τὴν ἀμοιβὴν καὶ μόνον οὐκ ὀνειδίζει λέγων, "Ὦ βέλτιστε Ἄπολλον, ἐγὼ μέν σου τὸν νεὼν τέως ἀστεφάνωτον ὄντα πολλάκις ἐστεφάνωσα, καὶ τοσαῦτά σοι μηρία ταύρων τε καὶ αἰγῶν ἔκαυσα ἐπὶ τῶν βωμῶν, σὺ δὲ ἀμελεῖς μου τοιαῦτα πεπονθότος καὶ παρ' οὐδὲν τίθεσαι τὸν εὐεργέτην." τοιγαροῦν οὕτω κατεδυσώπησεν αὐτὸν ἐκ τῶν λόγων, ὥστε ἁρπασάμενος τὰ τόξα

[1] MSS. add (before ἣν in γ, after ἣν in β) ἐν ἀρχῇ τῆς Ὁμήρου ποιήσεως, bracketed by Schmieder and subsequent editors.

The Ethiopians, on the other hand, may well be called happy and thrice-blessed, if Zeus is really paying them back for the kindness that they showed him in dining him for twelve days running, and that too when he brought along the other gods!

So nothing, it seems, that they do is done without compensation. They sell men their blessings, and one can buy from them health, it may be, for a calf, wealth for four oxen, a royal throne for a hundred, a safe return from Troy to Pylos for nine bulls, and a fair voyage from Aulis to Troy for a king's daughter! Hecuba, you know, purchased temporary immunity for Troy from Athena for twelve oxen and a frock. One may imagine, too, that they have many things on sale for the price of a cock or a wreath or nothing more than incense.

Chryses knew this, I suppose, being a priest and an old man and wise in the ways of the gods; so when he came away from Agamemnon unsuccessful, it was just as if he had loaned his good works to Apollo; he took him to task, demanded his due, and all but insulted him, saying: "My good Apollo, I have often dressed your temple with wreaths when it lacked them before, and have burned in your honour all those thighs of bulls and goats upon your altars, but you neglect me when I am in such straits and take no account of your benefactor."[1] Consequently, he so discomfited Apollo by his talk that he

[1] *Iliad* 1, 33 ff.

καὶ ἐπὶ τοῦ ναυστάθμου καθίσας ἑαυτὸν κατετόξευσε τῷ λοιμῷ τοὺς Ἀχαιοὺς αὐταῖς ἡμιόνοις καὶ κυσίν.

4 Ἐπεὶ δὲ ἅπαξ τοῦ Ἀπόλλωνος ἐμνήσθην, βούλομαι καὶ τὰ ἄλλα εἰπεῖν, ἃ περὶ αὐτοῦ οἱ σοφοὶ τῶν ἀνθρώπων λέγουσιν, οὐχ ὅσα περὶ τοὺς ἔρωτας ἐδυστύχησεν οὐδὲ τοῦ Ὑακίνθου τὸν φόνον οὐδὲ τῆς Δάφνης τὴν ὑπεροψίαν, ἀλλ' ὅτι καὶ καταγνωσθεὶς ἐπὶ τῷ τῶν Κυκλώπων θανάτῳ καὶ ἐξοστρακισθεὶς διὰ τοῦτο ἐκ τοῦ οὐρανοῦ, ἐπέμφθη εἰς τὴν γῆν ἀνθρωπίνῃ χρησόμενος τῇ τύχῃ· ὅτε δὴ καὶ ἐθήτευσεν ἐν Θετταλίᾳ παρὰ Ἀδμήτῳ καὶ ἐν Φρυγίᾳ παρὰ Λαομέδοντι, παρὰ τούτῳ μέν γε οὐ μόνος ἀλλὰ μετὰ τοῦ Ποσειδῶνος, ἀμφότεροι πλινθεύοντες ὑπ' ἀπορίας καὶ ἐργαζόμενοι τὸ τεῖχος· καὶ οὐδὲ ἐντελῆ τὸν μισθὸν ἐκομίσαντο παρὰ τοῦ Φρυγός, ἀλλὰ προσώφειλεν αὐτοῖς πλέον ἢ τριάκοντα, φασί, δραχμὰς Τρωϊκάς.

5 Ἦ γὰρ οὐ ταῦτα σεμνολογοῦσιν οἱ ποιηταὶ περὶ τῶν θεῶν καὶ πολὺ τούτων ἱερώτερα περί τε Ἡφαίστου καὶ Προμηθέως καὶ Κρόνου καὶ Ῥέας καὶ σχεδὸν ὅλης τῆς τοῦ Διὸς οἰκίας; καὶ ταῦτα παρακαλέσαντες τὰς Μούσας συνῳδοὺς ἐν ἀρχῇ τῶν ἐπῶν, ὑφ' ὧν δὴ ἔνθεοι γενόμενοι, ὡς τὸ εἰκός, ᾄδουσιν ὡς ὁ μὲν Κρόνος ἐπειδὴ τάχιστα ἐξέτεμε τὸν πατέρα τὸν Οὐρανόν, ἐβασίλευσέν τε ἐν αὐτῷ καὶ τὰ τέκνα κατήσθιεν ὥσπερ ὁ Ἀργεῖος Θυέστης ὕστερον· ὁ δὲ Ζεὺς[1] κλαπεὶς ὑπὸ τῆς Ῥέας ὑποβαλομένης τὸν λίθον εἰς τὴν Κρήτην ἐκτεθεὶς ὑπ' αἰγὸς ἀνετράφη καθάπερ ὁ Τήλεφος

[1] Θυέστης· ὕστερον δὲ ὁ Ζεὺς γ.

caught up his bow and arrows, sat himself down above the ships, and shot down the Achaeans with the plague, even to their mules and dogs.

Having once alluded to Apollo, I wish to mention something else that gifted men say about him, not his misfortunes in love, such as the slaying of Hyacinthus and the superciliousness of Daphne, but that when he was found guilty of killing the Cyclopes and was banished from Heaven on account of it, he was sent to earth to try the lot of a mortal. On this occasion he actually became a serf in Thessaly under Admetus and in Phrygia under Laomedon, where, to be sure, he was not alone, but had Poseidon with him; and both of them were so poor that they had to make bricks and work upon the wall;[1] what is more, they did not even get full pay from the Phrygian, who owed them, it is said, a balance of more than thirty Trojan drachmas!

Is it not true that the poets gravely tell these tales about the gods, and others, too, far more hallowed than these, about Hephaestus, Prometheus, Cronus, Rhea and almost the whole family of Zeus? Yet, in beginning their poems, they invite the Muses to join their song! Inspired, no doubt, by the Muses, they sing that as soon as Cronus had castrated his father Heaven, he became king there and devoured his own children, like the Argive Thyestes in later time; that Zeus, stolen away by Rhea, who put the stone in his place, and abandoned in Crete, was nursed by a nanny-goat (just as

[1] Of Troy.

ὑπὸ ἐλάφου καὶ ὁ Πέρσης Κῦρος ὁ πρότερος ὑπὸ τῆς κυνός, εἶτ' ἐξελάσας τὸν πατέρα καὶ εἰς τὸ δεσμωτήριον καταβαλὼν αὐτὸς ἔσχε τὴν ἀρχήν· ἔγημε δὲ πολλὰς μὲν καὶ ἄλλας, ὑστάτην δὲ τὴν ἀδελφὴν[1] κατὰ τοὺς Περσῶν καὶ[2] Ἀσσυρίων νόμους· ἐρωτικὸς δὲ ὢν καὶ εἰς τὰ ἀφροδίσια ἐκκεχυμένος[3] ῥᾳδίως ἐνέπλησε παίδων τὸν οὐρανόν, τοὺς μὲν ἐξ ὁμοτίμων ποιησάμενος, ἐνίους δὲ νόθους ἐκ τοῦ θνητοῦ καὶ ἐπιγείου γένους, ἄρτι μὲν ὁ γεννάδας γενόμενος χρυσός, ἄρτι δὲ ταῦρος ἢ κύκνος ἢ ἀετός, καὶ ὅλως ποικιλώτερος αὐτοῦ Πρωτέως· μόνην δὲ τὴν Ἀθηνᾶν ἔφυσεν ἐκ τῆς ἑαυτοῦ κεφαλῆς ὑπ' αὐτὸν ἀτεχνῶς τὸν ἐγκέφαλον συλλαβών· τὸν μὲν γὰρ Διόνυσον ἡμιτελῆ, φασίν, ἐκ τῆς μητρὸς ἔτι καιομένης ἁρπάσας ἐν τῷ μηρῷ φέρων κατώρυξε κᾆτα ἐξέτεμεν τῆς ὠδῖνος ἐνστάσης.

6 Ὅμοια δὲ τούτοις καὶ περὶ τῆς Ἥρας ᾄδουσιν, ἄνευ τῆς πρὸς τὸν ἄνδρα ὁμιλίας ὑπηνέμιον αὐτὴν παῖδα γεννῆσαι τὸν Ἥφαιστον, οὐ μάλα εὐτυχῆ τοῦτον, ἀλλὰ βάναυσον καὶ χαλκέα καὶ πυρίτην, ἐν καπνῷ τὸ πᾶν βιοῦντα καὶ σπινθήρων ἀνάπλεων οἷα δὴ καμινευτήν, καὶ οὐδὲ ἄρτιον τὼ πόδε· χωλευθῆναι γὰρ αὐτὸν ἀπὸ τοῦ πτώματος, ὁπότε ἐρρίφη ὑπὸ τοῦ Διὸς ἐξ οὐρανοῦ, καὶ εἴ γε μὴ οἱ Λήμνιοι καλῶς ποιοῦντες ἔτι φερόμενον αὐτὸν ὑπεδέξαντο, κἂν ἐτεθνήκει ἡμῖν ὁ Ἥφαιστος ὥσπερ ὁ Ἀστυάναξ ἀπὸ τοῦ πύργου καταπεσών.

[1] τὴν Ἥραν τὴν ἀδελφὴν β.
[2] τοῦτο καὶ β.
[3] ἐκκεχυμένος Cobet: κεχυμένος, MSS.

Telephus was nursed by a doe and the Persian, Cyrus the Elder, by a bitch) and then drove his father out, threw him into prison, and held the sovereignty himself; that, in addition to many other wives, he at last married his sister, following the laws of the Persians and the Assyrians; that, being passionate and prone to the pleasures of love, he soon filled Heaven with children, some of whom he got by his equals in station and some illegitimately of mortal, earthly stock, now turning into gold, this gallant squire, now into a bull or a swan or an eagle, and in short, showing himself more changeable than even Proteus; and that Athena was the only one to be born of his head, conceived at the very root of his brain, for as to Dionysus, they say, Zeus took him prematurely from his mother while she was still ablaze, implanted him hastily in his own thigh, and cut him out when labour came on.

Their rhapsodies about Hera are of similar tenor, that without intercourse with her husband she became the mother of a wind-child, Hephaestus, who, however, is not in great luck, but works at the blacksmith's trade over a fire, living in smoke most of the time and covered with cinders, as is natural with a forge-tender; moreover, he is not even straight-limbed, as he was lamed by his fall when Zeus threw him out of Heaven. In fact, if the Lemnians had not obligingly caught him while he was still in the air, we should have had our Hephaestus killed just like Astyanax when he fell from the battlements.[1]

[1] The notion that the Lemnians caught Hephaestus as he fell is Lucian's own contribution. He expects his audience to be aware that he is giving them a sly misinterpretation of Homer's ἄφαρ κομίσαντο πεσόντα (*Iliad*, 1, 594).

Καίτοι τὰ μὲν Ἡφαίστου μέτρια· τὸν δὲ Προμηθέα τίς οὐκ οἶδεν οἷα ἔπαθεν, διότι καθ' ὑπερβολὴν φιλάνθρωπος ἦν; καὶ γὰρ αὖ καὶ τοῦτον εἰς τὴν Σκυθίαν ἀγαγὼν ὁ Ζεὺς ἀνεσταύρωσεν ἐπὶ τοῦ Καυκάσου, τὸν ἀετὸν αὐτῷ παρακαταστήσας τὸ ἧπαρ ὁσημέραι κολάψοντα.

7 Οὗτος μὲν οὖν ἐξετέλεσε τὴν καταδίκην. ἡ Ῥέα δέ—χρὴ γὰρ ἴσως καὶ ταῦτα εἰπεῖν—πῶς οὐκ ἀσχημονεῖ καὶ δεινὰ ποιεῖ, γραῦς μὲν ἤδη καὶ ἔξωρος οὖσα καὶ τοσούτων μήτηρ θεῶν, παιδεραστοῦσα δὲ ἔτι καὶ ζηλοτυποῦσα καὶ τὸν Ἄττιν ἐπὶ τῶν λεόντων περιφέρουσα, καὶ ταῦτα μηκέτι χρήσιμον εἶναι δυνάμενον; ὥστε πῶς ἂν ἔτι μέμφοιτό τις ἢ τῇ Ἀφροδίτῃ ὅτι μοιχεύεται, ἢ τῇ Σελήνῃ πρὸς τὸν Ἐνδυμίωνα κατιούσῃ πολλάκις ἐκ μέσης τῆς ὁδοῦ;

8 Φέρε δὲ ἤδη τούτων ἀφέμενοι τῶν λόγων εἰς αὐτὸν ἀνέλθωμεν τὸν οὐρανὸν ποιητικῶς ἀναπτάμενοι κατὰ τὴν αὐτὴν Ὁμήρῳ καὶ Ἡσιόδῳ ὁδὸν καὶ θεασώμεθα ὅπως διακεκόσμηται τὰ ἄνω. καὶ ὅτι μὲν χαλκοῦς ἐστιν τὰ ἔξω, καὶ πρὸ ἡμῶν τοῦ Ὁμήρου λέγοντος ἠκούσαμεν· ὑπερβάντι δὲ καὶ ἀνακύψαντι μικρὸν εἰς τὸ ἄνω καὶ ἀτεχνῶς ἐπὶ τοῦ νώτου γενομένῳ φῶς τε λαμπρότερον φαίνεται καὶ ἥλιος καθαρώτερος καὶ ἄστρα διαυγέστερα καὶ τὸ πᾶν ἡμέρα καὶ χρυσοῦν τὸ δάπεδον. εἰσιόντων δὲ πρῶτα μὲν οἰκοῦσιν αἱ Ὧραι· πυλωροῦσι γάρ· ἔπειτα δ' ἡ Ἶρις καὶ ὁ Ἑρμῆς ὄντες ὑπηρέται καὶ ἀγγελιαφόροι τοῦ Διός, ἑξῆς δὲ τοῦ Ἡφαίστου τὸ χαλκεῖον ἀνάμεστον ἁπάσης τέχνης, μετὰ δὲ αἱ τῶν θεῶν

But Hephaestus came off quite well beside Prometheus. Who does not know what happened to him because he was too philanthropic? Taking him to Scythia, Zeus pegged him out on the Caucasus and posted an eagle at his side to peck at his liver every day.

Prometheus, then, received a sentence and served it out, but what about Rhea? One *must* surely speak of this also. Does not she misconduct herself and behave dreadfully? Although she is an old woman, past her best years, the mother of so many gods, nevertheless she still has a love affair with a boy and is jealous, and she takes Attis about with her behind her lions, in spite of the fact that he cannot be of any use to her now. So how can one find fault with Aphrodite for being unfaithful to her husband, or with Selene for going down to visit Endymion time and again in the middle of her journey?

Come, dismissing this topic, let us go up to Heaven itself, soaring up poet-fashion by the same route as Homer and Hesiod, and let us see how they have arranged things on high. That it is bronze on the outside we learned from Homer, who anticipated us in saying so. But when one climbs over the edge, puts up one's head a little way into the world above, and really gets up on the "back,"[1] the light is brighter, the sun is clearer, the stars are shinier, it is day everywhere, and the ground is of gold. As you go in, the Hours live in the first house, for they are the warders of the gate; then come Iris and Hermes, who are attendants and messengers of Zeus; next, there is the smithy of Hephaestus, filled with works of art of every kind, and after that,

[1] Plato, *Phaedrus* 247 B. Cf. p. 147.

οἰκίαι καὶ τοῦ Διὸς τὰ βασίλεια, ταῦτα πάντα περικαλλῆ τοῦ Ἡφαίστου κατασκευάσαντος.
9 "οἱ δὲ θεοὶ πὰρ Ζηνὶ καθήμενοι"—πρέπει γάρ, οἶμαι, ἄνω ὄντα μεγαληγορεῖν—ἀποσκοποῦσιν εἰς τὴν γῆν καὶ πάντη περιβλέπουσιν ἐπικύπτοντες εἴ ποθεν ὄψονται πῦρ ἀναπτόμενον ἢ ἀναφερομένην κνῖσαν "ἑλισσομένην περὶ καπνῷ." κἂν μὲν θύῃ τις, εὐωχοῦνται πάντες ἐπικεχηνότες τῷ καπνῷ καὶ τὸ αἷμα πίνοντες τοῖς βωμοῖς προσχεόμενον[1] ὥσπερ αἱ μυῖαι· ἢν δὲ οἰκοσιτῶσιν, νέκταρ καὶ ἀμβροσία τὸ δεῖπνον. πάλαι μὲν οὖν καὶ ἄνθρωποι συνειστιῶντο καὶ συνέπινον αὐτοῖς, ὁ Ἰξίων καὶ ὁ Τάνταλος· ἐπεὶ δὲ ἦσαν ὑβρισταὶ καὶ λάλοι, ἐκεῖνοι μὲν ἔτι καὶ νῦν κολάζονται, ἄβατος δὲ τῷ θνητῷ γένει καὶ ἀπόρρητος ὁ οὐρανός.

10 Τοιοῦτος ὁ βίος τῶν θεῶν. τοιγαροῦν καὶ οἱ ἄνθρωποι συνῳδὰ τούτοις καὶ ἀκόλουθα περὶ τὰς θρησκείας ἐπιτηδεύουσιν. καὶ πρῶτον μὲν ὕλας ἀπετέμοντο καὶ ὄρη ἀνέθεσαν καὶ ὄρνεα καθιέρωσαν καὶ φυτὰ ἐπεφήμισαν ἑκάστῳ θεῷ. μετὰ δὲ νειμάμενοι κατὰ ἔθνη σέβουσι καὶ πολίτας αὐτῶν ἀποφαίνουσιν, ὁ μὲν Δελφὸς τὸν Ἀπόλλω καὶ ὁ Δήλιος, ὁ δὲ Ἀθηναῖος τὴν Ἀθηνᾶν—μαρτυρεῖται γοῦν τὴν οἰκειότητα τῷ ὀνόματι—καὶ τὴν Ἥραν ὁ Ἀργεῖος καὶ ὁ Μυγδόνιος τὴν Ῥέαν καὶ τὴν Ἀφροδίτην ὁ Πάφιος. οἱ δ᾽ αὖ Κρῆτες οὐ γενέσθαι παρ᾽ αὐτοῖς οὐδὲ τραφῆναι μόνον τὸν Δία λέγουσιν, ἀλλὰ καὶ τάφον αὐτοῦ δεικνύουσιν· καὶ ἡμεῖς ἄρα τοσοῦτον ἠπατήμεθα χρόνον οἰόμενοι

[1] τοῖς βωμοῖς προσχεόμενον: a gloss? περιχεόμενον CA, editors since Dindorf.

the houses of the gods and the palace of Zeus, all very handsomely built by Hephaestus. "The gods, assembled in the house of Zeus"[1]—it is in order, I take it, to elevate one's diction when one is on high—look off at the earth and gaze about in every direction, leaning down to see if they can see fire being lighted anywhere, or steam drifting up to them "about the smoke entwined."[2] If anybody sacrifices, they all have a feast, opening their mouths for the smoke and drinking the blood that is spilt at the altars, just like flies; but if they dine at home, their meal is nectar and ambrosia. In days of old, men used to dine and drink with them—Ixion and Tantalus—but as they behaved shockingly and talked too much, they are still undergoing punishment to this day, and there is now no admission for human beings to Heaven, which is strictly private.

That is the way the gods live, and as a result, the practices of men in the matter of divine worship are harmonious and consistent with all that. First they fenced off groves, dedicated mountains, consecrated birds and assigned plants to each god. Then they divided them up, and now worship them by nations and claim them as fellow-countrymen ; the Delphians claim Apollo, and so do the Delians, the Athenians Athena (in fact, she proves her kinship by her name), the Argives Hera, the Mygdonians Rhea, the Paphians Aphrodite. As for the Cretans, they not only say that Zeus was born and brought up among them, but even point out his tomb. We were mistaken all this while, then, in thinking that thunder

[1] *Iliad* 4, 1. [2] *Iliad* 1, 317.

τὸν Δία βροντᾶν τε καὶ ὕειν καὶ τὰ ἄλλα πάντα ἐπιτελεῖν, ὁ δὲ ἐλελήθει πάλαι τεθνεὼς παρὰ Κρησὶ τεθαμμένος.

11 Ἔπειτα δὲ ναοὺς ἐγείραντες ἵνα αὐτοῖς μὴ ἄοικοι μηδὲ ἀνέστιοι δῆθεν ὦσιν, εἰκόνας αὐτοῖς ἀπεικάζουσιν παρακαλέσαντες ἢ Πραξιτέλην ἢ Πολύκλειτον ἢ Φειδίαν, οἱ δὲ οὐκ οἶδ' ὅπου[1] ἰδόντες ἀναπλάττουσι γενειήτην μὲν τὸν Δία, παῖδα δὲ εἰς ἀεὶ τὸν Ἀπόλλωνα καὶ τὸν Ἑρμῆν ὑπηνήτην καὶ τὸν Ποσειδῶνα κυανοχαίτην καὶ γλαυκῶπιν τὴν Ἀθηνᾶν. ὅμως δ' οὖν οἱ παριόντες εἰς τὸν νεὼν οὔτε τὸν ἐξ Ἰνδῶν ἐλέφαντα ἔτι οἴονται ὁρᾶν οὔτε τὸ ἐκ τῆς Θρᾴκης μεταλλευθὲν χρυσίον ἀλλ' αὐτὸν τὸν Κρόνου καὶ Ῥέας, εἰς τὴν γῆν ὑπὸ Φειδίου μετῳκισμένον καὶ τὴν Πισαίων ἐρημίαν ἐπισκοπεῖν κεκελευσμένον, ἀγαπῶντα εἰ διὰ πέντε ὅλων ἐτῶν θύσει τις αὐτῷ πάρεργον Ὀλυμπίων.

12 Θέμενοι δὲ βωμοὺς καὶ προρρήσεις καὶ περιρραντήρια προσάγουσι τὰς θυσίας, βοῦν μὲν ἀροτῆρα ὁ γεωργός, ἄρνα δὲ ὁ ποιμὴν καὶ αἶγα ὁ αἰπόλος, ὁ δέ τις λιβανωτὸν ἢ πόπανον, ὁ δὲ πένης ἱλάσατο τὸν θεὸν κύσας[2] μόνον τὴν ἑαυτοῦ δεξιάν.[3] ἀλλ' οἵ γε θύοντες—ἐπ' ἐκείνους γὰρ ἐπάνειμι—στεφανώσαντες τὸ ζῷον καὶ πολύ γε πρότερον ἐξετάσαντες εἰ ἐντελὲς εἴη, ἵνα μηδὲ τῶν ἀχρήστων τι κατασφάττωσιν, προσάγουσι τῷ βωμῷ καὶ φονεύουσιν ἐν ὀφθαλμοῖς τοῦ θεοῦ γοερόν τι μυκώμενον καὶ ὡς τὸ εἰκὸς εὐφημοῦν καὶ ἡμίφωνον ἤδη τῇ θυσίᾳ ἐπαυλοῦν. τίς οὐκ

[1] ὅπως γ. [2] κύσας Cobet: σείσας γ, φιλήσας β.
[3] τὴν αὐτοῦ δεξιὰν β.

and rain and everything else comes from Zeus; if we had but known it, he has been dead and buried in Crete this long time!

Then too they erect temples, in order that the gods may not be houseless and hearthless, of course; and they fashion images in their likeness, sending for a Praxiteles or a Polycleitus or a Phidias, who have caught sight of them somewhere and represent Zeus as a bearded man, Apollo as a perennial boy, Hermes with his first moustache, Poseidon with sea-blue hair and Athena with green eyes! In spite of all, those who enter the temple think that what they behold is not now ivory from India nor gold mined in Thrace, but the very son of Cronus and Rhea, transported to earth by Phidias and bidden to be overlord of deserted Pisa, thinking himself lucky if he gets a sacrifice once in four long years as an incident to the Olympic games.

When they have established altars and formulae and lustral rites, they present their sacrifices, the farmer an ox from the plough, the shepherd a lamb, the goatherd a goat, someone else incense or a cake; the poor man, however, propitiates the god by just kissing his own hand.[1] But those who offer victims (to come back to them) deck the animal with garlands, after finding out far in advance whether it is perfect or not, in order that they may not kill something that is of no use to them; then they bring it to the altar and slaughter it under the god's eyes, while it bellows plaintively—making, we must suppose, auspicious sounds, and fluting low music to accompany the sacrifice! Who would not suppose that

[1] Cf. *Saltat.* 17.

ἂν εἰκάσειεν ἥδεσθαι ταῦτα ὁρῶντας τοὺς θεούς;
13 *καὶ τὸ μὲν πρόγραμμά φησι μὴ παριέναι εἰς τὸ εἴσω τῶν περιρραντηρίων ὅστις μὴ καθαρός ἐστιν τὰς χεῖρας· ὁ δὲ ἱερεὺς αὐτὸς ἕστηκεν ᾑμαγμένος καὶ ὥσπερ ὁ* Κύκλωψ *ἐκεῖνος ἀνατέμνων καὶ τὰ ἔγκατα ἐξαιρῶν καὶ καρδιουλκῶν καὶ τὸ αἷμα τῷ βωμῷ περιχέων καὶ τί γὰρ οὐκ εὐσεβὲς ἐπιτελῶν; ἐπὶ πᾶσι δὲ πῦρ ἀνακαύσας ἐπέθηκε φέρων αὐτῇ δορᾷ τὴν αἶγα καὶ αὐτοῖς ἐρίοις τὸ πρόβατον· ἡ δὲ κνῖσα θεσπέσιος καὶ ἱεροπρεπὴς χωρεῖ ἄνω καὶ εἰς αὐτὸν τὸν οὐρανὸν ἠρέμα διασκίδναται.*

Ὁ *μέν γε* Σκύθης *πάσας τὰς θυσίας ἀφεὶς καὶ ἡγησάμενος ταπεινὰς αὐτοὺς τοὺς ἀνθρώπους τῇ* Ἀρτέμιδι *παρίστησι καὶ οὕτως ποιῶν ἀρέσκει τὴν θεόν.*

14 Ταῦτα *μὲν δὴ ἴσως μέτρια καὶ τὰ ὑπ'* Ἀσσυρίων *γιγνόμενα καὶ ὑπὸ* Φρυγῶν *καὶ* Λυδῶν, *ἢν δ' εἰς τὴν* Αἴγυπτον *ἔλθῃς, τότε δὴ τότε ὄψει πολλὰ τὰ σεμνὰ καὶ ὡς ἀληθῶς ἄξια τοῦ οὐρανοῦ, κριοπρόσωπον μὲν τὸν* Δία, *κυνοπρόσωπον δὲ τὸν βέλτιστον* Ἑρμῆν *καὶ τὸν* Πᾶνα *ὅλον τράγον καὶ ἶβίν τινα καὶ κροκόδειλον ἕτερον καὶ πίθηκον.*

εἰ δ' ἐθέλεις καὶ ταῦτα δαήμεναι, ὄφρ' εὖ εἰδῇς,

ἀκούσῃ πολλῶν σοφιστῶν καὶ γραμματέων καὶ προφητῶν ἐξυρημένων διηγουμένων,—πρότερον δέ, φησὶν ὁ λόγος, "θύρας δ' ἐπίθεσθε βέβηλοι"

the gods like to see all this? And although the notice says that no one is to be allowed within the holy-water who has not clean hands, the priest himself stands there all bloody, just like the Cyclops of old, cutting up the victim, removing the entrails, plucking out the heart, pouring the blood about the altar, and doing everything possible in the way of piety. To crown it all, he lights a fire and puts upon it the goat, skin and all, and the sheep, wool and all; and the smoke, divine and holy, mounts upward and gradually dissipates into Heaven itself.

The Scythians, indeed, reject all the sacrificial animals and think them too mean; they actually offer men to Artemis and by so doing gratify the goddess!

These practices are all very well, no doubt, and also those of the Assyrians and those of the Phrygians and Lydians; but if you go to Egypt, then, ah! then you will see much that is venerable and truly in keeping with Heaven—Zeus with the head of a ram, good Hermes with the head of a dog, Pan completely metamorphosed into a goat, some other god into an ibis, another into a crocodile, another into a monkey!

> Wouldst thou enquire the cause of these doings in
> order to know it,"[1]

you will hear plenty of men of letters and scribes and shaven prophets say—but first of all, as the saying goes, "Uninitiate, shut up your doors!"[2]—that

[1] *Iliad* 6, 150.

[2] An oft-quoted tag from a lost Orphic poem. Those who have not been initiated in the mysteries are required to go into their houses and close the doors, because the emblems of Dionysus are going to pass through the streets.

—ὡς ἄρα ὑπὸ τὸν πόλεμον[1] καὶ τῶν γιγάντων τὴν ἐπανάστασιν οἱ θεοὶ φοβηθέντες ἧκον εἰς τὴν Αἴγυπτον ὡς δὴ ἐνταῦθα λησόμενοι τοὺς πολεμίους· εἶθ' ὁ μὲν αὐτῶν ὑπέδυ τράγον, ὁ δὲ κριὸν ὑπὸ τοῦ δέους, ὁ δὲ θηρίον ἢ ὄρνεον· διὸ δὴ εἰσέτι καὶ νῦν φυλάττεσθαι τὰς τότε μορφὰς τοῖς θεοῖς. ταῦτα γὰρ ἀμέλει ἐν τοῖς ἀδύτοις ἀπόκειται γραφέντα πλεῖον ἢ πρὸ ἐτῶν μυρίων.

15 Αἱ δὲ θυσίαι καὶ παρ' ἐκείνοις αἱ αὐταί, πλὴν ὅτι πενθοῦσι τὸ ἱερεῖον καὶ κόπτονται περιστάντες ἤδη πεφονευμένον. οἱ δὲ καὶ θάπτουσι μόνον ἀποσφάξαντες.

Ὁ μὲν γὰρ Ἆπις, ὁ μέγιστος αὐτοῖς θεός, ἐὰν ἀποθάνῃ, τίς οὕτω περὶ πολλοῦ ποιεῖται τὴν κόμην ὅστις οὐκ ἀπεξύρησε καὶ ψιλὸν[2] ἐπὶ τῆς κεφαλῆς τὸ πένθος ἐπεδείξατο, κἂν τὸν Νίσου ἔχῃ πλόκαμον τὸν πορφυροῦν; ἔστι δὲ ὁ Ἆπις ἐξ ἀγέλης θεός, ἐπὶ τῷ προτέρῳ χειροτονούμενος ὡς πολὺ καλλίων καὶ σεμνότερος τῶν ἰδιωτῶν βοῶν.

Ταῦτα οὕτω γιγνόμενα καὶ ὑπὸ τῶν πολλῶν πιστευόμενα δεῖσθαί μοι δοκεῖ τοῦ μὲν ἐπιτιμήσοντος οὐδενός, Ἡρακλείτου δέ τινος ἢ Δημοκρίτου, τοῦ μὲν γελασομένου τὴν ἄγνοιαν αὐτῶν, τοῦ δὲ τὴν ἄνοιαν ὀδυρουμένου.

[1] τῶν πολεμίων γ. [2] ὑψηλὸν β.

on the eve of the war, the revolt of the giants, the gods were panic-stricken and came to Egypt, thinking that surely there they could hide from their enemies; and then one of them in his terror entered into a goat, another into a ram, and others into other beasts or birds; so of course the gods still keep the forms they took then. All this, naturally, is on record in the temples, having been committed to writing more than ten thousand years ago!

Sacrifices are the same there as with us, except that they mourn over the victim, standing about it and beating their breasts after it has been slain. In some cases they even bury it after simply cutting its throat.

And if Apis, the greatest of their gods, dies, who is there who thinks so much of his hair that he does not shave it off and baldly show his mourning on his head, even if he has the purple tress of Nisus?[1] But Apis is a god out of the herd, chosen to succeed the former Apis on the ground that he is far more handsome and majestic than the run of cattle!

Actions and beliefs like these on the part of the public seem to me to require, not someone to censure them, but a Heracleitus or a Democritus, the one to laugh at their ignorance, the other to bewail their folly.

[1] Nisus, king of Megara, had something in common with Samson, for as long as the purple tress remained where it belonged, his city was safe. Ovid (*Metam.* 8, 1–151) tells how his daughter robbed him of it, and became Scylla.

THE IGNORANT BOOK-COLLECTOR

This too is a diatribe, an excellent illustration of that sort of diatribe which made the word to us moderns synonymous with invective. It is far from a school exercise, but was directed against a real person, a Syrian (§ 19), evidently well enough known to Lucian's auditors. A scholiast (probably Bishop Arethas, who was himself a book-collector) remarks: "If I may guess, Lucian, you asked him for the loan of a book, and when you did not get it, requited him with this handsome token of your esteem!" It was written after the death of Peregrinus Proteus and during the reign of Marcus Aurelius, about 170 A.D.

ΠΡΟΣ ΤΟΝ ΑΠΑΙΔΕΥΤΟΝ ΚΑΙ ΠΟΛΛΑ ΒΙΒΛΙΑ ΩΝΟΥΜΕΝΟΝ

1 Καὶ μὴν ἐναντίον ἐστὶν οὗ ἐθέλεις ὃ νῦν ποιεῖς. οἴει μὲν γὰρ ἐν παιδείᾳ καὶ αὐτὸς εἶναί τις δόξειν σπουδῇ συνωνούμενος τὰ κάλλιστα τῶν βιβλίων· τὸ δέ σοι περὶ τὰ κάτω χωρεῖ, καὶ ἔλεγχος γίγνεται τῆς ἀπαιδευσίας πως τοῦτο. μάλιστα δὲ οὐδὲ τὰ κάλλιστα ὠνῇ, ἀλλὰ πιστεύεις τοῖς ὡς ἔτυχεν ἐπαινοῦσι καὶ ἕρμαιον εἶ τῶν τὰ τοιαῦτα ἐπιψευδομένων τοῖς βιβλίοις καὶ θησαυρὸς ἕτοιμος τοῖς καπήλοις αὐτῶν. ἢ πόθεν γάρ σοι διαγνῶναι δυνατόν, τίνα μὲν παλαιὰ καὶ πολλοῦ ἄξια, τίνα δὲ φαῦλα καὶ ἄλλως σαπρά, εἰ μὴ τῷ διαβεβρῶσθαι καὶ κατακεκόφθαι αὐτὰ τεκμαίροιο καὶ συμβούλους τοὺς σέας ἐπὶ τὴν ἐξέτασιν παραλαμβάνοις;[1] ἐπεὶ τοῦ ἀκριβοῦς ἢ ἀσφαλοῦς ἐν αὐτοῖς τίς ἢ ποία διάγνωσις;

2 Ἵνα δέ σοι δῶ αὐτὰ ἐκεῖνα κεκρικέναι, ὅσα ὁ Καλλῖνος εἰς κάλλος ἢ ὁ ἀοίδιμος Ἀττικὸς σὺν ἐπιμελείᾳ τῇ πάσῃ ἔγραψαν,[2] σοὶ τί ὄφελος, ὦ

Available in photographs: ΓΡΝ.

[1] παραλαμβάνοις Guyet: παραλαμβάνεις MSS.
[2] ἔγραψαν Herwerden: γράψαιεν MSS.

THE IGNORANT BOOK-COLLECTOR

Truly, what you are now doing is the reverse of what you are aiming to do. You expect to get a reputation for learning by zealously buying up the finest books, but the thing goes by opposites and in a way becomes proof of your ignorance. Indeed, you do not buy the finest; you rely upon men who bestow their praise hit-and-miss, you are a god-send to the people that tell such lies about books, and a treasure-trove ready to hand to those who traffic in them. Why, how can *you* tell what books are old and highly valuable, and what are worthless and simply in wretched repair[1]—unless you judge them by the extent to which they are eaten into and cut up, calling the book-worms into counsel to settle the question? As to their correctness and freedom from mistakes, what judgement have you, and what is it worth?

Yet suppose I grant you that you have selected the very *éditions de luxe* that were prepared by Callinus or by the famous Atticus with the utmost care.[2]

[1] Not old, though they look old.

[2] Both Atticus and Callinus are mentioned again as scribes in this piece (24); Callinus is not elsewhere mentioned, but Atticus is supposed to be the "publisher" of the Atticiana, editions which had great repute in antiquity. It is hardly likely that he is Cicero's friend.

θαυμάσιε, τοῦ κτήματος οὔτε εἰδότι τὸ κάλλος αὐτῶν οὔτε χρησομένῳ ποτὲ οὐδὲν μᾶλλον ἢ τυφλὸς ἄν τις ἀπολαύσειε κάλλους παιδικῶν; σὺ δὲ ἀνεῳγμένοις μὲν τοῖς ὀφθαλμοῖς ὁρᾷς τὰ βιβλία, καὶ νὴ Δία κατακόρως, καὶ ἀναγιγνώσκεις ἔνια πάνυ ἐπιτρέχων, φθάνοντος τοῦ ὀφθαλμοῦ τὸ στόμα· οὐδέπω δὲ τοῦτό μοι ἱκανόν, ἢν μὴ εἰδῇς τὴν ἀρετὴν καὶ κακίαν ἑκάστου τῶν ἐγγεγραμμένων καὶ συνίῃς ὅστις μὲν ὁ νοῦς σύμπασιν, τίς δὲ ἡ τάξις τῶν ὀνομάτων, ὅσα τε πρὸς τὸν ὀρθὸν κανόνα τῷ συγγραφεῖ ἀπηκρίβωται καὶ ὅσα κίβδηλα καὶ νόθα καὶ παρακεκομμένα.

3 Τί οὖν; φὴς καὶ ταὐτὰ[1] μὴ μαθὼν ἡμῖν εἰδέναι; πόθεν, εἰ μή ποτε παρὰ τῶν Μουσῶν κλῶνα δάφνης καθάπερ ὁ ποιμὴν ἐκεῖνος λαβών; Ἑλικῶνα μὲν γάρ, ἵνα διατρίβειν αἱ θεαὶ λέγονται, οὐδὲ ἀκήκοας οἶμαί ποτε, οὐδὲ τὰς αὐτὰς[2] διατριβὰς ἡμῖν ἐν παισὶν ἐποιοῦ· σοὶ καὶ μεμνῆσθαι Μουσῶν ἀνόσιον. ἐκεῖναι γὰρ ποιμένι μὲν οὐκ ἂν ὤκνησαν φανῆναι σκληρῷ ἀνδρὶ καὶ δασεῖ καὶ πολὺν τὸν ἥλιον ἐπὶ τῷ σώματι ἐμφαίνοντι, οἵῳ δὲ σοί—καί μοι πρὸς τῆς Λιβανίτιδος ἄφες ἐν τῷ παρόντι τὸ μὴ σύμπαντα σαφῶς εἰπεῖν—οὐδὲ ἐγγὺς γενέσθαι ποτ' ἂν εὖ οἶδ' ὅτι ἠξίωσαν, ἀλλ' ἀντὶ τῆς δάφνης μυρρίνῃ ἂν ἢ καὶ μαλάχης φύλλοις μαστιγοῦσαι ἀπήλλαξαν ἂν τῶν τοιούτων, ὡς μὴ

[1] ταὐτὰ Naber: ταῦτα MSS.
[2] τὰς αὐτὰς Marcilius: τοιαύτας MSS.

What good, you strange person, will it do you to own them, when you do not understand their beauty and will never make use of it one whit more than a blind man would enjoy beauty in favourites? To be sure you look at your books with your eyes open and quite as much as you like, and you read some of them aloud with great fluency, keeping your eyes in advance of your lips; but I do not consider that enough, unless you know the merits and defects of each passage in their contents, unless you understand what every sentence means, how to construe the words, what expressions have been accurately turned by the writer in accordance with the canon of good use, and what are false, illegitimate, and counterfeit.

Come now, do you maintain that without instruction you know as much as we? How can you, unless, like the shepherd of old,[1] you once received a branch of laurel from the Muses? Helicon, which the goddesses are said to haunt, you never even heard of, I take it, and your haunts in your boyhood were not the same as ours. That you should even mention the Muses is impious. They would not have shrunk from showing themselves to a shepherd, a hard-bitten, hairy man displaying rich tan on his body, but as for the like of you—in the name of your lady of Lebanon[2] dispense me for the present from giving a full description of you in plain language!—they would never have deigned, I am sure, to come near you, but instead of giving you laurel they would have scourged you with myrtle or sprays of mallow and would have made you keep your distance from those

[1] Hesiod: see the *Theogony* 29 ff.

[2] Aphrodite, perhaps, or Astarte; in later times there was a notorious cult of Aphrodite on Lebanon: Eusebius, *Vit. Constantini* 3, 53.

μιᾶναι μήτε τὸν Ὀλμειὸν μήτε τὴν τοῦ Ἵππου κρήνην, ἅπερ ἢ ποιμνίοις διψῶσιν ἢ ποιμένων στόμασι καθαροῖς πότιμα.

Καίτοι οὐδέ, εἰ καὶ πάνυ ἀναίσχυντος εἶ καὶ ἀνδρεῖος τὰ τοιαῦτα, τολμήσειας ἄν ποτε εἰπεῖν ὡς ἐπαιδεύθης ἢ ἐμέλησέ σοι πώποτε τῆς ἐν χρῷ πρὸς τὰ βιβλία συνουσίας ἢ ὡς διδάσκαλός σοι
4 ὁ δεῖνα ἢ τῷ δεῖνι συνεφοίτας. ἀλλ' ἑνὶ τούτῳ μόνῳ πάντα ἐκεῖνα ἀναδραμεῖσθαι νῦν ἐλπίζεις, τῷ κτᾶσθαι πολλὰ βιβλία. κατὰ δὴ ταῦτα, ἐκεῖνα ἔχε συλλαβὼν τὰ τοῦ Δημοσθένους ὅσα τῇ χειρὶ τῇ αὑτοῦ ὁ ῥήτωρ ἔγραψε, καὶ τὰ τοῦ Θουκυδίδου ὅσα παρὰ τοῦ Δημοσθένους καὶ αὐτὰ ὀκτάκις μεταγεγραμμένα εὑρέθη, καὶ ὅλως[1] ἅπαντα ἐκεῖνα ὅσα ὁ Σύλλας Ἀθήνηθεν εἰς Ἰταλίαν ἐξέπεμψε· τί ἂν πλέον ἐκ τούτου εἰς παιδείαν κτήσαιο, κἂν ὑποβαλόμενος αὐτὰ ἐπικαθεύδῃς ἢ συγκολλήσας καὶ περιβαλόμενος περινοστῇς; πίθηκος γὰρ ὁ πίθηκος, ἡ παροιμία φησί, κἂν χρύσεα ἔχῃ σύμβολα. καὶ σὺ τοίνυν βιβλίον μὲν ἔχεις ἐν τῇ χειρὶ καὶ ἀναγιγνώσκεις ἀεί, τῶν δὲ ἀναγιγνωσκομένων οἶσθα οὐδέν, ἀλλ' ὄνος λύρας ἀκούεις κινῶν τὰ ὦτα.

Ὡς εἴ γε τὸ κεκτῆσθαι τὰ βιβλία καὶ πεπαιδευμένον ἀπέφαινε τὸν ἔχοντα, πολλοῦ ἂν ὡ ἀληθῶς τὸ κτῆμα ἦν ἄξιον καὶ μόνων ὑμῶν τῶν πλουσίων, εἰ ὥσπερ ἐξ ἀγορᾶς ἦν πριάσθαι τοὺς

[1] εὑρέθη, καὶ ὅλως A.M.H.: εὑρέθη καλῶς MSS.; εὑρέθη καλῶς, καὶ Bekker, Dindorf.

---

[1] Of the copies of his own works and those of Thucydides written by Demosthenes we have no other notice; Sulla

regions, so as not to pollute either Olmeios or Hippocrene, whose waters only thirsty flocks or the clean lips of shepherds may drink.

No matter how shameless you are and how courageous in such matters, you would never dare to say that you have had an education, or that you ever troubled yourself to associate intimately with books, or that So-and-so was your teacher and you went to school with So-and-so. You expect to make up for all that now by one single expedient—by getting many books. On that theory, collect and keep all those manuscripts of Demosthenes that the orator wrote with his own hand, and those of Thucydides that were found to have been copied, likewise by Demosthenes, eight times over, and even all the books that Sulla sent from Athens to Italy.[1] What would you gain by it in the way of learning, even if you should put them under your pillow and sleep on them or should glue them together and walk about dressed in them? "A monkey is always a monkey," says the proverb, "even if he has birth-tokens of gold."[2] Although you have a book in your hand and read all the time, you do not understand a single thing that you read, but you are like the donkey that listens to the lyre and wags his ears.

If possessing books made their owner learned, they would indeed be a possession of great price, and only rich men like you would have them, since you could buy them at auction, as it were, outbidding us poor

took to Italy what was reported to have been the library of Aristotle: Plut. *Sulla* 26.

[2] These were trinkets put in the cradle or the clothing of a child when it was abandoned, as proof of good birth and as a possible means of identification later. Hyginus (187) calls them *insignia ingenuitatis*.

πένητας ἡμᾶς ὑπερβάλλοντας. τίς δὲ τοῖς ἐμπόροις καὶ τοῖς βιβλιοκαπήλοις ἤρισεν ἂν περὶ παιδείας τοσαῦτα βιβλία ἔχουσι καὶ πωλοῦσιν; ἀλλ' εἴ γε διελέγχειν ἐθέλεις, ὄψει μηδ' ἐκείνους πολύ σου τὰ εἰς παιδείαν ἀμείνους, ἀλλὰ βαρβάρους μὲν τὴν φωνὴν ὥσπερ σύ, ἀξυνέτους δὲ τῇ γνώσει, οἵους εἰκὸς εἶναι τοὺς μηδὲν τῶν καλῶν καὶ αἰσχρῶν καθεωρακότας. καίτοι σὺ μὲν δύο ἢ τρία παρ' αὐτῶν ἐκείνων πριάμενος ἔχεις, οἱ δὲ νύκτωρ καὶ μεθ' ἡμέραν διὰ χειρὸς ἔχουσιν αὐτά.
5 τίνος οὖν ἀγαθοῦ ὠνῇ ταῦτα, εἰ μὴ καὶ τὰς ἀποθήκας αὐτὰς τῶν βιβλίων ἡγῇ πεπαιδεῦσθαι τοσαῦτα περιεχούσας παλαιῶν ἀνδρῶν συγγράμματα;

Καί μοι, εἰ δοκεῖ, ἀπόκριναι· μᾶλλον δέ, ἐπεὶ τοῦτό σοι ἀδύνατον, ἐπίνευσον γοῦν ἢ ἀνάνευσον πρὸς τὰ ἐρωτώμενα. εἴ τις αὐλεῖν μὴ ἐπιστάμενος κτήσαιτο τοὺς Τιμοθέου αὐλοὺς ἢ τοὺς Ἰσμηνίου, οὓς ἑπτὰ ταλάντων ὁ Ἰσμηνίας ἐν Κορίνθῳ ἐπρίατο, ἆρ' ἂν διὰ τοῦτο καὶ αὐλεῖν δύναιτο, ἢ οὐδὲν ὄφελος αὐτῷ τοῦ κτήματος οὐκ ἐπισταμένῳ χρήσασθαι κατὰ τὴν τέχνην; εὖ γε ἀνένευσας· οὐδὲ γὰρ τοὺς Μαρσύου ἢ Ὀλύμπου κτησάμενος αὐλήσειεν ἂν μὴ μαθών. τί δ' εἴ τις τοῦ Ἡρακλέους τὰ τόξα κτήσαιτο μὴ Φιλοκτήτης ὢν ὡς δύνασθαι ἐντείνασθαί τε αὐτὰ καὶ ἐπίσκοπα τοξεῦσαι; τί σοι καὶ οὗτος δοκεῖ; ἆρ' ἂν ἐπιδείξασθαί τι ἔργον τοξότου ἄξιον; ἀνένευσας καὶ τοῦτο. κατὰ ταὐτὰ δὴ καὶ ὁ κυβερνᾶν οὐκ εἰδὼς καὶ ἱππεύειν μὴ μεμελετηκὼς εἰ ὁ μὲν ναῦν καλλίστην παραλάβοι, τοῖς πᾶσι καὶ εἰς κάλλος καὶ εἰς ἀσφάλειαν κάλ-

men. In that case, however, who could rival the dealers and booksellers for learning, who possess and sell so many books? But if you care to look into the matter, you will see that they are not much superior to you in that point; they are barbarous of speech and obtuse in mind like you—just what one would expect people to be who have no conception of what is good and bad. Yet you have only two or three books which they themselves have sold you, while they handle books night and day. What good, then, does it do you to buy them—unless you think that even the book-cases are learned because they contain so many of the works of the ancients!

Answer me this question, if you will—or better, as you are unable to answer, nod or shake your head in reply. If a man who did not know how to play the flute should buy the instrument of Timotheus or that of Ismenias,[1] for which Ismenias paid seven talents in Corinth, would that make him able to play, or would it do him no good to own it since he did not know how to use it as a musician would? You did well to shake your head. Even if he obtained the flute of Marsyas or Olympus, he could not play without previous instruction. And what if a man should get the bow of Heracles without being a Philoctetes so as to be able to draw it and shoot straight? What do you think about him? That he would make any showing worthy of an archer? You shake your head at this, too. So, of course, with a man who does not know how to steer, and one who has not practised riding; if the one should take the helm of a fine vessel, finely constructed in every detail both for beauty and for seaworthiness, and the other should

[1] Famous Theban flute-players of the fourth century B.C.; for Timotheus, see also Lucian's *Harmonides*.

λιστα ἐξειργασμένην, ὁ δὲ ἵππον κτήσαιτο Μῆδον ἢ κενταυρίδην ἢ κοππαφόρον, ἐλέγχοιτο ἄν, οἶμαι, ἑκάτερος οὐκ εἰδὼς ὅ τι χρήσαιτο ἑκατέρῳ. ἐπινεύεις καὶ τοῦτο; πείθου δὴ καὶ τοῦτό μοι ἐπίνευσον· εἴ τις ὥσπερ σὺ ἀπαίδευτος ὢν ὠνοῖτο πολλὰ βιβλία, οὐ σκώμματα οὗτος εἰς ἀπαιδευσίαν καθ' ἑαυτοῦ ἐκφέροι; τί ὀκνεῖς καὶ τοῦτο ἐπινεύειν; ἔλεγχος γάρ, οἶμαι, σαφὴς οὗτος, καὶ τῶν ὁρώντων ἕκαστος εὐθὺς τὸ προχειρότατον ἐκεῖνο ἐπιφθέγγεται, "τί κυνὶ καὶ βαλανείῳ;"

6 Καὶ ἐγένετό τις οὐ πρὸ πολλοῦ ἐν Ἀσίᾳ πλούσιος ἀνὴρ ἐκ συμφορᾶς ἀποτμηθεὶς τοὺς πόδας ἀμφοτέρους, ἀπὸ κρύους, οἶμαι, ἀποσαπέντας ἐπειδή ποτε διὰ χιόνος ὁδοιπορῆσαι συνέβη αὐτῷ. οὗτος τοίνυν τοῦτο μὲν ἐλεεινὸν ἐπεπόνθει, καὶ θεραπεύων τὴν δυστυχίαν ξυλίνους πόδας πεποίητο, καὶ τούτους ὑποδούμενος ἐβάδιζεν ἐπιστηριζόμενος ἅμα τοῖς οἰκέταις. ἐκεῖνο δὲ γελοῖον ἐποίει, κρηπῖδας γὰρ καλλίστας ἐωνεῖτο νεοτμήτους ἀεί, καὶ τὴν πλείστην πραγματείαν περὶ ταύτας εἶχεν, ὡς καλλίστοις ὑποδήμασι κεκοσμημένα εἴη αὐτῷ τὰ ξύλα.[1] οὐ ταὐτὰ οὖν καὶ σὺ ποιεῖς χωλὴν μὲν ἔχων καὶ συκίνην τὴν γνώμην, ὠνούμενος δὲ χρυσοῦς ἐμβάτας, οἷς μόλις ἄν τις καὶ ἀρτίπους ἐμπεριπατήσειεν;

7 Ἐπεὶ δὲ ἐν τοῖς ἄλλοις καὶ τὸν Ὅμηρον ἐπρίω πολλάκις, ἀναγνώτω σοί τις αὐτοῦ λαβὼν τὴν δευτέραν τῆς Ἰλιάδος ῥαψῳδίαν, ἧς τὰ μὲν ἄλλα

[1] τὰ ξύλα, οἱ πόδες δή MSS.: οἱ πόδες δή excised by Headlam.

---

[1] The "Centaur" horses probably came from Thessaly, the home of the Centaurs and a land of good horses. The

get an Arab or a "Centaur" or a "Koppa-brand,"[1] each would give proof, I have no doubt, that he did not know what to do with his property. Do you assent to this? Take my advice, now, and assent to this also; if an ignorant man like you should buy many books, would he not give rise to gibes at himself for his ignorance? Why do you shrink from assenting to this also? To do so is a clear give-away, I maintain, and everybody who sees it at once quotes that very obvious proverb: "What has a dog to do with a bath?"

Not long ago there was a rich man in Asia, both of whose feet had been amputated in consequence of an accident; they were frozen, I gather, when he had to make a journey through snow. Well, this of course was pitiable, and to remedy the mischance he had had wooden feet made for him, which he used to lace on, and in that way made shift to walk, leaning upon his servants as he did so. But he did one thing that was ridiculous: he used always to buy very handsome sandals of the latest cut and went to the utmost trouble in regard to them, in order that his timber toes might be adorned with the most beautiful footwear! Now are not you doing just the same thing? Is it not true that although you have a crippled, fig-wood[2] understanding, you are buying gilt buskins which even a normal man could hardly get about in?

As you have often bought Homer among your other books, have someone take the second book of his Iliad and read it to you. Do not bother about

"Koppa-brand" were marked ϙ, which in the alphabet of Corinth corresponded to K, and was used (on coins, for instance) as the abbreviation for Korinthos.

[2] The most worthless sort of wood.

μὴ ἐξετάζειν· οὐδὲν γὰρ αὐτῶν πρὸς σέ· πεποίηται δέ τις αὐτῷ δημηγορῶν παγγέλοιος ἄνθρωπος, διάστροφος τὸ σῶμα καὶ λελωβημένος. ἐκεῖνος τοίνυν ὁ Θερσίτης ὁ τοιοῦτος εἰ λάβοι τὴν Ἀχιλλέως πανοπλίαν, οἴει ὅτι αὐτίκα διὰ τοῦτο καὶ καλὸς ἅμα καὶ ἰσχυρὸς ἂν γένοιτο, καὶ ὑπερπηδήσεται μὲν τὸν ποταμόν, ἐπιθολώσει δὲ αὐτοῦ τὸ ῥεῖθρον τῷ φόνῳ τῶν Φρυγῶν, ἀποκτενεῖ δὲ τὸν Ἕκτορα καὶ πρὸ αὐτοῦ τὸν Λυκάονα καὶ τὸν Ἀστεροπαῖον, μηδὲ φέρειν ἐπὶ τῶν ὤμων τὴν μελίαν δυνάμενος; οὐκ ἂν εἴποις· ἀλλὰ καὶ γέλωτα ἂν ὀφλισκάνοι χωλεύων ὑπὸ τῇ ἀσπίδι καὶ ἐπὶ στόμα καταπίπτων ὑπὸ τοῦ βάρους καὶ ὑπὸ τῷ κράνει ὁπότε ἀνανεύσειε δεικνὺς τοὺς παραβλῶπας ἐκείνους αὐτοῦ ὀφθαλμοὺς καὶ τὸν θώρακα ἐπαίρων τῷ τοῦ μεταφρένου κυρτώματι καὶ τὰς κνημῖδας ἐπισυρόμενος, καὶ ὅλως αἰσχύνων ἀμφοτέρους, καὶ τὸν δημιουργὸν αὐτῶν καὶ τὸν δεσπότην. τὸ αὐτὸ δὴ καὶ σὺ πάσχων οὐχ ὁρᾷς, ὁπόταν τὸ μὲν βιβλίον ἐν τῇ χειρὶ ἔχῃς πάγκαλον, πορφυρᾶν μὲν ἔχον τὴν διφθέραν, χρυσοῦν δὲ τὸν ὀμφαλόν, ἀναγιγνώσκῃς δὲ αὐτὸ βαρβαρίζων καὶ καταισχύνων καὶ διαστρέφων, ὑπὸ μὲν τῶν πεπαιδευμένων καταγελώμενος, ὑπὸ δὲ τῶν συνόντων σοι κολάκων ἐπαινούμενος, οἳ καὶ αὐτοὶ πρὸς ἀλλήλους ἐπιστρεφόμενοι γελῶσι τὰ πολλά;

8 Θέλω γοῦν σοι διηγήσασθαί τι Πυθοῖ γενόμενον. Ταραντῖνος Εὐάγγελος τοὔνομα τῶν οὐκ ἀφανῶν ἐν τῷ Τάραντι ἐπεθύμησεν νικῆσαι Πύθια. τὰ μὲν οὖν τῆς γυμνῆς ἀγωνίας αὐτίκα ἐδόκει αὐτῷ ἀδύνατον εἶναι μήτε πρὸς ἰσχὺν μήτε

the rest of the book, for none of it applies to you; but he has a description of a man making a speech, an utterly ridiculous fellow, warped and deformed in body.[1] Now then, if that man, Thersites, should get the armour of Achilles, do you suppose that he would thereby at once become both handsome and strong; that he would leap the river, redden its stream with Trojan gore, and kill Hector—yes, and before Hector, kill Lycaon and Asteropaeus—when he cannot even carry the "ash tree" on his shoulders?[2] You will hardly say so. No, he would make himself a laughing-stock, limping under the shield, falling on his face beneath the weight of it, showing those squint eyes of his under the helmet every time he looked up, making the corselet buckle up with the hump on his back, trailing the greaves on the ground—disgracing, in short, both the maker of the arms and their proper owner. Do not you see that the same thing happens in your case, when the roll that you hold in your hands is very beautiful, with a slip-cover of purple vellum and a gilt knob, but in reading it you barbarize its language, spoil its beauty and warp its meaning? Men of learning laugh at you, while the toadies who live with you praise you—and they themselves for the most part turn to one another and laugh!

I should like to tell you of an incident that took place at Delphi. A man of Tarentum, Evangelus by name, a person of some distinction in Tarentum, desired to obtain a victory in the Pythian games. As far as the athletic competition was concerned, at the very outset that seemed to him to be impossible, as

[1] *Iliad* 2, 212. [2] Cf. *Iliad* 19, 387 ff.

πρὸς ὠκύτητα εὖ πεφυκότι, κιθάρᾳ δὲ καὶ ᾠδῇ ῥᾳδίως κρατήσειν ἐπείσθη ὑπὸ καταράτων ἀνθρώπων οὓς εἶχε περὶ αὐτὸν ἐπαινούντων καὶ βοώντων ὁπότε καὶ τὸ σμικρότατον ἐκεῖνος ἀνακρούσαιτο. ἧκεν οὖν εἰς τοὺς Δελφοὺς τοῖς τε ἄλλοις λαμπρὸς καὶ δὴ καὶ ἐσθῆτα χρυσόπαστον ποιησάμενος καὶ στέφανον δάφνης χρυσῆς κάλλιστον, ὡς ἀντὶ καρποῦ τῆς δάφνης σμαράγδους εἶναι ἰσομεγέθεις τῷ καρπῷ· τὴν μέν γε κιθάραν αὐτήν, ὑπερφυές τι χρῆμα εἰς κάλλος καὶ πολυτέλειαν, χρυσοῦ μὲν τοῦ ἀκηράτου πᾶσαν, σφραγῖσι δὲ καὶ λίθοις ποικίλοις κατακεκοσμημένην, Μουσῶν μεταξὺ καὶ Ἀπόλλωνος καὶ Ὀρφέως ἐντετορνευμένων, θαῦμα μέγα τοῖς ὁρῶσιν.

9 Ἐπεὶ δ' οὖν ποτε καὶ ἧκεν ἡ τοῦ ἀγῶνος ἡμέρα, τρεῖς μὲν ἦσαν, ἔλαχεν δὲ μέσος αὐτῶν ὁ Εὐάγγελος ᾄδειν· καὶ μετὰ Θέσπιν τὸν Θηβαῖον οὐ φαύλως ἀγωνισάμενον εἰσέρχεται ὅλος περιλαμπόμενος τῷ χρυσῷ καὶ τοῖς σμαράγδοις καὶ βηρύλλοις καὶ ὑακίνθοις· καὶ ἡ πορφύρα δὲ ἐνέπρεπε τῆς ἐσθῆτος, ἣ μεταξὺ τοῦ χρυσοῦ διεφαίνετο. τούτοις ἅπασι προεκπλήξας τὸ θέατρον καὶ θαυμαστῆς ἐλπίδος ἐμπλήσας τοὺς θεατάς, ἐπειδή ποτε καὶ ᾆσαι καὶ κιθαρίσαι πάντως ἔδει, ἀνακρούεται μὲν ἀνάρμοστόν τι καὶ ἀσύντακτον, ἀπορρήγνυσι δὲ τρεῖς ἅμα χορδὰς σφοδρότερον τοῦ δέοντος ἐμπεσὼν τῇ κιθάρᾳ, ᾄδειν δὲ ἄρχεται ἀπόμουσόν τι καὶ λεπτόν, ὥστε γέλωτα μὲν παρὰ πάντων γενέσθαι τῶν θεατῶν, τοὺς ἀθλοθέτας δὲ ἀγανακτήσαντας ἐπὶ τῇ τόλμῃ μαστιγώσαντας αὐτὸν ἐκβαλεῖν τοῦ θεάτρου· ὅτεπερ καὶ γελοιό-

he was not well endowed by nature either for strength or for speed; but in playing the lyre and singing he became convinced that he would win easily, thanks to detestable fellows whom he had about him, who applauded and shouted whenever he made the slightest sound in striking up. So he came to Delphi resplendent in every way; in particular, he had provided himself with a gold-embroidered robe and a very beautiful laurel-wreath of gold, which for berries had emeralds as large as berries. The lyre itself was something extraordinary for beauty and costliness, all of pure gold, ornamented with graven gems and many-coloured jewels, with the Muses and Apollo and Orpheus represented upon it in relief—a great marvel to all who saw it.[1]

When the day of the competition at last came, there were three of them, and Evangelus drew second place on the programme. So, after Thespis of Thebes had made a good showing, he came in all ablaze with gold and emeralds and beryls and sapphires. The purple of his robe also became him well, gleaming beside the gold. With all this he bedazzled the audience in advance and filled his hearers with wonderful expectations; but when at length he had to sing and play whether he would or no, he struck up a discordant, jarring prelude, breaking three strings at once by coming down upon the lyre harder than he ought, and began to sing in an unmusical, thin voice, so that a burst of laughter came from the whole audience, and the judges of the competition, indignant at his presumption, scourged him and turned him out of the theatre. Then indeed

[1] Compare the version of this story given in the *Rhetorica ad Herennium* 4, 47.

τατος ὤφθη δακρύων ὁ χρυσοῦς Εὐάγγελος καὶ ὑπὸ τῶν μαστιγοφόρων συρόμενος διὰ μέσης τῆς σκηνῆς καὶ τὰ σκέλη καθῃματωμένος ἐκ τῶν μαστίγων καὶ συλλέγων χαμάθεν τῆς κιθάρας τὰς σφραγῖδας· ἐξεπεπτώκεσαν γὰρ κἀκείνης συμμαστιγουμένης αὐτῷ.

10 Μικρὸν δὲ ἐπισχὼν μετ' αὐτὸν Εὔμηλός τις Ἠλεῖος εἰσέρχεται, κιθάραν μὲν παλαιὰν ἔχων, ξυλίνους δὲ κόλλοπας ἐπικειμένην, ἐσθῆτα δὲ μόγις σὺν τῷ στεφάνῳ δέκα δραχμῶν ἀξίαν· ἀλλ' οὗτός γε ᾄσας δεξιῶς καὶ κιθαρίσας κατὰ τὸν νόμον τῆς τέχνης ἐκράτει καὶ ἀνεκηρύττετο καὶ τοῦ Εὐαγγέλου κατεγέλα μάτην ἐμπομπεύσαντος τῇ κιθάρᾳ καὶ ταῖς σφραγῖσιν ἐκείναις. καὶ εἰπεῖν γε λέγεται πρὸς αὐτόν· "Ὦ Εὐάγγελε, σὺ μὲν χρυσῆν δάφνην περίκεισαι, πλουτεῖς γάρ, ἐγὼ δὲ ὁ πένης τὴν Δελφικήν. πλὴν τοῦτό γε μόνον ὤνησο τῆς σκευῆς, ὅτι μηδὲ ἐλεούμενος ἐπὶ τῇ ἥττῃ ἀπέρχῃ, ἀλλὰ μισούμενος προσέτι διὰ τὴν ἄτεχνόν σου ταύτην τρυφήν." περὶ πόδα δή σοι καὶ Εὐάγγελος οὗτος, παρ' ὅσον σοί γε οὐδ' ὀλίγον μέλει τοῦ γέλωτος τῶν θεατῶν.

11 Οὐκ ἄκαιρον δ' ἂν γένοιτο καὶ Λέσβιον μῦθόν τινα διηγήσασθαί σοι πάλαι γενόμενον. ὅτε τὸν Ὀρφέα διεσπάσαντο αἱ Θρᾷτται, φασὶ τὴν κεφαλὴν αὐτοῦ σὺν τῇ λύρᾳ εἰς τὸν Ἕβρον ἐμπεσοῦσαν ἐκβληθῆναι εἰς τὸν μέλανα κόλπον, καὶ ἐπιπλεῖν γε τὴν κεφαλὴν τῇ λύρᾳ, τὴν μὲν ᾄδουσαν θρῆνόν τινα ἐπὶ τῷ Ὀρφεῖ, ὡς λόγος,[1]

[1] Ὀρφεῖ, ὡς λόγος P: Ὀρφείῳ λόγῳ other MSS. Bekker's conjecture Ὀρφείῳ μόρῳ is anticipated rather than confirmed by a correction in Ψ.

that precious simpleton[1] Evangelus cut a comical figure with his tears as he was chivvied across the stage by the scourgers, his legs all bloody from their whips, gathering up the gems of the lyre—for they had dropped out when it shared his flogging.

After a moment's delay, a man named Eumelus, from Elis, came on, who had an old lyre, fitted with wooden pegs, and a costume that, including the wreath, was hardly worth ten drachmas; but as he sang well and played skilfully, he had the best of it and was proclaimed victor, so that he could laugh at Evangelus for the empty display that he had made with his lyre and his gems. Indeed, the story goes that he said to him: "Evangelus, you wear golden laurel, being rich; but I am poor and I wear the laurel of Delphi! However, you got at least this much by your outfit: you are going away not only unpitied for your defeat but hated into the bargain because of this inartistic lavishness of yours." There you have your own living image in Evangelus, except that you are not at all put out by the laughter of the audience.

It would not be out of place to tell you another story about something that happened in Lesbos long ago. They say that when the women of Thrace tore Orpheus to pieces, his head and his lyre fell into the Hebrus, and were carried out into the Aegean Sea; and that the head floated along on the lyre, singing a dirge (so the story goes) over Orpheus,

[1] The word χρυσοῦς, applied to a person, means "simpleton" (*Lapsus* 1). Here, of course, it also has a punning turn.

τὴν λύραν δὲ αὐτὴν ὑπηχεῖν τῶν ἀνέμων ἐμπιπτόντων ταῖς χορδαῖς, καὶ οὕτω μετ' ᾠδῆς προσενεχθῆναι τῇ Λέσβῳ, κἀκείνους ἀνελομένους τὴν μὲν κεφαλὴν καταθάψαι ἵναπερ νῦν τὸ Βακχεῖον αὐτοῖς ἐστι, τὴν λύραν δὲ ἀναθεῖναι εἰς τοῦ Ἀπόλλωνος τὸ ἱερόν, καὶ ἐπὶ πολύ γε σώ-
12 ζεσθαι αὐτήν. χρόνῳ δὲ ὕστερον Νέανθον τὸν τοῦ Πιττακοῦ τοῦ τυράννου ταῦτα ὑπὲρ τῆς λύρας πυνθανόμενον, ὡς ἐκήλει μὲν θηρία καὶ φυτὰ καὶ λίθους, ἐμελῴδει δὲ καὶ μετὰ τὴν τοῦ Ὀρφέως συμφορὰν μηδενὸς ἁπτομένου, εἰς[1] ἔρωτα τοῦ κτήματος ἐμπεσεῖν καὶ διαφθείραντα τὸν ἱερέα μεγάλοις χρήμασι πεῖσαι ὑποθέντα ἑτέραν ὁμοίαν λύραν δοῦναι αὐτῷ τὴν τοῦ Ὀρφέως. λαβόντα δὲ μεθ' ἡμέραν μὲν ἐν τῇ πόλει χρῆσθαι οὐκ ἀσφαλὲς οἴεσθαι εἶναι, νύκτωρ δὲ ὑπὸ κόλπου ἔχοντα μόνον προελθεῖν εἰς τὸ προάστειον καὶ προχειρισάμενον κρούειν καὶ συνταράττειν τὰς χορδὰς ἄτεχνον καὶ ἄμουσον νεανίσκον, ἐλπίζοντα μέλη τινὰ θεσπέσια ὑπηχήσειν τὴν λύραν ὑφ' ὧν πάντας καταθέλξειν καὶ κηλήσειν, καὶ ὅλως μακάριον ἔσεσθαι κληρονομήσαντα τῆς Ὀρφέως μουσικῆς· ἄχρι δὴ συνελθόντας τοὺς κύνας πρὸς τὸν ἦχον—πολλοὶ δὲ ἦσαν αὐτόθι—διασπάσασθαι αὐτόν, ὡς τοῦτο γοῦν ὅμοιον τῷ Ὀρφεῖ παθεῖν καὶ μόνους ἐφ' ἑαυτὸν συγκαλέσαι τοὺς κύνας. ὅτεπερ καὶ σαφέστατα ὤφθη ὡς οὐχ ἡ λύρα ἡ[2] θέλγουσα ἦν, ἀλλὰ ἡ τέχνη καὶ ἡ ᾠδή, ἃ μόνα ἐξαίρετα τῷ Ὀρφεῖ παρὰ τῆς μητρὸς ὑπῆρχεν· ἡ λύρα δὲ ἄλλως κτῆμα ἦν, οὐδὲν ἄμεινον τῶν ἄλλων βαρβίτων.

[1] εἰς Cobet: πρὸς MSS.
[2] ἡ Halm: not in MSS.

while the lyre itself gave out sweet sounds as the winds struck the strings. In that manner they came ashore at Lesbos to the sound of music, and the people there took them up, burying the head where their temple of Dionysus now stands and hanging up the lyre in the temple of Apollo, where it was long preserved. In after time, however, Neanthus, the son of Pittacus the tyrant, heard how the lyre charmed animals and plants and stones, and made music even after the death of Orpheus without any-one's touching it; so he fell in love with the thing, tampered with the priest, and by means of a generous bribe prevailed upon him to substitute another similar lyre, and give him the one of Orpheus. After securing it, he did not think it safe to play it in the city by day, but went out into the suburbs at night with it under his cloak, and then, taking it in hand, struck and jangled the strings, untrained and unmusical lad that he was, expecting that under his touch the lyre would make wonderful music with which he could charm and enchant everybody, and indeed that he would become immortal, inheriting the musical genius of Orpheus. At length the dogs (there were many of them there), brought together by the noise, tore him to pieces; so his fate, at least, was like that of Orpheus, and only the dogs answered his call. By that it became very apparent that it was not the lyre which had wrought the spell, but the skill and the singing of Orpheus, the only distinctive gifts that he had from his mother; while the lyre was just a piece of property, no better than any other stringed instrument.

13 Καὶ τί σοι τὸν Ὀρφέα ἢ τὸν Νέανθον λέγω, ὅπου καὶ καθ' ἡμᾶς αὐτοὺς ἐγένετό τις καὶ ἔτι ἐστίν, οἶμαι, ὃς τὸν Ἐπικτήτου λύχνον τοῦ Στωϊκοῦ κεραμεοῦν ὄντα τρισχιλίων δραχμῶν ἐπρίατο; ἤλπιζεν γὰρ οἶμαι κἀκεῖνος, εἰ τῶν νυκτῶν ὑπ' ἐκείνῳ τῷ λύχνῳ ἀναγιγνώσκοι, αὐτίκα μάλα καὶ τὴν Ἐπικτήτου σοφίαν ὄναρ ἐπικτήσεσθαι[1] καὶ ὅμοιος ἔσεσθαι τῷ θαυμαστῷ
14 ἐκείνῳ γέροντι. χθὲς δὲ καὶ πρῴην ἄλλος τις τὴν Πρωτέως τοῦ Κυνικοῦ βακτηρίαν, ἣν καταθέμενος ἥλατο εἰς τὸ πῦρ, ταλάντου κἀκεῖνος ἐπρίατο, καὶ ἔχει μὲν τὸ κειμήλιον τοῦτο καὶ δείκνυσιν ὡς Τεγεᾶται τοῦ Καλυδωνίου ὑὸς[2] τὸ δέρμα καὶ Θηβαῖοι τὰ ὀστᾶ τοῦ Γηρυόνου καὶ Μεμφῖται τῆς Ἴσιδος τοὺς πλοκάμους· αὐτὸς δὲ ὁ τοῦ θαυμαστοῦ κτήματος δεσπότης καὶ αὐτὸν σὲ τῇ ἀπαιδευσίᾳ καὶ βδελυρίᾳ ὑπερηκόντισεν. ὁρᾷς ὅπως κακοδαιμόνως διάκειται, βακτηρίας εἰς τὴν κεφαλὴν ὡς ἀληθῶς δεόμενος.

15 Λέγεται δὲ καὶ Διονύσιον τραγῳδίαν ποιεῖν φαύλως πάνυ καὶ γελοίως, ὥστε τὸν Φιλόξενον πολλάκις δι' αὐτὴν εἰς τὰς λατομίας ἐμπεσεῖν οὐ δυνάμενον κατέχειν τὸν γέλωτα. οὗτος τοίνυν πυθόμενος ὡς ἐγγελᾶται, τὸ Αἰσχύλου πυξίον εἰς ὃ ἐκεῖνος ἔγραφε σὺν πολλῇ σπουδῇ κτησάμενος καὶ αὐτὸς[3] ᾤετο ἔνθεος ἔσεσθαι καὶ κάτοχος ἐκ τοῦ πυξίου· ἀλλ' ὅμως ἐν αὐτῷ ἐκείνῳ μακρῷ γελοιότερα ἔγραφεν, οἷον κἀκεῖνο τό·

Δωρὶς τέθνηκεν[4] ἡ Διονυσίου γυνή.

[1] ἐπικτήσεσθαι Roeper: ἐπιστήσεσθαι MSS.
[2] ὑὸς Cobet: not in MSS.
[3] καὶ αὐτὸς Jacobs: αὐτὸ MSS.
[4] Δωρὶς τέθνηκεν C. F. Hermann: Δωρικόν· ἧκεν MSS.

But why do I talk to you of Orpheus and Neanthus, when even in our own time there was and still is, I think, a man who paid three thousand drachmas for the earthenware lamp of Epictetus the Stoic? He thought, I suppose, that if he should read by that lamp at night, he would forthwith acquire the wisdom of Epictetus in his dreams and would be just like that marvellous old man. And only a day or two ago another man paid a talent for the staff which Proteus the Cynic laid aside before leaping into the fire;[1] and he keeps this treasure and displays it just as the Tegeans do the skin of the Calydonian boar, the Thebans the bones of Geryon, and the Memphites the tresses of Isis. Yet the original owner of this marvellous possession surpassed even you yourself in ignorance and indecency. You see what a wretched state the collector is in: in all conscience he needs a staff—on his pate.

They say that Dionysius[2] used to write tragedy in a very feeble and ridiculous style, so that Philoxenus[3] was often thrown into the quarries on account of it, not being able to control his laughter. Well, when he discovered that he was being laughed at, he took great pains to procure the wax-tablets on which Aeschylus used to write, thinking that he too would be inspired and possessed with divine frenzy in virtue of the tablets. But for all that, what he wrote on those very tablets was far more ridiculous than what he had written before: for example,

> Doris, the wife of Dionysius,
> Is dead—

[1] Peregrinus; nicknamed Proteus because he changed his faith so readily. The story of his life and his voluntary death at Olympia is related in Lucian's *Peregrinus*.

[2] The Elder, Tyrant of Syracuse (431–367 B.C.).

[3] A contemporary poet.

καὶ πάλιν·

οἴμοι, γυναῖκα χρησίμην ἀπώλεσα.

καὶ τοῦτο γὰρ ἐκ τοῦ πυξίου, καὶ τό·

αὑτοῖς γὰρ ἐμπαίζουσιν οἱ μωροὶ βροτῶν.

Τοῦτο μέν γε πρὸς σὲ μάλιστα εὐστόχως ἂν εἰρημένον εἴη τῷ Διονυσίῳ, καὶ δι' αὐτὸ χρυσῶσαι 16 αὐτοῦ ἔδει ἐκεῖνο τὸ πυξίον. τίνα γὰρ ἐλπίδα καὶ αὐτὸς ἔχων εἰς[1] τὰ βιβλία καὶ ἀνατυλίττεις ἀεὶ καὶ διακολλᾷς καὶ περικόπτεις καὶ ἀλείφεις τῷ κρόκῳ καὶ τῇ κέδρῳ καὶ διφθέρας περιβάλλεις καὶ ὀμφαλοὺς ἐντίθης, ὡς δή τι ἀπολαύσων αὐτῶν; πάνυ γοῦν ἤδη βελτίων γεγένησαι διὰ τὴν ὠνήν, ὃς τοιαῦτα μὲν φθέγγῃ—μᾶλλον δὲ τῶν ἰχθύων ἀφωνότερος εἶ—βιοῖς δὲ ὡς οὐδ' εἰπεῖν καλόν, μῖσος δὲ ἄγριον, φασί, παρὰ πάντων ἔχεις ἐπὶ τῇ βδελυρίᾳ· ὡς εἰ τοιούτους ἀπειργάζετο τὰ βιβλία, φυγῇ φευκτέον ἂν ἦν ὅτι πορρωτάτω 17 ἀπ' αὐτῶν. δυοῖν δὲ ὄντοιν ἅττ' ἂν παρὰ τῶν παλαιῶν τις κτήσαιτο, λέγειν τε δύνασθαι καὶ πράττειν τὰ δέοντα ζήλῳ τῶν ἀρίστων καὶ φυγῇ τῶν χειρόνων, ὅταν μήτε ἐκεῖνα μήτε ταῦτα φαίνηταί τις παρ' αὐτῶν ὠφελούμενος, τί ἄλλο ἢ τοῖς μυσὶ διατριβὰς ὠνεῖται καὶ ταῖς τίλφαις οἰκήσεις καὶ πληγὰς ὡς ἀμελοῦσι τοῖς οἰκέταις;

18 Πῶς δὲ οὐ κἀκεῖνο αἰσχρόν, εἴ τις ἐν τῇ χειρὶ ἔχοντά σε βιβλίον ἰδών—ἀεὶ δέ τι πάντως ἔχεις

[1] <φυλάττ>εις? A.M.H.

[1] The few extant fragments of Dionysius' plays are given by Nauck, *Trag. Graec. Fragm.* pp. 793–796. Tzetzes

and again,

Alackaday, a right good wife I've lost!

—for that came from the tablet ; and so did this :

'Tis of themselves alone that fools make sport.[1]

The last line Dionysius might have addressed to you with especial fitness, and those tablets of his should have been gilded for it. For what expectation do you base upon your books that you are always unrolling them and rolling them up, glueing them, trimming them, smearing them with saffron and oil of cedar, putting slip-covers on them, and fitting them with knobs, just as if you were going to derive some profit from them? Ah yes, already you have been improved beyond measure by their purchase, when you talk as you do—but no, you are more dumb than any fish!—and live in a way that cannot even be mentioned with decency, and have incurred everybody's savage hatred, as the phrase goes, for your beastliness! If books made men like that, they ought to be given as wide a berth as possible. Two things can be acquired from the ancients, the ability to speak and to act as one ought, by emulating the best models and shunning the worst; and when a man clearly fails to benefit from them either in the one way or in the other, what else is he doing but buying haunts for mice and lodgings for worms, and excuses to thrash his servants for negligence?

Furthermore, would it not be discreditable if someone, on seeing you with a book in your hand (you always

(*Chil.* 5, 180) says that he repeatedly took second and third place in the competitions at Athens, and first with the *Ransom of Hector*. Amusing examples of his frigidity are given by Athenaeus (iii. p. 98 D).

—ἔροιτο οὗτινος ἢ ῥήτορος ἢ συγγραφέως ἢ ποιητοῦ ἐστι, σὺ δὲ ἐκ τῆς ἐπιγραφῆς εἰδὼς πρᾴως εἴποις τοῦτό γε· εἶτα, ὡς φιλεῖ τὰ τοιαῦτα ἐν συνουσίᾳ προχωρεῖν εἰς μῆκος λόγων, ὁ μὲν ἐπαινοῖ τι ἢ αἰτιῷτο τῶν ἐγγεγραμμένων, σὺ δὲ ἀποροίης καὶ μηδὲν ἔχοις εἰπεῖν; οὐκ εὔξῃ τότε χανεῖν σοι τὴν γῆν, κατὰ σεαυτοῦ ὁ Βελλεροφόντης περιφέρων τὸ βιβλίον;[1]

19 Δημήτριος δὲ ὁ Κυνικὸς ἰδὼν ἐν Κορίνθῳ ἀπαίδευτόν τινα βιβλίον κάλλιστον ἀναγιγνώσκοντα —τὰς Βάκχας οἶμαι τοῦ Εὐριπίδου, κατὰ τὸν ἄγγελον δὲ ἦν τὸν διηγούμενον τὰ τοῦ Πενθέως πάθη καὶ τὸ τῆς Ἀγαύης ἔργον—ἁρπάσας διέσπασεν αὐτὸ εἰπών, "Ἄμεινόν ἐστι τῷ Πενθεῖ ἅπαξ σπαραχθῆναι ὑπ' ἐμοῦ ἢ ὑπὸ σοῦ πολλάκις."

Ζητῶν δὲ ἀεὶ πρὸς ἐμαυτὸν οὔπω καὶ τήμερον εὑρεῖν δεδύνημαι τίνος ἕνεκα τὴν σπουδὴν ταύτην ἐσπούδακας περὶ τὴν ὠνὴν τῶν βιβλίων· ὠφελείας μὲν γὰρ ἢ χρείας τῆς ἀπ' αὐτῶν οὐδ' ἂν οἰηθείη τις τῶν καὶ ἐπ' ἐλάχιστόν σε εἰδότων, οὐ μᾶλλον ἢ φαλακρὸς ἄν τις πρίαιτο κτένας ἢ κάτοπτρον ὁ τυφλὸς ἢ ὁ κωφὸς αὐλητὴν ἢ παλλακὴν ὁ εὐνοῦχος ἢ ὁ ἠπειρώτης κώπην ἢ ὁ κυβερνήτης ἄροτρον. ἀλλὰ μὴ ἐπίδειξιν πλούτου σοι τὸ πρᾶγμα ἔχει καὶ βούλει τοῦτο ἐμφῆναι ἅπασιν, ὅτι καὶ εἰς τὰ μηδέν σοι χρήσιμα ὅμως ἐκ πολλῆς τῆς περιουσίας ἀναλίσκεις; καὶ μὴν ὅσα γε κἀμὲ Σύρον ὄντα εἰδέναι, εἰ μὴ σαυ-

[1] The letter that Bellerophon carried to the King of Lycia contained a request that he be put to death: *Iliad* 6, 155–195.

have one, no matter what), should ask what orator or historian or poet it was by, and you, knowing from the title, should easily answer that question; and if then—for such topics often spin themselves out to some length in conversation—he should either commend or criticise something in its contents, and you should be at a loss and have nothing to say? Would you not then pray for the earth to open and swallow you for getting yourself into trouble like Bellerophon by carrying your book about? [1]

When Demetrius, the Cynic, while in Corinth, saw an ignorant fellow reading a beautiful book (it was the Bacchae of Euripides, I dare say, and he was at the place where the messenger reports the fate of Pentheus and the deed of Agave),[2] he snatched it away and tore it up, saying: "It is better for Pentheus to be torn to tatters by me once for all than by you repeatedly."

Though I am continually asking myself the question, I have never yet been able to discover why you have shown so much zeal in the purchase of books. Nobody who knows you in the least would think that you do it on account of their helpfulness or use, any more than a bald man would buy a comb, or a blind man a mirror, or a deaf-mute a flute-player, or an eunuch a concubine, or a landsman an oar, or a seaman a plough. But perhaps you regard the matter as a display of wealth and wish to show everyone that out of your vast surplus you spend money even for things of no use to you? Come now, as far as I know—and I too am a Syrian[3]—if you had not

[2] 1041 ff.

[3] The implication is: "And therefore ought to know about your circumstances, if anyone knows."

τὸν φέρων ταῖς τοῦ γέροντος ἐκείνου διαθήκαις παρενέγραψας, ἀπωλώλεις ἂν ὑπὸ λιμοῦ ἤδη καὶ
20 ἀγορὰν προὐτίθεις τῶν βιβλίων. λοιπὸν οὖν δὴ ἐκεῖνο, πεπεισμένον ὑπὸ τῶν κολάκων ὡς οὐ μόνον καλὸς εἶ καὶ ἐράσμιος ἀλλὰ σοφὸς καὶ ῥήτωρ καὶ συγγραφεὺς οἷος οὐδ' ἕτερος, ὠνεῖσθαι τὰ βιβλία, ὡς ἀληθεύοις τοὺς ἐπαίνους αὐτῶν. φασὶ δὲ σὲ καὶ λόγους ἐπιδείκνυσθαι αὐτοῖς ἐπὶ δείπνῳ κἀκείνους χερσαίων βατράχων δίκην διψῶντας κεκραγέναι, ἢ μὴ πίνειν, ἢν μὴ διαρραγῶσι βοῶντες.

Καὶ γὰρ οὐκ οἶδ' ὅπως ῥᾷστος εἶ τῆς ῥινὸς ἕλκεσθαι, καὶ πιστεύεις αὐτοῖς ἅπαντα, ὅς ποτε κἀκεῖνο ἐπείσθης, ὡς βασιλεῖ τινι ὡμοιώθης τὴν ὄψιν, καθάπερ ὁ ψευδαλέξανδρος καὶ ὁ[1] ψευδοφίλιππος ἐκεῖνος κναφεὺς καὶ ὁ κατὰ τοὺς προπάτορας ἡμῶν ψευδονέρων καὶ εἴ τις ἄλλος τῶν
21 ὑπὸ τῷ ψευδο[2] τεταγμένων. καὶ τί θαυμαστὸν εἰ τοῦτο ἔπαθες, ἀνόητος καὶ ἀπαίδευτος ἄνθρωπος, καὶ προῄεις ἐξυπτιάζων καὶ μιμούμενος βάδισμα καὶ σχῆμα καὶ βλέμμα ἐκείνου ᾧ σεαυτὸν εἰκάζων ἔχαιρες, ὅπου καὶ Πύρρον φασὶ τὸν Ἠπειρώτην, τὰ ἄλλα θαυμαστὸν ἄνδρα, οὕτως ὑπὸ κολάκων ἐπὶ τῷ ὁμοίῳ ποτὲ διαφθαρῆναι ὡς πιστεύειν ὅτι ὅμοιος ἦν Ἀλεξάνδρῳ ἐκείνῳ; καίτοι τὸ τῶν μουσικῶν τοῦτο, δὶς διὰ πασῶν[3] τὸ

[1] ὁ Herwerden : not in MSS.
[2] τῷ ψευδο Sommerbrodt : τὸ ψεῦδος MSS.
[3] μουσικῶν τοῦτο, δὶς διὰ πασῶν ς : μυσῶν (μουσῶν Γ) τοῦτο διὰ πάντων MSS.

smuggled yourself into that old man's will with all speed, you would be starving to death by now, and would be putting up your books at auction! The only remaining reason is that you have been convinced by your toadies that you are not only handsome and charming but a scholar and an orator and a writer without peer, and you buy the books to prove their praises true. They say that you hold forth to them at dinner, and that they, like stranded frogs, make a clamour because they are thirsty, or else they get nothing to drink if they do not burst themselves shouting.

To be sure, you are somehow very easy to lead by the nose, and believe them in everything; for once you were even persuaded that you resembled a certain royal person in looks, like the false Alexander, the false Philip (the fuller), the false Nero in our grandfathers' time, and whoever else has been put down under the title "false."[1] And what wonder that you, a silly, ignorant fellow, were thus imposed upon and appeared in public holding your head high and imitating the gait and dress and glance of the man whom you delighted to make yourself resemble? Even Pyrrhus of Epirus, a marvellous man in other ways, was once, they say, so spoiled by toadies after the self-same fashion that he believed he was like the famous Alexander. Yet (to borrow a phrase from the musicians) the discrepancy

[1] Balas, in the second century B.C., claimed to be the brother of Antiochus V. Eupator on account of a strong resemblance in looks, and took the name of Alexander. At about the same time, after the defeat of Perses, Andriscus of Adramyttium, a fuller, claimed the name of Philip. The false Nero cropped up some twenty years after Nero's death, and probably in the East, as he had strong support from the Parthians, who refused to surrender him to Rome.

πρᾶγμα ἦν· εἶδον γὰρ καὶ τὴν τοῦ Πύρρου εἰκόνα· καὶ ὅμως ἐπέπειστο ἐκμεμάχθαι τοῦ Ἀλεξάνδρου τὴν μορφήν. ἀλλ' ἕνεκα μὲν δὴ τούτων ὕβρισταί μοι εἰς τὸν Πύρρον, ὅτι σὲ εἴκασα κατὰ τοῦτο αὐτῷ· τὸ δὲ ἀπὸ τούτου καὶ πάνυ σοι πρέπον ἂν εἴη. ἐπεὶ γὰρ οὕτω διέκειτο ὁ Πύρρος καὶ ταῦτα ὑπὲρ ἑαυτοῦ ἐπέπειστο, οὐδεὶς ὅστις οὐ συνετίθετο καὶ συνέπασχεν αὐτῷ, ἄχρι δή τις ἐν Λαρίσῃ πρεσβῦτις ξένη αὐτῷ τἀληθὲς εἰποῦσα ἔπαυσεν αὐτὸν τῆς κορύζης. ὁ μὲν γὰρ Πύρρος ἐπιδείξας αὐτῇ εἰκόνα Φιλίππου καὶ Περδίκκου καὶ Ἀλεξάνδρου καὶ Κασσάνδρου καὶ ἄλλων βασιλέων ἤρετο τίνι ὅμοιος εἴη, πάνυ πεπεισμένος ἐπὶ τὸν Ἀλέξανδρον ἥξειν αὐτήν, ἡ δὲ πολὺν χρόνον ἐπισχοῦσα, "Βατραχίωνι," ἔφη, "τῷ μαγείρῳ·" καὶ γὰρ ἦν τις ἐν τῇ Λαρίσῃ Βατραχίων μάγειρος τῷ Πύρρῳ ὅμοιος.

22 Καὶ σὺ δὴ ᾧτινι μὲν τῶν τοῖς ὀρχησταῖς συνόντων κιναίδων ἔοικας οὐκ ἂν εἴποιμι, ὅτι δὲ μανίαν ἐρρωμένην ἔτι καὶ νῦν μαίνεσθαι δοκεῖς ἅπασιν ἐπ' ἐκείνῃ τῇ εἰκόνι, πάνυ σαφῶς οἶδα. οὔκουν θαυμαστόν, εἰ ἀπίθανος οὕτως ζωγράφος ὢν καὶ τοῖς πεπαιδευμένοις ἐξομοιοῦσθαι ἐθέλεις, πιστεύων τοῖς τὰ τοιαῦτά σε ἐπαινοῦσι.

Καίτοι τί[1] ταῦτα ληρῶ; πρόδηλος γὰρ ἡ αἰτία τῆς περὶ τὰ βιβλία σπουδῆς, εἰ καὶ ὑπὸ νωθείας ἐγὼ μὴ πάλαι κατεῖδον· σοφὸν γάρ, ὡς γοῦν οἴει, τοῦτ' ἐπινενόηκας καὶ ἐλπίδας οὐ μικρὰς ἔχεις περὶ τοῦ πράγματος, εἰ βασιλεὺς μάθοι ταῦτα σοφὸς ἀνὴρ καὶ παιδείαν μάλιστα τιμῶν· εἰ δὲ ταῦτα ὑπὲρ σοῦ ἐκεῖνος ἀκούσειεν, ὡς ὠνῇ βιβλία

[1] καίτοι τί Fritzsche: καὶ ὅτι (καὶ τί) MSS.

was a matter of two octaves; for I have seen the portrait of Pyrrhus. But in spite of that he had acquired the conviction that he was a perfect replica of Alexander's beauty. To be sure, I have been uncomplimentary to Pyrrhus in comparing you with him in this matter, but what followed would be quite in character with you. When Pyrrhus was in this state of mind and had this conviction about himself, everyone without exception concurred with him and humoured him until an old foreign woman in Larissa told him the truth and cured him of drivelling. Pyrrhus showed her portraits of Philip, Perdiccas, Alexander, Cassander and other kings, and asked her whom he resembled, quite certain that she would fix upon Alexander; but, after delaying a good while, she said, "Batrachion, the cook": and as a matter of fact there was in Larissa a cook called Batrachion who resembled Pyrrhus.

As for you, I cannot say which of the profligates that hang about the actors in the pantomimes you resemble; I do know very well, however, that everyone thinks you are still downright daft over that likeness. It is no wonder, then, since you are such a failure at likenesses, that you want to make yourself resemble men of learning, believing those who praise you so.

But why do I talk beside the point? The reason for your craze about books is patent, even if I in my blindness failed to see it long ago. It is a bright idea on your part (you think so, anyhow), and you base no slight expectations upon the thing in case the emperor, who is a scholar and holds learning in especial esteem, should find out about it; if he should hear that you are buying books and making

καὶ συνάγεις πολλά, πάντα ἐν βραχεῖ παρ' αὐ-
23 *τοῦ ἔσεσθαί σοι νομίζεις. ἀλλ', ὦ κατάπυγον, οἴει τοσοῦτον μανδραγόραν κατακεχύσθαι αὐτοῦ ὡς ταῦτα μὲν ἀκούειν, ἐκεῖνα δὲ μὴ εἰδέναι, οἷος μέν σου ὁ μεθ' ἡμέραν βίος, οἷοι δέ σοι πότοι, ὁποῖαι δὲ νύκτες καὶ οἵοις καὶ ἡλίκοις συγκαθεύδεις; οὐκ οἶσθα ὡς ὦτα καὶ ὀφθαλμοὶ πολλοὶ βασιλέως; τὰ δὲ σὰ οὕτω περιφανῆ ἐστιν ὡς καὶ τυφλοῖς εἶναι καὶ κωφοῖς γνώριμα· εἰ γὰρ καὶ φθέγξαιο μόνον, εἰ γὰρ καὶ λουόμενος ἀποδύσαιο, μᾶλλον δὲ μὴ ἀποδύσῃ, εἰ δοκεῖ, οἱ δ' οἰκέται μόνον ἢν ἀποδύσωνταί σου, τί οἴει; μὴ αὐτίκα ἔσεσθαι πάντα σου πρόδηλα τὰ τῆς νυκτὸς ἀπόρρητα; εἰπὲ γοῦν μοι καὶ τόδε, εἰ Βάσσος ὁ ὑμέτερος ἐκεῖνος σοφιστὴς ἢ Βάταλος ὁ αὐλητὴς ἢ ὁ κίναιδος Ἡμιθέων ὁ Συβαρίτης, ὃς τοὺς θαυμαστοὺς ὑμῖν νόμους συνέγραψεν, ὡς χρὴ λεαίνεσθαι[1] καὶ παρατίλλεσθαι καὶ πάσχειν καὶ ποιεῖν ἐκεῖνα,—εἰ τούτων τις νυνὶ λεοντῆν περιβαλόμενος καὶ ῥόπαλον ἔχων βαδίζοι, τί οἴει φανεῖσθαι[2] τοῖς ὁρῶσιν; Ἡρακλέα εἶναι αὐτόν; οὔκ, εἴ γε μὴ χύτραις λημῶντες τυγχάνοιεν. μυρία γάρ ἐστι τὰ ἀντιμαρτυροῦντα τῷ σχήματι, βάδισμα καὶ βλέμμα καὶ φωνὴ καὶ τράχηλος ἐπικεκλασμένος καὶ ψιμύθιον καὶ μαστίχη καὶ φῦκος, οἷς ὑμεῖς κοσμεῖσθε, καὶ ὅλως κατὰ τὴν παροιμίαν, θᾶττον ἂν πέντε ἐλέφαντας ὑπὸ μάλης κρύψειας ἢ ἕνα κίναιδον. εἶτα ἡ λεοντῆ μὲν τὸν τοιοῦτον οὐκ ἂν ἔκρυψεν, σὺ δ' οἴει λήσειν*

[1] λεαίνεσθαι Markland : μαίνεσθαι MSS.
[2] φανεῖσθαι Cobet : φαίνεσθαι MSS.

a large collection, you think you will soon get all you want from him. But do you suppose, you rotter, that he is so steeped in mandragora as to hear that and yet not know how you pass your time during the day, what your drinking bouts are like, how you spend your nights, and in whose company? Do not you know that a monarch has many eyes and ears? And your doings are so conspicuous that even the blind and the deaf may know of them; for if you but speak, if you but bathe in public—or, if you choose, don't even do that—if your servants but bathe in public, do you not think that all your nocturnal arcana will be known at once? Answer me this question: if Bassus, that literary man who belonged to your following, or Battalus the flute-player, or the cinaedus Hemitheon of Sybaris, who wrote those wonderful regulations for you, which say that you must use cosmetics and depilatories and so forth—if one of those fellows should to-day walk about with a lion's skin on his back and a club in his hand, what do you suppose those who saw him would think? That he was Heracles? Not unless they were gravel-blind; for there are a thousand things in their appearance that would give the lie to their costume; the gait, the glance, the voice, the thin neck, the white lead and mastich and rouge that you beautify yourselves with; in short, to quote the proverb, it would be easier to conceal five elephants under your arm than a single cinaedus. Then if the lion's skin would not have hidden such as they, do you suppose that you will be undetected

σκεπόμενος βιβλίῳ; ἀλλ' οὐ δυνατόν· προδώσει γάρ σε καὶ ἀποκαλύψει τὰ ἄλλα ὑμῶν γνωρίσματα.

24 Τὸ δ' ὅλον ἀγνοεῖν μοι δοκεῖς ὅτι τὰς ἀγαθὰς ἐλπίδας οὐ παρὰ τῶν βιβλιοκαπήλων δεῖ ζητεῖν, ἀλλὰ παρ' αὐτοῦ καὶ τοῦ καθ' ἡμέραν βίου λαμβάνειν. σὺ δ' οἴει συνήγορον κοινὸν καὶ μάρτυρα ἔσεσθαί σοι τὸν Ἀττικὸν καὶ Καλλῖνον τοὺς βιβλιογράφους; οὔκ, ἀλλ' ὠμούς τινας ἀνθρώπους ἐπιτρίψοντάς σε, ἢν οἱ θεοὶ ἐθέλωσι, καὶ πρὸς ἔσχατον πενίας συνελάσοντας· δέον ἔτι νῦν σωφρονήσαντα ἀποδόσθαι μέν τινι τῶν πεπαιδευμένων τὰ βιβλία ταῦτα καὶ σὺν αὐτοῖς τὴν νεόκτιστον ταύτην οἰκίαν, ἀποδοῦναι δὲ τοῖς ἀνδραποδοκαπήλοις μέρος γοῦν ἀπὸ πολλῶν τῶν ὀφειλομένων.

25 Καὶ γὰρ κἀκεῖνα· περὶ δύο ταῦτα δεινῶς ἐσπούδακας, βιβλίων τε τῶν πολυτελῶν κτῆσιν καὶ μειρακίων τῶν ἐξώρων καὶ ἤδη καρτερῶν ὠνήν, καὶ τὸ πρᾶγμά σοι πάνυ σπουδάζεται καὶ θηρεύεται. ἀδύνατον δὲ πένητα ὄντα πρὸς ἄμφω διαρκεῖν. σκόπει τοίνυν ὡς ἱερὸν χρῆμα συμβουλή. ἀξιῶ γάρ σε ἀφέμενον τῶν μηδὲν προσηκόντων τὴν ἑτέραν νόσον θεραπεύειν καὶ τοὺς ὑπηρέτας ἐκείνους ὠνεῖσθαι, ὅπως μὴ ἐπιλειπόντων σε τῶν οἴκοθεν μεταστέλλοιό τινας τῶν ἐλευθέρων, οἷς ἀκίνδυνον ἀπελθοῦσιν, ἢν μὴ λάβωσιν ἅπαντα, ἐξαγορεῦσαι τὰ πραχθέντα ὑμῖν μετὰ τὸν πότον, οἷα καὶ πρῴην αἴσχιστα περὶ σοῦ διηγεῖτο ἐξελθὼν ὁ πόρνος, ἔτι καὶ δήγματα ἐπιδεικνύς. ἀλλ ἔγωγε καὶ μάρτυρας ἂν παρασχοίμην τοὺς τότε παρόντας ὡς ἠγανάκτησα καὶ ὀλίγου πληγὰς

behind a book? Impossible: the other earmarks of your sort will betray and reveal you.

You are completely unaware, it seems to me, that good expectations are not to be sought from the booksellers but derived from one's self and one's daily life. Do you expect to find public advocates and character-witnesses in the scribes Atticus and Callinus? No: you will find them heartless fellows, bent upon ruining you, if the gods so will it, and reducing you to the uttermost depths of poverty. Even now you ought to come to your senses, sell these books to some learned man, and your new house along with them, and then pay the slave dealers at least a part of the large sums you owe them.

For mark this, you have had a tremendous passion for two things, the acquisition of expensive books and the purchase of well-grown, vigorous slaves, and you are showing great zeal and persistence in the thing; but being poor, you cannot adequately manage both. See now what a precious thing advice is! I urge you to drop what does not concern you, cultivate your other weakness, and buy those menials of yours, so that your household may not be depleted and you may not for that reason have to send out for free men, who, if they do not get all they want, can safely go away and tell what you do after your wine. For instance, only the other day a vile fellow told a most disgraceful story about you when he came away, and even showed marks. I can prove by those who were there at the time that I was indignant and came near giving him a thrashing in my anger on your behalf,

ἐνέτριψα αὐτῷ χαλεπαίνων ὑπὲρ σοῦ, καὶ μάλισθ' ὅτε καὶ ἄλλον ἐπεκαλέσατο μάρτυρα τῶν ὁμοίων καὶ ἄλλον ταὐτὰ καὶ λόγοις διηγουμένους. πρὸς δὴ ταῦτα, ὦγαθέ, ταμιεύου τἀργύριον καὶ φύλαττε, ὡς οἴκοι καὶ κατὰ πολλὴν ἀσφάλειαν ταῦτα ποιεῖν καὶ πάσχειν ἔχῃς. ὥστε μὲν γὰρ μηκέτι ἐργάζεσθαι τίς ἂν μεταπείσειέ σε; οὐδὲ γὰρ κύων

26 ἅπαξ παύσαιτ' ἂν σκυτοτραγεῖν μαθοῦσα. τὸ δ' ἕτερον ῥᾴδιον, τὸ μηκέτι ὠνεῖσθαι βιβλία. ἱκανῶς πεπαίδευσαι, ἅλις σοι τῆς σοφίας. μόνον οὐκ ἐπ' ἄκρου τοῦ χείλους ἔχεις τὰ παλαιὰ πάντα. πᾶσαν μὲν ἱστορίαν οἶσθα, πάσας δὲ λόγων τέχνας καὶ κάλλη αὐτῶν καὶ κακίας καὶ ὀνομάτων χρῆσιν τῶν Ἀττικῶν· πάνσοφόν τι χρῆμα καὶ ἄκρον ἐν παιδείᾳ γεγένησαι διὰ τὸ πλῆθος τῶν βιβλίων. κωλύει γὰρ οὐδὲν κἀμέ σοι ἐνδιατρίβειν, ἐπειδὴ χαίρεις ἐξαπατώμενος.

27 Ἡδέως δ' ἂν καὶ ἐροίμην σε, τὰ τοσαῦτα βιβλία ἔχων τί μάλιστα ἀναγιγνώσκεις αὐτῶν; τὰ Πλάτωνος; τὰ Ἀντισθένους; τὰ Ἀρχιλόχου;[1] τὰ Ἱππώνακτος; ἢ τούτων μὲν ὑπερφρονεῖς, ῥήτορες δὲ μάλιστά σοι διὰ[2] χειρός; εἰπέ μοι, καὶ Αἰσχίνου τὸν κατὰ Τιμάρχου λόγον ἀναγιγνώσκεις; ἢ ἐκεῖνά γε πάντα οἶσθα καὶ γιγνώσκεις αὐτῶν ἕκαστον, τὸν δὲ Ἀριστοφάνην καὶ τὸν Εὔπολιν ὑποδέδυκας; ἀνέγνως καὶ τοὺς Βάπτας, τὸ δρᾶμα ὅλον; εἶτ' οὐδέν σου τἀκεῖ καθίκετο, οὐδ' ἠρυθρίασας γνωρίσας αὐτά; τοῦτο γοῦν καὶ μάλιστα θαυμάσειεν ἄν τις, τίνα ποτὲ ψυχὴν[3] ἔχων ἅπτῃ

[1] Ἀρχιλόχου Guyet : Ἀντιλόχου MSS.
[2] σοι διὰ Jacobitz : σοι τούτων διὰ MSS.
[3] ποτὲ ψυχὴν Gesner : ἀπὸ ψυχῆς MSS.

especially when he called upon one after another to corroborate his evidence and they all told the same story. In view of this, my friend, husband and save your money so that you may be able to misconduct yourself at home in great security; for who could persuade you now to change your ways? When a dog has once learned to gnaw leather, he cannot stop.[1] The other way is easier, not to buy books any longer. You are well enough educated; you have learning to spare; you have all the works of antiquity almost at the tip of your tongue; you know not only all history but all the arts of literary composition, its merits and defects, and how to use an Attic vocabulary; your many books have made you wondrous wise, consummate in learning. There is no reason why I should not have my fun with you, since you like to be gulled!

As you have so many books, I should like to ask you what you like best to read? Plato? Antisthenes? Archilochus? Hipponax? Or do you scorn them and incline to occupy yourself with the orators? Tell me, do you read the speech of Aeschines against Timarchus? No doubt you know it all and understand everything in it, but have you dipped into Aristophanes and Eupolis? Have you read the Baptae, the whole play?[2] Then did it have no effect upon you, and did you not blush when you saw the point of it? Indeed, a man may well wonder above all what the state of your soul is when you

[1] Cf. Horace, *Satires*, ii. 5, 83:
ut canis a corio nunquam absterrebitur uncto.

[2] The *Baptae* of Eupolis appears to have been a satire upon the devotees of Cotys (Cotytto), a Thracian goddess worshipped with orgiastic rites.

τῶν βιβλιων, ὁποίαις αὐτὰ χερσὶν ἀνελίττεις. πότε δὲ ἀναγιγνώσκεις; μεθ' ἡμέραν; ἀλλ' οὐδεὶς ἑώρακε τοῦτο ποιοῦντα. ἀλλὰ νύκτωρ; πότερον ἐπιτεταγμένος ἤδη ἐκείνοις ἢ πρὸ τῶν λόγων; ἀλλὰ πρὸς Κότυος[1] μηκέτι μὴ τολμήσῃς τοιοῦτο 28 μηδέν, ἄφες δὲ τὰ βιβλία καὶ μόνα ἐργάζου τὰ σαυτοῦ. καίτοι ἐχρῆν μηκέτι μηδὲ ἐκεῖνα, αἰδεσθῆναι δὲ τὴν τοῦ Εὐριπίδου Φαίδραν καὶ ὑπὲρ τῶν γυναικῶν ἀγανακτοῦσαν καὶ λέγουσαν,

οὐδὲ σκότον φρίσσουσι τὸν συνεργάτην
τέρεμνά τ' οἴκων μή ποτε φθογγὴν ἀφῇ.

εἰ δὲ πάντως ἐμμένειν τῇ ὁμοίᾳ νόσῳ διέγνωσται, ἴθι, ὠνοῦ μὲν βιβλία καὶ οἴκοι κατακλείσας ἔχε καὶ καρποῦ τὴν δόξαν τῶν κτημάτων. ἱκανόν σοι καὶ τοῦτο. προσάψῃ δὲ μηδέποτε μηδὲ ἀναγνῷς μηδὲ ὑπαγάγῃς τῇ γλώττῃ παλαιῶν ἀνδρῶν λόγους και ποιήματα μηδὲν δεινόν σε εἰργασμένα.

Οἶδα ὡς μάτην ταῦτά μοι λελήρηται καὶ κατὰ τὴν παροιμίαν Αἰθίοπα σμήχειν ἐπιχειρῶ· σὺ γὰρ ὠνήσῃ καὶ χρήσῃ εἰς οὐδὲν καὶ καταγελασθήσῃ πρὸς τῶν πεπαιδευμένων, οἷς ἀπόχρη ὠφελεῖσθαι οὐκ ἐκ τοῦ κάλλους τῶν βιβλίων οὐδ' ἐκ τῆς πολυτελείας αὐτῶν, ἀλλ' ἐκ τῆς φωνῆς καὶ 29 τῆς γνώμης τῶν γεγραφότων. σὺ δὲ οἴει θεραπεύσειν τὴν ἀπαιδευσίαν καὶ ἐπικαλύψειν τῇ δόξῃ ταύτῃ καὶ ἐκπλήξειν τῷ πλήθει τῶν βιβλίων, οὐκ εἰδὼς ὅτι καὶ οἱ ἀμαθέστατοι τῶν ἰατρῶν τὸ αὐτὸ σοὶ ποιοῦσιν, ἐλεφαντίνους νάρθηκας καὶ σικύας ἀργυρᾶς ποιούμενοι καὶ σμίλας χρυσοκολλήτους· ὁπόταν δὲ καὶ χρήσασθαι τούτοις δέῃ, οἱ μὲν

[1] πρὸς Κότυος Burmeister: πρὸ σκότους MSS.

lay hold of your books, and of your hands when you open them. When do you do your reading? In the daytime? Nobody ever saw you doing it. At night, then? When you have already given instructions to your henchmen, or before you have talked with them? Come, in the name of Cotys, never again dare to do such a thing. Leave the books alone and attend to your own affairs exclusively. Yet you ought not to do that, either; you ought to be put to shame by Phaedra in Euripides, who is indignant at women and says:

> "They shudder not at their accomplice, night,
> Nor chamber-walls, for fear they find a voice."[1]

But if you have made up your mind to cleave to the same infirmity at all costs, go ahead: buy books, keep them at home under lock and key, and enjoy the fame of your treasures—that is enough for you. But never lay hands on them or read them or sully with your tongue the prose and poetry of the ancients, that has done you no harm.

I know that in all this I am wasting words, and, as the proverb has it, trying to scrub an Ethiop white. You will buy them and make no use of them and get yourself laughed at by men of learning who are satisfied with the gain that they derive, not from the beauty of books or their expensiveness, but from the language and thought of their author. You expect to palliate and conceal your ignorance by getting a reputation for this, and to daze people by the number of your books, unaware that you are doing the same as the most ignorant physicians, who get themselves ivory pill-boxes and silver cupping-glasses and gold-inlaid scalpels; when the time comes to use

[1] *Hippolytus* 417 f.

οὐδὲ ὅπως χρὴ μεταχειρίσασθαι αὐτὰ ἴσασιν· παρελθὼν δέ τις εἰς τὸ μέσον τῶν μεμαθηκότων φλεβότομον εὖ μάλα ἠκονημένον ἔχων ἰοῦ τἆλλα μεστὸν ἀπήλλαξε τῆς ὀδύνης τὸν νοσοῦντα. ἵνα δὲ καὶ γελοιοτέρῳ τινὶ τὰ σὰ εἰκάσω, τοὺς κουρέας τούτους ἐπίσκεψαι, καὶ ὄψει τοὺς μὲν τεχνίτας αὐτῶν ξυρὸν καὶ μαχαιρίδας καὶ κάτοπτρον σύμμετρον ἔχοντας, τοὺς δὲ ἀμαθεῖς καὶ ἰδιώτας πλῆθος μαχαιρίδων προτιθέντας καὶ κάτοπτρα μεγάλα, οὐ μὴν λήσειν γε διὰ ταῦτα οὐδὲν εἰδότας. ἀλλὰ τὸ γελοιότατον ἐκεῖνο πάσχουσιν, ὅτι κείρονται μὲν οἱ πολλοὶ παρὰ τοῖς γείτοσιν αὐτῶν, πρὸς δὲ τὰ ἐκείνων κάτοπτρα προσελθόντες τὰς
30 κόμας εὐθετίζουσιν. καὶ σὺ τοίνυν ἄλλῳ μὲν δεηθέντι χρήσειας ἂν τὰ βιβλία, χρήσασθαι δὲ αὐτὸς οὐκ ἂν δύναιο. καίτοι οὐδὲ ἔχρησάς τινι βιβλίον πώποτε, ἀλλὰ τὸ τῆς κυνὸς ποιεῖς τῆς ἐν τῇ φάτνῃ κατακειμένης, ἣ οὔτε αὐτὴ τῶν κριθῶν ἐσθίει οὔτε τῷ ἵππῳ δυναμένῳ φαγεῖν ἐπιτρέπει.

Ταῦτα τό γε νῦν εἶναι ὑπὲρ μόνων τῶν βιβλίων παρρησιάζομαι πρὸς σέ, περὶ δὲ τῶν ἄλλων ὅσα κατάπτυστα καὶ ἐπονείδιστα ποιεῖς, αὖθις ἀκούσῃ πολλάκις.

them, however, they do not know how to handle them, but someone who has studied his profession comes upon the scene with a knife that is thoroughly sharp, though covered with rust, and frees the patient from his pain. But let me compare your case with something still more comical. Consider the barbers and you will observe that the master-craftsmen among them have only a razor and a pair of shears and a suitable mirror, while the unskilled, amateurish fellows put on view a multitude of shears and huge mirrors; but for all that, they cannot keep their ignorance from being found out. In fact, what happens to them is as comical as can be—people have their hair cut next door and then go to their mirrors to brush it. So it is with you: you might, to be sure, lend your books to someone else who wants them, but you cannot use them yourself. But you never lent a book to anyone; you act like the dog in the manger, who neither eats the grain herself nor lets the horse eat it, who can.

I give myself the liberty of saying this much to you for the present, just about your books; about your other detestable and ignominious conduct you shall often be told in future.

THE DREAM, OR LUCIAN'S CAREER

The *Dream* contains no hint that a lecture is to follow it, but its brevity, its structure—a parable followed by its application—and the intimacy of its tone show that it is an introduction similar to *Dionysus* and *Amber*. Read certainly in Syria, and almost certainly in Lucian's native city of Samosata, it would seem to have been composed on his first return to Syria, after the visit to Gaul that made him rich and famous; probably not long after it, for his return home is quite likely to have come soon after his departure from Gaul. It reads, too, as if it were written in the first flush of success, before his fortieth year.

Since it gives us a glimpse of his early history, and professes to tell us how he chose his career, it makes a good introduction to his works. For that reason it was put first in the early editions, and has found a place in a great many school readers, so that none of his writings is better known.

The amount of autobiography in it is not great. Lucian names no names, which might have given us valuable information as to his race, and he says nothing about his father except that he was not well off in the world. That his mother's father and brothers were sculptors, that he evinced his inheritance of the gift by his cleverness in modelling, and that he was therefore apprenticed to his uncle to learn the trade—all this is inherently probable, and interesting because it accounts for the seeing eye that made his pen-pictures so realistic. As to the dream, and his deliberate choice of a literary career on account of it, that is surely fiction. From what he does not say here, from what Oratory lets drop in the *Double Indictment*—that she found him wandering up and down Ionia, all but wearing native garb—we may guess that distaste for the sculptor's trade led him to run away from home without any very definite notion where he was going or what he should do, and that the dream, plainly inspired less by a thrashing than by the famous allegory of the sophist Prodicus, *Heracles at the Crossways* (Xenophon, *Memorabilia* 2, 1, 21), came to him in later years, while he meditated what he should say to those at home upon his return to them.

ΠΕΡΙ ΤΟΥ ΕΝΥΠΝΙΟΥ
ΗΤΟΙ
ΒΙΟΣ ΛΟΥΚΙΑΝΟΥ

1 Ἄρτι μὲν ἐπεπαύμην εἰς τὰ διδασκαλεῖα φοιτῶν ἤδη τὴν ἡλικίαν πρόσηβος ὤν, ὁ δὲ πατὴρ ἐσκοπεῖτο μετὰ τῶν φίλων ὅ τι καὶ διδάξαιτό με. τοῖς πλείστοις οὖν ἔδοξεν παιδεία μὲν καὶ πόνου πολλοῦ καὶ χρόνου μακροῦ καὶ δαπάνης οὐ μικρᾶς καὶ τύχης δεῖσθαι λαμπρᾶς, τὰ δ' ἡμέτερα μικρά τε εἶναι καὶ ταχεῖάν τινα τὴν ἐπικουρίαν ἀπαιτεῖν· εἰ δέ τινα τέχνην τῶν βαναύσων τούτων ἐκμάθοιμι, τὸ μὲν πρῶτον εὐθὺς ἂν αὐτὸς ἔχειν τὰ ἀρκοῦντα παρὰ τῆς τέχνης καὶ μηκέτ' οἰκόσιτος εἶναι τηλικοῦτος ὤν, οὐκ εἰς μακρὰν δὲ καὶ τὸν πατέρα εὐφρανεῖν ἀποφέρων ἀεὶ τὸ γιγνόμενον.

2 Δευτέρας οὖν σκέψεως ἀρχὴ προὐτέθη, τίς ἀρίστη τῶν τεχνῶν καὶ ῥᾴστη ἐκμαθεῖν καὶ ἀνδρὶ ἐλευθέρῳ πρέπουσα καὶ πρόχειρον ἔχουσα τὴν χορηγίαν καὶ διαρκῆ τὸν πόρον. ἄλλου τοίνυν ἄλλην ἐπαινοῦντος, ὡς ἕκαστος γνώμης ἢ ἐμπειρίας εἶχεν, ὁ πατὴρ εἰς τὸν θεῖον ἀπιδών,—παρῆν γὰρ ὁ πρὸς μητρὸς θεῖος, ἄριστος ἑρμογλύφος εἶναι δοκῶν[1]—"Οὐ θέμις," εἶπεν, "ἄλλην τέχνην

Available in photographs: ΓNZ.

[1] MSS. add καὶ (not in γ) λιθοξόος ἐν τοῖς μάλιστα εὐδοκίμοις: excised by Schmieder. Cf. 7.

THE DREAM
OR
LUCIAN'S CAREER

No sooner had I left off school, being then well on in my teens, than my father and his friends began to discuss what he should have me taught next. Most of them thought that higher education required great labour, much time, considerable expense, and conspicuous social position, while our circumstances were but moderate and demanded speedy relief; but that if I were to learn one of the handicrafts, in the first place I myself would immediately receive my support from the trade instead of continuing to share the family table at my age; besides, at no distant day I would delight my father by bringing home my earnings regularly.

The next topic for discussion was opened by raising the question, which of the trades was best, easiest to learn, suitable for a man of free birth, required an outfit that was easy to come by, and offered an income that was sufficient. Each praised a different trade, according to his own judgement or experience; but my father looked at my uncle (for among the company was my uncle on my mother's side, who had the reputation of being an excellent sculptor) and said: "It isn't right that any other

ἐπικρατεῖν σοῦ παρόντος, ἀλλὰ τοῦτον ἄγε"— δείξας ἐμέ—"δίδασκε παραλαβὼν λίθων ἐργάτην ἀγαθὸν εἶναι καὶ συναρμοστὴν καὶ ἑρμογλυφέα· δύναται γὰρ καὶ τοῦτο, φύσεώς γε, ὡς οἶσθα, ἔχων δεξιῶς." ἐτεκμαίρετο δὲ ταῖς ἐκ τοῦ κηροῦ παιδιαῖς· ὁπότε γὰρ ἀφεθείην ὑπὸ τῶν διδασκάλων, ἀποξέων ἂν τὸν κηρὸν ἢ βόας ἢ ἵππους ἢ καὶ νὴ Δί' ἀνθρώπους ἀνέπλαττον, εἰκότας,[1] ὡς ἐδόκουν τῷ πατρί· ἐφ' οἷς παρὰ μὲν τῶν διδασκάλων πληγὰς ἐλάμβανον, τότε δὲ ἔπαινος εἰς τὴν εὐφυίαν καὶ ταῦτα ἦν, καὶ χρηστὰς εἶχον ἐπ' ἐμοὶ τὰς ἐλπίδας ὡς ἐν βραχεῖ μαθήσομαι τὴν τέχνην, ἀπ' ἐκείνης γε τῆς πλαστικῆς.

3 Ἅμα τε οὖν ἐπιτήδειος ἐδόκει ἡμέρα τέχνης ἐνάρχεσθαι, κἀγὼ παρεδεδόμην τῷ θείῳ μὰ τὸν Δί' οὐ σφόδρα τῷ πράγματι ἀχθόμενος, ἀλλά μοι καὶ παιδιάν τινα οὐκ ἀτερπῆ ἐδόκει ἔχειν καὶ πρὸς τοὺς ἡλικιώτας ἐπίδειξιν, εἰ φαινοίμην θεούς τε γλύφων καὶ ἀγαλμάτια μικρά τινα κατασκευάζων ἐμαυτῷ τε κἀκείνοις οἷς προῃρούμην. καὶ τό γε πρῶτον ἐκεῖνο καὶ σύνηθες τοῖς ἀρχομένοις ἐγίγνετο. ἐγκοπέα γάρ τινά μοι δοὺς ὁ θεῖος ἐκέλευσεν ἠρέμα καθικέσθαι πλακὸς ἐν μέσῳ κειμένης, ἐπειπὼν τὸ κοινὸν "ἀρχὴ δέ τοι ἥμισυ παντός." σκληρότερον δὲ κατενεγκόντος ὑπ' ἀπειρίας κατεάγη μὲν ἡ πλάξ, ὁ δὲ ἀγανακτήσας σκυτάλην τινὰ πλησίον κειμένην λαβὼν οὐ πρᾴως οὐδὲ προτρεπτικῶς μου κατήρξατο, ὥστε δάκρυά μοι τὰ προοίμια τῆς τέχνης.

4 Ἀποδρὰς οὖν ἐκεῖθεν ἐπὶ τὴν οἰκίαν ἀφικνοῦμαι συνεχὲς ἀναλύζων καὶ δακρύων τοὺς ὀφθαλμοὺς

[1] εἰκότας Naber: εἰκότως MSS.

trade should have the preference while you are by Come, take this lad in hand"—with a gesture toward me—"and teach him to be a good stone-cutter, mason, and sculptor, for he is capable of it, since, as you know, he has a natural gift for it." He drew this inference from the way in which I had played with wax; for whenever my teachers dismissed me I would scrape the wax from my tablets and model cattle or horses or even men, and they were true to life, my father thought. I used to get thrashings from my teachers on account of them, but at that time they brought me praise for my cleverness, and good hopes were entertained of me, on the ground that I would soon learn the trade, to judge from that modelling.

So, as soon as it seemed to be a suitable day to begin a trade, I was turned over to my uncle, and I was not greatly displeased with the arrangement, I assure you; on the contrary, I thought it involved interesting play of a sort, and a chance to show off to my schoolmates if I should turn out to be carving gods and fashioning little figures for myself and for those I liked best. Then came the first step and the usual experience of beginners. My uncle gave me a chisel and told me to strike a light blow on a slab that lay at hand, adding the trite quotation. "Well begun, half done." But in my inexperience I struck too hard; the slab broke, and in a gust of anger he seized a stick that lay close by and put me through an initiation of no gentle or encouraging sort, so that tears were the overture to my apprenticeship.

I ran away from the place and came home sobbing continuously, with my eyes abrim with tears. I told

ὑπόπλεως, καὶ διηγοῦμαι τὴν σκυτάλην καὶ τοὺς μώλωπας ἐδείκνυον, καὶ κατηγόρουν πολλήν τινα ὠμότητα, προσθεὶς ὅτι ὑπὸ φθόνου ταῦτα ἔδρασε, μὴ αὐτὸν ὑπερβάλωμαι κατὰ τὴν τέχνην. ἀνακτησαμένης δὲ τῆς μητρὸς καὶ πολλὰ τῷ ἀδελφῷ λοιδορησαμένης, ἐπεὶ νὺξ ἐπῆλθεν κατέδαρθον ἔτι ἔνδακρυς καὶ τὴν σκυτάλην[1] ἐννοῶν.

5 Μέχρι μὲν δὴ τούτων γελάσιμα καὶ μειρακιώδη τὰ εἰρημένα· τὰ μετὰ ταῦτα δὲ οὐκέτι εὐκαταφρόνητα, ὦ ἄνδρες, ἀκούσεσθε, ἀλλὰ καὶ πάνυ φιληκόων ἀκροατῶν δεόμενα· ἵνα γὰρ καθ᾽ Ὅμηρον εἴπω,

θεῖός μοι ἐνύπνιον ἦλθεν ὄνειρος
ἀμβροσίην διὰ νύκτα,

ἐναργὴς οὕτως ὥστε μηδὲν ἀπολείπεσθαι τῆς ἀληθείας. ἔτι γοῦν καὶ μετὰ τοσοῦτον χρόνον τά τε σχήματά μοι τῶν φανέντων ἐν τοῖς ὀφθαλμοῖς παραμένει καὶ ἡ φωνὴ τῶν ἀκουσθέντων ἔναυλος· οὕτω σαφῆ πάντα ἦν.

6 Δύο γυναῖκες λαβόμεναι ταῖν χεροῖν εἷλκόν με πρὸς ἑαυτὴν ἑκατέρα μάλα βιαίως καὶ καρτερῶς· μικροῦ γοῦν με διεσπάσαντο πρὸς ἀλλήλας φιλοτιμούμεναι· καὶ γὰρ καὶ ἄρτι μὲν ἂν ἡ ἑτέρα ἐπεκράτει καὶ παρὰ μικρὸν ὅλον εἶχέ με, ἄρτι δ᾽ ἂν αὖθις ὑπὸ τῆς ἑτέρας εἰχόμην. ἐβόων δὲ πρὸς ἀλλήλας ἑκατέρα, ἡ μὲν ὡς αὐτῆς ὄντα με κεκτῆσθαι βούλοιτο, ἡ δὲ ὡς μάτην τῶν ἀλλοτρίων ἀντιποιοῖτο. ἦν δὲ ἡ μὲν ἐργατικὴ καὶ ἀνδρικὴ καὶ αὐχμηρὰ τὴν κόμην, τὼ χεῖρε τύλων ἀνάπλεως, διεζωσμένη τὴν ἐσθῆτα, τιτάνου

[1] σκυτάλην Steigerthal: νύκτα ὅλην MSS.

about the stick, showed the welts and charged my uncle with great cruelty, adding that he did it out of jealousy, for fear that I should get ahead of him in his trade. My mother comforted me and roundly abused her brother, but when night came on, I fell asleep, still tearful and thinking of the stick.

Up to this point my story has been humorous and childish, but what you shall hear next, gentlemen, is not to be made light of; it deserves a very receptive audience. The fact is that, to use the words of Homer,

"a god-sent vision appeared unto me in my slumber
Out of immortal night,"[1]

so vivid as not to fall short of reality in any way. Indeed, even after all this time, the figures that I saw continue to abide in my eyes and the words that I heard in my ears, so plain was it all.

Two women, taking me by the hands, were each trying to drag me toward herself with might and main; in fact, they nearly pulled me to pieces in their rivalry. Now one of them would get the better of it and almost have me altogether, and now I would be in the hands of the other. They shouted at each other, too, one of them saying, "He is mine, and you want to get him!" and the other: "It is no good your claiming what belongs to someone else." One was like a workman, masculine, with unkempt hair, hands full of callous places, clothing tucked up, and a heavy layer of

[1] *Iliad* 2, 56.

καταγέμουσα, οἷος ἦν ὁ θεῖος ὁπότε ξέοι τοὺς λίθους· ἡ ἑτέρα δὲ μάλα εὐπρόσωπος καὶ τὸ σχῆμα εὐπρεπὴς καὶ κόσμιος τὴν ἀναβολήν.

Τέλος δ' οὖν ἐφιᾶσί μοι δικάζειν ὁποτέρᾳ βουλοίμην συνεῖναι αὐτῶν. προτέρα δὲ ἡ σκληρὰ ἐκείνη καὶ ἀνδρώδης ἔλεξεν·

7 "Ἐγώ, φίλε παῖ, Ἑρμογλυφικὴ τέχνη εἰμί, ἣν χθὲς ἤρξω μανθάνειν, οἰκεία τέ σοι καὶ συγγενὴς οἴκοθεν·[1] ὅ τε γὰρ πάππος σου"—εἰποῦσα τοὔνομα τοῦ μητροπάτορος—"λιθοξόος ἦν καὶ τὼ θείω ἀμφοτέρω καὶ μάλα εὐδοκιμεῖτον δι' ἡμᾶς. εἰ δ' ἐθέλεις λήρων μὲν καὶ φληνάφων τῶν παρὰ ταύτης ἀπέχεσθαι,"—δείξασα τὴν ἑτέραν—"ἕπεσθαι δὲ καὶ συνοικεῖν ἐμοί, πρῶτα μὲν θρέψῃ γεννικῶς καὶ τοὺς ὤμους ἕξεις καρτερούς, φθόνου δὲ παντὸς ἀλλότριος ἔσῃ· καὶ οὔποτε ἄπει ἐπὶ τὴν ἀλλοδαπήν, τὴν πατρίδα καὶ τοὺς οἰκείους καταλιπών, οὐδὲ ἐπὶ λόγοις . . .[2] ἐπαινέσονταί σε πάντες.

8 "Μὴ μυσαχθῇς δὲ τοῦ σχήματος[3] τὸ εὐτελὲς μηδὲ τῆς ἐσθῆτος τὸ πιναρόν· ἀπὸ γὰρ τοιούτων ὁρμώμενος καὶ Φειδίας ἐκεῖνος ἔδειξε τὸν Δία καὶ Πολύκλειτος τὴν Ἥραν εἰργάσατο καὶ Μύρων ἐπῃνέθη καὶ Πραξιτέλης ἐθαυμάσθη. προσκυνοῦνται γοῦν οὗτοι μετὰ τῶν θεῶν. εἰ δὴ τούτων εἷς γένοιο, πῶς μὲν οὐ κλεινὸς αὐτὸς παρὰ πᾶσιν ἀνθρώποις ἔσῃ,[4] ζηλωτὸν δὲ καὶ τὸν πατέρα

[1] μητρόθεν Fritzsche, as in *Toxar.* 51.

[2] Lacuna noted by Bourdelot. At least ἀλλ' ἐπ' ἔργοις is necessary.

[3] σχήματος Bekker: σώματος MSS.

[4] ἔσῃ Dindorf: γένοιο MSS.

marble-dust upon her, just as my uncle looked when he cut stone. The other, however, was very fair of face, dignified in her appearance, and nice in her dress.

At length they allowed me to decide which of them I wanted to be with. The first to state her case was the hard-favoured, masculine one.

"Dear boy, I am the trade of Sculpture which you began to learn yesterday, of kin to you and related by descent; for your grandfather"—and she gave the name of my mother's father—"was a sculptor, and so are both your uncles, who are very famous through me. If you are willing to keep clear of this woman's silly nonsense"—with a gesture toward the other—"and to come and live with me, you will be generously kept and will have powerful shoulders, and you will be a stranger to jealousy of any sort; besides you will never go abroad, leaving your native country and your kinsfolk, and it will not be for mere words, either, that everyone will praise you.

"Do not be disgusted at my humble figure and my soiled clothing, for this is the way in which Phidias began, who revealed Zeus, and Polycleitus, who made Hera, Myron, whom men praise, and Praxiteles, at whom they marvel. Indeed, these men receive homage second only to the gods. If you become one of them, will you not yourself be famous in the sight of all mankind, make your

ἀποδείξεις, περίβλεπτον δὲ ἀποφανεῖς καὶ τὴν πατρίδα;"

Ταῦτα καὶ ἔτι τούτων πλείονα διαπταίουσα καὶ βαρβαρίζουσα πάμπολλα εἶπεν ἡ Τέχνη, μάλα δὴ σπουδῇ συνείρουσα καὶ πείθειν με πειρωμένη· ἀλλ᾽ οὐκέτι μέμνημαι· τὰ πλεῖστα γὰρ ἤδη μου τὴν μνήμην διέφυγεν.

Ἐπεὶ δ᾽ οὖν ἐπαύσατο, ἄρχεται ἡ ἑτέρα ὧδέ πως·

9 "Ἐγὼ δέ, ὦ τέκνον, Παιδεία εἰμὶ ἤδη συνήθης σοι καὶ γνωρίμη, εἰ καὶ μηδέπω εἰς τέλος μου πεπείρασαι. ἡλίκα μὲν οὖν τὰ ἀγαθὰ ποριῇ λιθοξόος γενόμενος, αὕτη προείρηκεν· οὐδὲν γὰρ ὅτι μὴ ἐργάτης ἔσῃ τῷ σώματι πονῶν κἀν τούτῳ τὴν ἅπασαν ἐλπίδα τοῦ βίου τεθειμένος, ἀφανὴς μὲν αὐτὸς ὤν, ὀλίγα καὶ ἀγεννῆ λαμβάνων, ταπεινὸς τὴν γνώμην, εὐτελὴς δὲ τὴν πρόοδον, οὔτε φίλοις ἐπιδικάσιμος οὔτε ἐχθροῖς φοβερὸς οὔτε τοῖς πολίταις ζηλωτός, ἀλλ᾽ αὐτὸ μόνον ἐργάτης καὶ τῶν ἐκ τοῦ πολλοῦ δήμου εἷς, ἀεὶ τὸν προὔχοντα ὑποπτήσσων καὶ τὸν λέγειν δυνάμενον θεραπεύων, λαγὼ βίον ζῶν καὶ τοῦ κρείττονος ἕρμαιον ὤν· εἰ δὲ καὶ Φειδίας ἢ Πολύκλειτος γένοιο καὶ πολλὰ θαυμαστὰ ἐξεργάσαιο, τὴν μὲν τέχνην ἅπαντες ἐπαινέσονται, οὐκ ἔστι δὲ ὅστις τῶν ἰδόντων, εἰ νοῦν ἔχοι, εὔξαιτ᾽ ἂν σοὶ ὅμοιος γενέσθαι· οἷος γὰρ ἂν ᾖς, βάναυσος καὶ χειρῶναξ καὶ ἀποχειροβίωτος νομισθήσῃ.

10 "Ἢν δ᾽ ἐμοὶ[1] πείθῃ, πρῶτον μέν σοι πολλὰ ἐπιδείξω παλαιῶν ἀνδρῶν ἔργα καὶ πράξεις θαυ-

[1] δ᾽ ἐμοὶ Lehmann: δέ μοι MSS.

father envied, and cause your native land to be admired?"

Sculpture said all this, and even more than this, with a great deal of stumbling and bad grammar, talking very hurriedly and trying to convince me: I do not remember it all, however, for most of it has escaped my memory by this time.

When she stopped, the other began after this fashion:

"My child, I am Education, with whom you are already acquainted and familiar, even if you have not yet completed your experience of me. What it shall profit you to become a sculptor, this woman has told you; you will be nothing but a labourer, toiling with your body and putting in it your entire hope of a livelihood, personally inconspicuous, getting meagre and illiberal returns, humble-witted, an insignificant figure in public, neither sought by your friends nor feared by your enemies nor envied by your fellow-citizens—nothing but just a labourer, one of the swarming rabble, ever cringing to the man above you and courting the man who can use his tongue, leading a hare's life, and counting as a godsend to anyone stronger. Even if you should become a Phidias or a Polycleitus and should create many marvellous works, everyone would praise your craftsmanship, to be sure, but none of those who saw you, if he were sensible, would pray to be like you; for no matter what you might be, you would be considered a mechanic, a man who has naught but his hands, a man who lives by his hands.

"If you follow my advice, first of all I shall show you many works of men of old, tell you their

μαστὰς καὶ λόγους αὐτῶν ἀπαγγελῶ, καὶ πάντων ὡς εἰπεῖν ἔμπειρον ἀποφανῶ, καὶ τὴν ψυχήν, ὅπερ σοι κυριώτατόν ἐστι, κατακοσμήσω πολλοῖς καὶ ἀγαθοῖς κοσμήμασι—σωφροσύνῃ, δικαιοσύνῃ, εὐσεβείᾳ, πρᾳότητι, ἐπιεικείᾳ, συνέσει, καρτερίᾳ, τῷ τῶν καλῶν ἔρωτι, τῇ πρὸς τὰ σεμνότατα ὁρμῇ· ταῦτα γάρ ἐστιν ὁ τῆς ψυχῆς ἀκήρατος ὡς ἀληθῶς κόσμος. λήσει δέ σε οὔτε παλαιὸν οὐδὲν οὔτε νῦν γενέσθαι δέον, ἀλλὰ καὶ τὰ μέλλοντα προόψει μετ' ἐμοῦ, καὶ ὅλως ἅπαντα ὁπόσα ἐστί, τά τε θεῖα τά τ' ἀνθρώπινα, οὐκ εἰς μακρὰν σε διδάξομαι.

11 "Καὶ ὁ νῦν πένης ὁ τοῦ δεῖνος, ὁ βουλευσάμενός τι περὶ ἀγεννοῦς οὕτω τέχνης, μετ' ὀλίγον ἅπασι ζηλωτὸς καὶ ἐπίφθονος ἔσῃ, τιμώμενος καὶ ἐπαινούμενος καὶ ἐπὶ τοῖς ἀρίστοις εὐδοκιμῶν καὶ ὑπὸ τῶν γένει καὶ πλούτῳ προὐχόντων ἀποβλεπόμενος, ἐσθῆτα μὲν τοιαύτην ἀμπεχόμενος,"—δείξασα τὴν ἑαυτῆς· πάνυ δὲ λαμπρὰν ἐφόρει—"ἀρχῆς δὲ καὶ προεδρίας ἀξιούμενος. κἄν που ἀποδημῇς, οὐδ' ἐπὶ τῆς ἀλλοδαπῆς ἀγνὼς οὐδ' ἀφανὴς ἔσῃ· τοιαῦτά σοι περιθήσω τὰ γνωρίσματα ὥστε τῶν ὁρώντων ἕκαστος τὸν πλησίον κινήσας δείξει σε τῷ δακτύλῳ, 'Οὗτος ἐκεῖνος' 12 λέγων. ἂν δέ τι σπουδῆς ἄξιον ᾖ τοὺς φίλους ἢ καὶ τὴν πόλιν ὅλην καταλαμβάνῃ, εἰς σὲ πάντες ἀποβλέψονται· κἄν πού τι λέγων τύχῃς, κεχηνότες οἱ πολλοὶ ἀκούσονται, θαυμάζοντες καὶ εὐδαιμονίζοντές σε τῆς δυνάμεως τῶν λόγων καὶ τὸν πατέρα τῆς εὐποτμίας.[1] ὃ δὲ λέγουσιν, ὡς ἄρα καὶ ἀθάνατοι γίγνονταί τινες ἐξ ἀνθρώπων,

[1] εὐπαιδίας Ψ^2 (conjectural?) and Hemsterhuys.

wondrous deeds and words, and make you conversant with almost all knowledge, and I shall ornament your soul, which concerns you most, with many noble adornments—temperance, justice, piety, kindliness, reasonableness, understanding, steadfastness, love of all that is beautiful, ardour towards all that is sublime; for these are the truly flawless jewels of the soul. Nothing that came to pass of old will escape you, and nothing that must now come to pass; nay, you will even foresee the future with me. In a word, I shall speedily teach you everything that there is, whether it pertains to the gods or to man.

"You who are now the beggarly son of a nobody, who have entertained some thought of so illiberal a trade, will after a little inspire envy and jealousy in all men, for you will be honoured and lauded, you will be held in great esteem for the highest qualities and admired by men preeminent in lineage and in wealth, you will wear clothing such as this"—she pointed to her own, and she was very splendidly dressed—"and will be deemed worthy of office and precedence. If ever you go abroad, even on foreign soil you will not be unknown or inconspicuous, for I will attach to you such marks of identification that everyone who sees you will nudge his neighbour and point you out with his finger, saying, 'There he is!' If anything of grave import befalls your friends or even the entire city, all will turn their eyes upon you; and if at any time you chance to make a speech, the crowd will listen open-mouthed, marvelling and felicitating you upon your eloquence and your father upon his good fortune. They say that some men become immortal. I shall bring this to pass

τοῦτό σοι περιποιήσω· καὶ γὰρ ἢν αὐτὸς ἐκ τοῦ βίου ἀπέλθῃς, οὔποτε παύσῃ συνὼν τοῖς πεπαιδευμένοις καὶ προσομιλῶν τοῖς ἀρίστοις. ὁρᾷς τὸν Δημοσθένην ἐκεῖνον, τίνος υἱὸν ὄντα ἐγὼ ἡλίκον ἐποίησα. ὁρᾷς τὸν Αἰσχίνην, ὡς τυμπανιστρίας υἱὸς ἦν, ἀλλ' ὅμως[1] αὐτὸν δι' ἐμὲ Φίλιππος ἐθεράπευεν. ὁ δὲ Σωκράτης καὶ αὐτὸς ὑπὸ τῇ Ἑρμογλυφικῇ ταύτῃ τραφείς, ἐπειδὴ τάχιστα συνῆκεν τοῦ κρείττονος καὶ δραπετεύσας παρ' αὐτῆς ηὐτομόλησεν ὡς ἐμέ, ἀκούεις ὡς παρὰ πάντων ᾄδεται.

13 "Ἀφεὶς δὲ αὖ τοὺς τηλικούτους καὶ τοιούτους ἄνδρας καὶ πράξεις λαμπρὰς καὶ λόγους σεμνοὺς καὶ σχῆμα εὐπρεπὲς καὶ τιμὴν καὶ δόξαν καὶ ἔπαινον καὶ προεδρίας καὶ δύναμιν καὶ ἀρχὰς καὶ τὸ ἐπὶ λόγοις εὐδοκιμεῖν καὶ τὸ ἐπὶ συνέσει εὐδαιμονίζεσθαι, χιτώνιόν τι πιναρὸν ἐνδύσῃ καὶ σχῆμα δουλοπρεπὲς ἀναλήψῃ καὶ μοχλία καὶ γλυφεῖα καὶ κοπέας καὶ κολαπτῆρας ἐν ταῖν χεροῖν ἕξεις κάτω νενευκὼς εἰς τὸ ἔργον, χαμαιπετὴς καὶ χαμαίζηλος καὶ πάντα τρόπον ταπεινός, ἀνακύπτων δὲ οὐδέποτε οὐδὲ ἀνδρῶδες οὐδὲ ἐλεύθερον οὐδὲν ἐπινοῶν, ἀλλὰ τὰ μὲν ἔργα ὅπως εὔρυθμα καὶ εὐσχήμονα ἔσται σοι προνοῶν, ὅπως δὲ αὐτὸς εὔρυθμός τε καὶ κόσμιος ἔσῃ, ἥκιστα πεφροντικώς, ἀλλ' ἀτιμότερον ποιῶν σεαυτὸν λίθων."

14 Ταῦτα ἔτι λεγούσης αὐτῆς οὐ περιμείνας ἐγὼ τὸ τέλος τῶν λόγων ἀναστὰς ἀπεφηνάμην, καὶ τὴν ἄμορφον ἐκείνην καὶ ἐργατικὴν ἀπολιπὼν

[1] ὅμως N marg., ς, vulg.: ὅπως MSS.

with you; for though you yourself depart from life, you will never cease associating with men of education and conversing with men of eminence. You know whose son Demosthenes was, and how great I made him. You know that Aeschines was the son of a tambourine girl, but for all that, Philip paid court to him for my sake. And Socrates himself was brought up under the tutelage of our friend Sculpture, but as soon as he understood what was better he ran away from her and joined my colours; and you have heard how his praises are sung by everyone.

"On the other hand, if you turn your back upon these men so great and noble, upon glorious deeds and sublime words, upon a dignified appearance, upon honour, esteem, praise, precedence, power and offices, upon fame for eloquence and felicitations for wit, then you will put on a filthy tunic, assume a servile appearance, and hold bars and gravers and sledges and chisels in your hands, with your back bent over your work; you will be a groundling, with groundling ambitions, altogether humble; you will never lift your head, or conceive a single manly or liberal thought, and although you will plan to make your works well-balanced and well-shapen, you will not show any concern to make yourself well-balanced and sightly; on the contrary, you will make yourself a thing of less value than a block of stone."

While these words were still on her lips, without waiting for her to finish what she was saying, I stood up and declared myself. Abandoning the ugly

μετέβαινον πρὸς τὴν Παιδείαν μάλα γεγηθώς, καὶ μάλιστα ἐπεί μοι καὶ εἰς νοῦν ἦλθεν ἡ σκυτάλη καὶ ὅτι πληγὰς εὐθὺς[1] οὐκ ὀλίγας ἀρχομένῳ μοι χθὲς ἐνετρίψατο. ἡ δὲ ἀπολειφθεῖσα τὸ μὲν πρῶτον ἠγανάκτει καὶ τὼ χεῖρε συνεκρότει καὶ τοὺς ὀδόντας συνέπριε· τέλος δέ, ὥσπερ τὴν Νιόβην ἀκούομεν, ἐπεπήγει καὶ εἰς λίθον μετεβέβλητο. εἰ δὲ παράδοξα ἔπαθε, μὴ ἀπιστήσητε· θαυματοποιοὶ γὰρ οἱ ὄνειροι.

15 Ἡ ἑτέρα δὲ πρός με ἀπιδοῦσα, "Τοιγαροῦν ἀμείψομαί σε," ἔφη, "τῆσδε τῆς δικαιοσύνης, ὅτι καλῶς τὴν δίκην ἐδίκασας, καὶ ἐλθὲ ἤδη, ἐπίβηθι τούτου τοῦ ὀχήματος,"—δείξασά τι ὄχημα ὑποπτέρων ἵππων τινῶν τῷ Πηγάσῳ ἐοικότων—"ὅπως εἰδῇς οἷα καὶ ἡλίκα μὴ ἀκολουθήσας ἐμοὶ ἀγνοήσειν ἔμελλες." ἐπεὶ δὲ ἀνῆλθον, ἡ μὲν ἤλαυνε καὶ ὑφηνιόχει, ἀρθεὶς δὲ εἰς ὕψος ἐγὼ ἐπεσκόπουν ἀπὸ τῆς ἕω ἀρξάμενος ἄχρι πρὸς τὰ ἑσπέρια[2] πόλεις καὶ ἔθνη καὶ δήμους, καθάπερ ὁ Τριπτόλεμος ἀποσπείρων τι εἰς τὴν γῆν. οὐκέτι μέντοι μέμνημαι ὅ τι τὸ σπειρόμενον ἐκεῖνο ἦν, πλὴν τοῦτο μόνον ὅτι κάτωθεν ἀφορῶντες ἄνθρωποι ἐπῄνουν καὶ μετ' εὐφημίας καθ' οὓς γενοίμην τῇ πτήσει παρέπεμπον.

16 Δείξασα δέ μοι τὰ τοσαῦτα κἀμὲ τοῖς ἐπαινοῦσιν ἐκείνοις ἐπανήγαγεν αὖθις, οὐκέτι τὴν αὐτὴν ἐσθῆτα ἐκείνην ἐνδεδυκότα ἣν εἶχον ἀφιπτάμενος, ἀλλά μοι ἐδόκουν εὐπάρυφός τις ἐπανήκειν. καταλαβοῦσα οὖν καὶ τὸν πατέρα ἑστῶτα καὶ

[1] ὁ θεῖος Hemsterhuys.
[2] τὰ ἑσπέρια Gronovius: τὰς ἑσπερίας MSS.

working-woman, I went over to Education with a right good will, especially when the stick entered my mind and the fact that it had laid many a blow upon me at the very outset the day before. When I abandoned Sculpture, at first she was indignant and struck her hands together and ground her teeth; but at length, like Niobe in the story, she grew rigid and turned to stone. Her fate was strange, but do not be incredulous, for dreams work miracles.

The other fixed her eyes upon me and said: "I will therefore repay you for the justice that you have done in judging this issue rightly: come at once and mount this car"—pointing to a car with winged horses resembling Pegasus—"in order that you may know what you would have missed if you had not come with me." When I had mounted she plied whip and reins, and I was carried up into the heights and went from the East to the very West, surveying cities and nations and peoples, sowing something broadcast over the earth like Triptolemus. I do not now remember what it was that I sowed; only that men, looking up from below, applauded, and all those above whom I passed in my flight sped me on my way with words of praise.

After all this had been shown to me and I to the men who applauded, she brought me back again, no longer dressed in the same clothing that I wore when I began the flight; I dreamed that I came back in princely purple. Finding my father standing and waiting, she pointed him out my clothing and the

περιμένοντα ἐδείκνυεν αὐτῷ ἐκείνη[1] τὴν ἐσθῆτα κἀμέ, οἷος ἥκοιμι, καί τι καὶ ὑπέμνησεν οἷα μικροῦ δεῖν περὶ ἐμοῦ ἐβουλεύσαντο.

Ταῦτα μέμνημαι ἰδὼν ἀντίπαις ἔτι ὤν, ἐμοὶ δοκεῖν ἐκταραχθεὶς πρὸς τὸν τῶν πληγῶν φόβον.

17 Μεταξὺ δὲ λέγοντος, "Ἡράκλεις," ἔφη τις, "ὡς μακρὸν τὸ ἐνύπνιον καὶ δικανικόν." εἶτ' ἄλλος ὑπέκρουσε, "Χειμερινὸς ὄνειρος, ὅτε[2] μήκισταί εἰσιν αἱ νύκτες, ἢ τάχα που τριέσπερος, ὥσπερ ὁ Ἡρακλῆς, καὶ αὐτός ἐστι. τί δ' οὖν ἐπῆλθεν αὐτῷ ληρῆσαι ταῦτα πρὸς ἡμᾶς καὶ μνησθῆναι παιδικῆς νυκτὸς καὶ ὀνείρων παλαιῶν καὶ γεγηρακότων; ἕωλος γὰρ ἡ ψυχρολογία. μὴ ὀνείρων τινὰς ὑποκριτὰς ἡμᾶς ὑπείληφεν;" οὔκ, ὠγαθέ· οὐδὲ γὰρ ὁ Ξενοφῶν ποτε διηγούμενος τὸ ἐνύπνιον, ὡς ἐδόκει αὐτῷ κεραυνὸς ἐμπεσὼν καίειν τὴν πατρῴαν οἰκίαν[3] καὶ τὰ ἄλλα,—ἴστε γάρ— οὐχ ὑπόκρισιν τὴν ὄψιν οὐδ' ὡς φλυαρεῖν ἐγνωκὼς αὐτὰ διεξῄει, καὶ ταῦτα ἐν πολέμῳ καὶ ἀπογνώσει πραγμάτων, περιεστώτων πολεμίων, ἀλλά τι καὶ χρήσιμον εἶχεν ἡ διήγησις.

18 Καὶ τοίνυν κἀγὼ τοῦτον τὸν ὄνειρον ὑμῖν διηγησάμην ἐκείνου ἕνεκα, ὅπως οἱ νέοι πρὸς τὰ βελτίω τρέπωνται καὶ παιδείας ἔχωνται, καὶ

[1] ἐκείνη ς, Allinson: ἐκείνην MSS.
[2] ὅτε Graevius (Z[1] ?): ὅτι MSS.
[3] <κεραυνὸς ἐμπεσὼν> καίειν τὴν πατρῴαν οἰκίαν A.M.H.: καὶ ἐν τῇ πατρῴᾳ οἰκίᾳ MSS.

guise in which I had returned, and even reminded him gently of the plans that they had narrowly escaped making for me.

That is the dream which I remember having had when I was a slip of a lad; it was due, I suppose, to my agitation on account of the fear inspired by the thrashing.

Even as I was speaking, "Heracles!" someone said, "what a long and tiresome dream!" Then someone else broke in: "A winter dream, when the nights are longest; or perhaps it is itself a product of three nights, like Heracles![1] What got into him to tell us this idle tale and to speak of a night of his childhood and dreams that are ancient and superannuated? It is flat to spin pointless yarns. Surely he doesn't take us for interpreters of dreams?" No, my friend; and Xenophon, too, when he told one time how he dreamed that a bolt of lightning, striking his father's house, set it afire, and all the rest of it—you know it—did not do so because he wanted the dream interpreted, nor yet because he had made up his mind to talk nonsense, particularly in time of war and in a desperate state of affairs, with the enemy on every side; no, the story had a certain usefulness.[2]

So it was with me, and I told you this dream in order that those who are young may take the better direction and cleave to education, above all if poverty

[1] The Alexandrians called Heracles "him of the three nights," because Zeus tripled the length of the night which he spent with Alcmene. See *Dial. of the Gods* 14 (vulg. 10).

[2] *Anabasis* 3, 1, 11. Lucian, perhaps confusing this with a later dream (4, 3, 7), evidently thinks that it was told to the soldiers to hearten them, but this is not the case. Xenophon was unable to interpret it until after the event, and did not tell it to anyone until he put it into his book.

μάλιστα εἴ τις αὐτῶν ὑπὸ πενίας ἐθελοκακεῖ καὶ πρὸς τὴν ἥττω ἀποκλίνει, φύσιν οὐκ ἀγεννῆ διαφθείρων. ἐπιρρωσθήσεται εὖ οἶδ' ὅτι κἀκεῖνος ἀκούσας τοῦ μύθου, ἱκανὸν ἑαυτῷ παράδειγμα ἐμὲ προστησάμενος, ἐννοῶν οἷος μὲν ὢν πρὸς τὰ κάλλιστα ὥρμησα καὶ παιδείας ἐπεθύμησα, μηδὲν ἀποδειλιάσας πρὸς τὴν πενίαν τὴν τότε, οἷος δὲ πρὸς ὑμᾶς ἐπανελήλυθα, εἰ καὶ μηδὲν ἄλλο, οὐδενὸς γοῦν τῶν λιθογλύφων ἀδοξότερος.

is making any one of them faint-hearted and inclining him toward the worse, to the detriment of a noble nature. He will be strengthened, I am very sure, by hearing the tale, if he takes me as an adequate example, reflecting what I was when I aspired to all that is finest and set my heart on education, showing no weakness in the face of my poverty at that time, and what I am now, on my return to you—if nothing more, at least quite as highly thought of as any sculptor.

THE PARASITE
PARASITIC AN ART

Ludwig Radermacher has shown that *The Parasite* owes its being to the age-long war of words between philosophy and rhetoric, and should be read in the light of controversial tracts such as the Rhetoric of Philodemus. Ever since the time of Plato and Isocrates, the two systems of education had been fighting for pupils, and philosophy had found it well worth her while to test the pretensions of her rival by investigating the nature and value of rhetoric. As usual, her schools did not agree in their results. The Stoics found rhetoric fruitful in her promise if cultivated under proper management; but most of the other schools would have naught of her. The leading voice of the opposition was that of Critolaus, the Peripatetic, who, debating against Diogenes the Stoic, tested rhetoric by the Stoic definition of an "art," and demonstrated to his own satisfaction that it was none.

The author of *The Parasite* makes fun of the question, still very much alive in his time, and of both parties to it by arguing that Parasitic is an art by the terms of the Stoic definition, and a better one than either rhetoric or philosophy. No other pursuit could have served his turn better than that of the parasite, who made a business of sponging, who, along with the cook, had been a standing butt of the New Comedy, and now had become the rival of the philosopher and the rhetorician for the favour of rich patrons.

The author of this clever comparison had the same standpoint as Lucian with reference to philosophy and rhetoric; he knows Lucian's writings; and the name of Tychiades is one of Lucian's masks. He is either Lucian himself or a conscious imitator. But the vocabulary, syntax, and style are so dissimilar as to seem another's, and even the humour has a different quality, for instance; "Aristotle only made a beginning in Parasitic, as in every other art!" Possibly Lucian wrote the piece in his extreme old age; but to my mind it is more likely to be the work of someone else. It is certainly prior to the *Ungrammatical Man*, which satirizes many words and expressions that occur in it. The text has come down to us through a single channel, and is exceptionally corrupt.

ΠΕΡΙ ΠΑΡΑΣΙΤΟΥ
ΟΤΙ ΤΕΧΝΗ Η ΠΑΡΑΣΙΤΙΚΗ

ΤΥΧΙΑΔΗΣ

1 Τί ποτε ἄρα, ὦ Σίμων, οἱ μὲν ἄλλοι ἄνθρωποι καὶ ἐλεύθεροι καὶ δοῦλοι τέχνην ἕκαστός τινα ἐπίστανται δι' ἧς αὐτοῖς τέ εἰσιν καὶ ἄλλῳ χρήσιμοι, σὺ δέ, ὡς ἔοικεν, ἔργον οὐδὲν ἔχεις δι' οὗ ἄν τι ἢ αὐτὸς ἀπόναιο ἢ ἄλλῳ μεταδοίης;

ΣΙΜΩΝ

Πῶς τοῦτο ἐρωτᾷς, ὦ Τυχιάδη; οὐδέπω οἶδα. πειρῶ δὴ σαφέστερον ἐρωτᾶν.

ΤΥΧΙΑΔΗΣ

Ἔστιν ἥντινα τυγχάνεις ἐπιστάμενος τέχνην, οἷον μουσικήν;

ΣΙΜΩΝ

Μὰ Δία.

ΤΥΧΙΑΔΗΣ

Τί δέ, ἰατρικήν;

ΣΙΜΩΝ

Οὐδὲ ταύτην.

ΤΥΧΙΑΔΗΣ

Ἀλλὰ γεωμετρίαν;

ΣΙΜΩΝ

Οὐδαμῶς.

Available in photographs: ΓPNZ.

THE PARASITE
PARASITIC AN ART

TYCHIADES

Why in the world is it, Simon, that while other men, both slave and free, each know some art by which they are of use to themselves and to someone else, you apparently have no work which would enable you to make any profit yourself or give away anything to anybody else?

SIMON

What do you mean by that question, Tychiades? I do not understand. Try to put it more clearly.

TYCHIADES

Is there any art that you happen to know? Music, for instance?

SIMON

No, indeed.

TYCHIADES

Well, medicine?

SIMON

Not that, either.

TYCHIADES

Geometry, then?

SIMON

Not by any means.

ΤΥΧΙΑΔΗΣ

Τί δέ, ῥητορικήν; φιλοσοφίας μὲν γὰρ τοσοῦτον ἀπέχεις ὅσον καὶ ἡ κακία.

ΣΙΜΩΝ

Ἐγὼ μέν, εἰ οἷόν τε εἶναι, καὶ πλεῖον. ὥστε μὴ δόκει[1] τοῦτο καθάπερ ἀγνοοῦντι ὀνειδίσαι· φημὶ γὰρ κακὸς εἶναι καὶ χείρων ἢ σὺ δοκεῖς.

ΤΥΧΙΑΔΗΣ

Ναί. ἀλλὰ ταύτας μὲν ἴσως τὰς τέχνας οὐκ ἐξέμαθες διὰ μέγεθος αὐτῶν καὶ δυσκολίαν, τῶν δὲ δημοτικῶν τινα, τεκτονικὴν ἢ σκυτοτομικήν; καὶ γὰρ οὐδὲ τἄλλα οὕτως ἔχει σοι, ὡς μὴ καὶ τοιαύτης ἂν δεηθῆναι τέχνης.

ΣΙΜΩΝ

Ὀρθῶς λέγεις, ὦ Τυχιάδη· ἀλλ' οὐδὲ γὰρ[2] τούτων οὐδεμιᾶς ἐπιστήμων εἰμί.

ΤΥΧΙΑΔΗΣ

Τίνος οὖν ἑτέρας;

ΣΙΜΩΝ

Τίνος; ὡς ἐγὼ οἶμαι, γενναίας· ἣν εἰ μάθοις, καὶ σὲ ἐπαινέσειν οἴομαι. ἔργῳ μὲν οὖν κατορθοῦν φημι ἤδη, εἰ δέ σοι καὶ λόγῳ,[3] οὐκ ἔχω εἰπεῖν.

ΤΥΧΙΑΔΗΣ

Τίνα ταύτην;

ΣΙΜΩΝ

Οὔπω μοι δοκῶ τοὺς περὶ ταύτην ἐκμεμελετηκέναι λόγους. ὥστε ὅτι τέχνην μέν τινα ἐπί-

[1] δόκει vulg.: δοκεῖν MSS.

[2] ἀλλ' οὐδὲ γὰρ A.M.H.: ἀλλ' οὐδὲ N, οὐδὲ γὰρ other MSS.

[3] εἰ δέ σοι καὶ λόγῳ A.M.H.: εἰ δὲ καὶ σοὶ (σύ, σὺν) λόγῳ MSS. Editors, except Jacobitz, omit σοι.

TYCHIADES

Well, rhetoric? For as to philosophy, you are as remote from that as vice itself is!

SIMON

Indeed, even more so, if possible. So don't suppose you have touched me with that taunt, as if I did not know it. I admit that I am vicious, and worse than you think!

TYCHIADES

Quite so. Well, it may be that although you have not learned those arts because of their magnitude and difficulty, you have learned one of the vulgar arts like carpentry or shoemaking; you are not so well off in every way as not to need even such an art.

SIMON

You are right, Tychiades; but I am not acquainted with any of these either.

TYCHIADES

What other art, then?

SIMON

What other? A fine one, I think. If you knew about it, I believe you would speak highly of it too. In practice, I claim to be successful at it already, but whether you will find me so in theory also I can't say.

TYCHIADES

What is it?

SIMON

I do not feel that I have yet thoroughly mastered the literature on that subject. So for the present

σταμαι, ὑπάρχει ἤδη σοι γιγνώσκειν καὶ μὴ διὰ τοῦτο χαλεπῶς μοι ἔχειν· ἥντινα δέ, αὖθις ἀκούσῃ.

ΤΥΧΙΑΔΗΣ

Ἀλλ' οὐκ ἀνέξομαι.

ΣΙΜΩΝ

Τό γε τῆς τέχνης παράδοξον ἴσως φανεῖταί σοι ἀκούσαντι.

ΤΥΧΙΑΔΗΣ

Καὶ μὴν διὰ τοῦτο σπουδάζω μαθεῖν.

ΣΙΜΩΝ

Εἰσαῦθις, ὦ Τυχιάδη.

ΤΥΧΙΑΔΗΣ

Μηδαμῶς, ἀλλ' ἤδη λέγε, εἰ μή περ ἄρα αἰσχύνῃ.

ΣΙΜΩΝ

Ἡ παρασιτική.

ΤΥΧΙΑΔΗΣ

2 Κᾆτα εἰ μὴ μαίνοιτό τις, ὦ Σίμων, τέχνην ταύτην φαίη ἄν;

ΣΙΜΩΝ

Ἔγωγε· εἰ δέ σοι μαίνεσθαι δοκῶ, τοῦ μηδεμίαν ἄλλην ἐπίστασθαι τέχνην αἰτίαν εἶναί μοι τὴν μανίαν δόκει καί με τῶν ἐγκλημάτων ἤδη ἀφίει. φασὶ γὰρ τὴν δαίμονα ταύτην τὰ μὲν ἄλλα χαλεπὴν εἶναι τοῖς ἔχουσι, παραιτεῖσθαι δὲ τῶν ἁμαρτημάτων αὐτοὺς ὥσπερ διδάσκαλον ἢ παιδαγωγὸν[1] τούτων ἀναδεχομένην εἰς αὑτὴν τὰς αἰτίας.

ΤΥΧΙΑΔΗΣ

Οὐκοῦν, ὦ Σίμων, ἡ παρασιτικὴ τέχνη ἐστί;

[1] παιδαγωγὸν Ψ (?), vulg.: παῖδα MSS. (πατέρα N).

you may know that I possess an art and need not be dissatisfied with me on that score; some other day you shall hear what art it is.

TYCHIADES

But I can't wait.

SIMON

The nature of the art will perhaps seem extraordinary when you hear it.

TYCHIADES

Truly, that is just why I am keen to know about it.

SIMON

Some other day, Tychiades.

TYCHIADES

Oh, no! Tell me now—unless you are ashamed!

SIMON

Parasitic.

TYCHIADES

Really, would anyone who was not insane call that an art, Simon?

SIMON

I do; and if you think I am insane, think also that my insanity is the reason for my not knowing any other art and acquit me of your charges at once. They say, you know, that this malign spirit, cruel in all else to those whom she inhabits, at least secures them remission of their sins, like a schoolmaster or a tutor, by taking the blame for them upon herself.

TYCHIADES

Well then, Simon, Parasitic is an art?

ΣΙΜΩΝ

Τέχνη γάρ, κἀγὼ ταύτης δημιουργός.

ΤΥΧΙΑΔΗΣ

Καὶ σὺ ἄρα παράσιτος;

ΣΙΜΩΝ

Πάνυ ὠνείδισας, ὦ Τυχιάδη.

ΤΥΧΙΑΔΗΣ

Ἀλλ' οὐκ ἐρυθριᾷς παράσιτον σαυτὸν καλῶν;

ΣΙΜΩΝ

Οὐδαμῶς· αἰσχυνοίμην γὰρ ἄν, εἰ μὴ λέγοιμι.

ΤΥΧΙΑΔΗΣ

Καὶ νὴ Δία ὁπόταν σε βουλώμεθα γνωρίζειν τῶν οὐκ ἐπισταμένων τῳ, ὅτε χρῄζοι μαθεῖν, ὁ παράσιτος δῆλον ὅτι φήσομεν εὖ λέγοντες;[1]

ΣΙΜΩΝ

Πολὺ μᾶλλον τοῦτο λέγοντες ἐμὲ ἢ Φειδίαν ἀγαλματοποιόν· χαίρω γὰρ τῇ τέχνῃ οὐδέν τι ἧττον ἢ Φειδίας ἔχαιρε τῷ Διί.

ΤΥΧΙΑΔΗΣ

Καὶ μὴν ἐκεῖνό μοι σκοποῦντι προοῖσται γέλως πάμπολυς.

ΣΙΜΩΝ

Τὸ ποῖον;

ΤΥΧΙΑΔΗΣ

Εἴ γε καὶ[2] ταῖς ἐπιστολαῖς ἄνωθεν ὥσπερ ἔθος ἐπιγράφοιμεν, Σίμωνι παρασίτῳ.

[1] εὖ λέγοντες A.M.H.: not in MSS. Dindorf supplies εὐφρανεῖτε after ἐμὲ, below.

[2] εἴ γε καὶ Hirschig: εἰ ξέσαι MSS.

SIMON

Indeed it is, and I am a craftsman in it.[1]

TYCHIADES

Then you are a parasite?

SIMON

That was a cruel thrust, Tychiades!

TYCHIADES

But do not you blush to call yourself a parasite?

SIMON

Not at all; I should be ashamed not to speak it out.

TYCHIADES

Then, by Zeus, when we wish to tell about you to someone who does not know you, when he wants to find out about you, of course we shall be correct in referring to you as "the parasite"?

SIMON

Far more correct in referring to me so than in referring to Phidias as a sculptor, for I take quite as much joy in my art as Phidias did in his Zeus.

TYCHIADES

I say, here is a point; as I think of it, a gale of laughter has come over me!

SIMON

What is it?

TYCHIADES

What if we should address you in due form at the top of our letters as "Simon the Parasite"!

[1] In the word δημιουργός there is an allusion to the definition of Rhetoric as Πειθοῦς δημιουργός.

ΣΙΜΩΝ

Καὶ μὴν ἂν ἐμοὶ μᾶλλον χαρίζοιο ἢ Δίωνι ἐπιγράφων φιλοσόφῳ.

ΤΥΧΙΑΔΗΣ

3 Ἀλλὰ σὺ μὲν ὅπως χαίρεις καλούμενος, οὐδὲν ἢ μικρόν μοι μέλει· σκοπεῖν δὲ δεῖ καὶ τὴν ἄλλην ἀτοπίαν.

ΣΙΜΩΝ

Τίνα μήν;

ΤΥΧΙΑΔΗΣ

Εἰ καὶ ταύτην ταῖς ἄλλαις τέχναις ἐγκαταλέξομεν, ὥστε ἐπειδὰν πυνθάνηταί τις, ὁποία τις αὕτη τέχνη ἐστί, λέγειν, οἷον γραμματικὴ ἢ[1] ἰατρική, παρασιτική.

ΣΙΜΩΝ

Ἐγὼ μέν, ὦ Τυχιάδη, πολὺ μᾶλλον ταύτην ἤ τινα ἑτέραν τέχνην φαίην ἄν. εἰ δέ σοι φίλον ἀκούειν, καὶ ὅπως οἴομαι λέγοιμι ἄν, καίπερ οὐ παντάπασιν ὤν, ὡς ἔφθην εἰπών, ἐπὶ τοῦτο παρεσκευασμένος.

ΤΥΧΙΑΔΗΣ

Οὐθέν, εἰ καὶ σμικρὰ λέγοις,[2] ἀληθῆ δέ, διοίσει.

ΣΙΜΩΝ

Ἴθι δὴ πρῶτον, εἴ σοι δοκεῖ, περὶ τῆς τέχνης, ἥτις ποτὲ οὖσα τυγχάνει τῷ γένει, σκοπῶμεν· οὑτωσὶ γὰρ ἐπακολουθήσαιμεν ἂν καὶ ταῖς κατ' εἶδος τέχναις, εἴπερ ἄρα ὀρθῶς μετέχοιεν[3] αὐτῆς.

[1] ἢ Fritzsche : not in MSS.
[2] λέγοις Jacobs : δὲ τοῖς (δέ τοι, δέοι) MSS.
[3] μετέχοιεν Gesner : μετέχοιμεν MSS.

SIMON

Why, you would do me greater pleasure than you would Dion by addressing him as "the Philosopher."[1]

TYCHIADES

Well, how it pleases you to be styled matters little or nothing to me; but you must consider the general absurdity of it.

SIMON

What absurdity, I should like to know?

TYCHIADES

If we are to list this among the other arts, so that when anybody enquires what art it is, we shall say "Parasitic," to correspond with Music and Rhetoric.[2]

SIMON

For my part, Tychiades, I should call this an art far more than any other. If you care to listen, I think I can tell you why, although, as I just said, I am not entirely prepared for it.

TYCHIADES

It will make no difference at all if you say little, as long as that little is true.

SIMON

Come now, first of all, if it please you, let us consider what an art is in general; for in that way we can go on to the individual arts and see if they truly come under that head.

[1] Dion of Syracuse, the friend of Plato.

[2] The examples in the Greek are "Grammar and Medicine," but it was necessary to choose English examples which retained the Greek ending.

ΤΥΧΙΑΔΗΣ

Τί ποτ' οὖν ἐστιν ἡ τέχνη; πάντως[1] ἐπίστασαι.

ΣΙΜΩΝ

Πάνυ μὲν οὖν.

ΤΥΧΙΑΔΗΣ

Μὴ τοίνυν ὄκνει λέγειν αὐτήν, εἴπερ οἶσθα.

ΣΙΜΩΝ

4 Τέχνη ἐστίν, ὡς ἐγὼ διαμνημονεύω σοφοῦ τινος ἀκούσας, σύστημα ἐκ καταλήψεων συγγεγυμνασμένων πρός τι τέλος εὔχρηστον τῷ βίῳ.

ΤΥΧΙΑΔΗΣ

Ὀρθῶς ἐκεῖνός γε εἰπὼν σύ τε ἀπομνημονεύσας.[2]

ΣΙΜΩΝ

Εἰ δὲ μετέχοι τούτων ἁπάντων ἡ παρασιτική, τί ἂν ἄλλο ἢ καὶ αὐτὴ τέχνη εἴη;

ΤΥΧΙΑΔΗΣ

Τέχνη γάρ, εἴπερ οὕτως ἔχοι.

ΣΙΜΩΝ

Φέρε δὴ καθ' ἕκαστον τοῖς τῆς τέχνης εἴδεσιν ἐφαρμόζοντες τὴν παρασιτικήν, εἰ συνᾴδει σκοπῶμεν ἢ[3] ὁ περὶ αὐτῆς λόγος, καθάπερ αἱ πονηραὶ χύτραι διακρουόμεναι, σαθρὸν ἀποφθέγγεται.[4] δεῖ τοίνυν[5] πᾶσαν τέχνην σύστημα ἐκ καταλήψεων

[1] πάντως Seiler: πάνυ ὡς MSS.

[2] σύ τε ἀπομνημονεύσας A.M.H.: οὗτος ἀπομνημονεύσας Γ[1]; οὕτως ἀπεμνημόνευσας Γ[2], other MSS. Cf. ὀρθῶς σύ γε λέγων 7.

[3] ἢ Fritzsche: καὶ MSS.

[4] σαθρὸν (Seager) ἀποφθέγγεται Fritzsche: μὴ σαπρὸν ἀποφθέγγωνται (ἀποφθέγγηται) MSS.

[5] MSS. (except ΓΩ) insert εἶναι καὶ ταύτην ὥσπερ καὶ.

TYCHIADES

What on earth is an art, then? Surely you know.

SIMON

To be sure.

TYCHIADES

Then do not hesitate to tell, if you do know.

SIMON

An art, I remember to have heard a learned man say,[1] is a complex of knowledges exercised in combination to some end useful to the world.

TYCHIADES

He was quite right in what he said, and you in your recollection of it.

SIMON

If Parasitic satisfies this definition completely, what other conclusion could there be than that it is an art?

TYCHIADES

It would be an art, of course, if it should really be like that.

SIMON

Now then, let us apply to Parasitic the individual characteristics of an art and see whether it is in harmony with them or whether its theory, like a good-for-nothing pot when you try its ring, sounds cracked.[2] Every art, then, must be a complex of

[1] The particular learned man who said it first is not known to us. It is the orthodox Stoic definition, quoted repeatedly by Sextus Empiricus. Cf. Quint. 2, 17, 41 : ille ab omnibus fere probatus finis . . . artem constare ex perceptionibus consentientibus et coexercitatis ad finem utilem vitae.

[2] Just so Critolaus had tested rhetoric and found it wanting : see Philodemus, *Rhetoric* 2 ; Sextus, *Against the Rhetoricians* ; and Quintilian 2, 17.

. . . πρῶτον[1] μὲν τὸ δοκιμάζειν καὶ διακρίνειν ὅστις ἂν ἐπιτήδειος γένοιτο τρέφειν αὐτόν, καὶ ὅτῳ παρασιτεῖν ἀρξάμενος οὐκ ἂν μεταγνοίη. ἢ τὸν μὲν ἀργυρογνώμονα τέχνην τινὰ φήσομεν ἔχειν, εἴπερ ἐπίσταται διαγιγνώσκειν τά τε κίβδηλα τῶν νομισμάτων καὶ τὰ μή, τοῦτον δὲ ἄνευ τέχνης διακρίνειν τούς τε κιβδήλους τῶν ἀνθρώπων καὶ τοὺς ἀγαθούς, καὶ ταῦτα οὐχ[2] ὥσπερ τῶν νομισμάτων καὶ τῶν ἀνθρώπων φανερῶν εὐθὺς ὄντων; αὐτὰ μέντοι ταῦτα[3] καὶ ὁ σοφὸς Εὐριπίδης καταμέμφεται λέγων·

> ἀνδρῶν δ' ὅτῳ χρὴ τὸν κακὸν διειδέναι,
> οὐδεὶς χαρακτὴρ ἐμπέφυκε σώματι.

ᾧ δὴ καὶ μείζων[4] ἡ τοῦ παρασίτου τέχνη, ἥ γε καὶ τὰ οὕτως ἄδηλα καὶ ἀφανῆ μᾶλλον τῆς μαντικῆς γνωρίζει τε καὶ οἶδεν.

5 Τὸ δέ γε ἐπίστασθαι λόγους λέγειν ἐπιτηδείους καὶ πράγματα πράττειν δι' ὧν οἰκειώσεται καὶ εὐνούστατον ἑαυτὸν τῷ τρέφοντι ἀποδείξει, ἆρ' οὐ συνέσεως καὶ καταλήψεως ἐρρωμένης εἶναί σοι δοκεῖ;

ΤΥΧΙΑΔΗΣ

Καὶ μάλα.

ΣΙΜΩΝ

Τὸ δέ γε ἐν ταῖς ἑστιάσεσιν αὐταῖς ὅπως παντὸς ἀπέλθοι πλέον ἔχων καὶ παρευδοκιμῶν τοὺς μὴ τὴν αὐτὴν αὐτῷ κεκτημένους τέχνην, ἄνευ τινὸς λόγου καὶ σοφίας πράττεσθαι[5] οἴει;

[1] Lacuna Fritzsche: supply εἶναι· ὧν τῷ παρασίτῳ A.M.H.
[2] οὐχ vulg.: not in MSS.
[3] ταῦτα vulg.: αὐτὰ MSS.
[4] μείζων vulg.: μεῖζον MSS.
[5] πράττεσθαι vulg.: πλάττεσθαι MSS.

knowledges; and of these, in the case of the parasite, first of all there is testing and deciding who would be suitable to support him, and whom he could begin to cultivate without being sorry for it later. Or do we care to maintain that assayers possess an art because they know how to distinguish between coins that are counterfeit and those that are not, but parasites discriminate without art between men that are counterfeit and those that are good, even though men are not distinguishable at once, like coins? Wise Euripides criticizes this very point when he says:

> "In men, no mark whereby to tell the knave
> Did ever yet upon his body grow."[1]

This makes the parasite's art even greater, since it is better than divination at distinguishing and recognising things so obscure and hidden.

As for knowing how to talk appropriately and to act in such a way as to become intimate and show himself extremely devoted to his patron, do not you think that this shows intelligence and highly-developed knowledge?

TYCHIADES

Yes, indeed.

SIMON

And at banquets, to go away with more than anybody else, enjoying greater favour than those who do not possess the same art—do you think that can be managed without some degree of theory and wisdom?

[1] Euripides, *Medea* 518.

ΤΥΧΙΑΔΗΣ

Οὐδαμῶς.

ΣΙΜΩΝ

Τί δέ, τὸ ἐπίστασθαι τὰς ἀρετὰς καὶ κακίας τῶν σιτίων καὶ τῶν ὄψων πολυπραγμοσύνην ἀτέχνου τινὸς εἶναί σοι δοκεῖ, καὶ ταῦτα τοῦ γενναιοτάτου Πλάτωνος οὑτωσὶ λέγοντος, "Τοῦ μέλλοντος ἑστιάσεσθαι μὴ μαγειρικοῦ ὄντος, σκευαζομένης θοίνης ἀκυροτέρα ἡ κρίσις";

6 Ὅτι γε μὴν οὐκ ἐκ καταλήψεως μόνον, ἀλλὰ συγγεγυμνασμένης ἐστὶν ἡ παρασιτική, μάθοις ἂν ἐνθένδε ῥᾳδίως· αἱ μὲν γὰρ τῶν ἄλλων τεχνῶν καταλήψεις καὶ ἡμέρας καὶ νύκτας καὶ μῆνας καὶ ἐνιαυτοὺς πολλάκις ἀσυγγύμναστοι μένουσιν, καὶ ὅμως οὐκ ἀπόλλυνται παρὰ τοῖς κεκτημένοις αἱ τέχναι, ἡ δὲ τοῦ παρασίτου κατάληψις[1] εἰ μὴ καθ' ἡμέραν εἴη ἐν γυμνασίᾳ, ἀπόλλυσιν οὐ μόνον, οἶμαι, τὴν τέχνην, ἀλλὰ καὶ αὐτὸν τὸν τεχνίτην.

7 Τό γε μὴν "πρός τι τέλος εὔχρηστον τῷ βίῳ" μὴ καὶ μανίας ᾖ[2] ζητεῖν. ἐγὼ γὰρ τοῦ φαγεῖν καὶ τοῦ πιεῖν οὐδὲν εὐχρηστότερον εὑρίσκω ἐν τῷ βίῳ, ὧν[3] οὐδὲ ζῆν γε ἄνευ ἔστιν.

ΤΥΧΙΑΔΗΣ

Πάνυ μὲν οὖν.

ΣΙΜΩΝ

8 Καὶ μὴν οὐδὲ τοιοῦτόν τί ἐστιν ἡ παρασιτικὴ ὁποῖον τὸ κάλλος καὶ ἡ ἰσχύς, ὥστε τέχνην μὲν μὴ δοκεῖν αὐτήν, δύναμιν δέ τινα τοιαύτην.

[1] Text Fritzsche: αἱ δὲ τοῦ παρασίτου καταλήψεις MSS.
[2] ᾖ Jacobitz: εἴη MSS.
[3] ὧν Hirschig: ὃν MSS. which (except Γ¹Ω) insert τούτου before ἄνευ

TYCHIADES

Not by any means.

SIMON

What about knowing the merits and defects of bake-stuffs and made dishes? Does that seem to you matter for an untrained man's bumptious inquisitiveness? Yet excellent Plato says: "When a man is about to partake of a banquet, if he be not versed in the art of cookery, his opinion of the feast in preparation is something deficient in weight."[1]

That Parasitic is based not only on knowledge, but on exercised knowledge, you may readily assure yourself from this fact: the knowledges that belong to the other arts often remain unexercised for days and nights and months and years, and yet the arts are not lost to those who possess them; but if the parasite's knowledge is not in exercise daily, not only the art, I take it, but the artist himself, is lost thereby!

And as to its being "directed to some end useful to the world," it would be crazy, don't you think, to investigate that point. I, for my part, cannot discover that anything in the world is more useful than eating and drinking, and in fact without them it is impossible to live at all!

TYCHIADES

Quite so.

SIMON

Again, Parasitic is not the same sort of thing as beauty and strength, so as to be considered a gift, like them, rather than an art.[2]

[1] Plato, *Theaetetus* 178 D.

[2] Again a thrust at Rhetoric, which some considered "vis tantum"; cf. Quintilian 2, 15, 2.

ΤΥΧΙΑΔΗΣ

Ἀληθῆ λέγεις.

ΣΙΜΩΝ

Ἀλλὰ μέντοι οὐδὲ ἀτεχνία ἐστίν· ἡ γὰρ ἀτεχνία οὐδέποτε οὐδὲν κατορθοῖ τῷ κεκτημένῳ. φέρε γάρ, εἰ ἐπιτρέψειας[1] σὺ σεαυτῷ ναῦν ἐν θαλάττῃ καὶ χειμῶνι μὴ ἐπιστάμενος κυβερνᾶν, σωθείης ἄν;[2]

<ΤΥΧΙΑΔΗΣ>

<Οὐδαμῶς.>

<ΣΙΜΩΝ>

<Τί δ', εἰ ἵππους ἐπιτραφθείη τις μὴ ἐπιστάμενος ἡνιοχεῖν;>

ΤΥΧΙΑΔΗΣ

Οὐδ' οὗτος.

ΣΙΜΩΝ

Τί δή ποτε, ἢ τῷ μὴ ἔχειν τέχνην, δι' ἧς δυνήσεται σώζειν ἑαυτόν;

ΤΥΧΙΑΔΗΣ

Καὶ μάλα.

ΣΙΜΩΝ

Οὐκοῦν καὶ παράσιτος ὑπὸ τῆς παρασιτικῆς, εἴπερ ἦν ἀτεχνία, οὐκ ἂν ἐσώζετο;

ΤΥΧΙΑΔΗΣ

Ναί.

ΣΙΜΩΝ

Οὐκοῦν τέχνῃ σώζεται, ἀτεχνίᾳ δὲ οὔ;

ΤΥΧΙΑΔΗΣ

Πάνυ μὲν οὖν.

[1] ἐπιτρέψειας Hirschig: ἐπιτρέψας MSS.
[2] Lacuna Fritzsche: supplemented partly by Fritzsche, partly by A.M.H.

TYCHIADES

You are right.

SIMON

But on the other hand, it is not want of art; for want of art never achieves anything for its possessor.[1] For example, if you should put yourself in command of a ship at sea in a storm without knowing how to steer, should you come safely through?

TYCHIADES

Not by any means.

SIMON

How about a man who should take horses in hand without knowing how to drive?

TYCHIADES

He would not come through, either.

SIMON

Why, pray, except because he does not possess the art by which he would be able to save himself?

TYCHIADES

To be sure.

SIMON

Then the parasite would not be saved by Parasitic if it were want of art?

TYCHIADES

True.

SIMON

Then it is art that saves him, and not want of art?

TYCHIADES

Quite so.

[1] Rhetoric is a want of art: cf. § 27, and Quint. 2, 15, 2.

ΣΙΜΩΝ

Τέχνη ἄρα ἐστὶν ἡ παρασιτική.

ΤΥΧΙΑΔΗΣ

Τέχνη, ὡς ἔοικεν.

ΣΙΜΩΝ

Καὶ μὴν κυβερνήτας μὲν ἀγαθοὺς ναυαγίᾳ περιπεσόντας[1] καὶ ἡνιόχους τεχνίτας ἐκπεσόντας τῶν δίφρων οἶδα ἐγὼ πολλάκις, καὶ τοὺς μὲν συντριβέντας, τοὺς δὲ καὶ πάμπαν διαφθαρέντας, παρασίτου δὲ ναυάγιον οὐδὲ εἷς ἔχοι τοιοῦτον εἰπεῖν.

Οὐκοῦν εἰ μήτε ἀτεχνία ἐστὶν ἡ παρασιτικὴ μήτε δύναμις, σύστημα δέ τι ἐκ καταλήψεων γεγυμνασμένων, τέχνη δῆλον ὅτι διωμολόγηται ἡμῖν σήμερον.

ΤΥΧΙΑΔΗΣ

9 Ὅσον ἐκ τούτου εἰκάζω· ἀλλ' ἐκεῖνο, ὅπως καὶ ὅρον ἡμῖν τινα γενναῖον ἀποδῷς τῆς παρασιτικῆς.

ΣΙΜΩΝ

Ὀρθῶς σύ γε λέγων. δοκεῖ γὰρ δή μοι οὕτως ἂν μάλιστα ὡρίσθαι· παρασιτική ἐστιν τέχνη ποτέων καὶ βρωτέων καὶ τῶν διὰ ταῦτα λεκτέων καὶ πρακτέων,[2] τέλος δὲ αὐτῆς τὸ ἡδύ.

ΤΥΧΙΑΔΗΣ

Ὑπέρευγέ μοι δοκεῖς ὁρίσασθαι τὴν σεαυτοῦ τέχνην· ἀλλ' ἐκεῖνο σκόπει, μὴ πρὸς ἐνίους τῶν φιλοσόφων μάχη σοι περὶ τοῦ τέλους ᾖ.

[1] ναυαγίᾳ περιπεσόντας Fritzsche: not in MSS.
[2] καὶ πρακτέων Fritzsche: not in MSS.

SIMON

Then Parasitic is an art?

TYCHIADES

It is, apparently.

SIMON

I assure you I know of many instances when good helmsmen have been wrecked and expert drivers thrown from their seats, and some had broken bones, while others were completely done for; but nobody can cite any such mishap in the case of a parasite.

Then if Parasitic is not want of art and not a gift, but a complex of knowledges exercised in combination, evidently we have reached an agreement to-day that it is an art.

TYCHIADES

As far as I can judge from what has been said. But wait a bit: give us a first-class definition of Parasitic.

SIMON

Right. It seems to me that the definition might best be expressed thus: Parasitic is that art which is concerned with food and drink and what must be said and done to obtain them, and its end is pleasure.

TYCHIADES

That, to my mind, is a tip-top definition of your art; but look out that you do not get into conflict with some of the philosophers over the end.[1]

[1] With the Epicureans, who claimed the same *summum bonum*, and the Stoics, who rejected it. The Stoics are met first, with the argument that not virtue but Parasitic is the consummation of happiness. The sense of τέλος shifts slightly, to prepare for its use in the citation from Homer.

ΣΙΜΩΝ

Καὶ μὴν ἀπόχρη γε εἴπερ ἔσται τὸ αὐτὸ τέλος
10 εὐδαιμονίας καὶ παρασιτικῆς. φανεῖται δὲ οὕτως· ὁ γὰρ σοφὸς Ὅμηρος τὸν τοῦ παρασίτου βίον θαυμάζων ὡς ἄρα μακάριος καὶ ζηλωτὸς εἴη μόνος, οὕτω φησίν·[1]

οὐ γὰρ ἔγωγέ τί φημι τέλος χαριέστερον εἶναι,
ἢ ὅτ' ἂν εὐφροσύνη μὲν ἔχῃ κάτα δῆμον ἅπαντα,
δαιτυμόνες δ' ἀνὰ δώματ' ἀκουάζωνται ἀοιδοῦ
ἥμενοι ἑξείης,[2] παρὰ δὲ πλήθωσι τράπεζαι
σίτου καὶ κρειῶν, μέθυ δ' ἐκ κρητῆρος ἀφύσσων
οἰνοχόος φορέῃσι καὶ ἐγχείῃ δεπάεσσι.

καὶ ὡς οὐχ ἱκανῶς ταῦτα θαυμάζων μᾶλλον τὴν αὑτοῦ γνώμην ποιεῖ φανερωτέραν εὖ λέγων·

τοῦτό τί μοι κάλλιστον ἐνὶ φρεσὶν εἴδεται εἶναι,

οὐχ ἕτερόν τι, ἐξ ὧν φησιν, ἢ τὸ παρασιτεῖν εὔδαιμον νομίζων. καὶ μὴν οὐδὲ τῷ τυχόντι ἀνδρὶ περιτέθεικε τούτους τοὺς λόγους, ἀλλὰ τῷ σοφωτάτῳ τῶν ὅλων. καίτοι γε εἴπερ ἐβούλετο Ὀδυσσεὺς τὸ κατὰ τοὺς Στωϊκοὺς ἐπαινεῖν τέλος, ἐδύνατο ταυτὶ λέγειν ὅτε τὸν Φιλοκτήτην ἀνήγαγεν ἐκ τῆς Λήμνου, ὅτε τὸ Ἴλιον ἐξεπόρθησεν, ὅτε τοὺς Ἕλληνας φεύγοντας κατέσχεν, ὅτε εἰς Τροίαν εἰσῆλθεν ἑαυτὸν μαστιγώσας καὶ κακὰ καὶ Στωϊκὰ ῥάκη ἐνδύς· ἀλλὰ τότε οὐκ εἶπε

[1] οὕτω φησίν Fritzsche: not in MSS.
[2] δαιτυμόνες—ἑξείης not in MSS.: supplied by Cobet.

SIMON

It will be quite sufficient if I can show that happiness and Parasitic have the same end, and that will be plain from this: wise Homer, admiring the life of a parasite on the ground that it alone is blessed and enviable, says:

"I for my own part hold that there is no end more delightful
Than when cheerfulness reigneth supreme over all of the people;
Banqueters down the long halls give ear to the bard as he singeth,
Sitting in regular order, and by each man is a table
Laden with bread and with meat; while the server from out of the great bowl
Dippeth the mead, and beareth and poureth it into the beakers."[1]

And as if this were not enough to express his admiration, he makes his own opinion more evident, rightly saying:—

"This is a thing that to me in my heart doth seem very goodly."[2]

From what he says, he counts nothing else happy but to be a parasite. And it was no ordinary man to whom he ascribed these words, but the wisest of them all. After all, if Odysseus had wished to commend the Stoic end, he could have said so when he brought Philoctetes back from Lemnos, when he sacked Troy, when he checked the Greeks in their flight, when he entered Troy after flogging himself and putting on wretched Stoic rags; but on those

[1] *Odyssey* 9, 5 ff. [2] *Odyssey* 9, 11.

τοῦτο τέλος χαριέστερον. ἀλλὰ μὴν καὶ ἐν τῷ τῶν Ἐπικουρείων βίῳ γενόμενος αὖθις παρὰ τῇ Καλυψοῖ, ὅτε αὐτῷ ὑπῆρχεν ἐν ἀργίᾳ τε βιοτεύειν καὶ τρυφᾶν καὶ βινεῖν τὴν Ἄτλαντος θυγατέρα καὶ κινεῖν πάσας τὰς λείας κινήσεις, οὐδὲ τότε[1] εἶπε τοῦτο τὸ τέλος χαριέστερον, ἀλλὰ τὸν τῶν παρασίτων βίον. ἐκαλοῦντο δὲ δαιτυμόνες οἱ παράσιτοι τότε. πῶς οὖν λέγει; πάλιν γὰρ ἄξιον ἀναμνησθῆναι τῶν ἐπῶν· οὐδὲν γὰρ οἷον ἀκούειν αὐτῶν πολλάκις[2] λεγομένων· "δαιτυμόνες καθήμενοι ἑξείης·" καί·

> παρὰ δὲ πλήθωσι τράπεζαι
> σίτου καὶ κρειῶν.

11 Ὅ γε μὴν Ἐπίκουρος σφόδρα ἀναισχύντως ὑφελόμενος τὸ τῆς παρασιτικῆς τέλος τῆς καθ' αὑτὸν εὐδαιμονίας τέλος αὐτὸ ποιεῖ. καὶ ὅτι κλοπὴ τὸ πρᾶγμά ἐστιν καὶ οὐδὲν Ἐπικούρῳ μέλει τὸ ἡδύ, ἀλλὰ τῷ παρασίτῳ, οὕτω μάθοις ἄν. ἔγωγε ἡγοῦμαι τὸ ἡδὺ πρῶτον μὲν τὸ τῆς σαρκὸς ἀόχλητον, ἔπειτα τὸ μὴ θορύβου καὶ ταραχῆς τὴν ψυχὴν ἐμπεπλῆσθαι. τούτων τοίνυν ὁ μὲν παράσιτος ἑκατέρων τυγχάνει, ὁ δὲ Ἐπίκουρος οὐδὲ θατέρου· ὁ γὰρ ζητῶν περὶ σχήματος γῆς καὶ κόσμων ἀπειρίας καὶ μεγέθους ἡλίου καὶ ἀποστημάτων καὶ πρώτων στοιχείων καὶ περὶ θεῶν, εἴτε εἰσὶν εἴτε οὐκ εἰσί, καὶ περὶ αὐτοῦ τοῦ τέλους ἀεὶ πολεμῶν καὶ διαφερόμενος πρός τινας οὐ μόνον ἐν ἀνθρωπίναις, ἀλλὰ καὶ ἐν

[1] οὐδὲ τότε vulg.: οὐδέποτε MSS.

[2] Text anonymous friend of Cobet's: οἷόν τε ἀκούειν αὐτῶν μὴ πολλάκις MSS.

occasions he did not call that a more delightful end! Moreover, after he had entered into the Epicurean life once more in Calypso's isle, when he had it in his power to live in idleness and luxury, to dally with the daughter of Atlas, and to enjoy every pleasurable emotion, even then he did not call that end more delightful, but the life of a parasite, who at that time was called a banqueter. What does he say, then? It is worth while to cite his verses once more, for there is nothing like hearing them said over and over: "banqueters sitting in regular order," and:

"by each man is a table
Laden with bread and with meat."

As to Epicurus, quite shamelessly filching the end of Parasitic, he makes it the end of his conception of happiness. That the thing is plagiarism, and that pleasure does not concern Epicurus at all, but does concern the parasite, you can assure yourself from this line of reasoning. I for my part consider that pleasure is first of all the freedom of the flesh from discomfort, and secondly, not having the spirit full of turbulence and commotion. Now then, each of these things is attained by the parasite, but neither by Epicurus. For with his inquiries about the shape of the earth, the infinitude of the universe, the magnitude of the sun, distances in space, primal elements, and whether the gods exist or not, and with his continual strife and bickering with certain persons about the end itself, he is involved not only in the troubles

κοσμικαῖς ἐστιν ὀχλήσεσιν. ὁ δὲ παράσιτος πάντα καλῶς ἔχειν οἰόμενος καὶ πεπιστευκὼς μὴ ἄλλως ταῦτα ἔχειν ἄμεινον ἢ ἔχει, μετὰ πολλῆς ἀδείας καὶ γαλήνης, οὐδενὸς αὐτῷ τοιούτου παρενοχλοῦντος, ἐσθίει καὶ κοιμᾶται ὕπτιος ἀφεικὼς τοὺς πόδας καὶ τὰς χεῖρας ὥσπερ Ὀδυσσεὺς τῆς Σχερίας[1] ἀποπλέων οἴκαδε.

12 Καὶ μὴν οὐχὶ κατὰ ταῦτα μόνον οὐδὲν προσήκει τὸ ἡδὺ τῷ Ἐπικούρῳ, ἀλλὰ καὶ κατ' ἐκεῖνα· ὁ γὰρ Ἐπίκουρος οὗτος, ὅστις ποτέ ἐστιν ὁ σοφός, ἤτοι φαγεῖν ἔχει ἢ οὔ· εἰ μὲν οὐκ ἔχει, οὐχ ὅπως ἡδέως ζήσεται,[2] ἀλλ' οὐδὲ ζήσεται· εἰ δὲ ἔχει, εἴτε παρ' ἑαυτοῦ εἴτε παρ' ἄλλου· εἰ μὲν οὖν παρ' ἄλλου τὸ φαγεῖν ἔχοι, παράσιτός ἐστι καὶ οὐχ ὃς[3] λέγει· εἰ δὲ παρ' ἑαυτοῦ, οὐχ ἡδέως ζήσεται.

ΤΥΧΙΑΔΗΣ

Πῶς οὐχ ἡδέως;

ΣΙΜΩΝ

Εἰ γὰρ ἔχοι τὸ φαγεῖν παρ' ἑαυτοῦ, πολλά τοι, ὦ Τυχιάδη, τὰ ἀηδέα[4] τῷ τοιούτῳ βίῳ παρακολουθεῖν ἀνάγκη· καὶ ἄθρει πόσα. δεῖ τὸν μέλλοντα βιώσεσθαι καθ' ἡδονὴν τὰς ἐγγιγνομένας ὀρέξεις ἁπάσας ἀναπληροῦν. ἢ τί φής;

ΤΥΧΙΑΔΗΣ

Κἀμοὶ δοκεῖ.

ΣΙΜΩΝ

Οὐκοῦν τῷ μὲν συχνὰ κεκτημένῳ ἴσως τοῦτο παρέχει, τῷ δὲ ὀλίγα καὶ μηδὲν οὐκέτι· ὥστε

[1] τῆς Σχερίας du Soul : τῆς σχεδίας MSS.
[2] ζήσεται Cobet : οὐ ζήσεται MSS.
[3] ὃς vulg. : ὡς MSS. [4] τὰ ἀηδέα A.M.H. : not in MSS.

of man but in those of the universe. The parasite, however, thinking that everything is all right and thoroughly convinced it would not be any better if it were other than as it is, eats and sleeps in great peace and comfort, with nothing of that sort annoying him, flat on his back, with his arms and legs flung out, like Odysseus sailing home from Scheria.[1]

Again, it is not only in this way that pleasure is foreign to Epicurus, but in another way. This Epicurus, whoever the learned gentleman is, either has or has not his daily bread. Now if he has not, it is not a question of living a life of pleasure; he will not even live! But if he has, he gets it either from his own larder or that of someone else. Now if he gets his daily bread from someone else, he is a parasite and not what he calls himself; but if he gets it from his own larder, he will not lead a life of pleasure.

TYCHIADES

Why not?

SIMON

If he gets his daily bread from his own larder, many are the unpleasantnesses which must needs attend such a life, Tychiades! Just see how many! A man who intends to shape his life by pleasure should satisfy all the desires that arise in him. What do you say to that?

TYCHIADES

I agree with you.

SIMON

Therefore the man of vast means no doubt has the opportunity of doing so, while the man of little or no means has not; consequently a poor

[1] Cf. *Odyssey* 13, 79, and 92.

πένης οὐκ ἂν σοφὸς γένοιτο οὐδὲ ἐφίκοιτο τοῦ τέλους, λέγω δὴ τοῦ ἡδέος. ἀλλ' οὐδὲ μὴν ὁ πλούσιος, ὁ παρὰ τῆς οὐσίας ἀφθόνως ταῖς ἐπιθυμίαις χορηγῶν, δυνήσεται τοῦδε ἐφικέσθαι. τί δή ποτε; ὅτι πᾶσα ἀνάγκη τὸν ἀναλίσκοντα τὰ ἑαυτοῦ πολλαῖς περιπίπτειν ἀηδίαις, τοῦτο μὲν τῷ μαγείρῳ κακῶς σκευάσαντι τὸ ὄψον μαχόμενον ἢ εἰ μὴ μάχοιτο φαῦλα παρὰ τοῦτο ἐσθίοντα τὰ ὄψα καὶ τοῦ ἡδέος ὑστεροῦντα,[1] τοῦτο δὲ τῷ οἰκονομοῦντι τὰ κατὰ τὴν οἰκίαν, εἰ μὴ καλῶς οἰκονομοίη, μαχόμενον. ἢ οὐχ οὕτως;

ΤΥΧΙΑΔΗΣ

Νὴ Δία, κἀμοὶ δοκεῖ.

ΣΙΜΩΝ

Τῷ μὲν οὖν Ἐπικούρῳ πάντα συμβαίνειν εἰκός, ὥστε οὐδέποτε τεύξεται τοῦ τέλους· τῷ δὲ παρασίτῳ οὔτε μάγειρός ἐστιν ᾧ χαλεπῆναι, οὔτε ἀγρὸς οὔτε οἶκος[2] οὔτε ἀργύρια, ὑπὲρ ὧν ἀπολλυμένων ἀχθεσθείη, ὥστε καὶ φάγοι καὶ πίοι μόνος οὗτος ὑπὸ μηδενός, ὧν ἐκείνους ἀνάγκη, ἐνοχλούμενος.

13 Ἀλλ' ὅτι μὲν τέχνη ἐστὶν ἡ παρασιτική, κἀκ τούτων καὶ τῶν ἄλλων ἱκανῶς δέδεικται. λοιπὸν ὅτι καὶ ἀρίστη δεικτέον, καὶ τοῦτο οὐχ ἁπλῶς, ἀλλὰ πρῶτον μέν, ὅτι κοινῇ πασῶν διαφέρει τῶν τεχνῶν, εἶτα ὅτι καὶ ἰδίᾳ ἑκάστης.

Κοινῇ μὲν οὖν ἁπασῶν οὕτω διαφέρει· πάσης γὰρ τέχνης ἀνάγκη προάγειν μάθησιν πόνον φό-

[1] ὑστεροῦντα Seager: ὑστερεῖν MSS.
[2] οἶκος A.M.H.: οἰκονόμος MSS. Cf. 53.

man cannot become an adept or attain the end, that is to say, pleasure. Even the rich man, however, who through his wealth ministers lavishly to his desires, cannot attain that. Why? Because quite inevitably, when a man spends his money, he becomes involved in many an unpleasantness, at one moment quarrelling with his cook for preparing the meat badly—or else if he does not quarrel, eating poor food on that account and coming short of his pleasure—and the next moment quarrelling with the man who manages his household affairs, if he does not manage them well. Is not that so?

TYCHIADES

Yes, by Zeus, I agree with you.

SIMON

Now Epicurus is likely to have all this happen to him, so that he will never reach the end. But the parasite has no cook with whom to lose his temper, nor lands nor house nor money over the loss of which to be vexed, so that he alone can eat and drink without being annoyed by any of the matters which inevitably annoy the rich.

That Parasitic is an art has been well enough demonstrated by means of this argument and the others. It remains to show that it is the best art, and not simply this, but first that it excels all the other arts put together, and then that it excels each of them individually.

It excels all put together for this reason. Every art has to be prefaced by study, hardships, fear and

βον πληγάς, ἅπερ οὐκ ἔστιν ὅστις οὐκ ἂν ἀπεύξαιτο· ταύτην δὲ τὴν τέχνην, ὡς ἔοικεν, μόνην ἔξεστι μαθεῖν ἄνευ πόνου. τίς γὰρ ἀπὸ δείπνου ποτὲ ἀπῆλθεν κλαίων, ὥσπερ τινὰς ἐκ τῶν διδασκάλων ὁρῶμεν, τίς δ' ἐπὶ δεῖπνον ἀπιὼν ὤφθη σκυθρωπός, ὥσπερ οἱ εἰς διδασκαλεῖα φοιτῶντες; καὶ μὴν ὁ μὲν παράσιτος ἑκὼν αὐτὸς ἐπὶ δεῖπνον ἔρχεται μάλα ἐπιθυμῶν τῆς τέχνης, οἱ δὲ τὰς ἄλλας τέχνας μανθάνοντες μισοῦσιν αὐτάς, ὥστε ἔνιοι δι' αὐτὰς ἀποδιδράσκουσι.

Τί δέ, οὐ κἀκεῖνο ἐννοῆσαί σε δεῖ, ὅτι καὶ τοὺς ἐν ἐκείναις ταῖς τέχναις προκόπτοντας οἱ πατέρες καὶ μητέρες τούτοις τιμῶσι μάλιστα, οἷς καθ' ἡμέραν καὶ τὸν παράσιτον, "Καλῶς νὴ Δία ἔγραψεν ὁ παῖς," λέγοντες, "δότε αὐτῷ φαγεῖν·" "Οὐκ ἔγραψεν ὀρθῶς, μὴ δότε;" οὕτω τὸ πρᾶγμα καὶ ἔντιμον καὶ ἐν τιμωρίᾳ μέγα φαίνεται.

14 Καὶ μὴν αἱ ἄλλαι τέχναι τὸ τέλος[1] ὕστερον τοῦτο ἔχουσι, μετὰ τὸ μαθεῖν καὶ τοὺς καρποὺς ἡδέως ἀπολαμβάνουσαι·[2] πολλὴ γὰρ "καὶ ὄρθιος οἶμος ἐς αὐτάς·"[3] ἡ δὲ παρασιτικὴ μόνη τῶν ἄλλων εὐθὺς ἀπολαύει τῆς τέχνης ἐν αὐτῷ τῷ μανθάνειν, καὶ ἅμα τε ἄρχεται καὶ ἐν τῷ τέλει ἐστίν.

Καὶ[4] μέντοι τῶν ἄλλων τεχνῶν οὐ τινές, ἀλλὰ πᾶσαι ἐπὶ μόνην τὴν τροφὴν γεγόνασιν, ὁ δὲ παράσιτος εὐθὺς ἔχει τὴν τροφὴν ἅμα τῷ ἄρξασθαι τῆς τέχνης. ἢ οὐκ ἐννοεῖς ὅτι ὁ μὲν γεωργὸς

[1] τέλος Fritzsche : not in MSS.
[2] ἀπολαμβάνουσαι A.M.H. : ἀπολαμβάνουσι MSS.
[3] αὐτάς vulg. : αὐτήν MSS.
[4] καὶ vulg. : αἱ MSS.

floggings, from which everyone would pray to be delivered. But this art alone, it seems, can be learned without hardships. Who ever went home from a dinner in tears, as we see some going home from their schools? Who ever set out for a dinner looking gloomy, like those who go to school? I promise you, the parasite goes to dinner of his own accord, with a right good will to exercise his art, while those who are learning the other arts hate them so much that some run away from home on account of them!

Again, should you not note that when pupils make progress in those arts, their fathers and mothers give them as special rewards what they give the parasite every day? "By Zeus, the boy has written nicely," they say; "give him something to eat!" "He has not written correctly; don't give him anything!" So highly is the thing esteemed, both as a reward and by way of punishment.

Again, the other arts attain to this end late, reaping their harvest of pleasure only after their apprenticeship; for "the road to them leadeth uphill" and is long.[1] Parasitic alone of them all derives profit from the art immediately, in the apprenticeship itself, and no sooner does it begin than it is at its end.

Moreover, the other arts, not merely in certain cases but in every case, have come into existence to provide support and nothing else, while the parasite has his support immediately, as soon as he enters upon his art. Do not you see that while the farmer

[1] The quotation is from Hesiod, *Works and Days* 290, and refers to the road that leads to virtue. The scholasticus, the grey-headed student, was a familiar figure; see Lucian's *Hermotimus*.

γεωργεῖ οὐ τοῦ γεωργεῖν ἕνεκα καὶ ὁ τέκτων τεκταίνεται οὐχὶ τοῦ τεκταίνεσθαι ἕνεκα, ὁ δὲ παράσιτος οὐχ ἕτερον μέν τι διώκει, ἀλλὰ τὸ αὐτὸ καὶ ἔργον μέν ἐστιν αὐτοῦ καὶ οὗ ἕνεκα γίγνεται;

15 Καὶ μὴν ἐκεῖνά γε οὐδείς ἐστιν ὅστις οὐκ ἐπίσταται, ὅτι οἱ μὲν τὰς λοιπὰς τέχνας ἐργαζόμενοι τὸν μὲν ἄλλον χρόνον ταλαιπωροῦσι, μίαν δὲ ἢ δύο μόνας τοῦ μηνὸς ἡμέρας ἱερὰς ἄγουσι,[1] καὶ εὐφραίνεσθαι λέγονται τότε· ὁ δὲ παράσιτος τοῦ μηνὸς τὰς τριάκονθ' ἡμέρας ἱερὰς ἄγει· πᾶσαι γὰρ αὐτῷ δοκοῦσιν εἶναι τῶν θεῶν.

16 Ἔτι οἱ μὲν βουλόμενοι τὰς ἄλλας τέχνας κατορθοῦν ὀλιγοσιτίαις καὶ ὀλιγοποσίαις χρῶνται καθάπερ οἱ νοσοῦντες, πολυποσίαις δὲ καὶ πολυσιτίαις οὐκ ἔστιν εὐφραινόμενον μανθάνειν.

17 Καὶ αἱ μὲν ἄλλαι τέχναι χωρὶς ὀργάνων οὐδαμῶς τῷ κεκτημένῳ ὑπηρετεῖν δύνανται· οὔτε γὰρ αὐλεῖν ἔνι χωρὶς αὐλῶν οὔτε ψάλλειν ἄνευ λύρας οὔτε ἱππεύειν ἄνευ ἵππου· αὕτη δὲ οὕτως ἐστὶν ἀγαθὴ καὶ οὐ βαρεῖα τῷ τεχνίτῃ, ὥστε ὑπάρχει καὶ μηδὲν ἔχοντι ὅπλον χρῆσθαι αὐτῇ.

18 Καὶ ὡς ἔοικεν ἄλλας τέχνας μανθάνομεν μισθὸν διδόντες, ταύτην δὲ λαμβάνοντες. ἔτι τῶν μὲν 19 ἄλλων τεχνῶν εἰσι διδάσκαλοί τινες, τῆς δὲ παρασιτικῆς οὐδείς, ἀλλ' ὥσπερ ἡ ποιητικὴ κατὰ Σωκράτη καὶ αὕτη τινὶ θείᾳ μοίρᾳ παραγίγνεται. 20 κἀκεῖνο δὲ σκόπει, ὅτι τὰς μὲν ἄλλας τέχνας

[1] MSS. add. καὶ αἱ πόλεις δὲ τὰς μὲν δι' ἔτους, τὰς δὲ ἐμμήνους ἑορτὰς διατελοῦσι, excised by A.M.H. as a comment. Note also διατελοῦσι for τελοῦσι, or ἐπιτελοῦσι.

does not farm for the sake of farming, nor the builder build for the sake of building, the parasite does not aim at something different; his work and its object are one and the same thing.

Everybody knows, too, that those who ply the rest of the arts drudge all the time except one or two days a month which they celebrate as holidays,[1] and are said to have their good time then. But the parasite celebrates thirty holidays a month, for he thinks that every day belongs to the gods.

Furthermore, those who wish to be successful in the other arts eat little and drink little, like invalids, and it is impossible to learn them while one is rejoicing the inner man with plenty of food and plenty of wine.

The other arts, moreover, cannot be of use to their possessor without tools, for it is impossible to pipe without a pipe or to strum without a lyre or to ride without a horse; but this one is so genial and presents so little difficulty to the artisan that even one who has no tools can follow it.

And we pay, it is likely, for our lessons in the other arts, but get paid in this one. Besides, the other arts have teachers, but Parasitic has none; like the Art of Poetry according to the definition of Socrates, it comes by some divine dispensation.[2] Reflect, too, that we cannot exercise the other arts

[1] The manuscripts add: "and the cities too hold some feasts once a year and others once a month."

[2] Plato, *Ion* 534 B–C.

ὁδεύοντες ἢ πλέοντες οὐ δυνάμεθα διαπράττεσθαι, ταύτῃ[1] δέ ἐστι χρῆσθαι καὶ ἐν ὁδῷ καὶ πλέοντι.

ΤΥΧΙΑΔΗΣ

21 *Πάνυ μὲν οὖν.*

ΣΙΜΩΝ

Καὶ μέντοι, ὦ Τυχιάδη, αἱ μὲν ἄλλαι τέχναι δοκοῦσί μοι ταύτης ἐπιθυμεῖν, αὕτη δὲ οὐδεμιᾶς ἑτέρας.

ΤΥΧΙΑΔΗΣ

Τί δέ, οὐχ οἱ τὰ ἀλλότρια λαμβάνοντες ἀδικεῖν σοι δοκοῦσι;

ΣΙΜΩΝ

Πῶς γὰρ οὔ;

ΤΥΧΙΑΔΗΣ

Πῶς οὖν ὁ παράσιτος τὰ ἀλλότρια λαμβάνων οὐκ ἀδικεῖ μόνος;

ΣΙΜΩΝ

22 *Οὐκ ἔχω λέγειν. καὶ μὴν τῶν ἄλλων τεχνῶν αἱ ἀρχαὶ φαῦλαί τινες καὶ εὐτελεῖς εἰσι, τῆς δὲ παρασιτικῆς ἀρχὴ πάνυ γενναία τις· τὸ γὰρ θρυλούμενον τοῦτο τῆς φιλίας ὄνομα οὐκ ἂν ἄλλο τι εὕροις ἢ ἀρχὴν παρασιτικῆς.*

ΤΥΧΙΑΔΗΣ

Πῶς λέγεις;

ΣΙΜΩΝ

Ὅτι οὐδεὶς ἐχθρὸν ἢ ἀγνῶτα ἄνθρωπον ἀλλ' οὐδὲ συνήθη μετρίως ἐπὶ δεῖπνον καλεῖ, ἀλλὰ δεῖ

[1] *ταύτῃ* vulg.: *αὐτῇ* MSS.

---

[1] This point is not dwelt upon here because the author proposes to use it with great effect later at the expense of philosophy (§§ 31 ff.).

while on a journey or a voyage, but this one can be plied both on the road and at sea.

TYCHIADES

Quite true.

SIMON

Moreover, Tychiades, it seems to me that the other arts stand in need of this one, but this one does not stand in need of any other.[1]

TYCHIADES

But, I say, don't you think that people who take what belongs to someone else do wrong?

SIMON

Certainly.

TYCHIADES

How is it, then, that the parasite is the only one that does not do wrong in taking what belongs to someone else?

SIMON

I can't say![2]—Again, in the other arts the first steps are shabby and insignificant, but in Parasitic the first step is a very fine one, for friendship, that oft-lauded word, is nothing else, you will find, than the first step in Parasitic.

TYCHIADES

What do you mean?

SIMON

That nobody invites an enemy or an unknown person to dinner; not even a slight acquaintance. A

[2] Fritzsche gives the two questions to Simon and the answers to Tychiades, at the expense of a little rewriting. Perhaps he is right, but it is rather too bad to lose the humorous effect of the "I can't say" in the mouth of Simon, followed by the change of subject.

πρότερον οἶμαι τοῦτον γενέσθαι φίλον, ἵνα κοινωνήσῃ σπονδῶν καὶ τραπέζης καὶ τῶν τῆς τέχνης ταύτης μυστηρίων. ἐγὼ γοῦν πολλάκις ἤκουσά τινων λεγόντων, "Ποταπὸς δὲ οὗτος φίλος[1] ὅστις οὔτε βέβρωκεν οὔτε πέπωκεν μεθ' ἡμῶν," δῆλον ὅτι τὸν συμπίνοντα καὶ συνεσθίοντα μόνον πιστὸν φίλον ἡγουμένων.

23 Ὅτι γε μὴν ἡ βασιλικωτάτη τῶν τεχνῶν ἔστιν αὕτη, μάθοις ἂν καὶ ἐκ τοῦδε οὐχ ἥκιστα· τὰς μὲν γὰρ λοιπὰς τέχνας οὐ μόνον κακοπαθοῦντες καὶ ἱδροῦντες, ἀλλὰ νὴ Δία καθήμενοι καὶ ἑστῶτες ἐργάζονται ὥσπερ ἀμέλει δοῦλοι τῶν τεχνῶν, ὁ δὲ παράσιτος μεταχειρίζεται τὴν αὑτοῦ τέχνην ὡς βασιλεὺς κατακείμενος.

24 Ἐκεῖνα μὲν γὰρ τί δεῖ λέγειν περὶ τῆς εὐδαιμονίας αὐτοῦ, ὅτι δὴ μόνος κατὰ τὸν σοφὸν Ὅμηρον "οὔτε φυτεύει χερσὶ φυτὸν οὔτε ἀροῖ, ἀλλὰ τά γ'[2] ἄσπαρτα καὶ ἀνήροτα πάντα" νέμεται;

25 Καὶ μὴν ῥήτορά τε καὶ γεωμέτρην καὶ χαλκέα οὐδὲν κωλύει τὴν ἑαυτοῦ τέχνην ἐργάζεσθαι ἐάν τε πονηρὸς ἐάν τε καὶ μωρὸς ᾖ, παρασιτεῖν δὲ οὐδεὶς δύναται ἢ μωρὸς ὢν ἢ πονηρός.

ΤΥΧΙΑΔΗΣ

Παπαί, οἷον χρῆμα ἀποφαίνῃ τὴν παρασιτικήν· ὥστε καὶ αὐτὸς ἤδη βούλεσθαι δοκῶ μοι παράσιτος εἶναι ἀντὶ τούτου ὅς εἰμι.

ΣΙΜΩΝ

26 Ὡς μὲν τοίνυν κοινῇ πασῶν[3] διαφερει, δε-

[1] οὗτος φίλος Cobet: οὗτος ὁ φίλος MSS.
[2] γ' Dindorf: not in MSS.
[3] πασῶν Jacobitz: πάντων MSS.

man must first, I take it, become a friend in order to share another's bowl and board, and the mystic rites of this art. Anyhow, I have often heard people say: "How much of a friend is he, when he has neither eaten nor drunk with us?" That is of course because they think that only one who has shared their meat and drink is a trusty friend.

That in truth it is the most royal of the arts, you can infer from this fact above all: men work at the rest of them not only with discomfort and sweat but actually sitting or standing, just as if they were slaves to the arts, while the parasite plies his art lying down, like a king!

What need is there, in speaking of his felicity, to mention that he alone, according to wise Homer, "neither planteth a plant with his hands nor plougheth, but all, without sowing or ploughing,"[1] supply him with pasture?

Again, there is nothing to hinder a rhetorician or a geometer or a blacksmith from working at his trade whether he is a knave or a fool, but nobody can be a parasite who is either a knave or a fool.

TYCHIADES

Goodness! What a fine thing you make out Parasitic to be! I myself already want to be a parasite, I think, rather than what I am.

SIMON

Well, that it excels all put together, I think I

[1] *Odyssey* 9, 108–109.

δεῖχθαί μοι δοκῶ. φέρε δὴ ὡς καὶ κατ' ἰδίαν ἑκάστης διαφέρει σκοπῶμεν. τὸ μὲν δὴ ταῖς βαναύσοις τέχναις παραβάλλειν αὐτὴν ἀνόητόν ἐστιν, καὶ μᾶλλόν πως καθαιροῦντος τὸ ἀξίωμα τῆς τέχνης. ὅτι γε μὴν τῶν καλλίστων καὶ μεγίστων τεχνῶν διαφέρει δεικτέον. ὡμολόγηται δὴ πρὸς πάντων τήν τε ῥητορικὴν καὶ τὴν φιλοσοφίαν, ἃς διὰ γενναιότητα καὶ ἐπιστήμας ἀποφαίνονταί τινες, . . . ἐπειδὰν[1] καὶ τούτων ἀποδείξαιμι τὴν παρασιτικὴν πολὺ κρατοῦσαν, δῆλον ὅτι[2] τῶν ἄλλων τεχνῶν δόξει προφερεστάτη καθάπερ ἡ Ναυσικάα τῶν θεραπαινίδων.

27 Κοινῇ μὲν οὖν ἀμφοῖν διαφέρει καὶ τῆς ῥητορικῆς καὶ τῆς φιλοσοφίας, πρῶτον κατὰ τὴν ὑπόστασιν· ἡ μὲν γὰρ ὑφέστηκεν, αἱ δὲ οὔ. οὔτε γὰρ τὴν ῥητορικὴν ἕν τι καὶ τὸ αὐτὸ νομίζομεν, ἀλλ' οἱ μὲν τέχνην, οἱ δὲ τοὐναντίον ἀτεχνίαν, ἄλλοι δὲ κακοτεχνίαν, ἄλλοι δὲ ἄλλο τι. ὁμοίως δὲ καὶ τὴν φιλοσοφίαν οὐ[3] κατὰ τὰ αὐτὰ καὶ ὡσαύτως ἔχουσαν, ἑτέρως μὲν γὰρ Ἐπικούρῳ δοκεῖ τὰ πράγματα ἔχειν, ἑτέρως δὲ τοῖς ἀπὸ τῆς Στοᾶς, ἑτέρως δὲ τοῖς ἀπὸ τῆς Ἀκαδημίας, ἑτέρως δὲ τοῖς ἀπὸ τοῦ Περιπάτου, καὶ ἁπλῶς ἄλλος ἄλλην ἀξιοῖ τὴν φιλοσοφίαν εἶναι· καὶ μέχρι γε νῦν οὔτε οἱ αὐτοὶ γνώμης κρατοῦσιν οὔτε αὐτῶν ἡ τέχνη μία φαίνεται. ἐξ ὧν δῆλον ὅ τι τεκμαίρεσθαι καταλείπεται. ἀρχὴν γάρ φημι μηδὲ[4] εἶναι τέχνην ἧς οὐκ ἔστιν ὑπόστασις. ἐπεὶ τί δή

[1] Lacuna Dindorf: ἐπειδὰν (ἐπειδὰν γοῦν) also is corrupt. μεγίστας εἶναι, ὥστε εἰ gives the required sense.
[2] δῆλον ὅτι vulg.: σχολῇ δῆλον ὅτι MSS.
[3] οὐ Cobet, Ψ (?): not in other MSS.
[4] μηδὲ vulg.: μήτε MSS.

have demonstrated. Come now, let us see how it excels each individually. To compare it with the vulgar arts is silly, and, in a way, more appropriate to someone who is trying to belittle its dignity. We must prove that it excels the finest and greatest of them. It is universally admitted that rhetoric and philosophy, which some people even make out to be sciences because of their nobility, are the greatest. Therefore, if I should prove that Parasitic is far superior to these, obviously it will appear preeminent among the other arts, like Nausicaa among her handmaidens.[1]

It excels both rhetoric and philosophy, in the first place in its objective reality; for it has this, and they have not. We do not hold one and the same view about rhetoric; some of us call it an art, some a want of art, others a depraved art, and others something else. So too with philosophy, which is not uniform and consistent; for Epicurus has on opinion about things, the Stoics another, the Academics another, the Peripatetics another; in brief, everybody claims that philosophy is something different, and up to now, at all events, it cannot be said either that the same men control opinion or that their art is one. By this it is clear what conclusion remains to be drawn. I maintain that there can be no art at all which has not objective reality. For how else can you

[1] *Odyssey* 6, 102–109.

ποτε ἀριθμητικὴ μὲν μία ἐστὶ καὶ ἡ αὐτὴ[1] καὶ δὶς δύο παρά τε[2] ἡμῖν καὶ παρὰ Πέρσαις τέσσαρά ἐστιν καὶ συμφωνεῖ ταῦτα καὶ παρὰ Ἕλλησι καὶ βαρβάροις, φιλοσοφίας δὲ πολλὰς καὶ διαφόρους ὁρῶμεν καὶ οὔτε τὰς ἀρχὰς οὔτε τὰ τέλη σύμφωνα πασῶν;

ΤΥΧΙΑΔΗΣ

Ἀληθῆ λέγεις· μίαν μὲν γὰρ τὴν φιλοσοφίαν εἶναι λέγουσιν, αὐτοὶ δὲ αὐτὴν[3] ποιοῦσι πολλάς.

ΣΙΜΩΝ

28 Καὶ μὴν καὶ τὰς μὲν ἄλλας τέχνας, εἰ καί τι κατὰ ταύτας ἀσύμφωνον εἴη, κἂν παρέλθοι τις συγγνώμης ἀξιώσας, ἐπεὶ μέσαι τε δοκοῦσι καὶ αἱ καταλήψεις αὐτῶν οὐκ εἰσὶν ἀμετάπτωτοι.[4] φιλοσοφίαν δὲ τίς ἂν καὶ[5] ἀνάσχοιτο μὴ μίαν εἶναι καὶ μηδὲ σύμφωνον αὐτὴν ἑαυτῇ μᾶλλον τῶν ὀργάνων; μία μὲν οὖν οὐκ ἔστι φιλοσοφία, ἐπειδὴ ὁρῶ καὶ ἄπειρον οὖσαν· πολλαὶ δὲ οὐ δύνανται εἶναι, ἐπειδήπερ ἡ σοφία[6] μία.

29 Ὁμοίως δὲ καὶ περὶ τῆς ὑποστάσεως τῆς ῥητορικῆς ταὐτὰ φαίη τις ἄν· τὸ γὰρ περὶ ἑνὸς προκειμένου ταὐτὰ μὴ λέγειν ἅπαντας, ἀλλὰ μάχην εἶναι φορᾶς ἀντιδόξου, ἀπόδειξις μεγίστη τοῦ μηδὲ ἀρχὴν εἶναι τοῦτο οὗ μία κατάληψις οὐκ ἔστιν· τὸ γὰρ ζητεῖν τό, τί μᾶλλον αὐτό[7]

[1] καὶ ἡ αὐτὴ vulg.: καὶ αὐτὴ MSS.
[2] τε vulg.: γε MSS.
[3] αὐτὴν Cobet's anonymous friend : αὐτὰς MSS.
[4] MSS. (except Ω) add : προσδεκτέος ἂν εἴη.
[5] ἂν καὶ vulg.: ἀναγκαῖαν MSS.

explain it that arithmetic is one and the same, and twice two is four not only here but in Persia, and all its doctrines are in tune not only in Greece but in strange lands, yet we see many different philosophies, all of them out of tune both in their beginnings and in their ends?

TYCHIADES

You are right: they say philosophy is one, but they themselves make it many.

SIMON

As far as the other arts are concerned, if there should be some discord in them, one might pass it over, thinking it excusable, since they are subordinate and their knowledges are not exempt from change. But who could endure that philosophy should not be one, and in better tune with itself than a musical instrument? Well now, philosophy is not one, for I see that it is infinitely many; yet it cannot be many, for wisdom is one.

The same can be said, too, of the objective reality of rhetoric. When all do not express the same views about one subject, but there is a battle royal of contradictory declarations, that is the greatest proof that the subject of which there is not a single definite conception does not exist at all; for to enquire whether it is this rather than that, and never to agree

[6] σοφία Cobet's friend: φιλοσοφία MSS.
[7] αὐτό Halm: αὐτῶν MSS.

ἐστιν, καὶ τὸ μηδέποτε ὁμολογεῖν ἓν[1] εἶναι, τοῦτο αὐτὴν ἀναιρεῖ τοῦ ζητουμένου τὴν οὐσίαν.

30 Ἡ μέντοι παρασιτικὴ οὐχ οὕτως ἔχει, ἀλλὰ καὶ ἐν Ἕλλησι καὶ βαρβάροις μία ἐστὶν καὶ κατὰ ταὐτὰ καὶ ὡσαύτως, καὶ οὐκ ἂν εἴποι τις ἄλλως μὲν τούσδε, ἑτέρως δὲ τούσδε παρασιτεῖν, οὐδέ εἰσιν ὡς ἔοικεν ἐν παρασίτοις[2] τινες οἷον Στωϊκοὶ ἢ Ἐπικούρειοι δόγματα ἔχοντες διάφορα, ἀλλὰ πᾶσι πρὸς ἅπαντας ὁμολογία τίς ἐστιν καὶ συμφωνία τῶν ἔργων καὶ τοῦ τέλους. ὥστε ἔμοιγε δοκεῖ ἡ παρασιτικὴ κινδυνεύειν κατά γε τοῦτο καὶ σοφία εἶναι.

ΤΥΧΙΑΔΗΣ

31 Πάνυ μοι δοκεῖς ἱκανῶς ταῦτα εἰρηκέναι. ὡς δὲ καὶ τὰ ἄλλα χείρων ἐστὶν ἡ φιλοσοφία τῆς σῆς τέχνης, πῶς ἀποδεικνύεις;

ΣΙΜΩΝ

Οὐκοῦν ἀνάγκη πρῶτον εἰπεῖν ὅτι φιλοσοφίας μὲν οὐδέποτε ἠράσθη παράσιτος, παρασιτικῆς δὲ πάμπολλοι ἐπιθυμήσαντες μνημονεύονται φιλόσοφοι, καὶ μέχρι γε νῦν ἐρῶσιν.

ΤΥΧΙΑΔΗΣ

Καὶ τίνας ἂν ἔχοις εἰπεῖν φιλοσόφους παρασιτεῖν σπουδάσαντας;

ΣΙΜΩΝ

Οὕστινας μέντοι, ὦ Τυχιάδη; οὓς καὶ σὺ γιγνώσκων ὑποκρίνῃ ἀγνοεῖν κἀμὲ κατασοφίζῃ ὡς[3]

[1] ἓν Fritzsche: ἂν Γ¹Ω, μιαν Γ², other MSS.
[2] ἐν παρασίτοις A.M.H.: παρασίτοις MSS. Cf. *Gallus* 27 fin. ἐν ἐκείνοις.
[3] κἀμὲ κατασοφίζῃ ὡς Fritzsche: κἀμὲ κατὰ Γ¹Ω, κἀμὲ ὡς Γ², other MSS.

that it is one, does away with the very existence of the subject that is questioned.

This is not the case, however, with Parasitic. Both among Greeks and among foreigners it is one and uniform and consistent, and nobody can say that it is practised in one way by this set of men and in another by that set. Nor are there, it seems, among parasites any sects like the Stoics or the Epicureans, holding different doctrines; no, there is concord among them all, and agreement in their works and in their end. So to my thinking Parasitic may well be, in this respect at least, actually wisdom.

TYCHIADES

It seems to me that you have put all this very well. But how do you prove that philosophy is inferior to your art in other ways?

SIMON

Well, it must first be mentioned that no parasite ever fell in love with philosophy; but it is on record that philosophers in great number have been fond of Parasitic, and even to-day they love it!

TYCHIADES

Why, what philosophers can you mention that have been eager to play parasite?

SIMON

What philosophers, Tychiades? Though you know them yourself, you pretend not to, and try to pull

τινος αὐτοῖς αἰσχύνης ἐντεῦθεν γιγνομένης, οὐχὶ τιμῆς.

ΤΥΧΙΑΔΗΣ

Οὐ μὰ τὸν Δία, ὦ Σίμων, ἀλλὰ καὶ σφόδρα ἀπορῶ οὕστινας καὶ εὕροις εἰπεῖν.

ΣΙΜΩΝ

Ὦ γενναῖε, σύ μοι δοκεῖς ἀνήκοος εἶναι καὶ τῶν ἀναγραψάντων τοὺς ἐκείνων βίους, ἐπεὶ πάντως ἂν καὶ ἐπιγνῶναι οὕστινας λέγω δύναιο.

ΤΥΧΙΑΔΗΣ

Καὶ μέντοι νὴ τὸν Ἡρακλέα ποθῶ δὴ ἀκούειν τίνες εἰσίν.

ΣΙΜΩΝ

Ἐγώ σοι καταλέξω αὐτοὺς ὄντας οὐχὶ τοὺς φαύλους, ἀλλ' ὡς[1] ἐγὼ δοκῶ, τοὺς ἀρίστους καὶ 32 οὓς ἥκιστα σὺ οἴει. Αἰσχίνης μέντοι ὁ Σωκρατικός, οὗτος ὁ τοὺς μακροὺς καὶ ἀστείους διαλόγους γράψας, ἧκέν ποτε εἰς Σικελίαν κομίζων αὐτούς, εἴ πως[2] δύναιτο δι' αὐτῶν γνωσθῆναι Διονυσίῳ τῷ τυράννῳ, καὶ τὸν Μιλτιάδην ἀναγνοὺς καὶ δόξας εὐδοκιμηκέναι λοιπὸν ἐκάθητο ἐν Σικελίᾳ παρασιτῶν Διονυσίῳ καὶ ταῖς Σωκράτους 33 διατριβαῖς ἐρρῶσθαι φράσας. τί δέ, καὶ Ἀρίστιππος ὁ Κυρηναῖος οὐχὶ τῶν δοκίμων φαίνεταί σοι φιλοσόφων;

ΤΥΧΙΑΔΗΣ

Καὶ πανυ.

ΣΙΜΩΝ

Καὶ οὗτος μέντοι κατὰ τὸν αὐτὸν χρόνον διέτριβεν ἐν Συρακούσαις παρασιτῶν Διονυσίῳ.

[1] ὡς Gesner: ὧν MSS. [2] εἴ πως Dindorf: ὅπως MSS.

the wool over my eyes, as if it brought them disgrace instead of honour!

TYCHIADES

No, by Zeus, Simon; I am very much at a loss as to whom you can find to mention.

SIMON

My dear fellow, you seem to be unfamiliar with their biographers, as otherwise you would certainly be able to recognize whom I mean.

TYCHIADES

Well, anyhow, by Heracles, I long to find out now who they are.

SIMON

I shall give you a list of them, and they are not the riff-raff, but in my opinion the best, and those whom you would least expect. Aeschines the Socratic, the man who wrote the long and witty dialogues, once went to Sicily, taking them with him, in the hope that through them he might be able to get acquainted with Dionysius the tyrant; and after he had read his "Miltiades" and was considered to have made a hit, he made himself at home in Sicily from then on, playing parasite to the tyrant and bidding adieu to the haunts of Socrates. And what about Aristippus of Cyrene? Is he not in your opinion one of the philosophers of distinction?

TYCHIADES

Very much so.

SIMON

But he too lived in Syracuse at about the same time, playing parasite to Dionysius. In fact, of all

πάντων γοῦν ἀμέλει τῶν παρασίτων αὐτὸς ηὐδοκίμει παρ' αὐτῷ· καὶ γὰρ ἦν πλέον τι τῶν ἄλλων πρὸς τὴν τέχνην εὐφυής, ὥστε τοὺς ὀψοποιοὺς ὁσημέραι ἔπεμπεν παρὰ τοῦτον ὁ Διονύσιος ὥς τι παρ' αὐτοῦ μαθησομένους.

Οὗτος μέντοι δοκεῖ καὶ κοσμῆσαι τὴν τέχνην 34 ἀξίως. ὁ δὲ Πλάτων ὑμῶν ὁ γενναιότατος καὶ αὐτὸς μὲν ἧκεν εἰς Σικελίαν ἐπὶ τούτῳ, καὶ ὀλίγας παρασιτήσας ἡμέρας τῷ τυράννῳ τοῦ παρασιτεῖν ὑπὸ ἀφυΐας ἐξέπεσε, καὶ πάλιν Ἀθήναζε ἀφικόμενος καὶ φιλοπονήσας καὶ παρασκευάσας ἑαυτὸν αὖθις δευτέρῳ στόλῳ ἐπέπλευσε τῇ Σικελίᾳ καὶ δειπνήσας πάλιν ὀλίγας ἡμέρας ὑπὸ ἀμαθίας ἐξέπεσε· καὶ αὕτη ἡ συμφορὰ Πλάτωνι περὶ Σικελίαν ὁμοία δοκεῖ γενέσθαι τῇ Νικίου.

ΤΥΧΙΑΔΗΣ

Καὶ τίς, ὦ Σίμων, περὶ τούτου λέγει;

ΣΙΜΩΝ

35 Πολλοὶ μὲν καὶ ἄλλοι, Ἀριστόξενος δὲ ὁ μουσικός, πολλοῦ λόγου ἄξιος.[1]

Εὐριπίδης μὲν γὰρ ὅτι Ἀρχελάῳ μέχρι μὲν τοῦ θανάτου παρεσίτει καὶ Ἀνάξαρχος Ἀλε-36 ξάνδρῳ πάντως ἐπίστασαι. καὶ Ἀριστοτέλης δὲ τῆς παρασιτικῆς ἤρξατο μόνον ὥσπερ καὶ τῶν ἄλλων τεχνῶν.

37 Φιλοσόφους μὲν οὖν, ὥσπερ ἦν, παρασιτεῖν[2] σπουδάσαντας ἔδειξα· παράσιτον δὲ οὐδεὶς ἔχει φράσαι φιλοσοφεῖν ἐθελήσαντα.

[1] MSS. add: καὶ αὐτὸς δὲ παράσιτος Νηλέως ἦν, excised by Cobet. Dindorf, referring it to Aristotle, sets it after τεχνῶν.
[2] παρασιτεῖν du Soul: παρασιτίᾳ MSS.

the parasites he was in highest favour with him, being, to be sure, somewhat more gifted for the art than the rest of them, so that Dionysius sent his cooks to him every day, to learn something from him.

Aristippus, indeed, appears to have been a worthy ornament to the art; but your most noble Plato also came to Sicily for this purpose, and after being parasite to the tyrant only a few days, was turned out of his place as parasite on account of ineptitude. Then, after going back to Athens and working hard and preparing himself, he cruised once more to Sicily on a second venture, and again, after only a few days of dining, was turned out on account of stupidity; and this "Sicilian disaster" of Plato's is considered equal to that of Nicias.

TYCHIADES

Why, who tells about this, Simon?

SIMON

A great many; among them, Aristoxenus the musician, who deserves great consideration.[1]

That Euripides was parasite to Archelaus until he died, and Anaxarchus to Alexander, you surely know. As to Aristotle, he only made a beginning in Parasitic, as in every other art.

I have shown that, as I said, philosophers have been eager to play parasite; but nobody can instance a parasite who has cared to practise philosophy.

[1] The MSS. add: "and he himself was parasite to Neleus." Both were pupils of Aristotle. Aristoxenus wrote a life of Plato, which was used by Diogenes Laertius.

38 Καὶ μέντοι εἰ ἔστιν εὔδαιμον τὸ μὴ πεινῆν μηδὲ διψῆν μηδὲ ῥιγοῦν, ταῦτα οὐδενὶ ἄλλῳ ὑπάρχει ἢ παρασίτῳ. ὥστε φιλοσόφους μὲν ἄν τις πολλοὺς καὶ ῥιγοῦντας καὶ πεινῶντας εὕροι, παράσιτον δὲ οὔ· ἢ οὐκ ἂν εἴη παράσιτος, ἀλλὰ δυστυχής τις καὶ[1] πτωχὸς ἄνθρωπος καὶ[1] φιλοσόφῳ ὅμοιος.

ΤΥΧΙΑΔΗΣ

39 Ἱκανῶς ταῦτά γε. ὅτι δὲ κατὰ τἄλλα[2] διαφέρει φιλοσοφίας καὶ ῥητορικῆς ἡ παρασιτικὴ πῶς ἐπιδεικνύεις;

ΣΙΜΩΝ

Εἰσίν, ὦ βέλτιστε, καιροὶ τοῦ τῶν ἀνθρώπων βίου, ὁ μέν τις εἰρήνης, οἶμαι, ὁ δ' αὖ πολέμου. ἐν δὴ τούτοις πᾶσα ἀνάγκη φανερὰς γίγνεσθαι τὰς τέχνας καὶ τοὺς ἔχοντας ταύτας ὁποῖοί τινές εἰσιν. πρότερον δέ, εἰ δοκεῖ, σκοπώμεθα τὸν τοῦ πολέμου καιρόν, καὶ τίνες ἂν εἶεν μάλιστα χρησιμώτατοι ἰδίᾳ τε ἕκαστος αὑτῷ καὶ κοινῇ τῇ πόλει.

ΤΥΧΙΑΔΗΣ

Ὡς οὐ μέτριον ἀγῶνα καταγγέλλεις τῶν ἀνδρῶν· καὶ ἔγωγε πάλαι γελῶ κατ' ἐμαυτὸν ἐννοῶν ποῖος ἂν εἴη συμβαλλόμενος παρασίτῳ φιλόσοφος.

ΣΙΜΩΝ

40 Ἵνα τοίνυν μὴ πάνυ θαυμάζῃς μηδὲ τὸ πρᾶγμά σοι δοκῇ χλεύης ἄξιον, φέρε προτυπωσώμεθα παρ' ἡμῖν αὐτοῖς ἠγγέλθαι μὲν αἰφνίδιον εἰς τὴν χώραν ἐμβεβληκέναι πολεμίους, εἶναι δὲ ἀνάγκην

[1] καὶ A.M.H.: ἢ MSS.
[2] τἄλλα Fritzsche: πολλὰ MSS.

Furthermore, if happiness lies in not hungering or thirsting or shivering, nobody has this in his power except the parasite. Consequently you can find many cold and hungry philosophers, but never a parasite; otherwise he would not be a parasite, but an unfortunate beggar fellow, resembling a philosopher.

TYCHIADES

You have been sufficiently explicit on that score. But how do you prove that Parasitic excels philosophy and rhetoric in other respects?

SIMON

There are seasons, my dear fellow, in the life of man, seasons of peace, I take it, and again seasons of war. Well, in those seasons it is absolutely inevitable that the arts and those who possess them should show what they are. First, if you please, let us consider the season of war, and what class of men would be above all most useful to themselves individually and to the state in general.

TYCHIADES

What a searching test of manhood you are announcing! I have long been laughing inwardly to think how a philosopher would look in comparison with a parasite.

SIMON

Then in order to prevent you from wondering too much and also from thinking it a laughing matter, let us imagine that right here in our city proclamation has been made that the enemy has unexpectedly invaded the country; that it is

ἐπεξιέναι καὶ μὴ περιορᾶν ἔξω δηουμένην τὴν γῆν, τὸν στρατηγὸν δὲ παραγγέλλειν ἅπαντας εἰς τὸν κατάλογον τοὺς ἐν ἡλικίᾳ, καὶ δὴ χωρεῖν τοὺς ἄλλους, ἐν δὲ δὴ τούτοις φιλοσόφους τινὰς καὶ ῥήτορας καὶ παρασίτους. πρῶτον τοίνυν ἀποδύσωμεν αὐτούς· ἀνάγκη γὰρ τοὺς μέλλοντας ὁπλίζεσθαι γυμνοῦσθαι πρότερον. θεῶ δὴ τοὺς ἄνδρας, ὦ γενναῖε, καθ' ἕκαστον καὶ δοκίμαζε τὰ σώματα. τοὺς μὲν τοίνυν αὐτῶν ὑπὸ ἐνδείας ἴδοις ἂν λεπτοὺς καὶ ὠχρούς, πεφρικότας, ὥσπερ ἤδη τραυματίας παρειμένους· ἀγῶνα μὲν γὰρ καὶ μάχην σταδιαίαν καὶ ὠθισμὸν καὶ κόνιν καὶ τραύματα μὴ γελοῖον ᾖ λέγειν δύνασθαι φέρειν ἀνθρώπους ὥσπερ ἐκείνους τινὸς δεομένους ἀναλήψεως.

41 ἄθρει δὲ πάλιν μεταβὰς τὸν παράσιτον ὁποῖός τις φαίνεται. ἆρ' οὐχ ὁ μὲν τὸ σῶμα πρῶτον πολὺς καὶ τὸ χρῶμα ἡδύς, οὐ μέλας δὲ οὐδὲ λευκός—τὸ μὲν γὰρ γυναικί, τὸ δὲ δούλῳ προσέοικεν—ἔπειτα θυμοειδής, δεινὸν βλέπων ὁποῖον ἡμεῖς, μέγα καὶ ὕφαιμον; οὐ γὰρ καλὸν δεδοικότα καὶ θῆλυν ὀφθαλμὸν εἰς πόλεμον φέρειν. ἆρ' οὐχ ὁ τοιοῦτος καλὸς μὲν γένοιτ' ἂν καὶ ζῶν ὁπλίτης, καλὸς δὲ καὶ εἰ ἀποθάνοι νεκρός;[1]

42 Ἀλλὰ τί δεῖ ταῦτα εἰκάζειν ἔχοντας αὐτῶν παραδείγματα; ἁπλῶς γὰρ εἰπεῖν, ἐν πολέμῳ τῶν πώποτε ῥητόρων ἢ φιλοσόφων οἱ μὲν οὐδὲ ὅλως ὑπέμειναν ἔξω τοῦ τείχους προελθεῖν, εἰ δέ τις καὶ ἀναγκασθεὶς παρετάξατο, φημὶ τοῦτον λείψαντα τὴν τάξιν ὑποστρέφειν.

[1] νεκρός A.M.H.: καλῶς MSS. Sommerbrodt excises καλῶς.

necessary to take the field against them and not allow the farm-lands outside the walls to be laid waste, that the commander has called to the colours all those of military age, and that of course everybody is going, including certain philosophers and rhetoricians and parasites. First, then, let us strip them to the skin; for those who are going to put on armour must first take off their clothes. Now inspect your men, sir, one by one, and give them a physical examination. Some of them you can see to be thin and pale through privation, shuddering, and as limp as if they had already been wounded. Surely it would be ridiculous to say that fighting, hand-to-hand combat, pushing, dust, and wounds can be borne by men like these, who need something to brace them up! Pass on, and now see how the parasite looks! In the first place, is he not generous in his proportions and pleasing in his complexion, neither dark nor fair of skin; for the one befits a woman, and the other a slave; and besides, has he not a spirited look, with a fiery glance like mine, high and bloodshot? It is not becoming, you know, to go into battle with a timorous and womanish eye. Would not such a man make a fine soldier in life and a fine corpse if he should die? [1]

But what is the good of guessing about all this, when we have historical examples? To put it briefly, in war, of all the rhetoricians and philosophers that ever were, some have not dared to go outside the walls at all, and if any one of them ever took the field under compulsion, he deserted his post, I maintain, and beat a retreat.

[1] Cf. Tyrtaeus 8, 29–30, and § 55.

ΤΥΧΙΑΔΗΣ

Ὡς θαυμάσια πάντα καὶ οὐδὲν ὑπισχνῇ μέτριον. λέγε δὲ ὅμως.

ΣΙΜΩΝ

Τῶν μὲν τοίνυν ῥητόρων Ἰσοκράτης οὐχ ὅπως εἰς πόλεμον ἐξῆλθέν ποτε, ἀλλ' οὐδ' ἐπὶ δικαστήριον ἀνέβη, διὰ δειλίαν, οἶμαι, ὅτι οὐδὲ τὴν φωνὴν διὰ τοῦτο εἶχεν ἔτι. τί δ'; [1] οὐχὶ Δημάδης μὲν καὶ Αἰσχίνης καὶ Φιλοκράτης ὑπὸ δέους εὐθὺς τῇ καταγγελίᾳ τοῦ Φιλίππου πολέμου τὴν πόλιν προὔδοσαν καὶ σφᾶς αὐτοὺς τῷ Φιλίππῳ καὶ διετέλεσαν Ἀθήνησιν ἀεὶ τὰ ἐκείνου πολιτευόμενοι, ὃς εἴ γε καὶ ἄλλος τις Ἀθηναίοις [2] κατὰ ταῦτα ἐπολέμει· κἀκεῖνος ἐν αὐτοῖς ἦν φίλος. Ὑπερίδης δὲ καὶ Δημοσθένης καὶ Λυκοῦργος, οἵ γε δοκοῦντες ἀνδρειότεροι κἀν ταῖς ἐκκλησίαις ἀεὶ θορυβοῦντες καὶ λοιδορούμενοι τῷ Φιλίππῳ, τι ποτε ἀπειργάσαντο γενναῖον ἐν τῷ πρὸς αὐτὸν πολέμῳ; καὶ Ὑπερίδης μὲν καὶ Λυκοῦργος οὐδὲ ἐξῆλθον, ἀλλ' οὐδὲ ὅλως ἐτόλμησαν μικρὸν ἔξω παρακῦψαι τῶν πυλῶν, ἀλλ' ἐντειχίδιοι ἐκάθηντο παρ' αὐτοῖς ἤδη πολιορκούμενοι γνωμίδια καὶ προβουλευμάτια συντιθέντες. ὁ δὲ δὴ κορυφαιότατος αὐτῶν, ὁ ταυτὶ λέγων ἐν ταῖς ἐκκλησίαις συνεχῶς· "Φίλιππος γὰρ ὁ Μακεδὼν ὄλεθρος, ὅθεν οὐδὲ ἀνδράποδον πρίαιτό τίς ποτε," τολμήσας

[1] τί δ' Fritzsche: not in MSS.

[2] ὃς—Ἀθηναίοις A.M.H.: ὡς—Ἀθηναῖος MSS.

TYCHIADES

What assertions, all surprising and none moderate! But say your say, nevertheless.

SIMON

Among the followers of rhetoric, Isocrates not only never went to war but never even went to court, through cowardice, I assume, as that is why he could not even keep his voice.[1] And did not Demades and Aeschines and Philocrates, through fright, directly upon the declaration of war against Philip, betray their city and themselves to Philip and continually direct public affairs at Athens in the interest of that man, who was waging war upon the Athenians at that time, if ever a man was; and he was their friend. Moreover, Hyperides and Demosthenes and Lycurgus, who put up a more courageous front and were always making an uproar and abusing Philip in the assemblies—what on earth did they do that was valiant in the war with him? Hyperides and Lycurgus did not even take the field—why, they did not even dare to show their heads just outside the gates, but safe within the walls, they sat at home as if the city were already besieged, framing trivial motions and petty resolutions! And as for the topmost of them, the man who was continually talking in the assembly about "Philip, the scoundrel from Macedon, where one could never even buy a decent slave!"[2] he did

[1] Every schoolboy knew—such was the interest in rhetoric—that Isocrates did not practise in the courts because his voice was too weak. The author pretends to think that its weakness must have been due to fright, and that therefore he was a terrible coward.

[2] Demosthenes, *Third Philippic* 31.

προελθεῖν εἰς τὴν Βοιωτίαν, πρὶν ἢ συμμῖξαι τὰ στρατόπεδα καὶ συμβαλεῖν εἰς χεῖρας ῥίψας τὴν ἀσπίδα ἔφυγεν. ἢ οὐδέπω ταῦτα πρότερον διήκουσας οὐδενός, πάνυ γνώριμα ὄντα οὐχ ὅπως Ἀθηναίοις, ἀλλὰ Θρᾳξὶ καὶ Σκύθαις, ὅθεν ἐκεῖνο τὸ κάθαρμα ἦν;

ΤΥΧΙΑΔΗΣ

43 Ἐπίσταμαι ταῦτα· ἀλλ' οὗτοι μὲν ῥήτορες καὶ λόγους λέγειν ἠσκηκότες, ἀρετὴν δὲ οὔ. τί δὲ περὶ τῶν φιλοσόφων λέγεις; οὐ γὰρ δὴ τούτους ἔχεις ὥσπερ ἐκείνους αἰτιᾶσθαι.

ΣΙΜΩΝ

Οὗτοι πάλιν, ὦ Τυχιάδη, οἱ περὶ τῆς ἀνδρείας ὁσημέραι διαλεγόμενοι καὶ κατατρίβοντες τὸ τῆς ἀρετῆς ὄνομα πολλῷ μᾶλλον τῶν ῥητόρων φανοῦνται δειλότεροι καὶ μαλακώτεροι. σκόπει δὴ οὕτως. πρῶτον μὲν οὐκ ἔστιν ὅστις εἰπεῖν ἔχοι φιλόσοφον ἐν πολέμῳ τετελευτηκότα· ἤτοι γὰρ οὐδὲ ὅλως ἐστρατεύσαντο, ἢ εἴπερ ἐστρατεύσαντο, πάντες ἔφυγον. Ἀντισθένης μὲν οὖν καὶ Διογένης καὶ Κράτης καὶ Ζήνων καὶ Πλάτων καὶ Αἰσχίνης καὶ Ἀριστοτέλης καὶ πᾶς οὗτος ὁ ὅμιλος οὐδὲ εἶδον παράταξιν· μόνος δὲ τολμήσας ἐξελθεῖν εἰς τὴν ἐπὶ Δηλίῳ [1] μάχην ὁ σοφὸς αὐτῶν Σωκράτης φεύγων ἐκεῖθεν ἀπὸ τῆς Πάρνηθος εἰς τὴν Ταυρέου

[1] ἐπὶ Δηλίῳ Gesner: ἐν τῇ πόλει MSS.

---

[1] The story that Demosthenes played the coward at Chaeronea was spread by his political enemies Aeschines (3, 244; 253) and Pytheas (Plut. *Demosth.* 20); see also Gellius 17, 21.

venture to join the advance into Boeotia, but before the armies joined battle and began to fight at close quarters he threw away his shield and fled![1] Has nobody ever told you that before? It is very well known, not only to the Athenians, but to the people of Thrace and Scythia, where that vagabond came from.[2]

TYCHIADES

I know all that. They were orators, however, who cultivated speech-making, not virtue. What have you to say about the philosophers? Surely you are not able to censure them as you did the others.

SIMON

They in turn, Tychiades, though they talk every day about courage and wear the word virtue smooth, will be found far more cowardly and effeminate than the orators. Look at it from this standpoint. In the first place, there is nobody that can mention a philosopher who died in battle; either they did not enter the service at all, or if they did, every one of them ran away. Antisthenes, Diogenes, Crates, Zeno, Plato, Aeschines, Aristotle, and all that motley array never even saw a line of battle. The only one who had the courage to go out for the battle at Delium, their wise Socrates, fled the field, fleeing for cover all the way from Parnes to the gymnasium of Taureas.[3]

[2] Cleobule, the mother of Demosthenes, was said to be Scythian on her mother's side (Aesch. 3, 171).

[3] As a matter of fact Socrates displayed conspicuous valour in the retreat from Delium (Plato, *Laches* 181 B). The allusion to the gymnasium of Taureas rests upon a hazy recollection of the opening of the *Charmides*, where Socrates says that he visited it on the morning after his return from Potidaea. Furthermore, there were no Spartan troops at Delium.

παλαίστραν κατέφυγεν. πολὺ γὰρ αὐτῷ ἀστειότερον ἐδόκει μετὰ τῶν μειρακυλλίων καθεζόμενον ὀαρίζειν καὶ σοφισμάτια προβάλλειν τοῖς ἐντυγχάνουσιν ἢ ἀνδρὶ Σπαρτιάτῃ μάχεσθαι.

ΤΥΧΙΑΔΗΣ

Ὦ γενναῖε, ταῦτα μὲν ἤδη καὶ παρ' ἄλλων ἐπυθόμην, οὐ μὰ Δία σκώπτειν αὐτοὺς καὶ ὀνειδίζειν βουλομένων· ὥστε οὐδέν τί μοι δοκεῖς χαριζόμενος τῇ σεαυτοῦ τέχνῃ καταψεύδεσθαι τῶν 44 ἀνδρῶν. ἀλλ' εἰ δοκεῖ ἤδη, φέρε καὶ σὺ τὸν παράσιτον ὁποῖός τίς ἐστιν ἐν πολέμῳ λέγε, καὶ εἰ καθόλως[1] λέγεται παράσιτός τις γενέσθαι τῶν παλαιῶν;

ΣΙΜΩΝ

Καὶ μήν, ὦ φιλότης, οὐδεὶς οὕτως[2] ἀνήκοος Ὁμήρου, οὐδ' ἂν πάμπαν ἰδιώτης τύχῃ, ὃς οὐκ ἐπίσταται παρ' αὐτῷ τοὺς ἀρίστους τῶν ἡρώων παρασίτους ὄντας. ὅ τε γὰρ Νέστωρ ἐκεῖνος, οὗ ἀπὸ τῆς γλώττης ὥσπερ μέλι ὁ λόγος ἀπέρρει,[3] αὐτοῦ τοῦ βασιλέως παράσιτος ἦν, καὶ οὔτε τὸν Ἀχιλλέα, ὅσπερ ἐδόκει τε καὶ ἦν τὸ σῶμα γενναιότατος, οὔτε τὸν Διομήδην οὔτε τὸν Αἴαντα ὁ Ἀγαμέμνων οὕτως ἐπαινεῖ τε καὶ θαυμάζει ὥσπερ τὸν Νέστορα. οὐδὲ γὰρ δέκα Αἴαντας εὔχεται γενέσθαι αὐτῷ οὔτε δέκα Ἀχιλλέας· πάλαι δ' ἂν ἑαλωκέναι τὴν Τροίαν, εἰ τοιούτους ὁποῖος ἦν οὗτος ὁ παράσιτος, καίπερ γέρων ὤν, στρατιώτας εἶχεν δέκα. καὶ τὸν Ἰδομενέα τὸν τοῦ Διὸς ἔγγονον παράσιτον Ἀγαμέμνονος ὁμοίως λέγει.

[1] καθόλως A.M.H.: καὶ ὅλως MSS.
[2] οὕτως Dindorf: not in MSS.
[3] ἀπέρρει vulg.: ἀπορρεῖ MSS.

He thought it far nicer to sit and philander with boys and propound petty sophistries to anyone who should come along than to fight with a Spartan soldier.

TYCHIADES

My excellent friend, I have already heard this from others, who certainly did not wish to ridicule or libel them; so I do not in the least think that you are belying them out of partiality to your own art. But if you are now willing, tell what the parasite is like in war, and whether anybody at all among the ancient heroes is said to have been a parasite.[1]

SIMON

Why, my dear friend, no one is so unfamiliar with Homer, even if he is completely unlettered, as not to know that in him the noblest of the heroes are parasites! The famous Nestor, from whose tongue speech flowed like honey, was parasite to the king himself; and neither Achilles, who seemed and was the finest in physique, nor Diomed nor Ajax was so lauded and admired by Agamemnon as Nestor. He does not pray to have ten of Ajax or ten of Achilles, but says that he would long ago have taken Troy if he had had ten soldiers like that parasite, old as he was.[2] Idomeneus, too, the son of Zeus, is similarly spoken of as parasite to Agamemnon.[3]

[1] The first orators were found in Homer; notably Odysseus, Nestor, Menelaus. Also the beginnings of philosophy (Philod. 2, frg. xxi). So the first parasites should be found there.
[2] *Iliad* 2, 371–374. [3] *Iliad* 4, 257–263.

ΤΥΧΙΑΔΗΣ

45 Ταῦτα μὲν καὶ αὐτὸς ἐπίσταμαι· οὔπω γε μὴν δοκῶ μοι γιγνώσκειν, πῶς δὴ τὼ ἄνδρε τῷ Ἀγαμέμνονι παράσιτοι ἦσαν.

ΣΙΜΩΝ

Ἀναμνήσθητι, ὦ γενναῖε, τῶν ἐπῶν ἐκείνων ὧνπερ αὐτὸς ὁ Ἀγαμέμνων πρὸς τὸν Ἰδομενέα λέγει.

ΤΥΧΙΑΔΗΣ

Ποίων;

ΣΙΜΩΝ

Σὸν δὲ πλεῖον δέπας αἰεὶ
ἕστηχ᾽ ὥσπερ ἐμοὶ πιέειν ὅτε θυμὸς ἀνώγοι.

ἐνταῦθα γὰρ τὸ αἰεὶ πλεῖον δέπας εἴρηκεν οὐχ ὅτι τὸ ποτήριον διὰ παντὸς πλῆρες ἑστήκει τῷ Ἰδομενεῖ καὶ μαχομένῳ καὶ καθεύδοντι, ἀλλ᾽ ὅτι αὐτῷ δι᾽ ὅλου τοῦ βίου μόνῳ συνδειπνεῖν ὑπῆρχεν τῷ βασιλεῖ, οὐχ ὥσπερ τοῖς λοιποῖς στρατιώταις πρὸς ἡμέρας τινὰς καλουμένοις.

Τὸν μὲν γὰρ Αἴαντα, ἐπεὶ καλῶς ἐμονομάχησεν τῷ Ἕκτορι, "εἰς Ἀγαμέμνονα δῖον ἄγον," φησίν, κατὰ τιμὴν ἀξιωθέντα ὀψὲ τοῦ παρὰ τῷ βασιλεῖ δείπνου. ὁ δὲ Ἰδομενεὺς καὶ ὁ Νέστωρ ὁσημέραι συνεδείπνουν τῷ βασιλεῖ, ὡς αὐτός φησιν. Νέστωρ δὲ παράσιτός μοι δοκεῖ τῶν βασιλέων μάλιστα τεχνίτης καὶ ἀγαθὸς γενέσθαι· οὐ γὰρ ἐπὶ τοῦ Ἀγαμέμνονος ἄρξασθαι τῆς τέχνης, ἀλλὰ ἄνωθεν ἐπὶ Καινέως καὶ Ἐξαδίου· δοκεῖ δὲ οὐδὲ ἂν

TYCHIADES

Of course I myself know all this, but I do not think that I yet see how the two men were parasites to Agamemnon.

SIMON

Remember, my friend, those lines that Agamemnon himself addresses to Idomeneus.

TYCHIADES

What lines?

SIMON

"Your beaker has always
Stood full, even as mine, to be drunk when the spirit should move you." [1]

For in saying there that the beaker "always stood full," he did not mean that Idomeneus' cup stood full under all circumstances, even when he fought or when he slept, but that he alone was privileged to eat with the king all the days of his life, unlike the rest of the soldiers, who were invited only on certain days.

As for Ajax, when he had fought gloriously in single combat with Hector, "they brought him to great Agamemnon," [2] Homer says, and by way of special honour, he was at last counted worthy of sharing the king's table. But Idomeneus and Nestor dined with the king daily, as he himself says. Nestor, indeed, in my opinion was the most workmanlike and efficient parasite among the kings; he began the art, not in the time of Agamemnon, but away back in the time of Caeneus and Exadius, [3]

[1] *Iliad* 4, 262–263. [2] *Iliad* 7, 312.
[3] Two generations earlier; *Iliad* 1, 250, 264.

παύσασθαι παρασιτῶν, εἰ μὴ ὁ Ἀγαμέμνων ἀπέθανεν.

ΤΥΧΙΑΔΗΣ

Οὑτοσὶ μὲν γενναῖος ὁ παράσιτος. εἰ δὲ καὶ ἄλλους τινὰς οἶσθα, πειρῶ λέγειν.

ΣΙΜΩΝ

46 *Τί οὖν, ὦ Τυχιάδη, οὐχὶ καὶ Πάτροκλος τοῦ Ἀχιλλέως παράσιτος ἦν, καὶ ταῦτα οὐδενὸς τῶν ἄλλων Ἑλλήνων φαυλότερος οὔτε τὴν ψυχὴν οὔτε τὸ σῶμα νεανίας ὤν; ἐγὼ γὰρ οὐδ' αὐτοῦ μοι δοκῶ τοῦ Ἀχιλλέως τεκμαίρεσθαι τοῖς ἔργοις αὐτοῦ χείρω εἶναι· τόν τε γὰρ Ἕκτορα ῥήξαντα τὰς πύλας καὶ παρὰ ταῖς ναυσὶν εἴσω μαχόμενον οὗτος ἐξέωσεν καὶ τὴν Πρωτεσιλάου ναῦν ἤδη καιομένην ἔσβεσεν, καίτοι ἐπεβάτευον αὐτῆς οὐχ οἱ φαυλότατοι, ἀλλ' οἱ τοῦ Τελαμῶνος Αἴας τε καὶ Τεῦκρος, ὁ μὲν ὁπλίτης ἀγαθός, ὁ δὲ τοξότης. καὶ πολλοὺς μὲν ἀπέκτεινε τῶν βαρβάρων, ἐν δὲ δὴ τούτοις καὶ Σαρπηδόνα τὸν παῖδα τοῦ Διός, ὁ παράσιτος τοῦ Ἀχιλλέως. καὶ ἀπέθανεν δὲ οὐχὶ τοῖς ἄλλοις ὁμοίως, ἀλλὰ τὸν[1] μὲν Ἕκτορα Ἀχιλλεὺς ἀπέκτεινεν, εἷς ἕνα, καὶ αὐτὸν τὸν Ἀχιλλέα Πάρις, τὸν δὲ παράσιτον θεὸς καὶ δύο ἄνθρωποι. καὶ τελευτῶν δὲ φωνὰς ἀφῆκεν οὐχ οἵας ὁ γενναιότατος Ἕκτωρ καὶ προσπίπτων τὸν Ἀχιλλέα καὶ ἱκετεύων ὅπως ὁ νεκρὸς αὐτοῦ τοῖς*

[1] ἀλλὰ τὸν Fritzsche : ἀλλ' αὐτόν MSS.

and by all appearances would never have stopped practising it if Agamemnon had not been killed.

TYCHIADES

He was a doughty parasite, I grant you. Try to name some more, if you know of any.

SIMON

What, Tychiades, was not Patroclus parasite to Achilles, and that too although he was quite as fine a young man, both in spirit and in physique, as any of the other Greeks? For my part I think I am right in concluding from his deeds that he was not even inferior to Achilles himself. When Hector broached the gates and was fighting within them beside the ships, it was he that thrust him out and extinguished the ship of Protesilaus, which was already in flames. Yet the fighters who manned that ship were not the most cowardly of all: they were the sons of Telamon, Ajax and Teucer, one of whom was a good spearman, the other a good archer. And he slew many of the barbarians, among them Sarpedon, the son of Zeus, this parasite of Achilles! In his death too, he was not to be compared with the others. Achilles slew Hector, man to man, and Paris slew Achilles himself, but it needed a god and two men to slay the parasite.[1] And in dying, the words that he uttered were not like those of noble Hector, who humbled himself before Achilles and besought that his body be given back to his family; no, they

[1] Apollo, Hector, and Euphorbus, Hector's squire; *Iliad* 16, 849–850.

οἰκείοις ἀποδοθῇ, ἀλλ' οἵας εἰκὸς ἀφεῖναι παράσιτον. τίνας δὴ ταύτας;

τοιοῦτοι δ' εἴπερ μοι ἐείκοσιν ἀντεβόλησαν,
πάντες κ' αὐτόθ' ὄλοντο ἐμῷ ὑπὸ δουρὶ δαμέντες.

ΤΥΧΙΑΔΗΣ

47 Ταῦτα μὲν ἱκανῶς· ὅτι δὲ μὴ φίλος ἀλλὰ παράσιτος ἦν ὁ Πάτροκλος τοῦ Ἀχιλλέως πειρῶ λέγειν.

ΣΙΜΩΝ

Αὐτόν, ὦ Τυχιάδη, τὸν Πάτροκλον ὅτι παράσιτος ἦν λέγοντά σοι παρέξομαι.

ΤΥΧΙΑΔΗΣ

Θαυμαστὰ λέγεις.

ΣΙΜΩΝ

Ἄκουε τοινυν αὐτῶν τῶν ἐπῶν·

μὴ ἐμὰ σῶν ἀπάνευθε τιθήμεναι ὀστέ', Ἀχιλλεῦ,
ἀλλ' ὁμοῦ, ὡς ἐτράφην περ ἐν ὑμετέροισι δόμοισι.

καὶ πάλιν ὑποβάς, "καὶ νῦν με δεξάμενος," φησίν, "ὁ Πηλεὺς

ἔτρεφεν ἐνδυκέως καὶ σὸν θεράποντ' ὀνόμηνε."

τουτέστι παράσιτον εἶχεν. εἰ μὲν τοίνυν φίλον ἐβούλετο τὸν Πάτροκλον λέγειν, οὐκ ἂν αὐτὸν ὠνόμαζεν θεράποντα· ἐλεύθερος γὰρ ἦν ὁ Πάτροκλος. τίνας τοίνυν λέγει τοὺς θεράποντας, εἰ

were the sort of words that a parasite would naturally utter. What were they, do you ask?

"Even if twenty such men had come in my way in the battle,
All would have met their death, laid low by my spear on the instant." [1]

TYCHIADES

Enough said as to that; but try to show that Patroclus was not the friend but the parasite of Achilles.

SIMON

I shall cite you Patroclus himself, Tychiades, saying that he was a parasite.

TYCHIADES

That is a surprising statement.

SIMON

Listen then to the lines themselves:

"Let my bones not lie at a distance from thine, O Achilles:
Let them be close to your side, as I lived in the house of our kindred." [2]

And again, farther on, he says: "And now Peleus took me in and
Kept me with kindliest care, and gave me the name of thy servant." [3]

That is, he maintained him as a parasite. If he had wanted to call Patroclus a friend, he would not have given him the name of servant, for Patroclus was a freeman. Whom, then, does he mean by

[1] *Iliad* 16, 847. [2] *Iliad* 23, 83. [3] *Iliad* 23, 89.

μήτε τοὺς δούλους μήτε τοὺς φίλους; τοὺς παρασίτους δῆλον ὅτι· ᾗ καὶ τὸν Μηριόνην τοῦ Ἰδομενέως καὶ αὐτὸν θεράποντα ὀνομάζει.[1]

Σκόπει δὲ ὅτι καὶ ἐνταῦθα τὸν μὲν Ἰδομενέα Διὸς ὄντα υἱὸν οὐκ ἀξιοῖ λέγειν "ἀτάλαντον Ἄρηϊ," Μηριόνην δὲ τὸν παράσιτον αὐτοῦ.

48 Τί δέ; οὐχὶ καὶ Ἀριστογείτων, δημοτικὸς ὢν καὶ πένης, ὥσπερ Θουκυδίδης φησί, παράσιτος ἦν Ἁρμοδίου; τί δέ; οὐχὶ καὶ ἐραστής; ἐπιεικῶς γὰρ οἱ παράσιτοι καὶ ἐρασταὶ τῶν τρεφόντων εἰσίν. οὗτος τοίνυν πάλιν ὁ παράσιτος τὴν Ἀθηναίων πόλιν τυραννουμένην εἰς ἐλευθερίαν ἀφείλετο, καὶ νῦν ἕστηκε χαλκοῦς ἐν τῇ ἀγορᾷ μετὰ τῶν παιδικῶν.

Οὗτοι μὲν δή, τοιοίδε ὄντες, μάλα ἀγαθοὶ παράσιτοι ἦσαν.

49 Σὺ δὲ δὴ ποῖόν τινα εἰκάζεις ἐν πολέμῳ τὸν παράσιτον; οὐχὶ πρῶτον μὲν ὁ τοιοῦτος ἀριστοποιησάμενος ἔξεισιν ἐπὶ τὴν παράταξιν, καθάπερ καὶ ὁ Ὀδυσσεὺς ἀξιοῖ; οὐ γὰρ ἄλλως ἐν πολέμῳ μάχεσθαι, φησίν, ἔστιν, εἰ καὶ[2] εὐθὺς ἅμα ἕῳ μάχεσθαι δέοι. καὶ ὃν ἄλλοι στρατιῶται χρόνον ὑπὸ δέους ὁ μέν τις ἀκριβῶς ἁρμόζει τὸ κράνος, ὁ δὲ θωράκιον ἐνδύεται, ὁ δὲ αὐτὸ τὸ δεινὸν ὑποπτεύων τοῦ πολέμου τρέμει, οὗτος δὲ ἐσθίει τότε μάλα φαιδρῷ τῷ προσώπῳ καὶ μετὰ τὴν ἔξοδον εὐθὺς ἐν πρώτοις διαγωνίζεται· ὁ δὲ τρέφων αὐτὸν ὄπισθεν ὑποτέτακται τῷ παρασίτῳ, κἀκεῖ-

[1] MSS. (except Γ) add *οὕτως οἶμαι καλουμένων τότε τῶν παρασίτων*, excised by Hirschig, Jacobitz.

[2] Text A.M.H.: *οὐ γὰρ ἀλλ' ἣν ἐν πολέμῳ μάχεσθαί φησιν ἑστιάσει καὶ* MSS.

servants, if not either friends or slaves? Parasites, evidently. In the same way he calls Meriones too a servant of Idomeneus.[1]

Observe also that in the same passage it is not Idomeneus, the son of Zeus, whom he thinks fit to call "unyielding in battle," but Meriones, his parasite.[2]

Again, was not Aristogeiton, who was a man of the people and a pauper, as Thucydides says, parasite to Harmodius?[3] Was he not his lover also? Naturally parasites are lovers of those who support them. Well, this parasite restored the city of Athens to freedom when she was in bondage to a tyrant, and now his statue stands in bronze in the public square along with that of his favourite.

Certainly these men, who were of such distinction, were very doughty parasites.

What is your own inference as to the character of the parasite in war? In the first place, does he not get his breakfast before he leaves his quarters to fall in, just as Odysseus thinks it right to do? Under no other circumstances, he says, is it possible to continue fighting in battle even if one should be obliged to begin fighting at the very break of day.[4] While the other soldiers in affright are adjusting their helmets with great pains, or putting on their breastplates, or quaking in sheer anticipation of the horrors of war, the parasite eats with a very cheerful visage; and directly after marching out he begins to fight in the first line. The man who supports him is posted in the second line, behind the parasite, who covers

[1] *Iliad* 13, 246.
[2] *Iliad* 13, 295.
[3] Thucydides 6, 54, 2.
[4] *Iliad* 19, 160–163.

νος αὐτὸν ὥσπερ ὁ Αἴας τὸν Τεῦκρον ὑπὸ τῷ σάκει καλύπτει, καὶ τῶν βελῶν ἀφιεμένων γυμνώσας ἑαυτὸν τοῦτον σκέπει· βούλεται γὰρ ἐκεῖνον μᾶλλον σώζειν ἢ ἑαυτόν.

50 Εἰ δὲ δὴ καὶ πέσοι παράσιτος ἐν πολέμῳ, οὐκ ἂν ἐπ᾽ αὐτῷ δήπου οὔτε λοχαγὸς οὔτε στρατιώτης αἰσχυνθείη μεγάλῳ τε ὄντι νεκρῷ καὶ ὥσπερ ἐν συμποσίῳ καλῷ καλῶς κατακειμένῳ. ὡς ἄξιόν γε φιλοσόφου νεκρὸν ἰδεῖν τούτῳ παρακείμενον, ξηρόν, ῥυπῶντα, μακρὸν πωγώνιον ἔχοντα, προτεθνηκότα τῆς μάχης, ἀσθενῆ ἄνθρωπον. τίς οὐκ ἂν καταφρονήσειε ταύτης τῆς πόλεως τοὺς ὑπασπιστὰς αὐτῆς οὕτως κακοδαίμονας ὁρῶν; τίς δὲ οὐκ ἂν εἰκάσαι, χλωροὺς καὶ κομήτας ὁρῶν ἀνθρωπίσκους κειμένους, τὴν πόλιν ἀποροῦσαν συμμάχων τοὺς ἐν τῇ εἱρκτῇ κακούργους ἐπιλῦσαι τῷ πολέμῳ;

Τοιοῦτοι μὲν ἐν πολέμῳ πρὸς ῥήτορας καὶ φιλο-
51 σόφους εἰσὶν οἱ παράσιτοι. ἐν εἰρήνῃ δὲ τοσούτῳ μοι δοκεῖ διαφέρειν[1] παρασιτικὴ φιλοσοφίας ὅσον αὐτὴ ἡ εἰρήνη πολέμου.

Καὶ πρῶτον, εἰ δοκεῖ, σκοπῶμεν τὰ τῆς εἰρήνης χωρία.

ΤΥΧΙΑΔΗΣ

Οὔπω συνίημι ὅ τι τοῦτό πως βούλεται, σκοπῶμεν δὲ ὅμως.

ΣΙΜΩΝ

Οὐκοῦν ἀγορὰν καὶ δικαστήρια καὶ παλαίστρας καὶ γυμνάσια καὶ κυνηγέσια καὶ συμπόσια ἔγωγε φαίην ἂν πόλεως χωρία.

[1] διαφέρειν vulg.; καὶ διαφέρειν MSS.

him with his shield as Ajax covered Teucer, and when missiles are flying exposes himself to protect his patron; for he prefers to save his patron rather than himself.

If a parasite should actually fall in battle, certainly neither captain nor private soldier would be ashamed of his huge body, elegantly reclining as at an elegant banquet. Indeed it would be worth one's while to look at a philosopher's body lying beside it, lean, squalid, with a long beard, a sickly creature dead before the battle! Who would not despise this city if he saw that her targeteers were such wretches? Who, when he saw pale, long-haired varlets lying on the field, would not suppose that the city for lack of reserves had freed for service the malefactors in her prison?

That is how parasites compare with rhetoricians and philosophers in war. In peace, it seems to me, Parasitic excels philosophy as greatly as peace itself excels war.

First, if you please, let us consider the strongholds of peace.

TYCHIADES

I do not understand what that means, but let us consider it all the same.

SIMON

Well, I should say that market-places, law-courts, athletic fields, gymnasia, hunting-parties and dinners were a city's strongholds.

ΤΥΧΙΑΔΗΣ

Πάνυ μὲν οὖν.

ΣΙΜΩΝ

Ὁ τοίνυν παράσιτος εἰς ἀγορὰν μὲν καὶ δικαστήρια οὐ πάρεισιν, ὅτι, οἶμαι, τοῖς συκοφάνταις πάντα τὰ χωρία ταῦτα μᾶλλον προσήκει καὶ ὅτι οὐδὲν μέτριόν ἐστιν τῶν ἐν τούτοις γιγνομένων, τὰς δὲ παλαίστρας καὶ τὰ γυμνάσια καὶ τὰ συμπόσια διώκει καὶ κοσμεῖ μόνος οὗτος. ἐπεὶ τίς ἐν παλαίστρᾳ φιλόσοφος ἢ ῥήτωρ ἀποδὺς ἄξιος συγκριθῆναι παρασίτου τῷ σώματι; ἢ τίς ἐν γυμνασίῳ τούτων ὀφθεὶς οὐκ αἰσχύνη μᾶλλον τοῦ χωρίου ἐστί; καὶ μὴν ἐν ἐρημίᾳ τούτων οὐδεὶς ἂν ὑποσταίη θηρίον ὁμόσε ἰόν, ὁ δὲ παράσιτος αὐτά τε ἐπιόντα μένει καὶ δέχεται ῥᾳδίως, μεμελετηκὼς αὐτῶν ἐν τοῖς δείπνοις καταφρονεῖν, καὶ οὔτε ἔλαφος οὔτε σῦς αὐτὸν ἐκπλήττει πεφρικώς, ἀλλὰ κἂν ἐπ' αὐτὸν ὁ σῦς τὸν ὀδόντα θήγῃ, καὶ ὁ παράσιτος ἐπὶ τὸν σῦν ἀντιθήγει. τοὺς μὲν γὰρ λαγὼς διώκει μᾶλλον τῶν κυνῶν. ἐν δὲ δὴ συμποσίῳ τίς ἂν καὶ ἁμιλλήσαιτο παρασίτῳ ἤτοι παίζοντι ἢ ἐσθίοντι; τίς δ' ἂν μᾶλλον εὐφράναι τοὺς συμπότας; πότερόν ποτε οὗτος ᾄδων καὶ σκώπτων, ἢ ἄνθρωπος μὴ γελῶν, ἐν τριβωνίῳ κείμενος, εἰς τὴν γῆν ὁρῶν, ὥσπερ ἐπὶ πένθος οὐχὶ συμπόσιον ἥκων; καὶ ἔμοιγε δοκεῖ, ἐν συμποσίῳ φιλόσοφος τοιοῦτόν ἐστιν οἷον ἐν βαλανείῳ κύων.

52 Φέρε δὴ ταῦτα ἀφέντες ἐπ' αὐτὸν ἤδη βαδίζωμεν τὸν βίον τοῦ παρασίτου, σκοποῦντες ἅμα καὶ παραβάλλοντες ἐκεῖνον.

Πρῶτον τοίνυν ἴδοι τις ἂν τὸν μὲν παράσιτον

TYCHIADES

To be sure.

SIMON

The parasite does not appear in the market-place or the courts because, I take it, all these points are more appropriate to swindlers, and because nothing that is done in them is good form; but he frequents the athletic fields, the gymnasia, and the dinners, and ornaments them beyond all others. On the athletic field what philosopher or rhetorician, once he has taken his clothes off, is fit to be compared with a parasite's physique? What one of them when seen in the gymnasium is not actually a disgrace to the place? In the wilds, too, none of them could withstand the charge of a beast; the parasite, however, awaits their attack and receives it easily, having learned to despise them at dinners; and neither stag nor bristling boar affrights him, but if the boar whets his tusks for him, the parasite whets his own for the boar! After a hare he is as keen as a hound. And at a dinner, who could compete with a parasite either in making sport or in eating? Who would make the guests merrier? He with his songs and jokes, or a fellow who lies there without a smile, in a short cloak, with his eyes upon the ground, as if he had come to a funeral and not to a banquet? In my opinion, a philosopher at a banquet is much the same thing as a dog in a bath-house!

Come now, let us dismiss these topics and forthwith turn to the parasite's way of living, considering at the same time and comparing with it that of the others.

In the first place, you can see that the parasite

ἀεὶ δόξης καταφρονοῦντα καὶ οὐδὲν αὐτῷ μέλον ὅ τι ἂν[1] οἱ ἄνθρωποι οἴωνται περὶ αὐτοῦ, ῥήτορας δὲ καὶ φιλοσόφους εὕροι τις ἂν οὐ τινάς, ἀλλὰ πάντας ὑπὸ τύφου καὶ δόξης τριβέντας, καὶ οὐ δόξης μόνον, ἀλλὰ καὶ ὃ τούτου αἴσχιόν ἐστιν, ὑπ᾽ ἀργυρίου. καὶ ὁ μὲν παράσιτος οὕτως ἔχει πρὸς ἀργύριον ὡς οὐκ ἄν τις οὐδὲ πρὸς τὰς ἐν τοῖς αἰγιαλοῖς ψηφῖδας ἀμελῶς ἔχοι, καὶ οὐδὲν αὐτῷ δοκεῖ διαφέρειν τὸ χρυσίον τοῦ πυρός. οἵ γε μὴν ῥήτορες, καὶ ὃ δεινότερόν ἐστιν, καὶ οἱ φιλοσοφεῖν φάσκοντες πρὸς αὐτὰ οὕτως διάκεινται κακοδαιμόνως, ὥστε τῶν μάλιστα νῦν εὐδοκιμούντων φιλοσόφων—περὶ μὲν γὰρ τῶν ῥητόρων τί δεῖ λέγειν;—ὁ μὲν δικάζων δίκην δώροις ἐπ᾽ αὐτῇ ἑάλω,[2] ὁ δὲ παρὰ βασιλέως ὑπὲρ τοῦ συνεῖναι μισθὸν αἰτεῖ καὶ οὐκ αἰσχύνεται ὅτι[3] πρεσβύτης ἀνὴρ διὰ τοῦτο ἀποδημεῖ καὶ μισθοφορεῖ καθάπερ Ἰνδὸς ἢ Σκύθης αἰχμάλωτος, καὶ οὐδὲ αὐτὸ τὸ ὄνομα αἰσχύνεται ὃ λαμβάνει.

53 Εὕροις δ᾽ ἂν οὐ μόνον ταῦτα περὶ τούτους, ἀλλὰ καὶ ἄλλα πάθη, οἷον λύπας καὶ ὀργὰς καὶ φθόνους καὶ παντοίας ἐπιθυμίας. ὅ γε μὴν παράσιτος ἔξωθεν τούτων ἐστὶν ἁπάντων· οὔτε γὰρ ὀργίζεται δι᾽ ἀνεξικακίαν καὶ ὅτι οὐκ ἔστιν αὐτῷ ὅτῳ ὀργισθείη· καὶ εἰ ἀγανακτήσειεν δέ ποτε, ἡ ὀργὴ αὐτοῦ χαλεπὸν μὲν οὐδὲ σκυθρωπὸν οὐδὲν ἀπεργάζεται, μᾶλλον δὲ γέλωτα, καὶ εὐφραίνει τοὺς συνόντας. λυπεῖταί γε μὴν ἥκιστα πάντων, τοῦτο

[1] ὅ τι ἂν Fritzsche: τί ἂν MSS. (τι ὢν Γ[2]: ὢν vulg.).
[2] MSS. (except ΓΩZ[1]) add ἀλλ᾽ ὁ μὲν (ἄλλος δὲ N) μισθὸν σοφιστεύων εἰσπράττεται τοὺς μανθάνοντας, excised by Jacobitz.
[3] ὅτι A.M.H.: ἔτι (εἴ τι) MSS.

always despises reputation and does not care at all what people think about him, but you will find that rhetoricians and philosophers, not merely here and there but everywhere, are harassed by self-esteem and reputation—yes, not only by reputation, but what is worse than that, by money! The parasite feels greater contempt for silver than one would feel even for the pebbles on the beach, and does not think gold one whit better than fire. The rhetoricians, however, and what is more shocking, those who claim to be philosophers, are so wretchedly affected by it that among the philosophers who are most famous at present—for why should we speak of the rhetoricians?—one was convicted of taking a bribe when he served on a jury, and another demands pay from the emperor as a private tutor; he is not ashamed that in his old age he resides in a foreign land on this account and works for wages like an Indian or Scythian prisoner of war—not even ashamed of the name that he gets by it.[1]

You will find too that they are subject to other passions as well as these, such as distress, anger, jealousy, and all manner of desires. The parasite is far from all this; he does not become angry because he is long-suffering, and also because he has nothing to get angry at; and if he should become indignant at any time, his temper does not give rise to any unpleasantness or gloom, but rather to laughter, and makes the company merry. He is least of all subject

[1] The allusion is uncertain. The emperor is probably Marcus Aurelius; if so, the philosopher may be Sextus of Chaeronea, or the Apollonius whom Lucian mentions in *Demonax* 31.

τῆς τέχνης παρασκευαζούσης αὐτῷ καὶ χαριζομένης, μὴ ἔχειν ὑπὲρ ὅτου λυπηθείη· οὔτε γὰρ χρήματά ἐστιν αὐτῷ οὔτε οἶκος οὔτε οἰκέτης οὔτε γυνὴ οὔτε παῖδες, ὧν διαφθειρομένων πᾶσα ἀνάγκη ἐστὶ λυπεῖσθαι τὸν ἔχοντα αὐτά.[1] ἐπιθυμεῖ δὲ οὔτε δόξης οὔτε χρημάτων, ἀλλ' οὐδὲ ὡραίου τινός.

ΤΥΧΙΑΔΗΣ

54 Ἀλλ', ὦ Σίμων, εἰκός γε ἐνδείᾳ τροφῆς λυπηθῆναι αὐτόν.

ΣΙΜΩΝ

Ἀγνοεῖς, ὦ Τυχιάδη, ὅτι ἐξ ἀρχῆς οὐδὲ παράσιτός ἐστιν οὗτος, ὅστις ἀπορεῖ τροφῆς· οὐδὲ γὰρ ἀνδρεῖος ἀπορίᾳ ἀνδρείας ἐστὶν ἀνδρεῖος, οὐδὲ φρόνιμος ἀπορίᾳ φρενῶν ἐστιν φρόνιμος· ἄλλως γὰρ οὐδὲ[2] παράσιτος ἂν εἴη. πρόκειται δὲ ἡμῖν περὶ παρασίτου ζητεῖν ὄντος, οὐχὶ μὴ ὄντος. εἰ δὲ[3] ὁ ἀνδρεῖος οὐκ ἄλλως ἢ παρουσίᾳ ἀνδρειότητος καὶ ὁ φρόνιμος παρουσίᾳ φρονήσεως, καὶ ὁ παράσιτος δὲ παρουσίᾳ τοῦ παρασιτεῖν παράσιτος ἔσται· ὡς εἴ γε τοῦτο μὴ ὑπάρχοι αὐτῷ, περὶ ἄλλου τινός, καὶ οὐχὶ παρασίτου, ζητήσομεν.

ΤΥΧΙΑΔΗΣ

Οὐκοῦν οὐδέποτε ἀπορήσει παράσιτος τροφῆς;

ΣΙΜΩΝ

Ἔοικεν· ὥστε οὔτ' ἐπὶ τούτῳ οὔτ' ἐπ' ἄλλῳ[4] ἐστὶν ὅτῳ λυπηθείη ἄν.

[1] MSS. add: ἐπεὶ ταῦτα ἀπόλλυνται, omitted by Lascaris.
[2] γὰρ οὐδὲ vulg.: γε οὔτε MSS.
[3] εἰ δὲ vulg.: εἰ δὲ μὴ MSS.
[4] οὔτ' ἐπὶ τούτῳ οὔτ' ἐπ' ἄλλῳ vulg.: ἐπὶ τούτῳ οὐκ ἐπ' ἄλλῳ MSS.

to distress, as his art supplies him gratuitously with the advantage of having nothing to be distressed about. For he has neither money nor house nor servant nor wife nor children, over which, if they go to ruin, it is inevitable that their possessor should be distressed. And he has no desires, either for reputation or money, or even for a beautiful favourite.

TYCHIADES

But, Simon, at least he is likely to be distressed by lack of food.

SIMON

You fail to understand, Tychiades, that *a priori* one who lacks food is not a parasite. A brave man is not brave if he lacks bravery, nor is a sensible man sensible if he lacks sense. On any other supposition the parasite would not exist; and the subject of our investigation is an existent, not a non-existent parasite. If the brave man is brave for no other reason than because he has bravery at his command, and the sensible man because he has sense at his command, so, too, the parasite is a parasite because he has food at his command; consequently, if this be denied him, we shall be studying some other sort of man instead of a parasite.

TYCHIADES

Then a parasite will never lack food?

SIMON

So it appears; therefore he cannot be distressed, either by that or by anything else whatsoever.

55 Καὶ μὴν καὶ πάντες ὁμοῦ καὶ φιλόσοφοι καὶ ῥήτορες φοβοῦνται μάλιστα. τούς γέ τοι πλείστους αὐτῶν εὕροι τις ἂν μετὰ ξύλου προϊόντας, οὐκ ἂν δή που, εἰ μὴ ἐφοβοῦντο, ὡπλισμένους, καὶ τὰς θύρας δὲ μάλα ἐρρωμένως ἀποκλείοντας, μή τις ἄρα νύκτωρ ἐπιβουλεύσειεν αὐτοῖς δεδιότας. ὁ δὲ τὴν θύραν τοῦ δωματίου προστίθησιν εἰκῇ, καὶ τοῦτο ὡς μὴ ὑπ' ἀνέμου ἀνοιχθείη, καὶ γενομένου ψόφου νύκτωρ οὐδέν τι μᾶλλον θορυβεῖται ἢ μὴ γενομένου, καὶ δι' ἐρημίας δὲ ἀπιὼν ἄνευ ξίφους ὁδεύει· φοβεῖται γὰρ οὐδὲν οὐδαμοῦ. φιλοσόφους δὲ ἤδη ἐγὼ πολλάκις εἶδον, οὐδενὸς ὄντος δεινοῦ, τόξα ἐνεσκευασμένους· ξύλα μὲν γὰρ ἔχουσιν καὶ εἰς βαλανεῖον ἀπιόντες καὶ ἐπ' ἄριστον.

56 Παρασίτου μέντοι οὐδεὶς ἔχοι κατηγορῆσαι μοιχείαν ἢ βίαν ἢ ἁρπαγὴν ἢ ἄλλο τι ἀδίκημα ἁπλῶς· ἐπεὶ ὅ γε τοιοῦτος οὐκ ἂν εἴη παράσιτος, ἀλλ' ἑαυτὸν ἐκεῖνος ἀδικεῖ. ὥστ' εἰ μοιχεύσας τύχοι, ἅμα τῷ ἀδικήματι καὶ τοὔνομα μεταλαμβάνει τοῦ ἀδικήματος. ὥσπερ γὰρ ὁ ἀγαθὸς φαῦλα ποιῶν διὰ τοῦτο οὐκ ἀγαθός,[1] ἀλλὰ φαῦλος εἶναι ἀναλαμβάνει, οὕτως, οἶμαι, καὶ ὁ παράσιτος, ἐάν τι ἀδικῇ, αὐτὸ μὲν τοῦτο ὅπερ ἐστὶν ἀποβάλλει, ἀναλαμβάνει δὲ ὃ ἀδικεῖ. ἀδικήματα δὲ τοιαῦτα ῥητόρων καὶ φιλοσόφων ἄφθονα οὐ μόνον ἴσμεν αὐτοὶ[2] γεγονότα καθ' ἡμᾶς, ἀλλὰ

[1] Text A.M.H.: ὥσπερ τὸ οὐκ ἀγαθός $\Gamma^1\Omega Z$, ὥσπερ οὐ τὸ ἀγαθός Γ^2, other MSS. ὥσπερ δὲ ὁ κακὸς οὐ τὸ ἀγαθὸς Jacobitz, ὥσπερ δὲ ὁ ἐξ ἀγαθοῦ φαῦλος οὐ τὸ ἀγαθός Fritzsche.

[2] αὐτοὶ Cobet: αὐτοῖς MSS.

Moreover, all the philosophers and rhetoricians, to a man, are particularly timid. At all events you will find that most of them appear in public with a staff—of course they would not have armed themselves if they were not afraid—and that they lock their doors very securely for fear that someone might plot against them at night. The parasite, however, casually closes the door of his lodgings, just to prevent it from being opened by the wind, and when a sound comes at night, he is no more disturbed than as if it had not come, and when he goes through unfrequented country he travels without a sword; for he does not fear anything anywhere. But I have often seen philosophers armed with bows and arrows when there was nothing to fear; and as for staves, they carry them even when they go to the bath and to luncheon.

Again, nobody could accuse a parasite of adultery or assault or larceny or any other offence at all, since a man of that character would be no parasite; he wrongs himself. Therefore if he should commit adultery, for instance, along with the offence he acquires the name that goes with it. Just as a good man who behaves badly thereby acquires the name of bad instead of good, so, I take it, if the parasite commits any offence, he loses his identity and becomes identified with his offence. But not only are we ourselves aware of such offences on the part of rhetoricians and philosophers committed without

κἀν τοῖς βιβλίοις ἀπολελειμμένα ὑπομνήματα ἔχομεν ὧν ἠδίκησαν. ἀπολογία μὲν γὰρ Σωκράτους ἐστὶν καὶ Αἰσχίνου καὶ Ὑπερίδου καὶ Δημοσθένους καὶ τῶν πλείστων σχεδόν τι ῥητόρων καὶ σοφῶν, παρασίτου δὲ οὐκ ἔστιν ἀπολογία οὐδ' ἔχει τις εἰπεῖν δίκην πρὸς παράσιτόν τινι γεγραμμένην.

57 Ἀλλὰ νὴ Δία ὁ μὲν βίος τοῦ παρασίτου κρείττων ἐστὶν τοῦ τῶν ῥητόρων καὶ τῶν φιλοσόφων, ὁ δὲ θάνατος φαυλότερος; πάνυ μὲν οὖν τοὐναντίον παρὰ πολὺ εὐδαιμονέστερος. φιλοσόφους μὲν γὰρ ἴσμεν ἅπαντας ἢ τοὺς πλείστους κακοὺς κακῶς ἀποθανόντας, τοὺς μὲν ἐκ καταδίκης, ἑαλωκότας ἐπὶ τοῖς μεγίστοις ἀδικήμασι, φαρμάκῳ, τοὺς δὲ καταπρησθέντας τὸ σῶμα ἅπαν, τοὺς δὲ ἀπὸ δυσουρίας φθινήσαντας, τοὺς δὲ φυγόντας. παρασίτου δὲ θάνατον οὐδεὶς ἔχει τοιοῦτον εἰπεῖν, ἀλλὰ τὸν εὐδαιμονέστατον φαγόντος καὶ πιόντος. εἰ δέ τις καὶ δοκεῖ βιαίῳ τετελευτηκέναι θανάτῳ, ἀπεπτήσας ἀπέθανεν.

ΤΥΧΙΑΔΗΣ

58 Ταῦτα μὲν ἱκανῶς διημίλληταί σοι τὰ πρὸς τοὺς φιλοσόφους ὑπὲρ τοῦ παρασίτου. λοιπὸν δὲ εἰ καλὸν καὶ λυσιτελές ἐστιν τὸ κτῆμα τοῦτο τῷ τρέφοντι, πειρῶ λέγειν· ἐμοὶ μὲν γὰρ δοκοῦσιν ὥσπερ εὐεργετοῦντες καὶ χαριζόμενοι τρέφειν αὐτοὺς οἱ πλούσιοι, καὶ εἶναι τοῦτο αἰσχύνην τῷ τρεφομένῳ.

ΣΙΜΩΝ

Ὡς ἠλίθιά γε σου, ὦ Τυχιάδη, ταῦτα, εἰ μὴ

number in our times, but we also possess records of their misdeeds left behind in books. And there are speeches in defence of Socrates, Aeschines, Hyperides, Demosthenes, and very nearly the majority of orators and sages, whereas there is no speech in defence of a parasite, and nobody can cite a suit that has been brought against a parasite.

Granted that the life of a parasite is better than that of a rhetorician or a philosopher, is his death worse? Quite to the contrary, it is happier by far. We know that most, if not all, of the philosophers died as wretchedly as they had lived; some died by poison, as a result of judicial sentence, after they had been convicted of the greatest crimes; some had their bodies completely consumed by fire; some wasted away through retention of urine; some died in exile.[1] But in the case of a parasite no one can cite any such death—nothing but the happy, happy death of a man who has eaten and drunk; and any one of them who is thought to have died by violence died of indigestion.

TYCHIADES

You have satisfactorily championed the cause of the parasite against the philosophers. Next try to explain whether he is a good and useful acquisition to his supporter; for to me it seems that the rich play the part of benefactors and philanthropists in supporting them, and that this is dishonourable to the man who receives support.

SIMON

How silly of you, Tychiades, not to be able to

[1] Socrates; Empedocles (and Peregrinus Proteus); Epicurus; Aristotle.

δύνασαι γινώσκειν ὅτι πλούσιος ἀνήρ, εἰ καὶ τὸ Γύγου χρυσίον ἔχοι, μόνος ἐσθίων πένης ἐστὶν καὶ προϊὼν ἄνευ παρασίτου πτωχὸς δοκεῖ, καὶ ὥσπερ στρατιώτης χωρὶς ὅπλων ἀτιμότερος καὶ ἐσθὴς ἄνευ πορφύρας καὶ ἵππος ἄνευ φαλάρων, οὕτω καὶ πλούσιος ἄνευ παρασίτου ταπεινός τις καὶ εὐτελὴς φαίνεται. καὶ μὴν ὁ μὲν πλούσιος κοσμεῖται ὑπ' αὐτοῦ, τὸν δὲ παράσιτον πλούσιος

59 οὐδέποτε κοσμεῖ. ἄλλως τε οὐδὲ ὄνειδος αὐτῷ ἐστιν, ὡς σὺ φής, τὸ παρασιτεῖν ἐκείνῳ, δῆλον ὅτι ὡς τινι κρείττονι χείρονα, ὅπου[1] γε μὴν τῷ πλουσίῳ τοῦτο λυσιτελές ἐστιν, τὸ τρέφειν τὸν παράσιτον, ᾧ γε μετὰ τοῦ κοσμεῖσθαι ὑπ' αὐτοῦ καὶ ἀσφάλεια πολλὴ ἐκ τῆς τούτου δορυφορίας ὑπάρχει· οὔτε γὰρ μάχῃ ῥᾳδίως ἄν τις ἐπιχειρήσαι τῷ πλουσίῳ τοῦτον ὁρῶν παρεστῶτα, ἀλλ' οὐδ' ἂν ἀποθάνοι φαρμάκῳ οὐδεὶς ἔχων παράσιτον. τίς γὰρ ἂν τολμήσειεν ἐπιβουλεῦσαί τινι τούτου προεσθίοντος καὶ προπίνοντος; ὥστε ὁ πλούσιος οὐχὶ κοσμεῖται μόνον, ἀλλὰ καὶ ἐκ τῶν μεγίστων κινδύνων ὑπὸ τοῦ παρασίτου σῴζεται. οὕτω μὲν[2] ὁ παράσιτος διὰ φιλοστοργίαν πάντα κίνδυνον ὑπομένει, καὶ οὐκ ἂν παραχωρήσειεν τῷ πλουσίῳ φαγεῖν μόνῳ,[3] ἀλλὰ καὶ ἀποθανεῖν αἱρεῖται συμφαγών.

ΤΥΧΙΑΔΗΣ

60 Πάντα μοι δοκεῖς, ὦ Σίμων, διεξελθεῖν ὑστερήσας οὐδὲν τῆς σεαυτοῦ τέχνης, οὐχ ὥσπερ αὐτὸς

[1] ὅπου vulg.: ὅπως MSS.
[2] οὕτω μὲν vulg.: αὖτε μὴν, ἅτε μὴν, ὅτι μὲν MSS.
[3] μόνῳ N: μόνον other MSS.

realise that a rich man, even if he has the wealth of Gyges, is poor if he eats alone; that if he takes the air without a parasite in his company he is considered a pauper, and that just as a soldier without arms, or a mantle without a purple border, or a horse without trappings is held in less esteem, so a rich man without a parasite appears low and cheap. Truly, he is an ornament to the rich man, but the rich man is never an ornament to the parasite. Furthermore, it is no disgrace to him to be the rich man's parasite, as you imply, evidently assuming that he is the inferior and the other a superior; since surely it is profitable for the rich man to support the parasite, seeing that, besides having him as an ornament, he derives great security from his service as bodyguard. In battle nobody would readily attack the rich man while he saw the other standing by, and in fact no one could die by poison who had a parasite; for who would dare to make an attempt on a man when a parasite tastes his meat and drink first? So the rich man not only is ornamented but is actually saved from the greatest perils by the parasite, who faces every danger on account of his affection, and will not suffer the rich man to eat alone, but chooses even to die from eating with him.

TYCHIADES

It seems to me, Simon, that you have treated of everything without being in any degree inadequate

ἔφασκες, ἀμελέτητος ὤν, ἀλλ᾽ ὥσπερ ἄν τις ὑπὸ τῶν μεγίστων γεγυμνασμένος. λοιπόν, εἰ μὴ αἴσχιον αὐτὸ τὸ ὄνομά ἐστι τῆς παρασιτικῆς, θέλω μαθεῖν.

ΣΙΜΩΝ

Ὅρα δὴ τὴν ἀπόκρισιν, ἐάν σοι ἱκανῶς λέγεσθαι δοκῇ, καὶ πειρῶ πάλιν αὐτὸς ἀποκρίνασθαι πρὸς τὸ ἐρωτώμενον ᾗ[1] ἄριστα οἴει. φέρε γάρ, τὸν σῖτον οἱ παλαιοὶ τί καλοῦσι;

ΤΥΧΙΑΔΗΣ

Τροφήν.

ΣΙΜΩΝ

Τί δὲ τὸ σιτεῖσθαι, οὐχὶ τὸ ἐσθίειν;

ΤΥΧΙΑΔΗΣ

Ναί.

ΣΙΜΩΝ

Οὐκοῦν καθωμολόγηται τὸ παρασιτεῖν ὅτι οὐκ ἄλλο ἐστίν;

ΤΥΧΙΑΔΗΣ

Τοῦτο γάρ, ὦ Σίμων, ἐστὶν ὃ αἰσχρὸν φαίνεται.

ΣΙΜΩΝ

61 Φέρε δὴ πάλιν ἀπόκριναί μοι, πότερόν σοι δοκεῖ διαφέρειν, καὶ προκειμένων ἀμφοῖν πότερον ἂν αὐτὸς ἕλοιο, ἆρά γε τὸ πλεῖν ἢ τὸ παραπλεῖν;

ΤΥΧΙΑΔΗΣ

Τὸ παραπλεῖν ἔγωγε.

[1] ᾗ vulg.: εἰ MSS.

to your art. You are not deficient in preparation, as you said you were; on the contrary, you are as thoroughly trained as one could be by the greatest masters. And now I want to know whether the very name of Parasitic is not discreditable.

SIMON

Note my answer and see if you think it is satisfactory, and try on your part to answer my question as you think best. Come, now, what about the noun from which it is derived? To what did the ancients apply it?

TYCHIADES

To food.

SIMON

And what about the simple verb, does it not mean "to eat"?

TYCHIADES

Yes.

SIMON

Then we have admitted, have we not, that to be a parasite is nothing but to eat with someone else?

TYCHIADES

Why, Simon, that is the very thing which seems discreditable!

SIMON

Come, then, answer me another question. Which seems to you to be the better, and which should you choose if both were open to you, to voyage or to voyage with someone else?

TYCHIADES

To voyage with someone else, for my part.

ΣΙΜΩΝ

Τί δέ, τὸ τρέχειν ἢ τὸ παρατρέχειν;

ΤΥΧΙΑΔΗΣ

Τὸ παρατρέχειν.

ΣΙΜΩΝ

Τί δέ, τὸ ἱππεύειν ἢ τὸ παριππεύειν;

ΤΥΧΙΑΔΗΣ

Τὸ παριππεύειν.

ΣΙΜΩΝ

Τί δέ, τὸ ἀκοντίζειν ἢ τὸ παρακοντίζειν;

ΤΥΧΙΑΔΗΣ

Τὸ παρακοντίζειν.

ΣΙΜΩΝ

Οὐκοῦν ὁμοίως ἂν ἕλοιο[1] καὶ τοῦ ἐσθίειν μᾶλλον τὸ παρασιτεῖν;

ΤΥΧΙΑΔΗΣ

Ὁμολογεῖν ἀνάγκη. καί σοι λοιπὸν ὥσπερ οἱ παῖδες ἀφίξομαι καὶ ἑῷος καὶ μετ᾽ ἄριστον μαθησόμενος τὴν τέχνην. σὺ δέ με αὐτὴν δίκαιος διδάσκειν ἀφθόνως, ἐπεὶ καὶ πρῶτος μαθητής σοι γίγνομαι. φασὶ δὲ καὶ τὰς μητέρας μᾶλλον τὰ πρῶτα φιλεῖν τῶν τέκνων.

[1] ἕλοιο Fritzsche: ἐθέλοιο Γ[1]Ω, θέλοις, θέλῃς other MSS.

SIMON

To run, or to run with someone else?

TYCHIADES

To run with someone else.

SIMON

To ride, or to ride with someone else?

TYCHIADES

To ride with someone else.

SIMON

To throw the javelin, or to throw it with someone else?

TYCHIADES

To throw it with someone else.

SIMON

Then, in like manner, should you not choose to eat with someone else, rather than just to eat?

TYCHIADES

I cannot but admit it. Hereafter I shall go to you like a schoolboy both in the morning and after luncheon to learn your art. You, for your part, ought to teach me ungrudgingly, for I shall be your first pupil. They say that mothers love their first children more.

THE LOVER OF LIES, OR THE DOUBTER

A conversation dealing with the supernatural, recently held at the house of Eucrates, is recounted by one of the chief participants, Tychiades, to his friend Philocles, to show how mendacious and how credulous people are.

To put ourselves in tune with Lucian and his audience requires very little effort, now that we too are inclined to believe in supernatural manifestations. To be sure, the other world manifested itself to men in those days through somewhat different channels; but the phenomena, then as now, were considered extremely well authenticated, and were credited by men of high standing. Take but one example, the younger Pliny. In a famous letter, which should be read in full (7, 27), he asks Licinius Sura for his opinion about *phantasmata*, citing as well vouched for by others the story of Curtius Rufus (told also by Tacitus: *Annals* 11, 21) and that of the haunted house, which we find in Lucian, and then relating two incidents that happened in his own family: in both cases a boy dreamed that his hair was being cut, and awoke in the morning to find it lying on the pillow beside him. Pliny does not seek a rationalistic explanation in the pranks of pages; he takes the incidents very seriously, and surely does not expect either Sura or the general public to do otherwise. Eucrates is Pliny's spiritual grandson.

Lucian's auditors, too, were credulous, and whether they fully believed such tales or not, anyhow they were eager to listen to them. Lucian for his part was uncommonly eager to repeat them because he was quite aware that he could do it very well. Was he to be debarred from that privilege simply because he did not believe in them? Not he! He could kill two birds with a single lucky stone, for he could tell what his audience craved to hear, and at the same time he and they could laugh at those who liked to tell and hear such stories. The inclusiveness of the satire is clearly shown in its last words. Both Tychiades and Philocles confess that they have been bitten with the prevailing mania.

ΦΙΛΟΨΕΥΔΗΣ Η ΑΠΙΣΤΩΝ

ΤΥΧΙΑΔΗΣ

1 Ἔχεις μοι, ὦ Φιλόκλεις, εἰπεῖν τί ποτε ἄρα ἐστὶν ὃ πολλοὺς[1] εἰς ἐπιθυμίαν τοῦ ψεύδους[2] προάγεται, ὡς αὐτούς τε χαίρειν μηδὲν ὑγιὲς λέγοντας καὶ τοῖς τὰ τοιαῦτα διεξιοῦσιν μάλιστα προσέχειν τὸν νοῦν;

ΦΙΛΟΚΛΗΣ

Πολλά, ὦ Τυχιάδη, ἐστὶν ἃ τοὺς ἀνθρώπους ἐνίους ἀναγκάζει τὰ ψευδῆ λέγειν εἰς τὸ χρήσιμον ἀποβλέποντας.

ΤΥΧΙΑΔΗΣ

Οὐδὲν πρὸς ἔπος ταῦτα, φασίν, οὐ γὰρ περὶ τούτων ἠρόμην ὁπόσοι τῆς χρείας ἕνεκα ψεύδονται· συγγνωστοὶ γὰρ οὗτοί γε, μᾶλλον δὲ καὶ ἐπαίνου τινὲς αὐτῶν ἄξιοι, ὁπόσοι ἢ πολεμίους ἐξηπάτησαν ἢ ἐπὶ σωτηρίᾳ τῷ τοιούτῳ φαρμάκῳ ἐχρήσαντο ἐν τοῖς δεινοῖς, οἷα πολλὰ καὶ ὁ Ὀδυσσεὺς ἐποίει τήν τε αὑτοῦ ψυχὴν ἀρνύμενος καὶ τὸν νόστον τῶν ἑταίρων. ἀλλὰ περὶ ἐκείνων, ὦ ἄριστε, φημὶ οἳ αὐτὸ ἄνευ τῆς χρείας τὸ ψεῦδος πρὸ πολλοῦ τῆς ἀληθείας τίθενται, ἡδόμενοι τῷ πράγματι καὶ ἐνδιατρίβοντες ἐπ᾽ οὐδεμιᾷ προφάσει ἀναγκαίᾳ. τούτους οὖν ἐθέλω εἰδέναι τίνος ἀγαθοῦ τοῦτο ποιοῦσιν.

Available in photographs: Γ, PN.

[1] τί ποτε ἄρα τοῦτό ἐστιν ὃ τοὺς πολλοὺς γ. [2] ψεύδεσθαι γ.

THE LOVER OF LIES, OR THE DOUBTER

TYCHIADES

Can you tell me, Philocles, what in the world it is that makes many men so fond of lying that they delight in telling preposterous tales themselves and listen with especial attention to those who spin yarns of that sort?

PHILOCLES

There are many reasons, Tychiades, which constrain men occasionally to tell falsehoods with an eye to the usefulness of it.

TYCHIADES

That has nothing to do with the case, as the phrase is, for I did not ask about men who lie for advantage. They are pardonable—yes, even praiseworthy, some of them, who have deceived national enemies or for safety's sake have used this kind of expedient in extremities, as Odysseus often did in seeking to win his own life and the return of his comrades.[1] No, my dear sir, I am speaking of those men who put sheer useless lying far ahead of truth, liking the thing and whiling away their time at it without any valid excuse. I want to know about these men, to what end they do this.

[1] An echo of *Odyssey* 1, 5.

ΦΙΛΟΚΛΗΣ

2 Ἦ που κατανενόηκας ἤδη τινὰς τοιούτους, οἷς ἔμφυτος ὁ ἔρως οὗτός ἐστι πρὸς τὸ ψεῦδος;

ΤΥΧΙΑΔΗΣ

Καὶ μάλα πολλοί εἰσιν οἱ τοιοῦτοι.

ΦΙΛΟΚΛΗΣ

Τί δ' οὖν ἄλλο ἢ ἄνοιαν χρὴ αἰτίαν εἶναι αὐτοῖς φάναι τοῦ μὴ τἀληθῆ λέγειν, εἴ γε τὸ χείριστον ἀντὶ τοῦ βελτίστου προαιροῦνται;

ΤΥΧΙΑΔΗΣ

Οὐδὲν οὐδὲ τοῦτο, ὦ Φιλόκλεις·[1] ἐπεὶ πολλοὺς ἂν ἐγώ σοι δείξαιμι συνετοὺς τἆλλα καὶ τὴν γνώμην θαυμαστοὺς οὐκ οἶδ' ὅπως ἑαλωκότας τούτῳ τῷ κακῷ καὶ φιλοψευδεῖς ὄντας, ὡς ἀνιᾶσθαί με, εἰ τοιοῦτοι ἄνδρες ἄριστοι τὰ πάντα ὅμως χαίρουσιν αὐτούς τε καὶ τοὺς ἐντυγχάνοντας ἐξαπατῶντες. ἐκείνους μὲν γὰρ τοὺς παλαιοὺς πρὸ ἐμοῦ σὲ χρὴ εἰδέναι, τὸν Ἡρόδοτον καὶ Κτησίαν τὸν Κνίδιον καὶ πρὸ τούτων τοὺς ποιητὰς καὶ τὸν Ὅμηρον αὐτόν, ἀοιδίμους ἄνδρας, ἐγγράφῳ τῷ ψεύσματι κεχρημένους, ὡς μὴ μόνους ἐξαπατᾶν τοὺς τότε ἀκούοντας σφῶν, ἀλλὰ καὶ μέχρις ἡμῶν διικνεῖσθαι τὸ ψεῦδος ἐκ διαδοχῆς ἐν καλλίστοις ἔπεσι καὶ μέτροις φυλαττόμενον. ἐμοὶ γοῦν πολλάκις αἰδεῖσθαι ὑπὲρ αὐτῶν ἔπεισιν, ὁπόταν Οὐρανοῦ τομὴν καὶ Προμηθέως δεσμὰ διηγῶνται καὶ Γιγάντων ἐπανάστασιν καὶ τὴν ἐν Αιδου πᾶσαν τραγῳδίαν, καὶ ὡς δι' ἔρωτα ὁ Ζεὺς ταῦρος ἢ κύκνος ἐγένετο καὶ ὡς ἐκ γυναικός τις εἰς ὄρνεον ἢ εἰς ἄρκτον μετέπεσεν, ἔτι δὲ

[1] οὐδὲν τοῦτο γ, omitting ὦ Φιλόκλεις.

PHILOCLES

Have you really noted any such men anywhere in whom this passion for lying is ingrained?

TYCHIADES

Yes, there are many such men.

PHILOCLES

What other reason, then, than folly may they be said to have for telling untruths, since they choose the worst course instead of the best?

TYCHIADES

That too has nothing to do with the case, Philocles, for I could show you many men otherwise sensible and remarkable for their intelligence who have somehow become infected with this plague and are lovers of lying, so that it irks me when such men, excellent in every way, yet delight in deceiving themselves and their associates. Those of olden time should be known to you before I mention them—Herodotus, and Ctesias of Cnidus, and before them the poets, including Homer himself—men of renown, who made use of the written lie, so that they not only deceived those who listened to them then, but transmitted the falsehood from generation to generation even down to us, conserved in the choicest of diction and rhythm. For my part it often occurs to me to blush for them when they tell of the castration of Uranus, and the fetters of Prometheus, and the revolt of the Giants, and the whole sorry show in Hades, and how Zeus turned into a bull or a swan on account of a love-affair, and how some woman changed into a bird or a

Πηγάσους καὶ Χιμαίρας καὶ Γοργόνας καὶ Κύκλωπας καὶ ὅσα τοιαῦτα, πάνυ ἀλλόκοτα καὶ τεράστια μυθίδια παίδων ψυχὰς κηλεῖν δυνάμενα ἔτι τὴν Μορμὼ καὶ τὴν Λάμιαν δεδιότων.

3 Καίτοι τὰ μὲν τῶν ποιητῶν ἴσως μέτρια, τὸ δὲ καὶ πόλεις ἤδη καὶ ἔθνη ὅλα[1] κοινῇ καὶ δημοσίᾳ ψεύδεσθαι πῶς οὐ γελοῖον; εἰ Κρῆτες μὲν τὸν Διὸς τάφον δεικνύντες οὐκ αἰσχύνονται, Ἀθηναῖοι δὲ τὸν Ἐριχθόνιον ἐκ τῆς γῆς ἀναδοθῆναί φασιν καὶ τοὺς πρώτους ἀνθρώπους ἐκ τῆς Ἀττικῆς ἀναφῦναι καθάπερ τὰ λάχανα, πολὺ σεμνότερον οὗτοί γε τῶν Θηβαίων, οἳ ἐξ ὄφεως ὀδόντων Σπαρτούς τινας ἀναβεβλαστηκέναι διηγοῦνται. ὃς δ' ἂν οὖν ταῦτα καταγέλαστα ὄντα μὴ οἴηται ἀληθῆ εἶναι, ἀλλ' ἐμφρόνως ἐξετάζων αὐτὰ Κοροίβου τινὸς ἢ Μαργίτου νομίζῃ[2] τὸ πείθεσθαι ἢ Τριπτόλεμον ἐλάσαι διὰ τοῦ ἀέρος ἐπὶ δρακόντων ὑποπτέρων ἢ Πᾶνα ἥκειν ἐξ Ἀρκαδίας σύμμαχον εἰς Μαραθῶνα ἢ Ὠρείθυιαν ὑπὸ τοῦ Βορέου ἁρπασθῆναι, ἀσεβὴς οὗτός γε[3] καὶ ἀνόητος αὐτοῖς ἔδοξεν οὕτω προδήλοις καὶ ἀληθέσι πράγμασιν ἀπιστῶν· εἰς τοσοῦτον ἐπικρατεῖ τὸ ψεῦδος.

ΦΙΛΟΚΛΗΣ

4 Ἀλλ' οἱ μὲν ποιηταί, ὦ Τυχιάδη, καὶ αἱ πόλεις δὲ συγγνώμης εἰκότως τυγχάνοιεν ἄν, οἱ μὲν τὸ ἐκ τοῦ μύθου τερπνὸν ἐπαγωγότατον ὂν ἐγκαταμιγνύντες τῇ γραφῇ, οὗπερ μάλιστα δέονται πρὸς τοὺς ἀκροατάς, Ἀθηναῖοι δὲ καὶ Θηβαῖοι

[1] πολλὰ γ.
[2] νομίζῃ Bekker: νομίζοι MSS.
[3] γε vulg.: τε γβ.

bear; yes, and of Pegasi, Chimaerae, Gorgons, Cyclopes, and so forth—very strange and wonderful fables, fit to enthrall the souls of children who still dread Mormo and Lamia.

Yet as far as the poets are concerned, perhaps the case is not so bad; but is it not ridiculous that even cities and whole peoples tell lies unanimously and officially? The Cretans exhibit the tomb of Zeus and are not ashamed of it, and the Athenians assert that Erichthonius sprang from the earth and that the first men came up out of the soil of Attica like vegetables; but at that their story is much more dignified than that of the Thebans, who relate that "Sown Men" grew up from serpents' teeth. If any man, however, does not think that these silly stories are true, but sanely puts them to the proof and holds that only a Coroebus or a Margites[1] can believe either that Triptolemus drove through the air behind winged serpents, or that Pan came from Arcadia to Marathon to take a hand in the battle, or that Oreithyia was carried off by Boreas, they consider that man a sacrilegious fool for doubting facts so evident and genuine; to such an extent does falsehood prevail.

PHILOCLES

Well, as far as the poets are concerned, Tychiades, and the cities too, they may properly be pardoned. The poets flavour their writings with the delectability that the fable yields, a most seductive thing, which they need above all else for the benefit of their readers; and the Athenians, Thebans and others, if

[1] Coroebus is known as a typical fool only from this passage, and the scholion upon it, which attributes to him a story told elsewhere of Margites, the hero of the lost mock-epic ascribed to Homer.

καὶ εἴ τινες ἄλλοι σεμνοτέρας ἀποφαίνοντες τὰς πατρίδας ἐκ τῶν τοιούτων. εἰ γοῦν τις ἀφέλοι τὰ μυθώδη ταῦτα ἐκ τῆς Ἑλλάδος, οὐδὲν ἂν κωλύσειε λιμῷ τοὺς περιηγητὰς αὐτῶν διαφθαρῆναι μηδὲ ἀμισθὶ τῶν ξένων τἀληθὲς ἀκούειν ἐθελησάντων. οἱ δὲ μηδεμιᾶς ἕνεκα αἰτίας τοιαύτης ὅμως χαίροντες τῷ ψεύσματι παγγέλοιοι εἰκότως δοκοῖεν ἄν.

ΤΥΧΙΑΔΗΣ

5 Εὖ λέγεις· ἐγώ γέ τοι παρὰ Εὐκράτους ἥκω σοι τοῦ πάνυ, πολλὰ τὰ ἄπιστα καὶ μυθώδη ἀκούσας· μᾶλλον δὲ μεταξὺ λεγομένων ἀπιὼν ᾠχόμην οὐ φέρων τοῦ πράγματος τὴν ὑπερβολήν, ἀλλά με ὥσπερ αἱ Ἐρινύες ἐξήλασαν πολλὰ τεράστια καὶ ἀλλόκοτα διεξιόντες.[1]

ΦΙΛΟΚΛΗΣ

Καίτοι, ὦ Τυχιάδη, ἀξιόπιστός τις ὁ Εὐκράτης ἐστίν, καὶ οὐδεὶς ἂν οὐδὲ πιστεύσειεν ὡς ἐκεῖνος οὕτω βαθὺν πώγωνα καθειμένος ἑξηκοντούτης ἀνήρ, ἔτι καὶ φιλοσοφίᾳ συνὼν τὰ πολλά, ὑπομείνειεν ἂν καὶ ἄλλου τινὸς ψευδομένου ἐπακοῦσαι παρών, οὐχ ὅπως αὐτός τι τολμῆσαι τοιοῦτον.

ΤΥΧΙΑΔΗΣ

Οὐ γὰρ οἶσθα, ὦ ἑταῖρε, οἷα μὲν εἶπεν, ὅπως δὲ αὐτὰ ἐπιστώσατο, ὡς δὲ καὶ ἐπώμνυτο τοῖς πλείστοις, παραστησάμενος τὰ παιδία, ὥστε με ἀποβλέποντα εἰς αὐτὸν ποικίλα ἐννοεῖν, ἄρτι μὲν ὡς μεμήνοι καὶ ἔξω εἴη τοῦ καθεστηκότος, ἄρτι δὲ ὡς γόης ὢν ἄρα τοσοῦτον χρόνον ἐλελήθει με

[1] διεξιόντος β.

any there be, make their countries more impressive by such means. In fact, if these fabulous tales should be taken away from Greece, there would be nothing to prevent the guides there from starving to death, as the foreigners would not care to hear the truth, even gratis! On the other hand, those who have no such motive and yet delight in lying may properly be thought utterly ridiculous.

TYCHIADES

You are quite right in what you say. For example, I come to you from Eucrates the magnificent, having listened to a great lot of incredible yarns; to put it more accurately, I took myself off in the midst of the conversation because I could not stand the exaggeration of the thing: they drove me out as if they had been the Furies by telling quantities of extraordinary miracles.

PHILOCLES

But, Tychiades, Eucrates is a trustworthy person, and nobody could ever believe that he, with such a long beard, a man of sixty, and a great devotee of philosophy too, would abide even to hear someone else tell a lie in his presence, let alone venturing to do anything of that sort himself.

TYCHIADES

Why, my dear fellow, you do not know what sort of statements he made, and how he confirmed them, and how he actually swore to most of them, taking oath upon his children, so that as I gazed at him all sorts of ideas came into my head, now that he was insane and out of his right mind, now that he was only a fraud, after all, and I had failed, in all these

ὑπὸ τῇ λεοντῇ γελοῖόν τινα πίθηκον περιστέλλων· οὕτως ἄτοπα διηγεῖτο.

ΦΙΛΟΚΛΗΣ

Τίνα ταῦτα πρὸς τῆς Ἑστίας, ὦ Τυχιάδη; ἐθέλω γὰρ εἰδέναι ἥντινα τὴν ἀλαζονείαν ὑπὸ τηλικούτῳ τῷ πώγωνι ἔσκεπεν.

ΤΥΧΙΑΔΗΣ

6 Εἰώθειν[1] μὲν καὶ ἄλλοτε, ὦ Φιλόκλεις, φοιτᾶν παρ᾽ αὐτόν, εἴ ποτε πολλὴν τὴν σχολὴν ἄγοιμι, τήμερον δὲ Λεοντίχῳ συγγενέσθαι δεόμενος—ἑταῖρος δέ μοι, ὡς οἶσθα—ἀκούσας τοῦ παιδὸς ὡς παρὰ τὸν Εὐκράτην ἕωθεν ἀπέλθοι νοσοῦντα ἐπισκεψόμενος, ἀμφοῖν ἕνεκα, ὡς καὶ τῷ Λεοντίχῳ συγγενοίμην κἀκεῖνον ἴδοιμι—ἠγνοήκειν γὰρ ὡς νοσοίη—παραγίγνομαι πρὸς αὐτόν.

Εὑρίσκω δὲ αὐτόθι τὸν μὲν Λεόντιχον οὐκέτι—ἐφθάκει γάρ, ὡς ἔφασκον, ὀλίγον προεξεληλυθὼς—ἄλλους δὲ συχνούς, ἐν οἷς Κλεόδημός τε ἦν ὁ ἐκ τοῦ Περιπάτου καὶ Δεινόμαχος ὁ Στωϊκὸς καὶ Ἴων, οἶσθα τὸν ἐπὶ τοῖς Πλάτωνος λόγοις θαυμάζεσθαι ἀξιοῦντα ὡς μόνον ἀκριβῶς καταvενοηκότα τὴν γνώμην τοῦ ἀνδρὸς καὶ τοῖς ἄλλοις ὑποφητεῦσαι δυνάμενον. ὁρᾷς οἵους ἄνδρας σοί φημι, πανσόφους καὶ παναρέτους, ὅ τι περ τὸ κεφάλαιον αὐτὸ ἐξ ἑκάστης προαιρέσεως, αἰδεσίμους ἅπαντας καὶ μονονουχὶ φοβεροὺς τὴν πρόσοψιν; ἔτι καὶ ὁ ἰατρὸς Ἀντίγονος παρῆν, κατὰ χρείαν, οἶμαι, τῆς νόσου ἐπικληθείς. καὶ ῥᾷον ἐδόκει ἤδη ἔχειν ὁ Εὐκράτης καὶ τὸ νόσημα τῶν συντρόφων ἦν· τὸ ῥεῦμα γὰρ εἰς τοὺς πόδας αὖθις αὐτῷ κατεληλύθει.

[1] εἴωθα γ.

years, to notice that his lion's skin covered a silly ape; so extravagant were the stories that he told.

PHILOCLES

What were they, Tychiades, in the name of Hestia?[1] I should like to know what sort of quackery he has been screening behind that great beard.

TYCHIADES

I used to visit him previously, Philocles, whenever I had a good deal of leisure; and to-day, when I wanted to find Leontichus, a close friend of mine, as you know, and was told by his boy that he had gone off to the house of Eucrates in the early morning to pay him a call because he was ill, I went there for two reasons, both to find Leontichus and to see Eucrates, for I had not known that he was ill.

I did not find Leontichus there, for he had just gone out a little while before, they said; but I found plenty of others, among whom there was Cleodemus the Peripatetic, and Deinomachus the Stoic, and Ion—you know the one that thinks he ought to be admired for his mastery of Plato's doctrines as the only person who has accurately sensed the man's meaning and can expound it to the rest of the world. You see what sort of men I am naming to you, all-wise and all-virtuous, the very fore-front of each school, every one venerable, almost terrible, to look at. In addition, the physician Antigonus was there, called in, I suppose, by reason of the illness. Eucrates seemed to be feeling better already, and the ailment was of a chronic character; he had had another attack of rheumatism in his feet.

[1] The oath amounts to "In the name of friendship."

Καθέζεσθαι οὖν με παρ' αὐτὸν ἐπὶ τῆς κλίνης ὁ Εὐκράτης ἐκέλευεν, ἠρέμα ἐγκλίνας τῇ φωνῇ εἰς τὸ ἀσθενικὸν ὁπότε εἶδέ με, καίτοι βοῶντος αὐτοῦ καὶ διατεινομένου τι μεταξὺ εἰσιὼν ἐπήκουον. κἀγὼ μάλα πεφυλαγμένως, μὴ ψαύσαιμι τοῖν ποδοῖν αὐτοῦ, ἀπολογησάμενος τὰ συνήθη ταῦτα, ὡς ἀγνοήσαιμι νοσοῦντα καὶ ὡς ἐπεὶ ἔμαθον δρομαῖος ἔλθοιμι, ἐκαθεζόμην πλησίον.

7 Οἱ μὲν δὴ ἐτύγχανον οἶμαι[1] περὶ τοῦ νοσήματος τὰ μὲν ἤδη πολλὰ προειρηκότες, τὰ δὲ καὶ τότε διεξιόντες, ἔτι δὲ καὶ θεραπείας τινὰς ἕκαστος ὑποβάλλοντες. ὁ γοῦν Κλεόδημος, "Εἰ τοίνυν," φησίν, "τῇ ἀριστερᾷ τις ἀνελόμενος χαμᾶθεν[2] τὸν ὀδόντα τῆς μυγαλῆς οὕτω φονευθείσης, ὡς προεῖπον, ἐνδήσειεν εἰς δέρμα λέοντος ἄρτι ἀποδαρέν, εἶτα περιάψειε περὶ τὰ σκέλη, αὐτίκα παύεται τὸ ἄλγημα."

"Οὐκ εἰς λέοντος," ἔφη ὁ Δεινόμαχος, "ἐγὼ ἤκουσα, ἐλάφου δὲ θηλείας ἔτι παρθένου καὶ ἀβάτου· καὶ τὸ πρᾶγμα οὕτω πιθανώτερον· ὠκὺ γὰρ ἡ ἔλαφος καὶ ἔρρωται μάλιστα ἐκ τῶν ποδῶν. ὁ δὲ λέων ἄλκιμος μέν, καὶ τὸ λίπος αὐτοῦ καὶ ἡ χεὶρ ἡ δεξιὰ καὶ αἱ τρίχες ἐκ τοῦ πώγωνος αἱ ὀρθαὶ μεγάλα δύνανται,[3] εἴ τις ἐπίσταιτο αὐτοῖς χρῆσθαι μετὰ τῆς οἰκείας ἐπῳδῆς ἑκάστῳ· ποδῶν δὲ ἴασιν ἥκιστα ἐπαγγέλλεται."

"Καὶ αὐτός," ἦ δ' ὃς ὁ Κλεόδημος, "οὕτω πάλαι ἐγίγνωσκον, ἐλάφου χρῆναι τὸ δέρμα εἶναι, διότι ὠκὺ ἔλαφος· ἔναγχος δὲ Λίβυς ἀνὴρ σοφὸς

[1] ἤδη γ.
[2] χαμᾶθεν Cobet: χαμάθεν Γ marg. χαμόθεν other β sources: χαμαὶ γ. [3] μεγάλα δύναιντο γ. But cf. *Pisc.* 6.

He bade me sit by him on the couch, letting his voice drop a little to the tone of an invalid when he saw me, although as I was coming in I heard him shouting and vigorously pressing some point or other. I took very good care not to touch his feet, and after making the customary excuses that I did not know he was ill and that when I learned of it I came in hot haste, sat down beside him.

It so happened that the company had already, I think, talked at some length about his ailment and were then discussing it further; they were each suggesting certain remedies, moreover. At any rate Cleodemus said: "Well then, if you take up from the ground in your left hand the tooth of the weasel which has been killed in the way I have already described and wrap it up in the skin of a lion just flayed, and then bind it about your legs, the pain ceases instantly."

"Not in a lion's skin, I was told," said Deinomachus, "but that of a hind still immature and unmated; and the thing is more plausible that way, for the hind is fleet and her strength lies especially in her legs. The lion is brave, of course, and his fat and his right fore-paw and the stiff bristles of his whiskers are very potent if one knew how to use them with the incantation appropriate to each; but for curing the feet he is not at all promising."

"I myself," said Cleodemus, "was of that opinion formerly, that it ought to be the skin of a hind because the hind is fleet; but recently a man from

τὰ τοιαῦτα μετεδίδαξέ με εἰπὼν ὠκυτέρους εἶναι τῶν ἐλάφων τοὺς λέοντας. Ἀμέλει, ἔφη, καὶ αἱροῦσιν αὐτὰς διώκοντες."

8 Ἐπῄνεσαν οἱ παρόντες ὡς εὖ εἰπόντος τοῦ Λίβυος. ἐγὼ δέ, "Οἴεσθε γάρ," ἔφην, "ἐπῳδαῖς τισιν τὰ τοιαῦτα παύεσθαι ἢ τοῖς ἔξωθεν παραρτήμασιν τοῦ κακοῦ ἔνδον διατρίβοντος;" ἐγέλασαν ἐπὶ τῷ λόγῳ καὶ δῆλοι ἦσαν κατεγνωκότες μου πολλὴν τὴν ἄνοιαν, εἰ μὴ ἐπισταίμην τὰ προδηλότατα καὶ περὶ ὧν οὐδεὶς ἂν εὖ φρονῶν[1] ἀντείποι μὴ οὐχὶ οὕτως ἔχειν. ὁ μέντοι ἰατρὸς Ἀντίγονος ἐδόκει μοι ἡσθῆναι τῇ ἐρωτήσει μου· πάλαι γὰρ ἠμελεῖτο, οἶμαι, βοηθεῖν ἀξιῶν τῷ Εὐκράτει μετὰ τῆς τέχνης οἴνου τε παραγγέλλων ἀπέχεσθαι καὶ λάχανα σιτεῖσθαι καὶ ὅλως ὑφαιρεῖν τοῦ τόνου.

Ὁ δ' οὖν Κλεόδημος ὑπομειδιῶν ἅμα, "Τί λέγεις," ἔφη, "ὦ Τυχιάδη; ἄπιστον εἶναί σοι δοκεῖ τὸ ἐκ τῶν τοιούτων γίγνεσθαί τινας ὠφελείας εἰς τὰ νοσήματα;" "Ἔμοιγε," ἦν δ' ἐγώ, "εἰ μὴ πάνυ κορύζης τὴν ῥῖνα μεστὸς εἴην, ὡς πιστεύειν τὰ ἔξω καὶ μηδὲν κοινωνοῦντα τοῖς ἔνδοθεν ἐπεγείρουσι τὰ νοσήματα μετὰ ῥηματίων, ὥς φατε, καὶ γοητείας τινὸς ἐνεργεῖν καὶ τὴν ἴασιν ἐπιπέμπειν προσαρτώμενα. τὸ δ' οὐκ ἂν γένοιτο, οὐδ' ἢν εἰς τοῦ Νεμείου λέοντος τὸ δέρμα ἐνδήσῃ τις ἑκκαίδεκα ὅλας μυγαλᾶς· ἐγὼ γοῦν αὐτὸν τὸν[2] λέοντα εἶδον πολλάκις χωλεύοντα ὑπ' ἀλγηδόνων ἐν ὁλοκλήρῳ τῷ αὑτοῦ δέρματι."

9 "Πάνυ γὰρ ἰδιώτης," ἔφη ὁ Δεινόμαχος, "εἶ καὶ τὰ τοιαῦτα οὐκ ἐμέλησέ σοι ἐκμαθεῖν ὅντινα

[1] οὐδεὶς φρονῶν γ. [2] τὸν vulg.: not in MSS.

Libya, well informed in such things, taught me better, saying that lions were fleeter than deer. 'No fear!' said he: 'They even chase and catch them!'"

The company applauded, in the belief that the Libyan was right in what he said. But I said, "Do you really think that certain incantations put a stop to this sort of thing, or external applications, when the trouble has its seat within?" They laughed at my remark and clearly held me convicted of great stupidity if I did not know the most obvious things, of which nobody in his right mind would maintain that they were not so. The doctor Antigonus, however, seemed to me to be pleased with my question, for he had been overlooked a long time, I suppose, when he wanted to aid Eucrates in a professional way by advising him to abstain from wine, adopt a vegetarian diet, and in general to "lower his pitch."

But Cleodemus, with a faint smile, said: "What is that, Tychiades? Do you consider it incredible that any alleviations of ailments are effected by such means?" "I do," said I, "not being altogether full of drivel, so as to believe that external remedies which have nothing to do with the internal causes of the ailments, applied as you say in combination with set phrases and hocus-pocus of some sort, are efficacious and bring on the cure. That could never happen, not even if you should wrap sixteen entire weasels in the skin of the Nemean lion; in fact I have often seen the lion himself limping in pain with his skin intact upon him!"

"You are a mere layman, you see," said Deinomachus, "and you have not made it a point to learn

τρόπον ὁμιλεῖ[1] τοῖς νοσήμασι προσφερόμενα, κἀμοὶ δοκεῖς οὐδὲ τὰ προφανέστατα ἂν παραδέξασθαι ταῦτα, τῶν ἐκ περιόδου πυρετῶν τὰς ἀποπομπὰς καὶ τῶν ἑρπετῶν τὰς καταθέλξεις καὶ βουβώνων ἰάσεις καὶ τἆλλα ὁπόσα καὶ αἱ γρᾶες ἤδη ποιοῦσιν. εἰ δὲ ἐκεῖνα γίγνεται ἅπαντα, τί δή ποτε οὐχὶ ταῦτα οἰήσῃ γίγνεσθαι ὑπὸ τῶν ὁμοίων;"

"Ἀπέραντα," ἦν δ' ἐγώ, "σὺ περαίνεις,[2] ὦ Δεινόμαχε, καὶ ἥλῳ, φασίν, ἐκκρούεις τὸν ἧλον· οὐδὲ γὰρ ἃ φὴς ταῦτα δῆλα μετὰ τοιαύτης δυνάμεως γιγνόμενα. ἢν γοῦν μὴ πείσῃς πρότερον ἐπάγων τῷ λόγῳ διότι φύσιν ἔχει οὕτω γίγνεσθαι, τοῦ τε πυρετοῦ καὶ τοῦ οἰδήματος δεδιότος ἢ ὄνομα θεσπέσιον ἢ ῥῆσιν βαρβαρικὴν καὶ διὰ τοῦτο ἐκ τοῦ βουβῶνος δραπετεύοντος, ἔτι σοι γραῶν μῦθοι τὰ λεγόμενά ἐστι."

10 "Σύ μοι δοκεῖς," ἦ δ' ὃς ὁ Δεινόμαχος, "τὰ τοιαῦτα λέγων οὐδὲ θεοὺς εἶναι πιστεύειν εἴ γε μὴ οἴει τὰς ἰάσεις οἷόν τε εἶναι ὑπὸ ἱερῶν ὀνομάτων γίγνεσθαι." "Τοῦτο μέν," ἦν δ' ἐγώ, "μὴ λέγε, ὦ ἄριστε· κωλύει γὰρ οὐδὲν καὶ θεῶν ὄντων ὅμως τὰ τοιαῦτα ψευδῆ εἶναι. ἐγὼ δὲ καὶ θεοὺς σέβω καὶ ἰάσεις αὐτῶν ὁρῶ καὶ ἃ εὖ ποιοῦσι τοὺς κάμνοντας ὑπὸ φαρμάκων καὶ ἰατρικῆς ἀνιστάντες· ὁ γοῦν Ἀσκληπιὸς αὐτὸς καὶ οἱ παῖδες αὐτοῦ ἤπια φάρμακα πάσσοντες ἐθεράπευον τοὺς νοσοῦντας, οὐ λεοντᾶς[3] καὶ μυγαλᾶς περιάπτοντες."

11 "Ἔα τοῦτον," ἔφη ὁ Ἴων, "ἐγὼ δὲ ὑμῖν θαυμά-

[1] ὠφελεῖ N Vat. 87.
[2] σὺ περαίνεις Fritzsche : σὺ παραινεῖς γ, ξυμπεραίνῃ β.
[3] λεοντᾶς Cobet : λέοντας MSS.

how such things agree with ailments when they are applied. I do not suppose you would accept even the most obvious instances—periodic fevers driven off, snakes charmed, swellings cured, and whatever else even old wives do. But if all that takes place, why in the world will you not believe that this takes place by similar means?"

"You are reasoning from false premises, Deinomachus," I replied, "and, as the saying goes, driving out one nail with another; for it is not clear that precisely what you are speaking of takes place by the aid of any such power. If, then, you do not first convince me by logical proof that it takes place in this way naturally, because the fever or the inflammation is afraid of a holy name or a foreign phrase and so takes flight from the swelling, your stories still remain old wives' fables."

"It seems to me," said Deinomachus, "that when you talk like that you do not believe in the gods, either, since you do not think that cures can be effected through holy names." "Don't say that, my dear sir!" I replied. "Even though the gods exist, there is nothing to prevent that sort of thing from being false just the same. For my part, I revere the gods and I see their cures and all the good that they do by restoring the sick to health with drugs and doctoring. In fact, Asclepius himself and his sons ministered to the sick by laying on healing drugs, not by fastening on lions' skins and weasels."[1]

"Never mind him," said Ion, "and I will tell you

[1] Cf. *Iliad* 4, 218; 11, 830.

σιόν τι διηγήσομαι. ἦν μὲν ἐγὼ μειράκιον ἔτι ἀμφὶ τὰ τετταρακαίδεκα ἔτη σχεδόν· ἧκεν δέ τις ἀγγέλλων τῷ πατρὶ Μίδαν τὸν ἀμπελουργόν, ἐρρωμένον εἰς τὰ ἄλλα οἰκέτην καὶ ἐργατικόν, ἀμφὶ πλήθουσαν ἀγορὰν ὑπὸ ἐχίδνης δηχθέντα κεῖσθαι ἤδη σεσηπότα τὸ σκέλος· ἀναδοῦντι γὰρ αὐτῷ τὰ κλήματα καὶ ταῖς χάραξι περιπλέκοντι προσερπύσαν τὸ θηρίον δακεῖν κατὰ τὸν μέγαν δάκτυλον, καὶ τὸ μὲν φθάσαι καὶ καταδῦναι αὖθις εἰς τὸν φωλεόν, τὸν δὲ οἰμώζειν ἀπολλύμενον ὑπ' ἀλγηδόνων.

"Ταῦτά τε οὖν ἀπηγγέλλετο καὶ τὸν Μίδαν ἑωρῶμεν αὐτὸν ἐπὶ σκίμποδος ὑπὸ τῶν ὁμοδούλων προσκομιζόμενον, ὅλον ᾠδηκότα, πελιδνόν, μυδῶντα ἐπιπολῆς,[1] ὀλίγον ἔτι ἐμπνέοντα. λελυπημένῳ δὴ τῷ πατρὶ τῶν φίλων τις παρών, 'Θάρρει,' ἔφη, 'ἐγὼ γάρ σοι ἄνδρα Βαβυλώνιον τῶν Χαλδαίων, ὥς φασιν, αὐτίκα μέτειμι, ὃς ἰάσεται τὸν ἄνθρωπον.' καὶ ἵνα μὴ διατρίβω λέγων, ἧκεν ὁ Βαβυλώνιος καὶ ἀνέστησε τὸν Μίδαν ἐπῳδῇ τινι ἐξελάσας τὸν ἰὸν ἐκ τοῦ σώματος, ἔτι καὶ προσαρτήσας τῷ ποδὶ νεκρᾶς[2] παρθένου λίθον ἀπὸ τῆς στήλης ἐκκολάψας.

"Καὶ τοῦτο μὲν ἴσως μέτριον· καίτοι ὁ Μίδας αὐτὸς ἀράμενος τὸν σκίμποδα ἐφ' οὗ ἐκεκόμιστο ᾤχετο εἰς τὸν ἀγρὸν ἀπιών· τοσοῦτον ἡ ἐπῳδὴ 12 ἐδυνήθη καὶ ὁ στηλίτης ἐκεῖνος λίθος. ὁ δὲ καὶ ἄλλα ἐποίησε θεσπέσια ὡς ἀληθῶς· εἰς γὰρ τὸν ἀγρὸν ἐλθὼν ἕωθεν, ἐπειπὼν ἱερατικά τινα ἐκ βίβλου παλαιᾶς ὀνόματα ἑπτὰ καὶ θείῳ καὶ δᾳδὶ καθαγνίσας τὸν τόπον περιελθὼν ἐς τρίς, ἐξεκά-

[1] τὴν ἐπιφάνειαν γ. [2] τεθνηκυίας γ.

a wonderful story. I was still a young lad, about fourteen years old, when someone came and told my father that Midas the vine-dresser, ordinarily a strong and industrious servant, had been bitten by a viper toward midday and was lying down, with his leg already in a state of mortification. While he was tying up the runners and twining them about the poles, the creature had crawled up and bitten him on the great toe; then it had quickly gone down again into its hole, and he was groaning in mortal anguish.

"As this report was being made, we saw Midas himself being brought up on a litter by his fellow-slaves, all swollen and livid, with a clammy skin and but little breath left in him. Naturally my father was distressed, but a friend who was there said to him: 'Cheer up: I will at once go and get you a Babylonian, one of the so-called Chaldeans, who will cure the fellow.' Not to make a long story of it, the Babylonian came and brought Midas back to life, driving the poison out of his body by a spell, and also binding upon his foot a fragment which he broke from the tombstone of a dead maiden.

"Perhaps this is nothing out of the common: although Midas himself picked up the litter on which he had been carried and went off to the farm, so potent was the spell and the fragment of the tombstone. But the Babylonian did other things that were truly miraculous. Going to the farm in the early morning, he repeated seven sacred names out of an old book, purified the place with sulphur and torches, going about it three times, and called out all the

λεσεν[1] ὅσα ἦν ἑρπετὰ ἐντὸς τῶν ὅρων. ἧκον οὖν ὥσπερ ἑλκόμενοι πρὸς τὴν ἐπῳδὴν ὄφεις πολλοὶ καὶ ἀσπίδες καὶ ἔχιδναι καὶ κεράσται καὶ ἀκοντίαι φρῦνοί τε καὶ φύσαλοι, ἐλείπετο δὲ εἷς δράκων παλαιός, ὑπὸ γήρως, οἶμαι, ἐξερπύσαι μὴ δυνάμενος ἢ παρακούσας τοῦ προστάγματος· ὁ δὲ μάγος οὐκ ἔφη παρεῖναι ἅπαντας, ἀλλ᾽ ἕνα τινὰ τῶν ὄφεων τὸν νεώτατον χειροτονήσας πρεσβευτὴν ἔπεμψεν ἐπὶ τὸν δράκοντα, καὶ μετὰ μικρὸν ἧκε κἀκεῖνος. ἐπεὶ δὲ συνηλίσθησαν,[2] ἐνεφύσησε μὲν αὐτοῖς ὁ Βαβυλώνιος, τὰ δὲ αὐτίκα μάλα κατεκαύθη ἅπαντα ὑπὸ τῷ φυσήματι, ἡμεῖς δὲ ἐθαυμάζομεν."

13 "Εἰπέ μοι, ὦ Ἴων," ἦν δ᾽ ἐγώ, "ὁ ὄφις δὲ ὁ πρεσβευτὴς ὁ νέος ἄρα καὶ ἐχειραγώγει τὸν δράκοντα ἤδη, ὡς φής, γεγηρακότα, ἢ σκίπωνα ἔχων ἐκεῖνος ἐπεστηρίζετο;"

"Σὺ μὲν παίζεις," ἔφη ὁ Κλεόδημος, "ἐγὼ δὲ καὶ αὐτὸς ἀπιστότερος ὢν σου πάλαι τὰ τοιαῦτα—ᾤμην γὰρ οὐδενὶ λόγῳ δυνατὸν γίγνεσθαι ἂν αὐτὰ—ὅμως ὅτε τὸ πρῶτον εἶδον πετόμενον τὸν ξένον τὸν βάρβαρον—ἐξ Ὑπερβορέων δὲ ἦν, ὡς ἔφασκεν—ἐπίστευσα καὶ ἐνικήθην ἐπὶ πολὺ ἀντισχών. τί γὰρ ἔδει ποιεῖν αὐτὸν ὁρῶντα διὰ τοῦ ἀέρος φερόμενον ἡμέρας οὔσης καὶ ἐφ᾽ ὕδατος βαδίζοντα καὶ διὰ πυρὸς διεξιόντα σχολῇ καὶ βάδην;" "Σὺ ταῦτα εἶδες," ἦν δ᾽ ἐγώ, "τὸν Ὑπερβόρεον ἄνδρα πετόμενον ἢ ἐπὶ τοῦ ὕδατος βεβηκότα;" "Καὶ μάλα," ἦ δ᾽ ὅς, "ὑποδεδεμένον γε καρβατίνας, οἷα μάλιστα ἐκεῖνοι ὑποδοῦνται. τὰ μὲν γὰρ σμικρὰ

[1] ἐξήλασεν γ.
[2] συνηλίσθησαν du Soul: συνηυλίσθησαν MSS.

reptiles that there were inside the boundaries. They came as if they were being drawn in response to the spell, snakes in great numbers, asps, vipers, horned snakes, darters, common toads, and puff-toads; one old python, however, was missing, who on account of his age, I suppose, could not creep out and so failed to comply with the command. The magician said that not all were there, and electing one of the snakes messenger, the youngest, sent him after the python, who presently came too. When they were assembled, the Babylonian blew on them and they were all instantly burned up by the blast, and we were amazed."

"Tell me, Ion," said I, "did the messenger snake, the young one, give his arm to the python, who you say was aged, or did the python have a stick and lean on it?"

"You are joking," said Cleodemus: "I myself was formerly more incredulous than you in regard to such things, for I thought it in no way possible that they could happen; but when first I saw the foreign stranger fly—he came from the land of the Hyperboreans, he said—, I believed and was conquered after long resistance. What was I to do when I saw him soar through the air in broad daylight and walk on the water and go through fire slowly on foot?" "Did you see that?" said I—"the Hyperborean flying, or stepping on the water?" "Certainly," said he, "with brogues on his feet such as people of that country commonly wear. As for the trivial

ταῦτα τί χρὴ καὶ λέγειν ὅσα ἐπεδείκνυτο, ἔρωτας ἐπιπέμπων καὶ δαίμονας ἀνάγων καὶ νεκροὺς ἑώλους ἀνακαλῶν καὶ τὴν Ἑκάτην αὐτὴν ἐναργῆ 14 παριστὰς καὶ τὴν Σελήνην καθαιρῶν;[1] ἐγὼ γοῦν διηγήσομαι ὑμῖν ἃ εἶδον γιγνόμενα ὑπ' αὐτοῦ ἐν Γλαυκίου τοῦ Ἀλεξικλέους.

"Ἄρτι γὰρ ὁ Γλαυκίας τοῦ πατρὸς ἀποθανόντος παραλαβὼν τὴν οὐσίαν ἠράσθη Χρυσίδος τῆς Δημέου γυναικός. ἐμοὶ δὲ διδασκάλῳ ἐχρῆτο πρὸς τοὺς λόγους, καὶ εἴ γε μὴ ὁ ἔρως ἐκεῖνος ἀπησχόλησεν αὐτόν, ἅπαντα ἂν ἤδη τὰ τοῦ Περιπάτου ἠπίστατο, ὃς καὶ ὀκτωκαιδεκαέτης ὢν ἀνέλυε καὶ τὴν φυσικὴν ἀκρόασιν μετεληλύθει εἰς τέλος. ἀμηχανῶν δὲ ὅμως τῷ ἔρωτι μηνύει μοι τὸ πᾶν, ἐγὼ δὲ ὥσπερ εἰκὸς ἦν, διδάσκαλον ὄντα, τὸν Ὑπερβόρεον ἐκεῖνον μάγον ἄγω παρ' αὐτὸν ἐπὶ μναῖς τέτταρσι μὲν τὸ παραυτίκα—ἔδει γὰρ προτελέσαι τι εἰς τὰς θυσίας—ἑκκαίδεκα δέ, εἰ τύχοι τῆς Χρυσίδος. ὁ δὲ αὐξομένην τηρήσας τὴν σελήνην—τότε γὰρ ὡς ἐπὶ τὸ πολὺ τὰ τοιαῦτα τελεσιουργεῖται—βόθρον τε ὀρυξάμενος ἐν ὑπαίθρῳ[2] τινὶ τῆς οἰκίας περὶ μέσας νύκτας ἀνεκάλεσεν ἡμῖν πρῶτον μὲν τὸν Ἀλεξικλέα τὸν πατέρα τοῦ Γλαυκίου πρὸ ἑπτὰ μηνῶν τεθνεῶτα· ἠγανάκτει δὲ ὁ γέρων ἐπὶ τῷ ἔρωτι καὶ ὠργίζετο, τὰ τελευταῖα δὲ ὅμως ἐφῆκεν αὐτῷ ἐρᾶν. μετὰ δὲ τὴν Ἑκάτην τε ἀνήγαγεν ἐπαγομένην τὸν Κέρβερον καὶ τὴν Σελήνην κατέσπασεν, πολύμορφόν τι θέαμα καὶ ἄλλοτε ἀλλοῖόν τι φανταζόμενον· τὸ μὲν γὰρ πρῶτον γυναικείαν μορφὴν ἐπεδείκνυτο, εἶτα βοῦς ἐγίγνετο πάγκαλος, εἶτα σκύλαξ

[1] κατασπᾶν γ. [2] αἰθρίῳ γ.

feats, what is the use of telling all that he performed, sending Cupids after people, bringing up supernatural beings, calling mouldy corpses to life, making Hecate herself appear in plain sight, and pulling down the moon? But after all, I will tell you what I saw him do in the house of Glaucias, son of Alexicles.

"Immediately after Glaucias' father died and he acquired the property, he fell in love with Chrysis, the wife of Demeas. I was in his employ as his tutor in philosophy, and if that love-affair had not kept him too busy, he would have known all the teachings of the Peripatetic school, for even at eighteen he was solving fallacies and had completed the course of lectures on natural philosophy.[1] At his wit's end, however, with his love-affair, he told me the whole story; and as was natural, since I was his tutor, I brought him that Hyperborean magician at a fee of four minas down (it was necessary to pay something in advance towards the cost of the victims) and sixteen if he should obtain Chrysis. The man waited for the moon to wax, as it is then, for the most part, that such rites are performed; and after digging a pit in an open court of the house, at about midnight he first summoned up for us Alexicles, Glaucias' father, who had died seven months before. The old gentleman was indignant over the love-affair and flew into a passion, but at length he permitted him to go on with it after all. Next he brought up Hecate, who fetched Cerberus with her, and he drew down the moon, a many-shaped spectacle, appearing differently at different times; for at first she exhibited the form of a woman, then she turned into a handsome bull, and then she looked like a puppy.

[2] Aristotle's *Physics*.

ἐφαίνετο. τέλος δ' οὖν ὁ Ὑπερβόρεος ἐκ πηλοῦ ἐρώτιόν τι ἀναπλάσας, Ἄπιθι, ἔφη, καὶ ἄγε Χρυσίδα. καὶ ὁ μὲν πηλὸς ἐξέπτατο, μετὰ μικρὸν δὲ ἐπέστη κόπτουσα τὴν θύραν ἐκείνη καὶ εἰσελθοῦσα περιβάλλει τὸν Γλαυκίαν ὡς ἂν ἐκμανέστατα ἐρῶσα καὶ συνῆν ἄχρι δὴ ἀλεκτρυόνων ἠκούσαμεν ᾀδόντων. τότε δὴ ἥ τε Σελήνη ἀνέπτατο εἰς τὸν οὐρανὸν καὶ ἡ Ἑκάτη ἔδυ κατὰ τῆς γῆς καὶ τὰ ἄλλα φάσματα ἠφανίσθη καὶ τὴν Χρυσίδα ἐξεπέμψαμεν περὶ αὐτό που σχεδὸν τὸ λυκαυγές. 15 εἰ ταῦτα εἶδες, ὦ Τυχιάδη, οὐκ ἂν ἔτι ἠπίστησας εἶναι πολλὰ ἐν ταῖς ἐπῳδαῖς χρήσιμα."

"Εὖ λέγεις," ἦν δ' ἐγώ· "ἐπίστευον γὰρ ἄν, εἴ γε εἶδον αὐτά, νῦν δὲ συγγνώμη, οἶμαι, εἰ μὴ τὰ ὅμοια ὑμῖν ὀξυδορκεῖν ἔχω.[1] πλὴν ἀλλ' οἶδα γὰρ τὴν Χρυσίδα ἣν λέγεις, ἐραστὴν γυναῖκα καὶ πρόχειρον, οὐχ ὁρῶ δὲ τίνος ἕνεκα ἐδεήθητε ἐπ' αὐτὴν τοῦ πηλίνου πρεσβευτοῦ καὶ μάγου τοῦ ἐξ Ὑπερβορέων καὶ Σελήνης αὐτῆς, ἣν εἴκοσι δραχμῶν ἀγαγεῖν εἰς Ὑπερβορέους δυνατὸν ἦν. πάνυ γὰρ ἐνδίδωσιν πρὸς ταύτην τὴν ἐπῳδὴν ἡ γυνὴ καὶ τὸ ἐναντίον τοῖς φάσμασιν πέπονθεν· ἐκεῖνα μὲν γὰρ ἢν ψόφον ἀκούσῃ χαλκοῦ ἢ σιδήρου, πέφευγε—καὶ ταῦτα γὰρ ὑμεῖς φατε—αὕτη δὲ ἂν ἀργύριόν που ψοφῇ, ἔρχεται πρὸς τὸν ἦχον. ἄλλως τε καὶ αὐτοῦ θαυμάζω τοῦ μάγου, εἰ δυνάμενος αὐτὸς ἐρᾶσθαι πρὸς τῶν πλουσιωτάτων γυναικῶν καὶ τάλαντα ὅλα παρ' αὐτῶν λαμβάνειν, ὁ δὲ τεττάρων μνῶν πάνυ σμικρολόγος ὢν[2] Γλαυκίαν ἐπέραστον ἐργάζεται."

[1] εἰ μή τις τὰ ὅμοια ὑμῖν ὀξυδερκεῖ β.
[2] τὸν μικρολόγον β (omitting πάνυ and ὢν).

Finally, the Hyperborean made a little Cupid out of clay and said: 'Go and fetch Chrysis.' The clay took wing, and before long Chrysis stood on the threshold knocking at the door, came in and embraced Glaucias as if she loved him furiously, and remained with him until we heard the cocks crowing. Then the moon flew up to the sky, Hecate plunged beneath the earth, the other phantasms disappeared, and we sent Chrysis home at just about dawn. If you had seen that, Tychiades, you would no longer have doubted that there is much good in spells."

"Quite so," said I, "I should have believed if I had seen it, but as things are I may perhaps be pardoned if I am not able to see as clearly as you. However, I know the Chrysis whom you speak of, an amorous dame and an accessible one, and I do not see why you needed the clay messenger and the Hyperborean magician and the moon in person to fetch her, when for twenty drachmas she could have been brought to the Hyperboreans! The woman is very susceptible to that spell, and her case is the opposite to that of ghosts; if they hear a chink of bronze or iron, they take flight, so you say, but as for her, if silver chinks anywhere, she goes toward the sound. Besides, I am surprised at the magician himself, if he was able to have the love of the richest women and get whole talents from them, and yet made Glaucias fascinating, penny-wise that he is, for four minas."

"Γελοῖα ποιεῖς," ἔφη ὁ Ἴων, "ἀπιστῶν ἅπασιν. 16 ἐγὼ γοῦν ἡδέως ἂν ἐροίμην σε, τί περὶ τούτων φῂς ὅσοι τοὺς δαιμονῶντας ἀπαλλάττουσι τῶν δειμάτων οὕτω σαφῶς ἐξᾴδοντες τὰ φάσματα. καὶ ταῦτα οὐκ ἐμὲ χρὴ λέγειν, ἀλλὰ πάντες ἴσασι τὸν Σύρον τὸν ἐκ τῆς Παλαιστίνης, τὸν ἐπὶ τούτῳ σοφιστήν, ὅσους παραλαβὼν καταπίπτοντας πρὸς τὴν σελήνην καὶ τὼ ὀφθαλμὼ διαστρέφοντας καὶ ἀφροῦ πιμπλαμένους τὸ στόμα ὅμως ἀνίστησι καὶ ἀποπέμπει ἀρτίους τὴν γνώμην, ἐπὶ μισθῷ μεγάλῳ ἀπαλλάξας τῶν δεινῶν. ἐπειδὰν γὰρ ἐπιστὰς κειμένοις ἔρηται ὅθεν εἰσεληλύθασιν εἰς τὸ σῶμα, ὁ μὲν νοσῶν αὐτὸς σιωπᾷ, ὁ δαίμων δὲ ἀποκρίνεται, ἑλληνίζων ἢ βαρβαρίζων ὁπόθεν[1] ἂν αὐτὸς ᾖ, ὅπως τε καὶ ὅθεν εἰσῆλθεν εἰς τὸν ἄνθρωπον· ὁ δὲ ὅρκους ἐπάγων, εἰ δὲ μὴ πεισθείη, καὶ ἀπειλῶν ἐξελαύνει τὸν δαίμονα. ἐγὼ γοῦν καὶ εἶδον ἐξιόντα μέλανα καὶ καπνώδη τὴν χρόαν."

"Οὐ μέγα," ἦν δ' ἐγώ, "τὰ τοιαῦτά σε ὁρᾶν, ὦ Ἴων, ᾧ γε καὶ αἱ ἰδέαι αὐταὶ φαίνονται ἃ ὁ πατὴρ ὑμῶν Πλάτων δείκνυσιν, ἀμαυρόν τι θέαμα ὡς πρὸς ἡμᾶς τοὺς ἀμβλυώττοντας."

17 "Μόνος γὰρ Ἴων," ἔφη ὁ Εὐκράτης, "τὰ τοιαῦτα εἶδεν, οὐχὶ δὲ καὶ ἄλλοι πολλοὶ δαίμοσιν ἐντετυχήκασιν οἱ μὲν νύκτωρ, οἱ δὲ μεθ' ἡμέραν; ἐγὼ δὲ οὐχ ἅπαξ ἀλλὰ μυριάκις ἤδη σχέδον τὰ τοιαῦτα τεθέαμαι· καὶ τὸ μὲν πρῶτον ἐταραττόμην πρὸς αὐτά, νῦν δὲ δὴ ὑπὸ τοῦ ἔθους οὐδέν τι

[1] ἢ ὅθεν γ.

"You act ridiculously," said Ion, "to doubt everything. For my part, I should like to ask you what you say to those who free possessed men from their terrors by exorcising the spirits so manifestly. I need not discuss this: everyone knows about the Syrian from Palestine, the adept in it,[1] how many he takes in hand who fall down in the light of the moon and roll their eyes and fill their mouths with foam; nevertheless, he restores them to health and sends them away normal in mind, delivering them from their straits for a large fee. When he stands beside them as they lie there and asks: 'Whence came you into his body?' the patient himself is silent, but the spirit answers in Greek or in the language of whatever foreign country he comes from, telling how and whence he entered into the man; whereupon, by adjuring the spirit and if he does not obey, threatening him, he drives him out. Indeed, I actually saw one coming out, black and smoky in colour." "It is nothing much," I remarked, "for you, Ion, to see that kind of sight, when even the 'forms'[2] that the father of your school, Plato, points out are plain to you, a hazy object of vision to the rest of us, whose eyes are weak."

"Why, is Ion the only one who has seen that kind of sight?" said Eucrates. "Have not many others encountered spirits, some at night and some by day? For myself, I have seen such things, not merely once but almost hundreds of times. At first I was disturbed by them, but now, of course, because of

[1] A scholiast takes this as a reference to Christ, but he is surely in error. The Syrian is Lucian's contemporary, and probably not a Christian at all. Exorcists were common then. [2] *i.e.* the "ideas."

παράλογον ὁρᾶν μοι δοκῶ, καὶ μάλιστα ἐξ οὗ μοι τὸν δακτύλιον ὁ Ἄραψ ἔδωκε σιδήρου τοῦ ἐκ τῶν σταυρῶν πεποιημένον καὶ τὴν ἐπῳδὴν ἐδίδαξεν τὴν πολυώνυμον, ἐκτὸς εἰ μὴ κἀμοὶ ἀπιστήσεις, ὦ Τυχιάδη." "Καὶ πῶς ἄν," ἦν δ' ἐγώ, "ἀπιστήσαιμι Εὐκράτει τῷ Δείνωνος, σοφῷ ἀνδρὶ καὶ μάλιστα ἐλευθερίῳ,[1] τὰ δοκοῦντά οἱ λέγοντι οἴκοι

18 παρ' αὑτῷ ἐπ' ἐξουσίας;" "Τὸ γοῦν περὶ τοῦ ἀνδριάντος," ἦ δ' ὃς ὁ Εὐκράτης, "ἅπασι τοῖς ἐπὶ τῆς οἰκίας ὅσαι νύκτες φαινόμενον καὶ παισὶ καὶ νεανίαις καὶ γέρουσι, τοῦτο οὐ παρ' ἐμοῦ μόνον ἀκούσειας ἂν ἀλλὰ καὶ παρὰ τῶν ἡμετέρων ἁπάντων." "Ποίου," ἦν δ' ἐγώ, "ἀνδριάντος;"

"Οὐχ ἑώρακας," ἔφη, "εἰσιὼν ἐν τῇ αὐλῇ ἀνεστηκότα πάγκαλον ἀνδριάντα, Δημητρίου ἔργον τοῦ ἀνθρωποποιοῦ;" "Μῶν τὸν δισκεύοντα," ἦν δ' ἐγώ, "φῄς, τὸν ἐπικεκυφότα κατὰ τὸ σχῆμα τῆς ἀφέσεως, ἀπεστραμμένον εἰς τὴν δισκοφόρον, ἠρέμα ὀκλάζοντα τῷ ἑτέρῳ, ἐοικότα συναναστησομένῳ μετὰ τῆς βολῆς;" "Οὐκ ἐκεῖνον," ἦ δ' ὅς, "ἐπεὶ τῶν Μύρωνος ἔργων ἓν καὶ τοῦτό ἐστιν, ὁ δισκοβόλος ὃν λέγεις· οὐδὲ τὸν παρ' αὐτόν φημι, τὸν διαδούμενον τὴν κεφαλὴν τῇ ταινίᾳ, τὸν καλόν, Πολυκλείτου γὰρ τοῦτο ἔργον. ἀλλὰ τοὺς μὲν ἐπὶ τὰ δεξιὰ εἰσιόντων ἄφες, ἐν οἷς καὶ τὰ Κριτίου καὶ[2] Νησιώτου πλάσματα ἕστηκεν, οἱ τυραννοκτόνοι· σὺ δὲ εἴ τινα παρὰ τὸ ὕδωρ τὸ ἐπιρρέον εἶδες προγάστορα, φαλαντίαν, ἡμίγυμνον τὴν ἀναβολήν, ἠνεμωμένον τοῦ πώγωνος τὰς τρίχας ἐνίας, ἐπίσημον τὰς φλέβας, αὐτοανθρώπῳ ὅμοιον, ἐκεῖ-

[1] ἐλευθερίῳ Fritzsche: ἐλευθερίως γ: μάλιστα καὶ ἐλευθέρῳ β.
[2] καὶ Ross: τοῦ MSS.

their familiarity, I do not consider that I am seeing anything out of the way, especially since the Arab gave me the ring made of iron from crosses and taught me the spell of many names. But perhaps you will doubt me also, Tychiades." "How could I doubt Eucrates, the son of Deinon," said I, "a learned and an uncommonly independent gentleman, expressing his opinions in his own home, with complete liberty?" "Anyhow," said Eucrates, "the affair of the statue was observed every night by everybody in the house, boys, young men and old men, and you could hear about it not only from me but from all our people." "Statue!" said I, "what do you mean?"

"Have you not observed on coming in," said he, "a very fine statue set up in the hall, the work of Demetrius, the maker of portrait-statues?" "Do you mean the discus-thrower," said I, "the one bent over in the position of the throw, with his head turned back toward the hand that holds the discus, with one leg slightly bent, looking as if he would spring up all at once with the cast?" "Not that one," said he, "for that is one of Myron's works, the discus-thrower you speak of. Neither do I mean the one beside it, the one binding his head with the fillet, the handsome lad, for that is Polycleitus' work. Never mind those to the right as you come in, among which stand the tyrant-slayers, modelled by Critius and Nesiotes; but if you noticed one beside the fountain, pot-bellied, bald on the forehead, half bared by the hang of his cloak, with some of the hairs of his beard wind-blown and his veins prominent, the image of a real man, that is the one I mean;

νον λέγω· Πέλλιχος ὁ Κορίνθιος στρατηγὸς εἶναι δοκεῖ."

19 "Νὴ Δί'," ἦν δ' ἐγώ, "εἶδόν τινα ἐπὶ δεξιὰ τοῦ κρουνοῦ,[1] ταινίας καὶ στεφάνους ξηροὺς ἔχοντα, κατακεχρυσωμένον πετάλοις τὸ στῆθος." "Ἐγὼ δέ," ὁ Εὐκράτης ἔφη, "ἐκεῖνα ἐχρύσωσα, ὁπότε μ' ἰάσατο διὰ τρίτης ὑπὸ τοῦ ἠπιάλου ἀπολλύμενον." "Ἦ γὰρ καὶ ἰατρός," ἦν δ' ἐγώ, "ὁ βέλτιστος ἡμῖν Πέλλιχος οὗτός ἐστιν;" "Μὴ σκῶπτε," ἦ δ' ὃς ὁ Εὐκράτης, "ἤ σε οὐκ εἰς μακρὰν μέτεισιν ὁ ἀνήρ· οἶδα ἐγὼ ὅσον δύναται οὗτος ὁ ὑπὸ σοῦ γελώμενος ἀνδριάς. ἦ οὐ νομίζεις τοῦ αὐτοῦ εἶναι καὶ ἐπιπέμπειν ἠπιάλους οἷς ἂν ἐθέλῃ, εἴ γε καὶ ἀποπέμπειν δυνατὸν αὐτῷ;" "Ἵλεως," ἦν δ' ἐγώ, "ἔστω ὁ ἀνδριὰς καὶ ἤπιος οὕτως ἀνδρεῖος ὤν. τί δ' οὖν καὶ ἄλλο ποιοῦντα ὁρᾶτε αὐτὸν ἅπαντες οἱ ἐν τῇ οἰκίᾳ;"

"Ἐπειδὰν τάχιστα," ἔφη, "νὺξ γένηται, ὁ δὲ καταβὰς ἀπὸ τῆς βάσεως ἐφ' ᾗ ἕστηκε περίεισιν ἐν κύκλῳ τὴν οἰκίαν, καὶ πάντες ἐντυγχάνομεν αὐτῷ ἐνίοτε καὶ ᾄδοντι, καὶ οὐκ ἔστιν ὅντινα ἠδίκησεν· ἐκτρέπεσθαι γὰρ χρὴ μόνον· ὁ δὲ παρέρχεται μηδὲν ἐνοχλήσας τοὺς ἰδόντας. καὶ μὴν καὶ λούεται τὰ πολλὰ καὶ παίζει δι' ὅλης τῆς νυκτός, ὥστε ἀκούειν τοῦ ὕδατος ψοφοῦντος." "Ὅρα τοίνυν," ἦν δ' ἐγώ, "μὴ οὐχὶ Πέλλιχος ὁ ἀνδριάς, ἀλλὰ Τάλως ὁ Κρὴς ὁ τοῦ Μίνωος ᾖ· καὶ

[1] Κρόνου γ.

he is thought to be Pellichus, the Corinthian general."[1]

"Yes," I said, "I saw one to the right of the spout, wearing fillets and withered wreaths, his breast covered with gilt leaves." "I myself put on the gilt leaves," said Eucrates, "when he cured me of the ague that was torturing me to death every other day." "Really, is our excellent Pellichus a doctor also?" said I. "Do not mock," Eucrates replied, "or before long the man will punish you. I know what virtue there is in this statue that you make fun of. Don't you suppose that he can send fevers upon whomsoever he will, since it is possible for him to send them away?" "May the manikin be gracious and kindly," said I, "since he is so manful. But what else does everyone in the house see him doing?"

"As soon as night comes," he said, "he gets down from the pedestal on which he stands and goes all about the house; we all encounter him, sometimes singing, and he has never harmed anybody. One has but to turn aside, and he passes without molesting in any way those who saw him. Upon my word, he often takes baths and disports himself all night, so that the water can be heard splashing." "See here, then," said I, "perhaps the statue is not Pellichus but Talos the Cretan, the son of Minos; he was a

[1] Probably the Pellichus named as the father of Aristeus, a Corinthian general in the expedition against Epidamnus in 434 B.C. The statue would thus be about contemporary with that of Simon by the same Demetrius of Alopece, which is mentioned in Aristophanes. It is surprisingly realistic for so early a period. Furtwängler thought the description inaccurate, but the statue may have been the work of some later Demetrius. Certainly its identification as a portrait of Pellichus was conjectural (δοκεῖ).

γὰρ ἐκεῖνος χαλκοῦς τις ἦν τῆς Κρήτης περίπολος. εἰ δὲ μὴ χαλκοῦ, ὦ Εὔκρατες, ἀλλὰ ξύλου πεποίητο, οὐδὲν αὐτὸν ἐκώλυεν οὐ Δημητρίου ἔργον εἶναι, ἀλλὰ τῶν Δαιδάλου τεχνημάτων· δραπετεύει γοῦν, ὡς φής, ἀπὸ τῆς βάσεως καὶ οὗτος."

20 "Ὅρα," ἔφη, "ὦ Τυχιάδη, μή σοι μεταμελήσῃ τοῦ σκώμματος ὕστερον. οἶδα ἐγὼ οἷα ἔπαθεν ὁ τοὺς ὀβολοὺς ὑφελόμενος οὓς κατὰ τὴν νουμηνίαν ἑκάστην τίθεμεν αὐτῷ." "Πάνδεινα ἐχρῆν," ἔφη ὁ Ἴων, "ἱερόσυλόν γε ὄντα. πῶς δ' οὖν αὐτὸν ἠμύνατο, ὦ Εὔκρατες; ἐθέλω γὰρ ἀκοῦσαι, εἰ καὶ ὅτι μάλιστα οὑτοσὶ Τυχιάδης ἀπιστήσει."

"Πολλοί," ἦ δ' ὅς, "ἔκειντο ὀβολοὶ πρὸ τοῖν ποδοῖν αὐτοῦ καὶ ἄλλα νομίσματα ἔνια ἀργυρᾶ πρὸς τὸν μηρὸν κηρῷ κεκολλημένα καὶ πέταλα ἐξ ἀργύρου, εὐχαί τινος ἢ μισθὸς ἐπὶ τῇ ἰάσει ὁπόσοι δι' αὐτὸν ἐπαύσαντο πυρετῷ ἐχόμενοι. ἦν δὲ ἡμῖν Λίβυς τις οἰκέτης κατάρατος, ἱπποκόμος· οὗτος ἐπεχείρησε νυκτὸς ὑφελέσθαι πάντα ἐκεῖνα καὶ ὑφείλετο καταβεβηκότα ἤδη τηρήσας τὸν ἀνδριάντα. ἐπεὶ δὲ ἐπανελθὼν τάχιστα ἔγνω περισεσυλημένος ὁ Πέλλιχος, ὅρα ὅπως ἠμύνατο καὶ κατεφώρασε τὸν Λίβυν· δι' ὅλης γὰρ τῆς νυκτὸς περιῄει ἐν κύκλῳ τὴν αὐλὴν ὁ ἄθλιος[1] ἐξελθεῖν οὐ δυνάμενος ὥσπερ εἰς λαβύρινθον ἐμπεσών, ἄχρι δὴ κατελήφθη ἔχων τὰ φώρια γενομένης ἡμέρας. καὶ τότε μὲν πληγὰς οὐκ ὀλίγας ἔλαβεν ἁλούς, οὐ πολὺν δὲ ἐπιβιοὺς χρόνον κακὸς κακῶς ἀπέθανεν μαστιγούμενος, ὡς ἔλεγεν, κατὰ τὴν νύκτα ἑκάστην, ὥστε καὶ μώλωπας εἰς τὴν

[1] ὁ ἄθλιος du Soul: ἄθλιος MSS.

bronze man, you know, and made the rounds in Crete. If he were made of wood instead of bronze, there would be nothing to hinder his being one of the devices of Daedalus instead of a work of Demetrius; anyhow, he is like them in playing truant from his pedestal, by what you say." "See here, Tychiades," said he, "perhaps you will be sorry for your joke later on. I know what happened to the man who stole the obols that we offer him on the first of each month." "It ought to have been something very dreadful," said Ion, "since he committed a sacrilege. How was he punished, Eucrates? I should like to hear about it, no matter how much Tychiades here is going to doubt it."

"A number of obols," he said, "were lying at his feet, and some other small coins of silver had been stuck to his thigh with wax, and leaves of silver, votive offerings or payment for a cure from one or another of those who through him had ceased to be subject to fever. We had a plaguy Libyan servant, a groom; the fellow undertook to steal and did steal everything that was there, at night, after waiting until the statue had descended. But as soon as Pellichus came back and discovered that he had been robbed, mark how he punished and exposed the Libyan! The unhappy man ran about the hall the whole night long unable to get out, just as if he had been thrown into a labyrinth, until finally he was caught in possession of the stolen property when day came. He got a sound thrashing then, on being caught, and he did not long survive the incident, dying a rogue's death from being flogged, he said, every night, so that welts showed on his body the

ἐπιοῦσαν φαίνεσθαι αὐτοῦ ἐπὶ τοῦ σώματος. πρὸς ταῦτα, ὦ Τυχιάδη, καὶ τὸν Πέλλιχον σκῶπτε κἀμὲ ὥσπερ τοῦ Μίνωος ἡλικιώτην παραπαίειν ἤδη δόκει." "Ἀλλ', ὦ Εὔκρατες," ἦν δ' ἐγώ, "ἔστ' ἂν χαλκὸς μὲν ὁ χαλκός, τὸ δὲ ἔργον Δημήτριος ὁ Ἀλωπεκῆθεν εἰργασμένος ᾖ, οὐ θεοποιός τις ἀλλ' ἀνθρωποποιὸς ὤν, οὔποτε φοβήσομαι τὸν ἀνδριάντα Πελλίχου, ὃν οὐδὲ ζῶντα πάνυ ἐδεδίειν ἂν ἀπειλοῦντά μοι."

21 Ἐπὶ τούτοις Ἀντίγονος ὁ ἰατρὸς εἶπε, "Κἀμοί, ὦ Εὔκρατες, Ἱπποκράτης ἐστὶ χαλκοῦς ὅσον πηχυαῖος τὸ μέγεθος· οὗτος ἐπειδὰν μόνον ἡ θρυαλλὶς ἀποσβῇ, περίεισιν τὴν οἰκίαν ὅλην ἐν κύκλῳ ψοφῶν καὶ τὰς πυξίδας ἀνατρέπων καὶ τὰ φάρμακα συγχέων καὶ τὴν θυίαν[1] περιτρέπων, καὶ μάλιστα ἐπειδὰν τὴν θυσίαν ὑπερβαλώμεθα, ἣν κατὰ τὸ ἔτος ἕκαστον αὐτῷ θύομεν." "Ἀξιοῖ γάρ," ἦν δ' ἐγώ, "καὶ ὁ Ἱπποκράτης ἤδη ὁ ἰατρὸς θύεσθαι αὐτῷ, καὶ ἀγανακτεῖ ἢν μὴ κατὰ καιρὸν ἐφ' ἱερῶν τελείων ἑστιαθῇ; ὃν ἔδει ἀγαπᾶν, εἴ τις ἐναγίσειεν αὐτῷ ἢ μελίκρατον ἐπισπείσειεν ἢ στεφανώσειε τὴν στήλην."[2]

22 "Ἄκουε τοίνυν," ἔφη ὁ Εὐκράτης, "—τοῦτο μὲν καὶ ἐπὶ μαρτύρων—ὃ πρὸ ἐτῶν πέντε εἶδον· ἐτύγχανε μὲν ἀμφὶ τρυγητὸν τοῦ ἔτους ὄν, ἐγὼ δὲ ἀνὰ τὸν ἀγρὸν μεσούσης ἡμέρας τρυγῶντας ἀφεὶς τοὺς ἐργάτας κατ' ἐμαυτὸν εἰς τὴν ὕλην ἀπῄειν μεταξὺ φροντίζων τι καὶ ἀνασκοπούμενος. ἐπεὶ δ' ἐν τῷ συνηρεφεῖ ἦν, τὸ μὲν πρῶτον ὑλαγμὸς ἐγένετο κυνῶν, κἀγὼ εἴκαζον Μνάσωνα τὸν υἱόν, ὥσπερ εἰώθει, παίζειν καὶ κυνηγετεῖν εἰς τὸ λάσιον

[1] θύραν γ.   [2] κεφαλὴν γ.

next day. In view of this, Tychiades, mock Pellichus and think me as senile as if I were a contemporary of Minos!" "Well, Eucrates," I said, "as long as bronze is bronze and the work a product of Demetrius of Alopece, who makes men, not gods, I shall never be afraid of the statue of Pellichus, whom I should not have feared very much even when he was alive if he threatened me."

Thereupon Antigonus, the physician, said, "I myself, Eucrates, have a bronze Hippocrates about eighteen inches high. As soon as the light is out, he goes all about the house making noises, turning out the vials, mixing up the medicines, and overturning the mortar, particularly when we are behindhand with the sacrifice which we make to him every year." "Has it gone so far," said I, "that even Hippocrates the physician demands sacrifice in his honour and gets angry if he is not feasted on unblemished victims at the proper season? He ought to be well content if anyone should bring food to his tomb or pour him a libation of milk and honey or put a wreath about his gravestone!"

"Let me tell you," said Eucrates, "—this, I assure you, is supported by witnesses—what I saw five years ago. It happened to be the vintage season of the year; passing through the farm at midday, I left the labourers gathering the grapes and went off by myself into the wood, thinking about something in the meantime and turning it over in my mind. When I was under cover, there came first a barking of dogs, and I supposed that my son Mnason was at his usual sport of following the hounds, and had

μετὰ τῶν ἡλικιωτῶν παρελθόντα. τὸ δ' οὐκ εἶχεν οὕτως, ἀλλὰ μετ' ὀλίγον σεισμοῦ τινος ἅμα γενομένου καὶ βοῆς οἷον ἐκ βροντῆς γυναῖκα ὁρῶ προσιοῦσαν φοβεράν, ἡμισταδιαίαν σχεδὸν τὸ ὕψος. εἶχεν δὲ καὶ δᾷδα ἐν τῇ ἀριστερᾷ καὶ ξίφος ἐν τῇ δεξιᾷ ὅσον εἰκοσάπηχυ, καὶ τὰ μὲν ἔνερθεν ὀφιόπους ἦν, τὰ δὲ ἄνω Γοργόνι ἐμφερής, τὸ βλέμμα φημὶ καὶ τὸ φρικῶδες τῆς προσόψεως, καὶ ἀντὶ τῆς κόμης τοὺς δράκοντας βοστρυχηδὸν καθεῖτο[1] εἰλουμένους περὶ τὸν αὐχένα καὶ ἐπὶ τῶν ὤμων ἐνίους ἐσπειραμένους. ὁρᾶτε," ἔφη, "ὅπως ἔφριξα, ὦ φίλοι, μεταξὺ διηγούμενος." καὶ ἅμα λέγων ἐδείκνυεν ὁ Εὐκράτης τὰς ἐπὶ τοῦ πήχεως τρίχας δῆθεν ὀρθὰς ὑπὸ τοῦ φόβου.

23 Οἱ μὲν οὖν ἀμφὶ τὸν Ἴωνα καὶ τὸν Δεινόμαχον καὶ τὸν Κλεόδημον κεχηνότες ἀτενὲς προσεῖχον αὐτῷ, γέροντες ἄνδρες ἑλκόμενοι τῆς ῥινός, ἠρέμα προσκυνοῦντες οὕτως ἀπίθανον κολοσσόν, ἡμισταδιαίαν γυναῖκα, γιγάντειόν τι μορμολύκειον. ἐγὼ δὲ ἐνενόουν μεταξὺ οἷοι ὄντες αὐτοὶ νέοις τε ὁμιλοῦσιν ἐπὶ σοφίᾳ καὶ ὑπὸ πολλῶν θαυμάζονται, μόνῃ τῇ πολιᾷ καὶ τῷ πώγωνι διαφέροντες τῶν βρεφῶν, τὰ δ' ἄλλα καὶ αὐτῶν ἐκείνων εὐαγωγό-24 τεροι πρὸς τὸ ψεῦδος. ὁ γοῦν Δεινόμαχος, "Εἰπέ μοι," ἔφη, "ὦ Εὔκρατες, οἱ κύνες δὲ τῆς θεοῦ πηλίκοι τὸ μέγεθος ἦσαν;"

"Ἐλεφάντων," ἦ δ' ὅς, "ὑψηλότεροι τῶν Ἰνδικῶν, μέλανες καὶ αὐτοὶ καὶ λάσιοι πιναρᾷ καὶ αὐχμώσῃ τῇ λάχνῃ.—ἐγὼ μὲν οὖν ἰδὼν ἔστην ἀναστρέψας ἅμα τὴν σφραγῖδα ἥν μοι ὁ Ἄραψ ἔδωκεν εἰς τὸ εἴσω τοῦ δακτύλου· ἡ Ἑκάτη δὲ

[1] περιεκεῖτο γ.

entered the thicket with his companions. This was not the case, however; but after a short time there came an earthquake and with it a noise as of thunder, and then I saw a terrible woman coming toward me, quite half a furlong in height. She had a torch in her left hand and a sword in her right, ten yards long; below, she had snake-feet, and above she resembled the Gorgon, in her stare, I mean, and the frightfulness of her appearance; moreover, instead of hair she had the snakes falling down in ringlets, twining about her neck, and some of them coiled upon her shoulders.—See," said he, "how my flesh creeps, friends, as I tell the story!" And as he spoke he showed the hairs on his forearm standing on end (would you believe it?) because of his terror!

Ion, Deinomachus, Cleodemus, and the rest of them, open-mouthed, were giving him unwavering attention, old men led by the nose, all but doing obeisance to so unconvincing a colossus, a woman half a furlong in height, a gigantic bugaboo! For my part I was thinking in the meantime: "They associate with young men to make them wise and are admired by many, but what are they themselves? Only their grey hair and their beard distinguishes them from infants, and for the rest of it, even infants are not so amenable to falsehood." Deinomachus, for instance, said: "Tell me, Eucrates, the dogs of the goddess—how big were they?"

"Taller than Indian elephants," he replied; "black, like them, with a shaggy coat of filthy, tangled hair.—Well, at sight of her I stopped, at the same time turning the gem that the Arab gave me to the inside of my finger, and Hecate, stamping

πατάξασα τῷ δρακοντείῳ ποδὶ τοὔδαφος ἐποίησεν χάσμα παμμέγεθες, ἡλίκον Ταρτάρειον τὸ βάθος· εἶτα ᾤχετο μετ' ὀλίγον ἁλλομένη εἰς αὐτό. ἐγὼ δὲ θαρρήσας ἐπέκυψα λαβόμενος δένδρου τινὸς πλησίον πεφυκότος, ὡς μὴ σκοτοδινιάσας ἐμπέσοιμι ἐπὶ κεφαλήν· εἶτα ἑώρων τὰ ἐν Ἅιδου ἅπαντα, τὸν Πυριφλεγέθοντα, τὴν λίμνην, τὸν Κέρβερον, τοὺς νεκρούς, ὥστε γνωρίζειν ἐνίους αὐτῶν· τὸν γοῦν πατέρα εἶδον ἀκριβῶς αὐτὰ ἐκεῖνα ἔτι ἀμπεχόμενον ἐν οἷς αὐτὸν κατεθάψαμεν."

"Τί δὲ ἔπραττον," ὁ Ἴων ἔφη, "ὦ Εὔκρατες, αἱ ψυχαί;" "Τί δ' ἄλλο," ἦ δ' ὅς, "ἢ κατὰ φῦλα καὶ φρήτρας μετὰ τῶν φίλων καὶ συγγενῶν διατρίβουσιν ἐπὶ τοῦ ἀσφοδέλου κατακείμενοι." "Ἀντιλεγέτωσαν νῦν[1] ἔτι," ἦ δ' ὃς ὁ Ἴων, "οἱ ἀμφὶ τὸν Ἐπίκουρον τῷ ἱερῷ Πλάτωνι καὶ τῷ περὶ τῶν ψυχῶν λόγῳ. σὺ δὲ μὴ καὶ τὸν Σωκράτην αὐτὸν καὶ τὸν Πλάτωνα εἶδες ἐν τοῖς νεκροῖς;" "Τὸν Σωκράτην ἔγωγε," ἦ δ' ὅς, "οὐδὲ τοῦτον σαφῶς, ἀλλὰ εἰκάζων[2] ὅτι φαλακρὸς καὶ προγάστωρ ἦν· τὸν Πλάτωνα δὲ οὐκ ἐγνώρισα· χρὴ γάρ, οἶμαι, πρὸς φίλους ἄνδρας τἀληθῆ λέγειν.

"Ἅμα δ' οὖν ἐγώ τε ἅπαντα ἱκανῶς ἑωράκειν, καὶ τὸ χάσμα συνῄει καὶ συνέμυε· καί τινες τῶν οἰκετῶν ἀναζητοῦντές με, καὶ Πυρρίας οὗτος ἐν αὐτοῖς, ἐπέστησαν οὔπω τέλεον μεμυκότος τοῦ χάσματος. εἰπέ, Πυρρία, εἰ ἀληθῆ λέγω." "Νὴ Δί'," ἔφη ὁ Πυρρίας, "καὶ ὑλακῆς δὲ ἤκουσα διὰ τοῦ χάσματος καὶ πῦρ τι ὑπέλαμπεν, ἀπὸ τῆς

[1] νῦν Cobet: οὖν MSS. [2] εἴκαζον β.

on the ground with her serpent foot, made a tremendous chasm, as deep as Tartarus; then after a little she leaped into it and was gone. I plucked up courage and looked over, taking hold of a tree that grew close by, in order that I might not get a dizzy turn and fall into it headlong. Then I saw everything in Hades, the River of Blazing Fire, and the Lake, and Cerberus, and the dead, well enough to recognise some of them. My father, for instance, I saw distinctly, still wearing the same clothes in which we buried him."

"What were the souls doing, Eucrates?" said Ion. "What else would they be doing," he said, "except lying upon the asphodel to while away the time, along with their friends and kinsmen by tribes and clans?" "Now let the Epicureans go on contradicting holy Plato," said Ion, "and his doctrine about the souls! But you did not see Socrates himself and Plato among the dead?" "Socrates I saw," he replied, "and even him not for certain but by guess, because he was bald and pot-bellied; Plato I could not recognise, for one must tell the truth to friends, I take it.

"No sooner had I seen everything sufficiently well than the chasm came together and closed up; and some of the servants who were seeking me, Pyrrhias here among them, came upon the scene before the chasm had completely closed. Tell them, Pyrrhias, whether I am speaking the truth or not." "Yes, by Heaven," said Pyrrhias, "and I heard barking, too, through the chasm and a gleam of fire was

δᾳδός μοι δοκεῖν."[1] κἀγὼ ἐγέλασα ἐπιμετρήσαντος τοῦ μάρτυρος τὴν ὑλακὴν καὶ τὸ πῦρ.

25 Ὁ Κλεόδημος δέ, "Οὐ καινά," εἶπεν, "οὐδὲ ἄλλοις ἀόρατα ταῦτα εἶδες, ἐπεὶ καὶ αὐτὸς οὐ πρὸ πολλοῦ νοσήσας τοιόνδε τι ἐθεασάμην· ἐπεσκόπει δέ με καὶ ἐθεράπευεν Ἀντίγονος οὗτος. ἑβδόμη μὲν ἦν ἡμέρα, ὁ δὲ πυρετὸς οἷος καῦσος σφοδρότατος. ἅπαντες δέ με ἀπολιπόντες ἐπ' ἐρημίας ἐπικλεισάμενοι τὰς θύρας ἔξω περιέμενον· οὕτω γὰρ αὐτὸς ἐκέλευσας, ὦ Ἀντίγονε, εἴ πως δυνηθείην εἰς ὕπνον τραπέσθαι. τότε οὖν ἐφίσταταί μοι νεανίας ἐγρηγορότι πάγκαλος λευκὸν ἱμάτιον περιβεβλημένος, εἶτα ἀναστήσας ἄγει διά τινος χάσματος εἰς τὸν Ἅιδην, ὡς αὐτίκα ἐγνώρισα Τάνταλον ἰδὼν καὶ Τιτυὸν καὶ Σίσυφον. καὶ τὰ μὲν ἄλλα τί ἂν ὑμῖν λέγοιμι; ἐπεὶ δὲ κατὰ τὸ δικαστήριον ἐγενόμην—παρῆν δὲ καὶ ὁ Αἰακὸς καὶ ὁ Χάρων καὶ αἱ Μοῖραι καὶ αἱ Ἐρινύες—ὁ μέν τις ὥσπερ βασιλεὺς (ὁ Πλούτων,[2] μοι δοκεῖ) καθῆστο ἐπιλεγόμενος τῶν τεθνηξομένων τὰ ὀνόματα, οὓς ἤδη ὑπερημέρους τῆς ζωῆς συνέβαινεν εἶναι. ὁ δὲ νεανίσκος ἐμὲ φέρων παρέστησεν αὐτῷ· ὁ δὲ Πλούτων ἠγανάκτησέν τε καὶ πρὸς τὸν ἀγαγόντα με, 'Οὔπω πεπλήρωται,' φησίν, 'τὸ νῆμα αὐτῷ, ὥστε ἀπίτω. σὺ δὲ δὴ τὸν χαλκέα Δημύλον ἄγε· ὑπὲρ γὰρ τὸν ἄτρακτον βιοῖ.' κἀγὼ ἄσμενος ἀναδραμὼν αὐτὸς μὲν ἤδη ἀπύρετος ἦν, ἀπήγγελλον δὲ ἅπασιν ὡς τεθνήξεται Δημύλος· ἐν γειτόνων δὲ ἡμῖν ᾤκει νοσῶν τι καὶ αὐτός, ὡς ἀπηγγέλλετο. καὶ μετὰ μικρὸν ἠκούομεν οἰμωγῆς ὀδυρομένων ἐπ' αὐτῷ."

[1] ὑπολάμπειν ἀπὸ τῆς δᾳδός μοι ἐδόκει γ. [2] Ἅιδης β.

shining, from the torch, I suppose." I had to laugh when the witness, to give good measure, threw in the barking and the fire!

Cleodemus, however, said, "These sights that you saw are not novel and unseen by anyone else, for I myself when I was taken sick not long ago witnessed something similar. Antigonus here visited and attended me. It was the seventh day, and the fever was like a calenture of the most raging type. Leaving me by myself and shutting the door, they all were waiting outside; for you had given orders to that effect, Antigonus, on the chance that I might fall asleep. Well, at that time there appeared at my side while I lay awake a very handsome young man, wearing a white cloak; then, raising me to my feet, he led me through a chasm to Hades, as I realised at once when I saw Tantalus and Ixion and Tityus and Sisyphus. Why should I tell you all the details? But when I came to the court—Aeacus and Charon and the Fates and the Furies were there—a person resembling a king (Pluto, I suppose) sat reading off the names of those about to die because their lease of life chanced to have already expired. The young man speedily set me before him; but Pluto was angry and said to my guide: 'His thread is not yet fully spun, so let him be off, and bring me the blacksmith Demylus, for he is living beyond the spindle.' I hastened back with a joyful heart, and from that time was free from fever; but I told everyone that Demylus would die. He lived next door to us, and himself had some illness, according to report. And after a little while we heard the wailing of his mourners."

26 "Τί θαυμαστόν;" εἶπεν ὁ Ἀντίγονος· "ἐγὼ γὰρ οἶδά τινα μετὰ εἰκοστὴν ἡμέραν ἧς[1] ἐτάφη ἀναστάντα, θεραπεύσας καὶ πρὸ τοῦ θανάτου καὶ ἐπεὶ ἀνέστη τὸν ἄνθρωπον." "Καὶ πῶς," ἦν δ' ἐγώ, "ἐν εἴκοσιν ἡμέραις οὔτ' ἐμύδησεν τὸ σῶμα οὔτε ἄλλως ὑπὸ λιμοῦ διεφθάρη; εἰ μή τινα Ἐπιμενίδην σύ γε ἐθεράπευες."

27 Ἅμα ταῦτα λεγόντων ἡμῶν ἐπεισῆλθον οἱ τοῦ Εὐκράτους υἱοὶ ἐκ τῆς παλαίστρας, ὁ μὲν ἤδη ἐξ ἐφήβων, ὁ δὲ ἕτερος ἀμφὶ τὰ πεντεκαίδεκα ἔτη, καὶ ἀσπασάμενοι ἡμᾶς ἐκαθέζοντο ἐπὶ τῆς κλίνης παρὰ τῷ πατρί· ἐμοὶ δὲ εἰσεκομίσθη θρόνος. καὶ ὁ Εὐκράτης ὥσπερ ἀναμνησθεὶς πρὸς τὴν ὄψιν τῶν υἱέων, "Οὕτως ὀναίμην," ἔφη, "τούτων"—ἐπιβαλὼν αὐτοῖν τὴν χεῖρα—"ἀληθῆ, ὦ Τυχιάδη, πρός σε ἐρῶ. τὴν μακαρῖτίν μου γυναῖκα τὴν τούτων μητέρα πάντες ἴσασιν ὅπως ἠγάπησα, ἐδήλωσα δὲ οἷς περὶ αὐτὴν ἔπραξα οὐ ζῶσαν μόνον, ἀλλὰ καὶ ἐπεὶ ἀπέθανεν, τόν τε κόσμον ἅπαντα συγκατακαύσας καὶ τὴν ἐσθῆτα ᾗ ζῶσα ἔχαιρεν. ἑβδόμῃ δὲ μετὰ τὴν τελευτὴν ἡμέρᾳ ἐγὼ μὲν ἐνταῦθα ἐπὶ τῆς κλίνης ὥσπερ νῦν ἐκείμην παραμυθούμενος τὸ πένθος· ἀνεγίγνωσκον γὰρ τὸ περὶ ψυχῆς τοῦ Πλάτωνος βιβλίον ἐφ' ἡσυχίας· ἐπεισέρχεται δὲ μεταξὺ ἡ Δημαινέτη αὐτὴ ἐκείνη καὶ καθίζεται πλησίον ὥσπερ νῦν Εὐκρατίδης οὑτοσί," δείξας τὸν νεώτερον τῶν υἱέων· ὁ δὲ αὐτίκα ἔφριξε μάλα παιδικῶς, καὶ πάλαι ἤδη ὠχρὸς ὢν[2] πρὸς τὴν διήγησιν. "Ἐγὼ δέ," ἦ δ' ὃς ὁ Εὐκράτης, "ὡς εἶδον, περιπλακεὶς αὐτῇ

[1] ᾗ β. [2] ἦν γ.

"What is there surprising in that?" said Antigonus: "I know a man who came to life more than twenty days after his burial, having attended the fellow both before his death and after he came to life." "How was it," said I, "that in twenty days the body neither corrupted nor simply wasted away from inanition? Unless it was an Epimenides[1] whom you attended."

While we were exchanging these words the sons of Eucrates came in upon us from the palaestra, one already of age, the other about fifteen years old, and after greeting us sat down upon the couch beside their father; a chair was brought in for me. Then, as if reminded by the sight of his sons, Eucrates said: "As surely as I hope that these boys will be a joy to me"—and he laid his hand upon them—"what I am about to tell you, Tychiades, is true. Everyone knows how I loved their mother, my wife of blessed memory; I made it plain by what I did for her not only while she was alive but even when she died, for I burned on the pyre with her all the ornaments and the clothing that she liked while she lived. On the seventh day after her death I was lying here on the couch, just as I am now, consoling my grief; for I was peacefully reading Plato's book about the soul. While I was thus engaged, Demaenete herself in person came in upon me and sat down beside me, just as Eucratides here is sitting now"—with a gesture toward the younger of his sons, who at once shuddered in a very boyish way; he had already been pale for some time over the story. "When I saw her," Eucrates continued, "I

[1] The Cretan priest who slept for forty years, or thereabouts.

ἐδάκρυον ἀνακωκύσας· ἡ δὲ οὐκ εἴα βοᾶν, ἀλλ' ᾐτιᾶτό με ὅτι τὰ ἄλλα πάντα[1] χαρισάμενος αὐτῇ θάτερον τοῖν σανδάλοιν χρυσοῖν ὄντοιν οὐ κατακαύσαιμι, εἶναι δὲ αὐτὸ ἔφασκεν ὑπὸ τῇ κιβωτῷ παραπεσόν. καὶ διὰ τοῦτο ἡμεῖς οὐχ εὑρόντες θάτερον μόνον ἐκαύσαμεν. ἔτι δὲ ἡμῶν διαλεγομένων κατάρατόν τι κυνίδιον ὑπὸ τῇ κλίνῃ ὂν Μελιταῖον ὑλάκτησεν, ἡ δὲ ἠφανίσθη πρὸς τὴν ὑλακήν. τὸ μέντοι σανδάλιον εὑρέθη ὑπὸ τῇ κιβωτῷ καὶ κατεκαύθη ὕστερον.

28 "Ἔτι ἀπιστεῖν τούτοις, ὦ Τυχιάδη, ἄξιον ἐναργέσιν οὖσιν καὶ κατὰ τὴν ἡμέραν ἑκάστην φαινομένοις;" "Μὰ Δί'," ἦν δ' ἐγώ· "ἐπεὶ σανδάλῳ γε χρυσῷ εἰς τὰς πυγὰς ὥσπερ τὰ παιδία παίεσθαι ἄξιοι ἂν εἶεν οἱ ἀπιστοῦντες καὶ οὕτως ἀναισχυντοῦντες πρὸς τὴν ἀλήθειαν."

29 Ἐπὶ τούτοις ὁ Πυθαγορικὸς Ἀρίγνωτος εἰσῆλθεν, ὁ κομήτης, ὁ σεμνὸς ἀπὸ τοῦ προσώπου, οἶσθα τὸν ἀοίδιμον ἐπὶ τῇ σοφίᾳ, τὸν ἱερὸν ἐπονομαζόμενον. κἀγὼ μὲν ὡς εἶδον αὐτὸν ἀνέπνευσα, τοῦτ' ἐκεῖνο ἥκειν μοι νομίσας πέλεκύν τινα κατὰ τῶν ψευσμάτων. "Ἐπιστομιεῖ γὰρ αὐτούς," ἔλεγον, "ὁ σοφὸς ἀνὴρ οὕτω τεράστια διεξιόντας." καὶ τὸ τοῦ λόγου, θεὸν ἀπὸ μηχανῆς ἐπεισκυκληθῆναί μοι τοῦτον ᾤμην ὑπὸ τῆς Τύχης· ὁ δὲ ἐπεὶ ἐκαθέζετο ὑπεκστάντος αὐτῷ τοῦ Κλεοδήμου, πρῶτα μὲν περὶ τῆς νόσου ἤρετο, καὶ ὡς ῥᾷον ἤδη ἔχειν ἤκουσεν παρὰ τοῦ Εὐκράτους, "Τί δέ," ἔφη, "πρὸς αὑτοὺς[2] ἐφιλοσοφεῖτε; μεταξὺ γὰρ

[1] πολλὰ β. [2] ἀλλήλους β.

caught her in my arms with a cry of grief and began to weep. She would not permit me to cry, however, but began to find fault with me because, although I had given her everything else, I had not burned one of her gilt sandals, which, she said, was under the chest, where it had been thrown aside. That was why we did not find it and burned only the one. We were continuing our conversation when a cursed toy dog that was under the couch, a Maltese, barked, and she vanished at his barking. The sandal, however, was found under the chest and was burned afterwards.

"Is it right, Tychiades, to doubt these apparitions any longer, when they are distinctly seen and a matter of daily occurrence?" "No, by Heaven," I said: "those who doubt and are so disrespectful toward truth deserve to be spanked like children, with a gilt sandal!"

At this juncture Arignotus the Pythagorean came in, the man with the long hair and the majestic face—you know the one who is renowned for wisdom, whom they call holy. As I caught sight of him, I drew a breath of relief, thinking: "There now, a broadaxe has come to hand to use against their lies. The wise man will stop their mouths when they tell such prodigious yarns." I thought that Fortune had trundled him in to me like a *deus ex machina*, as the phrase is. But when Cleodemus had made room for him and he was seated, he first asked about the illness, and when Eucrates told him that it was already less troublesome, said: "What were you debating among yourselves? As I came

εἰσιὼν ἐπήκουσα, καί μοι ἐδοκεῖτε[1] εἰς καλὸν διατεθήσεσθαι[2] τὴν διατριβήν."

"Τί δ' ἄλλο," εἶπεν ὁ Εὐκράτης, "ἢ τουτονὶ τὸν ἀδαμάντινον πείθομεν"—δείξας ἐμέ—"ἡγεῖσθαι δαίμονάς τινας εἶναι καὶ φάσματα καὶ νεκρῶν ψυχὰς περιπολεῖν ὑπὲρ γῆς καὶ φαίνεσθαι οἷς ἂν ἐθέλωσιν." ἐγὼ μὲν οὖν ἠρυθρίασα καὶ κάτω ἔνευσα αἰδεσθεὶς τὸν Ἀρίγνωτον. ὁ δέ, "Ὅρα," ἔφη, "ὦ Εὔκρατες, μὴ τοῦτό φησιν Τυχιάδης, τὰς τῶν βιαίως ἀποθανόντων μόνας ψυχὰς περινοστεῖν, οἷον εἴ τις ἀπήγξατο ἢ ἀπετμήθη τὴν κεφαλὴν ἢ ἀνεσκολοπίσθη ἢ ἄλλῳ γέ τῳ τρόπῳ τοιούτῳ ἀπῆλθεν ἐκ τοῦ βίου, τὰς δὲ τῶν κατὰ μοῖραν ἀποθανόντων οὐκέτι· ἢν γὰρ τοῦτο λέγῃ, οὐ πάνυ ἀπόβλητα φήσει." "Μὰ Δί'," ἦ δ' ὃς ὁ Δεινόμαχος, "ἀλλ' οὐδὲ ὅλως εἶναι τὰ τοιαῦτα οὐδὲ συνεστῶτα ὁρᾶσθαι οἴεται."

30 "Πῶς λέγεις," ἦ δ' ὃς ὁ Ἀρίγνωτος, δριμὺ ἀπιδὼν εἰς ἐμέ, "οὐδέν σοι τούτων γίγνεσθαι δοκεῖ, καὶ ταῦτα πάντων, ὡς εἰπεῖν, ὁρώντων;" "Ἀπολόγησαι,"[3] ἦν δ' ἐγώ, "ὑπὲρ ἐμοῦ, εἰ μὴ πιστεύω, διότι μηδὲ ὁρῶ μόνος τῶν ἄλλων· εἰ δὲ ἑώρων, καὶ ἐπίστευον ἂν δηλαδὴ ὥσπερ ὑμεῖς." "Ἀλλά," ἦ δ' ὅς, "ἤν ποτε εἰς Κόρινθον ἔλθῃς, ἐροῦ ἔνθα ἐστὶν ἡ Εὐβατίδου οἰκία, καὶ ἐπειδάν σοι δειχθῇ παρὰ τὸ Κράνειον, παρελθὼν εἰς αὐτὴν λέγε πρὸς τὸν θυρωρὸν Τίβειον ὡς ἐθέλοις

[1] δοκεῖτε γ.

[2] διατίθεσθαι β. διαθήσεσθαι Cobet, Fritzsche; but cf. *Scytha* 9 fin.

[3] ἀπολόγησαι A.M.H.: ἀπολογῇ γP (followed by a lacuna of 4 letters in P): ἀπολελόγησθε N Vat. 87.

in, I overheard you, and it seemed to me that you were on the point of giving a fine turn to the conversation!"

"We are only trying to persuade this man of adamant," said Eucrates, pointing at me, "to believe that spirits and phantoms exist, and that souls of dead men go about above ground and appear to whomsoever they will." I flushed and lowered my eyes out of reverence for Arignotus. "Perhaps, Eucrates," he said, "Tychiades means that only the ghosts of those who died by violence walk, for example, if a man hanged himself, or had his head cut off, or was crucified, or departed life in some similar way; and that those of men who died a natural death do not. If that is what he means, we cannot altogether reject what he says." "No, by Heaven," replied Deinomachus, "he thinks that such things do not exist at all and are not seen in bodily form."

"What is that you say?" said Arignotus, with a sour look at me. "Do you think that none of these things happen, although everybody, I may say, sees them?" "Plead in my defence," said I, "if I do not believe in them, that I am the only one of all who does not see them; if I saw them, I should believe in them, of course, just as you do." "Come," said he, "if ever you go to Corinth, ask where the house of Eubatides is, and when it is pointed out to you beside Cornel Grove, enter it and say to the doorman Tibius that you should like to see where the

ἰδεῖν ὅθεν τὸν δαίμονα ὁ Πυθαγορικὸς Ἀρίγνωτος ἀνορύξας ἀπήλασε καὶ πρὸς τὸ λοιπὸν οἰκεῖσθαι τὴν οἰκίαν ἐποίησεν."

31 "Τί δὲ τοῦτο ἦν, ὦ Ἀρίγνωτε;" ἤρετο ὁ Εὐκράτης. "Ἀοίκητος ἦν," ἦ δ' ὅς, "ἐκ πολλοῦ ὑπὸ δειμάτων, εἰ δέ τις οἰκήσειεν εὐθὺς ἐκπλαγεὶς ἔφευγεν, ἐκδιωχθεὶς ὑπό τινος φοβεροῦ καὶ ταραχώδους φάσματος. συνέπιπτεν οὖν ἤδη καὶ ἡ στέγη κατέρρει, καὶ ὅλως οὐδεὶς ἦν ὁ θαρρήσων παρελθεῖν εἰς αὐτήν.

"Ἐγὼ δὲ ἐπεὶ ταῦτα ἤκουσα, τὰς βίβλους λαβὼν—εἰσὶ δέ μοι Αἰγύπτιαι μάλα πολλαὶ περὶ τῶν τοιούτων—ἧκον εἰς τὴν οἰκίαν περὶ πρῶτον ὕπνον ἀποτρέποντος τοῦ ξένου καὶ μόνον οὐκ ἐπιλαμβανομένου, ἐπεὶ ἔμαθεν οἷ βαδίζοιμι, εἰς προὖπτον κακόν, ὡς ᾤετο. ἐγὼ δὲ λύχνον λαβὼν μόνος εἰσέρχομαι, καὶ ἐν τῷ μεγίστῳ οἰκήματι καταθεὶς τὸ φῶς ἀνεγίγνωσκον ἡσυχῇ χαμαὶ καθεζόμενος· ἐφίσταται δὲ ὁ δαίμων ἐπί τινα τῶν πολλῶν ἥκειν νομίζων καὶ δεδίξεσθαι κἀμὲ ἐλπίζων ὥσπερ τοὺς ἄλλους, αὐχμηρὸς καὶ κομήτης καὶ μελάντερος τοῦ ζόφου. καὶ ὁ μὲν ἐπιστὰς ἐπειρᾶτό μου, πανταχόθεν προσβάλλων εἴ ποθεν κρατήσειεν, καὶ ἄρτι μὲν κύων ἄρτι δὲ ταῦρος γιγνόμενος ἢ λέων. ἐγὼ δὲ προχειρισάμενος τὴν φρικωδεστάτην ἐπίρρησιν αἰγυπτιάζων τῇ φωνῇ συνήλασα κατᾴδων αὐτὸν εἴς τινα γωνίαν σκοτεινοῦ[1] οἰκήματος· ἰδὼν δὲ αὐτὸν οἷ κατέδυ, τὸ λοιπὸν ἀνεπαυόμην.

"Ἕωθεν δὲ πάντων ἀπεγνωκότων καὶ νεκρὸν εὑρήσειν με οἰομένων καθάπερ τοὺς ἄλλους, προ-

[1] μικροῦ τινος β. Perhaps σκοτεινὴν (Fritzsche) μικροῦ τινος.

Pythagorean Arignotus exhumed the spirit and drove it away, making the house habitable from that time on."

"What was that, Arignotus?" asked Eucrates. "It was uninhabitable," he replied, "for a long time because of terrors; whenever anyone took up his abode in it, he fled in panic at once, chased out by a fearful, terrifying phantom. So it was falling in and the roof was tumbling down, and there was nobody at all who had the courage to enter it.

"When I heard all this, I took my books—I have a great number of Egyptian works about such matters—and went into the house at bed-time, although my host tried to dissuade me and all but held me when he learned where I was going—into misfortune with my eyes open, he thought. But taking a lamp I went in alone; in the largest room I put down the light and was reading peacefully, seated on the ground, when the spirit appeared, thinking that he was setting upon a man of the common sort and expecting to affright me as he had the others; he was squalid and long-haired and blacker than the dark. Standing over me, he made attempts upon me, attacking me from all sides to see if he could get the best of me anywhere, and turning now into a dog, now into a bull or a lion. But I brought into play my most frightful imprecation, speaking the Egyptian language, pent him up in a certain corner of a dark room, and laid him. Then, having observed where he went down, I slept for the rest of the night.

"In the morning, when everybody had given up hope and expected to find me dead like the others,

ελθὼν ἀπροσδόκητος ἅπασι πρόσειμι τῷ Εὐβατίδῃ, εὖ ἀγγέλλων ὅτι καθαρὰν αὐτῷ καὶ ἀδείμαντον ἤδη ἐξῆν[1] τὴν οἰκίαν οἰκεῖν. παραλαβὼν οὖν αὐτόν τε καὶ τῶν ἄλλων πολλοὺς—εἵποντο γὰρ τοῦ παραδόξου ἕνεκα—ἐκέλευον ἀγαγὼν ἐπὶ τὸν τόπον οὗ καταδεδυκότα τὸν δαίμονα ἑωράκειν, σκάπτειν λαβόντας δικέλλας καὶ σκαφεῖα, καὶ ἐπειδὴ ἐποίησαν, εὑρέθη ὅσον ἐπ᾽ ὀργυιὰν κατορωρυγμένος τις νεκρὸς ἕωλος μόνα τὰ ὀστᾶ κατὰ σχῆμα συγκείμενος. ἐκεῖνον μὲν οὖν ἐθάψαμεν ἀνορύξαντες, ἡ οἰκία δὲ τὸ ἀπ᾽ ἐκείνου ἐπαύσατο ἐνοχλουμένη ὑπὸ τῶν φασμάτων."

32 Ὡς δὲ ταῦτα εἶπεν ὁ Ἀρίγνωτος, ἀνὴρ δαιμόνιος τὴν σοφίαν καὶ ἅπασιν αἰδέσιμος,[2] οὐδεὶς ἦν ἔτι τῶν παρόντων ὃς οὐχὶ κατεγίγνωσκέ μου πολλὴν τὴν ἄνοιαν τοῖς τοιούτοις ἀπιστοῦντος, καὶ ταῦτα Ἀριγνώτου λέγοντος. ἐγὼ δὲ ὅμως οὐδὲν τρέσας οὔτε τὴν κόμην οὔτε τὴν δόξαν τὴν περὶ αὐτοῦ, "Τί τοῦτ᾽," ἔφην, "ὦ Ἀρίγνωτε; καὶ σὺ τοιοῦτος ἦσθα, ἡ μόνη ἐλπὶς τῆς ἀληθείας—καπνοῦ μεστὸς καὶ ἰνδαλμάτων; τὸ γοῦν τοῦ λόγου ἐκεῖνο, ἄνθρακες ἡμῖν ὁ θησαυρὸς πέφηνε."

"Σὺ δέ," ἦ δ᾽ ὃς ὁ Ἀρίγνωτος, "εἰ μήτε ἐμοὶ πιστεύεις μήτε Δεινομάχῳ ἢ Κλεοδήμῳ τουτωῒ μήτε αὐτῷ Εὐκράτει, φέρε εἰπὲ τίνα περὶ τῶν τοιούτων ἀξιοπιστότερον ἡγῇ τἀναντία ἡμῖν λέγοντα;" "Νὴ Δί᾽," ἦν δ᾽ ἐγώ, "μάλα θαυμαστὸν ἄνδρα τὸν Ἀβδηρόθεν ἐκεῖνον Δημόκριτον, ὃς

[1] εὐαγγελιζόμενος αὐτῷ ὅτι καθαρὰν αὐτοῦ καὶ ἀδείμαντον ἤδη ἕξει γ. Lucian borrows εὖ ἀγγέλλω from Plato: cf. Rutherford, *New Phrynichus*, p. 335.

[2] θεσπέσιος εἶναι δοκῶν β.

I came forth to the surprise of all and went to Eubatides with the good tidings that he could now inhabit his house, which was purged and free from terrors. So, taking him along and many of the others too—they went with us because the thing was so amazing—I led them to the place where I had seen that the spirit had gone down and told them to take picks and shovels and dig. When they did so, there was found buried about six feet deep a mouldering body of which only the bones lay together in order. We exhumed and buried it; and the house from that time ceased to be troubled by the phantoms."

When Arignotus, a man of superhuman wisdom, revered by all, told this story, there was no longer any one of those present who did not hold me convicted of gross folly if I doubted such things, especially as the narrator was Arignotus. Nevertheless I did not blench either at his long hair or at the reputation which encompassed him, but said: "What is this, Arignotus? Were you, Truth's only hope, just like the rest—full of moonshine and vain imaginings? Indeed the saying has come true: our pot of gold has turned out to be nothing but coals."

"Come now," said Arignotus, "if you put no trust either in me or in Deinomachus or Cleodemus here or in Eucrates himself, tell whom you consider more trustworthy in such matters that maintains the opposite view to ours." "A very wonderful man," said I, "that Democritus who came from Abdera, who surely

οὕτως ἄρα ἐπέπειστο μηδὲν οἷόν τε εἶναι συστῆναι τοιοῦτον ὥστε, ἐπειδὴ καθείρξας ἑαυτὸν εἰς μνῆμα ἔξω πυλῶν ἐνταῦθα διετέλει γράφων καὶ συντάττων καὶ νύκτωρ καὶ μεθ' ἡμέραν, καί τινες τῶν νεανίσκων ἐρεσχελεῖν αὐτὸν βουλόμενοι καὶ δειματοῦν στειλάμενοι νεκρικῶς[1] ἐσθῆτι μελαίνῃ καὶ προσωπείοις εἰς τὰ κρανία μεμιμημένοις περιστάντες αὐτὸν περιεχόρευον ὑπὸ πυκνῇ τῇ βάσει ἀναπηδῶντες, ὁ δὲ οὔτε ἔδεισεν τὴν προσποίησιν αὐτῶν οὔτε ὅλως ἀνέβλεψεν πρὸς αὐτούς, ἀλλὰ μεταξὺ γράφων, 'Παύσασθε,' ἔφη, 'παίζοντες·' οὕτω βεβαίως ἐπίστευε μηδὲν εἶναι τὰς ψυχὰς ἔτι ἔξω γενομένας τῶν σωμάτων."

"Τοῦτο φής," ἦ δ' ὃς ὁ Εὐκράτης, "ἀνόητόν τινα ἄνδρα καὶ τὸν Δημόκριτον γενέσθαι, εἴ γε 33 οὕτως ἐγίγνωσκεν. ἐγὼ δὲ ὑμῖν καὶ ἄλλο διηγήσομαι αὐτὸς παθών, οὐ παρ' ἄλλου ἀκούσας· τάχα γὰρ ἂν καὶ σύ, ὦ Τυχιάδη, ἀκούων προσβιβασθείης πρὸς τὴν ἀλήθειαν τῆς διηγήσεως.

"Ὁπότε γὰρ ἐν Αἰγύπτῳ διῆγον ἔτι νέος ὤν, ὑπὸ τοῦ πατρὸς ἐπὶ παιδείας προφάσει ἀποσταλείς, ἐπεθύμησα εἰς Κοπτὸν ἀναπλεύσας ἐκεῖθεν ἐπὶ τὸν Μέμνονα ἐλθὼν ἀκοῦσαι τὸ θαυμαστὸν ἐκεῖνο ἠχοῦντα πρὸς ἀνίσχοντα τὸν ἥλιον. ἐκείνου μὲν οὖν ἤκουσα οὐ κατὰ τὸ κοινὸν τοῖς πολλοῖς ἄσημόν τινα φωνήν, ἀλλά μοι καὶ ἔχρησεν ὁ Μέμνων αὐτὸς ἀνοίξας γε τὸ στόμα ἐν ἔπεσιν ἑπτά, καὶ εἴ γε μὴ περιττὸν ἦν, αὐτὰ ἂν 34 ὑμῖν εἶπον τὰ ἔπη. κατὰ δὲ τὸν ἀνάπλουν ἔτυχεν ἡμῖν συμπλέων Μεμφίτης ἀνὴρ τῶν ἱερῶν γραμ-

[1] νεκροῖς ἐμφερεῖς β (ν. ἐμφερῶς N).

was thoroughly convinced that nothing of this kind can exist. He shut himself up in a tomb outside the gates, and constantly wrote and composed there by night and by day. Some of the young fellows, wishing to annoy and alarm him, dressed themselves up like dead men in black robes and masks patterned after skulls, encircled him and danced round and round, in quick time, leaping into the air. Yet he neither feared their travesty nor looked up at them at all, but as he wrote said: 'Stop your foolery!' So firmly did he believe that souls are nothing after they have gone out of their bodies."

"That," said Eucrates, "amounts to your saying that Democritus, too, was a foolish man, if he really thought so. But I will tell you another incident derived from my own experience, not from hearsay. Perhaps even you, Tychiades, when you have heard it, may be convinced of the truth of the story.

"When I was living in Egypt during my youth (my father had sent me travelling for the purpose of completing my education), I took it into my head to sail up to Koptos and go from there to the statue of Memnon in order to hear it sound that marvellous salutation to the rising sun. Well, what I heard from it was not a meaningless voice, as in the general experience of common people; Memnon himself actually opened his mouth and delivered me an oracle in seven verses, and if it were not too much of a digression, I would have repeated the very verses for you. But on the voyage up, there chanced to be sailing with us a man from Memphis, one of the scribes of the temple, wonderfully

ματέων,[1] θαυμάσιος τὴν σοφίαν καὶ τὴν παιδείαν πᾶσαν εἰδὼς τὴν Αἰγύπτιον· ἐλέγετο δὲ τρία καὶ εἴκοσιν ἔτη ἐν τοῖς ἀδύτοις ὑπόγειος ᾠκηκέναι μαγεύειν παιδευόμενος ὑπὸ τῆς Ἴσιδος."

"Παγκράτην," ἔφη ὁ Ἀρίγνωτος, "λέγεις ἐμὸν διδάσκαλον, ἄνδρα ἱερόν, ἐξυρημένον, ἐν ὀθονίοις, ἀεὶ νοήμονα, οὐ καθαρῶς ἑλληνίζοντα, ἐπιμήκη, σιμόν, πρόχειλον, ὑπόλεπτον τὰ σκέλη." "Αὐτόν," ἦ δ' ὅς, "ἐκεῖνον τὸν Παγκράτην· καὶ τὰ μὲν πρῶτα ἠγνόουν ὅστις ἦν, ἐπεὶ δὲ ἑώρων αὐτὸν εἴ ποτε ὁρμίσαιμεν τὸ πλοῖον ἄλλα τε πολλὰ τεράστια ἐργαζόμενον, καὶ δὴ καὶ ἐπὶ κροκοδείλων ὀχούμενον καὶ συννέοντα τοῖς θηρίοις, τὰ δὲ ὑποπτήσσοντα καὶ σαίνοντα ταῖς οὐραῖς, ἔγνων ἱερόν τινα ἄνθρωπον ὄντα, κατὰ μικρὸν δὲ φιλοφρονούμενος ἔλαθον ἑταῖρος αὐτῷ καὶ συνήθης γενόμενος, ὥστε πάντων ἐκοινώνει μοι τῶν ἀπορρήτων.

"Καὶ τέλος πείθει με τοὺς μὲν οἰκέτας ἅπαντας ἐν τῇ Μέμφιδι καταλιπεῖν, αὐτὸν δὲ μόνον ἀκολουθεῖν μετ' αὐτοῦ, μὴ γὰρ ἀπορήσειν ἡμᾶς τῶν διακονησομένων· καὶ τὸ μετὰ τοῦτο οὕτω διήγομεν. 35 ἐπειδὴ δὲ ἔλθοιμεν εἴς τι καταγώγιον, λαβὼν ἂν ὁ ἀνὴρ ἢ τὸν μοχλὸν τῆς θύρας ἢ τὸ κόρηθρον ἢ καὶ τὸ ὕπερον περιβαλὼν ἱματίοις ἐπειπών τινα ἐπῳδὴν ἐποίει βαδίζειν, τοῖς ἄλλοις ἅπασιν ἄνθρωπον εἶναι δοκοῦντα. τὸ δὲ ἀπιὸν ὕδωρ τε ἐμπίπλη[2] καὶ ὠψώνει καὶ ἐσκεύαζεν καὶ πάντα δεξιῶς ὑπηρέτει καὶ διηκονεῖτο ἡμῖν· εἶτα ἐπειδὴ ἅλις ἔχοι τῆς διακονίας, αὖθις κόρηθρον

[1] ἱερογραμματέων Fritzsche, Dindorf.
[2] ἐπίμπλη Γ²P : ἐπήντλει N.

learned, familiar with all the culture of the Egyptians. He was said to have lived underground for twenty-three years in their sanctuaries, learning magic from Isis."

"You mean Pancrates," said Arignotus, "my own teacher, a holy man, clean shaven, in white linen, always deep in thought, speaking imperfect Greek, tall, flat-nosed, with protruding lips and thinnish legs." "That self-same Pancrates," he replied: "and at first I did not know who he was, but when I saw him working all sorts of wonders whenever we anchored the boat, particularly riding on crocodiles and swimming in company with the beasts, while they fawned and wagged their tails, I recognised that he was a holy man, and by degrees, through my friendly behaviour, I became his companion and associate, so that he shared all his secret knowledge with me.

"At last he persuaded me to leave all my servants behind in Memphis and to go with him quite alone, for we should not lack people to wait upon us; and thereafter we got on in that way. But whenever we came to a stopping-place, the man would take either the bar of the door or the broom or even the pestle, put clothes upon it, say a certain spell over it, and make it walk, appearing to everyone else to be a man. It would go off and draw water and buy provisions and prepare meals and in every way deftly serve and wait upon us. Then, when he was through with its

τὸ κόρηθρον ἢ ὕπερον τὸ ὕπερον ἄλλην ἐπῳδὴν ἐπειπὼν ἐποίει ἄν.

"Τοῦτο ἐγὼ πάνυ ἐσπουδακὼς οὐκ εἶχον ὅπως ἐκμάθοιμι παρ' αὐτοῦ· ἐβάσκαινε γάρ,[1] καίτοι πρὸς τὰ ἄλλα προχειρότατος ὤν. μιᾷ δέ ποτε ἡμέρᾳ λαθὼν ἐπήκουσα τῆς ἐπῳδῆς, ἦν δὲ τρισύλλαβος σχεδόν, ἐν σκοτεινῷ ὑποστάς. καὶ ὁ μὲν ᾤχετο εἰς τὴν ἀγορὰν ἐντειλάμενος τῷ ὑπέρῳ ἃ ἔδει ποιεῖν. 36 ἐγὼ δὲ εἰς τὴν ὑστεραίαν ἐκείνου τι κατὰ τὴν ἀγορὰν πραγματευομένου λαβὼν τὸ ὕπερον σχηματίσας ὁμοίως, ἐπειπὼν τὰς συλλαβάς, ἐκέλευσα ὑδροφορεῖν. ἐπεὶ δὲ ἐμπλησάμενον τὸν ἀμφορέα ἐκόμισε, 'Πέπαυσο,' ἔφην, 'καὶ μηκέτι ὑδροφόρει, ἀλλ' ἴσθι αὖθις ὕπερον·' τὸ δὲ οὐκέτι μοι πείθεσθαι ἤθελεν, ἀλλ' ὑδροφόρει ἀεί, ἄχρι δὴ ἐνέπλησεν ἡμῖν ὕδατος τὴν οἰκίαν ἐπαντλοῦν. ἐγὼ δὲ ἀμηχανῶν τῷ πράγματι—ἐδεδίειν γὰρ μὴ ὁ Παγκράτης ἐπανελθὼν ἀγανακτήσῃ, ὅπερ καὶ ἐγένετο—ἀξίνην λαβὼν διακόπτω τὸ ὕπερον εἰς δύο μέρη· τὰ δέ, ἑκάτερον τὸ μέρος,[2] ἀμφορέας λαβόντα ὑδροφόρει καὶ ἀνθ' ἑνὸς δύο μοι ἐγεγένηντο οἱ διάκονοι. ἐν τούτῳ καὶ ὁ Παγκράτης ἐφίσταται καὶ συνεὶς τὸ γενόμενον ἐκεῖνα μὲν αὖθις ἐποίησε ξύλα, ὥσπερ ἦν πρὸ τῆς ἐπῳδῆς, αὐτὸς δὲ ἀπολιπών με λαθὼν οὐκ οἶδ' ὅποι ἀφανὴς ᾤχετο ἀπιών."

"Νῦν οὖν," ἔφη ὁ Δεινόμαχος, "οἶσθα κἂν ἐκεῖνο, ἄνθρωπον ποιεῖν ἐκ τοῦ ὑπέρου;" "Νὴ Δί'," ἦ δ' ὅς, "ἐξ ἡμισείας γε· οὐκέτι γὰρ εἰς τὸ ἀρχαῖον οἷόν τέ μοι ἀπάγειν αὐτό, ἢν ἅπαξ

[1] ἐφθόνει γὰρ αὐτοῦ β.   [2] ἑκάτερα κατὰ μέρος γ.

services, he would again make the broom a broom or the pestle a pestle by saying another spell over it.

"Though I was very keen to learn this from him, I could not do so, for he was jealous, although most ready to oblige in everything else. But one day I secretly overheard the spell—it was just three syllables—by taking my stand in a dark place. He went off to the square after telling the pestle what it had to do, and on the next day, while he was transacting some business in the square, I took the pestle, dressed it up in the same way, said the syllables over it, and told it to carry water. When it had filled and brought in the jar, I said, 'Stop! don't carry any more water: be a pestle again!' But it would not obey me now: it kept straight on carrying until it filled the house with water for us by pouring it in! At my wit's end over the thing, for I feared that Pancrates might come back and be angry, as was indeed the case, I took an axe and cut the pestle in two; but each part took a jar and began to carry water, with the result that instead of one servant I had now two. Meanwhile Pancrates appeared on the scene, and comprehending what had happened, turned them into wood again, just as they were before the spell, and then for his own part left me to my own devices without warning, taking himself off out of sight somewhere."

"Then you still know how to turn the pestle into a man?" said Deinomachus. "Yes," said he: "only half way, however, for I cannot bring it back to its original form if it once becomes a water-

γένηται ὑδροφόρος, ἀλλὰ δεήσει ἡμῖν ἐπικλυσθῆναι τὴν οἰκίαν ἐπαντλουμένην."

37 "Οὐ παύσεσθε," ἦν δ' ἐγώ, "τὰ τοιαῦτα τερατολογοῦντες γέροντες ἄνδρες; εἰ δὲ μή, ἀλλὰ κἂν τούτων γε τῶν μειρακίων ἕνεκα εἰς ἄλλον τινὰ καιρὸν ὑπερβάλλεσθε τὰς παραδόξους ταύτας καὶ φοβερὰς διηγήσεις, μή πως λάθωσιν ἡμῖν ἐμπλησθέντες δειμάτων καὶ ἀλλοκότων μυθολογημάτων. φείδεσθαι οὖν χρὴ αὐτῶν μηδὲ τοιαῦτα ἐθίζειν ἀκούειν, ἃ διὰ παντὸς τοῦ βίου συνόντα ἐνοχλήσει καὶ ψοφοδεεῖς ποιήσει ποικίλης τῆς δεισιδαιμονίας ἐμπιπλάντα."

38 "Εὖ γε ὑπέμνησας," ἦ δ' ὃς ὁ Εὐκράτης, "εἰπὼν τὴν δεισιδαιμονίαν. τί γάρ σοι, ὦ Τυχιάδη, περὶ τῶν τοιούτων δοκεῖ, λέγω δὴ χρησμῶν καὶ θεσφάτων καὶ ὅσα θεοφορούμενοί τινες ἀναβοῶσιν ἢ ἐξ ἀδύτων ἀκούεται ἢ παρθένος ἔμμετρα φθεγγομένη προθεσπίζει τὰ μέλλοντα; ἢ δηλαδὴ καὶ τοῖς τοιούτοις ἀπιστήσεις; ἐγὼ δὲ ὅτι μὲν καὶ δακτύλιόν τινα ἱερὸν ἔχω Ἀπόλλωνος τοῦ Πυθίου εἰκόνα ἐκτυποῦντα[1] τὴν σφραγῖδα καὶ οὗτος ὁ Ἀπόλλων φθέγγεται πρὸς ἐμέ, οὐ λέγω, μή σοι ἄπιστα δόξω περὶ ἐμαυτοῦ μεγαλαυχεῖσθαι· ἃ δὲ Ἀμφιλόχου[2] τε ἤκουσα ἐν Μαλλῷ, τοῦ ἥρωος ὕπαρ διαλεχθέντος[3] μοι καὶ συμβουλεύσαντος περὶ τῶν ἐμῶν, καὶ ἃ εἶδον αὐτός, ἐθέλω ὑμῖν εἰπεῖν, εἶτα ἑξῆς ἃ ἐν Περγάμῳ εἶδον καὶ ἃ ἤκουσα ἐν Πατάροις.

[1] ἐκτυποῦντα Fritzsche: ἐκτυποῦσαν γP: ἐκτυπούσης τῆς σφραγῖδος N Vat. 87.
[2] Ἀμφιλόχου P: ἐν Ἀμφιλόχου γN.
[3] ὕπαρ διαλεχθέντος Larcher: ὑπερδιαλεχθέντος MSS.

carrier, but we shall be obliged to let the house be flooded with the water that is poured in!"

"Will you never stop telling such buncombe, old men as you are?" said I. "If you will not, at least for the sake of these lads put your amazing and fearful tales off to some other time, so that they may not be filled up with terrors and strange figments before we realise it. You ought to be easy with them and not accustom them to hear things like this which will abide with them and annoy them their lives long and will make them afraid of every sound by filling them with all sorts of superstition."

"Thank you," said Eucrates, "for putting me in mind of superstition by mentioning it. What is your opinion, Tychiades, about that sort of thing—I mean oracles, prophecies, outcries of men under divine possession, voices heard from inner shrines, or verses uttered by a maiden who foretells the future? Of course you doubt that sort of thing also? For my own part, I say nothing of the fact that I have a holy ring with an image of Apollo Pythius engraved on the seal, and that this Apollo speaks to me: you might think that I was bragging about myself beyond belief. I should like, however, to tell you all what I heard from Amphilochus in Mallus,[1] when the hero conversed with me in broad day and advised me about my affairs, and what I myself saw, and then in due order what I saw at Pergamon and what I heard at Patara.

[1] A famous shrine in Cilicia. "After the death of his father Amphiaraus and his disappearance at Thebes, he (Amphilochus) was exiled from his own country and went to Cilicia, where he fared quite well, for he, like his father, foretold the future to the Cilicians and received two obols for each oracle."—*Alexander* 19.

"Ὁπότε γὰρ ἐξ Αἰγύπτου ἐπανήειν οἴκαδε ἀκούων τὸ ἐν Μαλλῷ τοῦτο μαντεῖον ἐπιφανέστατόν τε καὶ ἀληθέστατον εἶναι καὶ χρᾶν ἐναργῶς πρὸς ἔπος ἀποκρινόμενον οἷς ἂν ἐγγράψας τις εἰς τὸ γραμματεῖον παραδῷ τῷ προφήτῃ, καλῶς ἔχειν ἡγησάμην ἐν παράπλῳ πειραθῆναι τοῦ χρηστηρίου καί τι περὶ τῶν μελλόντων συμβουλεύσασθαι τῷ θεῷ—"

39 Ταῦτα ἔτι τοῦ Εὐκράτους λέγοντος ἰδὼν οἷ τὸ πρᾶγμα προχωρήσειν ἔμελλε καὶ ὡς οὐ μικρᾶς ἐνήρχετο τῆς περὶ τὰ χρηστήρια τραγῳδίας, οὐ δοκιμάσας[1] μόνος ἀντιλέγειν ἅπασιν, ἀπολιπὼν αὐτὸν ἔτι διαπλέοντα ἐξ Αἰγύπτου εἰς τὴν Μαλλόν—καὶ γὰρ συνίειν ὅτι μοι ἄχθονται παρόντι καθάπερ ἀντισοφιστῇ τῶν ψευσμάτων—"Ἀλλ' ἐγὼ ἄπειμι," ἔφην, "Λεόντιχον ἀναζητήσων· δέομαι γάρ τι αὐτῷ συγγενέσθαι. ὑμεῖς δὲ ἐπείπερ οὐχ ἱκανὰ ἡγεῖσθε τὰ ἀνθρώπινα εἶναι, καὶ αὐτοὺς ἤδη τοὺς θεοὺς καλεῖτε συνεπιληψομένους ὑμῖν τῶν μυθολογουμένων·" καὶ ἅμα λέγων ἐξῄειν. οἱ δὲ ἄσμενοι ἐλευθερίας λαβόμενοι εἱστίων, ὡς τὸ εἰκός, αὐτοὺς καὶ ἐνεφοροῦντο τῶν ψευσμάτων.

Τοιαῦτά σοι, ὦ Φιλόκλεις, παρὰ Εὐκράτει ἀκούσας περίειμι[2] νὴ τὸν Δία ὥσπερ οἱ τοῦ γλεύκους πιόντες ἐμπεφυσημένος τὴν γαστέρα ἐμέτου δεόμενος. ἡδέως δ' ἂν ποθεν ἐπὶ πολλῷ ἐπριάμην ληθεδανόν τι φάρμακον ὧν ἤκουσα, ὡς μή τι κακὸν ἐργάσηταί με ἡ μνήμη αὐτῶν ἐνοικουροῦσα· τέρατα γοῦν καὶ δαίμονας καὶ Ἑκάτας ὁρᾶν μοι δοκῶ.

[1] οὐ δοκεῖν οἰηθεὶς δεῖν β. [2] ἥκω β.

"When I was on my way home from Egypt I heard that this shrine in Mallus was very famous and very truthful, and that it responded clearly, answering word for word whatever one wrote in his tablet and turned over to the prophet. So I thought that it would be well to give the oracle a trial in passing and ask the god for some advice about the future—"

While Eucrates was still saying these words, since I could see how the business would turn out and that the cock-and-bull story about oracles upon which he was embarking would not be short, I left him sailing from Egypt to Mallus, not choosing to oppose everyone all alone: I was aware, too, that they were put out at my being there to criticise their lies. "I am going away," I said, "to look up Leontichus, for I want to speak to him about something. As for you, since you do not think that human experiences afford you a sufficient field, go ahead and call in the gods themselves to help you out in your romancing." With that I went out. They were glad to have a free hand, and continued, of course, to feast and to gorge themselves with lies.

There you have it, Philocles! After hearing all that at the house of Eucrates I am going about like a man who has drunk sweet must, with a swollen belly, craving an emetic. I should be glad if I could anywhere buy at a high price a dose of forgetfulness, so that the memory of what I heard may not stay with me and work me some harm. In fact, I think I see apparitions and spirits and Hecates!

ΦΙΛΟΚΛΗΣ

40 Καὶ αὐτός, ὦ Τυχιάδη, τοιοῦτόν τι ἀπέλαυσα τῆς διηγήσεως. φασί γέ τοι μὴ μόνον λυττᾶν καὶ τὸ ὕδωρ φοβεῖσθαι ὁπόσους ἂν οἱ λυττῶντες κύνες δάκωσιν, ἀλλὰ κἄν τινα ὁ δηχθεὶς ἄνθρωπος δάκῃ, ἴσα τῷ κυνὶ δύναται τὸ δῆγμα, καὶ τὰ αὐτὰ κἀκεῖνος φοβεῖται. καὶ σὺ τοίνυν ἔοικας αὐτὸς ἐν Εὐκράτους δηχθεὶς ὑπὸ πολλῶν ψευσμάτων μεταδεδωκέναι κἀμοὶ τοῦ δήγματος· οὕτω δαιμόνων μοι τὴν ψυχὴν ἐνέπλησας.

ΤΥΧΙΑΔΗΣ

Ἀλλὰ θαρρῶμεν, ὦ φιλότης, μέγα τῶν τοιούτων ἀλεξιφάρμακον ἔχοντες τὴν ἀλήθειαν καὶ τὸν ἐπὶ πᾶσι λόγον ὀρθόν, ᾧ χρωμένους ἡμᾶς μηδὲν μὴ ταράξῃ τῶν κενῶν καὶ ματαίων τούτων ψευσμάτων.[1]

[1] φασμάτων β.

PHILOCLES

Your story has had the same enjoyable effect upon me, Tychiades. They say, you know, that not only those who are bitten by mad dogs go mad and fear water, but if a man who has been bitten bites anyone else, his bite has the same effect as the dog's, and the other man has the same fears. It is likely, therefore, that having been bitten yourself by a multitude of lies in the house of Eucrates, you have passed the bite on to me; you have filled my soul so full of spirits!

TYCHIADES

Well, never mind, my dear fellow; we have a powerful antidote to such poisons in truth and in sound reason brought to bear everywhere. As long as we make use of this, none of these empty, foolish lies will disturb our peace.

THE JUDGEMENT OF THE GODDESSES

The judgement of Paris, reviewed by Lucian.

Since the first edition, it has always been printed as the twentieth of the *Dialogues of the Gods*, but in all the MSS. it is a separate piece and has a separate caption of its own, whereas in the *Dialogues of the Gods* the individual dialogues are headed merely by the names of their interlocutors. Then too it is longer than any of these, and although substantially of the same cloth, more markedly satirical than most of them.

In connection with Lucian's dialogue, it is well worth one's while to read Apuleius' detailed description of a pantomime on the same subject (*Metamorphoses* 10, 232). The strong contrast between the two treatments shows how little Lucian was influenced by the contemporary theatre.

ΘΕΩΝ ΚΡΙΣΙΣ

ΖΕΥΣ

1 Ἑρμῆ, λαβὼν τουτὶ τὸ μῆλον ἄπιθι εἰς τὴν Φρυγίαν παρὰ τὸν Πριάμου παῖδα τὸν βουκόλον—νέμει δὲ τῆς Ἴδης ἐν τῷ Γαργάρῳ—καὶ λέγε πρὸς αὐτόν, ὅτι "Σέ, ὦ Πάρι, κελεύει ὁ Ζεύς, ἐπειδὴ καλός τε αὐτὸς εἶ καὶ σοφὸς τὰ ἐρωτικά, δικάσαι ταῖς θεαῖς, ἥτις αὐτῶν ἡ καλλίστη ἐστίν· τοῦ δὲ ἀγῶνος τὸ ἆλθον ἡ νικῶσα λαβέτω τὸ μῆλον." ὥρα δὲ ἤδη καὶ ὑμῖν αὐταῖς ἀπιέναι παρὰ τὸν δικαστήν· ἐγὼ γὰρ ἀπωθοῦμαι τὴν δίαιταν ἐπ' ἴσης τε ὑμᾶς ἀγαπῶν, καὶ εἴ γε οἷόν τε ἦν, ἡδέως ἂν ἁπάσας νενικηκυίας ἰδών. ἄλλως τε καὶ ἀνάγκη, μιᾷ τὸ καλλιστεῖον ἀποδόντα πάντως ἀπεχθάνεσθαι ταῖς πλείοσιν. διὰ ταῦτα αὐτὸς μὲν[1] οὐκ ἐπιτήδειος ὑμῖν δικαστής, ὁ δὲ νεανίας οὗτος ὁ Φρὺξ ἐφ' ὃν ἄπιτε βασιλικὸς μὲν ἐστι καὶ Γανυμήδους τουτουὶ συγγενής, τὰ ἄλλα δὲ ἀφελὴς καὶ ὄρειος, κοὐκ ἄν τις αὐτὸν ἀπαξιώσειε τοιαύτης θέας.

ΑΦΡΟΔΙΤΗ

2 Ἐγὼ μέν, ὦ Ζεῦ, εἰ καὶ τὸν Μῶμον αὐτὸν ἐπιστήσειας ἡμῖν δικαστήν, θαρροῦσα βαδιοῦμαι πρὸς τὴν ἐπίδειξιν· τί γὰρ ἂν καὶ μωμήσαιτό μου; χρὴ δὲ καὶ ταύταις ἀρέσκειν τὸν ἄνθρωπον.

Available in photographs: Γ, PN. P contains only c. 16 ἐρασθῇς—end.

[1] αὐτὸς μὲν Fritzsche: μὲν αὐτὸς γβ.

THE JUDGEMENT OF THE GODDESSES

ZEUS

HERMES, take this apple; go to Phrygia, to Priam's son, the herdsman—he is grazing his flock in the foothills of Ida, on Gargaron—and say to him: "Paris, as you are handsome yourself, and also well schooled in all that concerns love, Zeus bids you be judge for the goddesses, to decide which of them is the most beautiful. As the prize for the contest, let the victor take the apple." (*To the* GODDESSES) You yourselves must now go and appear before your judge. I refuse to be umpire because I love you all alike and if it were possible, should be glad to see you all victorious. Moreover, it is sure that if I gave the guerdon of beauty to one, I should inevitably get into the bad graces of the majority. For those reasons I am not a proper judge for you, but the young Phrygian to whom you are going is of royal blood and near of kin to our Ganymede; besides, he is ingenuous and unsophisticated, and one cannot consider him unworthy of a spectacle such as this.

APHRODITE

For my part, Zeus, even if you should appoint Momus himself to be our judge, I would go and face the inspection confidently, for what could he carp at in me? The others, too, ought to be satisfied with the man.

ΗΡΑ

Οὐδ᾽ ἡμεῖς, ὦ Ἀφροδίτη, δέδιμεν, οὐδ᾽ ἂν ὁ Ἄρης ὁ σὸς ἐπιτραπῇ τὴν δίαιταν· ἀλλὰ δεχόμεθα καὶ τοῦτον, ὅστις ἂν ᾖ, τὸν Πάριν.

ΖΕΥΣ

Ἦ καὶ σοὶ ταῦτα, ὦ θύγατερ, συνδοκεῖ; τί φής; ἀποστρέφῃ καὶ ἐρυθριᾷς; ἔστι μὲν ἴδιον τὸ αἰδεῖσθαι τὰ τοιαῦτα ὑμῶν τῶν παρθένων· ἐπινεύεις δ᾽ ὅμως. ἄπιτε οὖν καὶ μὴ χαλεπήνητε τῷ δικαστῇ αἱ νενικημέναι μηδὲ κακὸν ἐντρίψησθε τῷ νεανίσκῳ· οὐ γὰρ οἷόν τε ἐπ᾽ ἴσης πάσας εἶναι καλάς.

ΕΡΜΗΣ

3 Προΐωμεν εὐθὺ τῆς Φρυγίας, ἐγὼ μὲν ἡγούμενος, ὑμεῖς δὲ μὴ βραδέως ἀκολουθεῖτέ μοι καὶ θαρρεῖτε. οἶδα ἐγὼ τὸν Πάριν. νεανίας ἐστὶ καλὸς καὶ τἄλλα ἐρωτικὸς καὶ τὰ τοιαῦτα κρίνειν ἱκανώτατος. οὐκ ἂν ἐκεῖνος δικάσειεν κακῶς.

ΑΦΡΟΔΙΤΗ

Τοῦτο μὲν ἅπαν ἀγαθὸν καὶ πρὸς ἐμοῦ λέγεις, τὸ δίκαιον ἡμῖν εἶναι τὸν δικαστήν· πότερα δὲ ἄγαμός ἐστιν οὗτος ἢ καὶ γυνή τις αὐτῷ σύνεστιν;

ΕΡΜΗΣ

Οὐ παντελῶς ἄγαμος, ὦ Ἀφροδίτη.

ΑΦΡΟΔΙΤΗ

Πῶς λέγεις;

ΕΡΜΗΣ

Δοκεῖ τις αὐτῷ συνοικεῖν Ἰδαία γυνή, ἱκανὴ μέν, ἀγροῖκος δὲ καὶ δεινῶς ὄρειος, ἀλλ᾽ οὐ σφόδρα προσέχειν αὐτῇ ἔοικε. τίνος δ᾽ οὖν ἕνεκα ταῦτα ἐρωτᾷς;

HERA

We are not afraid either, Aphrodite, not even if the arbitration is turned over to your own Ares. We accept this Paris, whoever he may be.

ZEUS

Is that your view too, daughter? What do you say? You turn away and blush? Of course, it is the way of a maid like you to be bashful in such matters, but you nod assent anyhow. Go, then, and do not get angry at your judge, those of you who are defeated, and do not inflict any harm on the lad. It is not possible for all of you to be equally beautiful.

HERMES

Let us make straight for Phrygia; I will lead the way, and you follow me without delaying. Be of good courage; I know Paris. He is young and handsome and in every way susceptible to love; just the sort to decide such questions. He would not judge amiss, not he.

APHRODITE

What you say is all to the good and in my favour, that our judge is just. Is he unmarried, or does some woman live with him?

HERMES

Not quite unmarried, Aphrodite.

APHRODITE

What do you mean by that?

HERMES

Apparently someone is living with him, a woman from Mount Ida, well enough, but countrified and terribly unsophisticated; however, he does not seem to think much of her.[1] But why do you ask?

[1] The reference is to Oenone.

ΑΦΡΟΔΙΤΗ

Ἄλλως ἠρόμην.

ΑΘΗΝΑ

4 Παραπρεσβεύεις, ὦ οὗτος, ἰδίᾳ πάλαι ταύτῃ κοινολογούμενος.

ΕΡΜΗΣ

Οὐδέν, ὦ Ἀθηνᾶ, δεινὸν οὐδὲ καθ' ὑμῶν, ἀλλ' ἤρετό με εἰ ἄγαμος ὁ Πάρις ἐστίν.

ΑΘΗΝΑ

Ὡς δὴ τί τοῦτο πολυπραγμονοῦσα;

ΕΡΜΗΣ

Οὐκ οἶδα· φησὶ δ' οὖν ὅτι ἄλλως ἐπελθόν, οὐκ ἐξεπίτηδες ἤρετο.

ΑΘΗΝΑ

Τί οὖν; ἄγαμός ἐστιν;

ΕΡΜΗΣ

Οὐ δοκεῖ.

ΑΘΗΝΑ

Τί δέ; τῶν πολεμικῶν ἐστιν αὐτῷ ἐπιθυμία καὶ φιλόδοξός τις, ἢ τὸ πᾶν βουκόλος;

ΕΡΜΗΣ

Τὸ μὲν ἀληθὲς οὐκ ἔχω εἰπεῖν, εἰκάζειν δὲ χρὴ νέον ὄντα καὶ τούτων ὀρέγεσθαι τυχεῖν καὶ βούλεσθαι ἂν πρῶτον αὐτὸν εἶναι κατὰ τὰς μάχας.

ΑΦΡΟΔΙΤΗ

Ὁρᾷς, οὐδὲν ἐγὼ μέμφομαι οὐδὲ ἐγκαλῶ σοι τὸ πρὸς ταύτην ἰδίᾳ λαλεῖν· μεμψιμοίρων γὰρ καὶ οὐκ Ἀφροδίτης τὰ τοιαῦτα.

APHRODITE

It was just a casual question.

ATHENA

I say, you are betraying your trust in talking to her privately all this while.

HERMES

It was nothing alarming, Athena, or against you and Hera; she asked me whether Paris is unmarried.

ATHENA

Why was she inquisitive about that?

HERMES

I don't know; she says, however, that she asked because it came into her head casually, and not because she had anything definite in view.

ATHENA

Well, what about it? Is he unmarried?

HERMES

Apparently not.

ATHENA

Tell me, does he covet success in war and is he fond of glory, or nothing but a herdsman?

HERMES

I can't say for certain, but it is fair to suppose that, being young, he yearns to acquire all that too, and would like to be first in war.

APHRODITE

You see, I am not making any complaint or reproaching you with talking confidentially to her; that is the way of fault-finders, not of Aphrodite!

ΕΡΜΗΣ

Καὶ αὕτη σχεδὸν τὰ αὐτά με ἤρετο· διὸ μὴ χαλεπῶς ἔχε μηδ' οἴου μειονεκτεῖν, εἴ τι καὶ
5 ταύτῃ κατὰ τὸ ἁπλοῦν ἀπεκρινάμην. ἀλλὰ μεταξὺ λόγων ἤδη πολὺ προϊόντες ἀπεσπάσαμεν τῶν ἀστέρων καὶ σχεδόν γε κατὰ τὴν Φρυγίαν ἐσμέν. ἐγὼ δὲ καὶ τὴν Ἴδην ὁρῶ καὶ τὸ Γάργαρον ὅλον ἀκριβῶς, εἰ δὲ μὴ ἐξαπατῶμαι, καὶ αὐτὸν ὑμῶν τὸν δικαστὴν τὸν Πάριν.

ΗΡΑ

Ποῦ δέ ἐστιν; οὐ γὰρ κἀμοὶ φαίνεται.

ΕΡΜΗΣ

Ταύτῃ, ὦ Ἥρα, πρὸς τὰ λαιὰ περισκόπει, μὴ πρὸς ἄκρῳ τῷ ὄρει, παρὰ δὲ τὴν πλευράν, οὗ τὸ ἄντρον, ἔνθα καὶ τὴν ἀγέλην ὁρᾷς.

ΗΡΑ

Ἀλλ' οὐχ ὁρῶ τὴν ἀγέλην.

ΕΡΜΗΣ

Πῶς φής; οὐχ ὁρᾷς βοΐδια κατὰ τὸν ἐμὸν οὑτωσὶ δάκτυλον ἐκ μέσων τῶν πετρῶν προερχόμενα καί τινα ἐκ τοῦ σκοπέλου καταθέοντα καλαύροπα ἔχοντα καὶ ἀνείργοντα μὴ πρόσω διασκίδνασθαι τὴν ἀγέλην;

ΗΡΑ

Ὁρῶ νῦν, εἴ γε ἐκεῖνός ἐστιν.

ΕΡΜΗΣ

Ἀλλὰ ἐκεῖνος. ἐπειδὴ δὲ πλησίον ἤδη ἐσμέν, ἐπὶ τῆς γῆς, εἰ δοκεῖ, καταστάντες βαδίζωμεν, ἵνα μὴ διαταράξωμεν αὐτὸν ἄνωθεν ἐξ ἀφανοῦς καθιπτάμενοι.

HERMES

She herself asked me practically the same questions; so do not be ill-tempered or think you are getting the worst of it if I answered her as I did you, in a straightforward way. But in the course of our conversation we have already left the stars far behind as we pressed on, and we are almost over Phrygia. Indeed I can see Ida and the whole of Gargaron plainly, and unless I am mistaken, even Paris himself, your judge.

HERA

Where is he? I do not see him.

HERMES

Look in this direction, Hera, to the left; not near the mountain-top, but on the side, where the cavern is, near which you see the herd.

HERA

But I do not see the herd.

HERMES

What? Don't you see tiny cattle over here in the direction of my finger, coming out from among the rocks, and someone running down from the cliff, holding a crook and trying to prevent the herd from scattering out ahead of him?

HERA

I see now—if that is really he.

HERMES

Yes, it is he. As we are near now, let us alight upon the earth and walk, if it is your pleasure, so that we may not alarm him by flying suddenly down from above.

ΗΡΑ

Εὖ λέγεις, καὶ οὕτω ποιῶμεν. ἐπεὶ δὲ καταβεβήκαμεν, ὥρα σοι, ὦ Ἀφροδίτη, προϊέναι καὶ ἡγεῖσθαι ἡμῖν τῆς ὁδοῦ· σὺ γὰρ ὡς τὸ εἰκὸς ἔμπειρος εἶ τοῦ χωρίου πολλάκις, ὡς λόγος, κατελθοῦσα πρὸς Ἀγχίσην.

ΑΦΡΟΔΙΤΗ

Οὐ σφόδρα, ὦ Ἥρα, τούτοις ἄχθομαι τοῖς σκώμμασιν.

ΕΡΜΗΣ

6 Ἀλλ' οὖν ἐγὼ ὑμῖν ἡγήσομαι· καὶ γὰρ αὐτὸς ἐνδιέτριψα τῇ Ἴδῃ, ὁπότε δὴ ὁ Ζεὺς ἤρα τοῦ μειρακίου τοῦ Φρυγός, καὶ πολλάκις δεῦρο ἦλθον ὑπ' ἐκείνου καταπεμφθεὶς εἰς ἐπισκοπὴν τοῦ παιδός. καὶ ὁπότε γε ἤδη ἐν τῷ ἀετῷ ἦν, συμπαριπτάμην αὐτῷ καὶ συνεκούφιζον τὸν καλόν, καὶ εἴ γε μέμνημαι, ἀπὸ ταυτησὶ τῆς πέτρας αὐτὸν ἀνήρπασεν. ὁ μὲν γὰρ ἔτυχε τότε συρίζων πρὸς τὸ ποίμνιον, καταπτάμενος δὲ ὄπισθεν αὐτοῦ ὁ Ζεὺς κούφως μάλα τοῖς ὄνυξι περιβαλὼν καὶ τῷ στόματι τὴν ἐπὶ τῇ κεφαλῇ τιάραν ἔχων ἀνέφερε τὸν παῖδα τεταραγμένον καὶ τῷ τραχήλῳ ἀπεστραμμένῳ εἰς αὐτὸν ἀποβλέποντα. τότε οὖν ἐγὼ τὴν σύριγγα λαβών, ἀποβεβλήκει γὰρ αὐτὴν ὑπὸ τοῦ δέους—ἀλλὰ γὰρ ὁ διαιτητὴς οὑτοσὶ 7 πλησίον, ὥστε προσείπωμεν αὐτόν. Χαῖρε, ὦ βουκόλε.

ΠΑΡΙΣ

Νὴ καὶ σύ γε, ὦ νεανίσκε. τίς δὲ ὢν δεῦρο ἀφῖξαι πρὸς ἡμᾶς; ἢ τίνας ταύτας ἄγεις τὰς γυναῖκας; οὐ γὰρ ἐπιτήδειαι ὀρεοπολεῖν, οὕτως γε οὖσαι καλαί.

HERA

You are right: let us do so . . . Now that we have descended, it is in order, Aphrodite, for you to go in front and lead the way for us. You are probably acquainted with the countryside, since by common report you often came down to visit Anchises.

APHRODITE

These jokes do not vex me greatly, Hera.

HERMES

No matter: I will lead you, for I myself spent some time on Ida when Zeus was in love with his Phrygian lad, and I often came here when he sent me down to watch the boy. Indeed, when he was in the eagle, I flew beside him and helped him to lift the pretty fellow, and if my memory serves me, it was from this rock just here that Zeus caught him up. You see, he chanced to be piping to his flock then, and Zeus, flying down behind him, grasped him very delicately in his talons, held in his beak the pointed cap which was on the boy's head, and bore him on high, terrified and staring at him with his head turned backwards. So then I took the syrinx, for he had let it fall in his fright—but here is your umpire close by, so let us speak to him. Good day, herdsman.

PARIS

Good day to you also, young man. But who are you, to have come here to see me, and who are these women whom you have with you? They are not of a sort to roam the mountains, being so beautiful.

ΕΡΜΗΣ

Ἀλλ' οὐ γυναῖκές εἰσιν, Ἥραν δέ, ὦ Πάρι, καὶ Ἀθηνᾶν καὶ Ἀφροδίτην ὁρᾷς· κἀμὲ τὸν Ἑρμῆν ἀπέστειλεν ὁ Ζεύς—ἀλλὰ τί τρέμεις καὶ ὠχριᾷς; μὴ δέδιθι· χαλεπὸν γὰρ οὐδέν. κελεύει δέ σε δικαστὴν γενέσθαι τοῦ κάλλους αὐτῶν· "Ἐπεὶ γάρ," φησί, "καλός τε αὐτὸς εἶ καὶ σοφὸς τὰ ἐρωτικά, σοὶ τὴν γνῶσιν ἐπιτρέπω." τοῦ δὲ ἀγῶνος τὸ ἆθλον εἴσῃ ἀναγνοὺς τὸ μῆλον.

ΠΑΡΙΣ

Φέρ' ἴδω τί καὶ βούλεται. "Ἡ καλή," φησίν, λαβέτω." πῶς ἂν οὖν, ὦ δέσποτα Ἑρμῆ, δυνηθείην ἐγὼ θνητὸς αὐτὸς καὶ ἀγροῖκος ὢν δικαστὴς γενέσθαι παραδόξου θέας καὶ μείζονος ἢ κατὰ βουκόλον; τὰ γὰρ τοιαῦτα κρίνειν τῶν ἁβρῶν μᾶλλον καὶ ἀστικῶν· τὸ δὲ ἐμόν, αἶγα μὲν αἰγὸς ὁποτέρα ἡ[1] καλλίων καὶ δάμαλιν ἄλλης δαμά-8 λεως, τάχ' ἂν δικάσαιμι κατὰ τὴν τέχνην· αὗται δὲ πᾶσαί τε ὁμοίως καλαὶ καὶ οὐκ οἶδ' ὅπως ἄν τις ἀπὸ τῆς ἑτέρας ἐπὶ τὴν ἑτέραν μεταγάγοι τὴν ὄψιν ἀποσπάσας· οὐ γὰρ ἐθέλει ἀφίστασθαι ῥᾳδίως, ἀλλ' ἔνθα ἂν ἀπερείσῃ τὸ πρῶτον, τούτου ἔχεται καὶ τὸ παρὸν ἐπαινεῖ· κἂν ἐπ' ἄλλο μεταβῇ, κἀκεῖνο καλὸν ὁρᾷ καὶ παραμένει, καὶ ὑπὸ τῶν πλησίον παραλαμβάνεται. καὶ ὅλως περικέχυταί μοι τὸ κάλλος αὐτῶν καὶ ὅλον περιείληφέ με καὶ ἄχθομαι, ὅτι μὴ καὶ αὐτὸς ὥσπερ ὁ Ἄργος ὅλῳ βλέπειν δύναμαι τῷ σώματι. δοκῶ δ' ἄν μοι καλῶς δικάσαι πάσαις ἀποδοὺς τὸ μῆλον. καὶ γὰρ αὖ καὶ τόδε, ταύτην μὲν εἶναι συμβέβηκεν

[1] ἡ Fritzsche: ᾗ γβ.

HERMES

They are not women; it is Hera and Athena and Aphrodite whom you see, Paris, and I am Hermes, sent by Zeus—but why do you tremble and turn pale? Don't be afraid; it is nothing terrible. He bids you be judge of their beauty, saying that as you are handsome yourself and also well schooled in all that concerns love, he turns over the decision to you. You will find out the prize for the contest if you read the writing on the apple.

PARIS

Come, let me see what it says; "The fairest may have me."—How could I, Lord Hermes, a mere mortal and a countryman, be judge of an extraordinary spectacle, too sublime for a herdsman? To decide such matters better befits dainty, city-bred folk. As for me, I could perhaps pass judgement as an expert between two she-goats, as to which is the more beautiful, or between two heifers; but these goddesses are all equally beautiful and I do not know how a man could withdraw his eyes from one and transfer them to another. They are not inclined to come away readily, but wherever one directs them first, they take firm hold and commend what is before them; and if they pass over to something else, they see that this too is beautiful and linger upon it, mastered by what is near. In short, their beauty encompasses and completely enthralls me, and I am distressed that I cannot see with my whole body as Argus did. I think I should pass a becoming judgement if I should give the apple to them all.—Another thing: one of them is Zeus' sister and wife,

τοῦ Διὸς ἀδελφὴν καὶ γυναῖκα, ταύτας δὲ θυγατέρας· πῶς οὖν οὐ χαλεπὴ καὶ οὕτως ἡ κρίσις;

ΕΡΜΗΣ

Οὐκ οἶδα· πλὴν οὐχ οἷόν τε ἀναδῦναι πρὸς τοῦ Διὸς κεκελευσμένον.

ΠΑΡΙΣ

9 Ἓν τοῦτο, ὦ Ἑρμῆ, πεῖσον αὐτάς, μὴ χαλεπῶς ἔχειν μοι τὰς δύο τὰς νενικημένας, ἀλλὰ μόνων τῶν ὀφθαλμῶν ἡγεῖσθαι τὴν διαμαρτίαν.

ΕΡΜΗΣ

Οὕτω φασὶ ποιήσειν· ὥρα δέ σοι ἤδη περαίνειν τὴν κρίσιν.

ΠΑΡΙΣ

Πειρασόμεθα· τί γὰρ ἂν καὶ πάθοι τις; ἐκεῖνο δὲ πρότερον εἰδέναι βούλομαι, πότερ' ἐξαρκέσει σκοπεῖν αὐτὰς ὡς ἔχουσιν, ἢ καὶ ἀποδῦσαι δεήσει πρὸς τὸ ἀκριβὲς τῆς ἐξετάσεως;

ΕΡΜΗΣ

Τοῦτο μὲν σὸν ἂν εἴη τοῦ δικαστοῦ, καὶ πρόσταττε ὅπῃ καὶ θέλεις.

ΠΑΡΙΣ

Ὅπῃ καὶ θέλω; γυμνὰς ἰδεῖν βούλομαι.

ΕΡΜΗΣ

Ἀπόδυτε, ὦ αὗται· σὺ δ' ἐπισκόπει· ἐγὼ δὲ ἀπεστράφην.

ΑΦΡΟΔΙΤΗ[1]

10 Καλῶς, ὦ Πάρι· καὶ πρώτη γε ἀποδύσομαι, ὅπως μάθῃς ὅτι μὴ μόνας ἔχω τὰς ὠλένας λευκὰς

[1] ΑΦΡΟΔΙΤΗ vulg.: ΗΡΑ MSS. editors since Jacobitz.

and the other two are his daughters! How, then, could the decision help being hazardous from that point of view also?

HERMES

I do not know; but it is impossible to escape carrying out what Zeus has commanded.

PARIS

Do me this one favour, Hermes: persuade them not to be angry with me, the two that are defeated, but to think that only my sight is at fault.

HERMES

They say they will do so, and now it is high time for you to get your judging done.

PARIS

I shall try; what else can one do? But first I want to know whether it will satisfy the requirements to look them over just as they are, or must I have them undress for a thorough examination?

HERMES

That is your affair, as you are the judge. Give your orders as you will.

PARIS

As I will? I want to see them naked.

HERMES

Undress, goddesses. Make your inspection, Paris. I have turned my back.

APHRODITE

Very well, Paris. I shall undress first, so that you may discover that I am not just "white-armed"

μηδὲ τῷ βοῶπις εἶναι μέγα φρονῶ, ἐπ' ἴσης δέ εἰμι πᾶσα καὶ ὁμοίως καλή.[1]

ΑΘΗΝΑ

Μὴ πρότερον ἀποδύσῃς αὐτήν, ὦ Πάρι, πρὶν ἂν τὸν κεστὸν ἀπόθηται—φαρμακὶς γάρ ἐστιν—μή σε καταγοητεύσῃ δι' αὐτοῦ. καίτοι γε ἐχρῆν μηδὲ οὕτω κεκαλλωπισμένην παρεῖναι μηδὲ τοσαῦτα ἐντετριμμένην χρώματα καθάπερ ὡς ἀληθῶς ἑταίραν τινά, ἀλλὰ γυμνὸν τὸ κάλλος ἐπιδεικνύειν.

ΠΑΡΙΣ

Εὖ λέγουσι τὸ περὶ τοῦ κεστοῦ, καὶ ἀπόθου.

ΑΦΡΟΔΙΤΗ

Τί οὖν οὐχὶ καὶ σύ, ὦ Ἀθηνᾶ, τὴν κόρυν ἀφελοῦσα ψιλὴν τὴν κεφαλὴν ἐπιδεικνύεις, ἀλλ' ἐπισείεις τὸν λόφον καὶ τὸν δικαστὴν φοβεῖς; ἢ δέδιας μή σοι ἐλέγχηται τὸ γλαυκὸν τῶν ὀμμάτων ἄνευ τοῦ φοβεροῦ βλεπόμενον;

ΑΘΗΝΑ

Ἰδού σοι ἡ κόρυς αὕτη ἀφῄρηται.

ΑΦΡΟΔΙΤΗ

Ἰδοὺ καί σοι ὁ κεστός.

[1] Most editors insert, with the Juntine edition, ΠΑΡ. Ἀπόδυθι καὶ σύ, ὦ Ἀφροδίτη, for which there is no MSS. authority. Giving the preceding speech to Aphrodite makes this unnecessary. Hemsterhuys' note should have settled the matter.

---

[1] Aphrodite, vexed at Hera for twitting her about Anchises, makes fun of her by implying that she has no other beauties than those habitually commended in her by Homer.

and vain of "ox-eyes," but that I am equally and uniformly beautiful all over.[1]

ATHENA

Do not let her undress, Paris, until she puts aside her girdle, for she is an enchantress; otherwise she may bewitch you with it.[2] And indeed she ought not to appear before you made up to that extent and bedaubed with all those colours, as if she were a courtesan in earnest: she ought to show her beauty unadorned.

PARIS

They are right about the girdle, so lay it aside.

APHRODITE

Then why do not you take off your helmet, Athena, and show your head bare, instead of tossing your plumes at the judge and frightening him? Are you afraid that you may be criticized for the green glare of your eyes if it is seen without trappings that inspire terror?[3]

ATHENA

There is the helmet for you: I have taken it off.

APHRODITE

There is the girdle for *you.*

[2] See *Iliad* 14, 214 ff.

[3] The word with which Homer describes the eyes of Athena had an uncomplimentary sense in Lucian's time. "Don't let it trouble you that her eyes are very green (πάνυ γλαυκούς), or that they squint and look at each other!" says a girl to her lover about a rival (*Dial. Mer.* 2, 1). And Hephaestus finds Athena very beautiful, but must except her eyes: "To be sure, she has green eyes, but the helmet makes even that a mark of beauty" (*Dial. Deor.* 13 (vulg. 8)). So *caesius* in Latin; cf. Lucretius 4, 1161.

ΗΡΑ

Ἀλλὰ ἀποδυσώμεθα.

ΠΑΡΙΣ

11 Ὦ Ζεῦ τεράστιε τῆς θέας, τοῦ κάλλους, τῆς ἡδονῆς. οἵα μὲν ἡ παρθένος, ὡς δὲ βασιλικὸν αὕτη καὶ σεμνὸν ἀπολάμπει καὶ ἀληθῶς ἄξιον τοῦ Διός, ἥδε[1] δὲ ὁρᾷ ἡδύ τι καὶ γλαφυρόν, καὶ προσαγωγὸν ἐμειδίασεν—ἀλλ' ἤδη μὲν ἅλις ἔχω τῆς εὐδαιμονίας· εἰ δοκεῖ δέ, καὶ ἰδίᾳ καθ' ἑκάστην ἐπιδεῖν βούλομαι, ὡς νῦν γε ἀμφίβολός εἰμι καὶ οὐκ οἶδα πρὸς ὅ τι ἀποβλέψω, πάντῃ τὰς ὄψεις περισπώμενος.

ΑΦΡΟΔΙΤΗ

Οὕτω ποιῶμεν.

ΠΑΡΙΣ

Ἄπιτε οὖν αἱ δύο· σὺ δέ, ὦ Ἥρα, περίμενε.

ΗΡΑ

Περιμενῶ, κἀπειδάν με ἀκριβῶς ἴδῃς, ὥρα σοι καὶ τἆλλα ἤδη σκοπεῖν εἰ καλά σοι, τὰ δῶρα τῆς ψήφου τῆς ἐμῆς. ἢν γάρ με, ὦ Πάρι, δικάσῃς εἶναι καλήν, ἁπάσης ἔσῃ τῆς Ἀσίας δεσπότης.

ΠΑΡΙΣ

Οὐκ ἐπὶ δώροις μὲν τὰ ἡμέτερα. πλὴν ἄπιθι· 12 πεπράξεται γὰρ ἅπερ ἂν δοκῇ. σὺ δὲ πρόσιθι ἡ Ἀθηνᾶ.

ΑΘΗΝΑ

Παρέστηκά σοι, καὶ ἤν με, ὦ Πάρι, δικάσῃς καλήν, οὔποτε ἥττων ἄπει ἐκ μάχης, ἀλλ' ἀεὶ

[1] ἥδε A.M.H.: ἡδέως Γ. The β MSS. read ὁρᾷ δὲ ἡδέως καὶ γλαφυρόν τι. Editors read ὡς δὲ ὁρᾷ ἥδε ἡδέως, καὶ γλάφυρόν τι (Juntine).

HERA

Come, let us undress.

PARIS

O Zeus, god of miracles! What a spectacle! What beauty! What rapture! How fair the maiden is! How royal and majestic and truly worthy of Zeus is the matron's splendour! How sweet and delicious is the other's gaze, and how seductively she smiled! But I have more than enough of bliss already; and if you please, I should like to examine each of you separately, for at present I am all at sea and do not know what to look at; my eyes are ravished in every direction.

APHRODITE

Let us do that.

PARIS

Then you two go away, and you, Hera, stay here.

HERA

Very well, and when you have examined me thoroughly, you must further consider whether the rewards of a vote in my favour are also beautiful in your eyes. If you judge me to be beautiful, Paris, you shall be lord of all Asia.

PARIS

My decisions are not to be influenced by rewards. But go; I shall do whatever seems best. Come, Athena.

ATHENA

I am at your side, and if you judge me beautiful, Paris, you shall never leave the field of battle

κρατῶν· πολεμιστὴν γάρ σε καὶ νικηφόρον ἀπεργάσομαι.

ΠΑΡΙΣ

Οὐδέν, ὦ Ἀθηνᾶ, δεῖ μοι πολέμου καὶ μάχης· εἰρήνη γάρ, ὡς ὁρᾷς, τὰ νῦν ἐπέχει τὴν Φρυγίαν τε καὶ Λυδίαν καὶ ἀπολέμητος ἡμῖν ἡ τοῦ πατρὸς ἀρχή. θάρρει δέ· οὐ μειονεκτήσεις γάρ, κἂν μὴ ἐπὶ δώροις δικάζωμεν. ἀλλ' ἔνδυθι ἤδη καὶ ἐπίθου τὴν κόρυν· ἱκανῶς γὰρ εἶδον. τὴν Ἀφροδίτην παρεῖναι καιρός.

ΑΦΡΟΔΙΤΗ

13 Αὕτη σοι ἐγὼ πλησίον, καὶ σκόπει καθ' ἓν ἀκριβῶς μηδὲν παρατρέχων, ἀλλ' ἐνδιατρίβων ἑκάστῳ τῶν μερῶν. εἰ δ' ἐθέλεις, ὦ καλέ, καὶ τάδε μου ἄκουσον. ἐγὼ γὰρ πάλαι ὁρῶσά σε νέον ὄντα καὶ καλὸν ὁποῖον οὐκ οἶδα εἴ τινα ἕτερον ἡ Φρυγία τρέφει, μακαρίζω μὲν τοῦ κάλλους, αἰτιῶμαι δὲ τὸ μὴ ἀπολιπόντα τοὺς σκοπέλους καὶ ταυτασὶ τὰς πέτρας κατ' ἄστυ ζῆν, ἀλλὰ διαφθείρειν τὸ κάλλος ἐν ἐρημίᾳ. τί μὲν γὰρ ἂν σὺ ἀπολαύσειας τῶν ὀρῶν; τί δ' ἂν ἀπόναιντο τοῦ σοῦ κάλλους αἱ βόες; ἔπρεπεν δὲ ἤδη σοι καὶ γεγαμηκέναι, μὴ μέντοι ἀγροῖκόν τινα καὶ χωρῖτιν, οἷαι κατὰ τὴν Ἴδην αἱ γυναῖκες, ἀλλά τινα ἐκ τῆς Ἑλλάδος, ἢ Ἀργόθεν ἢ ἐκ Κορίνθου ἢ Λάκαιναν οἵαπερ ἡ Ἑλένη ἐστίν, νέα τε καὶ καλὴ καὶ κατ' οὐδὲν ἐλάττων ἐμοῦ, καὶ τὸ δὴ μέγιστον, ἐρωτική. ἐκείνη γὰρ εἰ καὶ μόνον θεάσαιτό σε, εὖ οἶδα ἐγὼ ὡς ἅπαντα ἀπολιποῦσα καὶ παρασχοῦσα ἑαυτὴν ἔκδοτον ἕψεται καὶ συνοικήσει. πάντως δὲ καὶ σὺ ἀκήκοάς τι περὶ αὐτῆς.

defeated, but always victorious, for I shall make you a warrior and a conqueror.

PARIS

I have no use, Athena, for war and battle. As you see, peace reigns at present over Phrygia and Lydia, and my father's realm is free from wars. But have no fear; you shall not be treated unfairly, even if my judgement is not to be influenced by gifts. Dress yourself now, and put on your helmet, for I have seen enough. It is time for Aphrodite to appear.

APHRODITE

Here I am close by; examine me thoroughly, part by part, slighting none, but lingering upon each. And if you will be so good, my handsome lad, let me tell you this. I have long seen that you are young and more handsome than perhaps anyone else whom Phrygia nurtures. While I congratulate you upon your beauty, I find fault with you because, instead of abandoning these crags and cliffs and living in town, you are letting your beauty go to waste in the solitude. What joy can you get of the mountains? What good can your beauty do the kine? Moreover, you ought to have married by this time—not a country girl, however, a peasant, like the women about Ida, but someone from Greece, either from Argos or Corinth or a Spartan like Helen, who is young and beautiful and not a bit inferior to me, and above all, susceptible to love. If she but saw you, I know very well that, abandoning everything and surrendering without conditions, she would follow you and make her home with you. No doubt you yourself have heard something of her.

ΠΑΡΙΣ

Οὐδέν, ὦ Ἀφροδίτη· νῦν δὲ ἡδέως ἂν ἀκούσαιμί σου τὰ πάντα διηγουμένης.

ΑΦΡΟΔΙΤΗ

14 Αὕτη θυγάτηρ μέν ἐστι Λήδας ἐκείνης τῆς καλῆς ἐφ' ἣν ὁ Ζεὺς κατέπτη κύκνος γενόμενος.

ΠΑΡΙΣ

Ποία δὲ τὴν ὄψιν ἐστί;

ΑΦΡΟΔΙΤΗ

Λευκὴ μέν, οἵαν εἰκὸς ἐκ κύκνου γεγενημένην, ἁπαλὴ δέ, ὡς ἐν ᾠῷ τραφεῖσα, γυμνὰς τὰ πολλὰ καὶ παλαιστική, καὶ οὕτω δή τι περισπούδαστος ὥστε καὶ πόλεμον ἀμφ' αὐτῇ γενέσθαι, τοῦ Θησέως ἄωρον ἔτι ἁρπάσαντος. οὐ μὴν ἀλλ' ἐπειδήπερ εἰς ἀκμὴν κατέστη, πάντες οἱ ἄριστοι τῶν Ἀχαιῶν ἐπὶ τὴν μνηστείαν ἀπήντησαν, προεκρίθη δὲ Μενέλεως τοῦ Πελοπιδῶν γένους. εἰ δὴ θέλοις, ἐγώ σοι καταπράξομαι τὸν γάμον.

ΠΑΡΙΣ

Πῶς φής; τὸν τῆς γεγαμημένης;

ΑΦΡΟΔΙΤΗ

Νέος εἶ σὺ καὶ ἀγροῖκος, ἐγὼ δὲ οἶδα ὡς χρὴ τὰ τοιαῦτα δρᾶν.

ΠΑΡΙΣ

Πῶς; ἐθέλω γὰρ καὶ αὐτὸς εἰδέναι.

ΑΦΡΟΔΙΤΗ

15 Σὺ μὲν ἀποδημήσεις ὡς ἐπὶ θέαν τῆς Ἑλλάδος, κἀπειδὰν ἀφίκῃ εἰς τὴν Λακεδαίμονα, ὄψεταί σε ἡ Ἑλένη. τοὐντεῦθεν δὲ ἐμὸν ἂν εἴη τὸ ἔργον, ὅπως ἐρασθήσεταί σου καὶ ἀκολουθήσει.

PARIS

Nothing, Aphrodite, but I should be glad to hear you tell all about her now.

APHRODITE

In the first place, she is the daughter of that lovely Leda to whom Zeus flew down in the form of a swan.

PARIS

What is her appearance?

APHRODITE

She is white, as is natural in the daughter of a swan, and delicate, since she was nurtured in an egg-shell, much given to exercise and athletics, and so very much sought for that a war actually broke out over her because Theseus carried her off while she was still a young girl. Moreover, when she came to maturity, all the noblest of the Achaeans assembled to woo her, and Menelaus, of the line of Pelops, was given the preference. If you like, I will arrange the marriage for you.

PARIS

What do you mean? With a married woman?

APHRODITE

You are young and countrified, but I know how such things are to be managed.

PARIS

How? I too want to know.

APHRODITE

You will go abroad on the pretext of seeing Greece, and when you come to Sparta, Helen will see you. From that time on it will be my look-out that she falls in love with you and follows you.

ΠΑΡΙΣ

Τοῦτο αὐτὸ καὶ ἄπιστον εἶναί μοι δοκεῖ, τὸ ἀπολιποῦσαν τὸν ἄνδρα ἐθελῆσαι βαρβάρῳ καὶ ξένῳ συνεκπλεῦσαι.

ΑΦΡΟΔΙΤΗ

Θάρρει τούτου γε ἕνεκα. παῖδε γάρ μοι ἐστὸν δύο καλώ, Ἵμερος καὶ Ἔρως, τούτω σοι παραδώσω ἡγεμόνε τῆς ὁδοῦ γενησομένω· καὶ ὁ μὲν Ἔρως ὅλος παρελθὼν εἰς αὐτὴν ἀναγκάσει τὴν γυναῖκα ἐρᾶν, ὁ δ' Ἵμερος αὐτῷ σοι περιχυθεὶς τοῦθ' ὅπερ ἐστίν, ἱμερτόν τε θήσει καὶ ἐράσμιον. καὶ αὐτὴ δὲ συμπαροῦσα δεήσομαι καὶ τῶν Χαρίτων ἀκολουθεῖν· καὶ οὕτως ἅπαντες αὐτὴν ἀναπείσομεν.

ΠΑΡΙΣ

Ὅπως μὲν ταῦτα χωρήσει, ἄδηλον, ὦ Ἀφροδίτη· πλὴν ἐρῶ γε ἤδη τῆς Ἑλένης καὶ οὐκ οἶδ' ὅπως καὶ ὁρᾶν αὐτὴν οἴομαι καὶ πλέω εὐθὺ τῆς Ἑλλάδος καὶ τῇ Σπάρτῃ ἐπιδημῶ καὶ ἐπάνειμι ἔχων τὴν γυναῖκα—καὶ ἄχθομαι ὅτι μὴ ταῦτα ἤδη πάντα ποιῶ.

ΑΦΡΟΔΙΤΗ

16 Μὴ πρότερον ἐρασθῇς, ὦ Πάρι, πρὶν ἐμὲ τὴν προμνήστριαν καὶ νυμφαγωγὸν ἀμείψασθαι τῇ κρίσει· πρέποι γὰρ ἂν κἀμὲ νικηφόρον ὑμῖν συμπαρεῖναι καὶ ἑορτάζειν ἅμα καὶ τοὺς γάμους καὶ τὰ ἐπινίκια. πάντα γὰρ ἔνεστί σοι—τὸν ἔρωτα, τὸ κάλλος, τὸν γάμον—τουτουὶ τοῦ μήλου πρίασθαι.

ΠΑΡΙΣ

Δέδοικα μή μου ἀμελήσῃς μετὰ τὴν κρίσιν.

PARIS

That is just the thing that seems downright incredible to me, that she should be willing to abandon her husband and sail away with a foreigner and a stranger.

APHRODITE

Be easy on that score; I have two beautiful pages, Desire and Love; these I shall give you to be your guides on the journey. Love will enter wholly into her heart and compel the woman to love you, while Desire will encompass you and make you what he is himself, desirable and charming. I myself shall be there too, and I shall ask the Graces to go with me; and in this way, by united effort, we shall prevail upon her.

PARIS

How this affair will turn out is uncertain, Aphrodite; but, anyhow, I am in love with Helen already; somehow or other I think I see her; I am sailing direct to Greece, visiting Sparta, coming back again with the woman—and it irks me not to be doing all this now!

APHRODITE

Do not fall in love, Paris, until you have requited me, your match-maker and maid of honour, with the decision. It would be only fitting that when I am there with you, I too should be triumphant, and that we should celebrate at the same time your marriage and my victory. It is in your power to buy everything—her love, her beauty, and her hand—at the price of this apple.

PARIS

I am afraid you may dismiss me from your mind after the decision.

ΑΦΡΟΔΙΤΗ

Βούλει οὖν ἐπομόσομαι;

ΠΑΡΙΣ

Μηδαμῶς, ἀλλ' ὑπόσχου πάλιν.

ΑΦΡΟΔΙΤΗ

Ὑπισχνοῦμαι δή σοι τὴν Ἑλένην παραδώσειν γυναῖκα, καὶ ἀκολουθήσειν γέ σοι αὐτὴν καὶ ἀφίξεσθαι παρ' ὑμᾶς εἰς τὴν Ἴλιον· καὶ αὐτὴ παρέσομαι καὶ συμπράξω τὰ πάντα.

ΠΑΡΙΣ

Καὶ τὸν Ἔρωτα καὶ τὸν Ἵμερον καὶ τὰς Χάριτας ἄξεις;

ΑΦΡΟΔΙΤΗ

Θάρρει, καὶ τὸν Πόθον καὶ τὸν Ὑμέναιον ἔτι πρὸς τούτοις παραλήψομαι.

ΠΑΡΙΣ

Οὐκοῦν ἐπὶ τούτοις δίδωμι τὸ μῆλον· ἐπὶ τούτοις λάμβανε.

APHRODITE

Do you want me to take an oath?

PARIS

Not at all; but promise once again.

APHRODITE

I do promise that I will give you Helen to wife, and that she shall follow you and come to your people in Troy; and I myself will be there and help in arranging it all.

PARIS

And shall you bring Love and Desire and the Graces?

APHRODITE

Have no fear; I shall take with me Longing and Wedlock as well.

PARIS

Then on these conditions I award you the apple: take it on these conditions.

ON SALARIED POSTS IN GREAT HOUSES

A Hogarthian sketch of the life led by educated Greeks who attached themselves to the households of great Roman lords—and ladies. Lucian feigns to be advising a young friend, whom he dubs Timocles (Master Ambitious), against such a career—a most effective stratagem, since by giving him a pretext for his criticism, it relieves him from all semblance of personal animus and even enables him to appear sympathetic toward the varlets while he dusts their jackets.

In after years, when Lucian went into the Roman civil service in Egypt, this essay rose up to haunt him, and he had to write his *Apology* in order to lay its ghost.

ΠΕΡΙ ΤΩΝ ΕΠΙ ΜΙΣΘΩΙ ΣΥΝΟΝΤΩΝ

1 Καὶ τί σοι πρῶτον, ὦ φιλότης, ἢ τί ὕστατον, φασί, καταλέξω τούτων ἃ πάσχειν ἢ ποιεῖν ἀνάγκη τοὺς ἐπὶ μισθῷ συνόντας κἀν ταῖς τῶν εὐδαιμόνων τούτων φιλίαις ἐξεταζομένους—εἰ χρὴ φιλίαν τὴν τοιαύτην αὐτῶν δουλείαν ἐπονομάζειν; οἶδα γὰρ πολλὰ καὶ σχεδὸν τὰ πλεῖστα τῶν συμβαινόντων αὐτοῖς, οὐκ αὐτὸς μὰ Δία τοῦ τοιούτου πειραθείς, οὐ γὰρ ἐν ἀνάγκῃ μοι ἡ πεῖρα ἐγεγένητο, μηδέ, ὦ θεοί, γένοιτο· ἀλλὰ πολλοὶ τῶν εἰς τὸν βίον τοῦτον ἐμπεπτωκότων ἐξηγόρευον πρός με, οἱ μὲν ἔτι ἐν τῷ κακῷ ὄντες, ἀποδυρόμενοι ὁπόσα καὶ ὁποῖα ἔπασχον, οἱ δὲ ὥσπερ ἐκ δεσμωτηρίου τινὸς ἀποδράντες οὐκ ἀηδῶς μνημονεύοντες ὧν ἐπεπόνθεσαν· ἀλλὰ γὰρ εὐφραίνοντο ἀναλογιζόμενοι οἵων ἀπηλλάγησαν.

Ἀξιοπιστότεροι δὲ ἦσαν οὗτοι διὰ πάσης, ὡς εἰπεῖν, τῆς τελετῆς διεξεληλυθότες καὶ πάντα ἐξ ἀρχῆς εἰς τέλος ἐποπτεύσαντες. οὐ παρέργως οὖν οὐδὲ ἀμελῶς ἐπήκουον αὐτῶν καθάπερ ναυαγίαν τινὰ καὶ σωτηρίαν αὑτῶν παράλογον διηγουμένων, οἷοί εἰσιν οἱ πρὸς τοῖς ἱεροῖς ἐξυρημένοι τὰς κεφαλὰς συνάμα πολλοὶ τὰς τρικυμίας καὶ ζάλας καὶ ἀκρωτήρια καὶ ἐκβολὰς καὶ ἱστοῦ κλά-

Available in photographs: Γ, UN.

ON SALARIED POSTS IN GREAT HOUSES

"Where shall I make a beginning," my friend, "and where make an end of relating"[1] all that must be done and suffered by those who take salaried posts and are put on trial in the friendship of our wealthy men—if the name of friendship may be applied to that sort of slavery on their part? I am familiar with much, I may say most, of their experiences, not because I myself have ever tried anything of that kind, for it never became a necessity for me to try it, and, ye gods! I pray it never may; but many of those who have blundered into this existence have talked to me freely, some, who were still in their misery, bewailing the many bitter sufferings which they were then undergoing, and others, who had broken jail, as it were, recalling not without pleasure those they had undergone; in fact they joyed in recounting what they had escaped from.

These latter were the more trustworthy because they had gone through all the degrees of the ritual, so to speak, and had been initiated into everything from beginning to end. So it was not without interest and attention that I listened to them while they spun yarns about their shipwreck and unlooked-for deliverance, just like the men with shaven heads who gather in crowds at the temples and tell of third waves, tempests, headlands, strandings, masts carried

[1] Cf. *Odyssey* 9, 14.

σεις καὶ πηδαλίων ἀποκαυλίσεις διεξιόντες, ἐπὶ πᾶσι δὲ τοὺς Διοσκούρους ἐπιφαινομένους,—οἰκεῖοι γὰρ τῆς τοιαύτης τραγῳδίας οὗτοί γε—ἤ τιν᾽ ἄλλον ἐκ μηχανῆς θεὸν ἐπὶ τῷ καρχησίῳ καθεζόμενον ἢ πρὸς τοῖς πηδαλίοις ἑστῶτα καὶ πρός τινα ᾐόνα μαλακὴν ἀπευθύνοντα τὴν ναῦν, οἷ προσενεχθεῖσα ἔμελλεν αὐτὴ μὲν ἠρέμα καὶ κατὰ σχολὴν διαλυθήσεσθαι, αὐτοὶ δὲ ἀσφαλῶς ἀποβήσεσθαι χάριτι καὶ εὐμενείᾳ τοῦ θεοῦ.

Ἐκεῖνοι μὲν οὖν τὰ πολλὰ ταῦτα πρὸς τὴν χρείαν τὴν παραυτίκα ἐπιτραγῳδοῦσιν ὡς παρὰ πλειόνων λαμβάνοιεν, οὐ δυστυχεῖς μόνον ἀλλὰ 2 καὶ θεοφιλεῖς τινες εἶναι δοκοῦντες· οἱ δὲ τοὺς ἐν ταῖς οἰκίαις χειμῶνας καὶ τὰς τρικυμίας καὶ νὴ Δία πεντακυμίας τε καὶ δεκακυμίας, εἰ οἷόν τε εἰπεῖν, διηγούμενοι, καὶ ὡς τὸ πρῶτον εἰσέπλευσαν, γαληνοῦ ὑποφαινομένου τοῦ πελάγους, καὶ ὅσα πράγματα παρὰ τὸν πλοῦν ὅλον ὑπέμειναν ἢ διψῶντες ἢ ναυτιῶντες ἢ ὑπεραντλούμενοι τῇ ἅλμῃ, καὶ τέλος ὡς πρὸς πέτραν τινὰ ὕφαλον ἢ σκόπελον ἀπόκρημνον περιρρήξαντες τὸ δύστηνον σκαφίδιον ἄθλιοι κακῶς ἐξενήξαντο γυμνοὶ καὶ πάντων ἐνδεεῖς τῶν ἀναγκαίων—ἐν δὴ τούτοις καὶ τῇ τούτων διηγήσει ἐδόκουν μοι τὰ πολλὰ οὗτοι ὑπ᾽ αἰσχύνης ἐπικρύπτεσθαι, καὶ ἑκόντες εἶναι ἐπιλανθάνεσθαι αὐτῶν.

Ἀλλ᾽ ἔγωγε κἀκεῖνα καὶ εἴ τιν᾽[1] ἄλλα ἐκ τοῦ λόγου συντιθεὶς εὑρίσκω προσόντα ταῖς τοιαύταις συνουσίαις, οὐκ ὀκνήσω σοι πάντα, ὦ καλὲ Τιμόκλεις, διεξελθεῖν· δοκῶ γάρ μοι ἐκ πολλοῦ ἤδη κατανενοηκέναι σε τούτῳ τῷ βίῳ ἐπιβουλεύοντα,

[1] εἴ τιν᾽ Halm: ἔστιν γ, τινα N.

away, rudders broken, and to cap it all, how the Twin Brethren appeared (they are peculiar to this sort of rhodomontade), or how some other *deus ex machina* sat on the masthead or stood at the helm and steered the ship to a soft beach where she might break up gradually and slowly and they themselves get ashore safely by the grace and favour of the god.

Those men, to be sure, invent the greater part of their tragical histories to meet their temporary need, in order that they may receive alms from a greater number of people by seeming not only unfortunate but dear to the gods; but when the others told of household tempests and third waves—yes, by Zeus, fifth and tenth waves, if one may say so—and how they first sailed in, with the sea apparently calm, and how many troubles they endured through the whole voyage by reason of thirst or sea-sickness or inundations of brine, and finally how they stove their unlucky lugger on a submerged ledge or a sheer pinnacle and swam ashore, poor fellows, in a wretched plight, naked and in want of every necessity—in these adventures and their account of them it seemed to me that they concealed the greater part out of shame, and voluntarily forgot it.

For my part I shall not hesitate to tell you everything, my dear Timocles, not only their stories but whatever else I find by logical inference to be characteristic of such household positions; for I think I detected long ago that you are entertaining designs

3 καὶ πρῶτόν γε ὁπηνίκα περὶ τῶν τοιούτων ὁ λόγος ἐνέπεσεν, εἶτα ἐπῄνεσέ τις τῶν παρόντων τὴν τοιαύτην μισθοφοράν, τρισευδαίμονας εἶναι λέγων οἷς μετὰ τοῦ φίλους ἔχειν τοὺς ἀρίστους Ῥωμαίων καὶ δειπνεῖν δεῖπνα πολυτελῆ καὶ ἀσύμβολα καὶ οἰκεῖν ἐν καλῷ καὶ ἀποδημεῖν μετὰ πάσης ῥᾳστώνης καὶ ἡδονῆς ἐπὶ λευκοῦ ζεύγους, εἰ τύχοι, ἐξυπτιάζοντας, προσέτι καὶ μισθὸν τῆς φιλίας καὶ ὧν εὖ πάσχουσιν τούτων λαμβάνειν οὐκ ὀλίγον ἐστίν· ἀτεχνῶς γὰρ ἄσπορα καὶ ἀνήροτα τοῖς τοιούτοις τὰ πάντα φύεσθαι. ὁπότε οὖν ταῦτα καὶ τὰ τοιαῦτα ἤκουες, ἑώρων ὅπως ἐκεχήνεις πρὸς αὐτὰ καὶ πάνυ σφόδρα πρὸς τὸ δέλεαρ ἀναπεπταμένον παρεῖχες τὸ στόμα.

Ὡς οὖν τό γε ἡμέτερον εἰσαῦθίς ποτε ἀναίτιον ᾖ μηδὲ ἔχῃς[1] λέγειν ὡς ὁρῶντές σε τηλικοῦτο μετὰ τῆς καρίδος ἄγκιστρον καταπίνοντα οὐκ ἐπελαβόμεθα οὐδὲ πρὶν ἐμπεσεῖν τῷ λαιμῷ περιεσπάσαμεν οὐδὲ προεδηλώσαμεν, ἀλλὰ περιμείναντες ἐξ ἑλκομένου[2] καὶ ἐμπεπηγότος ἤδη συρόμενον καὶ πρὸς ἀνάγκην ἀγόμενον ὁρᾶν, ὅτ᾽ οὐδὲν ὄφελος ἑστῶτες ἐπεδακρύομεν· ὅπως μὴ ταῦτα λέγῃς ποτέ, πάνυ εὔλογα, ἢν λέγηται, καὶ ἄφυκτα ἡμῖν, ὡς οὐκ ἀδικοῦμεν μὴ προμηνύσαντες, ἄκουσον ἐξ ἀρχῆς ἁπάντων, καὶ τὸ δίκτυόν τε αὐτὸ καὶ τῶν κύρτων τὸ ἀδιέξοδον ἔκτοσθεν ἐπὶ σχολῆς, ἀλλὰ

[1] ἔχῃς Fritzsche: ἔχοις MSS.
[2] ἐξ ἑλκομένου A.M.H.: ἐξελκομένου MSS.

upon that life. I detected it first one time when our conversation turned to that theme, and then someone of the company praised this kind of wage-earning, saying that men were thrice happy when, besides having the noblest of the Romans for their friends, eating expensive dinners without paying any scot, living in a handsome establishment, and travelling in all comfort and luxury, behind a span of white horses, perhaps, with their noses in the air,[1] they could also get no inconsiderable amount of pay for the friendship which they enjoyed and the kindly treatment which they received; really everything grew without sowing and ploughing for such as they. When you heard all that and more of the same nature, I saw how you gaped at it and held your mouth very wide open for the bait.

In order, then, that as far as I am concerned I may be free from blame in future and you may not be able to say that when I saw you swallowing up that great hook along with the bait I did not hold you back or pull it away before it got into your throat or give you forewarning, but waited until I saw you dragged along by it and forcibly haled away when at last it was pulled and had set itself firmly, and then, when it was no use, stood and wept—in order that you may not say this, which would be a very sound plea if you should say it, and impossible for me to controvert on the ground that I had done no wrong by not warning you in advance—listen to everything at the outset; examine the net itself and the impermeability of the pounds beforehand, from the outside at

[1] That this is the meaning of ἐξυπτιάζοντες, and not "lolling at ease," is clear from *Book-Collector* 21 and *Downward Journey* 16.

μὴ ἔνδοθεν ἐκ τοῦ μυχοῦ προεπισκόπησον, καὶ τοῦ ἀγκίστρου δὲ τὸ ἀγκύλον καὶ τὴν εἰς τὸ ἔμπαλιν τοῦ σκόλοπος ἀναστροφὴν καὶ τῆς τριαίνης τὰς ἀκμὰς εἰς τὰς χεῖρας λαβὼν καὶ πρὸς τὴν γνάθον πεφυσημένην ἀποπειρώμενος, ἢν μὴ πάνυ ὀξέα μηδὲ ἄφυκτα μηδὲ ἀνιαρὰ ἐν τοῖς τραύμασι φαίνηται βιαίως σπῶντα καὶ ἀμάχως ἀντιλαμβανόμενα, ἡμᾶς μὲν ἐν τοῖς δειλοῖς καὶ διὰ τοῦτο πεινῶσιν ἀνάγραφε, σεαυτὸν δὲ παρακαλέσας θαρρεῖν ἐπιχείρει τῇ ἄγρᾳ, εἰ θέλεις, καθάπερ ὁ λάρος ὅλον περιχανὼν τὸ δέλεαρ.

4 Ῥηθήσεται δὲ ὁ πᾶς λόγος τὸ μὲν ὅλον ἴσως διὰ σέ, πλὴν ἀλλ᾽ οὔ γε περὶ τῶν φιλοσοφούντων ὑμῶν μόνον, οὐδὲ ὁπόσοι σπουδαιοτέραν τὴν προαίρεσιν προείλοντο ἐν τῷ βίῳ, ἀλλὰ καὶ περὶ γραμματιστῶν καὶ ῥητόρων καὶ μουσικῶν καὶ ὅλως τῶν ἐπὶ παιδείαις συνεῖναι καὶ μισθοφορεῖν ἀξιουμένων. κοινῶν δὲ ὡς ἐπίπαν ὄντων καὶ ὁμοίων τῶν συμβαινόντων ἅπασι, δῆλον ὡς οὐκ ἐξαίρετα μέν, αἰσχίω δὲ τὰ αὐτὰ ὄντα γίγνεται τοῖς φιλοσοφοῦσιν, εἰ τῶν ὁμοίων τοῖς ἄλλοις ἀξιοῖντο καὶ μηδὲν αὐτοὺς σεμνότερον οἱ μισθοδόται ἄγοιεν. ὅ τι δ᾽ ἂν οὖν ὁ λόγος αὐτὸς ἐπιὼν ἐξευρίσκῃ, τούτου τὴν αἰτίαν μάλιστα μὲν οἱ ποιοῦντες αὐτοί, ἔπειτα δὲ οἱ ὑπομένοντες αὐτὰ δίκαιοι ἔχειν· ἐγὼ δὲ ἀναίτιος, εἰ μὴ ἀληθείας καὶ παρρησίας ἐπιτίμιόν τί ἐστιν.

Τοὺς μέντοι τοῦ ἄλλου πλήθους, οἷον γυμναστάς τινας ἢ κόλακας, ἰδιώτας καὶ μικροὺς τὰς γνώμας καὶ ταπεινοὺς αὐτόθεν ἀνθρώπους, οὔτε ἀποτρέπειν ἄξιον τῶν τοιούτων συνουσιῶν, οὐδὲ γὰρ ἂν πεισθεῖεν, οὔτε μὴν αἰτιᾶσθαι καλῶς ἔχει μὴ ἀπολειπομένους τῶν μισθοδοτῶν εἰ καὶ πάνυ

your leisure, not from the inside after you are in the fyke; take in your hands the bend of the hook and the barb of its point, and the tines of the harpoon; puff out your cheek and try them on it, and if they do not prove very keen and unescapable and painful in one's wounds, pulling hard and gripping irresistibly, then write me down a coward who goes hungry for that reason, and, exhorting yourself to be bold, attack your prey if you will, swallowing the bait whole like a gull!

The whole story will be told for your sake, no doubt, in the main, but it will concern not only students of philosophy like yourself, and those who have chosen one of the more strenuous vocations in life, but also grammarians, rhetoricians, musicians, and in a word all who think fit to enter families and serve for hire as educators. Since the experiences of all are for the most part common and similar, it is clear that the treatment accorded the philosophers, so far from being preferential, is more contumelious for being the same, if it is thought that what is good enough for the others is good enough for them, and they are not handled with any greater respect by their paymasters. Moreover, the blame for whatever the discussion itself brings out in its advance ought to be given primarily to the men themselves who do such things and secondarily to those who put up with them. I am not to blame, unless there is something censurable in truth and frankness.

As to those who make up the rest of the mob, such as athletic instructors and parasites, ignorant, petty-minded, naturally abject fellows, it is not worth while to try to turn them away from such household positions, for they would not heed, nor indeed is it proper to blame them for not leaving their paymasters,

πολλὰ ὑβρίζοιντο ὑπ' αὐτῶν, ἐπιτήδειοι γὰρ καὶ οὐκ ἀνάξιοι τῆς τοιαύτης διατριβῆς· ἄλλως τε οὐδὲ σχοῖεν ἄν τι ἄλλο πρὸς ὅ τι χρὴ ἀποκλίναντας αὐτοὺς παρέχειν αὑτοὺς ἐνεργούς,[1] ἀλλ' ἤν τις αὐτῶν ἀφέλῃ τοῦτο, ἄτεχνοι αὐτίκα καὶ ἀργοὶ καὶ περιττοί εἰσιν. οὐδὲν οὖν οὔτ' αὐτοὶ δεινὸν πάσχοιεν ἂν οὔτ' ἐκεῖνοι ὑβρισταὶ δοκοῖεν εἰς τὴν ἀμίδα, φασίν, ἐνουροῦντες· ἐπὶ γάρ τοι τὴν ὕβριν ταύτην ἐξ ἀρχῆς παρέρχονται εἰς τὰς οἰκίας, καὶ ἡ τέχνη φέρειν καὶ ἀνέχεσθαι τὰ γιγνόμενα. περὶ δὲ ὧν προεῖπον τῶν πεπαιδευμένων ἄξιον ἀγανακτεῖν καὶ πειρᾶσθαι ὡς ἔνι μάλιστα μετάγειν αὐτοὺς καὶ πρὸς ἐλευθερίαν ἀφαιρεῖσθαι.

5 Δοκῶ δέ μοι καλῶς ἂν ποιῆσαι, εἰ τὰς αἰτίας ἀφ' ὧν ἐπὶ τὸν τοιοῦτον βίον ἀφικνοῦνταί τινες προεξετάσας δείξαιμι οὐ πάνυ βιαίους οὐδ' ἀναγκαίας· οὕτω γὰρ ἂν αὐτοῖς ἡ ἀπολογία προαναιροῖτο καὶ ἡ πρώτη ὑπόθεσις τῆς ἐθελοδουλείας. οἱ μὲν δὴ πολλοὶ τὴν πενίαν καὶ τὴν τῶν ἀναγκαίων χρείαν προθέμενοι ἱκανὸν τοῦτο προκάλυμμα οἴονται προβεβλῆσθαι τῆς πρὸς τὸν βίον τοῦτον αὐτομολίας, καὶ ἀποχρῆν αὐτοῖς νομίζουσιν εἰ λέγοιεν ὡς συγγνώμης ἄξιον ποιοῦσιν τὸ χαλεπώτατον τῶν ἐν τῷ βίῳ, τὴν πενίαν, διαφυγεῖν ζητοῦντες· εἶτα ὁ Θέογνις πρόχειρος καὶ πολὺ τό,

πᾶς γὰρ ἀνὴρ πενίῃ δεδμημένος

[1] ἄλλως τε οὐδὲ σχοῖεν ἂν πρὸς ὅ τι ἄλλο ἀποκλίναντες παρέχοιεν αὑτοὺς ἐνεργοὺς Hartman.

however much they may be insulted by them, for they are adapted to this kind of occupation and not too good for it. Besides, they would not have anything else to which they might turn in order to keep themselves busy, but if they should be deprived of this, they would be without a trade at once and out of work and superfluous. So they themselves cannot suffer any wrong nor their employers be thought insulting for using a pot, as the saying goes, for a pot's use. They enter households in the first instance to encounter this insolence, and it is their trade to bear and tolerate it. But in the case of the educated men whom I mentioned before, it is worth while to be indignant and to put forth every effort to bring them back and redeem them to freedom.

It seems to me that I should do well to examine in advance the motives for which some men go into this sort of life and show that they are not at all urgent or necessary. In that way their defence and the primary object of their voluntary slavery would be done away with in advance. Most of them plead their poverty and their lack of necessities, and think that in this way they have set up an adequate screen for their desertion to this life. They consider that it quite suffices them if they say that they act pardonably in seeking to escape poverty, the bitterest thing in life. Then Theognis comes to hand, and time and again we hear:

"All men held in subjection to Poverty,"[1]

[1] Theognis 173 ff.:

Ἄνδρ' ἀγαθὸν πενίη πάντων δάμνησι μάλιστα,
καὶ γήρως πολιοῦ, Κύρνε, καὶ ἠπιάλου,
ἣν δὴ χρὴ φεύγοντα καὶ ἐς βαθυκήτεα πόντον
ῥιπτεῖν καὶ πετρέων, Κύρνε. κατ' ἠλιβάτων.
καὶ γὰρ ἀνὴρ πενίῃ δεδμημένος οὔτε τι εἰπεῖν
οὔθ' ἕρξαι δύναται, γλῶσσα δέ οἱ δέδεται.

καὶ ὅσα ἄλλα δείματα ὑπὲρ τῆς πενίας οἱ ἀγεννέστατοι τῶν ποιητῶν ἐξενηνόχασιν.

Ἐγὼ δ' εἰ μὲν ἑώρων αὐτοὺς φυγήν τινα ὡς ἀληθῶς τῆς πενίας εὑρισκομένους ἐκ τῶν τοιούτων συνουσιῶν, οὐκ ἂν ὑπὲρ τῆς ἄγαν ἐλευθερίας ἐμικρολογούμην πρὸς αὐτούς· ἐπεὶ δὲ—ὡς ὁ καλός που ῥήτωρ ἔφη—τοῖς τῶν νοσούντων σιτίοις ἐοικότα λαμβάνουσι, τίς ἔτι μηχανὴ μὴ οὐχὶ καὶ πρὸς τοῦτο κακῶς βεβουλεῦσθαι δοκεῖν αὐτούς, ἀεὶ μενούσης αὐτοῖς ὁμοίας τῆς ὑποθέσεως τοῦ βίου; πενία γὰρ εἰσαεὶ καὶ τὸ λαμβάνειν ἀναγκαῖον καὶ ἀπόθετον οὐδὲν οὐδὲ περιττὸν εἰς φυλακήν, ἀλλὰ τὸ δοθέν, κἂν δοθῇ, κἂν ἀθρόως ληφθῇ, πᾶν ἀκριβῶς καὶ τῆς χρείας ἐνδεῶς καταναλίσκεται. καλῶς δὲ εἶχε μὴ τοιαύτας τινὰς ἀφορμὰς ἐπινοεῖν αἳ τὴν πενίαν τηροῦσι παραβοηθοῦσαι μόνον αὐτῇ, ἀλλ' αἳ τέλεον ἐξαιρήσουσιν, καὶ ὑπέρ γε τοῦ τοιούτου καὶ εἰς βαθυκήτεα πόντον ἴσως ῥιπτεῖν, εἰ δεῖ, ὦ Θέογνι, καὶ πετρέων, ὡς φής, κατ' ἠλιβάτων. εἰ δέ τις ἀεὶ πένης καὶ ἐνδεὴς καὶ ὑπόμισθος ὢν οἴεται πενίαν αὐτῷ τούτῳ διαπεφευγέναι, οὐκ οἶδα πῶς ὁ τοιοῦτος οὐκ ἂν δόξειεν ἑαυτὸν ἐξαπατᾶν.

6 Ἄλλοι δὲ πενίαν μὲν αὐτὴν οὐκ ἂν φοβηθῆναι οὐδὲ καταπλαγῆναί φασιν, εἰ ἐδύναντο τοῖς ἄλλοις ὁμοίως πονοῦντες ἐκπορίζειν τὰ ἄλφιτα, νῦν δέ, πεπονηκέναι γὰρ αὐτοῖς τὰ σώματα ἢ ὑπὸ γήρως ἢ ὑπὸ νόσων, ἐπὶ τήνδε ῥᾴστην οὖσαν τὴν μισθοφορὰν ἀπηντηκέναι. φέρ' οὖν ἴδωμεν εἰ ἀληθῆ λέγουσιν καὶ ἐκ τοῦ ῥᾴστου, μὴ πολλὰ μηδὲ πλείω τῶν ἄλλων ποιοῦσι, περιγίγνεται αὐτοῖς τὰ διδόμενα· εὐχῇ γὰρ ἂν ἐοικότα εἴη ταῦτά γε, μὴ

and all the other alarming statements about poverty that the most spiritless of the poets have put forth.

If I saw that they truly found any refuge from poverty in such household positions, I should not quibble with them in behalf of excessive liberty; but when they receive what resembles "the diet of invalids," as our splendid orator once said,[1] how can one avoid thinking that even in this particular they are ill advised, inasmuch as their condition in life always remains the same? They are always poor, they must continue to receive, there is nothing put by, no surplus to save: on the contrary, what is given, even if it is given, even if payment is received in full, is all spent to the last copper and without satisfying their need. It would have been better not to excogitate any such measures, which keep poverty going by simply giving first aid against it, but such as will do away with it altogether—yes, and to that end perhaps even to plunge into the deep-bosomed sea if one must, Theognis, and down precipitous cliffs, as you say. But if a man who is always poor and needy and on an allowance thinks that thereby he has escaped poverty, I do not know how one can avoid thinking that such a man deludes himself.

Others say that poverty in itself would not frighten or cow them if they could get their daily bread by working like the rest, but as things are, since their bodies have been debilitated by old age or by illnesses, they have resorted to this form of wage-earning, which is the easiest. Come, then, let us see if what they say is true and they secure their gifts easily, without working much, or any more than the rest. It would indeed be a godsend to get money readily

[1] Demosthenes 3, 33.

πονήσαντα μηδὲ καμόντα ἕτοιμον ἀργύριον λαβεῖν. τὸ δ' ἐστὶ καὶ ῥηθῆναι κατ' ἀξίαν ἀδύνατον· τοσαῦτα πονοῦσιν καὶ κάμνουσιν ἐν ταῖς συνουσίαις, ὥστε πλείονος ἐνταῦθα καὶ ἐπὶ τοῦτο μάλιστα τῆς ὑγιείας δεῖσθαι, μυρίων ὄντων ὁσημέραι τῶν ἐπιτριβόντων τὸ σῶμα καὶ πρὸς ἐσχάτην ἀπόγνωσιν καταπονούντων. λέξομεν δὲ αὐτὰ ἐν τῷ προσήκοντι καιρῷ, ἐπειδὰν καὶ τὰς ἄλλας αὐτῶν δυσχερείας διεξίωμεν· τὸ δὲ νῦν εἶναι ἱκανὸν ἦν ὑποδεῖξαι ὡς οὐδ' οἱ διὰ ταύτην λέγοντες αὑτοὺς ἀποδίδοσθαι τὴν πρόφασιν ἀληθεύοιεν ἄν.

7 Λοιπὸν δὴ καὶ ἀληθέστατον μέν, ἥκιστα δὲ πρὸς αὐτῶν λεγόμενον, ἡδονῆς ἕνεκα καὶ τῶν πολλῶν καὶ ἀθρόων ἐλπίδων εἰσπηδᾶν αὐτοὺς εἰς τὰς οἰκίας, καταπλαγέντας μὲν τὸ πλῆθος τοῦ χρυσοῦ καὶ τοῦ ἀργύρου, εὐδαιμονήσαντας δὲ ἐπὶ τοῖς δείπνοις καὶ τῇ ἄλλῃ τρυφῇ, ἐλπίσαντας δὲ ὅσον αὐτίκα χανδὸν οὐδενὸς ἐπιστομίζοντος πίεσθαι τοῦ χρυσίου. ταῦτα ὑπάγει αὐτοὺς καὶ δούλους ἀντὶ ἐλευθέρων τίθησιν—οὐχ ἡ τῶν ἀναγκαίων χρεία, ἣν ἔφασκον, ἀλλ' ἡ τῶν οὐκ ἀναγκαίων ἐπιθυμία καὶ ὁ τῶν πολλῶν καὶ πολυτελῶν ἐκείνων ζῆλος. τοιγαροῦν ὥσπερ δυσέρωτας αὐτοὺς καὶ κακοδαίμονας ἐρασταὶ ἔντεχνοί τινες καὶ τρίβωνες ἐρώμενοι παραλαβόντες ὑπεροπτικῶς περιέπουσιν, ὅπως ἀεὶ ἐρασθήσονται αὐτῶν θεραπεύοντες, ἀπολαῦσαι δὲ τῶν παιδικῶν ἀλλ' οὐδὲ μέχρι φιλήματος ἄκρου μεταδιδόντες· ἴσασι γὰρ ἐν τῷ τυχεῖν τὴν διάλυσιν τοῦ ἔρωτος γενησομένην. ταύτην οὖν ἀποκλείουσιν καὶ ζηλοτύπως φυλάττουσιν· τὰ δὲ ἄλλα ἐπ' ἐλπίδος ἀεὶ τὸν ἐραστὴν ἔχουσιν. δεδίασι γὰρ μὴ αὐτὸν ἡ ἀπό-

without toiling and moiling. As a matter of fact, the thing cannot even be put into adequate words. They toil and moil so much in their household positions that they need better health there and need health more than anything else for that occupation, since there are a thousand things every day that fret the body and wear it down to the lowest depths of despair. We shall speak of these at the proper time, when we recount their other hardships. For the present it is enough to indicate that those who allege this reason for selling themselves are not telling the truth either.

One motive remains, which is exceedingly genuine but not mentioned at all by them, namely, that they plunge into these households for the sake of pleasure and on account of their many extravagant expectations, dazzled by the wealth of gold and silver, enraptured over the dinners and the other forms of indulgence, and assured that they will immediately drink gold in copious draughts, and that nobody will stop their mouths. That is what seduces them and makes them slaves instead of freemen—not lack of necessaries, as they alleged, but desire for unnecessaries and envy of that abundance and luxury. Therefore, like unsuccessful and unhappy lovers, they fall into the hands of shrewd, experienced minions who treat them superciliously, taking good care that they shall always love them, but not permitting them to enjoy the objects of their affection even to the extent of a meagre kiss ; for they know that success will involve the dissolution of love. So they hold that under lock and key and guard it jealously, but otherwise they keep their lover always hopeful, since they fear that despair may wean him

γνωσις ἀπαγάγῃ τῆς ἄγαν ἐπιθυμίας καὶ ἀνέραστος αὐτοῖς γένηται· προσμειδιῶσιν οὖν καὶ ὑπισχνοῦνται καὶ ἀεὶ εὖ[1] ποιήσουσι καὶ χαριοῦνται καὶ ἐπιμελήσονται πολυτελῶς. εἶτ' ἔλαθον ἄμφω γηράσαντες, ἔξωροι γενόμενοι καὶ οὗτος τοῦ ἐρᾶν κἀκεῖνος τοῦ μεταδιδόναι. πέπρακται δ' οὖν αὐτοῖς οὐδὲν ἐν ἅπαντι τῷ βίῳ πέρα τῆς ἐλπίδος.

8 Τὸ μὲν δὴ δι' ἡδονῆς ἐπιθυμίαν ἅπαντα ὑπομένειν οὐ πάνυ ἴσως ὑπαίτιον, ἀλλὰ συγγνώμη εἴ τις ἡδονῇ χαίρει καὶ τοῦτο ἐξ ἅπαντος θεραπεύει ὅπως μεθέξει αὐτῆς. καίτοι αἰσχρὸν ἴσως καὶ ἀνδραποδῶδες ἀποδόσθαι διὰ ταύτην ἑαυτόν· πολὺ γὰρ ἡδίων ἡ ἐκ τῆς ἐλευθερίας ἡδονή. ὅμως δ' οὖν ἐχέτω τινὰ συγγνώμην αὐτοῖς, εἰ ἐπιτυγχάνοιτο· τὸ δὲ δι' ἡδονῆς ἐλπίδα μόνον πολλὰς ἀηδίας ὑπομένειν γελοῖον οἶμαι καὶ ἀνόητον, καὶ ταῦτα ὁρῶντας ὡς οἱ μὲν πόνοι σαφεῖς καὶ πρόδηλοι καὶ ἀναγκαῖοι, τὸ δὲ ἐλπιζόμενον ἐκεῖνο, ὁτιδήποτέ ἐστιν τὸ ἡδύ, οὔτε ἐγένετό πω τοσούτου χρόνου, προσέτι δὲ οὐδὲ γενήσεσθαι ἔοικεν, εἴ τις ἐκ τῆς ἀληθείας λογίζοιτο. οἱ μέν γε τοῦ Ὀδυσσέως ἑταῖροι γλυκύν τινα τὸν λωτὸν ἐσθίοντες ἠμέλουν τῶν ἄλλων καὶ πρὸς τὸ παρὸν ἡδὺ τῶν καλῶς ἐχόντων κατεφρόνουν· ὥστε οὐ πάντη ἄλογος αὐτῶν ἡ λήθη τοῦ καλοῦ, πρὸς τῷ ἡδεῖ ἐκείνῳ τῆς ψυχῆς διατριβούσης. τὸ δὲ λιμῷ συνόντα παρεστῶτα ἄλλῳ τοῦ λωτοῦ ἐμφορουμένῳ μηδὲν

[1] εὖ Bekker: not in MSS.

from his overmastering desire, and that he may grow out of love for them. They smile upon him, then, and make promises, and are always on the point of being good to him, and generous, and lavish with their attentions. Then before they know it, they both are old, the one has passed the season for loving, the other for yielding to love. Consequently they have done nothing in all their life except to hope.

Now to put up with everything on account of desire for pleasure is perhaps not altogether blameworthy, even excusable, if a man likes pleasure and makes it his aim above all else to partake of it. Yet perhaps it is shameful and ignoble for him to sell himself on that account; for the pleasure of freedom is far sweeter. Nevertheless, let us grant that he would be excusable in a measure, if he obtained it. But to put up with many unpleasantnesses just on account of the hope of pleasure is ridiculous in my opinion and senseless, particularly when men see that the discomforts are definite and patent in advance and inevitable, while the pleasure that is hoped for, whatever it is, has never yet come in all the past, and what is more, is not even likely to come in the future, if one should figure the matter out on the basis of hard fact. The companions of Odysseus neglected all else because they were eating the lotus and found it sweet, and they contemned what was honourable because they contrasted it with their immediate pleasure; therefore it was not entirely unreasonable of them to forget honour while their souls dwelt upon that sweetness. But for a man in hunger to stand beside another who eats his fill of lotus without giving him any, and to be chained

μεταδιδόντι ὑπὸ ἐλπίδος μόνης τοῦ κἂν αὐτὸν παραγεύσασθαί ποτε δεδέσθαι, τῶν καλῶς καὶ ὀρθῶς ἐχόντων ἐπιλελησμένον, Ἡράκλεις, ὡς καταγέλαστον καὶ πληγῶν τινων Ὁμηρικῶν ὡς ἀληθῶς δεόμενον.

9 Τὰ μὲν τοίνυν πρὸς τὰς συνουσίας αὐτοὺς ἄγοντα καὶ ἀφ᾽ ὧν αὐτοὺς φέροντες ἐπιτρέπουσι τοῖς πλουσίοις χρῆσθαι πρὸς ὅ τι ἂν ἐθέλωσιν, ταῦτά ἐστιν ἢ ὅτι ἐγγύτατα τούτων, πλὴν εἰ μὴ κἀκείνων τις μεμνῆσθαι ἀξιώσειεν τῶν καὶ μόνῃ τῇ δόξῃ ἐπαιρομένων τοῦ συνεῖναι εὐπατρίδαις τε καὶ εὐπαρύφοις ἀνδράσιν· εἰσὶν γὰρ οἳ καὶ τοῦτο περίβλεπτον καὶ ὑπὲρ τοὺς πολλοὺς νομίζουσιν, ὡς ἔγωγε τοὐμὸν ἴδιον οὐδὲ βασιλεῖ τῷ μεγάλῳ αὐτὸ μόνον συνεῖναι καὶ συνὼν ὁρᾶσθαι μηδὲν χρηστὸν ἀπολαύων τῆς συνουσίας δεξαίμην ἄν.

10 Τοιαύτης δὲ αὐτοῖς τῆς ὑποθέσεως οὔσης, φέρε ἤδη πρὸς ἡμᾶς αὐτοὺς ἐπισκοπήσωμεν οἷα μὲν πρὸ τοῦ εἰσδεχθῆναι καὶ τυχεῖν ὑπομένουσιν, οἷα δὲ ἐν αὐτῷ ἤδη ὄντες πάσχουσιν, ἐπὶ πᾶσι δὲ ἥτις αὐτοῖς ἡ καταστροφὴ τοῦ δράματος γίγνεται. οὐ γὰρ δὴ ἐκεῖνό γε εἰπεῖν ἐστιν, ὡς εἰ καὶ πονηρὰ ταῦτα, εὔληπτα γοῦν καὶ οὐ πολλοῦ δεήσει τοῦ πόνου, ἀλλὰ θελῆσαι δεῖ μόνον, εἶτά σοι πέπρακται τὸ πᾶν εὐμαρῶς· ἀλλὰ πολλῆς μὲν τῆς διαδρομῆς δεῖ,[1] συνεχοῦς δὲ τῆς θυραυλίας, ἕωθέν τε ἐξανιστάμενον περιμένειν ὠθούμενον καὶ ἀποκλειόμενον καὶ ἀναίσχυντον ἐνίοτε

[1] δεῖ ς, du Soul: not in best MSS.

to the spot, forgetful of all that is honourable and right, by the mere hope that he himself may get a taste some day—Heracles! how ridiculous and in very truth deserving of a proper Homeric thrashing![1]

Well, the motives which attract them to these household positions, which cause them to put themselves eagerly into the power of the rich to treat as they will, are these or as near as may be to these, unless one should think it worth while to mention also those men who are impelled by the mere name of associating with men of noble family and high social position. There are people who think that even this confers distinction and exalts them above the masses, just as in my own case, were it even the Great King, merely to associate with him and to be seen associating with him without getting any real benefit out of the association would not be acceptable to me.

So much for their object. Let us now consider between ourselves what they put up with before they are received and gain their end, and what they endure when they are fairly in the thing, and to cap the climax, what the outcome of the drama proves to be. For surely it cannot be said that even if all this is unworthy, at least it is easy to get and will not call for much trouble; that you need only wish, and then the whole thing is accomplished for you without any effort. No, it calls for much running hither and thither, and for continual camping on doorsteps; you must get up early and wait about; meanwhile you are elbowed, you are kept locked out, you are sometimes thought impudent and annoying, you are

[1] Like that bestowed upon Thersites by Odysseus (*Iliad* 2, 199, 265).

καὶ ὀχληρὸν δοκοῦντα καὶ ὑπὸ θυρωρῷ κακῶς συρίζοντι καὶ ὀνομακλήτορι Λιβυκῷ ταττόμενον καὶ μισθὸν τελοῦντα τῆς μνήμης τοῦ ὀνόματος. καὶ μὴν καὶ ἐσθῆτος ὑπὲρ τὴν ὑπάρχουσαν δύναμιν ἐπιμεληθῆναι χρὴ πρὸς τὸ τοῦ θεραπευομένου ἀξίωμα, καὶ χρώματα αἱρεῖσθαι οἷς ἂν ἐκεῖνος ἥδηται, ὡς μὴ ἀπᾴδῃς μηδὲ προσκρούῃς βλεπόμενος, καὶ φιλοπόνως ἕπεσθαι, μᾶλλον δὲ ἡγεῖσθαι, ὑπὸ τῶν οἰκετῶν προωθούμενον καὶ ὥσπερ τινὰ πομπὴν ἀναπληροῦντα.

Ὁ δὲ οὐδὲ προσβλέπει πολλῶν ἑξῆς ἡμερῶν. 11 ἢν δέ ποτε καὶ τὰ ἄριστα πράξῃς, καὶ ἴδῃ σε καὶ προσκαλέσας ἔρηταί τι ὧν ἂν τύχῃ, τότε δὴ τότε πολὺς μὲν ὁ ἱδρώς, ἀθρόος δὲ ὁ ἴλιγγος καὶ τρόμος ἄκαιρος καὶ γέλως τῶν παρόντων ἐπὶ τῇ ἀπορίᾳ. καὶ πολλάκις ἀποκρίνασθαι δέον, "Τίς ἦν ὁ βασιλεὺς τῶν Ἀχαιῶν," ὅτι "Χίλιαι νῆες ἦσαν αὐτοῖς," λέγεις. τοῦτο οἱ μὲν χρηστοὶ αἰδῶ ἐκάλεσαν, οἱ δὲ τολμηροὶ δειλίαν, οἱ δὲ κακοήθεις ἀπαιδευσίαν. σὺ δ' οὖν ἐπισφαλεστάτης πειραθεὶς τῆς πρώτης φιλοφροσύνης ἀπῆλθες καταδικάσας σεαυτοῦ πολλὴν τὴν ἀπόγνωσιν.

Ἐπειδὰν δὲ

> πολλὰς μὲν ἀΰπνους νύκτας ἰαύσῃς
> ἤματα δ' αἱματόεντα

διαγάγῃς, οὐ μὰ Δία τῆς Ἑλένης ἕνεκα οὐδὲ τῶν Πριάμου Περγάμων, ἀλλὰ τῶν ἐλπιζομένων πέντε ὀβολῶν, τύχῃς δὲ καὶ τραγικοῦ τινος θεοῦ συνιστάντος, ἐξέτασις τοὐντεῦθεν εἰ οἶσθα τὰ μαθήματα. καὶ τῷ μὲν πλουσίῳ ἡ διατριβὴ οὐκ

subordinate to a door-man with a vile Syrian accent and to a Libyan master of ceremonies, and you tip them for remembering your name. Moreover you must provide yourself with clothing beyond the means at your command, to correspond with the dignity of the man whom you are cultivating, and choose whatever colours he likes in order that you may not be out of harmony or in discord when he looks at you, and you must follow him zealously, or rather, lead the way, shoved on by the servants and filling out a guard of honour, as it were.

But your man does not even look at you for many days on end. And if ever you have a rare stroke of luck—if he sees you, calls you up and asks you a casual question, then, ah! then you sweat profusely, your head swims confusedly, you tremble inopportunely, and the company laughs at you for your embarrassment. Many a time, when you should reply to the question: "Who was the king of the Achaeans," you say, "They had a thousand ships!" Good men call this modesty, forward men cowardice, and unkind men lack of breeding. So, having found the beginning of friendly relations very unstable footing, you go away doomed by your own verdict to great despair.

When "many a sleepless night you have pillowed" and have lived through "many a blood-stained day," [1] not for the sake of Helen or of Priam's Trojan citadel, but the five obols that you hope for, and when you have secured the backing of a tragedy god,[2] there follows an examination to see if you are learned in the arts. For the rich man that way of

[1] *Iliad* 9, 325.

[2] Some person, as opportune and powerful as a *deus ex machina*, to press your suit.

ἀηδὴς ἐπαινουμένῳ καὶ εὐδαιμονιζομένῳ, σοὶ δὲ ὁ ὑπὲρ τῆς ψυχῆς ἀγὼν καὶ ὑπὲρ ἅπαντος τοῦ βίου τότε προκεῖσθαι δοκεῖ· ὑπεισέρχεται γὰρ εἰκότως τὸ μηδ' ὑπ' ἄλλου ἂν καταδεχθῆναι πρὸς τοῦ προτέρου ἀποβληθέντα καὶ δόξαντα εἶναι ἀδόκιμον. ἀνάγκη τοίνυν εἰς μυρία διαιρεθῆναι τότε, τοῖς μὲν ἀντεξεταζομένοις φθονοῦντα,—τίθει γὰρ καὶ ἄλλους εἶναι τῶν αὐτῶν ἀντιποιουμένους—αὐτὸν δὲ πάντα ἐνδεῶς εἰρηκέναι νομίζοντα, φοβούμενον δὲ καὶ ἐλπίζοντα καὶ πρὸς τὸ ἐκείνου πρόσωπον ἀτενίζοντα καὶ εἰ μὲν ἐκφαυλίζοι τι τῶν λεγομένων, ἀπολλύμενον, εἰ δὲ μειδιῶν ἀκούοι, 12 γεγηθότα καὶ εὔελπιν καθιστάμενον. εἰκὸς δὲ πολλοὺς εἶναι τοὺς ἐναντία σοι φρονοῦντας καὶ ἄλλους ἀντὶ σοῦ τιθεμένους, ὧν ἕκαστος ὥσπερ ἐκ λόχου τοξεύων λέληθεν. εἶτ' ἐννόησον ἄνδρα ἐν βαθεῖ πώγωνι καὶ πολιᾷ τῇ κόμῃ ἐξεταζόμενον εἴ τι οἶδεν ὠφέλιμον, καὶ τοῖς μὲν δοκοῦντα εἰδέναι, τοῖς δὲ μή.

Μέσος ἐν τοσούτῳ χρόνος, καὶ πολυπραγμονεῖταί σου ἅπας ὁ παρεληλυθὼς βίος, κἂν μέν τις ἢ πολίτης ὑπὸ φθόνου ἢ γείτων ἔκ τινος εὐτελοῦς αἰτίας προσκεκρουκὼς ἀνακρινόμενος εἴπῃ μοιχὸν ἢ παιδεραστήν, τοῦτ' ἐκεῖνο, ἐκ τῶν Διὸς δέλτων ὁ μάρτυς, ἂν δὲ πάντες ἅμα ἑξῆς ἐπαινῶσιν, ὕποπτοι καὶ ἀμφίβολοι καὶ δεδεκασμένοι. χρὴ τοίνυν πολλὰ εὐτυχῆσαι καὶ μηδὲν ὅλως ἐναντιωθῆναι· μόνως γὰρ ἂν οὕτως κρατήσειας.

Εἶεν· καὶ δὴ εὐτύχηταί σοι πάντα εὐχῆς[1] μειζόνως· αὐτός τε γὰρ ἐπῄνεσε τοὺς λόγους καὶ

[1] εὐχῆς du Soul: εὐτυχὴς (—ῆς, —εῖς) MSS.

passing time is not unpleasant, since he is praised and felicitated, but you feel that you have then before you the struggle for your life and for your entire existence, for the thought of course steals into your mind that no one else would receive you if you were rejected by his predecessor and considered unacceptable. So you cannot help being infinitely distracted then; for you are jealous of your rivals (let us suppose that there are others competing with you for the same object); you think that everything you yourself have said has been inadequate, you fear, you hope, you watch his face with straining eyes; if he scouts anything you say, you are in distress, but if he smiles as he listens, you rejoice and become hopeful. No doubt there are many who side against you and favour others in your stead, and each of them stealthily shoots at you, so to speak from ambush. Then too imagine a man with a long beard and grey hair undergoing examination to see if he knows anything worth while, and some thinking that he does, others that he does not!

Then a period intervenes, and your whole past life is pried into. If a fellow-countryman out of jealousy or a neighbour offended for some insignificant reason says, when questioned, that you are a follower of women or boys, there they have it! the witness speaks by the book of Zeus; but if all with one accord commend you, they are considered questionable, dubious, and suborned. You must have great good fortune, then, and no opposition at all; for that is the only way in which you can win.

Well, suppose you have been fortunate in everything beyond your fondest hopes. The master himself has commended your discussions, and those of

τῶν φίλων οἱ ἐντιμότατοι καὶ οἷς μάλιστα πιστεύει τὰ τοιαῦτα οὐκ ἀπέτρεψαν· ἔτι δὲ καὶ ἡ γυνὴ βούλεται, οὐκ ἀντιλέγει δὲ οὔτε ὁ ἐπίτροπος οὔτε ὁ οἰκονόμος· οὐδέ τις ἐμέμψατό σου τὸν βίον, ἀλλὰ πάντα ἵλεω καὶ πανταχόθεν αἴσια τὰ ἱερά.

13 κεκράτηκας οὖν, ὦ μακάριε, καὶ ἔστεψαι τὰ Ὀλύμπια, μᾶλλον δὲ Βαβυλῶνα εἴληφας ἢ τὴν Σάρδεων ἀκρόπολιν καθῄρηκας, καὶ ἕξεις τὸ τῆς Ἀμαλθείας κέρας καὶ ἀμέλξεις ὀρνίθων γάλα. δεῖ δή σοι ἀντὶ τῶν τοσούτων πόνων μέγιστα ἡλίκα γενέσθαι τἀγαθά, ἵνα μὴ φύλλινος μόνον ὁ στέφανος ᾖ, καὶ τόν τε μισθὸν οὐκ εὐκαταφρόνητον ὁρισθῆναι καὶ τοῦτον ἐν καιρῷ τῆς χρείας ἀπραγμόνως ἀποδίδοσθαι καὶ τὴν ἄλλην τιμὴν ὑπὲρ τοὺς πολλοὺς ὑπάρχειν, πόνων δὲ ἐκείνων καὶ πηλοῦ καὶ δρόμων καὶ ἀγρυπνιῶν ἀναπεπαῦσθαι, καὶ τοῦτο δὴ τὸ τῆς εὐχῆς, ἀποτείναντα τὼ πόδε καθεύδειν, μόνα ἐκεῖνα πράττοντα ὧν ἕνεκα τὴν ἀρχὴν παρελήφθης καὶ ὧν ἔμμισθος εἶ. ἐχρῆν μὲν οὕτως, ὦ Τιμόκλεις, καὶ οὐδὲν ἂν ἦν μέγα κακὸν ὑποκύψαντα φέρειν τὸν ζυγὸν ἐλαφρόν τε καὶ εὔφορον καὶ τὸ μέγιστον, ἐπίχρυσον ὄντα. ἀλλὰ πολλοῦ, μᾶλλον δὲ τοῦ παντὸς δεῖ· μυρία γάρ ἐστιν ἀφόρητα ἐλευθέρῳ ἀνδρὶ ἐν αὐταῖς ἤδη ταῖς συνουσίαις γιγνόμενα. σκέψαι δὲ αὐτὸς ἑξῆς[1] ἀκούων, εἴ τις ἂν αὐτὰ ὑπομεῖναι δύναιτο παιδείᾳ κἂν ἐπ' ἐλάχιστον

14 ὡμιληκώς. ἄρξομαι δὲ ἀπὸ τοῦ πρώτου δείπνου,

[1] τὰ ἑξῆς? ἑξῆς ἕκαστα Fritzsche.

his friends whom he holds in the highest esteem and trusts most implicitly in such matters have not advised him against you. Besides, his wife is willing, and neither his attorney nor his steward objects, nor has anyone criticized your past; everything is propitious and from every point of view the omens are good. You have won, then, lucky man, and have gained the Olympic crown—nay, you have taken Babylon or stormed the citadel of Sardis; you shall have the horn of Plenty and fill your pails with pigeon's milk. It is indeed fitting that in return for all your labours you should have the very greatest of blessings, in order that your crown may not be mere leaves; that your salary should be set at a considerable figure and paid you when you need it, without ado; that in other ways you should be honoured beyond ordinary folk; that you should get respite from your former exertions and muddiness and running about and loss of sleep, and that in accordance with your prayer you should "sleep with your legs stretched out,"[1] doing only what you were engaged for at the outset and what you are paid for. That ought to be the way of it, Timocles, and there would be no great harm in stooping and bearing the yoke if it were light and comfortable and, best of all, gilded! But the case is very different—yes, totally different. There are thousands of things insupportable to a free man that take place even after one has entered the household. Consider for yourself, as you hear a list of them, whether anyone could put up with them who is even to the slightest degree cultured. I shall begin, if you like, with the first dinner which will be

[1] A proverbial expression for "taking it easy."

ἢν δοκῇ, ὅ σε εἰκὸς δειπνήσειν τὰ προτέλεια τῆς μελλούσης συνουσίας.

Εὐθὺς οὖν πρόσεισιν παραγγέλλων τις ἥκειν ἐπὶ τὸ δεῖπνον, οὐκ ἀνομίλητος οἰκέτης, ὃν χρὴ πρῶτον ἵλεων ποιήσασθαι, παραβύσαντα εἰς τὴν χεῖρα, ὡς μὴ ἀδέξιος εἶναι δοκῇς, τοὐλάχιστον πέντε δραχμάς· ὁ δὲ ἀκκισάμενος καί, "Ἄπαγε, παρὰ σοῦ δὲ ἐγώ;" καί, "Ἡράκλεις, μὴ γένοιτο," ὑπειπὼν τέλος ἐπείσθη, καὶ ἄπεισί σοι πλατὺ ἐγχανών. σὺ δὲ ἐσθῆτα καθαρὰν προχειρισάμενος καὶ σεαυτὸν ὡς κοσμιώτατα σχηματίσας λουσάμενος ἥκεις, δεδιὼς μὴ πρὸ τῶν ἄλλων ἀφίκοιο· ἀπειρόκαλον γάρ, ὥσπερ καὶ τὸ ὕστατον ἥκειν φορτικόν. αὐτὸ οὖν τηρήσας τὸ μέσον τοῦ καιροῦ εἰσελήλυθας, καί σε πάνυ ἐντίμως ἐδέξατο, καὶ παραλαβών τις κατέκλινε μικρὸν ὑπὲρ τοῦ πλουσίου μετὰ δύο που σχεδὸν τῶν παλαιῶν

15 φίλων. σὺ δ' ὥσπερ εἰς[1] τοῦ Διὸς τὸν οἶκον παρελθὼν πάντα τεθαύμακας καὶ ἐφ' ἑκάστῳ τῶν πραττομένων μετέωρος εἶ· ξένα γάρ σοι καὶ ἄγνωστα πάντα· καὶ ἥ τε οἰκετεία εἰς σὲ ἀποβλέπει καὶ τῶν παρόντων ἕκαστος ὅ τι πράξεις ἐπιτηροῦσιν, οὐδὲ αὐτῷ δὲ ἀμελὲς τῷ πλουσίῳ τοῦτο, ἀλλὰ καὶ προεῖπέ τισι τῶν οἰκετῶν ἐπισκοπεῖν εἴ πως[2] εἰς τοὺς παῖδας ἢ εἰς τὴν γυναῖκα πολλάκις ἐκ περιωπῆς ἀποβλέψεις. οἱ μὲν γὰρ τῶν συνδείπνων ἀκόλουθοι ὁρῶντες ἐκπεπληγμένον εἰς τὴν ἀπειρίαν τῶν δρωμένων ἀποσκώπτουσι, τεκμήριον[3] τοῦ μὴ παρ' ἄλλῳ

[1] εἰς Coraës: not in MSS.
[2] εἴ πως Fritzsche: ὅπως MSS. adding εἰ before πολλάκις.
[3] τεκμήριον Cobet: τεκμήριον ποιούμενοι MSS.

given you, no doubt, as a formal prelude to your future intimacy.

Very soon, then, someone calls, bringing an invitation to the dinner, a servant not unfamiliar with the world, whom you must first propitiate by slipping at least five drachmas into his hand casually so as not to appear awkward. He puts on airs and murmurs: "Tut, tut! *I* take money from *you?*" and: "Heracles! I hope it may never come to that!"; but in the end he is prevailed upon and goes away with a broad grin at your expense. Providing yourself with clean clothing and dressing yourself as neatly as you can, you pay your visit to the bath and go, afraid of getting there before the rest, for that would be gauche, just as to come last would be ill-mannered. So you wait until the middle moment of the right time, and then go in. He receives you with much distinction, and someone takes you in charge and gives you a place at table a little above the rich man, with perhaps two of his old friends. As though you had entered the mansion of Zeus, you admire everything and are amazed at all that is done, for everything is strange and unfamiliar to you. The servants stare at you, and everybody in the company keeps an eye on you to see what you are going to do. Even the rich man himself is not without concern on this score; he has previously directed some of the servants to watch whether you often gaze from afar at his sons or his wife. The attendants of your fellow-guests, seeing that you are impressed, crack jokes about your unfamiliarity with what is doing and conjecture

πρότερόν σε δεδειπνηκέναι τὸ καινὸν εἶναί σοι τὸ χειρόμακτρον τιθέμενοι.

῞Ωσπερ οὖν εἰκός, ἰδίειν τε ἀνάγκη ὑπ᾽ ἀπορίας καὶ μήτε διψῶντα πιεῖν αἰτεῖν τολμᾶν, μὴ δόξῃς οἰνόφλυξ τις εἶναι, μήτε τῶν ὄψων παρατεθέντων ποικίλων καὶ πρός τινα τάξιν ἐσκευασμένων εἰδέναι ἐφ᾽ ὅ τι πρῶτον ἢ δεύτερον τὴν χεῖρα ἐνέγκῃς· ὑποβλέπειν οὖν εἰς τὸν πλησίον δεήσει κἀκεῖνον ζηλοῦν καὶ μανθάνειν τοῦ δείπνου τὴν 16 ἀκολουθίαν. τὰ δ᾽ ἄλλα ποικίλος εἶ καὶ θορύβου πλέως τὴν ψυχήν, πρὸς ἕκαστα τῶν πραττομένων ἐκπεπληγμένος, καὶ ἄρτι μὲν εὐδαιμονίζεις τὸν πλούσιον τοῦ χρυσοῦ καὶ τοῦ ἐλέφαντος καὶ τῆς τοσαύτης τρυφῆς, ἄρτι δὲ οἰκτείρεις σεαυτόν, ὡς τὸ μηδὲν ὢν εἶτα ζῆν ὑπολαμβάνεις. ἐνίοτε δὲ κἀκεῖνο εἰσέρχεταί σε, ὡς ζηλωτόν τινα βιώσῃ τὸν βίον ἅπασιν ἐκείνοις ἐντρυφήσων καὶ μεθέξων αὐτῶν ἐξ ἰσοτιμίας· οἴει γὰρ εἰσαεὶ Διονύσια ἑορτάσειν. καί που καὶ μειράκια ὡραῖα διακονούμενα καὶ ἠρέμα προσμειδιῶντα γλαφυρωτέραν ὑπογράφει σοι τὴν μέλλουσαν διατριβήν, ὥστε συνεχῶς τὸ Ὁμηρικὸν ἐκεῖνο ἐπιφθέγγεσθαι,

οὐ νέμεσις Τρῶας καὶ ἐϋκνήμιδας Ἀχαιούς

πολλὰ πονεῖν καὶ ὑπομένειν ὑπὲρ τῆς τοσαύτης εὐδαιμονίας.

Φιλοτησίαι τὸ ἐπὶ τούτῳ, καὶ σκύφον εὐμεγέθη

that you have never before dined anywhere because your napkin is new.[1]

As is natural, then, you inevitably break out in a cold sweat for perplexity; you do not dare to ask for something to drink when you are thirsty for fear of being thought a toper, and you do not know which of the dishes that have been put before you in great variety, made to be eaten in a definite order, you should put out your hand to get first, or which second; so you will be obliged to cast stealthy glances at your neighbour, copy him, and find out the proper sequence of the dinner. In general, you are in a chaotic state and your soul is full of agitation, for you are lost in amazement at everything that goes on. Now you call Dives lucky for his gold and his ivory and all his luxury, and now you pity yourself for imagining that you are alive when you are really nothing at all. Sometimes, too, it comes into your head that you are going to lead an enviable life, since you will revel in all that and share in it equally; you expect to enjoy perpetual Bacchic revels. Perhaps, too, pretty boys waiting upon you and faintly smiling at you paint the picture of your future life in more attractive colours, so that you are forever quoting that line of Homer:

> "Small blame to the fighters of Troy and the bright-greaved men of Achaea" [2]

that they endure great toil and suffering for such happiness as this.

Then come the toasts, and, calling for a large bowl,

[1] Guests brought their own napkins.

[2] Said of Helen by the Trojan elders; *Iliad* 3, 156. They continue:

> "That for a woman like this they long have endured tribulations."

τινὰ αἰτήσας προὔπιέν σοι τῷ διδασκάλῳ, ἢ ὁτιδήποτε προσειπών· σὺ δὲ λαβών, ὅτι μέν τί σε καὶ αὐτὸν ὑπειπεῖν ἔδει ἠγνόησας ὑπ' ἀπειρίας,
17 καὶ ἀγροικίας δόξαν ὦφλες. ἐπίφθονος δ' οὖν ἀπὸ τῆς προπόσεως ἐκείνης πολλοῖς τῶν παλαιῶν φίλων γεγένησαι, καὶ πρότερον ἐπὶ τῇ κατακλίσει λυπήσας[1] τινὰς αὐτῶν, ὅτι τήμερον ἥκων προὐκρίθης ἀνδρῶν πολυετῆ δουλείαν ἠντληκότων. εὐθὺς οὖν καὶ τοιοῦτός τις ἐν αὐτοῖς περὶ σοῦ λόγος· "Τοῦτο ἡμῖν πρὸς τοῖς ἄλλοις δεινοῖς ἐλείπετο, καὶ τῶν ἄρτι εἰσεληλυθότων εἰς τὴν οἰκίαν δευτέρους εἶναι, καὶ μόνοις τοῖς Ἕλλησι τούτοις ἀνέῳκται ἡ Ῥωμαίων πόλις· καίτοι τί ἐστιν ἐφ' ὅτῳ προτιμῶνται ἡμῶν; οὐ[2] ῥημάτια δύστηνα λέγοντες οἴονταί τι παμμέγεθες ὠφελεῖν;" ἄλλος δέ, "Οὐ γὰρ εἶδες ὅσα μὲν ἔπιεν, ὅπως δὲ τὰ παρατεθέντα συλλαβὼν κατέφαγεν; ἀπειρόκαλος ἄνθρωπος καὶ λιμοῦ πλέως, οὐδ' ὄναρ λευκοῦ ποτε ἄρτου ἐμφορηθείς, οὔτι γε Νομαδικοῦ ἢ Φασιανοῦ ὄρνιθος, ὧν μόλις τὰ ὀστᾶ ἡμῖν καταλέλοιπεν." τρίτος ἄλλος, "Ὦ μάταιοι," φησίν, "πέντε οὐδ' ὅλων ἡμερῶν ὄψεσθε αὐτὸν ἐνταῦθά που ἐν ἡμῖν τὰ ὅμοια ποτνιώμενον· νῦν μὲν γὰρ ὥσπερ τὰ καινὰ τῶν ὑποδημάτων ἐν τιμῇ τινι καὶ ἐπιμελείᾳ ἐστίν, ἐπειδὰν δὲ πατηθῇ πολλάκις καὶ ὑπὸ τοῦ πηλοῦ ἀναπλασθῇ, ὑπὸ τῇ κλίνῃ ἀθλίως ἐρρίψεται κόρεων ὥσπερ ἡμεῖς ἀνάπλεως."

Ἐκεῖνοι μὲν οὖν τοιαῦτα πολλὰ περὶ σοῦ στρέ-

[1] λυπήσας Bekker: ἐλύπησας MSS.
[2] οἳ Naber.

he drinks your health, addressing you as "the professor" or whatever it may be. You take the bowl, but because of inexperience you do not know that you should say something in reply, and you get a bad name for boorishness. Moreover, that toast has made many of his old friends jealous of you, some of whom you had previously offended when the places at table were assigned because you, who had only just come, were given precedence over men who for years had drained the dregs of servitude. So at once they begin to talk about you after this fashion: "That was still left for us in addition to our other afflictions, to play second fiddle to men who have just come into the household, and it is only these Greeks who have the freedom of the city of Rome. And yet, why is it that they are preferred to us? Isn't it true that they think they confer a tremendous benefit by turning wretched phrases?" Another says: "Why, didn't you see how much he drank, and how he gathered in what was set before him and devoured it? The fellow has no manners, and is starved to the limit; even in his dreams he never had his fill of white bread, not to speak of guinea fowl or pheasants, of which he has hardly left us the bones!" A third observes: "You silly asses, in less than five days you will see him here in the midst of us making these same complaints. Just now, like a new pair of shoes, he is receiving a certain amount of consideration and attention, but when he has been used again and again and is smeared with mud, he will be thrown under the bed in a wretched state, covered with vermin like the rest of us."

Well, as I say, they go on about you indefinitely in

φουσι, καί που ἤδη καὶ πρὸς διαβολάς τινες
18 αὐτῶν παρασκευάζονται. τὸ δ' οὖν συμπόσιον
ὅλον ἐκεῖνο σόν ἐστιν καὶ περὶ σοῦ οἱ πλεῖστοι
τῶν λόγων. σὺ δ' ὑπ' ἀηθείας πλέον τοῦ ἱκανοῦ
ἐμπιὼν οἴνου λεπτοῦ καὶ δριμέος, πάλαι τῆς
γαστρὸς ἐπειγούσης, πονηρῶς ἔχεις, καὶ οὔτε
προεξαναστῆναί σοι καλὸν οὔτε μένειν ἀσφαλές.
ἀποτεινομένου τοίνυν τοῦ πότου καὶ λόγων ἐπὶ
λόγοις γιγνομένων καὶ θεαμάτων ἐπὶ θεάμασι
παριόντων—ἅπαντα γὰρ ἐπιδείξασθαί σοι τὰ
αὑτοῦ βούλεται—κόλασιν οὐ μικρὰν ὑπομένεις
μήτε ὁρῶν τὰ γιγνόμενα μήτε ἀκούων εἴ τις ᾄδει
ἢ κιθαρίζει πάνυ τιμώμενος μειρακίσκος, ἀλλ'
ἐπαινεῖς μὲν ὑπ' ἀνάγκης, εὔχῃ δὲ ἢ σεισμῷ συμ-
πεσεῖν ἐκεῖνα πάντα ἢ πυρκαϊάν τινα προσαγ-
γελθῆναι, ἵνα ποτὲ καὶ διαλυθῇ τὸ συμπόσιον.

19 Τοῦτο μὲν δή σοι τὸ πρῶτον, ὦ ἑταῖρε, καὶ
ἥδιστον ἐκεῖνο δεῖπνον, οὐκ ἔμοιγε τοῦ θύμου καὶ
τῶν λευκῶν ἁλῶν ἥδιον ὁπηνίκα βούλομαι καὶ
ὁπόσον ἐλευθέρως ἐσθιομένων.

Ἵνα γοῦν σοι τὴν ὀξυρεγμίαν τὴν ἐπὶ τούτοις
παρῶ καὶ τὸν ἐν τῇ νυκτὶ ἔμετον, ἕωθεν δεήσει
περὶ τοῦ μισθοῦ συμβῆναι ὑμᾶς, ὁπόσον τε καὶ
ὁπότε τοῦ ἔτους χρὴ λαμβάνειν. παρόντων οὖν
ἢ[1] δύο ἢ τριῶν φίλων προσκαλέσας σε καὶ καθί-
ζεσθαι κελεύσας ἄρχεται λέγειν· "Τὰ μὲν ἡμέτερα ὁποῖά ἐστιν ἑώρακας ἤδη, καὶ ὡς τῦφος ἐν
αὐτοῖς οὐδὲ εἷς, ἀτραγῴδητα δὲ καὶ πεζὰ πάντα
καὶ δημοτικά, χρὴ δέ σε οὕτως ἔχειν ὡς ἁπάντων

[1] καὶ? Cobet excises.

that vein, and perhaps even then some of them are getting ready for a campaign of slander. Anyhow, that whole dinner-party is yours, and most of the conversation is about you. For your own part, as you have drunk more than enough subtle, insidious wine because you were not used to it, you have been uneasy for a long time and are in a bad way: yet it is not good form to leave early and not safe to stay where you are. So, as the drinking is prolonged and subject after subject is discussed and entertainment after entertainment is brought in (for he wants to show you all his wealth!), you undergo great punishment; you cannot see what takes place, and if this or that lad who is held in very great esteem sings or plays, you cannot hear; you applaud perforce while you pray that an earthquake may tumble the whole establishment into a heap or that a great fire may be reported, so that the party may break up at last.

So goes, then, my friend, that first and sweetest of dinners, which to me at least is no sweeter than thyme and white salt eaten in freedom, when I like and as much as I like.

To spare you the tale of the flatulency that follows and the sickness during the night, early in the morning you two will be obliged to come to terms with one another about your stipend, how much you are to receive and at what time of year. So with two or three of his friends present, he summons you, bids you to be seated, and opens the conversation: "You have already seen what our establishment is like, and that there is not a bit of pomp and circumstance in it, but everything is unostentatious, prosaic, and ordinary. You must feel that we shall have everything in

ἡμῖν κοινῶν ἐσομένων· γελοῖον γὰρ εἰ τὸ κυριώτατον, τὴν ψυχήν σοι τὴν ἐμαυτοῦ ἢ καὶ νὴ Δία τῶν παίδων"—εἰ παῖδες εἶεν αὐτῷ παιδεύσεως δεόμενοι—"ἐπιτρέπων τῶν ἄλλων μὴ ἐπ᾽ ἴσης ἡγοίμην δεσπότην. ἐπεὶ δὲ καὶ ὡρίσθαι τι δεῖ, —ὁρῶ μὲν τὸ μέτριον καὶ αὔταρκες τοῦ σοῦ τρόπου καὶ συνίημι ὡς οὐχὶ μισθοῦ ἐλπίδι προσελήλυθας ἡμῶν τῇ οἰκίᾳ, τῶν δὲ ἄλλων ἕνεκα, τῆς εὐνοίας τῆς παρ᾽ ἡμῶν καὶ τιμῆς, ἣν παρὰ πᾶσιν ἕξεις· ὅμως δ᾽ οὖν καὶ ὡρίσθω τι,—σὺ δ᾽ αὐτὸς ὅ τι καὶ βούλει λέγε, μεμνημένος, ὦ φίλτατε, κἀκείνων ἅπερ ἐν ἑορταῖς διετησίοις εἰκὸς ἡμᾶς παρέξειν· οὐ γὰρ ἀμελήσομεν οὐδὲ τῶν τοιούτων, εἰ καὶ μὴ νῦν αὐτὰ συντιθέμεθα· πολλαὶ δέ, οἶσθα, τοῦ ἔτους αἱ τοιαῦται ἀφορμαί. καὶ πρὸς ἐκεῖνα τοίνυν ἀποβλέπων μετριώτερον δῆλον ὅτι ἐπιβαλεῖς ἡμῖν τὸν μισθόν. ἄλλως τε καὶ πρέπον ἂν εἴη τοῖς πεπαιδευμένοις ὑμῖν κρείττοσιν εἶναι χρημάτων."

20 Ὁ μὲν ταῦτα εἰπὼν καὶ ὅλον σε διασείσας ταῖς ἐλπίσι τιθασὸν ἑαυτῷ πεποίηκε, σὺ δὲ πάλαι τάλαντα καὶ μυριάδας ὀνειροπολήσας καὶ ἀγροὺς ὅλους καὶ συνοικίας συνίῃς μὲν ἠρέμα τῆς μικρολογίας, σαίνεις δὲ ὅμως τὴν ὑπόσχεσιν καὶ τό, "Πάντα ἡμῖν κοινὰ ἔσται," βέβαιον καὶ ἀληθὲς ἔσεσθαι νομίζεις, οὐκ εἰδὼς ὅτι τὰ τοιαῦτα

χείλεα μέν τ᾽ ἐδίην᾽, ὑπερῴην δ᾽ οὐκ ἐδίηνε.

τελευταῖον δ᾽ ὑπ᾽ αἰδοῦς αὐτῷ ἐπέτρεψας. ὁ δὲ

common; for it would be ridiculous if I trusted you with what is most important, my own soul or that of my children"—suppose he has children who need instruction—"and did not consider you equally free to command everything else. But there should be some stipulation. I recognise, to be sure, that you are temperate and independent by nature, and am aware that you did not join our household through hope of pay but on account of the other things, the friendliness that we shall show you and the esteem which you will have from everyone. Nevertheless, let there be some stipulation. Say yourself what you wish, bearing in mind, my dear fellow, what we shall probably give you on the annual feast-days. We shall not forget such matters, either, even though we do not now reckon them in, and there are many such occasions in the year, as you know. So, if you take all that into consideration, you will of course charge us with a more moderate stipend. Besides, it would well become you men of education to be superior to money."

By saying this and putting you all in a flutter with expectations, he has made you submissive to him. You formerly dreamed of thousands and millions and whole farms and tenements, and you are somewhat conscious of his meanness; nevertheless, you welcome his promise with dog-like joy, and think his "We shall have everything in common" reliable and truthful, not knowing that this sort of thing

"Wetteth the lips, to be sure, but the palate it
leaveth unwetted."[1]

In the end, out of modesty, you leave it to him. He

[1] *Iliad* 22, 495.

αὐτὸς μὲν οὔ φησιν ἐρεῖν, τῶν φίλων δέ τινα τῶν παρόντων κελεύει μέσον ἐλθόντα τοῦ πράγματος εἰπεῖν ὃ μήτ' αὐτῷ γίγνοιτ' ἂν βαρὺ καὶ πρὸς ἄλλα τούτων ἀναγκαιότερα δαπανῶντι μήτε τῷ ληψομένῳ εὐτελές. ὁ δὲ ὠμογέρων τις ἐκ παίδων κολακείᾳ σύντροφος, "Ὡς μὲν οὐκ εὐδαιμονέστατος εἶ," φησίν, "τῶν ἐν τῇ πόλει ἁπάντων, ὦ οὗτος, οὐκ ἂν εἴποις, ᾧ γε τοῦτο πρῶτον ὑπῆρχεν ὃ πολλοῖς πάνυ γλιχομένοις μόλις ἂν γένοιτο παρὰ τῆς Τύχης· λέγω δὲ ὁμιλίας ἀξιωθῆναι καὶ ἑστίας κοινωνῆσαι καὶ εἰς τὴν πρώτην οἰκίαν τῶν ἐν τῇ Ῥωμαίων ἀρχῇ καταδεχθῆναι· τοῦτο γὰρ ὑπὲρ τὰ Κροίσου τάλαντα καὶ τὸν Μίδου πλοῦτον, εἰ σωφρονεῖν οἶσθα. ἰδὼν[1] δὲ πολλοὺς τῶν εὐδοκίμων ἐθελήσαντας ἄν, εἰ καὶ προσδιδόναι δέοι, μόνης τῆς δόξης ἕνεκα συνεῖναι τούτῳ καὶ ὁρᾶσθαι περὶ αὐτὸν ἑταίρους καὶ φίλους εἶναι δοκοῦντας, οὐκ ἔχω ὅπως σε τῆς εὐποτμίας μακαρίσω, ὃς καὶ προσλήψῃ μισθὸν τῆς τοιαύτης εὐδαιμονίας. ἀρκεῖν οὖν νομίζω, εἰ μὴ πάνυ ἄσωτος εἶ, τοσόνδε τι·"—εἰπὼν ἐλάχιστον καὶ μάλιστα

21 πρὸς τὰς σὰς ἐκείνας ἐλπίδας. ἀγαπᾶν δ' ὅμως ἀναγκαῖον· οὐ γὰρ οὐδ' ἂν φυγεῖν ἔτι σοι δυνατὸν ἐντὸς ἀρκύων γενομένῳ. δέχῃ τοίνυν τὸν χαλινὸν μύσας καὶ τὰ πρῶτα εὐάγωγος εἶ πρὸς αὐτὸν οὐ πάνυ περισπῶντα οὐδὲ ὀξέως νύττοντα, μέχρι ἂν λάθῃς τέλεον αὐτῷ συνήθης γενόμενος.

Οἱ μὲν δὴ ἔξω ἄνθρωποι τὸ μετὰ τοῦτο ζηλοῦσί σε ὁρῶντες ἐντὸς τῆς κιγκλίδος διατρίβοντα καὶ ἀκωλύτως εἰσιόντα καὶ τῶν πάνυ

[1] ἰδὼν Gesner: εἶδον MSS.

himself refuses to say, but tells one of the friends who are present to intervene in the business and name a sum that would be neither burdensome to him, with many other expenses more urgent than this, nor paltry to the recipient. The friend, a sprightly old man, habituated to flattery from his boyhood, says: "You cannot say, sir, that you are not the luckiest man in the whole city. In the first place you have been accorded a privilege which many who covet it greatly would hardly be able to obtain from Fortune; I mean in being honoured with his company, sharing his hospitality, and being received into the first household in the Roman Empire. This is better than the talents of Croesus and the wealth of Midas, if you know how to be temperate. Perceiving that many distinguished men, even if they had to pay for it, would like, simply for the name of the thing, to associate with this gentleman and be seen about him in the guise of companions and friends, I cannot sufficiently congratulate you on your good luck, since you are actually to receive pay for such felicity. I think, then, that unless you are very prodigal, about so and so much is enough"—and he names a very scanty sum, in striking contrast to those expectations of yours. You must be content, however, for it would not even be possible for you to get away, now that you are in the paddock. So you take the bit with your eyes shut, and in the beginning you answer his touch readily, as he does not pull hard or spur sharply until you have imperceptibly grown quite used to him.

People on the outside envy you after that, seeing that you live within the pale and enter without let and have become a notable figure in the inner circle.

τινὰ ἔνδον γεγενημένον· σὺ δὲ αὐτὸς οὐδέπω ὁρᾷς οὗτινος ἕνεκα εὐδαίμων αὐτοῖς εἶναι δοκεῖς. πλὴν ἀλλὰ χαίρεις γε καὶ σεαυτὸν ἐξαπατᾷς καὶ ἀεὶ τὰ μέλλοντα βελτίω γενήσεσθαι νομίζεις. τὸ δ' ἔμπαλιν ἢ σὺ ἤλπισας γίγνεται καὶ ὡς ἡ παροιμία φησίν, ἐπὶ Μανδροβούλου χωρεῖ τὸ πρᾶγμα, καθ' ἑκάστην, ὡς εἰπεῖν, τὴν ἡμέραν ἀποσμικρυ-

22 νόμενον καὶ εἰς τοὐπίσω ἀναποδίζον. ἠρέμα οὖν καὶ κατ' ὀλίγον, ὥσπερ ἐν ἀμυδρῷ τῷ φωτὶ τότε πρῶτον διαβλέπων, ἄρχῃ κατανοεῖν ὡς αἱ μὲν χρυσαῖ ἐκεῖναι ἐλπίδες οὐδὲν ἀλλ' ἢ φῦσαί τινες ἦσαν ἐπίχρυσοι, βαρεῖς δὲ καὶ ἀληθεῖς καὶ ἀπαραίτητοι καὶ συνεχεῖς οἱ πόνοι. "Τίνες οὗτοι;" ἴσως ἐρήσῃ με· "οὐχ ὁρῶ γὰρ ὅ τι τὸ ἐπίπονον ἐν ταῖς τοιαύταις συνουσίαις ἐστὶν οὐδ' ἐπινοῶ ἅτινα ἔφησθα τὰ καματηρὰ καὶ ἀφόρητα." οὐκοῦν ἄκουσον, ὦ γενναῖε, μὴ εἰ κάματος ἔνεστιν ἐν τῷ πράγματι μόνον ἐξετάζων, ἀλλὰ καὶ τὸ αἰσχρὸν καὶ ταπεινὸν καὶ συνόλως δουλοπρεπὲς οὐκ ἐν παρέργῳ τῆς ἀκροάσεως τιθέμενος.

23 Καὶ πρῶτόν γε μέμνησο μηκέτι ἐλεύθερον τὸ ἀπ' ἐκείνου μηδὲ εὐπατρίδην σεαυτὸν οἴεσθαι. πάντα γὰρ ταῦτα, τὸ γένος, τὴν ἐλευθερίαν, τοὺς προγόνους ἔξω τοῦ ὀδοῦ καταλείψων ἴσθι ἐπειδὰν ἐπὶ τοιαύτην σαυτὸν λατρείαν ἀπεμπολήσας εἰσίῃς· οὐ γὰρ ἐθελήσει σοι ἡ Ἐλευθερία συνεισελθεῖν ἐφ' οὕτως ἀγεννῆ πράγματα καὶ ταπεινὰ εἰσιόντι. δοῦλος οὖν, εἰ καὶ πάνυ ἀχθέσῃ τῷ ὀνόματι, καὶ οὐχ ἑνός, ἀλλὰ πολλῶν δοῦλος ἀναγ-

You yourself do not yet see why you seem to them to be fortunate. Nevertheless, you are joyous and delude yourself, and are always thinking that the future will turn out better. But the reverse of what you expected comes about: as the proverb has it, the thing goes Mandrobulus-wise,[1] diminishing every day, almost, and dropping back. Slowly and gradually, therefore, as if you could then distinguish things for the first time in the indistinct light, you begin to realize that those golden hopes were nothing but gilded bubbles, while your labours are burdensome and genuine, inexorable and continuous. "What are they?" perhaps you will ask me: "I do not see what there is in such posts that is laborious, nor can I imagine what those wearisome and insupportable things are that you spoke of."[2] Listen, then, my worthy friend, and do not simply try to find out whether there is any weariness in the thing, but give its baseness and humility and general slavishness more than incidental consideration in the hearing.

First of all, remember never again from that time forward to think yourself free or noble. All that—your pride of race, your freedom, your ancient lineage—you will leave outside the threshold, let me tell you, when you go in after having sold yourself into such service; for Freedom will refuse to enter with you when you go in for purposes so base and humble. So you will be a slave perforce, however distasteful you may find the name, and not the slave of one man but of many; and you will

[1] "This Mandrobulus once found a treasure in Samos and dedicated to Hera a golden sheep, and in the second year one of silver, and in the third, one of bronze." Scholia.

[2] In chapter 13.

καίως ἔσῃ καὶ θητεύσεις κάτω νενευκὼς ἕωθεν εἰς ἑσπέραν "ἀεικελίῳ ἐπὶ μισθῷ." καὶ ἅτε δὴ μὴ ἐκ παίδων τῇ Δουλείᾳ συντραφείς, ὀψιμαθήσας δὲ καὶ πόρρω που τῆς ἡλικίας παιδευόμενος πρὸς αὐτῆς οὐ πάνυ εὐδόκιμος ἔσῃ οὐδὲ πολλοῦ ἄξιος τῷ δεσπότῃ· διαφθείρει γάρ σε ἡ μνήμη τῆς ἐλευθερίας ὑπιοῦσα καὶ ἀποσκιρτᾶν ἐνίοτε ποιεῖ καὶ δι' αὐτὸ ἐν τῇ δουλείᾳ πονηρῶς ἀπαλλάττειν.

Πλὴν εἰ μὴ ἀποχρῆν σοι πρὸς ἐλευθερίαν νομίζεις τὸ μὴ Πυρρίου μηδὲ Ζωπυρίωνος υἱὸν εἶναι, μηδὲ ὥσπερ τις Βιθυνὸς ὑπὸ μεγαλοφώνῳ τῷ κήρυκι ἀπημπολῆσθαι. ἀλλ' ὁπόταν, ὦ βέλτιστε, τῆς νουμηνίας ἐπιστάσης ἀναμιχθεὶς τῷ Πυρρίᾳ καὶ τῷ Ζωπυρίωνι προτείνῃς τὴν χεῖρα ὁμοίως τοῖς ἄλλοις οἰκέταις καὶ λάβῃς ἐκεῖνο ὁτιδήποτε ἦν τὸ γιγνόμενον, τοῦτο ἡ πρᾶσίς ἐστι. κήρυκος γὰρ οὐκ ἔδει ἐπ' ἄνδρα ἑαυτὸν ἀποκηρύξαντα καὶ μακρῷ χρόνῳ μνηστευσάμενον ἑαυτῷ τὸν δεσπότην.

24 Εἶτ', ὦ κάθαρμα, φαίην ἄν, καὶ μάλιστα πρὸς τὸν φιλοσοφεῖν φάσκοντα, εἰ μέν σέ τις ἢ πλέοντα καταποντιστὴς συλλαβὼν ἢ λῃστὴς ἀπεδίδοτο, ᾤκτειρες ἂν σεαυτὸν ὡς παρὰ τὴν ἀξίαν δυστυχοῦντα, ἢ εἴ τίς σου λαβόμενος ἦγε δοῦλον εἶναι λέγων, ἐβόας ἂν τοὺς νόμους καὶ δεινὰ ἐποίεις καὶ ἠγανάκτεις καί, "Ὦ γῆ καὶ θεοί," μεγάλῃ τῇ φωνῇ ἐκεκράγεις ἄν, σεαυτὸν δὲ ὀλίγων ἕνεκα ὀβολῶν ἐν τούτῳ τῆς ἡλικίας, ὅτε καὶ εἰ φύσει δοῦλος ἦσθα, καιρὸς ἦν πρὸς ἐλευθερίαν ἤδη ὁρᾶν, αὐτῇ

drudge from morn till night with hanging head, "for shameful hire." [1] Since you were not brought up in the company of Slavery from your boyhood but made her acquaintance late and are getting your schooling from her at an advanced age, you will not be very successful or highly valuable to your master. The memory of your freedom, stealing over you, plays the mischief with you, sometimes causing you to be skittish, and for that reason to come off badly in slavery.

Perhaps, however, you think it quite enough to establish your freedom that you are not the son of a Pyrrhias or a Zopyrion, and that you have not been sold in the market like a Bithynian by a loud-voiced auctioneer. But, my excellent friend, when the first of the month arrives and side by side with Pyrrhias and Zopyrion you stretch out your hand like the rest of the servants and take your earnings, whatever they are—that is sale! There was no need of an auctioneer in the case of a man who put himself up at auction and for a long time solicited a master.

Ah, scurvy outcast (that would be my language, above all to a self-styled philosopher), if a wrecker or a pirate had taken you at sea and were offering you for sale, would you not pity yourself for being ill-fated beyond your deserts; or if someone had laid hands upon you and were haling you off, saying that you were a slave, would you not invoke the law and make a great stir and be wrathful and shout "Heavens and Earth!" at the top of your voice? Then just for a few obols, at that age when, even if you were a slave by birth, it would be high

[1] Either a variation upon Homer (cf. *Odyssey* 19, 341: *Iliad* 13, 84, 21, 444-5), or a quotation from a lost epic.

ἀρετῇ καὶ σοφίᾳ φέρων ἀπημπόληκας, οὐδὲ τοὺς πολλοὺς ἐκείνους λόγους αἰδεσθεὶς οὓς ὁ καλὸς Πλάτων ἢ ὁ Χρύσιππος ἢ Ἀριστοτέλης διεξεληλύθασι τὸ μὲν ἐλευθέριον ἐπαινοῦντες, τὸ δουλοπρεπὲς δὲ διαβάλλοντες; καὶ οὐκ αἰσχύνῃ κόλαξιν ἀνθρώποις καὶ ἀγοραίοις καὶ βωμολόχοις ἀντεξεταζόμενος καὶ ἐν τοσούτῳ πλήθει Ῥωμαϊκῷ[1] μόνος ξενίζων τῷ τρίβωνι καὶ πονηρῶς τὴν Ῥωμαίων φωνὴν βαρβαρίζων, εἶτα δειπνῶν δεῖπνα θορυβώδη καὶ πολυάνθρωπα συγκλύδων τινῶν καὶ τῶν πλείστων μοχθηρῶν; καὶ ἐν αὐτοῖς ἐπαινεῖς φορτικῶς καὶ πίνεις πέρα τοῦ μετρίως ἔχοντος. ἕωθέν τε ὑπὸ κώδωνι ἐξαναστὰς ἀποσεισάμενος τοῦ ὕπνου τὸ ἥδιστον συμπεριθεῖς ἄνω καὶ κάτω ἔτι τὸν χθιζὸν ἔχων πηλὸν ἐπὶ τοῖν σκελοῖν. οὕτως ἀπορία μέν σε θέρμων ἔσχεν ἢ τῶν ἀγρίων λαχάνων, ἐπέλιπον δὲ καὶ αἱ κρῆναι ῥέουσαι τοῦ ψυχροῦ ὕδατος, ὡς ἐπὶ ταῦτά σε ὑπ' ἀμηχανίας ἐλθεῖν; ἀλλὰ δῆλον ὡς οὐχ ὕδατος οὐδὲ θέρμων, ἀλλὰ πεμμάτων καὶ ὄψου καὶ οἴνου ἀνθοσμίου ἐπιθυμῶν ἑάλως, καθάπερ ὁ λάβραξ αὐτὸν μάλα δικαίως τὸν ὀρεγόμενον τούτων λαιμὸν διαπαρείς. παρὰ πόδας τοιγαροῦν τῆς λιχνείας ταύτης τἀπίχειρα, καὶ ὥσπερ οἱ πίθηκοι δεθεὶς κλοιῷ τὸν τράχηλον ἄλλοις μὲν γέλωτα παρέχεις, σεαυτῷ δὲ δοκεῖς τρυφᾶν, ὅτι ἔστι σοι τῶν ἰσχάδων ἀφθόνως ἐντραγεῖν. ἡ δὲ ἐλευθερία καὶ τὸ εὐγενὲς αὐτοῖς φυλέταις καὶ φράτερσι φροῦδα πάντα καὶ οὐδὲ μνήμη τις αὐτῶν.

25 Καὶ ἀγαπητὸν εἰ μόνον τὸ αἰσχρὸν προσῆν τῷ

[1] ἀστεικῷ N: ἀστικῷ Dindorf, edd.

time for you to look forward at last to liberty, have you gone and sold *yourself*, virtue and wisdom included? Had you no respect, either, for all those wonderful sermons that your noble Plato and Chrysippus and Aristotle have preached in praise of freedom and in censure of servility? Are you not ashamed to undergo comparison with flatterers and loafers and buffoons; to be the only person in all that Roman throng who wears the incongruous cloak of a scholar and talks Latin with a villainous accent; to take part, moreover, in uproarious dinners, packed with human flotsam that is mostly vile? At these dinners you are vulgar in your compliments, and you drink more than is discreet. Then in the morning, roused by a bell, you shake off the sweetest of your sleep and run about town with the pack, up hill and down dale, with yesterday's mud still on your legs. Were you so in want of lupines and herbs of the field, did even the springs of cold water fail you so completely, as to bring you to this pass out of desperation? No, clearly it was because you did not want water and lupines, but cates and meat and wine with a bouquet that you were caught, hooked like a pike in the very part that hankered for all this—in the gullet—and it served you quite right! You are confronting, therefore, the rewards of this greediness, and with your neck in a collar like a monkey you are a laughing-stock to others, but seem to yourself to be living in luxury because you can eat figs without stint. Liberty and noblesse, with all their kith and kin, have disappeared completely, and not even a memory of them abides.

Indeed, it would be lucky for you if the thing

πράγματι, δοῦλον ἀντ' ἐλευθέρου δοκεῖν, οἱ δὲ πόνοι μὴ κατὰ τοὺς πάνυ τούτους οἰκέτας. ἀλλ' ὅρα εἰ μετριώτερά σοι προστέτακται τῶν Δρόμωνι καὶ Τιβείῳ προστεταγμένων. ὧν μὲν γὰρ ἕνεκα, τῶν μαθημάτων ἐπιθυμεῖν φήσας, παρείληφέ σε, ὀλίγον αὐτῷ μέλει. "Τί γὰρ κοινόν," φασί, "λύρᾳ καὶ ὄνῳ;" πάνυ γοῦν,—οὐχ ὁρᾷς;—ἐκτετήκασι τῷ πόθῳ τῆς Ὁμήρου σοφίας ἢ τῆς Δημοσθένους δεινότητος ἢ τῆς Πλάτωνος μεγαλοφροσύνης, ὧν ἤν τις ἐκ τῆς ψυχῆς ἀφέλῃ τὸ χρυσίον καὶ τὸ ἀργύριον καὶ τὰς περὶ τούτων φροντίδας, τὸ καταλειπόμενόν ἐστι τῦφος καὶ μαλακία καὶ ἡδυπάθεια καὶ ἀσέλγεια καὶ ὕβρις καὶ ἀπαιδευσία. δεῖται δή σου ἐπ' ἐκεῖνα μὲν οὐδαμῶς, ἐπεὶ δὲ πώγωνα ἔχεις βαθὺν καὶ σεμνός τις εἶ τὴν πρόσοψιν καὶ ἱμάτιον Ἑλληνικὸν εὐσταλῶς περιβέβλησαι καὶ πάντες ἴσασί σε γραμματικὸν ἢ ῥήτορα ἢ φιλόσοφον, καλὸν αὐτῷ δοκεῖ ἀναμεμῖχθαι καὶ τοιοῦτόν τινα τοῖς προϊοῦσι καὶ προπομπεύουσιν αὐτοῦ· δόξει γὰρ ἐκ τούτου καὶ φιλομαθὴς τῶν Ἑλληνικῶν μαθημάτων καὶ ὅλως περὶ παιδείαν φιλόκαλος. ὥστε κινδυνεύεις, ὦ γενναῖε, ἀντὶ τῶν θαυμαστῶν λόγων τὸν πώγωνα καὶ τὸν τρίβωνα μεμισθωκέναι.

Χρὴ οὖν σε ἀεὶ σὺν αὐτῷ ὁρᾶσθαι καὶ μηδέποτε ἀπολείπεσθαι, ἀλλὰ ἕωθεν ἐξαναστάντα παρέχειν σεαυτὸν ὀφθησόμενον ἐν τῇ θεραπείᾳ καὶ μὴ λιπεῖν τὴν τάξιν. ὁ δὲ ἐπιβάλλων ἐνίοτέ σοι τὴν χεῖρα, ὅ τι ἂν τύχῃ ληρεῖ, τοῖς ἐντυγχάνουσιν

involved only the shame of figuring as a slave instead of a free man, and the labour was not like that of an out-and-out servant. But see if what is required of you is any more moderate than what is required of a Dromo or a Tibius! To be sure, the purpose for which he engaged you, saying that he wanted knowledge, matters little to him; for, as the proverb says, "What has a jackass to do with a lyre?" Ah, yes, can't you see? they are mightily consumed with longing for the wisdom of Homer or the eloquence of Demosthenes or the sublimity of Plato, when, if their gold and their silver and their worries about them should be taken out of their souls, all that remains is pride and softness and self-indulgence and sensuality and insolence and ill-breeding! Truly, he does not want you for that purpose at all, but as you have a long beard, present a distinguished appearance, are neatly dressed in a Greek mantle, and everybody knows you for a grammarian or a rhetorician or a philosopher, it seems to him the proper thing to have a man of that sort among those who go before him and form his escort; it will make people think him a devoted student of Greek learning and in general a person of taste in literary matters So the chances are, my worthy friend, that instead of your marvellous lectures it is your beard and mantle that you have let for hire.

You must therefore be seen with him always and never be missing; you must get up early to let yourself be noted in attendance, and you must not desert your post. Putting his hand upon your shoulder now and then, he talks nonsense at random,

ἐπιδεικνύμενος ὡς οὐδὲ ὁδῷ βαδίζων ἀμελής ἐστι τῶν Μουσῶν, ἀλλ' εἰς καλὸν τὴν ἐν τῷ περιπάτῳ
26 διατίθεται σχολήν. σὺ δ' ἄθλιος τὰ μὲν παραδραμών, τὰ δὲ βάδην ἄναντα πολλὰ καὶ κάταντα —τοιαύτη γάρ, ὡς οἶσθα, ἡ πόλις—περιελθὼν ἱδρωκώς τε καὶ πνευστιῶν, κἀκείνου ἔνδον τινὶ τῶν φίλων πρὸς ὃν ἦλθεν διαλεγομένου, μηδὲ ὅπου καθίζῃς ἔχων ὀρθὸς ὑπ' ἀπορίας ἀναγιγνώσκεις τὸ βιβλίον προχειρισάμενος.

Ἐπειδὰν δὲ ἄσιτόν τε καὶ ἄποτον ἡ νὺξ καταλάβῃ, λουσάμενος πονηρῶς ἀωρὶ περὶ αὐτό που σχεδὸν τὸ μεσονύκτιον ἥκεις ἐπὶ τὸ δεῖπνον, οὐκέθ' ὁμοίως ἔντιμος οὐδὲ περίβλεπτος τοῖς παροῦσιν, ἀλλ' ἤν τις ἄλλος ἐπεισέλθῃ νεαλέστερος, εἰς τοὐπίσω σύ· καὶ οὕτως εἰς τὴν ἀτιμοτάτην γωνίαν ἐξωσθεὶς κατάκεισαι μάρτυς μόνον τῶν παραφερομένων, τὰ ὀστᾶ, εἰ ἐφίκοιτο μέχρι σοῦ, καθάπερ οἱ κύνες περιεσθίων ἢ τὸ σκληρὸν τῆς μαλάχης φύλλον ᾧ τὰ ἄλλα συνειλοῦσιν, εἰ ὑπεροφθείη ὑπὸ τῶν προκατακειμένων, ἄσμενος ὑπὸ λιμοῦ παροψώμενος.[1]

Οὐ μὴν οὐδὲ ἡ ἄλλη ὕβρις ἄπεστιν, ἀλλ' οὔτε ᾠὸν ἔχεις μόνος—οὐ γὰρ ἀναγκαῖόν ἐστιν καὶ σὲ τῶν αὐτῶν ἀεὶ τοῖς ξένοις καὶ ἀγνώστοις ἀντιποιεῖσθαι· ἀγνωμοσύνη γὰρ δὴ[2] τοῦτό γε—οὔτε ἡ ὄρνις ὁμοία ταῖς ἄλλαις, ἀλλὰ τῷ μὲν πλησίον παχεῖα καὶ πιμελής, σοὶ δὲ νεοττὸς ἡμίτομος ἢ φάττα τις ὑπόσκληρος, ὕβρις ἄντικρυς καὶ ἀτιμία. πολλάκις δ' εἰ[3] ἐπιλίποι ἄλλου τινὸς αἰφνιδίως

[1] παροψώμενος Jensius: παραψόμενος MSS. (παραψάμενος U).
[2] δὴ Fritzsche: σὴ MSS.
[3] δ' εἰ U[2]: δὲ other MSS., all except N continuing ἐπειλίποι.

showing those who meet him that even when he takes a walk he is not inattentive to the Muses but makes good use of his leisure during the stroll. For your own part, poor fellow, now you run at his side, and now you forge about at a foot's pace, over many ups and downs (the city is like that, you know), until you are sweaty and out of breath, and then, while he is indoors talking to a friend whom he came to see, as you have no place to sit down, you stand up, and for lack of employment read the book with which you armed yourself.

When night overtakes you hungry and thirsty, after a wretched bath you go to your dinner at an unseasonable hour, in the very middle of the night; but you are no longer held in the same esteem and admiration by the company. If anyone arrives who is more of a novelty, for you it is "Get back!" In this way you are pushed off into the most unregarded corner and take your place merely to witness the dishes that are passed, gnawing the bones like a dog if they get as far as you, or regaling yourself with gratification, thanks to your hunger, on the tough mallow leaves with which the other food is garnished, if they should be disdained by those nearer the head of the table.

Moreover, you are not spared other forms of rudeness. You are the only one that does not have an egg. There is no necessity that you should always expect the same treatment as foreigners and strangers: that would be unreasonable! Your bird, too, is not like the others; your neighbour's is fat and plump, and yours is half a tiny chick, or a tough pigeon—out-and-out rudeness and contumely! Often, if there is a shortage when another guest appears of

ἐπιπαρόντος, ἀράμενος ὁ διάκονος τὰ σοὶ παρακείμενα φέρων ἐκείνῳ παρατέθεικεν ὑποτονθορύσας, "Σὺ γὰρ ἡμέτερος εἶ." τεμνομένου μὲν γὰρ ἐν τῷ μέσῳ ἢ συὸς ὑπογαστρίου ἢ ἐλάφου, χρὴ ἐκ παντὸς ἢ τὸν διανέμοντα ἵλεων ἔχειν ἢ τὴν Προμηθέως μερίδα φέρεσθαι, ὀστᾶ κεκαλυμμένα τῇ πιμελῇ. τὸ γὰρ τῷ μὲν ὑπὲρ σὲ τὴν λοπάδα παρεστάναι ἔστ' ἂν ἀπαγορεύσῃ ἐμφορούμενος, σὲ δὲ οὕτω ταχέως παραδραμεῖν, τίνι φορητὸν ἐλευθέρῳ ἀνδρὶ κἂν ὁπόσην αἱ ἔλαφοι τὴν χολὴν ἔχοντι; καίτοι οὐδέπω ἐκεῖνο ἔφην, ὅτι τῶν ἄλλων ἥδιστόν τε καὶ παλαιότατον οἶνον πινόντων μόνος σὺ πονηρόν τινα καὶ παχὺν πίνεις, θεραπεύων ἀεὶ ἐν ἀργύρῳ ἢ χρυσῷ πίνειν, ὡς μὴ ἐλεγχθείης ἀπὸ τοῦ χρώματος οὕτως ἄτιμος ὢν συμπότης. καὶ εἴθε γε κἂν ἐκείνου εἰς κόρον ἦν πιεῖν, νῦν δὲ πολλάκις αἰτήσαντος ὁ παῖς "οὐδ' ἀΐοντι ἔοικεν."

27 Ἀνιᾷ δή σε πολλὰ καὶ ἀθρόα καὶ σχεδὸν τὰ πάντα, καὶ μάλιστα ὅταν σε παρευδοκιμῇ κίναιδός τις ἢ ὀρχηστοδιδάσκαλος ἢ Ἰωνικὰ συνείρων Ἀλεξανδρεωτικὸς ἀνθρωπίσκος. τοῖς μὲν γὰρ τὰ ἐρωτικὰ ταῦτα διακονουμένοις καὶ γραμματίδια ὑπὸ κόλπου διακομίζουσιν πόθεν σύ γ' ἰσότιμος; κατακείμενος τοιγαροῦν ἐν μυχῷ τοῦ συμποσίου καὶ ὑπ' αἰδοῦς καταδεδυκὼς στένεις ὡς τὸ εἰκὸς καὶ σεαυτὸν οἰκτείρεις καὶ αἰτιᾷ τὴν Τύχην οὐδὲ ὀλίγα σοι τῶν χαρίτων ἐπιψεκάσασαν. ἡδέως δ' ἄν μοι δοκεῖς καὶ ποιητὴς γενέσθαι τῶν ἐρωτικῶν

a sudden, the waiter takes up what you have before you and quickly puts it before him, muttering: "You are one of us, you know." Of course when a side of pork or venison is cut at table, you must by all means have especial favour with the carver or else get a Prometheus-portion, bones hidden in fat. That the platter should stop beside the man above you until he gets tired of stuffing himself, but speed past you so rapidly—what free man could endure it if he had even as much resentment as a deer? And I have not yet mentioned the fact that while the others drink the most delectable and oldest of wines, you alone drink one that is vile and thick, taking good care always to drink out of a gold or silver cup so that the colour may not convict you of being such an unhonoured guest. If only you might have your fill, even of that! But as things are, though you ask for it repeatedly, the page "hath not even the semblance of hearing"! [1]

You are annoyed, indeed, by many things, a great many, almost everything; most of all when your favour is rivalled by a cinaedus or a dancing-master or an Alexandrian dwarf who recites Ionics. [2] How could you be on a par, though, with those who render these services to passion and carry notes about in their clothing? So, couched in a far corner of the dining-room and shrinking out of sight for shame, you groan, naturally, and commiserate yourself and carp at Fortune for not besprinkling you with at least a few drops of the amenities. You would be glad, I think, to become a composer of

[1] *Iliad* 23, 430.

[2] Anacreontics, Sotadeans, and in general, the "erotic ditties" mentioned below.

ᾀσμάτων ἢ κἂν ἄλλου ποιήσαντος δύνασθαι ᾄδειν ἀξίως·[1] ὁρᾷς γὰρ οἷ τὸ προτιμᾶσθαι καὶ εὐδοκιμεῖν ἐστιν. ὑποσταίης δὲ ἄν, εἰ καὶ μάγον ἢ μάντιν ὑποκρίνασθαι δέοι τῶν κλήρους πολυταλάντους καὶ ἀρχὰς καὶ ἀθρόους τοὺς πλούτους ὑπισχνουμένων· καὶ γὰρ αὖ καὶ τούτους ὁρᾷς εὖ φερομένους ἐν ταῖς φιλίαις καὶ πολλῶν ἀξιουμένους. κἂν ἕν τι οὖν τούτων ἡδέως ἂν γένοιο, ὡς μὴ ἀπόβλητος καὶ περιττὸς εἴης· ἀλλ' οὐδὲ πρὸς ταῦτα ὁ κακοδαίμων πιθανὸς εἶ. τοιγαροῦν ἀνάγκη μειοῦσθαι καὶ σιωπῇ ἀνέχεσθαι ὑποιμώζοντα καὶ ἀμελούμενον.

28 Ἢν μὲν γὰρ κατείπῃ σοῦ τις ψιθυρὸς οἰκέτης, ὡς μόνος οὐκ ἐπῄνεις τὸν τῆς δεσποίνης παιδίσκον ὀρχούμενον ἢ κιθαρίζοντα, κίνδυνος οὐ μικρὸς ἐκ τοῦ πράγματος. χρὴ οὖν χερσαίου βατράχου δίκην διψῶντα κεκραγέναι, ὡς ἐπίσημος ἔσῃ ἐν τοῖς ἐπαινοῦσι καὶ κορυφαῖος ἐπιμελούμενον· πολλάκις δὲ καὶ τῶν ἄλλων σιωπησάντων αὐτὸν ἐπειπεῖν ἐσκεμμένον τινὰ ἔπαινον πολλὴν τὴν κολακείαν ἐμφανιοῦντα.

Τὸ μὲν γὰρ λιμῷ συνόντα καὶ νὴ Δία γε διψῶντα μύρῳ χρίεσθαι καὶ στεφανοῦσθαι τὴν κεφαλήν, ἠρέμα καὶ γελοῖον· ἔοικας γὰρ τότε στήλῃ ἑώλου τινὸς νεκροῦ ἄγοντος ἐναγίσματα· καὶ γὰρ ἐκείνων καταχέαντες μύρον καὶ τὸν στέφανον ἐπιθέντες αὐτοὶ πίνουσι καὶ εὐωχοῦνται τὰ παρεσκευασμένα.

29 Ἢν μὲν γὰρ καὶ ζηλότυπός τις ᾖ καὶ παῖδες εὔμορφοι ὦσιν ἢ νέα γυνὴ καὶ σὺ μὴ παντελῶς πόρρω Ἀφροδίτης καὶ Χαρίτων ᾖς, οὐκ ἐν εἰρήνῃ

[1] δεξιῶς Jacobs.

erotic ditties, or at all events to be able to sing them properly when somebody else had composed them: for you see where precedence and favour go! You would put up with it if you had to act the part of a magician or a soothsayer, one of those fellows who promise legacies amounting to many thousands, governorships, and tremendous riches; you see that they too get on well in their friendships and are highly valued. So you would be glad to adopt one of those rôles in order not to be entirely despicable and useless; but even in them, worse luck, you are not convincing. Therefore you must needs be humble and suffer in silence, with stifled groans and amid neglect.

If a whispering servant accuse you of being the only one who did not praise the mistress's page when he danced or played, there is no little risk in the thing. So you must raise your thirsty voice like a stranded frog, taking pains to be conspicuous among the claque and to lead the chorus; and often when the others are silent you must independently let drop a well-considered word of praise that will convey great flattery.

That a man who is famished, yes, and athirst, should be perfumed with myrrh and have a wreath on his head is really rather laughable, for then you are like the gravestone of an ancient corpse that is getting a feast to his memory. They drench the stones with myrrh and crown them with wreaths, and then they themselves enjoy the food and drink that has been prepared!

If the master is of a jealous disposition and has handsome sons or a young wife, and you are not wholly estranged from Aphrodite and the Graces,

τὸ πρᾶγμα οὐδὲ ὁ κίνδυνος εὐκαταφρόνητος. ὦτα γὰρ καὶ ὀφθαλμοὶ βασιλέως πολλοί, οὐ μόνον τἀληθῆ ὁρῶντες, ἀλλ' ἀεί τι καὶ προσεπιμετροῦντες, ὡς μὴ νυστάζειν δοκοῖεν. δεῖ οὖν ὥσπερ ἐν τοῖς Περσικοῖς δείπνοις κάτω νεύοντα κατακεῖσθαι, δεδιότα μή τις εὐνοῦχός σε ἴδῃ προσβλέψαντα μιᾷ τῶν παλλακίδων, ἐπεὶ ἄλλος γε εὐνοῦχος ἐντεταμένον πάλαι τὸ τόξον ἔχων ἃ μὴ θέμις ὁρῶντα ἕτοιμος κολάσαι,[1] διαπείρας τῷ οἰστῷ μεταξὺ πίνοντος τὴν γνάθον.

30 Εἶτα ἀπελθὼν τοῦ δείπνου μικρόν τι κατέδαρθες· ὑπὸ δὲ ᾠδὴν ἀλεκτρυόνων ἀνεγρόμενος, "Ὦ δείλαιος ἐγώ," φής, "καὶ ἄθλιος, οἵας τὰς πάλαι διατριβὰς ἀπολιπὼν καὶ ἑταίρους καὶ βίον ἀπράγμονα καὶ ὕπνον μετρούμενον τῇ ἐπιθυμίᾳ καὶ περιπάτους ἐλευθερίους εἰς οἷον βάραθρον φέρων ἐμαυτὸν ἐνσέσεικα. τίνος ἕνεκα, ὦ θεοί, ἢ τίς ὁ λαμπρὸς οὗτος μισθός ἐστιν; οὐ γὰρ καὶ ἄλλως μοι πλείω τούτων ἐκπορίζειν δυνατὸν ἦν καὶ προσῆν τὸ ἐλεύθερον καὶ τὸ πάντα ἐπ' ἐξουσίας; νῦν δὲ τὸ τοῦ λόγου, λέων κρόκῃ δεθείς, ἄνω καὶ κάτω περισύρομαι, τὸ πάντων οἴκτιστον, οὐκ εὐδοκιμεῖν εἰδὼς οὐδὲ κεχαρισμένος εἶναι δυνάμενος. ἰδιώτης γὰρ ἔγωγε τῶν τοιούτων καὶ ἄτεχνος, καὶ μάλιστα παραβαλλόμενος ἀνδράσι τέχνην τὸ πρᾶγμα πεποιημένοις, ὥστε[2] καὶ ἀχάριστός εἰμι καὶ ἥκιστα συμποτικός, οὐδ' ὅσον γέλωτα ποιῆσαι δυνάμενος. συνίημι δὲ ὡς καὶ ἐνοχλῶ πολλάκις βλεπόμενος, καὶ μάλισθ' ὅταν

[1] ἕτοιμος κολάσαι Bekker: not in MSS.
[2] ὥστε ς, edd.: ὡς δὲ MSS.

your situation is not peaceful or your danger to be taken lightly. The king has many ears and eyes, which not only see the truth but always add something more for good measure, so that they may not be considered heavy-lidded. You must therefore keep your head down while you are at table, as at a Persian dinner, for fear that an eunuch may see that you looked at one of the concubines; for another eunuch, who has had his bow bent this long time, is ready to punish you for eyeing what you should not, driving his arrow through your cheek just as you are taking a drink.

Then, after you have left the dinner-party, you get a little bit of sleep, but towards cock-crow you wake up and say: "Oh, how miserable and wretched I am! To think what I left—the occupations of former days, the comrades, the easy life, the sleep limited only by my inclination, and the strolls in freedom—and what a pit I have impetuously flung myself into! Why, in heaven's name? What does this splendid salary amount to? Was there no other way in which I could have earned more than this and could have kept my freedom and full independence? As the case stands now, I am pulled about like a lion leashed with a thread, as the saying is, up hill and down dale; and the most pitiful part of it all is that I do not know how to be a success and cannot be a favourite. I am an outsider in such matters and have not the knack of it, especially when I am put in comparison with men who have made an art of the business. Consequently I am unentertaining and not a bit convivial; I cannot even raise a laugh. I am aware, too, that it often actually annoys him to look at me, above all when he

ἡδίων αὐτὸς αὑτοῦ εἶναι θέλῃ· σκυθρωπὸς γὰρ αὐτῷ δοκῶ. καὶ ὅλως οὐκ ἔχω ὅπως ἁρμόσωμαι πρὸς αὐτόν. ἢν μὲν γὰρ ἐπὶ τοῦ σεμνοῦ φυλάττω ἐμαυτόν, ἀηδὴς ἔδοξα καὶ μονονουχὶ φευκτέος· ἢν δὲ μειδιάσω καὶ ῥυθμίσω τὸ πρόσωπον εἰς τὸ ἥδιστον, κατεφρόνησεν εὐθὺς καὶ διέπτυσεν, καὶ τὸ πρᾶγμα ὅμοιον δοκεῖ ὥσπερ ἂν εἴ τις κωμῳδίαν ὑποκρίναιτο τραγικὸν προσωπεῖον περικείμενος. τὸ δ' ὅλον, τίνα ἄλλον ὁ μάταιος ἐμαυτῷ βιώσομαι βίον τὸν παρόντα τοῦτον ἄλλῳ βεβιωκώς;"

31 Ἔτι σου ταῦτα διαλογιζομένου ὁ κώδων ἤχησεν, καὶ χρὴ τῶν ὁμοίων ἔχεσθαι καὶ περινοστεῖν καὶ ἑστάναι, ὑπαλείψαντά γε πρότερον τοὺς βουβῶνας καὶ τὰς ἰγνύας, εἰ θέλεις διαρκέσαι πρὸς τὸν ἆθλον. εἶτα δεῖπνον ὅμοιον καὶ εἰς τὴν αὐτὴν ὥραν περιηγμένον. καί σοι τὰ τῆς διαίτης πρὸς τὸν πάλαι βίον ἀντίστροφα, καὶ ἡ ἀγρυπνία δὲ καὶ ὁ ἱδρὼς καὶ ὁ κάματος ἠρέμα ἤδη ὑπορύττουσιν, ἢ φθόην ἢ περιπνευμονίαν ἢ κώλου ἄλγημα ἢ τὴν καλὴν ποδάγραν ἀναπλάττοντες. ἀντέχεις δε ὅμως, καὶ πολλάκις κατακεῖσθαι δέον, οὐδὲ τοῦτο συγκεχώρηται· σκῆψις γὰρ ἡ νόσος καὶ φυγὴ τῶν καθηκόντων ἔδοξεν. ὥστ' ἐξ ἁπάντων ὠχρὸς ἀεὶ καὶ ὅσον οὐδέπω τεθνηξομένῳ ἔοικας.

32 Καὶ τὰ μὲν ἐν τῇ πόλει ταῦτα. ἢν δέ που καὶ ἀποδημῆσαι δέῃ, τὰ μὲν ἄλλα ἐῶ· ὕοντος δὲ πολλάκις ὕστατος ἐλθὼν—τοιοῦτο γάρ σοι ἀποκεκλήρωται καὶ τὸ ζεῦγος—περιμένεις ἔστ' ἂν οὐκέτ' οὔσης καταγωγῆς τῷ μαγείρῳ σε ἢ τῷ τῆς δεσποίνης κομμωτῇ συμπαραβύσωσιν, οὐδὲ τῶν φρυγάνων δαψιλῶς ὑποβαλόντες.

wishes to be merrier than his wont, for I seem to him gloomy. I cannot suit him at all. If I keep to gravity, I seem disagreeable and almost a person to run away from; and if I smile and make my features as pleasant as I can, he despises me outright and abominates me. The thing makes no better impression than as if one were to play a comedy in a tragic mask! All in all, what other life shall I live for myself, poor fool, after having lived this one for another?"

While you are still debating these matters the bell rings, and you must follow the same routine, go the rounds and stand up; but first you must rub your loins and knees with ointment if you wish to last the struggle out! Then comes a similar dinner, prolonged to the same hour. In your case the diet is in contrast to your former way of living; the sleeplessness, too, and the sweating and the weariness gradually undermine you, giving rise to consumption, pneumonia, indigestion, or that noble complaint, the gout. You stick it out, however, and often you ought to be abed, but this is not permitted. They think illness a pretext, and a way of shirking your duties. The general consequences are that you are always pale and look as if you were going to die any minute.

So it goes in the city. And if you have to go into the country, I say nothing of anything else, but it often rains; you are the last to get there—even in the matter of horses it was your luck to draw that kind!—and you wait about until for lack of accommodation they crowd you in with the cook or the mistress's hairdresser without giving you even a generous supply of litter for a bed!

33 Οὐκ ὀκνῶ δέ σοι καὶ διηγήσασθαι ὅ μοι Θεσμόπολις οὗτος ὁ Στωϊκὸς διηγήσατο συμβὰν αὐτῷ πάνυ γελοῖον καὶ νὴ Δί' οὐκ ἀνέλπιστον ὡς ἂν καὶ ἄλλῳ ταὐτὸν συμβαίη. συνῆν μὲν γὰρ πλουσίᾳ τινὶ καὶ τρυφώσῃ γυναικὶ τῶν ἐπιφανῶν ἐν τῇ πόλει. δεῆσαν δὲ καὶ ἀποδημῆσαί ποτε, τὸ μὲν πρῶτον ἐκεῖνο παθεῖν ἔφη γελοιότατον, συγκαθέζεσθαι γάρ[1] αὐτῷ παραδεδόσθαι φιλοσόφῳ ὄντι κίναιδόν τινα τῶν πεπιττωμένων τὰ σκέλη καὶ τὸν πώγωνα περιεξυρημένων· διὰ τιμῆς δ' αὐτὸν ἐκείνη, ὡς τὸ εἰκός, ἦγεν. καὶ τοὔνομα δὲ τοῦ κιναίδου ἀπεμνημόνευεν· Χελιδόνιον γὰρ καλεῖσθαι. τοῦτο τοίνυν πρῶτον ἡλίκον, σκυθρωπῷ καὶ γέροντι ἀνδρὶ καὶ πολιῷ τὸ γένειον—οἶσθα δὲ ὡς βαθὺν πώγωνα καὶ σεμνὸν ὁ Θεσμόπολις εἶχεν—παρακαθίζεσθαι φῦκος ἐντετριμμένον καὶ ὑπογεγραμμένον τοὺς ὀφθαλμοὺς καὶ διασεσαλευμένον τὸ βλέμμα καὶ τὸν τράχηλον ἐπικεκλασμένον, οὐ χελιδόνα μὰ Δί', ἀλλὰ γῦπά τινα περιτετιλμένον τὰ πτερά·[2] καὶ εἴ γε μὴ πολλὰ δεηθῆναι αὐτοῦ, καὶ τὸν κεκρύφαλον ἔχοντα ἐπὶ τῇ κεφαλῇ ἂν συγκαθίζεσθαι. τὰ δ' οὖν ἄλλα παρ' ὅλην τὴν ὁδὸν μυρίας τὰς ἀηδίας ἀνασχέσθαι ὑπᾴδοντος καὶ τερετίζοντος, εἰ δὲ μὴ ἐπεῖχεν αὐτός, ἴσως ἂν καὶ ὀρχουμένου ἐπὶ τῆς ἀπήνης.

34 Ἕτερον δ' οὖν τι καὶ τοιοῦτον αὐτῷ προσταχθῆναι. καλέσασα γὰρ αὐτὸν ἡ γυνή, "Θεσμόπολι," φησίν, "οὕτως ὄναιο, χάριν οὐ μικρὰν

[1] γὰρ Fritzsche : παρ' MSS.

[2] Text Halbertsma, de Jong : περιτετιλμένον τοῦ πώγωνος τὰ πτερά MSS.

I make no bones of telling you a story that I was told by our friend Thesmopolis, the Stoic, of something that happened to him which was very comical, and it is not beyond the bounds of possibility that the same thing may happen to someone else. He was in the household of a rich and self-indulgent woman who belonged to a distinguished family in the city. Having to go into the country one time, in the first place he underwent, he said, this highly ridiculous experience, that he, a philosopher, was given a favourite to sit by, one of those fellows who have their legs depilated and their beards shaved off; the mistress held him in high honour, no doubt. He gave the fellow's name; it was Dovey![1] Now what a thing that was, to begin with, for a stern old man with a grey beard (you know what a long, venerable beard Thesmopolis used to have) to sit beside a fellow with rouged cheeks, underlined eyelids, an unsteady glance, and a skinny neck—no dove, by Zeus, but a plucked vulture! Indeed, had it not been for repeated entreaties, he would have worn a hair-net on his head. In other ways too Thesmopolis suffered numerous annoyances from him all the way, for he hummed and whistled and no doubt would even have danced in the carriage if Thesmopolis had not held him in check.

Then too, something else of a similar nature was required of him. The woman sent for him and said: "Thesmopolis, I am asking a great favour of you;

[1] Chelidonion: Little Swallow.

αἰτούσῃ δὸς μηδὲν ἀντειπὼν μηδὲ ὅπως ἐπὶ πλεῖόν σου δεήσομαι περιμείνας." τοῦ δέ, ὅπερ εἰκὸς ἦν, ὑποσχομένου πάντα πράξειν, "Δέομαί σου τοῦτο," ἔφη, "χρηστὸν ὁρῶσά σε καὶ ἐπιμελῆ καὶ φιλόστοργον, τὴν κύνα ἣν οἶσθα τὴν Μυρρίνην ἀναλαβὼν εἰς τὸ ὄχημα φύλαττέ μοι καὶ ἐπιμελοῦ ὅπως μηδενὸς ἐνδεὴς ἔσται· βαρύνεται γὰρ ἡ ἀθλία τὴν γαστέρα καὶ σχεδὸν ὡς ἐπίτεξ ἐστίν· οἱ δὲ κατάρατοι οὗτοι καὶ ἀπειθεῖς οἰκέται οὐχ ὅπως ἐκείνης, ἀλλ' οὐδ' ἐμοῦ αὐτῆς πολὺν ποιοῦνται λόγον ἐν ταῖς ὁδοῖς. μὴ τοίνυν τι σμικρὸν οἰηθῇς εὖ ποιήσειν με τὸ περισπούδαστόν μοι καὶ ἥδιστον κυνίδιον διαφυλάξας." ὑπέσχετο ὁ Θεσμόπολις πολλὰ ἱκετευούσης καὶ μονονουχὶ καὶ δακρυούσης. τὸ δὲ πρᾶγμα παγγέλοιον ἦν, κυνίδιον ἐκ τοῦ ἱματίου προκῦπτον μικρὸν ὑπὸ τὸν πώγωνα καὶ κατουρῆσαν πολλάκις, εἰ καὶ μὴ ταῦτα ὁ Θεσμόπολις προσετίθει, καὶ βαΰζον λεπτῇ τῇ φωνῇ—τοιαῦτα γὰρ τὰ Μελιταῖα—καὶ τὸ γένειον τοῦ φιλοσόφου περιλιχμώμενον, καὶ μάλιστα εἴ τι τοῦ χθιζοῦ αὐτῷ ζωμοῦ ἐγκατεμέμικτο. καὶ ὅ γε κίναιδος, ὁ σύνεδρος, οὐκ ἀμούσως ποτὲ καὶ εἰς τοὺς ἄλλους τοὺς παρόντας ἐν τῷ συμποσίῳ ἀποσκώπτων, ἐπειδή ποτε καὶ ἐπὶ τὸν Θεσμόπολιν καθῆκε τὸ σκῶμμα, "Περὶ δὲ Θεσμοπόλιδος," ἔφη, "τοῦτο μόνον εἰπεῖν ἔχω, ὅτι ἀντὶ Στωϊκοῦ ἤδη Κυνικὸς ἡμῖν γεγένηται." τὸ δ' οὖν κυνίδιον καὶ τετοκέναι ἐν τῷ τρίβωνι τῷ τοῦ Θεσμοπόλιδος ἐπυθόμην.

35 Τοιαῦτα ἐντρυφῶσι, μᾶλλον δὲ ἐνυβρίζουσι τοῖς συνοῦσι, κατὰ μικρὸν αὐτοὺς χειροήθεις τῇ ὕβρει παρασκευάζοντες. οἶδα δ' ἐγὼ καὶ ῥήτορα

please do it for me without making any objections or waiting to be asked repeatedly." He promised, as was natural, that he would do anything, and she went on: "I ask this of you because I see that you are kind and thoughtful and sympathetic—take my dog Myrrhina (you know her) into your carriage and look after her for me, taking care that she does not want for anything. The poor thing is unwell and is almost ready to have puppies, and these abominable, disobedient servants do not pay much attention even to me on journeys, let alone to her. So do not think that you will be rendering me a trivial service if you take good care of my precious, sweet doggie." Thesmopolis promised, for she plied him with many entreaties and almost wept. The situation was as funny as could be: a little dog peeping out of his cloak just below his beard, wetting him often, even if Thesmopolis did not add that detail, barking in a squeaky voice (that is the way with Maltese dogs, you know), and licking the philosopher's beard, especially if any suggestion of yesterday's gravy was in it! The favourite who had sat by him was joking rather wittily one day at the expense of the company in the dining-room, and when in due course his banter reached Thesmopolis, he remarked: "As to Thesmopolis, I can only say that our Stoic has finally gone to the dogs!"[1] I was told, too, that the doggie actually had her puppies in the cloak of Thesmopolis.

That is the way they make free with their dependants, yes, make game of them, gradually rendering them submissive to their effrontery. I know a sharp-

[1] *i.e.* had become a Cynic.

τῶν καρχάρων ἐπὶ τῷ δείπνῳ κελευσθέντα μελετήσαντα μὰ τὸν Δί' οὐκ ἀπαιδεύτως, ἀλλὰ πάνυ τορῶς καὶ συγκεκροτημένως· ἐπῃνεῖτο γοῦν μεταξὺ πινόντων οὐ πρὸς ὕδωρ μεμετρημένον, ἀλλὰ πρὸς οἴνου ἀμφορέας λέγων, καὶ τοῦτο ὑποστῆναι τὸ τόλμημα ἐπὶ διακοσίαις δραχμαῖς ἐλέγετο.

Ταῦτα μὲν οὖν ἴσως μέτρια. ἦν δὲ ποιητικὸς αὐτὸς ἢ συγγραφικὸς ὁ πλούσιος ᾖ, παρὰ τὸ δεῖπνον τὰ αὑτοῦ ῥαψῳδῶν, τότε καὶ μάλιστα διαρραγῆναι χρὴ ἐπαινοῦντα καὶ κολακεύοντα καὶ τρόπους ἐπαίνων καινοτέρους ἐπινοοῦντα. εἰσὶ δ' οἳ καὶ ἐπὶ κάλλει θαυμάζεσθαι ἐθέλουσιν, καὶ δεῖ Ἀδώνιδας αὐτοὺς καὶ Ὑακίνθους ἀκούειν, πήχεως ἐνίοτε τὴν ῥῖνα ἔχοντας. σὺ δ' οὖν ἂν μὴ ἐπαινῇς, εἰς τὰς λιθοτομίας τὰς Διονυσίου εὐθὺς ἀφίξῃ ὡς καὶ φθονῶν καὶ ἐπιβουλεύων αὐτῷ. χρὴ δὲ καὶ σοφοὺς καὶ ῥήτορας εἶναι αὐτούς, κἂν εἴ τι σολοικίσαντες τύχωσιν, αὐτὸ τοῦτο[1] τῆς Ἀττικῆς καὶ τοῦ Ὑμηττοῦ μεστοὺς δοκεῖν τοὺς λόγους καὶ νόμον εἶναι τὸ λοιπὸν οὕτω λέγειν.

36 Καίτοι φορητὰ ἴσως τὰ τῶν ἀνδρῶν. αἱ δὲ οὖν[2] γυναῖκες—καὶ γὰρ αὖ καὶ τόδε ὑπὸ τῶν γυναικῶν σπουδάζεται, τὸ εἶναί τινας αὐταῖς πεπαιδευμένους μισθοῦ ὑποτελεῖς[3] συνόντας καὶ

[1] αὐτὸ τοῦτο edd.: αὐτὸ τὸ MSS. Perhaps something more has been lost.

[2] δὲ οὖν Seager: δὴ οὖν MSS.

[3] μισθοῦ ὑποτελεῖς = ὑπομίσθους. Cobet and Fritzsche emend.

tongued rhetorician who made a speech by request at dinner in a style that was not by any means uncultivated, but very finished and studied. He was applauded, however, because his speech, which was delivered while they were drinking, was timed by flasks of wine instead of measures of water! And he took this venture on, it was said, for two hundred drachmas.[1]

All this is not so bad, perhaps. But if Dives himself has a turn for writing poetry or prose and recites his own compositions at dinner, then you must certainly split yourself applauding and flattering him and excogitating new styles of praise. Some of them wish to be admired for their beauty also, and they must hear themselves called an Adonis or a Hyacinthus, although sometimes they have a yard of nose. If you withhold your praise, off you go at once to the quarries of Dionysius because you are jealous and are plotting against your master. They must be philosophers and rhetoricians, too, and if they happen to commit a solecism, precisely on that account their language must seem full of the flavour of Attica and of Hymettus, and it must be the law to speak that way in future.

After all, one could perhaps put up with the conduct of the men. But the women—! That is another thing that the women are keen about—to have men of education living in their households on a salary

[1] It was not the fashion at ancient banquets for guests to make speeches. In consenting to deliver a selection from his repertory, the rhetorician put himself on a par with a professional entertainer. This was bad enough, but he made things still worse by allowing the company to time his speech with a substitute for a water-clock which they improvised out of a flask of wine.

τῷ φορείῳ ἑπομένους· ἓν γάρ τι καὶ τοῦτο τῶν ἄλλων καλλωπισμάτων αὐταῖς δοκεῖ, ἢν λέγηται ὡς πεπαιδευμέναι τέ εἰσιν καὶ φιλόσοφοι καὶ ποιοῦσιν ᾄσματα οὐ πολὺ τῆς Σαπφοῦς ἀποδέοντα—διὰ δὴ ταῦτα μισθωτοὺς καὶ αὗται περιάγονται ῥήτορας καὶ γραμματικοὺς καὶ φιλοσόφους, ἀκροῶνται δ' αὐτῶν—πηνίκα; γελοῖον γὰρ καὶ τοῦτο—ἤτοι μεταξὺ κομμούμεναι καὶ τὰς κόμας παραπλεκόμεναι ἢ παρὰ τὸ δεῖπνον· ἄλλοτε γὰρ οὐκ ἄγουσι σχολήν. πολλάκις δὲ καὶ μεταξὺ τοῦ φιλοσόφου τι διεξιόντος ἡ ἅβρα προσελθοῦσα ὤρεξε παρὰ τοῦ μοιχοῦ γραμμάτιον, οἱ δὲ περὶ σωφροσύνης ἐκεῖνοι λόγοι ἑστᾶσι περιμένοντες, ἔστ' ἂν ἐκείνη ἀντιγράψασα τῷ μοιχῷ ἐπαναδράμῃ πρὸς τὴν ἀκρόασιν.

37 Ἐπειδὰν δέ ποτε διὰ μακροῦ τοῦ χρόνου Κρονίων ἢ Παναθηναίων ἐπιστάντων πέμπηταί τί σοι ἐφεστρίδιον ἄθλιον ἢ χιτώνιον ὑπόσαθρον, ἐνταῦθα μάλιστα πολλὴν δεῖ καὶ μεγάλην γενέσθαι τὴν πομπήν. καὶ ὁ μὲν πρῶτος εὐθὺς ἔτι σκεπτομένου[1] παρακούσας τοῦ δεσπότου προδραμὼν καὶ προμηνύσας ἀπέρχεται μισθὸν οὐκ ὀλίγον τῆς ἀγγελίας προλαβών. ἕωθεν δὲ τρισκαίδεκα ἥκουσιν κομίζοντες, ἕκαστος ὡς πολλὰ εἶπε καὶ ὡς ὑπέμνησε καὶ ὡς ἐπιτραπεὶς τὸ κάλλιον ἐπελέξατο διεξιών. ἅπαντες δ' οὖν ἀπαλλάττονται λαβόντες, ἔτι καὶ βρενθυόμενοι ὅτι μὴ πλείω ἔδωκας.

38 Ὁ μὲν γὰρ μισθὸς αὐτὸς κατὰ δυ' ὀβολοὺς ἢ τέτταρας, καὶ βαρὺς αἰτῶν σὺ καὶ ὀχληρὸς δοκεῖς. ἵνα δ' οὖν λάβῃς, κολακευτέος μὲν αὐτὸς

[1] ἔτι σκεπτομένου ς, edd.: ἐπισκεπτομένου MSS.

and following their litters. They count it as one among their other embellishments if it is said that they are cultured and have an interest in philosophy and write songs not much inferior to Sappho's. To that end, forsooth, they too trail hired rhetoricians and grammarians and philosophers about, and listen to their lectures—when? it is ludicrous!—either while their toilet is being made and their hair dressed, or at dinner; at other times they are too busy! And often while the philosopher is delivering a discourse the maid comes up and hands her a note from her lover, so that the lecture on chastity is kept waiting until she has written a reply to the lover and hurries back to hear it.

At last, after a long lapse of time, when the feast of Cronus[1] or the Panathenaic festival comes, you are sent a beggarly scarf or a flimsy undergarment. Then by all means there must be a long and impressive procession. The first man, who has overheard his master still discussing the matter, immediately runs and tells you in advance, and goes away with a generous fee for his announcement, paid in advance. In the morning a baker's dozen of them come bringing it, and each one tells you: "I talked about it a great deal!" "I jogged his memory!" "It was left to me, and I chose the finest one!" So all of them depart with a tip, and even grumble that you did not give more.

As to your pay itself, it is a matter of two obols, or four, at a time, and when you ask for it you are a bore and a nuisance. So, in order to get it you

[1] The Greek festival that corresponded to the Roman Saturnalia.

καὶ ἱκετευτέος, θεραπευτέος δὲ καὶ ὁ οἰκονόμος, οὗτος μὲν κατ'[1] ἄλλον θεραπείας τρόπον·[2] οὐκ ἀμελητέος δὲ οὐδὲ ὁ σύμβουλος καὶ φίλος. καὶ τὸ ληφθὲν ἤδη προωφείλετο ἱματιοκαπήλῳ ἢ ἰατρῷ ἢ σκυτοτόμῳ τινί. ἄδωρα[3] οὖν σοι τὰ δῶρα καὶ ἀνόνητα.

39 Πολὺς δὲ ὁ φθόνος, καί που καὶ διαβολή τις ἠρέμα ὑπεξανίσταται πρὸς ἄνδρα ἤδη τοὺς κατὰ σοῦ λόγους ἡδέως ἐνδεχόμενον· ὁρᾷ γὰρ ἤδη σὲ μὲν ὑπὸ τῶν συνεχῶν πόνων ἐκτετρυχωμένον καὶ πρὸς τὴν θεραπείαν σκάζοντα καὶ ἀπηυδηκότα, τὴν ποδάγραν δὲ ὑπανιοῦσαν. ὅλως γὰρ ὅπερ ἦν νοστιμώτατον ἐν σοὶ ἀπανθισάμενος καὶ τὸ ἐγκαρπότατον τῆς ἡλικίας καὶ τὸ ἀκμαιότατον τοῦ σώματος ἐπιτρίψας καὶ ῥάκος σε πολυσχιδὲς ἐργασάμενος ἤδη περιβλέπει, σὲ μὲν οἷ τῆς κόπρου ἀπορρίψει φέρων, ἄλλον δὲ ὅπως τῶν δυναμένων τοὺς πόνους καρτερεῖν προσλήψεται. καὶ ἤτοι μειράκιον αὐτοῦ ὅτι ἐπείρασάς ποτε[4] ἢ τῆς γυναικὸς ἅβραν παρθένον γέρων ἀνὴρ διαφθείρεις ἢ ἄλλο τι τοιοῦτον ἐπικληθείς, νύκτωρ ἐγκεκαλυμμένος ἐπὶ τράχηλον ὠσθεὶς ἐξελήλυθας, ἔρημος ἁπάντων καὶ ἄπορος, τὴν βελτίστην ποδάγραν αὐτῷ γήρᾳ παραλαβών, καὶ ἃ μὲν τέως ᾔδεις ἀπομαθὼν ἐν τοσούτῳ χρόνῳ, θυλάκου δὲ μείζω τὴν γαστέρα ἐργασάμενος, ἀπλήρωτόν τι καὶ ἀπαραίτητον κακόν. καὶ γὰρ ὁ λαιμὸς ἀπαιτεῖ τὰ[5] ἐκ τοῦ ἔθους καὶ ἀπομανθάνων αὐτὰ ἀγανακτεῖ.

[1] κατ' A.M.H.: καὶ MSS.
[2] Text ς, edd.: ἄλλος . . . τρόπος MSS.
[3] ἄδωρα vulg.: ἄωρα MSS.
[4] ποτε ς: τότε MSS.
[5] τὰ Lehmann: not in MSS.

must flatter and wheedle the master and pay court to his steward too, but in another way; and you must not neglect his friend and adviser, either. As what you get is already owing to a clothier or doctor or shoemaker, his gifts are no gifts and profit you nothing.[1]

You are greatly envied, however, and perhaps some slanderous story or other gradually gets afoot by stealth and comes to a man who by now is glad to receive charges against you, for he sees that you are used up by your unbroken exertions and pay lame and exhausted court to him, and that the gout is growing upon you. To sum it up, after garnering all that was most profitable in you, after consuming the most fruitful years of your life and the greatest vigour of your body, after reducing you to a thnig of rags and tatters, he is looking about for a rubbish-heap on which to cast you aside unceremoniously, and for another man to engage who can stand the work. Under the charge that you once made overtures to a page of his, or that, in spite of your age, you are trying to seduce an innocent girl, his wife's maid, or something else of that sort, you leave at night, hiding your face, bundled out neck and crop, destitute of everything and at the end of your tether, taking with you, in addition to the burden of your years, that excellent companion, gout. What you formerly knew you have forgotten in all these years, and you have made your belly bigger than a sack, an insatiable, inexorable curse. Your gullet, too, demands what it is used to, and dislikes to unlearn its lessons.

[1] An allusion to Sophocles, *Ajax* 665: ἐχθρῶν ἄδωρα δῶρα κοὐκ ὀνήσιμα.

40 Καί σε οὐκ ἄν τις ἄλλος δέξαιτο ἔξωρον ἤδη γεγονότα καὶ τοῖς γεγηρακόσιν ἵπποις ἐοικότα, ὧν οὐδὲ τὸ δέρμα ὁμοίως χρήσιμον. ἄλλως τε καὶ ἡ ἐκ τοῦ ἀπωσθῆναι διαβολὴ πρὸς τὸ μεῖζον εἰκαζομένη μοιχὸν ἢ φαρμακέα σε ἤ τι τοιοῦτον ἄλλο δοκεῖν ποιεῖ· ὁ μὲν γὰρ κατήγορος καὶ σιωπῶν ἀξιόπιστος, σὺ δὲ Ἕλλην καὶ ῥᾴδιος τὸν τρόπον καὶ πρὸς πᾶσαν ἀδικίαν εὔκολος. τοιούτους γὰρ ἅπαντας ἡμᾶς εἶναι οἴονται, καὶ μάλα εἰκότως· δοκῶ γάρ μοι καὶ τῆς τοιαύτης δόξης αὐτῶν, ἣν ἔχουσι περὶ ἡμῶν, κατανενοηκέναι τὴν αἰτίαν. πολλοὶ γὰρ εἰς τὰς οἰκίας παρελθόντες ὑπὲρ τοῦ μηδὲν ἄλλο χρήσιμον εἰδέναι μαντείας[1] καὶ φαρμακείας ὑπέσχοντο καὶ χάριτας ἐπὶ τοῖς ἐρωτικοῖς καὶ ἐπαγωγὰς τοῖς ἐχθροῖς, καὶ ταῦτα πεπαιδεῦσθαι λέγοντες καὶ τρίβωνας ἀμπεχόμενοι καὶ πώγωνας οὐκ εὐκαταφρονήτους καθειμένοι. εἰκότως οὖν τὴν ὁμοίαν περὶ πάντων ὑπόνοιαν ἔχουσιν, οὓς ἀρίστους ᾤοντο τοιούτους ὁρῶντες, καὶ μάλιστα ἐπιτηροῦντες αὐτῶν τὴν ἐν τοῖς δείπνοις καὶ τῇ ἄλλῃ συνουσίᾳ κολακείαν καὶ τὴν πρὸς τὸ κέρδος δουλοπρέπειαν.

41 Ἀποσεισάμενοι δὲ αὐτοὺς μισοῦσι, καὶ μάλα εἰκότως, καὶ ἐξ ἅπαντος ζητοῦσιν ὅπως ἄρδην ἀπολέσωσιν, ἢν δύνωνται· λογίζονται γὰρ ὡς ἐξαγορεύσουσιν αὐτῶν τὰ πολλὰ ἐκεῖνα τῆς φύσεως ἀπόρρητα ὡς ἅπαντα εἰδότες ἀκριβῶς καὶ γυμνοὺς αὐτοὺς ἐπωπτευκότες. τοῦτο τοίνυν ἀποπνίγει αὐτούς· ἅπαντες γὰρ ἀκριβῶς ὅμοιοί

[1] μαγείας Valckenaer, which has been generally adopted; but cf. 27 μάγον ἢ μάντιν.

Nobody else would take you in, now that you have passed your prime and are like an old horse whose hide, even, is not as serviceable as it was. Besides, the scandal of your dismissal, exaggerated by conjecture, makes people think you an adulterer or poisoner or something of the kind. Your accuser is trustworthy even when he holds his tongue, while you are a Greek, and easy-going in your ways and prone to all sorts of wrong-doing. That is what they think of us all, very naturally. For I believe I have detected the reason for that opinion which they have of us. Many who have entered households, to make up for not knowing anything else that was useful, have professed to supply predictions, philtres, love-charms, and incantations against enemies; yet they assert they are educated, wrap themselves in the philosopher's mantle, and wear beards that cannot lightly be sneered at. Naturally, therefore, they entertain the same suspicion about all of us on seeing that men whom they considered excellent are that sort, and above all observing their obsequiousness at dinners and in their other social relations, and their servile attitude toward gain.

Having shaken them off, they hate them, very naturally, and endeavour in every way to destroy them outright if possible; for they expect them to betray the many hidden mysteries of their make-up, inasmuch as they are thoroughly acquainted with everything and have looked upon them unveiled. That sticks in their throat, because they are all exactly like

εἰσιν τοῖς καλλίστοις τούτοις βιβλίοις, ὧν χρυσοῖ μὲν οἱ ὀμφαλοί, πορφυρᾶ δὲ ἔκτοσθεν ἡ διφθέρα, τὰ δὲ ἔνδον ἢ Θυέστης ἐστὶν τῶν τέκνων ἑστιώμενος ἢ Οἰδίπους τῇ μητρὶ συνὼν ἢ Τηρεὺς δύο ἀδελφὰς ἅμα ὀπυίων. τοιοῦτοι καὶ αὐτοί εἰσι, λαμπροὶ καὶ περίβλεπτοι, ἔνδον δὲ ὑπὸ τῇ πορφύρᾳ πολλὴν τὴν τραγῳδίαν σκέποντες· ἕκαστον γοῦν αὐτῶν ἢν ἐξειλήσῃς, δρᾶμα οὐ μικρὸν εὑρήσεις Εὐριπίδου τινὸς ἢ Σοφοκλέους, τὰ δ' ἔξω πορφύρα εὐανθὴς καὶ χρυσοῦς ὁ ὀμφαλός. ταῦτα οὖν συνεπιστάμενοι αὑτοῖς, μισοῦσι καὶ ἐπιβουλεύουσιν εἴ τις ἀποστὰς ἀκριβῶς κατανενοηκὼς αὐτοὺς ἐκτραγῳδήσει καὶ πρὸς πολλοὺς ἐρεῖ.

42 Βούλομαι δ' ὅμως ἔγωγε ὥσπερ ὁ Κέβης ἐκεῖνος εἰκόνα τινὰ τοῦ τοιούτου βίου σοι γράψαι, ὅπως εἰς ταύτην ἀποβλέπων εἰδῇς εἴ σοι παριτητέον ἐστὶν εἰς αὐτήν. ἡδέως μὲν οὖν Ἀπελλοῦ τινος ἢ Παρρασίου ἢ Ἀετίωνος ἢ καὶ Εὐφράνορος ἂν ἐδεήθην ἐπὶ τὴν γραφήν· ἐπεὶ δὲ ἄπορον νῦν εὑρεῖν τινα οὕτως γενναῖον καὶ ἀκριβῆ τὴν τέχνην, ψιλὴν ὡς οἷόν τέ σοι ἐπιδείξω τὴν εἰκόνα.

Καὶ δὴ γεγράφθω προπύλαια μὲν ὑψηλὰ καὶ ἐπίχρυσα καὶ μὴ κάτω ἐπὶ τοῦ ἐδάφους, ἀλλ' ἄνω τῆς γῆς ἐπὶ λόφου κείμενα, καὶ ἡ ἄνοδος ἐπὶ πολὺ καὶ ἀνάντης καὶ ὄλισθον ἔχουσα, ὡς πολλάκις ἤδη πρὸς τῷ ἄκρῳ ἔσεσθαι ἐλπίσαντας ἐκτραχηλισθῆναι διαμαρτόντος τοῦ ποδός. ἔνδον δὲ ὁ Πλοῦτος αὐτὸς καθήσθω χρυσοῦς ὅλος, ὡς δοκεῖ, πάνυ εὔμορφος καὶ ἐπέραστος. ὁ δὲ ἐραστὴς μόλις ἀνελθὼν καὶ πλησιάσας τῇ θύρᾳ τεθηπέτω ἀφορῶν εἰς τὸ χρυσίον. παραλαβοῦσα δ' αὐτὸν

the finest of papyrus rolls, of which the knobs are of gold and the slip-cover of purple, but the content is either Thyestes feasting on his children or Oedipus married to his mother, or Tereus debauching two sisters at once. They too are splendid and universally admired, but inside, underneath their purple, they hide a deal of tragedy; in fact if you unroll any one of them, you will find an ample drama by an Euripides or a Sophocles, while on the outside there is a gaudy purple laticlave and a golden bulla. Conscious of all this, they hate and plot against any renegade who, having become thoroughly familiar with them, is likely to expose the plot and tell it broadcast.

I desire, nevertheless, in imitation of Cebes,[1] to paint you a picture of this career that we have discussed, so that you may look at it and determine whether you should enter it. I should gladly have requisitioned an Apelles, or Parrhasius, or Aetion, or Euphranor to paint it, but since it is impossible nowadays to find anyone so excellent and so thoroughly master of his craft, I shall show you the picture as best I can in unembellished prose.

Imagine painted a lofty, golden gateway, not down on the level ground but above the earth on a hill; the slope is long and steep and slippery, so that many a time those who hoped soon to be at the summit have broken their necks by a slip of the foot. Within, let Wealth himself be sitting, all golden, seemingly, very beautiful and fascinating; and let his lover, after ascending with great toil, draw near the door and gaze spellbound at the gold. Let Hope, herself

[1] Reputed author of the *Tabula*, a description of an imaginary allegorical painting representing human life.

ἡ Ἐλπίς, εὐπρόσωπος καὶ αὕτη καὶ ποικίλα ἀμπεχομένη, εἰσαγέτω σφόδρα ἐκπεπληγμένον τῇ εἰσόδῳ. τοὐντεῦθεν δὲ ἡ μὲν Ἐλπὶς ἀεὶ προηγείσθω, διαδεξάμεναι δ' αὐτὸν ἄλλαι γυναῖκες, Ἀπάτη καὶ Δουλεία, παραδότωσαν τῷ Πόνῳ, ὁ δὲ πολλὰ τὸν ἄθλιον καταγυμνάσας τελευτῶν ἐγχειρισάτω αὐτὸν τῷ Γήρᾳ ἤδη ὑπονοσοῦντα καὶ τετραμμένον τὴν χρόαν. ὑστάτη δὲ ἡ Ὕβρις ἐπιλαβομένη συρέτω πρὸς τὴν Ἀπόγνωσιν. ἡ δὲ Ἐλπὶς τὸ ἀπὸ τούτου ἀφανὴς ἀποπτέσθω, καὶ μηκέτι καθ' οὓς εἰσῆλθε τοὺς χρυσοῦς θυρῶνας, ἔκ τινος δὲ ἀποστρόφου καὶ λεληθυίας ἐξόδου ἐξωθείσθω γυμνὸς προγάστωρ ὠχρὸς γέρων, τῇ ἑτέρᾳ μὲν τὴν αἰδῶ σκέπων, τῇ δεξιᾷ δὲ αὐτὸς ἑαυτὸν ἄγχων. ἀπαντάτω δ' ἐξιόντι ἡ Μετάνοια δακρύουσα εἰς οὐδὲν ὄφελος καὶ τὸν ἄθλιον ἐπαπολλύουσα.

Τοῦτο μὲν ἔστω τὸ τέλος τῆς γραφῆς. σὺ δ' οὖν, ὦ ἄριστε Τιμόκλεις, αὐτὸς ἤδη ἀκριβῶς ἐπισκοπῶν ἕκαστα ἐννόησον, εἴ σοι καλῶς ἔχει παρελθόντα[1] εἰς τὴν εἰκόνα κατὰ ταύτας τὰς θύρας ἐκείνης τῆς[2] ἔμπαλιν αἰσχρῶς οὕτως ἐκπεσεῖν. ὅ τι δ' ἂν πράττῃς, μέμνησο τοῦ σοφοῦ λέγοντος ὡς θεὸς ἀναίτιος, αἰτία δὲ ἑλομένου.

[1] παρελθόντα A.M.H.: προσελθόντα MSS.
[2] ἐκείνης τῆς Bourdelot: ἐκείνην τὴν MSS.

fair of face and gaily dressed, take him in charge and conduct him within, tremendously impressed by his entrance. Then let Hope keep always in advance of him, and let other women, Deceit and Servitude, receive him successively and pass him on to Toil, who, after breaking the wretch with hard labour, shall at length deliver him, now sickly and faded, to Old Age. Last of all, let Insolence lay hold of him and drag him along to Despair; let Hope then fly away and vanish, and instead of the golden portal by which he entered, let him be ejected by some remote and secret postern, naked, paunchy, pale, and old, screening his nakedness with his left hand and throttling himself with his right; and on the way out, let him be met by Repentance, weeping to no avail and helping to make an end of the poor man.

Let that be the conclusion of the painting. The rest, my dear Timocles, is up to you; examine all the details with care and make up your mind whether it suits you to enter the pictured career by these doors and be thrown out so disgracefully by that one opposite. Whatever you do, remember the words of the philosopher: "God is not at fault; the fault is his who maketh the choice." [1]

[1] Plato *Republic* 10, 617 E.

INDEX

INDEX

INDEX

INDEX

INDEX

INDEX

INDEX

LTSS Lineberger Memorial Library
3 5898 00118 0062